Stephen R. Donaldson is a no.1 bestselling fantasy author all around the world. With – amongst others – his Thomas Covenant series, he has dominated the charts and the awards for over 20 years. He was born in Cleveland, Ohio, in 1947, and made his debut in 1977 with his first Thomas Covenant novel.

Stephen Donaldson

THE REED STEPHENS NOVELS

The Man Who Killed His Brother

The Man Who Risked His Partner

The Man Who Tried To Get Away

ORION

The Man Who Killed His Brother © Reed Stephens 1980
First published in Great Britain 1982 by Fontana Paperbacks
The Man Who Risked His Partner © Reed Stephens 1984
First published in Great Britain 1985 by Fontana Paperbacks
The Man Who Tried To Get Away © Reed Stephens 1990
First published in Great Britain 1990 by Collins

The Reed Stephens Novels © Stephen Donaldson 2001

First published in Great Britain in 2001 by Orion Books
an imprint of The Orion Publishing Group
Orion House, 5 Upper St Martin's Lane, London WC2H 9EA

A CIP catalogue record for this book is available
from the British Library

ISBN (hardback) 0 75284 689 2
ISBN (trade paperback) 075284 690 6

Typeset by Deltatype Ltd, Birkenhead, Merseyside

Printed and bound in Great Britain by
Clays Ltd, St Ives plc

Contents

An introduction to
REED STEPHENS

Readers unfamiliar with the name 'Stephen R. Donaldson' can safely skip this introduction. Perhaps they should. Unencumbered by expectations, they can consider the novels in this volume without fear of feeling misled.

Readers who *do* recognize my name, on the other hand, may have a question or two they would like answered.

The first, obviously, is: *Reed Stephens*? What's *that* about?

Well, it wasn't *my* idea. I'm perfectly willing to stand behind my own work. In fact, I actively desire to stand behind it. Nevertheless my publishers at the time insisted on a pseudonym.

As a writer, I was discovered by Lester del Rey at Ballantine Books in the mid-70s. And, of course, I was discovered for the books which have been the foundation of my career ever since: 'The Chronicles of Thomas Covenant the Unbeliever'. In retrospect, I doubt that Lester was surprised to hear that my next novel was a mystery, *The Man Who Killed His Brother* (which, by the way, I originally called *City of Day/ City of Night*). He came from a generation of writers who often tackled a variety of genres. By time-honoured tradition, however, he and his contemporaries had used different pen-names for different categories of fiction. Naturally I was expected to follow his example.

At the same time, his wife, the inestimable publisher Judy-Lynn del Rey, believed whole-heartedly in 'category publishing'. Put simply, her philosophy was this: you can't sell cars and stoves and call them both Buick; buyers will get confused. By extension, you can't sell fantasies and mysteries and call them both Donaldson for the same reason: readers will get confused.

She and her husband were in perfect agreement. Ballantine Books required a pseudonym as a condition of publication. And I was young,

1

newly published, eager to get my work into print. With regret, I agreed.

I chose the name Reed Stephens because it reminded me of mine (the 'R' stands for Reeder, my mother's maiden name). During the next fifteen years or so I produced two more mystery novels like the first purportedly written by Reed Stephens – or, as I came to call him, 'poor ol' Reed'. Sadly *his* career never took off, and in time all three of his books went out of print. This volume, kindly issued by Orion Books, represents their first appearance in nearly ten years.

So much for practical matters. On a deeper level, readers acquainted with 'The Chronicles of Thomas Covenant', 'Mordant's Need', and the *Gap* sequence may well wonder: why mysteries?

In answer, let me say first that my mystery novels – the three included here and one forthcoming – have occupied a consistent place in the cycle or rhythm of my creative life. My pattern for nearly twenty-five years has been this: I write an epic (e.g. my first Covenant trilogy); I collapse from exhaustion; I gradually recover energy – not to mention morale – by producing a few short stories; that recovery enables me to write a mystery novel; and some time during the process of the mystery I discover that I've committed myself – internally – to another epic. The first Covenant trilogy; prostration; some short fiction; *The Man Who Killed His Brother*; the second Covenant trilogy; more prostration; some short fiction; *The Man Who Risked His Partner*; 'Mordant's Need'; still more prostration; more short fiction; *The Man Who Tried to Get Away*; the *Gap* sequence; massive prostration; still more short fiction; and now the forthcoming new book, *The Man Who Fought Alone*.

Even *I* have to wonder what's up next.

But the foregoing only demonstrates that I feel a need to write mystery novels for some reason. What that reason might be is a more complex subject.

As it happens, I find mysteries extremely arduous to write, primarily because they don't play to my strengths. I suppose I could claim that their function is to make me feel that writing another epic will be comparatively easy. After all, I can't afford to remember the previous bout of prostration too vividly.

However, the guy who wrote the novels included here – not to mention all those epics – obviously can't be satisfied by such a superficial explanation.

So . . .

I used to believe that I wrote about Mick 'Brew' Axbrewder and Ginny Fistoulari in order to ground myself; to consolidate the creative gains of the immediately preceding epic by drawing those gains into a fictionalized contemporary reality so that I – as a person as well as a writer – would have a solid foundation on which to begin the next epic. A nice theory, as far as it goes. It may even contain some truth. But it no longer satisfies me.

An explanation I now prefer goes like this: I write mystery novels in order to stretch myself, both creatively and artistically, so that I'll be better prepared for my next epic. Precisely because mystery fiction doesn't play to my strengths, it forces me to expand the range of my skills, which will in turn – I devoutly hope – ensure that whatever I tackle next will go beyond anything I've written previously.

Again, a nice theory, as far as it goes. It contains considerable truth. If I weren't the kind of man who writes books like these, I'd accept it at face value and stop probing.

Unfortunately, any still deeper explanation will draw the reader into some rather murky autobiographical waters. So be warned: any information gleaned from what now follows will be inherently misleading, its relevance oblique at best and almost certainly obscure; and any interpretation of these novels based on that information isn't likely to turn out well.

Put simply – by which I mean inaccurately – Mick Axbrewder is founded on a real person. At least I *hope* he's a real person. Of course, I'm referring to myself. Brew is a stand-in, of a sort. Or an attempt to exorcize personal demons. A simulacrum designed to help me extend my understanding of myself.

When I say this, I'm not referring to anything as obvious as Brew's troubles with alcohol – although I've had my share. Nor do I refer to his problematic relationship with Ginny – although it would be a kindness to describe some of my experiences with relationships as problematic. Rather I'm thinking of those characteristics and quests which Brew shares imperfectly with Thomas Covenant (and with Covenant's indirect obverse, Angus Thermopyle): the inability to compromise combined with the rather flawed grasp on what the real issues are; the almost autonomic yearning for personal integrity; the emphasis on pain, struggle, and self-doubt as the only viable road to that integrity.

However, I *do* mean 'imperfectly'. Although Brew shares those characteristics and quests, they don't carry him as far as Covenant goes. Perhaps because he hasn't yet been granted the sheer narrative space necessary for his personal journey, Brew's victories and validations fall short of Covenant's. In effect, Brew resembles me more than I resemble Covenant.

Hence the importance of placing him in a setting, a 'reality', which more closely resembles mine. And hence, also, the role of the 'puzzle', the mystery, in Brew's story. As I do, he wrestles with conundrums of passion and responsibility, and feels entirely flummoxed by them. As I do, he finds that intuition and knowledge together, the unexpected leap of imagination triggered by the unanticipated bit of information, are his only means to penetrate the mystery which he has undertaken to untangle – and which, not at all coincidentally, he *must* untangle in order to understand himself.

In an odd way, Mick Axbrewder exists to help me keep up with my own work. Without him, characters like Thomas Covenant (and Terisa Morgan, and Morn Hyland, and – less directly – Angus Thermopyle) might well exceed my ability to write about them.

By revealing all this, however, I do *not* mean to imply that the novels in this volume can't (or – shudder – shouldn't) stand on their own; that they can't be read and enjoyed without autobiographical information or a knowledge of my other work. I believe they can. If I didn't, I wouldn't publish them. My sense of creative ethics would forbid it. Characters like Covenant, Angus, and Brew so obviously serve my own needs that I wouldn't consider offering them to readers if I were not convinced that their stories have an integrity, a value, entirely apart from their relevance to my own.

A brief textual note in conclusion: these three novels have been very slightly revised since their original publication. Readability was my own concern. I made no attempt to up-date their themes or settings, to make the stages of Brew's journey more consistent with my own present reality. I've smoothed and tightened the prose; but I've left everything else alone.

THE MAN WHO
KILLED HIS BROTHER

– to *Barbara*, *Jim* and *Debbie*
the best siblings I could wish for

Part One
Tuesday Night / Wednesday

Chapter One

I was sitting at the bar of the Hegira that night when Ginny came in.
The barkeep, an ancient sad-eyed patriarch named José, had just
poured me another drink, and I was having one of those rare
moments any serious drunk can tell you about. A piece of real quiet.
José's cheeks bristled because he didn't shave very often, and his apron
was dingy because it didn't get washed very often, and his fingernails
had little crescents of grime under them. The glass he poured for me
wasn't all that clean. But the stuff he poured was golden-amber and
beautiful, like distilled sunlight, and it made the whole place soothing
as sleep – which drunks know how to value because they don't get
much of it.

It made the dull old fly-brown *santos* against the wall behind the
bottles look like the saints knew what they were doing and it made the
drinkers at the tables look peaceful and happy. It made the men
playing pool in the back of the room look like they were moving in
slow motion, flowing through the air as if it were syrup. It made José
look wise and patient behind his stubble and his groggy eyes. It was
one of those rare moments when everything is in the right place, and
there's a soft gold light shining on it, and you feel like you're being
healed. It never lasts – but you always think it will, if you just stay
where you are and don't stop drinking.

By the curious logic of the drunk, I felt I'd earned it. After all, I'd
been drinking most of the time for several days now, just trying to
create that amber glow for myself. So when Ginny walked in the door
– when every head in the bar turned to stare at her – I didn't know
which to feel first, surprise or resentment. There wasn't any doubt she
was looking for me.

I had the right to be surprised. For one thing, she had no business walking into the Hegira like that – especially at night. The Hegira is down in the old part of Puerta del Sol, on Eighth Street between Oak and Maple. Cities are like that. The old parts – where the descendants and countrymen of the founders live – have street names like 'Eighth' and 'Oak'. The rich suburbs – half of them built in the last ten years – have flashier names like 'tenochtitlan' and 'montezuma'. And in the old part of town women don't go into bars at all. When the Chicano and Mestizo and Indian women want their men to come out, they stand on the sidewalk and send in their children.

As Ginny pushed her way through the door, scanned the room, and came striding over towards me, the quiet buzz of voices stopped. José's eyes went blank and empty – you could tell if she spoke to him he was going to say he didn't speak English. The men with the pool cues stood very still, as if they were waiting to start a different kind of game.

But I also had another reason to be surprised. This wasn't the way Ginny was supposed to come looking for me. She came looking for me often enough – I would've probably drunk myself to death by now if she hadn't been so faithful about it – but this wasn't the way. We had a system worked out, and she was breaking it.

What the system did was let me get ready. She didn't bother me in the morning, when I was taking those first stiff drinks, trying to push the sickness back down my throat where it belonged. She didn't bother me during the day, when I was drinking slow and steady to control the shakes. She didn't bother me in the afternoon, when I started to hit the bottle harder because the stuff didn't seem to be having any effect. She didn't bother me in the evening, when I went to places like the Hegira looking for amber and comfort. She didn't bother me when I left whatever bar it was and bought a bottle and wandered away into the night to pay the price.

No, we had a system.

When I was ready for her, I knew where to go at night with my bottle. One of the benches in a cheap little park down on Tin Street. It was still in the old part of town, which meant the city didn't water the grass and the cops didn't roust drunks who spent the night there. And when the sun came up I'd be sitting on that bench, waiting – just waiting because I was too sick to hope. And then I'd see her walking over to me. She always came from the east – the sun was always behind her, so I couldn't see her face. She always said, 'Brew.' (My name is Mick Axbrewder, but not even my enemies call me Mick.) I always said, 'Ginny.' And then she always said, 'I need you.'

That's when I knew I was going to get sober and go back to work.

Sometimes I said, 'What do you need me for? I'm a drunk.' But that was just a variation. She never gave me a straight answer. I wouldn't have known what do to with a straight answer.

So I was surprised when she walked into the Hegira looking for me. But I resented it, too. I was having one of those rare moments, and she took it away from me. And I wasn't ready.

But Ginny Fistoulari isn't the kind of woman who lets things like that stand in her way. She's tall – about the only time she doesn't look tall is when I'm standing beside her – and five years younger than I am, with the kind of lean and ready look about her you see in a good racehorse. Her eyes are the same colour grey as the .357 Smith & Wesson she carries in her purse, but other than that you wouldn't know she's tough as rivets unless you look at her up close. From a few feet away she's just an attractive blonde with a nice mouth, delicate nostrils, and a perfect chin.

Up close you can see her nose was broken once – broken the way a nose gets broken when somebody clips it with a crowbar. The clown who did it didn't live to regret it. She shot him three times in the face. For that the commission almost took away her licence. She's tough the way you have to be tough in order to spend your time getting involved in the messy side of other people's problems. As a result, she's reasonably successful. Fistoulari Investigations can afford to refuse surveillance cases and domestic problems, even if it isn't making her rich.

Maybe she would've made more money if she hadn't insisted on dragging me back to work every time one of her cases got hard. Maybe in the long run she could've had pricier clients if that big goon working for her (me) wasn't always in trouble with the cops for carrying out investigations without a licence. I don't know. When I was sober, I never asked her why she put up with me. I just did the work. She didn't have any use for my gratitude.

But this time I wasn't grateful. I wasn't ready. When I saw her striding straight at me as if the Hegira and all its patrons didn't exist, I wanted to tell her to go to hell. I could see from the way the men watched her that I was never going to be welcome in the Hegira again. And I resented that – a bar where you can get amber and quiet is hard to find. The words were right there in my mind. *Go to hell, Ginny Fistoulari.*

If I'd said that, she probably would've turned around and walked away and never come back. So it was a good thing I kept my mouth shut.

But I had to do something. I swung away from her and went back to my drink. The stuff was there waiting for me. It was the right colour, even if the feeling was gone. I wrapped my fist around the glass and raised it in the direction of my face.

Ginny's hand came down hard on my wrist, slapped the glass back to the counter so hard the stuff spilled all over my fingers. Which isn't easy to do to me, even when I'm not expecting it.

If anyone else had done it – anyone at all – I would've taken their hand off. At the wrist. People don't do that kind of thing to me – just like they don't call me Mick.

Only this wasn't anyone else. It was Ginny Fistoulari. I couldn't even try to get her hand off of me. I was doing everything I was capable of when I worked up enough energy to be mad.

'God damn it, Ginny –'

She came right back at me. 'God damn it, Brew' – she had one of those voices that can do anything, melt in your mouth or tear your skin off your bones – 'you're going to come with me, or I swear to God I'll let you have it right here.' At the moment she sounded like being pistol-whipped. She didn't shout – she didn't have to. When she used that tone on me, there was no question about which one of us was in charge.

So much for my being mad. I've never been able to be mad at her at the same time she was mad at me. Which is probably a good thing. But this time I didn't have the vaguest idea *why* she was mad at me.

I didn't want to have any ideas. I wanted to drink. Without looking at her, I said, 'I'm not ready.'

Her voice practically jumped at me. 'I don't give a flying fuck at the moon whether you're ready or not. You're going to come with me.'

That reached me. Ginny doesn't talk that way very often. Only when she's furious. I turned, met her eyes.

She didn't look furious. The anger was just in her voice, not in her face. Instead, she was worried. Her nostrils were flaring and pale, and there were lines at the corners of her eyes that showed only when she's worried. And her eyes were wet. They looked like they might overflow any second now.

I couldn't remember the last time I'd seen her look so concerned. Concerned about me. All of a sudden my throat was dry, and I could barely scrape the words out. 'What's the matter?'

Anybody else, and the tears would've been running down her cheeks. But not her. She was Ginny Fistoulari, private investigator. Licensed by the state to work on other people's misery. Human trouble and pain did a lot of different things to her, but they didn't make her cry. She just looked straight at me through the wet and said with all the anger gone out of her voice, 'Your niece is missing.'

I heard her, but something about it didn't penetrate. 'Alathea?' Of course I had a niece, my dead brother's daughter. Her mother hated me. Alathea was another one of those people I was responsible for without being able to do anything about it. And on top of that I liked her. But I couldn't seem to remember what she looked like. 'Missing?'

I couldn't call up an image. All I got was her name – and a blank wall of dread. 'What're you talking about?'

Ginny didn't flinch. 'Lona called me today. I've been looking for you ever since. Alathea has been missing for a week.'

I went on staring at her. Then it got through to me. Alathea was missing. Her mother had called Ginny. Ginny had come looking for me. We had work to do.

There were things about it that didn't make sense. But right then they didn't matter. Not with Alathea missing, and Ginny looking at me like that. I fumbled some money on to the bar, got off my stool and started for the door. I didn't know how much I owed because I didn't know how much I'd had to drink, but José didn't even blink at me so I must've paid him enough – or else he was just glad to get a woman out of his bar without trouble. I stumbled once, then Ginny took my arm. I didn't say goodbye to the Hegira. Together we went out into the night.

Chapter Two

Ginny took me back to my apartment to get me sobered up. I didn't have a car, and she'd left hers at my apartment, so we had to walk.

I live in one of those run-down apartment houses on the edge of the old part of town. The place was just far enough from the centre to have been named La Cienga Apartments, but still close enough to be in danger of being torn down for urban renewal every time the city fathers felt like they had to make some kind of choice between 'modern' and 'quaint'. In Puerta del Sol those words are really two different names for 'profitable' – the city is growing, and people like to come for a visit, so it's just a question of whether money is going to be made from redeveloping real estate or from tourism.

Right then I didn't give a damn. They could blow up the place or sell tickets to my bedroom for all I cared. I was in one of those horrible 'between' places any drunk can tell you about – too drunk to cope, not drunk enough to be anesthetized. I was half-blind with dread and my mind kept repeating, *Alathea Alathea Alathea.* I wanted Ginny to talk to me, tell me what was going on. But she just hung on to my arm and dragged me along and didn't say a thing.

The walk must've done me some good. She didn't have to carry me upstairs.

At least I was spared the embarrassment of a messy apartment. I'm tidy enough when I'm sober, and I hardly ever visit my apartment when I'm drinking. The place smelled musty and it needed dusting, but it wasn't a mess.

I was a mess. Getting sober is something I usually do for myself. It's not a pretty business, and you don't like having people watch. With Ginny there I kept noticing things that didn't usually bother me – like the fact that I couldn't put one foot in front of the other. Or that I stank. How many days had I been wearing these clothes? I had no idea. I needed a drink, and I didn't like having Ginny see it.

She didn't give me any choice. Before I could get past Alathea's name to try do something for myself, she had me undressed, God knows how. When you're six foot five and two hundred and forty pounds, other people usually can't just take your clothes away from you. Then she prised me into the shower. She slammed on the water and left me there as if she wanted me to drown. But after a while she came back, scrubbed me, got me out of the shower and into an old bathrobe. Then she began pouring coffee down me.

That lasted for a while. Then the coffee and the other stuff started to do a little dance inside me, and I threw up for a while. After that I felt better. I was about to tell Ginny about Alathea when I fell asleep.

It was dawn before she woke me up and began treating me again. Orange juice, coffee, toast, vitamin pills of all kinds. She's a vitamin freak – carries whole bottles in her purse, along with her .357. She even got me shaved. But it was close to nine before I was in any condition to go anywhere. All that time she didn't say a word. And I didn't ask any questions. I was too sick.

I was going to be sicker. Already I wanted a drink so bad it brought tears to my eyes – and this was just the beginning. Shame is an awkward thing to live with, and having Ginny there, having her see me like this, made me ashamed on top of all the other remorse and responsibility. And there aren't many cures for it. Sometimes work is one of them. But the only one you can actually count on is alcohol.

But Alathea was missing. When Ginny asked me if I was ready to go, I didn't answer right away. I went over to the dresser in the bedroom half of the apartment and got out my gun, a .45 automatic, which is about the only gun I've ever found that doesn't feel like a toy in my hand. I checked it over, made sure it was loaded, then strapped on the shoulder holster and put the .45 under my left arm. Then I looked Ginny in the eye as steadily as I could and said, 'Alathea is my niece. My brother's daughter. She's thirteen years old – and beside the fact she's one of those cute kids that makes you happy just to look at her, she also happens to like me. For some reason, Lona has never told her exactly what happened to her father. She thinks I'm just her nice old Uncle Brew. And besides that, she's solid as a rock. Half the time these days when things get too much for Lona, Alathea carries her – which is one hell of a job for a thirteen-year-old, and she does it beautifully. It doesn't matter whether I'm ready or not. Let's go.'

For a second there, Ginny almost smiled. The lines of worry around her eyes faded. She seemed to shake herself, and then it was as if she hadn't been up most of the night taking care of me. She didn't look tired anymore. 'That's more like it,' she said, mostly to herself. She handed me a jacket, and a minute later I was walking down the stairs.

Talk is cheap. I wasn't ready, and it showed. I almost didn't make it down the stairs. My knees felt like mush, and the stairwell kept trying to stand on edge. There was a little voice in the back of my head saying, *You need a drink you need a drink you need a drink.* It wasn't easy to ignore, even with Ginny watching me.

But I didn't figure out why she was acting so much like she was worried about me until she took my arm to steer me towards her car. Of course she knew all about the connection between me and Alathea. Now she thought something serious had happened to my niece. She was afraid of what knowing that would do to me. She knew killing Richard had pushed me right to the edge. She was afraid whatever happened to Alathea would push me over.

I wanted to ask her about that. Ask, hell! I wanted to drag it out of her. But I put it off. Just climbing into her Olds left me weak as an old man. And I'd forgotten my sunglasses. Already the sun was beating down on the streets like bricks out of the dry thin blue sky. Made my eyes hurt. If it hadn't been for the tinted glass in the Olds, I might not have survived as far as Lona's house.

Lona Axbrewder, my brother's widow. I wasn't exactly her favourite person. There was one question I had to ask. When we parked in front of the house, I stayed where I was for a minute, trying not to hold my head in my hands. Then I said, 'Why did she call you? You know how she feels about me.'

'Ask her yourself,' Ginny said. 'I'm not a mind reader.' But her voice was stiff, and I'd heard that stiffness before. It meant she knew the answer and didn't want to tell me.

'Maybe,' I muttered to myself. Maybe I would ask her. I was in no condition to know what I was going to do. I had enough problems just getting the door open and climbing out on to the sidewalk.

Lona lives down on Mission Street in a neighbourhood that's only about two levels up from my apartment building. None of the houses for blocks in all directions are new, none of them look big enough to have more than two bedrooms, and none of them are out of spitting range from the house next door. But it's a nice enough neighbourhood, and people don't spit. Lona's house is adobe, but that squat brown shape is softened by rose trellises that frame the top and sides of the front door. She must've watered those roses twice a day to make them look so nice.

I spent a minute standing on the sidewalk, looking around. Trees along the walk cut out a lot of the sun, and after the glare of the roads and traffic it was restful in a way just to stand there, looking. The whole place was restful – shade, trees, grass, tidy brown houses. It looked like the kind of place where nothing ever happens. I didn't want to move – didn't want to find out any different.

But Ginny took my arm again, and before I knew it we were standing in front of the door, and the door was opening, and Lona was telling us to come in. Then the door shut behind us, and my retreat was cut off. I felt like I'd made a fatal mistake. The voice in my head started to shout, You need a *drink*! It sounded desperate.

Dumbly, I let Ginny steer me. We followed Lona into the living room and sat down.

I couldn't see very clearly. The room was too dark – she had all the shades pulled down and didn't turn on any lights. That made the air dim and cool and comforting, which was nice. It almost seemed like she did it for my benefit, as if she had any reason in the world to give a good goddamn how I felt. But it didn't let me read her face. I wanted to know how hard she was taking this thing. That would tell me a lot.

The outlines I could do from memory. She was small and vague and somehow brittle, like most wives of cops I've ever met. They don't start out that way. It just happens to them because they're afraid of losing their husbands, and they can't share the danger – or even the strain – and they can't feel good about it because nobody loves a cop. It's like living with a man who has some kind of terminal disease. She had medium-length brown hair and a habit of pushing both hands through it, pulling it away from her temples as if she were trying to drag some horrible grimace off her face. Even before she lost her husband she used to make me nervous. Now she could've made me scream with no trouble at all.

She sat Ginny and me down on the Naugahyde couch across from the TV, then asked us if we wanted any coffee. Ginny said, 'Yes, thanks,' before I could even think about the question. Lona pushed her hands through her hair, then left us alone.

I suppose I should have been thinking about Alathea – as a way of fighting off the need – but I was too strung out to have any control over my thoughts. I was sitting exactly where I used to sit when Richard and I watched football together. I knew from memory that there was a picture of him sitting on top of the TV, staring at me with that lopsided grin of his. Richard Axbrewder, my younger brother. Rick and Mick. It was when he died that people stopped calling me Mick.

Died, hell. I killed him, and half the city knows it. The papers didn't exactly play it down. One of them had it right there on the front page, PRIVATE INVESTIGATOR KILLS COP. BROTHER SHOOTS BROTHER. There's no way I can pretend I didn't do it.

It happened five years ago, when Ginny and I were partners. I remember everything about it. I was sitting at a table by the window in Norman's, which is one of those downtown bars that caters to the business-man-getting-off-work trade. It just happened to be right across from the First Puerta del Sol National Bank. I was having a few drinks – exactly six, according to the testimony of the barkeep – and trying to make up my mind about whether I wanted or had the nerve to ask Ginny to marry me. Not an unpleasant kind of indecision, and I had enough stuff in me to glow while I thought about it. It was almost dark outside, but the streetlights hadn't come on yet so I couldn't see very well, and the air was dim and relaxed.

Then I heard gunfire. I snapped a look out the window and saw a man running away from the bank in my direction. He was carrying a bag of some kind and waving a gun over his shoulder, shooting at something behind him. There was a cop chasing him. I jumped to the conclusion he'd just robbed the bank.

I was out the door and on the sidewalk in no time. I had the .45 in my hand. I shouted at the man to stop. When he pointed his gun at me, I fired a couple of times. He kept running, but the cop chasing him went down.

It turned out the man was a purse-snatcher. Richard had already been chasing him for three blocks. If the snatcher hadn't had a gun, I would've been indicted for manslaughter. As it was, the commission read the results of my blood-alcohol test, charged me with 'negligence', and took away my licence. For good.

The cops were not amused. For a while, a bunch of them used to roust me every time we ran across each other. I spent a lot of time in the drunk tank in those days, while bruises I couldn't remember getting turned black-and-blue on my ribs and face. Probably that was where I got in the habit of not letting anybody touch me. But after a couple of years they let it ride. Then I got into trouble only when some cop got the bright idea I was working for Ginny without a licence. But that's pretty hard to prove, because I was careful and I never got caught doing the kinds of things you're not allowed to do without a licence. So far I've been able to get away with it.

So what? So now I don't drink in bars like Norman's any more. I go down to the old part of town, where they don't care what I look like or smell like as long as my money's green and my Spanish doesn't sound like it came out of a textbook in some Anglo school. When I'm not working on a case for Ginny, I'm drunk. When I am working on a case, I'm sober. She's the one friend I've got, and everybody who remembers Richard hates me. Except Alathea. She doesn't know I shot her father.

Or at least she *didn't* know. Maybe she was missing because she ran away when she found out the truth – the truth her mother hadn't told her.

I was trembling deep down inside my gut. When Lona brought the coffee, I had to hold the cup with both hands to keep from spilling it. While I drank it down, she stood right in front of me as if she was waiting until I finished to start screaming at me. But she just refilled my cup, then put the pot down where Ginny could reach it, and went to sit in the armchair beside the TV. Her hands she knotted in her lap, as if she was trying to keep them out of trouble.

When she spoke, her face was aimed at me, and her voice was brittle. 'Will you take the case?'

'Of course,' Ginny said smoothly. Her tone was sympathetic-neutral. Gentle but businesslike. The kind of tone she uses when she doesn't want a client to break down. 'But I have to ask you a lot of questions.'

'Yes.' Lona sounded small and far away. The light was so dim I couldn't even see her lips move – her voice could've come from anywhere in the room. All of a sudden, I knew for a fact it was serious. Lona wouldn't have me sitting in front of her like this if it wasn't serious. She kept the room dark so I couldn't see the need in her face.

The trembling climbed up through my bones. I had to clamp my forearms between my knees to keep from shivering.

'How long has she been gone?' Ginny asked.

'Eight days.' Her voice was as brittle as it could get. Brittleness was the only defence she had left. 'Last week Tuesday she went to school and didn't come home.'

'Did you call the school?'

'Yes. That evening. First I called some of her friends, but they didn't know where she was. They said they hadn't seen her since PE. So then I called the school. She goes to Mountain Junior High. It's just five blocks up the street. They said after fifth period she wasn't in any of her classes. Fifth period was PE. They thought she must've gotten sick and gone home. But she didn't come home. She didn't.' Lona was insistent. 'I don't have anywhere to go on Tuesdays and I was here all the time.'

'I understand,' Ginny said. As smooth as Vaseline. 'What did you do after you called the school?'

'I waited – I waited a while.' Her hands were starting to twist in her lap. One of them went up to push at her hair, but she jerked it back down again. 'As long as I could stand. Then I called the police.'

'You called the police.' Ginny was good at neutral sympathy.

I wasn't. Alcohol is a jealous comforter, and it doesn't like to let go. Right then my nerves had had all the abstinence they could stand, and now they were going to get even with me. I was going into withdrawal. I was shaking all over. My head was shivering on my neck – my brains rattled in my skull. The need was using a vice to squeeze sweat out of my forehead. My jaws hurt because I was grinding my teeth, but I had to do something to keep from groaning out loud. I had to have something to hang on to, and the only thing in reach was Lona's voice.

'Yes,' she said, in the same small brittle voice. 'I talked to Missing Persons. Sergeant Encino. I've talked to him half a dozen times, but he doesn't help. He says he wants to help, but he doesn't. The first–' for a second her voice shuddered as if she was about to lose control, but she didn't 'the first time I talked to him, he said she'd probably be home in a couple of days. He said kids are like that, they run away, and then they come home. He gets cases like that all the time. He said – he said it's department policy that they don't even start looking for runaways for three days. It's about impossible to find runaways because most of them are trying hard not to be found, and anyway most of them come home in three days. That's what he said.

'If I wanted the police to start looking for her right away, he said, I'd have to go down and swear out a complaint against her. File charges against her! He advised me not to do that. If I did, he said, the police would start looking for her right away, but if they found her they wouldn't bring her home. It's not against the law to run away and they couldn't bring her home against her will. They'd put her in some kind of juvenile shelter – he called it a JINS facility – where she could run away again whenever she wanted, and I wouldn't get her back until a judge in juvenile court ruled on my complaint.

'I said, What if she hasn't run away? What if something happened to

20

her?' But he just told me to try not to worry, and to call him when she came home.'

She dug out a handkerchief and blew her nose. Then she went on. 'So I did what he told me. I tried to wait. He's a police officer, isn't he? He works for Missing Persons, doesn't he? He knows what he's talking about, doesn't he?' She was talking to Ginny now, asking Ginny to tell her she'd done the right thing.

But after a minute, she aimed herself at me again. 'I tried to wait. But I couldn't. I called him again Wednesday, and Wednesday night. I asked him to check the hospitals. Maybe she was hurt. Maybe she was in a hospital, and the doctors couldn't call me because they didn't know who she was and she was hurt too bad to tell them.

'He told me I didn't have to worry about that. He said the hospitals always call the police when they have a patient they can't identify and they hadn't had any calls like that recently.

'I wanted to call the hospitals myself, but I didn't. I waited. I used to do a lot of waiting when Richard was alive.'

I was dripping sweat, and my head almost split open when she said his name.

'I tried to do it again, but it wasn't the same. He was a grown man. He was doing what he wanted to do. She's a child. A child!'

'What happened then?' Ginny asked. She might as well have been living in another world. Lona was talking to me. She and I were tied together in that dim room by fear and need. Ginny's questions were just cues, promptings.

'Thursday in the mail I got a letter from her.' She didn't offer to show it to us. 'It said, 'Dear Mom, I'm not going to be coming home for a while. I've got something to work out. It might take a long time. Don't worry. I'll be all right. Love Al– Al–'

But she couldn't say the name. For a long minute she didn't go on. I could feel her eyes on me, but I wasn't looking at her. I was looking at the place where the sweat was dropping from my face on to my pants and sinking in, making a dark patch in the material – just watching the sweat fall and hanging on to her voice.

'What did you do after you got the note?'

With an effort, Lona got started again. 'I– I called Sergeant Encino. What else could I do? I asked him to help me. He told me I'd have to file a complaint. Even though she's just a child.' She didn't shout, but the protest in her voice was so strong it almost made me lose my grip.

Ginny asked softly, 'Did you do it?'

'No.'

'You don't believe the note.' It was just a statement of fact.

'No!' She was so vehement I looked up at her. 'She wouldn't run away from me. Never!'

'I appreciate that, Mrs Axbrewder, but it doesn't prove anything. Can you tell me why you're so sure?'

The question didn't faze her. She'd thought about it a lot since Missing Persons had asked her the same thing. 'Because she wasn't the kind of girl who runs away from problems. If she had something bothering her, something she hadn't told me – which I don't believe – she wouldn't have to run away from it. Her father taught her–' then she faltered, but only for a second 'her father taught her to stand her ground.'

I believed her. I was in pain from head to foot – I wanted to pound my hands on my knees, just to distract myself from the hurting inside – but I believed her. If Alathea had run away because she found out about me and her father, found out her mother had never told her the truth, then the note didn't fit. She would have been angry, and it wasn't an angry note. And I couldn't think of anything else in the world she would run away from. She wasn't the kind of kid who gets herself into trouble she can't handle. She had too much common sense.

Lona was right, the note didn't fit at all. There had to be something wrong with it. Something. But I was in no condition to figure out what. I wanted more coffee – wanted to try to trick my nerves into thinking the stuff was on its way – but I couldn't control my shakes enough to even pick up the cup. Something inside me was at breaking point. If this withdrawal went on much longer, I was going to be a basket case.

Ginny must've been thinking along the same lines because she asked, 'What about the handwriting? Do you recognize it?'

'It's hers,' Lona said carefully, 'but it's different from usual. She has such neat writing, she's always gotten As in penmanship, and this is so messy. It looks like she wrote it while she was riding in a car over a rough road.'

'How about a postmark?'

'Sergeant Encino asked me about that. It was mailed right here in town.'

Suddenly I passed over the crest and the crisis began to recede. You never know if the first one is going to be the worst or the easiest, but this one was beginning to let go of me. The pain ran out of me like dirty dishwater. It left me feeling like I'd been bedridden half my life, but at least I was able to get my voice back. Without looking at Lona, or unclenching myself at all for fear the need might turn around and come back at me before I had the chance to recover, I asked her, 'How was the note signed?'

She didn't answer. I could feel the air of the living room pleading with me, raging at me, hating me, but she didn't answer.

My voice grated in my throat. 'How did she sign her name?'

A long time passed. Finally Lona pulled herself together enough to say faintly, 'Alathea.'

Alathea. That was it. Proof this whole thing was serious – that there was trouble worse than just a runaway thirteen-year-old. It was a minute or two before I realized I hadn't said what I was thinking out loud. From somewhere inside I mustered up the strength to say, 'She never called herself Alathea. Everyone else did, but she didn't. She called herself "Thea". That's what her father called her, and she never called herself anything else.'

'That's right,' Lona said. Just echoing what she heard in my voice. She knew it was true. It just hadn't occurred to her.

'All right.' Ginny said. 'I can accept that.' Back-to-business Ginny Fistoulari. 'We'll take the case on that basis. I don't know what else I'll need from you, but I'd like to start with a list of her friends. Names, addresses, phone numbers for everyone you can think of.'

'Sergeant Encino asked that. I thought you'd want a copy.' She got up and handed Ginny a sheet of paper, then went back to her chair. She never turned her face away from me the whole time. We weren't finished with each other yet.

But Ginny wasn't finished either. Maybe she didn't like being left out of the silence. She stood it for half a minute, then said, 'I've just got one more question, Mrs Axbrewder. Alathea disappeared last week Tuesday. Why did you wait more than a week to call me?'

'Sergeant Encino told me to wait and try not to worry. He told me she'd come back when she was ready. I thought I was doing what Richard – what Richard would want me to do. But then I read, in yesterday's paper – I read about that Christie girl.' She was under too much strain. Her brittleness was starting to crack. 'Since she didn't come home, I've been reading the paper every day. Every word. I've been looking for some kind of news that would tell me what happened.

'Yesterday I read about that poor Christie girl. Carol Christie. The paper said' – she was right on the edge – 'she ran away from home three months ago, and on Monday they found her body in the river. She was just thirteen, the same age as my Alathea.' Her hands were jammed into her hair, pulling at the sides of her head as if that was the only way she could keep herself from crying. 'The same age.'

I didn't have anything else to offer, so I gave her something to get mad about, hoping it would help her hang on to herself. 'But why us, Lona? Why me? If you have to have a detective, you could've called some of Richard's friends on the force. They would've referred you to someone you could trust.'

'Because you owe me!' Her sudden vehemence was as physical as a fist. 'You took my husband away from me! You owe me my daughter back!'

'We'll do our best.' Ginny came between Lona and me as if she were afraid we were about to start hitting each other. 'There are no guarantees in this business, but we'll do everything we can. Which is more than the police are doing.

'Now.' Ginny was on her feet, and I joined her. Force of habit. I didn't actually feel strong enough to stand. And I sure didn't want to tower over Lona like that. It was a cheap advantage, and with her I didn't want any cheap advantages. But I've been following Ginny so long now, taking orders from her, I hardly ever think about it any more. 'There's one thing we have to settle before we can get started. My fee.'

'There doesn't have to be any fee,' I said, ashamed money had ever been mentioned.

'Mrs Axbrewder has to pay something,' Ginny snapped. 'If she doesn't, I can't call her my client. And if she isn't my client, I don't have any legal standing. Anybody who wants to can tell me to stuff it.'

There was no help for it. Lona was looking at me, and I had to say, 'She's right, Lona.'

She didn't say anything for a long minute. When she found her voice again, she wasn't angry any more, just weak and helpless and at the end of her rope. 'I don't have much,' she said. 'Richard's pension is so small. And my job – I work as much as I can, cleaning house for some of the neighbours. It's hardly enough to pay for clothes.' Then she said, 'I have a hundred dollars.'

Ginny said, 'Fifty will be plenty.' Fifty bucks would just about pay two days' rent on her office. 'If I get in trouble with the commission I can always tell them it was only an advance.'

The commission frowns on private investigators who work cheap. The same kind of argument doctors and lawyers use – people who work cheap are presumed to be shoddy and unscrupulous. Unprofessional. If I still had a licence, I'd be in danger of losing it twice a day.

Lona shuffled out of the room and came back a minute later with the money. Ginny took it without counting it and gave her a receipt. Before I could think of anything else to say, Ginny and I were out on the walk again and Lona had closed the door behind us. In the whole time I hadn't had one good look at her face.

Ginny made straight for the car, but I dawdled along for a moment. Though the sun was getting hotter, in the shade of the trees it was still bearable. I wasn't eager to sear my butt on the vinyl of the Olds. And I wasn't satisfied, either. There were things I needed to know.

'All right,' I said at Ginny's back. 'Spill it.'

She stopped, then turned around, looking blank. 'Spill what?'

But she couldn't fool me with that. Her face has more than one kind of blank, and this wasn't the right kind. Besides, she'd turned around too quickly – like she was expecting me to say something.

'You know what I'm talking about.'

She came back toward me a couple of steps. 'When you've been drinking I never know what you're talking about.'

That was a cheap shot, and she knew it. As soon as she said it, she winced in regret. But I sloughed it off. It just confirmed she knew something she wasn't telling. So I said, 'The hell you don't. You're scared of this case, Fistoulari. You're scared of it because of me. You're afraid something about it is going to get to me. I want to know why.'

'You heard her.' Ginny nodded at the house. 'She didn't tell me any secrets.'

'Yeah,' I growled. 'First you're worried about me, and then you won't tell me why. If you've got so goddamn little confidence in me, why didn't you just leave me out of it? You don't need me to find a runaway.'

Now she came close and looked right up at me. 'She's your niece. You've got a right to be involved. Besides, I thought you'd want–'

'Don't say it. Of course I want to help find her.' For a minute I glanced around the neighbourhood, looking for suggestions. Then I locked on to her again. Something about that broken nose of hers did funny things to my insides. Sometimes I wanted to kiss it so bad I had to grit my teeth. Now I wanted to hit it. 'Maybe I'm asking the wrong question. Let's be professional about it. It's just a case. Like any other case. There's just one thing wrong with it. You don't do missing persons. Why start now?'

'She's your–'

I didn't let her finish. 'Don't do me any favours.'

That got through to her. All of a sudden, her eyes went cold and narrow, and her nostrils flared. Just for a second, her voice had the soft hot sound of an acetylene torch. 'That's cute, Axbrewder. All right, you want it? You got it. I read the papers, too. I read about Carol Christie. There's one little fact your sister-in-law neglected to mention. According to her parents, Carol Christie was an excellent swimmer.'

An excellent swimmer. Oh, hell. You don't have to be an excellent swimmer to be safe in the Flat River. If you're half as tall as I am, you don't have to know how to swim at all.

'When a reporter asked the cops if they had any reason to think she might've been killed,' she went on, 'they didn't deny it.'

I scanned the neighbourhood one more time. It still looked like the kind of place where nothing ever happened. It was too tidy, and there was too much sunshine.

I turned my back on it and followed Ginny to the Olds.

Chapter Three

While she started the engine, I pulled down the sunshade to give my aching head a little protection. Then, more to let her know I was still with her than to satisfy my curiosity, I asked, 'Where do we go from here?'

She glanced over at me. 'How long has it been since you had a full meal?'

That was the kind of question she usually asked me. I shrugged. She didn't need an answer.

As we pulled away from the kerb, she muttered, 'You ought to be more careful. If you don't get regular meals, it'll stunt your growth.'

I suppose I should've at least grinned. She was just trying to clear the air. But I didn't have the energy for it. The little strength I had I was using to think about thirteen-year-old girls who end up dead in the river for no good reason. As far as I knew, there was zero connection between Carol Christie and Alathea, but just knowing something like that could happen to my niece gave me a cold pain in the stomach.

And maybe there was a connection. In this business, things like that happen all the time. Accidents happen by themselves – crimes have a way of tying themselves together. I was in no mood to grin at bad jokes, even when I knew why Ginny was making them.

We didn't have to go far to find food. In a few blocks, we were in one of those small business sections that looks like someone just dropped a bunch of white concrete bricks out of the sky and ran away before anybody could catch him and make him clean it up. Pawnshops, grocery stores, insurance offices, and gas stations stood facing every which way. With all that sun on them, they were blinding – I could hardly tell them apart. But Ginny's eyes handle brightness better than mine, and after a couple of minutes she pulled into a Muchoburger that was just opening up. We went inside, ordered cheeseburgers and about a gallon of coffee, then sat down at one of the tables.

We didn't talk while we waited for the food, and after that I was too busy eating half-raw hamburger and the vitamin pills that Ginny handed out like my life depended on them. When she'd had enough to eat, she got down to business.

'We need to talk to this Sergeant Encino. But he probably doesn't come on duty until mid-afternoon, so we've got five or six hours to do our homework. I suppose we could start with this list of Alathea's friends, but I'd rather wait until they get home from school, so they can't check what they're saying with each other – just in case there's something going on that they want to keep secret.'

I nodded. My stomach didn't much like what I was putting in it. But I liked it better than the dread.

'Any suggestions?'

She was just being polite. She knew what our choices were as well as I did. But she was usually polite when we were just starting a case. That was generally the only time when she wasn't way ahead of me. As soon as she had a handle on what was happening, she wouldn't waste time being polite.

Anyway, I owed her some politeness myself. And if she was giving me a choice, I wanted to use it. There were some things I wasn't ready for yet, so I said, 'We might as well go to the school while we're out this way. It's closer than your office.'

That must have been what she wanted to do herself. She said, 'Good enough,' and went to pay the check. I finished up, drank down as much of that coffee as I could stand. Then we got in the car and drove to Mountain Junior High over on the corner of Mission and Natividad.

It wasn't the best junior high in the city – the best ones are called middle schools – but it was far enough from the old part of town to be better than the worst. It didn't look like a converted warehouse, and it wasn't cramped into a plot of ground too small to hold that many kids, and it didn't have a chain link fence around it. In fact, it had several buildings built around one another, and there was a small gymnasium and a ragged playing field. It was the sort of place where some kids would be perfectly happy – and some would get started on drugs.

We went in and found our way to the main office, where Ginny showed her ID to a secretary and asked to see the principal. The secretary informed us the principal was 'out'. But when she heard why we were here, she told us the vice-principal was really the person we ought to talk to. Vice-Principal Rumsfeld was 'in'.

She was a taut little woman with a severe hairstyle and an air of terminal fatigue, worn out by burdens. You could tell by the tension compressing her lips that she was responsible for 'discipline', and had long since used up whatever tolerance she was born with.

Her office suited her. It was stark and forbidding, and the chairs were uncomfortable. Probably in her career she'd seen thousand of kids squirming on those chairs. Probably Ginny and I didn't look much different to her than those kids.

'You want to know about Alathea Axbrewder.' She sounded like a blunt instrument. 'There's nothing I can tell you. She came to school last week Tuesday, but didn't attend any of her classes after fifth period. That was physical education. She hasn't been here since. In the old days, we had truant officers who tracked down runaways, but now the police are supposed to handle it. They do a poor job.'

'What about Alathea herself?' At times like this, Ginny was a model of diplomacy. She could be firm, even insistent, without sounding pushy or irritating people.

'What do you want to know about her? She was a good student, bright and pleasant. Her teachers liked her, and she didn't get into trouble. She seemed more grown up than most girls her age. That happens quite often when a child loses a parent. The added pressure forces them to mature more rapidly.'

'She doesn't sound like the kind of girl who runs away.'

Vice-Principal Rumsfeld's lips got tighter, and her hairdo suddenly seemed even more severe. 'What kind of girl is that, Ms Fistoulari? All kinds of children run away.'

'At thirteen?'

'They run away because they are in pain. No one is immune to pain – not even children.'

The stiffness in her voice made me revise my opinion of her. She wasn't the Wicked Witch of the West. She was tired because she was the school's disciplinarian, and she didn't like her job. I said softly, 'That bothers you.'

'It *concerns* me, Mr Axbrewder. A society that can't care for its children is in very serious trouble. I do what is in my power here, but I'm a poor substitute for a healthy family or a constructive sense of life. When a child like Alathea runs away, she places herself entirely beyond my reach.'

'Ms Rumsfeld,' I said, 'Alathea didn't run away.'

She looked at me sharply. 'Do you have some reason to believe that?'

'She's my niece. I know her pretty well.'

'Your confidence is misplaced. Alathea isn't the first young girl to run away, and won't be the last. I admit that in the past most runaways were boys. Perhaps as boys they believed they were expected to be adventuresome. But in recent years, more and more girls have done the same. Twelve- and thirteen-year-olds, Mr Axbrewder.'

'How recently is that?' Ginny asked.

'I can't say – I've only been aware of it for the last year or so. Fortunately, Alathea is the first from our school, but other junior high and middle schools have had more than their share.'

'Can you give us any details?' Ginny was groping – but that's normal. At the beginning of a case, you have to look under every rock you find.

'I don't have any,' Ms Rumsfeld said. 'I don't see what possible use they could be to you, but if you feel compelled to look for them, the school board may be willing to help you.' She was dismissing us. 'In a case as serious as a runaway, the board receives copies of all reports as a matter of course. In fact, they have copies of all our files on every student.'

Ginny and I stood up. Ginny thanked her for her time and turned to open the door. I said, 'When we find out what happened to her, we'll let you know.'

'Don't find out what happened to her,' the vice-principal snapped. 'Find her. Bring her back.'

'We'll try,' Ginny said. She ushered me out of the door, and we went back to the Olds.

Sitting in the car, she said, 'Maybe she did run away.'

'Maybe none of them ran away,' I countered.

After a minute she said, 'Right.' She put the Olds in gear, and we headed in the direction of her office.

Fistoulari Investigations is in the Murchison Building, one of the three buildings in Puerta del Sol that stands more than five storeys tall. It's on the other side of the city from Mountain Junior High, but the new freeway makes it fairly easy to get to. We had the Olds parked in the basement garage and were on our way up in the elevator before noon.

We hadn't been working on it very long, but so far I had the distinct impression that we weren't getting anywhere. If something had happened to Alathea, it was a secret, and we didn't know who could tell us what it was. So we had to start trying to eliminate the obvious.

The Murchison Building isn't cheap, but it isn't as expensive as it looks. It sits in what used to be the business centre of Puerta del Sol, a good three miles down Paseo Grande from the ritzy real estate where the banks live these days. The owners have always had trouble attracting tenants, and the place is never more than two-thirds occupied. Which is why Ginny can afford to operate there, along with a handful of half-reputable lawyers, some chancy doctors, and a few insurance companies that may or may not have any assets. The elevator and the halls are carpeted, but the lighting is bad so you can't see that they don't clean very often. Too many of the walls have the kind of smudges you would expect to find in places where people get arrested regularly – the kind sweaty palms make while the rest of the body is being frisked.

But Ginny's office is in good condition. FISTOULARI INVESTIGATIONS is neatly lettered on the door, and inside the air-conditioning works. The waiting room has a plastic potted plant, a side table covered with old magazines, and only three chairs. But three chairs is about all it needs – most people won't even bother to wait in a private investigator's office if someone else is already there. And the office itself is at least comfortable. It holds Ginny's desk and files, a large sofa, a couple of roomy chairs, two phones, and a picture window looking out towards the valley of the Flat River. The carpet is clean because I keep it that way. The walls are bare except for a couple of framed diplomas and the display copy of Ginny's licence – all part of making the place look 'professional'.

Fortunately, there was no one in the waiting room so she didn't have to juggle clients. We went into the office, and I started up the electric coffeepot while she went through her mail. After she'd read it all – and thrown most of it into the wastebasket – we went to work.

On the phones.

Ginny called the school board and set up an appointment to see the chairman the following afternoon. Then she went down the list of Alathea's friends, asking the parents' permission to visit their homes and talk to their kids. Calling for permission is a nice touch, when you can afford it – forestalls a certain number of complaints to the commission. I used the other phone to eliminate at least some of the obvious.

Didn't take either of us very long. I'd never worked on a runaway before, but I knew a place that was in the business of telling people like me where to look. Tel-a-Help. Basically, it's a referral agency for all the social services in San Reno County, including state and federal bureaus. They gave me five different numbers – The State Bureau of Children's Services, the National Runaway Hotline, the National Drug

Abuse Hotline, the San Reno County Crisis Hotline, and the police. I thanked them politely before crossing the police off my list.

I wanted to cross off the National Drug Abuse number, too – but I didn't. Couldn't afford to. It was one of the obvious possibilities I had to check, and I had a sick feeling about it. So I did that number first. It's one of those toll-free 800 numbers. The way my head felt, you'd have thought I was about to pass out from anoxia – but I gave them my spiel and listened to their answer. 'We're a confidential information service, Mr Axbrewder. We can't give out the names of the young people who call us. But we always urge runaways to call their parents, and no reputable drug treatment facility or social service agency in the country would accept a thirteen-year-old girl without making some effort to contact her parents.' When I hung up, I was practically gasping for breath.

The Bureau of Children's Services and the Crisis Hotline gave me variations on the same answer – confidentiality, always urging the runaways to get in touch with their parents, etc. In five minutes I was starting to understand Lona's outrage at the new laws and the public machinery that exist for the 'benefit' of runaways – which seems to mean, 'protect them from their parents'.

But the National Runaway Hotline – another 800 number – was an improvement. Part of their business was to pass messages back and forth between kids and parents. And whenever possible they got the name of any runaway who called so that they could at least assure the parents their child was safe. All the names and messages were fed into a computer so that they could be retrieved instantly.

No one named Alathea – or Thea – Axbrewder had ever called the National Runaway Hotline.

I almost hung up – but snatched back the receiver and asked, 'Did you ever get a call from a girl named Carol Christie?'

That was the wrong thing to say. All at once the voice at the other end of the line turned distant and suspicious. 'Why do you ask, Mr. Axbrewder? Is she a relative of yours?'

I didn't have any other way out, so I said, 'She's dead. I'm worried about Alathea, and I'm trying to find some kind of pattern.'

The voice was silent for a minute. Then it said carefully, 'There's no Carol Christie in the computer.'

'All right,' I said. 'It was a dumb question. Tell me this. Out of all the kids who run away, how many call you? What percentage?'

'We don't have any reliable figures, but our best estimate is only about twenty per cent. We're not as well known as we need to be.'

'Thanks.'

I hung up the phone, looked at Ginny. In spite of the AC I was sweating. But I wasn't due for another crisis yet – and if one was coming there wasn't anything I could do about it anyway, so I just tried to shove it out of my mind. When Ginny put down her phone, I asked, 'What've you got?'

She pushed her list away from her. 'We're going to be busy this evening. How about you?'

'Nothing.' I sounded disgusted to myself.

'Relax,' she said. 'If you found her this fast, you wouldn't know what to do with yourself for the rest of the day.' She was jollying me – but her eyes had that worried look in them again. She gave me the impression that she was asking herself how long I could hold out without a drink.

I got up, went and faced her across the desk, and said, 'I don't like it when you look at me like that. Let's go talk to Carol Christie's parents.'

I was half hoping she had something better in mind. I wasn't feeling any readier to visit them than when the idea first occurred to me. It was like calling the Drug Abuse Hotline – something in me was afraid of it. But we had to do it. We were looking for some kind of pattern, and we wouldn't know if there was any connection between Carol Christie and Alathea unless we checked it out.

Ginny knew that as well as I did. She said, 'Good idea,' and pushed herself out of her chair. She looked in Tuesday's paper for the names of the Christies, then got their address out of the phone book. Five minutes later, we were back in the Olds.

The Christies lived quite a ways out, in what they call the North Valley. Puerta del Sol lays down its inhabitants horizontally instead of stacking them vertically, so it's a sprawling place. And the way the population's growing these days, there are suburbs and even industries sitting on ground that was neglected dirt ten years ago. The city spreads in all directions, but mostly north and south along the valley of the Flat River, where water is a little easier to come by.

Mr and Mrs Christie lived all the way out at the northern tip of the sprawl. Where the cowboy-money lives. Half the people out there wear old Stetsons and plaid shirts and faded jeans and dusty boots, and if you met them on the street you wouldn't know they're solid gold on the hoof. Most of them probably get their money from things like real estate, but the way they dress you would think they got rich just by looking so by-God Western. Before we were within five miles of the

Christies', every house we passed was an ersatz ranch, with a split rail fence, three acres of ground, and two horses.

When we got to where we were going, we found that the Christies ran a stables, complete with riding lessons, trails, and about thirty of the mangiest-looking horses I'd ever seen. They used a converted horse trailer for an office. When we went inside, we found Mary Christie there, working on a set of books.

She looked up as we came in and said, 'Howdy, folks. What can we do for y'all?' Her cowboy-twang was stretched pretty thin over an accent that sounded like it probably came from Boston. But she was dressed right in not-too-new, not-too-clean, let's-go-muck-out-the-stalls clothes, with a red bandanna knotted around her neck.

Ginny said, 'Mrs Christie?' Her professional voice made it sound like she had every right in the world to be standing there asking personal questions. 'I'm Ginny Fistoulari.' She flipped her ID out of her purse and showed Mrs Christie the photocopy of her licence. 'This is Mr Axbrewder. We'd like to ask you and your husband a few questions.'

It didn't take much to make Mary Christie forget about horses. Ginny's ID was enough. She practically jumped to her feet, went to a window behind her and jerked out, 'John!' There was an edge in her voice that sounded like panic at first, but I put it down to strain. It was only two days ago that her daughter had turned up dead. Then she came and stood in front of us with her arms clutched across her stomach as if she wanted to hide it. 'Questions about what? What do you want?' Her twang had deserted her.

Ginny said evenly, 'We'd like to talk to you about your daughter, Carol.'

'Why?' She was as jumpy as a hop-head. 'What has it got to do with you?' Then she was at the window again. 'John!'

Now I knew it wasn't just strain. Mrs Christie was afraid of something.

From outside, a man's voice – real cowboy, this time – answered, 'Ah'm comin'.' Ten seconds later he was in the trailer with us.

He was tall and rangy, like a cowboy is supposed to be, with a grizzled, weather-bitten face and a cigarette stuck in his teeth. His battered old hat was pulled down tight on his head, probably so it wouldn't fall off when he was riding. He scanned Ginny and me, then asked slowly, 'Now, what's all this-here ruckus about?'

'They want to know about Carol,' Mary Christie said quickly – too quickly. 'They want to ask questions about her.'

At that, her husband's eyes narrowed until he was practically squinting at us. Deliberately he took the cigarette out of his mouth, threw it through the doorway. Then he said, 'Naw, they don't want to ask no questions. They was just leavin'.' If he was worried about the fact I was three inches taller and seventy pounds heavier than he was, he didn't show it.

But I didn't need Ginny to tell me this was no time for muscle. I just stood my ground and let her handle it.

She said, 'We have good reason for asking.' If it came down to a bluff, she could match John Christie any day. 'We don't want to pry into anything that doesn't concern us, but we're working on a case that's remarkably similar to Carol's.' Remarkably similar, hell. Both girls were thirteen – period. 'If you help us, we might be able to prevent the same thing from happening again.'

She made it sound practically inevitable. But Mr Christie wasn't having any. 'You said one thing right,' he drawled. 'You ain't gonna pry. There ain't no case on Carol. She was a good li'l girl, and you ain't gonna dig up no dirt on her. If other folks want to let their young'uns screw around, it ain't no concern of mine.'

Ginny faced him squarely. 'Nobody said anything about dirt. That was your idea.' Then she asked harshly, 'If Carol was such a good swimmer, how did she happen to drown?'

Christie felt that. For a second, his eyes went out of focus. His hands twitched as if he was getting ready to swing at Ginny. I shifted into position to block him. But instead of moving, he just said in a dead voice, 'Get the hell outta here.'

Ginny considered him for a moment, then turned to Mary Christie. The woman was staring back at her with something like nausea in her face. Sharply Ginny said, 'All right. Let it happen to other girls. Why should you care? There's just one thing I have to know.' She knew how to be tough. 'Did she write to you at all after she ran away? Was there a note?'

John Christie barked, 'Mary!' For a minute she just stood there, squirming with indecision and grief. Then, abruptly, she jerked open one of the desk drawers, fumbled for a sheet of paper, and handed it to Ginny.

Ginny gave it to me without looking at it. If John Christie wanted it back, it was safer with me. I put it in my pocket.

'Thank you, Mrs Christie,' Ginny said softly. 'I hope you won't regret helping us.' Then she went to the door. 'Come on, Brew. Mr Christie thinks we should leave.'

I followed her out, half expecting Christie to jump me as I went past him. But he didn't. He slammed the door behind us, and a second later we heard him yelling, 'God damn it, woman! You want the whole fuckin' world to know?' We could hear him until we got into the Olds and shut the doors.

I didn't say anything. I just took out the note, and we looked at it together.

It said, 'Dear Mom and Dad, I have to go away for a while. I have a problem, and I have to take care of it myself. It might take a long time. Don't worry about me. Love, Carol.'

It was written on half a sheet of good twenty-pound bond, but the handwriting was a mess.

Chapter Four

We didn't say anything. We didn't have to. We both knew what to do next. Ginny started up the Olds, and we headed back into the city. Hurrying. We wanted to get to Lona.

It was after four o'clock when we reached her house, so we didn't waste any time. Ginny was better at this kind of thing than I was. I waited in the car while she went to talk to Lona.

Even that way, it took a while. Lona didn't want to let go of her note. It was the last tangible thing she had from Alathea. But we needed the original – a copy wouldn't do us any good. I was relieved to see it in Ginny's hand when she came back to the Olds.

With her sitting beside me, we compared the notes. The similarity of the wording made my stomach ache, but Ginny was looking at other things. She compared the writing quickly, pointed out that the ink and scripts were different, then started to examine the paper.

Lona's note was written on half a sheet of twenty-pound bond.

Both sheets had been neatly torn – not cut – along one edge.

When Ginny held them up to the sun, we could see that they both had the same watermark.

I said, 'Sonofabitch.' Something deep in my chest was trembling. I was overdue for another withdrawal crisis.

'This doesn't prove anything,' Ginny said stiffly. 'There's a lot of this kind of paper around. It's a big company. It doesn't prove anything unless these notes came from the same sheet.' She put the notes up against the sun again, then said, 'No chance. Look what happens when I put the torn edges together.'

I looked. The watermarks were facing in opposite directions. The top third of the mark on Lona's note was cut off – and it wasn't completed anywhere on the other sheet.

'Terrific.' I could taste bile in my mouth. The lining of my stomach wanted alcohol. Wanted to be numb. 'Two thirteen-year-olds run away from home and write notes that say almost exactly the same thing on the same kind of paper, with the same kind of bad handwriting. Of course it's just a coincidence. Why didn't I think of that?'

'I didn't say it was a coincidence,' she replied with elaborate patience. Just letting Axbrewder know she wasn't senile yet. 'I said it wasn't proof.' Then she grinned – a shark's grin, eager and dangerous. 'That's the difference between us and the police. We don't need proof.' She threw the Olds into gear. 'Let's go talk to Encino.'

We were on the trail now – I could see it in her eyes.

I left it to her. I was thinking about the Christies. They were scared about something – and anything that could worry John Christie would probably frighten Lona to death.

We went down Mission, then crossed over on Gypsum until we hit Paseo Grande and turned right. A couple of miles down Paseo Grande we came to the new Municipal Building – the pride of the mayor, the joy of half a dozen construction companies, the flower of a couple of architects, and the treasure of the bank that floated the loan. I didn't know anyone else who liked it.

From the outside, it looks like a country club for millionaires. An ordinary citizen can no more walk in there and feel comfortable than fly to the moon. All those fountains and flowerbeds might've been a good idea, but unfortunately the main part of the building hangs over the fountains and flowers and walkways. A square mountain of white concrete leans on the back of your neck – from some angles you can't even see what holds it up – so by the time you get to the doors and start climbing to wherever you have to go, you already feel intimidated. And of course there's no parking. Official cars have a private garage – ordinary citizens have to scramble for what they can get.

We were lucky – we only had to walk a couple of blocks.

Inside, there isn't a scrap of carpet or one warm soft colour in the whole place. It looks like a brand-new abattoir. Since there aren't any windows, and the blank fluorescent lighting is always the same, you can't tell whether it's day or night.

I suppose I should've been used to it. I'd been in the City Gaol, up on the top floor of the police department wing, at least a couple of times. But I was always at a disadvantage here. I could never remember the names of the cops who rousted me when I was drunk. I couldn't remember anything about them, except they always looked short. But they knew who I was. The whole situation gave me a definite paranoid feeling.

But I figured I should be pretty safe in Missing Persons. They didn't have any reason to know me. So I just kept my coat buttoned and my hands at my sides, hiding the .45 under my left arm, and followed Ginny – trying to ignore the fact that I could feel another withdrawal attack coming on.

The sergeant at the front desk issued us passes and told us where to go in the dull mumble of a man who'd spent too many years repressing a secret yen to *really* tell people where to go. We did what he told us and a couple of corridors later we were at a glass door. The glass was safety plate with steel mesh sandwiched into it, and it said MISSING PERSONS across the top. We went in.

A Formica counter stood so close to the entrance that the door almost hit it when it opened. Behind the counter, there were four desks and a row of filing cabinets. That was all. Missing Persons wasn't a very big item in the police budget.

Three cops sat at the desks, two women and a man. The man was a sergeant, so he out-ranked the women. Of course, they made us wait. Cops always make you wait as long as they can. It's in the Officers Handbook. Eventually, however, one of the women, Policewoman Rand, asked us what we wanted. Ginny asked for Sergeant Encino, using her I'm-an-important-citizen-don't-mess-with-me voice. The man found himself off his butt and standing in front of us faster than he wanted to.

He was short, barely tall enough to stare at Ginny's clavicles. He had dark olive skin that complemented his dark blue uniform, and his close-cut black hair was so tidy that you would think he trained it with a whip. His moustache was assertive but not aggressive. And he had Chicano eyes – sad, world-weary, and arrogant. Sure enough, both the name-tag pinned over his left shirt pocket and the ID clipped to his right shirt pocket said, 'Sgt Raul Encino, Missing Persons'.

Ginny introduced herself, flashed her licence, mentioned my name. Encino looked back at her with his face blank. That's also in the Handbook – treat everyone like two of them and a sandwich would be just about right for lunch. 'What can I do for you?' He had just enough accent to make what he said sound more interesting than it really was.

'Information,' Ginny said crisply. 'We're trying to find a young girl named Alathea Axbrewder. Her mother reported her missing eight days ago.'

Encino's expression was perfect, as noncommittal as a rock. 'Mrs

Axbrewder chose to make no complaint. We look for her daughter, of course. Each patrol officer has a description. But without a complaint–' He gave us a delicate Chicano shrug. 'You understand, it is not against the law to run away from home. The girl is a minor, so we have our eyes open for her. But in a city so big as Puerta del Sol, we are unlikely to find her. Also she has possibly left the city. The sheriff's office has been informed. What more do you want?'

With just a hint of sarcasm, Ginny said, 'You assume she ran away.'

'Why not? As I have said, the city is big. Girls disappear each week. Do you think she has been kidnapped? That is doubtful. For what purpose? There has been no demand for ransom.'

That was true enough. Any hint of kidnapping, any hint at all, and this whole situation would've been different. For one thing, Lona would've had the FBI camped in her living room. But that didn't faze Ginny. In the same light-acid tone, she said, 'I don't know whether I'm talking about kidnapping or not. I haven't gotten that far yet. What I'm interested in right now is thirteen-year-old girls who disappear and then turn up dead.' She was trying to irritate Encino, nag him into defending himself. Maybe spring loose some spontaneous information.

I could see the muscles along his jaw tighten, but he didn't change his ground. 'Is Alathea Axbrewder dead?'

'Carol Christie is.'

He blinked. As far as the rest of his face was concerned, he was sound asleep. 'Of what interest is Carol Christie to you?'

'There's a connection between her and Alathea.'

'Are the parents of Carol Christie your clients?'

Ginny could've refused to answer that. She had a right to protect her client. But I guess she didn't see any point to it. She said, 'I've been retained by Lona Axbrewder.'

'Then the death of Carol Christie is of no concern to you.'

'I said there's a connection.' Ginny let herself start to sound angry. She took out the notes and put them down on the counter in front of Encino. 'Both Alathea and Carol wrote to their parents after disappearing. If you look at them, you'll see that they were written on the same kind of paper. The sheets were torn in half the same way. What they say is almost identical, and the handwriting is similar.'

'That's most ingenious.' Encino didn't even glance at the notes. 'Unfortunately the truth remains. Carol Christie's death can be of no concern to you. The rights of your client do not include her. Mr Christie and his wife desire privacy.'

'Says who?'

'Their wishes were made known to the investigating officer, Detective-Lieutenant Acton.'

Investigating officer, huh? Ginny was getting somewhere. Now we knew there was enough wrong with Carol Christie's death to interest the cops.

But she didn't stop to chew it over. She had Encino backing up, and she kept at him.

'That's wonderful. The Christies don't want people to know what really happened to their daughter, so the cops clamp a lid on it. Having money is good for something after all. I just wonder what you and Acton are getting out of it.'

Encino's composure split for a second. *'Hija de la puta.'* Before he could get it back, I reached for him. I was going to knot my fist in the front of his nice blue uniform and shake him up good. But Ginny stopped me with an elbow that almost caved in my ribs. I could feel blood pounding in my face.

The sergeant had his blankness back in place, but he couldn't keep the rasp out of his voice. 'Go away. You Anglos, you're all the same. A girl runs away and is later found dead. There's an investigation, and everything is kept with great propriety, even from the papers, to avoid distress for the family. But someone hires private investigators, and because they can't do their jobs they accuse the police. It's like that everywhere. And why? Because the girl is white. Anglo. If a Chicano girl runs away, and the mother asks for help, you Anglos say, "What do you expect? Look for her in the brothels." And if that Chicano girl is found dead, then the papers print every rumour they hear about her, true or false.' His sneer twisted his whole face. 'Go away. You interfere with my work.'

My pulse was still racing, but I heard him. I picked up the notes, pulled open the door, said to Ginny, 'Come on.' But she was really mad now. Leaning over the counter, she thrust her face at Encino. 'I work for whoever asks me,' she said very softly. 'I don't have any control over who asks. I just take whatever they ask and give it my best shot. That's *my* work.'

Encino jerked his head contemptuously. *'Muy bravo.'*

I took Ginny's arm, dragged her out into the corridor and shut the door behind us. She threw off my hand. Stalked along for a minute in silence. Then she said, 'That sonofabitch.'

I said, 'He has a point.'

'He has orders. Somebody told him to put a lid on Carol Christie. It's not my fault he doesn't like it.' Then she asked, 'How come you're so sympathetic all of a sudden? Two minutes ago you wanted to take his head off for him.'

I didn't have a good answer to that, so I just said, 'I spend a lot of time in the old part of town. Probably he's a good cop.'

'A good cop,' she snorted. She didn't say anything more until we got into the elevator. Then she muttered, 'You big ape, you've got to learn to keep your temper.'

'Dear God,' I said. 'Did I lose my temper? I'm pitifully sorry. It's never happened to me before.'

She said, 'Aw, shut up.' But she didn't sound so angry any more. After a minute, she asked, 'What was that he called me?'

'*Hija de la puta.* Daughter of a whore.'

She considered that briefly, then grinned. 'It sounds nastier in Spanish.' When the elevator doors opened, she led the way out.

Following her toward the exit, I had a wild urge to put my arms around her and kiss the back of her neck. But when we walked out into the late afternoon, the sun hit me in the eyes like a hammer. Suddenly my head was reeling for a drink. It was coming, and there was nothing I could do about it. Except get a drink. My nerves pleaded for the stuff. *Get a drink get a drink get a drink.* Feel the alcohol flow like bliss through the sore lining of my stomach straight into my blood.

Usually when I go sober, I have three big withdrawal crises – along with half a dozen or so smaller ones – before my body gives up on pain and starts looking for other arguments. So far this time I'd only had one. One coming on, and after that at least one more to go. With the sun in my eyes, and my brain aching, I didn't think I was going to make it.

I didn't realize I was just standing there with my fingers clamped over my face until Ginny came back for me. She put her hands on my arm. 'It's that bad?'

'All of a sudden. Doesn't usually come on this fast.'

She said, 'Is there anything I can do?' But she knew there wasn't. She'd done everything anybody could do when she came looking for me in the first place.

I said, 'Take me home.'

She shook my arm. 'No chance. We've got all those friends of Alathea's to go see, remember? We're late already.'

I said it again. 'Take me home.'

'Brew,' she whispered, 'I don't want to leave you alone.'

With an effort, I pulled my hands off my face. I must've looked pretty fierce, because she winced. 'I want to be alone. It's bad enough when I'm alone. This morning was easy. It's going to get worse. Do you think I like having you watch me fall apart?'

That reached her. It didn't ease the tight worry in her face, but it got me what I wanted. She took me home.

By the time she got me up to my apartment, the pressure in my skull was squeezing sweat out of my face like beads of thirst. I shook like a cripple. It was all I could do to get across the room and sit down on the convertible couch I use for a bed.

This one was going to be a sonofabitch.

Had it ever been this bad before? I couldn't remember. Probably not. Every time is always the worst.

Ginny sat down beside me for a while. She looked like she wanted to hold my hand. 'Are you going to be all right?'

From somewhere, I dredged up the energy to say, 'There's nothing here. I never keep the stuff in my apartment.'

'That isn't what I asked. I asked you if you're going to be all right.'

I said, 'You go on.' If she didn't leave soon I was going to scream. 'Talk to Alathea's friends. I'm going to sit here. As long as I have to. Then I'll get something to eat. Then I'll go to bed. Pick me up in the morning.'

'All right.' She didn't like it, but she swallowed it. 'I'll make sure the answering service knows where I am.' A minute later she was gone.

A minute after that, I wanted to cry out, *Ginny*!

But this mess was one I'd made for myself, and I was going to have to live with it. So I just sat where I was, and watched the sunlight in the room get dimmer.

Soon there were red hot bugs crawling along my nerves, ticks and chiggers and cockroaches of need, and at one point I thought I could hear high-pitched mewling sounds coming from somewhere in the vicinity of my face. But I just sat where I was and waited. Waited for the sun to set. Waited for night. There was a cure for this, and I was going to go get it. Never mind what I'd told Ginny. I was going to go as soon as it was dark. As soon as I recovered enough control over myself to move.

I hung on for the sake of the dark. After a while there was no more light in the room, and the pressure eased a bit. Not much – this was going to be a long one. But enough so that I could tell my arms and legs what to do with some hope of having them listen to me.

I lurched into the kitchen and drank what felt like about a gallon of water. Then I left my apartment, struggled down the long stairs to the street, and went shambling in the direction of the old part of town.

Looking for that cure.

Chapter Five

The cure I had in mind was an old Mestizo named Manolo. Somewhere in the old part of town, he would be sitting alone in the corner of a bar, sipping a glass of anisette, and looking for all the world like the last remains of some long-dead grandee's noble family. He'd be sitting there like a sleepwalker, and if you saw him you'd be afraid to wake him up for fear the shock might fuddle what was left of his wits. But all the time he'd be as alert as a cat, soaking up little bits and hints of rumours, facts, information, as if he took them in through his pores. He knew a world of secrets. And if you asked him the right questions – or if you asked them the right way, or maybe if he trusted you for some reason – he'd tell you one or two of them.

There was a good chance he'd be able to tell me the secret of Carol Christie, and I knew how to ask.

I had an idea in my head that made my nerves crawl as bad as the DTs, and this was the only way I knew to check it out.

I'm not like Ginny – I'm not a puzzle solver. For instance, it might never have occurred to me to compare the watermarks of those two notes. My brain doesn't work that way. I get where I'm going – wherever that is – by intuition and information. In a city like Puerta del Sol, there are a lot of information dealers, and I know at least half of them. And I'm not talking about stool pigeons, punks who shill for the cops.

Like most independent businessmen, old Manolo was a specialist. Next to el Señor himself, Manolo knew more than anybody in the city about who's doing what to whom and how in the grubby world of drugs. The cops could put away most of the pushers in the state if they just knew what old Manolo knew.

I was doing my best not to think too much about Alathea. I didn't dare. I was already too jittery – if I stopped to consider what I was thinking, I might not be able to stop myself until I ended up at the bottom of a bottle somewhere. No, all I wanted to know was how a good swimmer ends up drowning in the Flat River.

It was the kind of question you had to ask at night. People like old Manolo don't exist during the day. When the sun comes up, they evaporate, and all you can find of them is what they leave behind – a rank, sodden body snoring away like a ruin on a pallet full of fleas somewhere, as empty of answers as an old beer can.

But I didn't get the chance to ask. I wasn't more than five blocks away from my apartment, just turning on to Eighth Street on my way toward the Hegira and all the other bars where Manolo might be drinking his anisette, when things started to get out of hand.

Down from the corner of Eighth and Sycamore, there are a couple of abandoned buildings with a long dirty alley between them. They're close enough to the old part of town so even the cops don't walk into an alley like that unless they have backup on the way. I was just about to cross in front of that alley when the screaming started.

A woman screaming, terror and pain. Somewhere back in the semi-darkness of the alley.

My body is faster than my brain, and by the time the woman screamed again, before I'd even thought about it, I was headed toward the sound as fast as I could run.

Probably I should've pulled the .45 out where I could use it, but when you're as big as I am, you get in the habit of thinking you don't need a weapon. Anyway, I had good reason not to trust the way I handle a gun.

This time – for once – it turned out I'd done the right thing. The only reason the woman didn't get hurt worse was that I got there so fast. The man had already torn off most of her clothes, and he had her on her back in the dirt. She fought like fury, but he was much too strong for her.

He should've heard me coming – I'm not exactly light on my feet – but he must've been too far gone. Holding her down, he sprawled himself between her legs and started to thrust at her.

I was moving too fast to land on him without hurting her, so instead I caught hold of the back of his shirt with both hands as I went past and used his weight to pivot me to a stop. I was ecstatic with rage – the pressure inside me was exploding. Frustration and dread and all the long pain of trying to fight my way off the stuff came to a head in a second, and I went happily crazy.

45

The man wasn't small, but for all the good his size did him he might as well have been. My momentum lifted him bodily into the air, and as I pivoted I swung him around and slammed him against the wall of the building. When he bounced back at me, I saw he had a switchblade, but even that didn't slow me down. I blocked it aside, grabbed him again, wheeled, and threw him face first into the other wall as if I were trying to demolish the building.

Before he could turn, bring his knife around, I got him. With a long swing that came all the way up from my shoes, I hit him in the small of the back, just on the left side of his spine.

A gasp of pain broke out of him. His knife skittered away into the dark somewhere. He spun around and flipped forward, fell on his face, then jerked on to his side, arching his back as if he were trying to get away from the pain. His legs went rigid, and he kept pushing with them, slowly skidding his body in a circle.

There was a high keening noise in my ears, like the sound of blood rushing through my head, and I had a terrible urge to haul off and kick him. I wanted to do it. I could already feel the jolt of my toe hitting his back. But I didn't. He'd had enough.

Instead I turned away and went to see about the woman.

She huddled, sobbing, against one of the walls. She had her knees pulled up tight in front of her, and she clutched the remains of her clothes about her desperately, as if those scraps were all that was left of her. Her face was pressed against her knees. She didn't look up when I spoke to her.

I hunkered down in front of her. Not knowing what else to do, I put one hand on her arm.

She flinched away so violently that I had to draw back. But at least the movement made her lift her head. I saw she was Chicano. It's hard to tell the age of young Chicano women – when they first stop being kids they look too old for their years, and later on they look too young – but I didn't think she was more than seventeen. Not pretty, but beautiful. Either the bad light or the tears made her eyes look dark as bruises.

'Hush, child,' I said to her gently in Spanish. 'The harm is past. I am Señor Axbrewder. My name is known in many places. Are you injured?'

She didn't say anything. But she made an effort and finally managed to swallow her sobs. In answer to my question, she shook her head.

The man on the ground behind me groaned.

Her eyes jumped fearfully toward him, but I said, 'Do not fear. He is hurt, and will not harm you now.' This time when I touched her arm she looked back at me and didn't flinch.

'That is well,' she said in English. Strength was starting to come back into her face. There was a dignity in her tone, perhaps in the way she spoke English, that touched me more than any amount of crying. 'He is a pig, and I spit on him.'

I liked her English so much I switched to it myself. 'We'll do better than spit on him. The rape laws around here are pretty tough.' That's one advantage of living in a state where some of the old Spanish traditions and values still carry weight. 'We'll put him in gaol. He won't get out until he's too old to even think about doing something like this again.'

She nodded her head once, sharply. 'Yes.'

'Good.'

I got up to check on the man. He was groaning louder and moving around a bit now, but he wasn't going anywhere. He was a white dude – an Anglo all dolled up in the kind of cowboy-tourist finery no self-respecting Westerner would wear. That made him a hit-and-run rapist, the kind that never gets caught because by the time the cops go looking for them they're already in some other part of the country, bragging about how those 'Mex chicks' couldn't get enough of them. 'Not this time, ace,' I muttered at him. Then I went back to the woman and asked her name.

She said, 'Theresa Sanguillan.'

'Well, Theresa Sanguillan.' All of a sudden, I was trembling – reaction, I guess – and I had to fake a hearty tone to keep my voice from quavering. 'I'm afraid you've got a long night ahead of you. We'd better get on with it.'

She didn't respond. The brief look she cast down at her clothes said more than enough.

I groped mentally for a second, then shrugged off my jacket and handed it to her.

Her eyes snagged momentarily on the butt of the .45 under my left arm, but then she took the jacket. I turned my back and went to look for the knife. I found it a few feet away, snapped it closed and dropped it into my pocket. Then I started to rouse the dude.

While I was shaking him to his feet and she was getting herself covered as best she could, I asked her how she'd happened to run into this clown.

I liked her – she had spunk. Now that her fear was over, she was just mad. But it was a controlled mad, cold and vehement. I was glad about that, because it meant she wasn't going to back out on me, refuse to press charges. In a tight, even voice, she told me she worked as a domestic out in the Heights, where a lot of professional people live. She was on her way home to her mother and two younger sisters, but the bus she had to take didn't go into the old part of town, so every evening she had to walk this way home in the dark. The Anglo had been on the bus with her, and when she got off he followed her, giving her some sort of speech about how girls weren't safe on the streets alone at night. It only took him three blocks to start treating her like a hooker, and when she gave him to understand that he was mistaken, he turned nasty.

The whole thing made me want to hit him again. While I was getting him up, I saw his penis still hanging out of his open fly. I was tempted to leave him that way. But on second thoughts, for the sake of Theresa Sanguillan's dignity, I tucked him in and zipped him up. Then I lifted him to his feet and dragged him along. The three of us went out to the street.

In that part of town, you can't find a unit at night if you go looking for it with a bloodhound. I didn't feel much like lugging the dude all the way back to Cuevero Road in hopes of spotting a cop or a working phone booth, so we went on down Eighth Street and turned in at the first bar we came to. The few lethargic drinkers in the place looked at us with only momentary interest despite our far-from-tidy appearance. The barkeep knew me and let us use his phone. First I called the cops. Then Theresa called a friend who had a phone, so the friend could take a message to her mother. Then we went back outside to wait. It would've been nice to sit down in the bar for a rest, but considering the shape I was in, I didn't want to stay in such close proximity to all those bottles.

It was an easier decision than it should've been, almost twenty-four hours since my last drink. I was wearing my white armour – knight rescues maiden – which helped. But that was only part of it. Vanity is no match for alcohol. If it were, half the distilleries in the country would go out of business. No, the main thing was that I was working, doing something I believed in. While we stood out there on the sidewalk I almost didn't regret that I wasn't back in the bar having a drink.

I passed the time by shaking the dude every time he started to fade or shutting him up whenever he started to groan, and by asking Theresa questions – simple questions, the kind she could answer without having to forget that she was mad. After about five minutes

48

the cops arrived. There were two of them in the unit, and they drove up quietly, trying not to attract attention.

Once they heard what had happened they didn't seem very eager to make an arrest. They inspected Theresa and the dude and me, and shuffled their feet, and asked us a bunch of questions without writing any of the answers down, generally making it clear that they wanted us to forget the whole thing. I suppose I could understand their situation – in this city, Anglo versus Chicano was every cop's nightmare. But I wasn't having any. Theresa Sanguillan and I were citizens, the dude had committed a crime, and we had a right to have him arrested. I handed over the knife, and finally the cops gave in. They piled us into the back of their unit and took us over to the Municipal Building.

The building is just as bad at night as it is during the day. It's always disorienting. During the day you have the impression that the sun set hours ago, and at night you end up thinking it's noon outside. But this time I didn't let it bother me. As long as Theresa had her chin up, I didn't intend to let anything get in my way. I knew it could turn out to be messy, but I didn't care.

The so-called 'arresting officers' took us to the duty room where all the detectives had their desks. The person who designed the room was either a drunk or a real joker – the place looked like the embalming room of a mortuary. For a while we were ground along by the usual routine of police work. The arresting officers made a statement to one of the detectives. He tried to ask the dude a few questions, but the dude was hurting too bad to make sense, so the detective put him in the tank to wait for a doctor. Then a couple of detectives took Theresa and me to opposite sides of the room – so we couldn't check our answers with each other – and made us tell our stories a few times. After that, we were given the opportunity to sit around and wait.

The cops do stuff like that on purpose. They try to put pressure on the people filing the charges. Most of them don't actually want the people to back out, but from a cop's point of view, if a victim is going to back out, the sooner the better. Saves wasted effort and frustration later on. So they give you a chance to reconsider. A long chance.

While we were waiting, we saw the doctor come in. He examined the dude, then went away muttering to himself. A few minutes later, two paramedics arrived with a stretcher and carted the dude off on it. Theresa watched them go, but the anger in her eyes stayed.

After another half-hour or so, a different detective came over and introduced himself as Captain Cason. He was a short, fleshy man with hands like shovels and eyes so flat and pale that from the side they looked like the eyes of a blind man. His voice had a particular rasp with which I was all too familiar – the hoarseness of a man who does a lot of interrogating. He took Theresa across the duty room into his office and shut the door.

They were in there a long time. When they came out, she looked shell-shocked, like she was about to faint away right there on the floor. I had a sick taste in my mouth as I hurried toward her.

Cason tried to stop me. He put himself between us, steered her over to a nearby desk and told the detective there to arrange a ride home for her. Then he took my arm and tugged me in the direction of his office.

I slapped his hand off and stepped around him. For one second Theresa looked straight at me. Her face was as pale as if she were bleeding internally, but there was a hot red spot of colour on each cheekbone, and her lips were tight. Her dark intense eyes didn't flinch. Half her anger was aimed at me.

Cason barked, 'Axbrewder!' But I ignored him long enough to say tell her in Spanish, 'I will put him in prison by myself if you do not speak against him.' Then I turned away. Cason was getting ready to muscle me, and I didn't want that to happen. I said to him, 'Tell your detective I want my jacket back.' Then I strode straight into his office and dropped myself into one of the chairs.

He followed me in, shut the door and sat down. He put his hands on the desk and kept them there as if they were too heavy to carry around. Or maybe he just didn't want me to forget how strong they were. With that harsh rasp of his, he demanded, 'What did you say to her?'

The bad taste in my mouth was getting worse, but I made an effort to keep my vocabulary polite. 'The opposite of what you said.'

'Huh?'

'You told her I wasn't going to testify for her.' That was what I'd seen in her eyes. I didn't need her to explain it. 'You tried to scare her off by telling her she'd have to carry this alone in court. You must've had a fine old time describing how ugly a rape trial can get.'

'Is that so?' Cason growled. For a second there, he didn't sound quite so sure of himself. Then he rallied. 'Well, I've got news for you, smart-ass. You aren't going to testify.'

'How do you figure that?' I said, hoping there wasn't something important about all this that he knew and I didn't.

'You're a known alcoholic. You were in the part of town where you do your drinking. The arresting officers found you outside a bar. Who's going to believe a thing you say?'

'That's cute.' The taste in my mouth made me sound like him. 'The only problem is that I'm sober.'

'Is that a fact?' he drawled. 'How do you propose to convince a jury?'

I almost laughed at him. 'You're wasting my time. I'll call you as a character witness. Even you won't be able to explain why you didn't give me a blood-alcohol test.' He blinked at that a couple of times, but didn't say anything. 'Come on, Captain,' I went on. 'You're playing games with me. Why don't you cut out the bullshit and tell me what's really going on?'

His fingertips began to touch each other lightly. 'The man's name is Charles Saunders, and he's from Cleveland. We're trying to get in touch with his wife. The doctor says he may have a ruptured kidney.' Then his hands jumped into fists. 'Goddamn it, Axbrewder! Haven't you ever heard of minimum force?'

'Minimum force'?' I countered. 'What's that?'

'He could sue you for every penny you ever had!'

'Is that a fact?' Deliberately I imitated Cason's tone.

'We can probably get you off the hook if you let this thing drop.'

I felt like it was my turn to get angry, but I held back. 'So let him sue me. That's my problem. I don't give a shit what he does as long as he does it in gaol.'

'Smart-ass!' Cason barked. 'I wish you still had a licence, so I could get it pulled for this.'

'Yeah, well, I appreciate your consideration. But I'm just a private citizen. I saw a crime being committed, and I intervened. I went in hard because there wasn't time for anything else. He had a knife. I didn't have a chance to ask him if he was going to use it.' I tried not to sound too angry, but I couldn't swallow all of it. 'What the hell's the matter with you, anyway? You like rape? You want clowns like this Saunders running around loose?'

'Shut up, Axbrewder,' he said softly, 'or I'll stuff it down your throat.'

'Just what we need around here,' I shot back. 'More police brutality.'

'All right.' He was furious. 'That's enough. You want to be cute? I'll give it to you straight. This Sanguillan' – he made her name into an insult – 'is just another Mex chippy who tried to back out when she didn't get enough money. It happens all the time. That's why she was out on the street alone at night. Saunders just got sucked in. He's a tourist here, and he deserves an even break. A ruptured kidney is a hell of a price to pay for not having enough cash on him. This won't go any further. You're not going to testify.'

'Because he's Anglo,' I said carefully.

'If that's the way you want to put it.' His hands were flat on the desk, as if everything was settled.

I got to my feet. 'Theresa Sanguillan has a perfectly respectable job as a domestic in the Heights. That'll be easy to prove. She was on the street at night alone because that's the only way she can get home. But even if she *is* "just another Mex chippy", it doesn't make any difference. She was being *raped*!' I couldn't stop myself. I hammered my fist on to the top of his desk so hard that a couple of files fell off on to the floor. 'If you try to sit on this, I'll go to the DA.' District Attorney Martinez was notoriously unsympathetic with racist cops. 'He might like to find out how many rape investigations you've quashed since you got your promotion.'

Captain Cason was standing behind his desk, and his hands were twitching, and he was saying, 'You sonofabitch, you–!' But I wasn't listening. I'd had enough of him. I threw open the door and went out into the duty room.

I'd been in there longer than I thought. Theresa was gone, and my jacket waited for me on the corner of a desk. Everybody in the duty room stared at me, but I ignored them. I shoved my arms into my coat, moving fast to hide the way I was shaking. Then I stalked out of the room.

I was in no mood to be interfered with, so when a woman in the corridor behind me called my name, I didn't pay any attention. No, thanks – not interested. I've had enough. But she was determined. 'Mr Axbrewder!' I could hear her hurrying to catch up with me. Oh, hell. I gritted my teeth, shoved my hands into the pockets of my jacket so that she wouldn't see them tremble, and turned to face her.

Policewoman Rand, from Missing Persons.

'Mr Axbrewder,' she repeated, 'Sergeant Encino wants to see you.'

Encino. Just what I needed. Another racist, like Cason, only on the opposite side of the fence. I didn't feel like putting up with him. I had my mouth open to tell Policewoman Rand where Sergeant Encino could stuff it when my right hand found a piece of paper in my jacket pocket. I shut up long enough to take it out and look at it.

It was just a scrap of paper. On one side there was something in Spanish that looked like a grocery list. On the other side, in awkward childlike handwriting, it said, 'I am indebted to you. Theresa Maria Sanguillan y Garcia.'

That made a difference, somehow. All of a sudden, Cason didn't seem to be worth the emotion I was spending on him. I folded the note neatly, put it back in my pocket. Then I asked Policewoman Rand, 'Where is he?'

She nodded back down the corridor. 'In the office.'

'All right,' I said. 'I'll go see him.'

She didn't come with me, but continued on the way I'd been going. Maybe it was time for her coffee break. I went back to Missing Persons alone.

Encino was the only one there. As soon as he saw me come in, he got up from his desk and came to stand at the counter, facing me. We stared at each over for a moment across the Formica. Then he said, 'I hear that you have stopped a rape tonight.'

That took me by surprise. I nodded stupidly.

His sad eyes didn't waver. 'I hear that the woman is Chicano.'

I didn't say anything to that either. Something was going on here – I couldn't even guess what it was. As a way of answering him, I took out my scrap of paper and let him see it.

'Ah.' He read it, then looked back up at me. He was too good at hiding his emotions – I couldn't find anything in his face. After a moment, he said, 'So you have spoken with Captain Cason.'

For the sake of not acting like an idiot, I mustered up enough voice to growl, 'Yeah.'

Carefully Encino asked, 'What have you said to him?'

It was none of his business, but I was glad to tell him anyway. 'I told him to blow it out his ass.'

Suddenly Encino's whole face smiled. He was so happy that even his hair looked like it was grinning. He turned serious again a few seconds later, but by then everything between us was different.

'Señor Axbrewder,' he said formally, 'I've been unjust. Men such as Cason' – he said the name bitterly – 'blind me. Accept my apologies.'

Before I could respond, he went back to his desk, picked up a stack of manila folders, and brought them over to the counter.

'The truth is that you upset me when you said there is a connection between Alathea Axbrewder and Carol Christie. I had not considered that. So I have been reading the files for two years back. I found these.' He tapped the stack of folders. Then he shrugged. 'They were investigated. There is no apparent connection.'

He didn't let me interrupt him. 'I can't permit you to read these. But' – he sighed eloquently – 'I must leave the office for a short time. How can I know what happens behind my back? Please use my desk.'

Five seconds later, he was gone, and I was alone with his files.

Now I was more than just surprised. But I didn't have time for it. I wanted to read those files, and I didn't know how long the office would be empty. I grabbed up the stack, straightened it in front of me, and got started.

There were seven folders. Carol Christie's was on the top, and I took it first.

Before I finished it, I felt so weak that I feared I was going to fall down. I couldn't help myself – I had to go sit in Encino's chair.

After Carol Christie's, I read the other six files straight through. Then I went back to the beginning and started over again. This time I took notes. Halfway through, Sergeant Encino came back. But he was alone, and I didn't stop.

By the time I finished, I was dripping sweat on his blotter. My shirt was soaked and sticking to my back, along with most of my jacket. I didn't ask Encino's permission to use his phone – I just grabbed it and dialled as well as I could with my hands shaking like cowards. I held on while Ginny's answering service tracked her down. When she answered, they patched me through.

'Brew,' she started, 'what's wrong?'

I brushed past her anxiety. 'I'm at Missing Persons. You've got to get down here.'

'Why? What's happened?'

'There are seven of them,' I said. 'Not counting Alathea. I don't care what the cops say, this is no accident.'

'Make sense, Brew! Seven what?'

'Seven thirteen-year-olds. No, five. Two of them were twelve.' I knew I wasn't getting through to her, but I couldn't help myself. I was too upset to pull it together.

'What the bloody hell are you talking about?'

I pushed the phone against the side of my head as hard as I could, trying to make that damn inanimate plastic steady me. I wanted to howl, but I couldn't get enough air into my lungs. 'Carol Christie didn't drown because she couldn't swim. She didn't drown. She OD'ed on heroin. And that's not all. Before she drowned, she–' But I couldn't say it over the phone. Carol Christie was only thirteen. Just like Alathea. There are some things you can hardly say out loud at all.

'I'm on my way,' Ginny told me. 'I'll be there in fifteen minutes.' Then the line went dead, leaving me with nothing but an empty phone to hang on to.

Part Two
Wednesday Night / Thursday

Chapter Six

Ginny made good time, but it was long enough for me to get a grip on myself. I couldn't afford to fall apart just because this case had turned messy all of a sudden. Alathea needed help in the worst way. So I muttered curses at myself for a while, and finally managed to give Sergeant Encino his desk back. By the time Ginny arrived, I was standing at the counter where I belonged.

She came in so fast that she almost hit me with the door. Her eyes jumped back and forth between Encino and me, trying to figure out what was going on. She was on the alert, ready to explode. But I didn't say anything for a moment or two. I was so glad to see her that I wanted to hug her. Just having her there made me feel steadier. She'd know what to do, know how to cope.

'All right,' she panted, out of breath from hurry and anxiety. 'What's going on?'

It was still a tough question, but I could handle it now. 'After we talked this afternoon, Sergeant Encino went through his files for the past couple of years. He found six more young white girls like Carol Christie who ran away from home and later turned up dead. All seven of them were heroin addicts. In one way or another, they all died as a result of overdoses.' I faltered for a second, groping for courage, then went on.

'According to the medical examiner, they all showed signs of "intensive sexual activity".'

That's how the coroner put it in all seven reports. In each case, he'd concluded that these twelve- and thirteen-year-old girls supported their addictions by prostitution.

Ginny took it in like a sponge. Whenever she's listening really hard, she doesn't react to what she hears – she just concentrates on absorbing it. When I stopped, she asked in a flat voice, 'Have you got the details?'

I showed her my sheaf of notes.

She nodded sharply, then turned to Encino. 'Were these cases investigated?'

'Of course. Yes.'

'And?'

He shrugged. 'No connection was found.'

'No connection?' she snapped. 'They're identical!'

If he resented her attitude, he didn't show it. 'Drugs, yes. Prostitution, running away from home. But drugs are available everywhere. For a young girl to get drugs, she needs money. Especially for heroin. It's common. What connection is there?'

I said, 'He's right.' I didn't agree with him, but he had a good point. 'These seven girls lived in different parts of town. They went to five different schools. According to their friends, none of them knew each other. Their parents don't have anything in common.' When I thought about it, the individual investigations looked pretty thorough. 'None of them went to the same church or belonged to the same club or had the same family doctor.'

Ginny didn't even glance at me. 'Who did the investigations?'

'Detective-Lieutenant Acton,' Encino said.

'All of them?' she demanded.

He nodded.

'Is he a good cop?' I asked.

Encino thought for a moment. 'He's Anglo – but not like Captain Cason. He's hard on drugs. It's said he searches for the pushers who supplied these children.'

Ginny started to ask another question, but I stopped her with a nudge. Policewoman Rand was coming through the door behind us. I didn't know which racial or political faction she belonged to, but I didn't want to risk getting Encino in trouble for helping us. In Puerta del Sol, the police department is like the city – so fragmented, broken up into groups that can't stand one another, it's a wonder they get any work done at all. About the only time I've ever seen the cops stick together is when one of them gets killed.

Maybe Rand was on the wrong side. Encino's tone changed suddenly as he said, 'No, it's impossible. I've done everything I can. No more.'

Two hints were more than enough for Ginny. 'If that's the way you want it,' she sighed in her aggrieved-citizen voice. 'We'll get a subpoena if we have to.' That was a nice touch. It kept Encino in the clear as far as Policewoman Rand was concerned. I liked it so much that I almost made the mistake of grinning. 'Come on, Brew. Let's get out of here.'

We turned to go, but the door was already in use. A short dried-up little man practically ran into the office. He had thin grey-and-black hair sticking up in all directions, a stiff moustache covering his mouth, and a face that looked like it'd been redesigned by a pair of cleats long ago. His eyes bulged as if they were about to fall out. He didn't react to us – I don't think he even saw us – but I knew who he was. One of Ginny's less-successful competitors, a private investigator named Ted Hangst. Mostly because he didn't have any choice about it, he worked in the grubby world of 'domestic relations', spying for people who were jealous, greedy, or malicious enough to pay him. I seemed to remember hearing somewhere that his wife had run off and left him a few years back.

He almost jumped the counter to confront Sergeant Encino as he thrust half a sheet of paper on to the counter. His hands shook. 'See! I told you she didn't run away.'

Ginny and I froze.

There was no triumph in his voice – just urgency and fear. 'Read it!'

Encino scanned the paper, then turned his sad eyes back to Ted. 'It says that she has run away, Mr Hangst.'

'She didn't run away!' he insisted. 'This proves it. Listen.' He held the note trembling in front of his face.

'Dear Dad, I won't be coming home for a while – maybe for a long time. Don't worry about me. There's something I have to work out. Love, Mittie.' He slapped the paper down on the counter. 'See?'

Without inflection, Encino repeated, 'It says that she has run away.'

'No!' His whole body twitched with frustration. 'Mittie didn't write this. It says, 'Dear Dad.' She never called me Dad. She always called me Pop. That proves she didn't write this. She didn't run away. She was kidnapped!'

'For what purpose?' the sergeant asked. 'Not for ransom. So why?'

'I don't know.' He was close to crying. 'It doesn't make sense.' Then he recovered his determination. 'You've got to help me. I can't get anywhere alone. There are too many things that could've happened. I can't do it alone.'

Encino leaned closer to Ted. 'Mr Hangst, I sympathize. We will look for your daughter. We understand the importance. But truthfully there is little we can do.' He stopped Ted's response with a short gesture. 'For now, you should perhaps speak to Mr Axbrewder.'

'Axbrewder?' Ted turned, saw Ginny and me. 'Oh.' He nodded at us, swallowing hard. 'Brew. Ginny.'

At once Ginny said, 'We're working on a case that sounds a lot like what happened to your daughter. We'd like to talk to you about it.'

Ted said, 'Oh,' again, weakly. He looked back at Encino. But before he could add anything, Ginny took his arm and started him toward the door. 'Sergeant Encino understands the situation,' she said reassuringly. 'I'm sure he'll do everything he can.'

Policewoman Rand was taking in all of this, so I didn't try to thank Encino. I just followed Ginny and Ted out into the corridor and closed the door behind me.

'Where shall we go?' she asked me over the top of his head.

'Somewhere we can eat.' I hadn't had any food for close to fourteen hours, and I was feeling it.

Ted didn't resist. He looked like he'd used up all his energy or resolution just going to see Encino. Now he mumbled along beside Ginny like an empty shell. We took him out of the Municipal Building into the night.

The streetlights are bright in that part of town, and you don't see many stars. But streetlights don't fool anybody. They just make the shadows look more dangerous. The people on the streets – there're always a few – moved as if they had secrets they were trying to hide. The cars that went by were going either too slow or too fast.

Night is the only time when I feel like I understand the city.

We went to a twenty-four-hour diner. After we'd ordered a good-sized pile of food, Ginny asked Ted to show us his note. He took it out without even a question – he looked like he was numb with shock. She scanned it, held it up to the light, then handed it to me.

It was a half sheet of good twenty-pound bond, neatly torn along one edge. The handwriting scrawled every which way. I held the paper up to the light and looked through it. It had part of the same watermark that was on the two notes in my pocket. I dug them out and gave them to Ginny.

She compared them from several angles, studied all three of them against the light, then handed Lona's and Ted's notes back to me.

With the torn edges together, they matched perfectly. Ted's note held the top third of the watermark missing from Lona's. There couldn't be any doubt about it – both these notes came from the same sheet of paper.

Sonofabitch! It was all I could do to contain myself. Fortunately the food began to arrive. I shut myself up by shovelling things into my mouth while Ginny told Ted about Alathea.

Just to look at him, you wouldn't have thought he heard a word she said. But when she asked him, 'How long ago did Mittie disappear?' he blinked suddenly, and tears started running down his cheeks. It was hard to watch. His eyes were gushing, but he didn't let out a whimper. A couple minutes passed before he finally answered faintly, 'Three days.'

Five – no, six – days after Alathea turned up missing.

For no reason in the world that I was aware of, I found myself thinking, *The bastard's getting greedy.* More time had passed between the disappearances of the other seven girls.

Then Ginny asked, 'How old was she?'

He had to struggle to make himself audible. 'Thirteen.' Then he covered his face with both hands. 'She's all I have.'

When Ginny looked over at me, her eyes were glittering the way they'd glittered after she'd shot the punk who broke her nose. 'I'm ready to hear the details now,' she said flatly. I glanced at Ted, but she answered, 'He has a right to hear this.'

He must've been paying attention despite his grief. He pulled out a dirty handkerchief, blew his nose hard. Then he fixed his watery eyes on me and didn't let go.

I put my notes on the table beside my plate and started to recite. The basic facts were simple enough.

Two years ago, Marisa Lutt, a seventh-grader at Ensenada Middle School up in the Heights, failed to return home from school. Her parents filed a complaint almost immediately. Five days later, they reported receiving a letter from her, asking them not to worry. Her description – 'very attractive' – was given to all police units. A detective spoke to her friends, her parents, and their friends, but failed to trace her. Three months later, she was killed by a truck while walking in the middle of the southbound interstate. The ME found evidence of massive heroin addiction, which he described as being of recent origin. He also found evidence of intensive sexual activity. The coroner concluded that she'd turned to prostitution to earn money for heroin. Death accidental as a consequence of an overdose. Investigation in progress to determine where she obtained her drugs. She was thirteen years old.

Twenty-two months ago, Esther Hannibal, a seventh-grader at Matthew Pilgrim Junior High down in the southeast part of town, failed to return home from school. Her parents reported her missing, but refused to file a complaint and didn't call again. Her description – 'good-looking' – was given to all patrol units. Five months later, she fell off the roof of an abandoned building in the old part of town and died a few hours later of internal injuries. The ME found evidence of massive heroin addiction, which he described as being of recent origin. He also found evidence of intensive sexual activity. The coroner concluded that she'd turned to prostitution to earn money for heroin. Death accidental as a consequence of an overdose. Investigation in progress to determine where she obtained her drugs. She was thirteen.

Eighteen months ago, Ruth Ann Larsen, a sixth-grader at North Valley Middle School, failed to return home from school. Her parents were frantic initially and didn't hesitate to file a complaint. Four days later, however, they withdrew the complaint. Her description – 'mature for her age' – was given to all patrol units. Three months later, she was found dead in the bottom of a construction pit out on the east side of the city. The ME was getting in a rut. Ditto the coroner. And the investigation. She was twelve.

Sixteen months ago, May-Belle Podhorentz, a seventh-grader at South Valley Junior High, failed to return home from school. Her parents reported her missing but were unwilling to file a complaint at first. However, three days later they received a letter from her, asking them not to worry. They asserted that the letter didn't fit their daughter and must have been written under duress. They then filed a complaint. Her description – 'lovely' – was given to all patrol units. A detective spoke to friends, and so forth and so on. Six months later, she crashed in a hang glider at night and was killed instantly. ME and coroner as usual. Investigation as usual. She was thirteen.

Eleven months ago, Rosalynn Swift, a sixth-grader at Matthew Pilgrim Junior High, failed to attend school after missing half her classes the previous day. The school reported her to the police. When questioned, her mother said that she hadn't come home the previous day. Her mother reported her as 'a no-good chippy who's only interested in boys' and refused to file a complaint. The school filed instead. Her description – 'cute and well-developed' – was given to all patrol units. Investigation went nowhere. Six months later her body was uncovered by a plough in the city dump while sanitation workers were redistributing garbage. The ME reported death by suffocation about a month previously. The rest of the report was as usual. She was twelve.

Seven months ago, Dottie Ann Consciewitz, a seventh-grader at

Alsatia Junior High, failed to return home from school. Her parents filed a complaint immediately, claiming that she'd been kidnapped by her uncle in Detroit. Three days later, they received a letter asking them not to worry. This they showed to the police as evidence that her uncle had kidnapped her. They claimed she couldn't have written such a letter without his help. She was described as 'beautiful'. The Detroit police were unable to locate either her or her uncle. Five months later she was found in an empty apartment on the south side of the city. Death by electrocution – bad wiring on an electric hot plate. The ME and the coroner had nothing new to say. The investigation went nowhere. She was thirteen.

Three months ago, Carol Christie, a seventh-grader at North Valley Middle School, failed to return home from school. Her parents reported her missing. They appeared distressed, and her father filed a complaint without her mother's approval. Her description – 'healthy and pretty' – was given to all patrol units. A detective and so on, without success. Her father called the police frequently to complain. Several times he made vague threats. Three months later – Monday this week – her body was found floating in the Flat River. Although she'd apparently been in the water for several hours, the ME found little or no water in her lungs. The cause of death was a heavy overdose of heroin. The rest of his report was the same as the other six. Likewise the coroner's findings. Investigation still in progress. She was thirteen.

Ginny didn't react to any of it. She was just absorbing data. But a change came over Ted while he listened. Gradually he went rigid. Before I was finished, he'd turned so pale that I was afraid he'd have a coronary. He looked like a man whose whole life was falling apart. So he surprised me when he said in a tight flat voice, 'You tell it as if all those girls were tied together – as if this is some kind of sick conspiracy. I don't know about that. What does it have to do with Mittie? She isn't a junkie. And she isn't a wh–' for a second, he couldn't get the word out 'a whore.'

'Neither is Alathea,' I growled.

'We don't know for sure that there *is* any connection,' Ginny said. Her voice was abstract, and she didn't look at either of us. She was just thinking out loud. 'All we know for sure is that both Mittie's and Alathea's notes came from the same sheet of paper – which happens to be the same kind of paper Carol Christie's note was on. Those three notes say almost exactly the same thing. If there were anything more solid than that, the cops would've found it by now. Obviously there're a lot of differences. But there're a lot of similarities, too. They were all in the same kind of trouble before they died. They all overlap by about a month – each one died a month after the next one disappeared.'

Except for Alathea and Mittie, I said to myself. But I didn't interrupt her.

'And they all disappeared from school. None of them ran away at night, or after school, or over the weekend, or during the summer. Also none of them seem to have been on the stuff for very long.'

'Three to six months,' I agreed.

'I didn't know it was that easy to get,' she muttered. 'I didn't know a kid could buy enough of it to actually kill herself in three months – or even six.' Suddenly she was angry. 'Who the bloody hell supplies children like that?'

I was about to say that was what Acton reportedly wanted to find out, but Ted distracted me. He didn't look like he'd heard what Ginny just said. He was fumbling for his wallet. He got out a picture, showed it to Ginny and me. 'And they were all cute.'

He was right about that. I could vouch for Alathea. And Mittie looked very nice in her picture. It was hard to believe she was actually Ted's daughter.

For a while none of us said anything. Ginny was staring at a burnt-out light bulb in the ceiling, and I concentrated on eating. Judging from past experience, this would probably be the last food I could hold down until after the next withdrawal crisis. I didn't know when it was going to come – but it sure as hell was going to come. After that maybe being sober would get a little easier for a while.

Ted didn't eat anything. He was fidgeting under the silence. Finally he asked in a thin voice, 'What're you going to do?'

Ginny's thoughts came down off the ceiling with a jerk. 'The first thing we're going to do is try to get a look at some more notes.'

Ted nodded. For a moment his lips trembled. Then he said, 'I want to help.'

'I'm counting on it.' The glitter was back in her eyes. 'If Mittie and Alathea really are tied in to Carol Christie and the rest of these girls, we need to move fast. Where did Mittie go to school?'

'Alsatia Junior High.'

'All right. You take the Consciewitz girl. Give him the address, Brew.' I got out a pen and wrote down the address on one of the napkins. When Ginny starts to give orders, she doesn't kid around. 'The report on her mentioned a letter. I want that letter – the letter itself, not a copy. I want to know when they got it. I want to know where it was postmarked. I want to know why they think Dottie Ann didn't write it.

'Then go to the school. I'm not sure what I'm looking for there, so ask them about everything you can think of. Try to find out exactly where and when Dottie and Mittie left school. When you've got all that, call my answering service. We'll figure out where to go from there.'

Watching him, you'd have thought that she'd just given him a transfusion. A little blood came back into his face, and some of the rigid way he held himself relaxed. It was just what he needed – somebody to give him orders, make him feel like he was doing something to help Mittie. But he had something else going on, too. There was something distant in his eyes that didn't match the rest of him. Just for a second he gave me the distinct impression that he had ideas he wasn't telling us. Then he left the table to pay his bill. A minute later he hurried out of the diner. The impression faded as soon as he was gone.

I turned back to Ginny. 'You found out something from Alathea's friends.'

'Maybe.' She started getting money out of her purse. 'I'm not sure. I want to take another look at her school. She disappeared after fifth period, PE, right?'

'Right.'

'Well, her sixth period class was Home Ec. Apparently she was the only kid in that PE class who had Home Ec. afterwards. So she always went from one to the other alone. The gym and the Home Ec. classroom are on opposite sides of the school, and she didn't have much time to get from one to the other, so she took a shortcut outside the buildings. As far as her friends know, she's the only one who took that shortcut between fifth and sixth periods.'

'So whatever happened to her happened on that shortcut.'

Ginny nodded. 'Seems that way. We'll check it out tomorrow.' Then she got to her feet. 'Right now I'm going to take you home. You need sleep. If your eyes sink any further back in your head, you might swallow them.'

I couldn't argue with that. I'd been running on nothing but nervous tension for hours now – I did need sleep. And I always have an easier time relaxing when Ginny is in one of her take-charge moods. Spares me having to make decisions for myself. I waited for her to pay the bill, then followed her out to the Olds.

By then it was after midnight, and the night was darker than ever.

But that suited me, too. It's hard to work on cases like this during the day. Sunlight makes everything about them seem unreal. At night there's always somebody somewhere who knows the secret. It's just a question of finding the right person and asking the right questions.

And something else kept me from feeling quite so scared for Alathea. The other girls on that list took at least three months to end up dead. Alathea had only been missing for nine days.

On the drive back to my apartment, I told Ginny how Encino had happened to change his mind about letting us see his files. That must've made a difference to her, because when she said good night she didn't look anywhere near as worried as she had earlier. She looked like a woman who knew she was on the right track.

Chapter Seven

The next morning, the phone pounded me awake around eight. It took me a long time to get to it. As soon as I sat up in bed, I had a blinding headache and every muscle in my body hurt as if I'd just gone fifteen rounds with a brick wall. That told me something, but for a while I couldn't remember what it was. All I could remember was the fine sharp taste of whiskey. Remember it, hell – I *wanted* it. For a while there it was worth more to me than love or money.

That explained why I hurt so bad. I'd slept through the first half of a crisis. My muscles ached from clenching, and my poor sodden brain was yowling with thirst. I was drenched in sweat.

The phone went on hammering at me, but I ignored it. I lumbered into the kitchen, thanking all the gods who watch over slobs like me that I'd had enough foresight to make up a jug of frozen orange juice before I went to bed. I drank about a quart of that while the phone went on ringing. Then I answered it.

'Brew?' It was Ginny. 'Are you – no, forget that. Did I wake you up?'

That was an old question, and I answered it by force of habit. 'No, I had to get up to answer the phone anyway.' I didn't have enough brains with me to think of anything original.

She didn't even pretend to laugh. 'How soon can you get ready to go? We've got work to do.'

'Come pick me up,' I said. 'I'll be ready by then.'

'We don't have time for that. We've got six sets of parents, five schools, and a school board to talk to. You'll have to rent a car.'

'All right.' Her tone was infectious. Just listening to her made me feel like she and I actually lived in the same world. 'What do you want me to do?'

'There's no point in you going to any of the schools. If they have any sense, they won't talk to anybody until they see a licence. Why don't you start with John and Mary Christie?'

'They'll never forgive me.'

'I don't give a good goddamn. I want to know more about that note. I want to know what makes them so edgy.'

I said, 'They'll tell me.' People generally tell me what I want to know – one way or another.

'They'd better,' she said. Then she went on giving me orders. 'When you're through there, go see that other family up in the North Valley, the Larsons. If you finish early, call my service. Otherwise I'll meet you at the school board at one. We have an appointment to talk to the chairman.'

'Right.' It sounded simple enough. It even sounded good to have her give me things to do alone. A big improvement over having her worried about me. 'Anything else?'

'Yes. I need the addresses of those two girls who went to Matthew Pilgrim Junior High. I'll concentrate on the southeast – try to see the parents and talk to the school before I meet you.'

I left the phone to dig out my notes, then gave her the addresses for the Hannibals and Mrs Swift. A moment later, she said, 'That leaves two.'

'Marisa Lutt and May-Belle Podhorentz.'

'Maybe we can check them out this afternoon.'

She made sure I knew where the school board was. Then she hung up.

Work. I had work to do. I spent a minute trying to stretch some of the soreness out of my muscles. Then I got dressed.

Breakfast and the rest of the orange juice did a lot to soak the worst of the pain out of my head. By a quarter of nine I was practically functional. More out of duty than conviction, I strapped on my shoulder holster and checked over the .45. Then I made sure I had all the right papers with me – my notes and *the* notes – grabbed up my sunglasses and went out to start batting my head against the morning.

As it happens, there's a cheap rent-a-relic agency about ten blocks from my apartment. By the time I walked the distance, I felt steadier physically, and they were open for business. I ended up with a middle-aged Torino. I wasn't very comfortable – some cars just aren't designed to fit the human body, no matter what size it is. But it had four wheels and an engine, which was all I needed. Before long I was on my way out toward the North Valley again.

I avoided what was left of rush-hour traffic by taking old roads up along the river, but still it took me quite a while to reach the horsy area where the Christies lived. By then I was sweating in the heat. And the sun beat down on me in an almost insulting way – which didn't do anything for my mood, either. When the Torino bounced into the parking lot for the Christies' riding stables, I was ready to be as tough as necessary.

I went through the office door fast, aiming to take John and Mary by surprise. But the only one I surprised was Mrs Christie. Her husband wasn't there.

When she saw me, she almost jumped out of her shirt. But she didn't yell for John. Instead she asked, 'What do you want?' and her voice trembled. Which told me that Mr Christie was somewhere out of range – maybe on one of the trails, or doing business in town. In a way, that was unfortunate. I was primed to throw my weight around, and it wouldn't take any weight at all to make Mrs Christie talk. Nerves or fear or whatever had already put enough pressure on her.

So I sat down in a chair by the desk, crossed my legs, and said in the least threatening voice I could muster on such short notice, 'I want to ask you a few questions about Carol.'

'Go away.' She had to hug herself to keep from shouting. 'I can't talk to you. John doesn't want me to talk to you. He'll be back any minute. I'll call the police.'

The way her eyes groped around the room as if she were praying for some kind of miracle told me that she was lying about her husband coming back. I countered with a lie of my own. 'The cops know I'm here. They know we're working on this case.'

'I don't want to talk to you.' Somewhere she found the determination to sound defiant. 'I don't have to talk to you.'

I said, 'That's true, Mrs. Christie.' Calm, unthreatening. 'But if you'll listen to me for a minute, I think you'll find you want to talk. You're afraid of something, and it isn't going to go away until this case is solved. This may be hard for you to believe, but I'm trying to help you.

'You see, I know what happened to Carol. I know she didn't drown. I know she died from an overdose of heroin. I know how she earned the money for drugs.' Abruptly Mary Christie dropped into a chair and put her hands over her face. 'There's no reason why you shouldn't answer my questions.'

I gave her a minute to absorb that. Then I went on.

'Carol isn't the only one, Mrs Christie. For two years now, the same thing has been happening to twelve- and thirteen-year-old girls everywhere in the city. Right now it's happening to my niece. That's why I need to talk to you.'

She didn't look up, but slowly she took her hands away from her face. I could tell by the way her shoulders sagged that she was giving in. She was under too much strain to fight me and her fear at the same time.

Very gently, I eased her into it. 'How long after Carol disappeared did you get her note?'

She took a deep, shuddering breath. 'It was three days. We were worried sick.'

'I can believe it. Did you happen to notice the postmark?'

'John did. It surprised him. It was mailed here in town.'

'Why did that surprise him?'

'He – we both thought Carol had gone somewhere else. She has a lot of friends living in other parts of the state. We thought she must have gone to visit one of them.'

'I understand. Mrs Christie, did anything about the note bother you? Was there anything that didn't sound like her?'

'No,' she said. Then, a moment later, 'Yes – sort of. Carol didn't write letters. We used to send her to camp every summer, and she never wrote to us. And when she got back she didn't write to her friends. She didn't like to write. She liked to use the phone – she liked to call people. But she wouldn't write. One year she got in trouble at camp because the counsellors wanted her to write a letter home like the rest of the girls, and she wouldn't.' Finally she looked up at me. Her face was full of distress. 'She loved us, that wasn't it. She didn't write to anybody. She didn't like to write.'

I wanted to tell her that I understood, that I believed her. But the way she was looking at me gave me an opening I couldn't afford to miss. 'Mrs Christie,' I said softly, 'what're you so afraid of?'

'I– we–' For a moment she choked on it. But by now it was too late. She couldn't stop herself. 'John says we might lose our business. He says if people find out what happened to Carol, they'll think we had something to do with it and stop coming here. They won't want their children to associate with us. But he's just saying that. He doesn't care about it. Carol was a *good* girl. He wants people to remember her the way she was, before – before she ran away.'

I waited a moment, then said, 'But that isn't it, either.'

'No. No. We're both so – so ashamed. We don't want anybody to know. We failed her somehow. There must've been some way we could've been better parents. So she wouldn't have had to run away. That hurts. I keep wanting it to go away, and it doesn't.

'And that – that policeman. Detective Acton?' She looked at me, expecting me to recognize the name. 'He th– threatened us. He said somebody is supplying drugs to young girls – all through the city – and the parents are the first suspects. He said he wanted to believe we were innocent, but he needed to keep what happened quiet, out of the papers and everything so nobody would know about it, and if we told anybody, talked to anybody, he would know we were deliberately interfering with his investigation. He was – awful. He looked like he liked hurting us.

'I haven't been able to sleep for nights. I keep having this nightmare that Carol is drowning and screaming for help, and I'm running frantically to try to get to her, but before I can get there Detective Acton comes out of the water and pushes her head down, and all the time he has the most terrible grin.' Again she covered her face. 'Oh, my baby!'

I didn't say anything. There was nothing I could say. The world is full of pains no stranger can comfort. The only thing I could do for her was find out the truth about Carol.

And keep my eyes open for a chance to give Detective-Lieutenant Acton what he had coming.

I left the trailer, closed the door quietly behind me, and went back to my rented Torino.

When I eased myself into the seat, I almost scalded my back on the vinyl upholstery. The sun had made it hot enough to fry eggs. I spat a few curses, but that didn't accomplish anything. The heat was just another item on a long list of things I couldn't do anything about. I started the engine, then tramped down on the accelerator and slewed out of the parking lot on to the road. For a few minutes I concentrated on speed, trying to build up enough wind to ventilate the car. Then I settled back, got a better grip on myself, and began to look for the Larsens' address.

It shouldn't have been hard to find, but I didn't know the North Valley very well, and for some reason Lujan Street didn't seem to be where I thought it was. Finally I had to stop at a small corner grocery store – the kind of glittering artificial place you find in moneyed neighbourhoods, the kind that stocks more caviar than macaroni – to ask directions. Sure enough, Lujan Street turned out to be just about where I thought it was. However, *I* wasn't where I thought I was.

It was late in the morning when I finally parked in front of the

Larsen mansion. It wasn't new. In fact, it had the Victorian look of a converted funeral home. But it sure as hell was big. I had to trek half a dozen blocks to reach the porch and ring the doorbell. Along the way, I passed five or six kids' bikes standing to one side.

About that time, the name 'Bjorn Larsen' began to sound vaguely familiar.

A solid matronly woman – who turned out to be Magda Larsen – answered the doorbell and invited me into the house. The front hall was only twice the size of my apartment, and it was decorated, if that's the right word, with four massive iron sculptures as tall as I am. Two flanked the door, one stood beside the staircase, and one guarded the entrance to the living room. That explained it. Ruth Ann Larsen's father was Bjorn Larsen, the famous sculptor – one of Puerta del Sol's few certifiable claims to being an 'art centre'.

Magda Larsen steered me into the living room, and a few moments later we were joined by her husband. He was as thickly built as she was, and as brawny as a steeplejack. He had a pair of welding goggles pushed back on his head and wore an asbestos apron over his T-shirt and jeans. The contrast between his clean hands and grimy forearms showed that he'd just taken off his work gloves.

'This is Mr Axbrewder,' Mrs. Larsen said. 'He wants to talk to us about our daughter.' Virtually a repeat of what I'd told her at the door. Her tone was non-committal, almost distant, but her husband stuck out his hand as if he were prepared to welcome anybody she let into the house. 'Pleased to meet you, Mr Axbrewder. Have a seat?' He waved me toward an overstuffed sofa that looked like it ate people for lunch. All the furniture in the room was like that – deep, sturdy, and made to last.

I sat down at one end of the sofa. Magda joined me at the other, and Bjorn took a chair near her, unselfconsciously courteous about placing himself so I could talk to both of them at once. 'Which daughter did you have in mind?' he asked directly, 'Risa or Natalie?'

Their openness made me hesitate. Neither of them had the vaguest notion what I had to say – and neither of them was the least bit afraid of it. I had a sudden desire to just tell them that I'd made a mistake and walk away. Somehow the complete frankness in their eyes made me feel like a child molester – me with all my grim, guilty secrets. I had to make an effort to say, 'Ruth Ann.'

In a way, that announcement didn't make any difference. Mrs Larsen gave a faint gasp and went pale. Blood flushed through her husband's face. But neither of them tried to hide their reactions – or to attack me with them. When Larsen spoke, he didn't sound either embarrassed or hostile.

'Ruth Ann died a miserable and senseless death. Magda and I will never understand it. What is your interest in her?'

Now that I was started, it was easier to go on. 'I'm a private investigator. My niece has disappeared, and I'm trying to find her. It's possible she's going through the same thing that happened to your daughter. If you'd answer some questions for me, it might help me find her.'

Bjorn Larsen looked at his wife. She was shaking her head. He turned back to me. 'Ruth Ann has been dead for more than a year. Fifteen months now. What do you think our daughter and your niece have in common?'

That was tough to answer. His politeness gave me more trouble than almost any amount of hostility. After groping for a minute, I said, 'It works better if I don't tell you. If I told you what I'm looking for, I'd be putting ideas into your head, and anything you said after that might not be completely candid. Naturally you'll react to whatever I say.'

'I see.' He folded his arms across his chest and considered me gravely.

'That policeman' – Magda Larsen was talking to her husband – 'that Lieutenant Acton. He told us not to speak to anybody.'

Bjorn nodded. 'You see our problem, Mr Axbrewder.'

'Yeah.' I saw it, all right – and I didn't much like what I was seeing. 'But that was fifteen months ago. We know things now that Acton didn't know then. Look.' My voice was rougher than I intended, but I had to appeal to them somehow. 'I didn't find out about this from the papers. I know exactly how miserable and senseless Ruth Ann's death was. What I'm trying to do is prevent the same thing from happening again, to another vulnerable little girl.'

Again Larsen looked at his wife. She'd produced a Kleenex from somewhere and was using it to wipe her eyes. 'Ah, Bjorn,' she sighed, 'tell him. Of all people we should be willing to do whatever we can to prevent such things.'

Larsen accepted that without argument. 'Very well, Mr Axbrewder. Ask your questions.'

'Thanks. I won't take much of your time.' But then I had to pause for a few seconds, pull my scattered brains together. The living room was starting to get hot, but neither of the Larsens looked like they felt it. Both of them watched me, curious to see what sort of questions I'd produce. I took a deep breath.

'When Ruth Ann didn't come home from school that day, you were very concerned.'

'That's true,' Larsen said. 'She was always a very responsible child. If she were going to a friend's home after school, if she were to be late for any reason, she was very faithful about letting us know.'

'So when you realized she was missing, you called the police and filed a complaint.'

'Yes. We were reluctant to file the complaint. But we were very concerned, and the police didn't appear to take the situation seriously enough. We filed the complaint in an effort to produce action.'

'Then four days later you withdrew the complaint.'

'Why, yes.' He seemed momentarily confused. 'Yes, we did.'

'Why was that?'

'Well, you see—' He faltered. 'As I say, she was a very responsible girl. We knew that she wouldn't run away without very good reasons. Four days after she disappeared, we received a letter from her. Really, it was just a short note. She assured us that she was all right, and said that she would come home as soon as she had dealt with some problem bothering her. Under the circumstances, we felt it would be a violation of her privacy if the police were to bring her home against her will. We withdrew the complaint.' He said this with such unselfconscious dignity that I couldn't argue with him. It was on the tip of my tongue to say that twelve-year-old girls have more important needs than privacy. But I didn't.

He must have seen some of what I was thinking on my face, because he added, 'Children have the same rights as any other person. So many children grow up to be spoiled, irresponsible, or unproductive because they are treated "like children"', which means that their parents are more interested in their own desires for power than in their children's autonomy.'

That shook me up. Ruth Ann Larsen had turned to prostitution to support her drug habit, and her parents hadn't even tried to look for her. But my expression didn't make a dent on her father. He believed in his own integrity.

For some reason, so did I. Instead of shouting at him, I just said, 'All right. There's only one thing that really matters. Do you still have her note?'

'I will get it,' Mrs Larsen said. She rose out of the sofa, left her husband and me staring at each other. I didn't much care for the view, so I spent my time looking around the room until she came back.

She handed me an envelope. It had a clear Puerta del Sol postmark.

Inside I found a half sheet of good twenty-pound bond, neatly torn along one edge. The handwriting scrawled all over the place.

It said, 'Dear Mom and Dad, I have to be away for a while, but there's nothing to worry about. I'll be fine. I have a problem to work on. I'll be back when I'm done. Love, Ruth Ann.'

Sure enough, the paper had the same watermark as the other notes.

All of a sudden, my throat was so dry that I could hardly swallow. I needed a *drink*. It took me a moment to work enough moisture into my mouth to ask, 'Is – is there anything about this that – seems unusual to you? Out of place? Does it sound like her?'

Larsen said immediately, 'Of course. It's her writing.'

But his wife didn't hesitate either. 'No. It isn't like her. It says, "Dear Mom and Dad." Our children don't call us by those names. Since she was a little girl she has called us "Bjorn" and "Magda".'

I was cold and shivering inside. Whoever had dictated those notes hadn't even bothered to get them right.

I didn't ask the Larsens if I could have their note. I just took it and left. What else can you do with parents who trust their children too much to protect them?

Chapter Eight

I still needed a drink. Sometimes being sober is like drowning. After a certain point, you know you're going to have to breathe, no matter what. But you don't – not until you pass out. I didn't go to a bar, I went to meet Ginny.

It was a long drive back to the middle of town, but when I got near Central High, where the school board has its offices, I was still a bit early so I stopped to grab a quick lunch. That made it 12.45 when I pulled into the Central High parking lot.

Central isn't the newest high school in the city, but it is sure as hell the biggest and most bewildering. You could hide a football field in there and never find it again because the school was built in huge square sections that interlock and form a maze. They had to make it a high school because nobody younger than a freshman could find their way around in it. I was lucky I hadn't gone to school there. I've never been very good at mazes.

A couple of minutes later, Ginny wheeled her Olds into the lot and parked it a few spaces down from my rented Torino. I was glad to see her. The sun on all those parked cars gave the day a glare of futility. Everybody in the whole city could go crazy, rape each other and drop dead, and it wouldn't make one damn bit of difference to the sun. Ginny was a good antidote for that kind of thinking.

I walked over to join her. Maybe it was just wishful thinking, but I thought she looked glad to see me, too. I caught her making a sneaky effort to check my breath. Then her face relaxed into a smile. For a second there, I almost hugged her. Sometimes her smile does funny things to me.

Then she said, 'What've you got?' and we were back to business.

I showed her the Larsens' note and told her about my morning. I didn't leave anything out. Talking about good old Detective-Lieutenant Acton didn't do my blood pressure any favours, but I've never worried much about my arteries anyway.

She absorbed what I had to say, considered it briefly. Then she told me what she'd come up with.

'Mrs Swift is a real charmer. I must've gotten her out of bed. She came to the door looking like the wrath of God, wearing one of those polyester bathrobes, turquoise-and-pink paisley. Gave me a headache just to look at her. She acted like she'd invented bitchiness all by herself. All she could say about her daughter was that she was "no good". Ungrateful little slut, running off and leaving her poor mother all alone like that. I had to lean on her to get anything else.'

I grinned. 'Wish I'd seen that.'

'It wasn't fun. And hardly worth the effort. She finally admitted getting a letter, though, some time after her daughter ran away. She doesn't remember when, and she doesn't remember what it said. She tore it up as soon as she read it. She does remember the cops coming to see her, especially after Rosalynn turned up dead. But she claims she doesn't remember who they were or what they wanted.'

She paused, then said, 'I don't know, Brew. Maybe Rosalynn Swift doesn't fit the pattern. If I were her, I'd run away from that woman seven days a week.'

'Yeah, but don't cross her off the list yet. She went the same route as the others.'

Ginny thought a minute before she said, 'Right.'

'What about the Hannibals?'

'Better.' She made the transition with a jerk. '*Much* better. I caught them both at home. He works the evening shift down at the paper mill, so he was just having breakfast when I got there. He's a feisty little man who likes to fly off the handle, but his heart's in the right place. Mrs Hannibal is as steady as a rock, so she keeps him in line. At first they didn't want to talk. Some cop told them not to, they don't remember his name. After all, it was a year and a half ago. But after I explained what we were trying to do, they changed their minds.

'Judging from what they told me, I'd say that when Esther disappeared they were nearly paralysed with anger and fear. Furious at her for running away, and at the same time terrified that something had happened to her. It was all they could do to report her missing. They just couldn't bring themselves to swear out a complaint. Mr Hannibal probably spent half his time shouting and the other half in a cold sweat. Then they got a letter from her telling them not to worry, she was all right. That gave them an out, an excuse to do nothing.

'Looking back on it, they're pretty bitter about themselves. Esther's death gave them a real shock, which probably explains why they were willing to help me in the end. They say they've changed their whole attitude toward their other children. To prove it, they gave me Esther's letter.'

Ginny handed it to me, envelope and all.

It had a local postmark. The handwriting was barely legible. The note was on a half sheet of good twenty-pound bond, neatly torn along one edge. It said, 'Dear Mom and Dad, I'm not going to be coming home for a while. Maybe for a long time. I've got something to work out. Don't worry, I'll be all right. Love, Esther.' The watermark matched the others.

While I studied it, Ginny went on, 'I asked them if there was anything about this that bothered them. At first they couldn't think of anything, but then they said there was one thing. One of the many things that made them ashamed of themselves. Esther always came home from school for lunch, which she always complained about because her friends ate in the school cafeteria. But the Hannibals only live three blocks from the school, and anyway they couldn't afford school lunches.

'The day she disappeared, she didn't come home for lunch. The Hannibals didn't think much about it. They assumed a friend gave her lunch, or she bought her own out of her allowance. Now they feel like they failed her by not realizing something was wrong. As if there was anything they could've done.' Abruptly Ginny's voice went stiff with anger. 'Heaven help the bastard who's responsible for this when I get my hands on him.'

I knew how she felt. But we have a reciprocal relationship – when one of us gets mad, the other tries to stay calm. I said, 'If Ted doesn't get to him first.' Which wasn't much of a contribution, but it was all I had. 'How's he doing, anyway? Has he called in?'

She calmed down again so fast it was almost scary. 'He called while I was at the Hannibals. He didn't want to talk about it over the phone, he just wanted me to give him more to do. I told him to check out May-Belle Podhorentz and South Valley Junior High. He's supposed to meet us back at the office in a couple of hours.'

It was one o'clock when we headed into Central High's monster building and began hunting for the school board wing. The kids must've all been in class, because we saw only one or two. As we walked along the hollow corridors, I asked Ginny if she'd learned anything at Matthew Pilgrim Junior High.

'It probably doesn't mean anything,' she said, 'but both Rosalynn Swift and Esther Hannibal disappeared at times when they were routinely alone. Esther was there for her last period before lunch, and gone afterward. As for Rosalynn, apparently she had a tendency to get in trouble. Nothing serious. Just trying to get attention. So as a form of punishment she was assigned to clean up the math classroom every day right after lunch, while the other kids were free. Alone. She'd been doing it for about a month – and doing a good job of it, according to the math teacher – when she disappeared. Just didn't show up for her next class. Nobody saw her leave, which isn't surprising since the math room is in the corner of the building furthest away from the playground and the cafeteria.

'The people I talked to were fairly helpful, but they made it clear that I ought to be talking to the school board instead of bothering them. They kept assuring me the board had all the information I needed. I got the impression they want the board to decide for them whether or not we have any legal right to pry into all this.'

'Sounds familiar,' I muttered. At Alathea's school, Vice-Principal Rumsfeld had given me pretty much the same impression.

Then we found what we were looking for, a frosted-glass door in the middle of a blank wall. The lettering on the glass said,

PUERTA DEL SOL BOARD OF EDUCATION
PAUL M. STRETTO, CHAIRMAN
JULIAN Z. KIRKE, SECRETARY

Ginny pulled open the door, and I followed her in.

The rooms inside reminded me of the Municipal Building – no windows, no comfortable colours, everything artificial. Beyond the counter in front of us was a room that looked too small for the ten or twelve desks and thirty or so filing cabinets squeezed into it. At the desks, women in various stages of energy or desperation hacked away at typewriters, scrawled on files, answered phones. Two or three of them in particular had a frightened air, as if someone I couldn't see stood over them with a cat-o'-nine-tails.

We found out why. Before we had time to introduce ourselves to the secretary who did double duty as receptionist, a man came out of an office at the back of the room. He had light blond hair, sleepy eyes, and a mouth so sharp and strong that it looked like he ate steel for breakfast every morning. He wasn't in a hurry, but somehow he gave the impression that he was pouncing.

He said, 'Sondra.' Although he didn't raise his voice, it cut through the work noise in the room, and a woman two desks away from him flinched. She was young and pretty. After I'd noticed that, I realized that all the secretaries who looked particularly miserable were young and pretty.

The man went over and held a sheet of paper in front of her. He handled the paper gently enough, but in some strange way his manner made the movement look like an act of violence. 'Type it again,' he said. 'This time, get it right.' His tone held enough sarcasm to draw blood.

He'd started back to his office when he noticed Ginny and me standing at the counter. He turned toward us. 'It looks like Sally is asleep on the job again.' The secretary-receptionist flushed and bit her lip. 'What can I do for you?' the man asked.

'I'm Ginny Fistoulari,' Ginny said. 'This is Mr Axbrewder.' If you didn't know her, you would've thought that she hadn't felt a thing. But I could hear the underlying bite in her voice. 'We have an appointment with Mr Stretto.'

'He's expecting you,' the man said. 'This way.' We passed around the counter and followed him toward a door in the opposite corner. As we crossed the room, I caught a look at the name-plate on the door of the man's office. It said, 'JULIAN Z. KIRKE, SECRETARY'.

Then we were in a corridor that ran between more offices and ended up in a big place that looked like a corporate boardroom. Long dark-wood table, heavy matching armchairs. Soft indirect lighting. Picture window along one wall overlooking the glare of the parking lot. It was a far cry from the sweatshop where those harried secretaries worked. Kirke guided us into the room and introduced us to Chairman Paul Stretto.

He looked like the kind of man the Republicans run for president – strong lines in his face, a mane of silver hair, resonant baritone voice, just a hint of well-earned fat on his tall frame. He sat at the head of the table as if he'd been born there. At first I couldn't figure out what he was doing in a lowly job like Board of Education chairman when he could've been elected mayor tomorrow – with a little help from TV. But as we shook hands I got a closer look at him. He was younger than he seemed, and the fine silver of his hair came out of a jar. Probably he was saving mayor for later. After which he'd take a crack at governor.

He gestured Ginny and me toward chairs as if he were offering to knight us. He asked Kirke to stay. 'Things always run better around here,' he explained, 'when Julian knows what's going on.'

No doubt. I was already sure that Paul M. Stretto was just office-sitting on his way to better things. Kirke was the man who actually ran the school board.

When we were all seated around the head of the table, Stretto said, 'Now, what can we do for you?' He sounded full to the gills with professional bonhomie.

'Mr Stretto,' Ginny began, 'we're private investigators.' She showed him the photocopy of her licence. 'We've been retained to find two young girls who ran away from home early last week. In the process, we've learned that quite a few girls of junior high age have run away recently – in the past two years, to be more exact. Some of those cases bear a striking resemblance to the ones we're working on. It might help us find these girls if we could see some of your files.'

'I see.' She'd taken him by surprise – most people don't expect visits from private investigators – and he made a great show of thinking hard about it. Which led him to the unsurprising conclusion that he was out of his depth. 'What do you think, Julian?'

Before Kirke could answer, however, Stretto said to us, 'Julian is the expert on our files. We're in the process of a major overhaul of our record system. Our goal is to computerize the files completely so that Puerta del Sol's entire school system will share a network linked to a central server here. Everything will be available by computer anywhere in the system.

'But' – he smiled warmly – 'that's a few years in the future. Right now, Julian is busy getting our files ready for computerization. It's a huge job. First he had to get copies of everything from each individual school. And now he has to put all that data in a usable form. Fortunately he's an expert at it. That's why the board hired him.'

Kirke listened to all this without any particular show of respect, but at least he didn't interrupt. On the other hand, he didn't waste time when the chairman finally finished his little speech. Right away, he asked Ginny, 'Do you have consent from the parents?'

'Not in writing,' she said evenly. 'We've spoken to them, that's all.'

'We'd be violating the confidentiality of our students if we opened our files without some kind of written permission.'

'That's right,' Stretto said. Nobody even looked at him.

'In any case,' Kirke went on, 'I don't think it would be worth your trouble.' His voice held just a hint of a sneer. 'What could you possibly find? From our point of view, all runaways are the same. They're all having trouble of some kind. They all miss school for a while. Eventually most of them return. If some of them have something in common, you wouldn't find it in our files.'

Innocent as sugar, Ginny asked, 'You don't keep any record of the runaways who end up dead?'

'Dead?' Stretto demanded. 'Are these girls dead?'

Now she let him feel some of the bite in her tone. 'In the past two years, seven junior-high girls in this school system have run away from home and died.'

'But' – the chairman was groping – 'what does that have to do with us?'

'Those seven girls are connected in some way. And they're connected to the girls we're looking for. We want to find them before the same thing happens to them. We can't afford to overlook anything – and one possibility is that there are facts buried away in your files that could help us.'

'This is very upsetting.' Stretto looked upset. 'Of course we want to help in any way we can.' Probably because he didn't have any better ideas, he latched on to what Kirke had said earlier. 'If you'll get written consent from the parents, we'll show you everything we have.'

'We don't have time to do that,' Ginny snapped. 'Those seven girls died as a direct result of whatever made them run away. The process has already started for two more.' She was laying it on thick. 'Every delay could be fatal.' I wanted to applaud.

'I'm sorry, Ms Fistoulari.' If you could trust his face, Paul Stretto really was sorry. 'There's nothing I can do.' But if he wanted us to believe him, he blew it a second later by turning to Kirke and asking, 'Is there, Julian?'

Kirke said, 'No.' He made the word sound like he'd chewed it out of pig iron.

Ginny considered for a moment. Then she said, 'Give me the notes, Brew.'

I dug them out and handed them over.

'Mr Stretto,' she said grimly, 'we have reason to believe that these girls didn't just die. They may have been killed. Murdered.' She stressed the word. 'Each girl sent her parents a note. I have some of them here, and I'd like you to read them.'

One by one, she put the Christie, Larsen, and Hannibal notes in front of him.

He was confused, but her tone didn't leave him any choice. He read them, then read them again.

'Now please read these two,' she said as she showed him Alathea's note, and Mittie's. 'They were written by the girls we're trying to find.'

He read them too, but he seemed to have difficulty understanding what they said.

'They're all written on the same kind of paper,' Ginny observed roughly. 'The watermarks are identical.'

A minute later I was surprised to see a change come over Mr Paul M. Stretto, Chairman of the Board of Education. All of a sudden, he didn't look like a man who just happened to have an electable face. He looked like he'd earned it. 'Julian,' he said in a completely different tone, 'get Martha and Astin in here.'

If all this made any impression on Kirke, he didn't show it. He just got up and left the room. When he came back, he had a man and a woman in tow. The man looked worn out, like a pencil that's been sharpened too often, but the woman bristled with energy.

Stretto introduced us. The man was Astin Greenling, Curriculum Vice-Chairman for the board. The woman was Martha Scurvey, Budget Vice-Chairman. Aside from Stretto and Kirke, they were the only full-time members of the board. The other elected members served part-time.

Stretto gave Greenling and Scurvey a quick summary covering most of the facts, then handed them the notes.

Neither of them seemed to grasp the significance of what they read. Greenling muttered, 'You'd think we didn't teach penmanship at all.' Scurvey gave a sigh that puffed out her cheeks. 'If this kind of thing gets out, we're in trouble. We already have a hard enough time selling our budget to the legislature.'

'I didn't call you in here for your opinions,' Stretto rapped out. Under his hair-paint, he must've been a secretly decisive man. Or else he was doing a damn good imitation. 'I simply want witnesses so that there won't be any confusion. These notes have convinced me that Ms Fistoulari is right. As of now, I'm instructing Julian to give her our complete cooperation. I don't know what's happening to these girls, but I want it to stop.'

There was silence in the room. Then Scurvey said, 'Wouldn't it be better to call the police?'

'Leave that to me, Martha,' the chairman answered.

Finally I figured out what he was doing. He was putting on a show for two influential – i.e., voting – members of the board. A display of power to consolidate his position. When a diplomat does it, it's called statesmanship. But it was a gift horse, and I didn't look it in the mouth. All I cared about was getting to see those files.

Stretto dismissed us. I picked up the notes, and we followed Kirke back down the hall to his office. There I gave him our list of names. Mostly because I didn't like him, I watched him carefully for a reaction to any of the names, but I didn't spot one. For all he cared, apparently, I'd read them out of the phone book. He wrote them down, then left us in his office.

He came back with the files fast enough to prove that he knew his job. But he didn't leave us alone while we read them.

It took us half an hour to go through them all. I hated to admit it, even to myself, but as far as I could see, Kirke was right. The files didn't do us any good. I took a few notes – the girls' schedules on the days they disappeared, the names of their teachers, things like that – but the information didn't help. If Ginny found anything interesting, she didn't say so. But I didn't expect her to, not with Kirke hovering over us.

When we were finished, she thanked him – which I thought wasn't called for – and led the way out of his office. As I followed her through the door, he stopped me. He stood up close and whispered so that Ginny couldn't hear him, 'Do you always tag along behind her like this?'

'Like what?'

He shook his head, dismissed the question. 'You're wasting your time. By the time they reach junior high, most girls are nothing but little whores. There's nothing special about the ones that run away. Did you know that we're having a near-epidemic of VD among the junior-high boys?'

I wrapped my left hand around his upper arm and dug my fingers in until his face turned white. 'Watch your mouth,' I whispered back at him. 'You're talking about my niece.'

I gave his arm an extra squeeze to remember me by, then hurried after Ginny. I was grinning, but I wasn't amused.

Once we were outside the office and on our way back to the parking lot, Ginny asked me, 'What was that all about?'

'Kirke didn't much like the way he got overruled.'

She nodded sharply. 'Sonofabitch.'

I agreed with her. But the main thing bothering me was the feeling that it was all wasted. We weren't getting anywhere.

84

Chapter Nine

We didn't talk about it. Ginny had a pinched look between her eyes, the one that meant she was thinking hard. I had no idea what she was thinking about, but I learned long ago to leave her alone when she looks like that.

I didn't even ask her where we were going. She headed straight for her Olds, opened the door and got in. I wedged myself into my Torino and followed.

We ended up at Mountain Junior High, where we had another session with Vice-Principal Rumsfeld. She wasn't exactly overjoyed to see us again, but this time Ginny had a much clearer idea of what she wanted to know, and the vice-principal wasn't the kind of woman who could turn us down if there was any chance at all of helping one of her students. She took us to meet Alathea's PE teacher, and the two of them showed us Alathea's shortcut between her fifth and sixth periods.

'We don't normally allow our students outside the school buildings unsupervised,' Ms Rumsfeld said sternly, 'but I understand that this was something of a special case.'

'Alathea had an awkward schedule,' the PE teacher said. 'She had a hard time getting from the gym to her next class before it started. She asked permission to take this shortcut. I didn't see any reason to turn her down. She was a very dependable girl.'

Very dependable. Yes. That's what I had to keep in mind. I didn't know any of the seven dead girls. For all I knew, every one of them might've been a raving lunatic. But I knew Alathea. She wasn't crazy, or on drugs, or a whore.

With the vice-principal and the PE teacher guiding us, we needed about five seconds to see why Alathea had wanted to use the outside route. For someone in a hurry, it was much easier than going through the buildings. But it was also a perfect place to disappear from, if that's what you had in mind. The buildings stood close to the street, and on that side most of them – the gym, the auditorium, one end of the library – didn't have any windows. Alathea hadn't just been alone, she'd been out of sight.

Which fit with what Ginny'd learned about Rosalynn Swift and Esther Hannibal. But it didn't mean anything to me. If you wanted to run away from school, would you do it when you were surrounded by kids and teachers, or when you were alone?

But Ginny seemed satisfied with whatever it was we'd learned. She thanked Ms Rumsfeld and the PE teacher, told them we wouldn't bother them again if we could help it. Then we left.

This time she led me all the way down Paseo Grande to the Murchison Building. Back to her office.

Ted was there waiting for us. He looked like he'd spent the day in a dryer at the Laundromat – he looked hot, thirsty, and about two sizes smaller. But his eyes weren't bulging the way they had last night. They were sunken and sizzling, as if they were being cooked from inside by whatever he was thinking.

He didn't say anything until we were settled in Fistoulari Investigations' back room. Then he confronted Ginny. Standing in front of her with his hands on his hips, he looked like the losing end of a cockfight, plucked half to death and still ready to peck anything in sight. 'You're wasting my time,' he said.

That surprised her. She looked at him hard. 'I thought you wanted to help.' Even sitting down, she was practically his size.

'I want to find Mittie. This way isn't getting me anywhere.'

Well, off and on I'd been thinking the same thing myself, but for some reason it irritated me to hear him say it. Apparently I felt that nobody but me was allowed to disagree with Ginny – which makes even less sense when you think about it. But I didn't get a chance to argue with him. She was working on what he said faster than I was. 'Why not? Didn't you get anything?' she asked.

'Oh, I got what you wanted, all right.' He took two half sheets of paper out of his pocket and tossed them on the desk. 'I know we're in a grubby business, but it isn't supposed to be this bad. Nailing people who screw around, clearing people who don't, that's what we're supposed to do. Not this. It was bad enough talking to those Consciewitz people. They're lunatics – all that stuff about an "uncle in Detroit" – but they miss their daughter so much it's making them sick. They were practically desperate to make me take their note. They say it proves she didn't run away, I don't know how, their explanations didn't make any sense. As far as I can tell, believing she didn't run away is the only thing that stops them from killing themselves.

'But May-Belle Podhorentz' parents – My God, Ginny! I practically had to extort that note out of them. It's the only piece of her they had left. After what happened to her, they had to put up with some half-wit cop who gave them a bunch of shit. They spent ten months being eaten alive by fear and shame and God knows what else. Then I came along. Next time, just ask me to rape the rest of their kids. It'll be easier.'

Ginny still hadn't even glanced at the notes on her desk. But if Ted made her mad, she kept it to herself. She just held her eyes on him and asked, 'Did they say if they thought May-Belle's note was written under duress?'

'They didn't say, and I didn't ask. I was too ashamed of myself.'

She considered for a moment, then said, 'All right. I don't really need that. What about the schools?'

'Nothing,' Ted rasped. 'May-Belle Podhorentz and Dottie Ann Consciewitz were just like Mittie. They disappeared when nobody was watching them.'

Ginny sat up straighter in her chair. 'What do you mean?'

'What do you think I mean? None of them walked away from their friends or disappeared in the middle of a class or snuck out the back way during lunch. They all waited until they were alone. May-Belle was a piano student. One of the practice rooms was assigned to her during her third period. She didn't show up for her fourth-period class. Dottie Ann liked PE, and she had a job in the gym during fifth period. She sorted uniforms and equipment. Alone. She didn't make it to sixth period. And Mittie–'

He started to shout. 'It was the same goddamn thing with Mittie!' He couldn't help himself. 'What the hell do you care? What does all this prove? We're not getting anywhere, and you know it!'

Ginny never flinched. 'I think that what we're doing is pretty obvious. What else would you suggest?'

That stopped him. But not because he didn't have ideas of his own. His expression reminded me of the way he'd left the diner the night before. He had something in mind, no question about it. Whatever it was, however, he stopped because he didn't want to say it out loud.

'Spill it, Ted,' I said softly. 'We're all in this together.'

He didn't move a muscle.

I went on, 'And you need us. You don't have a client. You can't hire yourself to look for your own daughter. You'll lose your licence.'

I knew a thing or two about losing a licence.

Then he turned to face me. His cheeks were as pale as frostbite. 'I don't give a shit about that,' he said. 'I don't want any of this to be true.'

I held his eyes.

Thickly he asked, 'What do you think about – about prostitution? Where does that fit in?'

'Isn't it obvious?' I was trying to guess what he really had in mind. 'That's probably the only thing the coroner was right about. They have to get money somewhere. How else are girls that age going to do it?'

Something like a spasm of rage or disgust jumped across Ted's face. He turned on his heel and left the office.

Ginny stared after him for a long time, frowning grimly. Then she picked up the notes he'd left on her desk. She read them, studied them, checked the watermarks, then handed them to me.

They fitted the pattern exactly – paper, watermark, torn edge, handwriting, everything. When I compared them with the notes we already had, I saw that May-Belle Podhorentz' was word-for-word identical with Mittie's.

After all, sixteen months is a long time for whatever bastard dictated these notes to remember exactly what they said.

'I should have told him what we've got,' Ginny said. Still thinking about Ted.

'He didn't want to hear it.' That was my first reaction. Then I said, 'Besides, we haven't got anything.'

'That depends on what you're looking for,' she replied in a musing tone. 'Things are starting to fit together.'

'Oh, good.' Being sober doesn't do much for my temper. 'Now if the fit just made sense, we'd be getting somewhere.'

It was her turn to stay calm. 'We *are* getting somewhere. If Maria Lutt's parents have a note like these, we'll have a case that can stand up under any kind of pressure – even if that fucker Acton tries to get us out of the way.'

'That isn't what I meant.' Even I knew how important those notes were.

She looked at the ceiling for a moment, then said, 'I take it you didn't notice anything interesting in what Ted told us? About how Mittie, May-Belle, and Dottie Ann disappeared?'

'It's the same story as Alathea,' I said sourly. 'I knew all that already. I read it in Kirke's files. So what?'

'I'm going to have to check it out with the other schools. This is too iffy to take chances with. But I think there's something important in those files. According to them, these girls didn't just run away from school – they ran away *during* school. Never after or before. During. And every one of them was alone on a regular basis at some point in the school day. Being alone didn't happen by accident on a particular day.'

'Which proves what?' She was on the edge of something, I could feel it. But I didn't have the dimmest notion what it was. I was like Ted – I had ideas of my own, and they didn't seem to relate to what Ginny was thinking.

'I don't know yet. Files don't always give a very clear picture of what really happens.'

That was true enough. But it still didn't mean anything to me. Even if the other files checked out with the schools themselves, that only showed that every one of the girls had a regular chance to run away. Opportunity, nothing more.

I used to know some cops, back in the days when I was still on speaking terms with some of them, who believed that opportunity creates crime. People do things for the simple reason that they get the chance. Wives shoot their husbands because there's a gun in the house. Kids become junkies because drugs exist. Responsible executives take money out of the till and blow it in Las Vegas because Las Vegas is there. Opportunity. Those cops used to talk about preventing crime by getting rid of opportunity.

I think that's a crock of manure. In my opinion, people commit gratuitous crimes, crimes they aren't forced into, the way a starving man sometimes feels forced to steal, or a woman whose husband is cheating on her sometimes feels forced to shoot him, for the sake of power. If they can get away with it, it puts them on top of the world.

But right then I wasn't so sure of anything. If Ginny wanted to blame it on opportunity, I wasn't going to argue with her. I didn't have anything better to offer. Instead I said, 'There's plenty of daylight left. What do you want me to do while I've still got wheels?'

'Marisa Lutt,' she said without hesitation. 'Let's make sure we've got everything. I'm tempted to call Encino, ask him to go further back than two years. But I'm half afraid to find out if there're any more of these cases. And I got the impression that he's going to work on it anyway. Maybe he didn't know about the notes before, but he does now. He'll probably call us himself if he finds anything we need to know.'

I agreed with that. 'You're going to do the rest of the schools?'

'Yes. Ensenada and North Valley. I think that covers it, doesn't it?'

I made a quick mental check. 'That's it.'

'OK.' She got to her feet. 'Call my answering service when you're finished. Then you might as well get rid of that clunker.'

'Yeah.' I heaved myself up out of the chair. Collected all the notes and stuffed them in my pocket. This time I went out first. I wasn't trying to prove anything, no matter what Kirke had said. It was her office, and she had to lock up after me.

Alone again, I dug the Torino out of the garage and headed in the direction of the Heights. The Lutts lived in one of those newish suburbs where all the houses look nice even though they're crammed together on lots you can hardly lie down crosswise on, and all the streets and even the developments have cute irrelevant names. The Lutts' development was called Sherwood Forest – in this part of the world, of all places – and they lived on Friar Tuck Road between Little John Street and Maid Marian Lane. As first impressions go, it didn't raise my expectations about Carson and Lillian Lutt, but I suppose with real estate prices being what they are you pretty much have to live wherever you find a house you can afford. If I wasn't mistaken, Sherwood Forest's big selling point was that the houses were less expensive than they looked. That, and a chance to send your junior-high kids to Ensenada Middle School.

I parked in the street, even though that left precious little room for the rest of the traffic, and went up the walk to the Lutts' front door. Paint and trim aside, their place was identical to every fourth house on the block. And they had one chest-high piñon growing out of their front lawn, just like every other property in sight.

Unfortunately you can't tell what's going on inside a house from the outside. When Carson Lutt opened the door, it took me just one second to be sure that he was drunk.

He looked me up and down blearily, as if I were some kind of obnoxious consequence of his drinking, then said, 'What the hell do you want?' His voice was smeared around the edges in a way that showed he wasn't really very good at drinking. It takes practice to learn how to speak clearly when you're full of booze.

I groaned to myself. The smell of his breath made me as thirsty as a dog. And I was already in no mood to put up with a belligerent drunk.

I had to make a special effort not to sound too hostile myself. 'My name is Axbrewder. I'd like to talk to you about your daughter.'

'That punk?' he snorted. 'What's she done now?'

'Nothing as far as I know.'

'Oh.' That seemed to surprise him. For a minute he forgot to be angry at me. 'Come on in.' He waved me into the house and shut the door. 'Have a drink.'

'No, thanks.' The living room looked better than I'd expected. Whoever decorated it had spent enough money to make the atmosphere soothing and the furniture comfortable, but stopped before the place looked like those implausible pictures in home decorating magazines. It was the kind of room where you'd expect a quietly successful businessman and his wife to give quiet parties for friends they actually enjoyed.

Well, Lillian Lutt was sitting there on the couch quietly enough – but if she'd looked any more miserable you could've stuck her head on a pole and used her to ward off evil spirits. She had a tall glass in her hands, the kind you use for heavy drinking. It took me a couple of seconds to pull myself together enough to add, 'I'm on the wagon today.'

Carson Lutt peered at me. 'Did I hear you say no?'

'Offer him a drink, Carson,' Lillian Lutt said from the couch. 'I hate to drink alone.'

'You're not drinking alone,' he said. 'I'm drinking with you.'

'That's nice.' She almost smiled.

'Have a drink,' he said to me. 'I'm serious.'

I said, 'So am I. I don't want a drink. I want to talk about your daughter.'

'What's she done now?' Mrs Lutt asked. The pain in her face was terrible to look at.

'Nothing,' I snapped. The smell of all that alcohol made my nerves jumpy. My control wasn't as good as it should've been. 'She's been dead a little too long for that.'

That took a minute to sink in. Lillian gave me one straight look as if she were about to scream, then got up and walked out of the room.

'All right, you, whatever your name is.' Suddenly Lutt's voice was clear and sharp and determined. 'Get out of here.'

'Tell me about Marisa first.'

He didn't even blink. 'You're a lot bigger than I am. I don't think I can throw you out. But I'm going to try. And I'm going to keep trying until you' – his voice jumped into a yell – '*get the hell out of here!*'

I didn't have anything to say to that. It was his house. And I understood what he was doing with his pain. So I just shrugged and let myself out the front door.

But I didn't leave. Instead I sat down on the front porch and tried to think of a way to handle the situation.

Part of me wanted to go back and accept his offer. I had a feeling that he'd tell me everything I wanted to know and more if I just had a few drinks with him. People who aren't used to being drunk are like that. But I wasn't ready to pay that much for the answers to a few questions. Once I got started, I wouldn't stop. On the other hand, I was seriously tempted to go back into the house and pound on him for a while.

I was still considering my non-existent options when a kid came up the driveway toward the house. She looked to be about nine or ten – a cute kid with straight blond hair, braces, and one of those loose-jointed tomboy bodies that promises a lot of future development. She stopped in front of me, studied me gravely for a long minute.

Not having any better ideas, I said, 'Hi.'

'Hi,' she said. Then abruptly, 'Are they drunk again?'

That sounded like a dangerous question, and I was leery of it. But the seriousness in her child-face demanded an honest answer. Finally I said, 'I think so.'

'Oh, damn.' She made *damn* sound as innocent as sunlight. All at once, she dropped herself onto the porch beside me and put her chin on her knees. 'They're going to blame it on me.'

'Why would they do that?'

'I'm late. When I'm late, they always use it as an excuse. They say they're worried sick about me.' Her sarcasm underlined the hurt in her voice.

I waited a moment. Then I said, 'But you don't think that's the real reason.'

'Of course not.' This time I heard real bitterness. 'I come home late because I know they're going on one of their binges. I stay away as late as I can.'

I nodded. 'It must be rough.'

'Yeah.' She stared in front of her as if her whole future were a desert. 'They think I'm going to turn out like Marisa.'

All of a sudden, the Lutts went *click* in my head and started to make sense. Now I knew what they were going through. I'd seen a lot of it in the last two days. Your thirteen-year-old daughter suddenly runs away for no reason in the world, and when she turns up dead months later you're told she's a junky whore. So who do you blame? It must be your fault. She's a little too young for you to pin it all on her, but to save your soul you can't think what you did wrong. Pretty soon you start to think that you did everything wrong. You can't trust yourself any more – and that means you can't trust anybody. Not even your ten-year-old.

'That's why they drink,' I said quietly. 'Because of what happened to her.'

'Yeah,' she assented. 'And then that pig came. The cop. At first I thought you were him. He was big, too. I didn't hear what he said, but when he was gone Mom was crying and couldn't stop, and Dad looked like he was going to be sick.'

I was thinking fast now – and what I came up with disgusted me. I felt rotten just considering it. But I didn't see any other way. After a minute I said, 'My name is Brew.'

She looked over at me, made an effort to smile. 'I'm Denise.'

'Denise,' I said carefully, 'I'm a private investigator. I'm trying to find a girl who ran away from home. Just like Marisa. Right now, it looks like they're connected. The same thing is going to happen to this girl unless I can find her in time. But I'm not getting anywhere, and I need help. Your parents – well, they're too upset to understand why I need to talk to them.'

She peered at me intensely. 'You can ask me. I know all about it. They didn't want me to hear, but I listened at the door.' She was eager to help. Probably her own self-respect wasn't exactly in great shape. She needed to do something, make a positive contribution in some way.

I gave her the best smile I could muster. 'There's just one thing I really need. After she ran away, Marisa wrote your parents a note. That's where the connection is. In the note. I need it.'

For a second while she looked at me, her eyes brightened. Then she jumped up. 'I know where it is.' Before I could regret what I'd gotten her into, she hurried into the house.

She wasn't gone long. I heard shouts as if her parents were yelling at her. Then she came back out and handed me a piece of paper.

A half sheet of good twenty-pound bond, neatly torn along one edge. What the messy handwriting had to say wasn't more than three words different than Alathea's note. By this time I could recognize the watermark at fifty paces.

I got to my feet. Talking fast so that I could finish before either of the Lutts came out after Denise, I said, 'Now listen. When your parents are sober, I want you to tell them about me. Tell them Marisa didn't run away. She was kidnapped. I don't know how or why, but I'm going to find out. I'm going to nail whoever did it. Your parents don't have any reason to hate themselves. And they don't have any reason to be worried about you.'

If Ginny had been there, she would've tried to stop me during that whole speech. I didn't have any business making promises like that, and I knew it. But I felt dirty about the way I'd used Denise, gotten her in trouble with her parents when she already had more than she could handle. I had to give her something in return.

If it turned out that I couldn't keep my promises, I could always go back to drinking. One shame more or less wouldn't make any difference. Alcohol doesn't care about details like that.

Chapter Ten

Rush-hour traffic slowed me down, so by the time I'd returned the Torino and walked back down Cuevero to my apartment I needed supper. I didn't feel much like cooking for myself, but in my neighbourhood there aren't any restaurants that don't have bars attached, so I didn't have much choice. I fixed whatever was left in the refrigerator and ate as much of it as I could stand. Then I called Ginny's service and left a message telling her everything I knew.

Afterwards I spent about an hour cleaning my apartment, which is something I do whenever I'm feeling particularly grimy inside – and trying not to think about it. You'd be surprised how much cleaning you can do in a one-room efficiency apartment if you really put your mind to it.

By then it was dark outside. But not dark enough to suit me. Looking for chores to pass the time, I stripped the .45 and cleaned it. It didn't need much. In the past few years, I'd probably cleaned the damn thing three times for every shot I fired. But it's another job that can take a while if you go into it with the right attitude.

When I was done, I took a long shower.

The night still felt too early, but I couldn't stomach any more waiting. After my shower, I got dressed, loaded the .45 and stuffed it into my shoulder holster, and went out.

Looking for Manolo, the information dealer.

I'd spent the whole day doing what Ginny wanted me to do. Now I wanted to check out an idea of my own.

Manolo was the man who could help me.

Most of the traffic had died out on Eighth Street. I could smell the alleys as I walked past them, hear the jukeboxes in the bars. Women shouted at their children, husband, loan sharks. Young studs swaggered in the road, catcalling at every girl they saw. Grizzled patriarchal Indians, Chicanos, Mestizos tried their best to walk in straight lines. Couples stood and necked in doorways and around corners. I didn't pass five Anglos between Cuevero and the centre of the old city, where Paseo Grande would've continued on if it hadn't turned into a pitiful narrow thoroughfare called Coal Street. For the first time today, I felt like I knew what I was doing. Things can happen at night.

Not that my search promised to be easy. Old Manolo was a man of regular habits – and he made it his regular habit to be wherever the listening was good. Which on any given night could be any one of twenty different places. Sometimes he seemed to be everywhere and nowhere, and you had to know the history and fate of every bottle of anisette in the city to find him. Not a very reassuring prospect, but I didn't see any way around it.

I was trying to decide where to start when I got lucky. A kid came running toward me down the sidewalk, and I recognized him before he got to me. His name was Pablo. I knew him because I'd met his family two years ago, when Ginny and I were working on a protection-racket case. He was in a hurry, and there was a strange bulge under his shirt. He had a packet of some kind tucked into the front of his pants.

Apparently he was running for a numbers racket.

I suppose you could say that's a relatively harmless way for a kid to hustle a few bucks. He was a messenger boy, nothing more. And anyway it was none of my business. But that didn't stop me. I caught his arm as he went past and swung him to a halt. '*Hola*, Pablo. There is no dignity in such haste,' I said in Spanish.

'I must run, Señor.' He didn't even look at me. He was trying to break my grip without making a production out of it. Probably afraid of attracting attention. 'If I go and come swiftly, I will be given a dollar.'

'A man does not run to do the bidding of those who are themselves not men enough to do their own running.' Stern Uncle Axbrewder. If Ginny heard me, she would've had real trouble keeping a straight face.

Now he looked at me. 'Ay, Señor Axbrewder?'

'It is I myself, Pablo.'

Then he put on a whine. 'Señor Axbrewder, my arm is being broken.'

'An arm will mend, Pablo, when it is the self-esteem which breaks, mending is not done easily.'

'Yes, Señor. For what have I been stopped?'

Well, I could see that I wasn't getting through to him. I got down off my high horse. 'I wish to have speech with old Manolo the drinker of anisette. Where is he to be found?'

'God knows, Señor.'

'That is very true. But a cunning boy like Pablo has surely taken thought on the matter.'

He twisted against me for another moment. Then he gave up. 'It is possible that he takes his anisette in the place of Juan Cideño.'

I said, 'Gracias, Pablo,' and let him go.

He stared at me for a moment as if I were as crazy as all Anglos. Then he turned and started running again.

Like I said – lucky. Juan Cideño's bar wasn't more than a block from where I stood.

On the inside, it resembled the Hegira. Its major distinction was a life-sized poster of Raul Ramirez on the wall opposite the bar. The poster wasn't old, but stale air and smoke had stained it until Ramirez seemed like a champion from another generation.

Old Manolo sat in a booth at the back.

His eyes were closed – he looked sound asleep. Even knowing him the way I did, I half expected him to topple slowly to the floor and start snoring. But there was a small glass of anisette on the table between his hands, and after a few seconds he picked it up delicately with his fingertips, tucked it under his gray walrus moustache, and took a sip. Then he set the glass down, swallowed, and went back to looking like he was asleep.

I glanced around the bar, just making sure there wasn't anyone nearby who might be offended if he happened to overhear me. None of el Señor's men, for example, would take kindly to the questions I wanted to ask. Then I went over to the barkeep. Old Manolo is like an oracle – there are ceremonies you have to perform if you want answers from him. I bought a bottle of anisette and took it over to his booth.

Hoping he wouldn't try to make me drink it with him. Wondering what I was going to say.

He spared me the effort of finding an opening line. When I arrived at his table, he said without opening his eyes, '*Hola*, Señor Axbrewder. Have you come to sit with an old man and tell him interesting tales? That would be very welcome.'

His English was distinct. But I answered in Spanish. '*Hola*, Manuel Sevilla y Acclara de los Maestos.' Speaking Spanish with him was part of the ritual, like knowing his proper name. 'Alas, all my tales are poor things in comparison to your own legendary knowledge.' I was trying to figure out how he'd known who I was without opening his eyes. 'Yet I would sit with you, and share speech, if I am not an intrusion.'

He nodded as if he knew exactly what I had in mind. 'You bear with you a thing more precious than many tales. Please sit.'

Huh? I said to myself. But then I figured it out. He was talking about the bottle. He must have heard me buy it, recognized my voice. I kept forgetting just how good he was at picking up on everything around him.

I said, 'Gracias,' and slid into the booth. Then I unscrewed the top of the bottle and refilled his glass.

He nodded again, smiling faintly under his moustache. But a moment later his eyes opened, and he looked at me with an air of mild surprise. His eyeballs were a muddy colour, as if they'd been stained by all the secrets he carried around in his head. 'You do not accompany me, Señor?' he asked. When I didn't answer right away, he went on, 'Perhaps tequila would be of more pleasure to you. Not all are equally enamored with anisette.'

He was being perfectly magnanimous. But his graciousness cut both ways. He was offering me a chance to get out of being rude – and warning me that I'd better take him up on it.

'Unhappily, I must decline,' I said carefully. 'I am like other Anglos. Drink plays upon my wits discourteously.' That was like admitting a failure of manhood, but I couldn't think of an alternative. 'The matter before me is urgent. I must practise great sobriety if I am to speak clearly, and to hear what is said to me without confusion.' I shrugged as eloquently as I could.

Old Manolo considered for some time. But he didn't close his eyes. Finally he made up his mind. 'It is said of you, Señor Axbrewder, that you suffer an infirmity of the heart, arising from the greatly-to-be-regretted death of your brother. Such things must be understood and accepted.' Solemnly he took a sip of his anisette.

Deep inside me, I gave a sigh of relief. He wasn't offended. The oracle was still open.

I didn't say anything. I knew better.

He didn't keep me waiting long. He scanned my face for a moment, then said, 'You spoke of urgency. Is it permitted to enquire concerning this matter?'

'Señor Sevilla, the young daughter of my brother's widow has gone from her home.'

'Ah,' he said politely. 'That is to be regretted. But many girls both young and old have gone from their homes, Señor. The world has become corrupt in every place. Girls no longer honour their homes, or the wishes of their parents. What can be done? The world pays no heed to the sorrow of parents.'

'That is very true. But I have cause to think that the corruption does not lie in this widow's daughter. Hear what I have learned in seeking her.' Speaking formally, precisely, I told him about the seven dead girls. I described the connection between them and Alathea. When I was finished, I said, 'Such evil does not befall so many young girls by chance. It is deliberately done. My thought is that for each the corruption comes from one source, one supplier of drugs. I must find that man if I am to save my dead brother's child.'

Old Manolo had closed his eyes while I was speaking. Now he was silent for a long time. I didn't rush him. Information-dealing is a touchy profession. He was alive after all these years because he was cautious and selective. But by the time he decided to speak, my knuckles were white from clutching the edge of the table.

'Señor,' he said softly, not opening his eyes, 'I think perhaps you have made the acquaintance of my son's wife's father's sister's daughter. You were not properly introduced. So few things are now done properly in the world. But her name will be known to you. She is Theresa Maria Sanguillan y Garcia.'

He paused, and I said, 'I have been given the honour of knowing her name.'

'Then you will understand that I wish to assist.'

'I believe it.' His family was in my debt. That meant something to him.

'Unhappily, I can offer you nothing. Indeed, the fate of these young girls has been known to me. But the supplier, he who works this evil – that one is not known.'

I was trembling. 'Señor Sevilla, it is said that no grain or gram of heroin passes from hand to hand in Puerta del Sol without your knowledge. In the matter of drugs, all tales come to your ears.'

'I hear much,' old Manolo assented. 'No man hears all.'

'Can it be that el Señor has such evil dealings, and there is no talk of them? Or that men talk of the dealings of el Señor, and you do not hear?'

At that, he opened his eyes. I half expected him to be offended, but he wasn't. There was nothing in his gaze but sadness. 'Señor Axbrewder, the knowledge you seek is dark and mysterious. I can shed no light upon it. But I ask you to believe that no hint of this knowledge has touched my ears. That in itself is knowledge for you, is it not?'

When I didn't answer, he went on, 'I will speak further. There are many drugs, and much passing among hands. But in the matter of heroin, all passing begins in the hands of el Señor. That is his pride, and the source of his great wealth. I do not speak this to mislead you. El Señor is a man of honour, placing great value upon his family and his children, and the purity of his daughters. Such corrupting of young girls is a terrible evil, and he would in no way permit it.'

'These girls are Anglo,' I said. 'Does el Señor's honour extend itself to Anglos?'

'In truth, it does. He has no love for Anglos. That cannot be denied. But I speak absolutely. This corrupting of young girls does not come through him.'

Well, probably that wasn't the whole story. If the bastard I wanted was cutting into el Señor's profits, el Señor would've slapped him down long ago. So I could assume that those profits weren't in any danger. Which fitted with what old Manolo was saying. Apparently Alathea's kidnapper made his own clientele out of people el Señor didn't want.

But that didn't help me any. I was still stuck. I couldn't keep the bitterness out of my voice as I said, 'El Señor controls all heroin in Puerta del Sol – and yet he does not supply these girls. Still they die from heroin. What, then, can I do? My brother's widow's daughter will surely die also.'

Manolo poured himself another drink, then recapped the bottle and stuck it in the pocket of his coat. He emptied his glass and got to his feet. My audience was over – he was going somewhere else. But before he left, he bent close to me and whispered so that no one in the bar could overhear him, 'Possibly you must go to el Señor himself. If you wish to have speech with him, you must know his name. It is Hector Jesus Fria de la Sancha.'

A minute later he was gone.

I stayed where I was. Go to el Señor for help. Sure. That sounded like a polite way of telling me to go to hell. El Señor was what the newspapers probably would have called 'the crime-czar of Puerta del Sol', if they'd known of his existence. A man of honour. Oh, absolutely. He would chew me up into little pieces and spit me in the gutter. No thanks. I wasn't that desperate. Not yet.

So I didn't go looking for el Señor, even though I knew where to find him. I left the bar and started for home. Feeling like shit. Because I'd failed Alathea. I'd played the only hand I had, and lost. Now the only thing left was to be Ginny's errand boy while she tried to crack this case her own way.

My depression must've showed in the way I walked, because this time the *muchachos* felt free to notice me – which they don't usually do, even when I'm drunk. Most of the time I'm a little too big for them. But not tonight. They weren't exactly aggressive about it, but they whistled from across the street and muttered obscure Spanish insults at my back as I went past. The whole community seemed to know that I hadn't been able to get what I needed out of old Manolo.

When you're in that kind of mood, it's hard to stay away from the stuff. Alcohol is the only magic in the world. When you're working, you're trying to change things around you so that you fit into them better. But when you're drinking, the fit comes from inside. And if it isn't real, at least it's easier than straining to figure out puzzles when no one will tell you the secret. On my way home I had a tough time staying out of the bars.

But I did stay out of them – for Alathea. Because the one thing alcohol would never do was help me find her. Until she was found, being Ginny's errand boy was better than nothing, and it was probably about all I was good for.

I ignored the bars. I ignored the *muchachos* and their insults. I just lumbered my way up Eighth Street in the direction of home.

As I approached my apartment building, I noticed a long black Buick parked at the corner of a side street. All the lights were off, but the motor ran softly. Three men sat inside.

Just when I got abreast of the car, its doors thunked open, and the men got out. They wore neat businessmen's suits, with crisp businessmen's ties and shiny businessmen's shoes. At that time of night in that neighbourhood, they might as well have worn sandwich boards saying, 'Plain-clothes Cops'. They were all big, and the biggest one was a chunky individual about my size and maybe thirty pounds heavier. He said, 'Axbrewder,' in the kind of voice you'd expect if you taught a bulldozer to talk.

The muscle with him stayed back and didn't say anything – and the light was bad, so there was a chance I might not recognize them if I saw them again. But the goon with the diesel voice I got a good look at. He had a jaw hard and square enough to set rivets, a nose that could moonlight as a can opener, and a forehead that looked like it was made out of reinforced concrete. He flashed his badge at me and said, 'Detective-Lieutenant Acton.'

But he wasn't trying to introduce himself, or even prove he was a cop. He just wanted to get close to me. As he put the badge away, his other hand came up to my chest and shoved.

I wasn't braced for it, and it wasn't exactly a gesture of undying friendship. He got his weight into it. It sent me backward, smacking me hard against the wall of the building.

I was already rebounding at him when I saw that his backups had their guns out. Acton grinned like the blade of a plough, and suddenly I could picture him writing his report. 'Shot while resisting arrest.'

I stopped with a jerk.

'Acton,' I said, trying not to show how much breath he'd knocked out of me. 'What a pleasant surprise. I've been wanting to talk to you.'

'Is that a fact?' His hand came up again, but this time he just poked me with one finger. He aimed to jab me in the solar plexus, which is a nice way to hurt someone when you don't want to leave any marks. He missed, but that didn't stop him. 'Well, I want to talk to you, too' – he poked again – 'Mick.'

Mick. Instantly a wind began to blow inside my head, and my balance shifted. Nobody calls me Mick. Nobody. Not since my brother died. The night seemed to congeal at Acton's back, and I lost sight of the two cops with the guns. My chest was so full of rage and pressure that it felt like my ribs were going to crack.

'What's the matter, Mick?' Poke. 'Don't you like being called "Mick"?' Poke. Any second now, he was going to rupture my self-control, and then I'd have to take his face off with my bare hands.

But then his partners registered on me again. They had guns. If I touched Acton, they'd probably beat me half to death before they threw me in gaol. Ordinarily I wouldn't have cared much about being locked up, but if it happened now I wouldn't be able to help find Alathea. Right this minute, she was somewhere in the city prostituting herself to get money for drugs. If we didn't find her, she was going to end up dead.

Just holding the knowledge in hurt so bad that I thought I was going to pass out. But I stood there. Let Acton do whatever he had in mind.

He must've seen me make the decision, because he eased off with his finger. 'That's nice, Mick. That's a good boy. Swallow your pride. A drunk like you should be used to it by now.'

I didn't say anything.

'Give me the notes, Mick.'

The notes – that surprised me. Who the fuck told him about the notes? But I was already clenched, and I didn't show anything. Through my teeth, I said, 'I don't have them.' If I'd opened my jaws, I wouldn't have been able to hold in my rage.

'Where are they, Mick?'

'The safe. Fistoulari Investigations.'

'Ah, that's too bad.' He never stopped grinning. 'That means I'll have to get a warrant. What a shame. It's a good thing you're a liar, Mick.'

I couldn't do anything about it. I had to stand there while he searched me. When he found the notes, he glanced through them, counted them, then stuffed them into his coat pocket.

I stopped looking at him. Instead I stared into the darkness past his shoulder. That grin of his was going to give me nightmares.

'Now, Mick. I'm going to let you have a little friendly advice. Get off my case. Stay off it. I hate your guts, Mick, and if you get in my way I'll slap you down so hard you'll have to reach up to touch bottom.'

Staring into the darkness was a good way to watch his shoulder muscles. If he intended to hit me again, I wanted to know about it. 'Why?'

He laughed, but it wasn't because there was anything funny. 'Rick Axbrewder was a good cop. He was also a friend of mine.'

I shrugged. What else could I do? 'How did you know about the notes?'

He stepped closer, and I almost flinched. But he didn't hit me. His tone was soft and bitter as he said, 'That bastard Stretto lit a fire under the commissioner. Now the commissioner wants my hide. I'm in trouble because I didn't make the connection with those notes. So I'm warning you. This is the last time a punk drunk like you is going to make me look bad.'

'I don't have to,' I said. 'You're already doing it to yourself. Why did you scare the Christies like that?'

That did it. His shoulder bunched, and he swung at me hard, fingers stiff, gouging for my solar plexus. I blocked it as best I could, but his fingers still dug deep into my gut.

I hunched over, staggered back to get out of the way of another hit. However, he didn't swing again. He and his goons got back into their car and drove off, roaring the engine and squealing the tyres to convince me that they meant business.

For a couple of minutes, I stayed where I was, almost retching. Then I went the rest of the way to Cuevero Road, and struggled up the stairs to my apartment.

Losing the notes made me a whole lot sicker than just one jab in the stomach. But there was no way around it – I had to face Ginny. While I was still mad enough to make decisions, I yanked up the phone and called her service. As it turned out, she was at home, and they patched me through.

'Brew. What's happening?'

Almost puking with self-disgust, I told her, 'I just had a run-in with Acton. He took the notes.'

My fault entirely. A Mongoloid idiot could've warned me to take better care of the evidence.

She must've heard most of the story in my voice. She didn't ask me how it happened. Or how I could've been so stupid. She asked, 'Are you all right?'

'I'm not in gaol.'

'Thank God for small blessings.' Somehow she made her tone just right for my mood. 'How did he even find out about them?'

'Stretto. It seems he went to the commissioner. Apparently he doesn't think the cops are doing their job. The commissioner took it out on Acton.'

'Surprise, surprise,' Ginny muttered. 'I wasn't sure the illustrious Mr Stretto had that much in him.'

'Anyway' – I gritted my teeth and said it – 'I've pretty well blown our case. Now we've got nothing.'

'He's a cop,' she snapped. 'What could you do, eat the damn things?'

'I shouldn't have been carrying them around.'

She dismissed that without hesitation. 'Forget about it. They were safe enough. We just didn't know Acton was going to get desperate. Anyway,' she went on before I could object, 'we don't need them now.'

I said, 'Huh?' Always the brilliant conversationalist.

'Acton won't destroy them. Too many people know about them. And I've already got what I need out of them.'

'Which is what?'

'Brew, I finished checking out the other schools.' My head must've been clearing – I finally started to hear the vibration of excitement in her voice. 'I'll spare you the details. The point is that everything fits. Every one of these girls disappeared from school at a time when they were scheduled to be alone.'

'You already knew that. It's in the school board files.'

'Exactly!'

'Exactly what? It still doesn't prove anything. Why call attention to yourself running away when you've got a perfect chance to sneak off every day of the week?'

'Well, that's true, of course,' she admitted, 'if you look at it that way. Let me ask you a different question, Brew. Is there any proof in those notes? Proof the girls didn't write them, or wrote them under duress? I'm talking about hard evidence, the kind that stands up in court.'

I thought about it for a long time. Then I said, 'No.'

'Damn right. As far as we know, they were all addressed correctly. But that's minor. The main thing is that all the notes were addressed to the right parents.'

I said, 'Huh?' again. It was getting to be a habit.

'Marisa Lutt wrote, 'Dear Mom and Dad.' So did Esther Hannibal. So did Ruth Ann Larsen, May-Belle Podhorentz, Dottie Ann Consciewitz, Carol Christie. We don't know about Rosalynn Swift. But Alathea wrote, 'Dear Mom.' Mittie wrote, 'Dear Dad.''

It still didn't mean anything to me. 'So what? Most kids know how many parents they have. If they've only got one, they can usually tell if it's male or female.'

'Of course! That's the point!' She was hot on a trail I couldn't see. 'Just look at it from the other side. We know those notes are wrong. We have good reason to believe they were all dictated by the same person. Well, nine girls who live in nine different neighbourhoods and go to six different schools aren't going to end up having the same person dictate their notes by accident. So what does that tell you?'

'Kidnapping.' I grated. I already knew that.

'Right! But if that's true, then the girls didn't run away at all. So it isn't a question of figuring out why the girls ran away while they were alone. The question is, how did the kidnapper know they were going to be alone? How did he know they were going to be somewhere that he could get at them without being seen? For that matter, how did he know he could get them to come with him? And how did he know their addresses? How did he know how many parents they had?'

I said, 'Research?' Feeling like an idiot.

'Now you're getting it. Tell me, Brew. If you wanted to research nine different girls in six different schools, and find out the answers to all these questions, where would you go?'

That was it. Finally I understood. 'The school board. The files.' She was right, I could feel it. The bastard we were looking for got his information from those files. It was the only answer that made sense.

Maybe he was even on the board.

Part Three
Thursday Night / Friday

Chapter Eleven

Of course, it all rested on the assumption that the girls were being kidnapped. I had no problem with that. But it had one crucial flaw.

There didn't seem to be any payoff. No ransom demands. And in any case, half the families involved couldn't have scraped up a self-respecting ransom to save their souls.

Which brought me back to drugs. Some pusher in town was hot for new business. A very particular kind of new business.

Some pusher old Manolo had never heard of.

There must've been a hell of a lot of money in it to make it worth a possible kidnapping rap. Or a hell of a lot of hate. The kind of hate that makes serial killers.

I didn't say anything to Ginny about that. Instead I said, 'That's going to be a big job. How many people are in the school board these days? Twenty?'

She said, 'Fifteen.'

'And then there are all those secretaries. And on top of that, some people from the individual schools may have access to the general files. You're talking about thirty suspects.' Or more. 'Where do we start?'

'By whittling down the list.'

I said, 'Oh.' Heavy on the sarcasm. The sense that we were finally getting somewhere made me feel a little better about Alathea, but it didn't do much for my opinion of myself. 'That shouldn't be too hard. We'll just call people up and ask them how they feel about stuffing dope down thirteen-year-old girls.'

'So we'll have to work at it,' she said evenly. 'Where did you get the idea it was supposed to be easy?' When I didn't answer, she went on,

'There's a lot we can do, but to save time we'll start with the obvious, the full-time people. Stretto, Scurvey, Greenling, and the secretaries.'

I couldn't argue with her, so I asked, 'What about Acton?'

'I'll check on him tonight. Find out if he was lying about the commissioner. If he was telling the truth, we'll have to assume he's in the clear – and Stretto, too, for that matter. Until we know more, anyway.'

I couldn't argue with that either. If Stretto was involved, he wouldn't have called the commissioner. As for Acton – if he was dealing drugs, we'd put him in a real bind. As long as the commissioner knew about those notes, Acton couldn't risk destroying them. *If* the commissioner knew. After chewing it around for a minute, I asked, 'What do you want me to do?'

'Get some sleep,' she said promptly. 'At this point, there's nothing more we *can* do until morning. Get a cab and come to the office tomorrow early. By then I'll have something set up.'

After that, it was too late to argue. I didn't have anything else to offer. It was her case now. When she hung up, I went to bed.

And I went right to sleep. Being sober makes you more tired than you'd expect. But I spent the whole night dreaming about amber, and the next morning I was up with the birds. My face ached as if I'd been grinding my teeth for hours. Nevertheless I ignored it, ignored the feeling of stupidity that filled my chest, ignored the dry wish for alcohol in my mouth. Some day I'd have to find a way to feel proud of being sober, but right then I wasn't up to it. By 8 a.m. I was out on Cuevero Road looking for a cab.

Which was not a good time of day for cabs, but I finally found one. Then it wasn't long until I was riding up the elevator of the Murchison Building to Ginny's office.

She was there already. When I went into her back room, I found her on the phone. I dropped into a chair. Whoever she was talking to, it didn't take her long. A couple of minutes later, we had an appointment with somebody or other for 9.30.

'That was Dr Sandoval,' she said. 'Camilla Sandoval, paediatrician. How long has it been since you voted?'

I shrugged. How can you answer a question like that?

'Well, you probably don't know she represents your district on the Board of Education. This is her fifth term – she's very popular. One of the part-time members.' She looked at me sharply, as if she expected me to be surprised. 'Your friend Encino speaks highly of her.'

If she wanted a reaction out of me, she was going to be

disappointed. We errand boys try to keep our opinions to ourselves. Especially when we're ashamed of our own bitterness. I got out my pocketknife and pretended to clean my fingernails, letting her hang for a moment before I asked, 'What else did he have to say?'

She frowned, but she didn't look serious about it. I wasn't fooling her any. 'Not much about Dr Sandoval. But he told me a little something about Acton and the commissioner. Apparently Acton was giving it to you straight. Encino wasn't there, but when the commissioner personally goes to see a lieutenant instead of sending for him, and chews him out in front of half the duty room, word gets around pretty fast. Stretto called the commissioner, all right. We can count on it.'

'Politicians,' I muttered, mostly to myself. They know how to talk to each other. If I'd gone to the commissioner with those notes myself, I would've gotten in trouble for "obstructing an official investigation". Paul M. Stretto makes one phone call, and all of a sudden the air's full of shit. 'So scratch the chairman of the board. Put Acton on the back burner. What's next?'

Ginny frowned again. This time she meant it. 'We've got a lot of ground to cover, and everything we do takes time. I can't find Ted, so I bit the bullet and hired some help. I called fat-ass Smithsonian.'

All things considered, that probably shouldn't have surprised me. We had between ten and thirty suspects lined up, and every passing day put Alathea in that much more trouble. But Ginny is an independent cuss, and she doesn't like farming out work to other agencies. And of all the private investigators I know, Lawrence Smithsonian is the one she actively hates. He isn't all that fat, but he as sure as hell *looks* fat, probably because his fees are overweight. And on top of that, his way of condescending to Ginny sends her blood pressure through the roof. Hiring his help probably cost her a pound of flesh. I had to stare at her for a while before I recovered enough to ask, 'Why him?'

'Because he knows money.' She was practically spitting. 'He can learn more about the personal finances of our suspects in one morning than we could in a week. He'll start with the full-time board members and the secretaries, try to find out if any of them are getting rich in private, or living over their heads, or gambling with money they haven't earned, or rolling too high on the stock market. Anything. He has half the bank presidents in this town in his back pocket. I think he blackmails them.'

After a minute I said, 'Lona can't pay you.'

'I know that.' She wasn't thinking about money. She was still steaming about Smithsonian.

'I can't either.'

That made her look at me. 'Who asked you?'

I got up, went over to her. Cupped her head with both my hands and kissed her on the mouth.

She didn't kiss me back. She just sat there and took it. When I stopped, she looked at me like the barrel of a gun and said, 'The next time you do that, you better mean it.'

Well, I meant it all right. My shoulders were trembling, and my pulse beat in my head so loud that I could hardly hear her. But that wasn't what she was getting at. What she had in mind was something even more serious than the way I felt about her. We'd been through it before. She wanted me to quit drinking. Completely. For ever.

That was something I couldn't do. I wasn't worth it.

I went back to my chair and sat down, trying to hold myself so that she couldn't see me shake. When I thought I could control my voice, I asked, 'When is he going to call back?'

'When he finds something. Or this afternoon. Whichever comes first.'

'And in the mean time?'

'We'll go talk to Dr Sandoval. Then we'll go back to the school board and see what we can run down this time.' Her composure was too perfect. I'd confused her and probably hurt her – which was something I had definitely not meant to do. While she got herself ready to leave, I spent a few minutes trying to think of a new way to curse myself.

She was still holding up her wall of businesslike professionalism as we rode the elevator down to the garage and took the Olds out into the morning glare. But after that she unbent enough to tell me what her plans were. They sounded reasonable, and if they worked, we could probably cross half the people off our list today. I let it go at that. I'd already pushed my luck too far with her.

The office of Dr Camilla Sandoval was on the opposite side of the old part of town from where I lived. It was in a squat dull-red adobe structure that looked like it moonlighted as a bordello. Already the waiting room was full of mothers with babies in various stages of stupor or hysteria. Most of them were either Chicano or Indian, and all together they gave a pretty good capsule summary of what life was like in the old part of Puerta del Sol. After half an hour in that room, Ginny and I'd seen every degree of squalor, sickness, flamboyance,

112

passivity, colour, resentment, joy, hunger, love, and rage. A real education, if you can stand to hear babies squall. And see mothers hit them.

When Ginny told the nurse we had an appointment for 9.30, she just shrugged and gestured at all the people ahead of us. It looked like it was going to be a long wait, and I didn't see any way around it. In this part of the world, the Anglos have spent the past hundred and fifty years or so barging in line ahead of Chicanos and Indians, and I didn't want to add to the resentment in those faces. But in situations like this Ginny has a thicker skin than I do. She stood it for that first half hour. Then she dug some paper and a pen out of her purse, wrote a long note, and gave it to the nurse. Her way of presenting it didn't leave the nurse much choice. Three minutes later, Dr Sandoval called us in to see her.

She was a chunky little woman, too small to be a football player and too big to be a fireplug. If she was married, she didn't advertise it by wearing a ring. In fact, she didn't wear any jewellery at all. Her manner was tough, but it was a particular kind of tough, the kind that can look pain straight in the face and make it hurt less without being hurt herself. Or without showing it, anyway. By the time she asked Ginny and me to have a seat in the square cubicle she used for an office, I liked her.

She sat down behind her desk and studied us for a second. Then she picked up Ginny's note and slapped it with the back of her hand. 'Nine junky whores,' she said, 'thirteen or younger. Seven of them dead. What do you want from me? Do you think they were my patients?'

'Dr Sandoval' – Ginny matched her tone evenly – 'we're private investigators.' She flipped the photocopy of her licence on to the desk. 'We've been hired to find the two girls who are still alive. I don't think you know anything about them. That's why we want to talk to you. We want to ask you some questions about the people you work with on the Board of Education.'

That was confusing enough to short-circuit some of Dr Sandoval's hostility. She didn't exactly retreat, but she eased back a bit. 'I don't understand.'

'I know it's complicated,' Ginny said, 'and I can't tell you much without violating the confidence of my clients. But I can tell you this. We have reason to believe these girls were kidnapped. And we suspect the kidnapper has some sort of connection with the school board. We'd like you to give us background information about a few of the people who work there.'

Now that the first surprise was over, Dr Sandoval had started to fume. 'This is insane. Do you understand what you're saying? Perhaps you don't know what the school board does. It exists to help children, to provide them with an education. Not all the members are idealists, of course, but they believe in education. We all believe in children. What you suggest is inconceivable.'

Ginny didn't falter. 'Criminals come in all disguises, Dr Sandoval.'

'I repeat. It is inconceivable.'

'Then you believe Paul Stretto is pure as the driven snow?'

The doctor hesitated. Not a long hesitation, but a hesitation none the less. When it was over, she answered the question with a question. 'If you're right,' she asked, 'why aren't the police involved in this?'

'They are,' Ginny drawled. 'It wouldn't surprise me a bit if you have cops on your doorstep before the day's over. The only difference is, they're trying to catch a pusher. We're trying to find two little girls.'

'I see.' She scanned both of us, and after a minute she looked like she really did see. 'I have patients waiting. Please be as quick as you can.'

Ginny's gaze didn't shift an inch. 'Paul Stretto?'

'Mr Stretto is a politician. I doubt that he has so much as glanced at a textbook since fifth grade. He is on his way to an exalted career as a public servant.' Her mouth twisted sourly around the words. 'I can't believe that he would risk his future by involving himself in kidnapping.'

'Maybe he has friends who just ask him for information.'

'How would I know that?'

'Have you heard any rumours?'

'The rumour,' Dr Sandoval said, 'is that Paul Stretto wants to be president. Of the United States.'

'All right,' Ginny said, 'how about Astin Greenling?'

'That man is the salt of the earth.' No hesitation at all. 'His life has been very unhappy, but he burns himself out every day struggling to provide the children of this city with a decent education. Every year when the levies are voted down, the budget cuts always come out of curriculum. He'll have heart failure some day if he doesn't stop trying to raise the quality of education with less money every year.'

'You say unhappy? In what way?'

'His wife has leukemia.' Dr Sandoval's tone made it clear that she didn't intend to say anything more about Astin Greenling's unhappy life.

Ginny nodded. She was thinking the same thing I was. Treating leukemia costs money. Reams of money. But she didn't make any comment. Money was Smithsonian's job. Instead she went on down the list. 'What can you tell us about Martha Scurvey?'

The doctor frowned, took a moment to decide on an answer. Then she said, 'I don't like her personally. But since she was elected budget vice-chairman last year, our accounting procedures have started to climb out of the Dark Ages. And she seems to have a talent for procurement. She gets lower prices for our supplies. I have to respect that. It takes a little pressure off Astin.'

'How long has she served on the board?'

'Just a year.' Dr Sandoval was sardonic. 'For some reason, most people don't seem to know that the full-time members of the Board of Education are elected by the city at large. As far as I know, she's never been elected for anything before.'

I sighed to myself and mentally crossed Martha Scurvey off the list. She hadn't been on the board when the first four girls disappeared. But Ginny went right on, not wasting the doctor's time. 'And Julian Kirke?'

'He isn't an elected officer. We hired him. The board decided to get into this business of computerizing the files – which, incidentally, I've resisted every step of the way. It's expensive, and I think the money should be spent on the children. But quality education doesn't have as much prestige as computers. Machines have more dignity than human beings.'

I liked her more and more all the time.

'But that's beside the point,' she went on. 'When I was out-voted, the board looked for someone who could handle the nuts and bolts of this grand system. They found Julian. He's a data-management expert, and had a good job with NCR, but they didn't promote him fast enough to keep him. I think he is a petty tyrant, but that doesn't prevent him from doing a good job. The fact is, in his hands the whole project has been less expensive than I thought it would be.'

'How long ago did you hire him?'

'Two and a half, maybe three years.'

'All right, Doctor,' Ginny said briskly. 'Just a couple more questions. How much do you know about the secretaries who work under Mr Kirke?'

'Very little. That's his department. I'm not involved with it. It's my impression that he's pretty hard on them. For that matter, he's barely civil to me. But they do good work.' She sighed. 'Our correspondence looks professional now. Finally.'

I wanted to think about that for a while. I didn't know whether Kirke was a perfectionist or just a cantankerous sonofabitch. But it was going to have to wait. Ginny was asking, 'How many people have access to those files?'

'In theory, everybody in the school system. They aren't intended to be secret. They're supposed to help the schools run better. But the process hasn't reached that point yet. In practice, the files are primarily accessible to the full-time people. When the rest of us want information, we ask Julian or one of the secretaries.'

Ginny glanced at me, looking for more questions. But I didn't have any. This was her type of investigation, not mine. If it'd been up to me, I would've told the doctor exactly what we were looking for and asked her for some kind of intuitive answer. Her intuitions I would've trusted. So I shook my head, and Ginny got to her feet.

Without seeming rude about it, Dr Sandoval ushered us out quickly. About a minute after we stood up, we were past the resentment of all those mothers and in the Olds. By then the doctor was probably examining her next patient.

I pushed my sunglasses on to my face, but they didn't help much. While Ginny started up the Olds, I muttered at her, 'That was fun. What did we get out of it?'

She jerked around to me. 'That's a cheap shot.'

I looked away. I couldn't face her.

'I know. I just said it because I feel useless. It's my niece we're trying to find, and you're spending money like it was water, not to mention working your tail off, and my contribution is nil.'

'Stop that,' she snapped. 'You know what we got out of it. Now when we go to talk to these people, we'll have a handle on who we're talking to.'

'How will that help?' Trying to sound neutral.

With grim patience, she said, 'We'll finally be able to put on some pressure. Maybe we can get our kidnapper to make a mistake.'

I couldn't argue with that. It was something to do. It might even work. So I just sat there while Ginny stamped down on the accelerator and took the Olds squealing out of Dr Sandoval's parking lot on to the highway.

Chapter Twelve

I knew that Ginny and I were headed for a showdown.

I wasn't looking forward to it. It was a guaranteed no-win situation for me. In this day and age, there's no way to talk about shame and guilt without making it sound like self-pity. That's why people with any integrity keep their goddamn mouths shut. A nice trick, if you can do it.

But the fireworks weren't going to start yet. We didn't have time for them. We were on our way back to big Central High and the school board to take a crack at one of Ginny's plans.

When we got close to the school, we started hunting for a phone booth. Ginny's idea was to begin with Kirke. She didn't have anything particular against him – she just wanted to take advantage of the way he treated his secretaries. I had to admit it was a good idea. If he felt the pressure, it might shake him up a bit. And if he didn't, he might pass the joy on to someone who did.

When we found a phone, Ginny said, 'I'll give you ten minutes.'

'Should be enough. How long can you keep him?'

She got out of the Olds, and I slid over into the driver's seat. 'I'll try for half an hour,' she said, 'but I can't guarantee it.'

I put the car in gear. 'That's OK. If he catches me, it'll just make someone more nervous.'

She said, 'Right,' and I drove off.

I parked in the Central High lot and went into the building. Ten minutes didn't turn out to be too much time. It was between class breaks, and the halls were full of kids, half of them apparently trying to run into me. On top of that, with all the kids coming and going every which way, I missed a turn and had to ask directions. And the whole time I had to fight this crazy impulse to stop what I was doing and just

117

go hunting for Alathea. Seeing so many young girls made me feel more desperate than ever. What with one thing and another, it took me more than eight minutes to reach the Board of Education door.

From there I went back down the hall and tucked myself around a corner where I could watch the door without much chance of being seen. Then I waited.

Exactly three minutes later, Kirke left the office. He looked a little more awake than he had the day before, and he was moving fast. Not hurrying, really. Just going like a man who couldn't afford to waste any time. Ginny knew how to get results over the phone.

When he disappeared around a corner, I gave him a minute for second thoughts, then went to the door and let myself in.

The front room hadn't changed. It still reminded me of the police duty-room in the Municipal Building. But it was busier. Several kids at the counter occupied the attention of five secretaries. Fortunately the one I wanted wasn't one of them. I was looking for the secretary that Kirke had chewed out in front of Ginny and me the day before.

She sat at her desk with a harried look on her face.

I caught her eye, and she came over to the counter. I said, 'Sondra?' She nodded. My face didn't register with her, so I said, 'My name's Axbrewder. I was here yesterday.'

'Oh yes, I remember.' For a moment her expression relaxed, and she turned pretty, the way she was born to look. She leaned toward me and said softly so that the kids couldn't hear, 'You're the private detective.' Word gets around.

'That's right.' I took a stab at trying to look charming, but for some reason my smile didn't feel right, so I dropped it. 'I'd like to talk to you.'

The way she turned her eyes up at me conveyed the impression that she gave my smile credit for good intentions. 'What about?'

'I can't tell you here. Can you take a break or something? I'll buy you a cup of coffee.'

At that her face closed like a shutter. 'I can't.'

'Oh, come on.' Axbrewder at his most persuasive. 'Kirke won't catch you. My partner has him, and she won't let him go for at least half an hour. And if he comes back sooner, I can cover you.' I was prepared to try almost anything. 'He'd look better with his nose sticking out his ear, don't you think?'

Well, I was right about one thing, anyway. Kirke had been leaning on her hard. Too hard. Even timid people have limits, and Sondra had just reached hers. Her smile looked brittle and vaguely feverish, but it was a smile. 'Where shall we go?'

This time my own smile was a lot more genuine. 'How about the cafeteria?'

'OK.' She went to her desk and got her purse, then said to one of the other secretaries in a determined little voice, 'I'm going to take my break now.' A minute later she was guiding me down the hall in the direction of the cafeteria.

I kept my mouth shut for a while, giving her a chance to feel as indignant and defiant and maybe scared as she wanted. But when we'd poured ourselves some coffee and found a table in the oversized mausoleum they called the cafeteria, I got started.

'How long have you worked here, Sondra?'

'About a year.' She was so preoccupied with the risk she took that she seemed to have forgotten I had a particular reason for wanting to talk to her.

'A year,' I repeated, crossing her off my list. 'How do you like it?'

She grimaced. 'It's a job. I don't have much choice. I've got to work somewhere.'

'But you don't get along with Kirke.'

'Who does?' Defiance had the upper hand at the moment.

'What's his problem?'

Bitterly she said, 'He thinks secretaries shouldn't make mistakes. He thinks secretaries shouldn't be human. And,' she added after a moment, 'he doesn't like women.'

I scanned her with what I hoped was an appreciative gleam in my eyes. 'He's a little confused.'

She rewarded me with another smile. If her colour hadn't been so high already, she might've blushed.

I took a slug of my coffee, then fought down an almost overwhelming desire to throw up. What could they have made the stuff out of, Clorox? When the impulse to puke passed, I asked carefully, 'Sondra, how much do you know about this new filing system Kirke is working on?'

'Not much.' The coffee didn't seem to faze her. She must've been used to it. 'He only lets three of us touch it, and I'm not one of them. Just Mabel, Joan, and Connie. The rest of us do ordinary office work. Letters, transcripts, reports, newsletters, stuff like that.'

'What do you do if you need something in those files? Say you need to look up the records for a kid who goes to Ensenada Middle School.'

'Usually I ask Mabel. Or Connie or Joan, if Mabel isn't around.'

119

'I see.' I pushed my coffee away. Just looking at it made my stomach queasy. 'Besides them and Kirke, who knows how to use the files?'

'Well,' she considered, 'there's Mr Greenling – he's nice – and Mrs Scurvey. Mr Stretto never touches anything. If he wants something, he asks Mr Kirke for it. I think that's all.'

'None of the other people on the board?'

'No.' She was sure.

'What about people from other schools? What if the vice-principal of Mountain Junior High, for instance, wants to know something?'

'They ask for it, and Mabel or Connie or Joan gets it for them. Or maybe Mr Kirke. Those files aren't easy to use. They're sort of in-between, you know? You don't just look in a filing cabinet alphabetically and pull out what you want. They're getting ready to be put in a computer, so they aren't handy. Mabel says they're all in pieces, cross-indexed every which way. Besides' – her tone went sour again – 'Mr Kirke doesn't like other people to touch them.'

'That figures.' I paused for a moment, trying to guess how far I could go with her without losing her spontaneity. Then I said, 'Would you mind telling me a little more about Mabel and Connie and Joan?'

'Like what?' She must've felt giddy with courage. She sure as hell wasn't feeling suspicious.

'Well, take Mabel. What's her last name?'

'Allson. Mabel Allson.'

'What's she like? Is she married?'

'I like her. She's the only one who ever stands up to Mr Kirke. I think it's because she doesn't need the job. Her husband is a bank president. Flat Valley Savings and Loan, I think. She works because she likes it.'

'How about Connie?'

'Connie Mousse.' Sondra giggled. 'We call her the Moose. She's a frustrated old maid. She hates everything. She works here because she likes hating it. If she had a husband, she wouldn't need the job, she could hate him instead.'

'And Joan?'

'She's Joan Phillips. We get along OK, I guess, but I don't feel close to her. All she ever talks about is her fiancé. Jon, what's his name? Jon Gren, that's it. I ought to know all about him by now. He's a second-year intern at University Hospital. They're going to get married when he graduates.'

She said some more, but all of a sudden I wasn't listening. I was thinking, *intern*. Who else besides pushers know where to get drugs?

Doctors, that's who. Not Camilla Sandoval. It would be too risky for her. There was a hell of a lot of junk involved, and all the records would be in her name. But how about a second-year intern in a major hospital? If he knew what he was doing, he could rip off any drug he wanted by the pound.

'Sondra,' I said, 'you're a delight. I haven't been delighted in a long time, and I need it. But we're just about out of time.' I fished out one of Ginny's cards and handed it to her. 'You can get me with that number. If there's ever anything I can do for you, call. Day or night, it doesn't matter. Especially give me a call if Kirke hassles you about talking to me. I'll make a pretzel out of him.'

She smiled bravely. But the mention of Kirke brought back her fear, her smile betrayed a hint of the old despair.

'I mean it,' I said. 'Nobody pushes my friends around.'

'All right, Mr Axbrewder,' she said brightly. She was determined to carry it off. 'I'll keep that in mind.'

It wasn't until we were on our way back to her office that I remembered there was something else I had to ask her. 'Just one more thing, Sondra. People like Mabel, Joan, Connie – how long have they worked here?'

'I'm not sure. Longer than I have. I know it's been a long time for Mabel. The Moose has been here for ever. And Joan – I don't know, maybe a couple of years.'

I thanked her again and we went back through the school board door. The whole time I'd been with her, she hadn't once asked what all these questions were about. When she sat down at her desk, her face was white and her hands shook.

Apparently I'd underestimated just how scared she was of Kirke.

I found it a little hard to understand. He wasn't back yet, and unless someone ratted on her, he wouldn't know that she'd been talking with me. But she seemed to think he'd know. Just know.

Then he came back. Stalked into the office so quickly that he almost hit me with the door. We glared at each other for a second. A hot red spot marked each of his pale cheeks, and his chain-saw mouth was gripped tight. Ginny had put pressure on him, all right.

'I just finished telling your partner where to stick it,' he rasped. 'What the hell do you want?'

I grinned unkindly. 'I'm waiting for her. When she gets here, we want to talk to Mr Greenling.'

Kirke turned on his heel. The kids were gone now. He had a room full of women at desks to consider. But he homed in on Sondra as if she'd sent up a flare. He had a good eye. There was something scared in the way she hunched over her work, not looking at anything except the paper in her typewriter, and he spotted it. At once he went over to her, stood beside her. He didn't say anything. All he did was drum lightly on the desktop with his fingers. And watch her fall apart. The shaking of her hands got worse. Her fingers tangled, and in a minute she'd made a hopeless snarl out of what she was typing.

'When Miss Fistoulari gets here,' he said, 'take her and Mr Axbrewder to see Mr Greenling.' He made it sound like a form of torture. Then he went into his private office and closed the door.

'Nice guy,' I said to the room.

It might as well have been empty. Nobody even glanced at me.

'Thanks,' I said. 'I think I'll wait outside.'

Stepping into the hall, I closed the door behind me. Mostly for my own protection. I couldn't stand the reproach of Sondra's hunched shoulders.

Before long Ginny came down the hall. There was a fighting flare to her nostrils, but mostly she was just alert and ready, like she'd gone the distance with him, and he hadn't laid a glove on her.

'This better be worth it,' I growled. 'That man is a solid-gold bastard.'

She considered for a moment, then shrugged. 'We'll find out.'

'What did you get out of him?' I asked.

'Not much. I don't know whether he's tough or not, but he's hostile as all hell. At first I couldn't figure it out. I wasn't hassling him in the beginning. But then it hit me. He hates women. According to him, he left his job at NCR because his boss was a woman. "All women are bitches" – that's a direct quote.' A fighting light shone in her eyes. 'That's when I cut into him.'

'I guess you did.' Sondra had just said the same thing. 'He's taking it out on his secretaries.'

'That's their problem.' She was in no mood to sympathize. 'If they don't like it, let them stand up for themselves.'

For a minute we stood there scowling at each other – or rather scowling past each other. Then she asked, 'How about you?'

I shook myself, made an effort to haul my insides into some semblance of order. Then I told her about Mabel, Connie, and Joan – and Jon Gren.

She wasn't as impressed as I'd expected by the news about Joan Phillips' intern boyfriend. 'You're assuming that if somebody is leaking those files, they're leaking to somebody they know personally. That doesn't have to be true. It could be pure business. They're just doing it for money.'

'At the moment, that doesn't matter,' I countered. 'The point is, it gives us a place to work.' She nodded, and I went on, 'Anyway, our list is down to five, three secretaries, Kirke, and Greenling. And it isn't even lunch time yet.'

She looked at me sharply. 'You're feeling better.'

'I'm making a contribution.'

'Glad to hear it.'

Her tone was sardonic, but I knew that it wasn't aimed at me. Sardonic was just her way of keeping herself distant, objective. She was working. She didn't have time to worry about my poor dismal ego. I wanted to kiss her again, but I knew better.

'Who do you want to tackle next?' she asked.

'We have an appointment with Mr Greenling.' Axbrewder playing at formality.

'Let's go.'

I opened the door for her, mainly to remind her I wasn't Julian Kirke, and followed her back into the office.

Sondra's face had that swollen almost-crying look, and she wasn't willing to meet my eyes. But she came over to us right away and guided us down the back hall to Astin Greenling's office. In a minute we were standing in a room that would've made a perfectly comfortable broom closet if it hadn't been crammed to the ceiling with files and textbooks. In a tired voice, the curriculum vice-chairman offered us seats. When I sat down, my back was jammed against a bookcase and my knees were pushing the edge of his desk.

He looked vaguely more rumpled than he had the day before, but other than that he seemed pretty much the same. He gave the impression that he was too obsessed with and exhausted by his work to get dressed in the morning without help. No matter what Dr Sandoval said about him, he belonged on the list. He looked like a moral wreck. There aren't very many people in the world so good that they wouldn't sell their own mothers into slavery – if you got them tired enough and desperate enough. Especially if they needed the money for some 'good' reason.

But he didn't make any effort to put us off, didn't tell us how busy he was. He didn't say anything at all. He just sat behind his desk and looked at us with those exhausted eyes, waiting for us to let him know why we were there.

Ginny took a few moments deciding what approach to use. Then she said, 'When Mr Stretto showed you those notes yesterday, the only thing you had to contribute was an inane comment about "penmanship". Didn't you understand what you were reading?'

Apparently she'd decided on the hard-headed approach.

Greenling made an aimless gesture with his hands. 'It doesn't have anything to do with me.' He didn't sound hopeless. For him hopeless was so long ago that he didn't remember what it felt like any more.

'I disagree.' To hear her, you would've thought she'd already made up her mind about this case. 'There are only five people in this entire school system who could've kidnapped those girls. You're one of them.'

'Kid–?' If she'd suddenly ripped off her clothes and jumped him right then and there, he couldn't have been more surprised. 'Kid–?' He couldn't even get the word out. Probably his reaction would've been the same if he were innocent or guilty. It's amazing how hard it can be to tell the difference in this lousy world of ours.

'That's not all,' she went on. 'Of those five people, you're the only one who has a motive.'

'Motive?' He was gaping like a fish. 'I–? Motive?'

'You need the money. For your wife.'

'Wife' was the magic word. It transformed him. Not all at once. He had to struggle with it for a minute. I watched with a kind of nauseated fascination while terrible things went on inside him. He looked like an alcoholic going through withdrawal. Then it was over. His eyes burned, and all the lines of his face were sharper. In a tight voice, he said, 'Get out. My wife is dying. Get out of here.'

Ginny didn't flinch. 'How are you paying for it, Mr Greenling?'

But he didn't flinch either. 'We have security guards. I didn't want them. The money for these things always seems to come out of curriculum. But now I'm glad we have them. Get out!'

Ginny studied him for a moment. Then she got to her feet. She'd done what we came for – she'd turned up the heat. There wasn't any point in trying to call Greenling's bluff. And right then he didn't look like a bluffer.

'We're going to find those girls, Mr Greenling,' she said evenly. 'Whoever kidnapped them we're going to nail to the wall.'

Then she left the room.

I stayed where I was. Sometimes that works. Sometimes when people get mad at her they're willing to talk to me. Innocent people, usually. When she was gone, I said, 'Come on, Greenling. Save yourself some grief. Tell me how you pay for it.'

He picked up his phone, pushed a button. When a voice answered, he said, 'Connie, get Security. Now.'

I didn't argue with him. It was his play. He could call it any way he wanted. I wedged my way out of his closet and closed the door behind me.

Ginny was waiting for me in the hall. I said, 'Nothing,' and she nodded. But she wasn't really paying attention. She was on some other trail. She had a hunting look in her face.

After a moment she said, 'Did you see it?'

'See what?'

'Over on the right side of his desk. A stack of paper. Probably for notes. White stuff. Half sheets.

'They looked like they'd been torn along one edge.'

Chapter Thirteen

I said, 'I don't believe it. That man is as innocent as the day he was born. Even if he has something to be guilty about, he's still innocent.'

She looked at me – not challenging, just questioning. 'What makes you say that?'

I was about to answer, *Because I've been there and I ought to know.* But I couldn't say that to her, not the way things were going today. So instead I said, 'He's got too much dignity.' It was lame, but I didn't have anything better to offer at the moment.

Ginny said, 'Dignity covers a multitude of sins. I'd rather have proof.'

'Yeah? I thought you were the one who said we didn't need proof.'

She grinned quickly. 'That's true. But I wouldn't turn it down if you offered it to me.'

I loved that grin. 'What're we waiting for? Let's go find some.'

'Right.' She went about three steps down the hall, then knocked at a door with a sign on it saying:

MRS MARTHA SCURVEY
Budget Vice-chairman

From inside, a woman's voice snapped. 'Go away. I'm busy.'

Ginny opened the door, stuck her head in, then looked back at me with a sudden ferocity in her grin. She gestured for me to follow her.

'I told you to go away!' the woman said angrily.

When I got into the office – which was about the same size as Greenling's, but a hell of a lot neater – I found out why. The air was thick with sweet grey smoke. Martha Scurvey sat stiffly behind her desk with a hash pipe in her hands. Probably she didn't want anyone to come in until the air-conditioning cleared the air. Or maybe until she smoked a cigar to cover the odour.

'I'll tell you what, Ms Scurvey,' Ginny offered. 'You give us a little of your time, and we'll forget what that stuff smells like.' I could hear the grin in her voice.

'That's blackmail.' Martha Scurvey was angry enough to pluck chickens, but she was also under complete control. A dangerous combination. She must've had a lot of charm on tap, or she wouldn't be sitting where she was. At the moment, however, it didn't show. The only thing she showed was stainless steel. I wondered where she picked up the hash habit. Offhand, she didn't look like the kind of woman who needed it.

'Not at all,' Ginny said smoothly. 'Just persuasion. The only thing we're interested in is a little talk.'

Ms Scurvey didn't want to talk. She wanted us to get the hell out of her life. But she knew how to concede without losing face. With a gesture that might've looked gracious if her eyes had backed it up, she offered us chairs. While we seated ourselves, she stashed her pipe, pouch, and matches in a briefcase, which she locked. Then she leaned her elbows on the desk and said, 'I prefer Mrs not Ms. I'm a married woman, and proud of it.'

That sounded as phony as her graciousness. How she felt about her marriage was irrelevant. She was just trying to get on top of the situation.

Ginny let her try. 'Certainly, Mrs Scurvey. We're not here to give you any trouble. As far as we know, you're in the clear.'

I had to admire her. Ginny plays control games as well as anyone. Mrs Scurvey had already been outmanoeuvred, and she didn't even know it. 'In the clear?' she asked. 'I don't understand.'

After that I stopped listening for a minute. I was distracted.

In a neat stack off to one side of her desk, Mrs Scurvey had a pile of white writing paper. A handy size for notes – full sheets torn neatly in half. From where I sat, the paper looked like good twenty-pound bond.

I felt a childish urge to nudge Ginny and point, but I resisted it. Instead I shifted my weight, sneaked a couple of deep breaths, and went back to paying attention.

Ginny was saying, '. . . your opinion of Mr Greenling?'

Mrs Scurvey looked at her hands, checked her fingernails. 'He's conscientious – very conscientious – but hopelessly out of date. His ideas of education have yet to reach the twentieth century. I'd love to do a strict cost-analysis of his department, but he won't let me touch it. I'm expected to take his word for everything. At present.' She made it clear that Astin Greenling wouldn't have the power to turn her down much longer.

'Do you know about his wife?'

'He doesn't talk about her, and I don't ask. I've heard she's ill. That's more than I want to know.'

'What about Paul Stretto?'

'Paul is a forward-thinking educator with a keen appreciation for economic reality. He's brought this school system a long way toward facing the facts of life and doing the job it's supposed to do.'

I was glad Ginny didn't ask what kind of job that was. The smugness in Mrs Scurvey's tone made my scalp itch. I didn't like what it implied about her relationship with Stretto. Fortunately Ginny wasn't interested in theories of education. Instead of pursuing Stretto, she asked, 'How do you feel about Julian Kirke?'

'Personally, I think he's odious. Professionally, he does great work. His new filing system will save us thousands of dollars a year – once he gets it into the computer.'

'Do you see him socially, know anything about him?'

Mrs Scurvey gave Ginny a withering stare and said, 'No.' Kirke was probably too low for her. He wasn't chairman of anything.

'Who works on the files with him?'

'Three of his girls,' she said stiffly. 'Mabel, Joan, and – and Connie? I think that's her name.'

'What do you know about them?'

'What should I know about them? They're his girls. Ask him.'

'Do they ever do any work for you?'

'Just routine typing.'

'They don't help you with the files?'

'When I want something out of the files, I get it myself.' Mrs Scurvey was running out of endurance. Her tone would've curdled milk. All of a sudden, I guessed that she didn't smoke hash because she liked it. She smoked it because she needed it. She was brittle inside and didn't want anybody to know.

Before I could think about it, I asked her, 'How long has your husband been dead, Mrs Scurvey?'

Milk, hell. She practically curdled me. 'That's none of your business.'

Which told me what I wanted to know. Now she made sense to me. Her high-pressure approach to her job, her relationship with Stretto, the hash – she was running away from grief. I half wanted to ask Ginny to leave her alone. A married woman, and proud of it. It's a hard life when you lose everything that used to tell you who you are.

But Ginny was almost through anyway. 'Just one practical question, Mrs Scurvey. What's the phone setup around here?'

'The phone–? I don't understand.'

'If I wanted to call you, could I reach you directly, or would I have to go through one of the secretaries?'

'Through the secretaries.'

'And when you want to make a call?'

Mrs Scurvey sighed. 'Through the secretaries.'

'So they can make calls that you don't know about, but you can't make or receive any calls that they don't know about. Right?'

Mrs Scurvey was hugging herself with her arms. 'Are you finished?'

'Yes, I'm finished,' Ginny said. 'Just let me make a note of that.' Before Mrs Scurvey could stop her – if Mrs Scurvey wanted to stop her – she reached over and took a sheet off the stack of white paper. She got a pen out of her purse, scribbled something on one end of the sheet, then put it and the pen back in her purse.

'Thanks for your time. We're sorry we troubled you.'

'Come on, Brew.' Thirty seconds later, we were out of the school board offices and walking down the halls of Central High.

I wanted to see that sheet of paper. But Ginny didn't seem to be in any hurry to look at it, so I asked her, 'What was all that about the phones?'

'Just fishing,' she said. 'Whoever we're looking for doesn't work alone. One way or another, I think there have to be at least two of them. It's hard for me to picture somebody who works here moonlighting as a pusher successfully. Too many things could go wrong. I figure we're looking for somebody who gets the information, then passes it to somebody else. Somebody else who handles the girls.'

I stopped her. 'They wouldn't be stupid enough to call each other at work.'

'That depends.' She pushed open a door, and we went out into the glare of the parking lot. The asphalt swam with heat. 'Greenling or Scurvey wouldn't because their calls go through the secretaries. But that doesn't apply to the secretaries.'

When we reached the Olds, she put her purse on the hood and took out the sheet of paper.

Sure enough, it was twenty-pound bond. Neatly torn along one edge. The watermark matched all the other notes.

'Damn it,' Ginny muttered under her breath.

'For sure.' I couldn't figure out what Martha Scurvey was doing with paper like this. She wasn't supposed to be one of our suspects. She'd only been on the board a year.

But Ginny was cursing something else. 'I should've grabbed a sheet from Greenling too. I wasn't thinking.' She stuffed the note angrily back into her purse. 'I swear to God, Brew,' she rasped, not looking at me, 'some days I don't know what I use for brains.'

The frustration in her voice surprised me. I tended to get so involved in my own inadequacies that I sometimes forgot she's human, too. Judging from the sound of things, finding this paper in Martha Scurvey's office must've broken one of Ginny's intricate logical chains. Ruined a theory or two and left her feeling stupid. 'Don't complain to me,' I said quietly. 'I'm the guy who lost the notes, remember? I didn't even see that paper on Greenling's desk.'

'Yes, well,' she said, jerking open the door of the Olds, 'That's a big consolation.'

That crack irked me. But I didn't snap back. Reciprocity – it was my turn to stay cool. I got into the passenger seat, watched her while she took us out of the parking lot in the direction of her office. When I got tired of looking at her scowl, I said, 'So who cares about your brains? It's your body I'm interested in.'

For a second there I thought she was going to let go of the wheel and clobber me. But then suddenly the scowl broke. She threw back her head and laughed.

'Ah, Brew,' she sighed after a minute, 'if I ever figure out what to do with you, you're going to be in big trouble.'

'Take your time,' I said. 'I can wait.'

We chuckled together, and while it lasted I felt better.

About a mile from the Murchison Building we stopped for a quick lunch. As we ate, Ginny looked at me abruptly and asked, 'How did you know Mrs Scurvey's husband was dead?'

'Intuition,' I said. 'She doesn't have any kids. She's having an affair with Mr Paul M. Stretto. I don't know how I knew. It just came to me.'

'Are you sure you didn't figure it out from the name on her door? It didn't say, "Mrs George-or-whatever Scurvey". It said, "Mrs Martha".'

'That,' I said flatly, 'never occurred to me.'

She shook her head. 'You're not a well man. You ought to see a doctor. Maybe there's a treatment for it.'

I didn't try for a come-back. Her eyes were focused somewhere else, and her voice had an abstract sound. She wasn't even listening to herself. Instead she was groping for something, some kind of link that would tie this case together. I knew better than to distract her.

When we were finished eating, we went on to her office.

While she called her answering service, I started a pot of coffee. But after that I didn't have anything to do except sit and watch her think some more. I didn't mind at first. Ginny thinking is Ginny making progress. But after half an hour or so I started to get restless. I was just about to interrupt her when she reached a decision. Without warning, she came back from wherever it was she'd been and pulled the phone toward her. 'The hell with him,' she muttered. 'I can't wait any longer.'

There was a kind of suppressed violence in the way she dialled, and when she started talking her face was knotted in a grimace, but she managed to keep her voice tolerably smooth. Once she got past the people who fronted for him to Smithsonian himself, she put the call on the speaker so that I could hear him too.

Even over that tinny amplifier he had the kind of voice that makes you want to wash your hands. Oily and sticky. You'd have to be a bank president to like it. 'What's the matter, Fistoulari?' he asked. 'No patience? I told you I'd call at three. You can't crack this case without me?'

Ginny picked up a metal letter opener, set the point in the blotter on her desk, and slowly twirled it with her fingers. 'Of course not, Lawrence.' Somehow she kept the acid out of her tone. 'You know I'm helpless without you.'

'That's probably true.' He couldn't have sounded more self-satisfied if he'd just been propositioned by Miss America. Ginny stopped twirling the letter opener and began slowly pushing it into the blotter. The expression on her face said, *Why am I talking to this asshole?* 'Under the circumstances,' he went on, 'I won't keep you hanging. I have most of the information anyway. The only one I'm not satisfied about is this Stretto character.'

'What have you got on him?'

'Nothing you want. For a politician, he looks pretty clean. But I always double-check politicians. He keeps a higher profile than he can afford on Board of Education money, but right now it looks like it comes out of his campaign organization. Rumour is that it's clean money. Maybe it was born clean, and maybe somebody washed it. I'll know later on, probably by tomorrow.'

Well, it was still possible that Stretto supplied files to someone who supplied him with money. But I didn't believe it. He'd been too quick to call the commissioner.

'How about the others?' Ginny asked.

'Scurvey and Kirke are clean. Martha Scurvey is a society broad' – the letter opener was starting to bend – 'and she probably has more cash in her purse than she gets paid in a year. Her husband was Matthew Scurvey, the computer biggie. He left her enough to buy her own public school, if she wants it.' He paused, then said, 'It's possible she's one of Stretto's private contributors.'

'I already know that,' Ginny said. With malice aforethought. But she kept her voice bland.

'Yeah?' Smithsonian growled. He didn't like it when people already knew what he was telling them. 'Then maybe you already know about Kirke, too.'

'Not a thing. I can't get close to him.'

'Well, then.' Smithsonian mollified. 'He's clean. He lives within his means – which aren't that much, let me tell you. His apartment has a certain amount of class, and he drives a car with a hefty price-tag. A Citroen-Maseratti. But his bank financed the car. Take the payments on that, plus rent and taxes, out of his salary, and you still have enough for food, with something left over for a trip to Mexico every once in a while. Unless you're trying to support a little action on the side. He isn't. Absolutely no money he can't account for.'

Ginny absorbed that for a minute. So did I. I hated to cross Kirke off the list, but at the moment I didn't see any way around it. About the only thing I was sure of in this mess was that whoever was kidnapping these girls and pumping them full of junk was making money out of it. Considering what can happen to you if you're convicted for kidnapping, it had to be a *lot* of money.

Then Ginny asked, 'What about Astin Greenling?'

'Ah, Mr Greenling,' Smithsonian said, 'The man with the sick wife. I took a good look at him. Medical expenses cause more crime in this country than anybody knows about. You can bet he doesn't pay his bills with his salary. And the kind of hospitalization the Board carries is nothing special. I was a little surprised to learn that in fact Mr Greenling does pay his bills.

'How? you ask. I'll tell you how.' Smithsonian was enjoying himself. 'That sucker is up to his ass in loan sharks.'

'Loan sharks.' Ginny sat up straight, tossed the letter opener aside. I could almost see her thinking, *How does he pay them back? Maybe he pays them with something besides money. Maybe he pays them with information.* 'How long has that been going on?'

'About two years.' Smithsonian chuckled. 'I don't know why they haven't broken his arms yet.'

'After two years? How do you think he's handling it?'

'Hard to tell without actually talking to him. No doubt every time one of them gets nasty he goes to another and borrows enough to save his skin for a while. If that's what he's doing, he's digging himself a hole they'll bury him in.'

'All right, Lawrence,' Ginny said. 'You're giving me exactly what I want. Now I have some more names for you.'

'More?' he barked. 'You think you're my only client? I don't have better things to do than this—?'

Ginny cut him off. 'I'll pay. Whatever it is. Just send me a bill.'

'Believe it, Fistoulari. I'll send you a bill.' He paused to give us a chance to feel like we were being threatened, then said, 'So tell me the names.'

'Mabel Allson,' Ginny said promptly. 'Connie Mousse. Joan Phillips. They're all secretaries for the board. And Jon Gren.' She spelled out the names for him. 'Gren is Joan Phillips' fiancé. An intern at University Hospital.'

'Do not call me,' he said heavily. 'I'll call you. Tomorrow. Around noon.' He paused again, probably waiting for Ginny to tell him how wonderful he was. When she didn't say anything, he hung up with a bang.

She switched off the speaker, and we stared at each other for a minute. Or rather I stared at her, and she looked through me into empty space. I stood it as long as I could. Then I got up. 'Let's go.'

Her gaze didn't shift an inch. 'Where?'

'Back to the school board. Or over to Greenling's house, talk to his wife. Somewhere. We can't just sit here.'

She wasn't listening. 'I've missed something. There's something here. Something that gives it all away. But I can't pick it up. Damn and blast! What's the matter with me?'

I said, 'You're trying too hard.'

I don't know why I bothered. It didn't register with her at all. 'I'm going blind,' she insisted. 'It's right here in front of me, but I can't see it.'

I didn't see it either, so I took a deep breath and said, 'Acton.'

That reached her. She looked up, and her eyes came into focus on my face. 'What did you say?'

'Acton.'

'What is that? More intuition?'

'No. I'm just trying to shake you up a little. You're in a rut. You've got Greenling on the brain.'

She leaned back in her chair, put her hands behind her head. 'You still don't believe he's the one?'

'Who, me? Do you think I'm crazy? Of course he's the one. Who else could it be?'

Her eyes narrowed, until I almost couldn't see the fighting gleam in them. 'All right, ace. Maybe I'm in a rut. She's your niece. What do you think we should be doing?'

'I think we should go shake down Jon Gren.'

'Wonderful. Try it with my blessing. Only there's one thing you ought to keep in mind. Hospitals don't keep heroin around. Morphine, yes. Heroin, no. He's just Joan Phillips' fiancé – that's all you've got on him.'

What could I say to that? 'Well then, let's talk to Mrs Greenling.' Trying not to sound defensive. No point in telling her that she'd just shot down the only theory I had.

She sighed. 'That may be a good idea.' Reluctantly she got to her feet. 'So why do I feel like you're asking me to go hurt a sick woman?'

Under other circumstances, that would've made me mad. After all the things I'd done in the past three days without helping Alathea even a little bit, I was in no mood for her to turn finicky. But I was saved by the phone.

She snatched it up. 'Fistoulari Investigations.'

While she listened, all the blood drained out of her face and something else took its place – something that looked like murder. Then she said, 'Hang on. We'll be right there.'

She put the receiver down.

If I hadn't known better, I might've thought that it was me she wanted to kill.

In a tight voice, she said, 'That was Lona. She's over at University Hospital. The cops just brought in Alathea. She's still alive, but she's in a coma. OD.'

Maybe she wanted some kind of reaction from me. Maybe there was something she wanted me to say. I didn't know, and I didn't care. I was already on my way out to the elevator.

Chapter Fourteen

I hit the call button for the elevator, hit it again, pounded the damn thing. Finally the lights of the floor indicator started to move. They were slow, slow. By the time the doors opened, Ginny ran down the hall to catch up with me.

'Sorry,' she muttered under her breath as she hurried into the elevator. She must've thought I was holding it for her. 'Had to call my answering service.'

I ignored her. I was thinking, Coma. Alathea. In a coma. Bastards bastards bastards.

'They'll get her out of it,' Ginny said. 'Doctors know more about these things than they used to. She'll be able to tell us everything we want.'

'Leave me alone.' I looked at her, let her see I meant it. 'That isn't what I need.'

For a second I feared that she would ask me just what it was I did need. But then the elevator opened into the basement, and we both hustled towards the Olds.

I wasn't driving, I didn't have anything to do, I was helpless. The sun shone cheerfully, the traffic took its own sweet time, and the man who designed the sequencing of the stop lights was a maniac – and there was nothing anyone could do about any of it. I just sat staring through the windshield with my hands clenched on my knees, trying to hold myself together while Ginny wrestled with things she couldn't change. I'd forgotten my sunglasses.

She made good time. She must've because I was still in one piece when she slammed the Olds into a parking space in the University Hospital lot. We hit the asphalt together. But when I started to run, she caught my arm, held me back so that we walked towards the entrance together.

I let her do it. When Ginny gives orders, I obey.

University Hospital is a tall building built in two square sections. For five storeys the sections have a common wall, then the east wing goes on up for another five storeys. They built the place out of red brick, and when the sun catches it at the right time of day, it looks like blood. The emergency entrance is on the ground floor of the west wing, and with all the security guards they have around, it looks more like a top-secret military installation than a place where urgent hurts are treated. At least during the day. At night, with lights in all those windows, it looks a bit more comforting.

We went in, asked a guard for directions, and got ourselves pointed toward the waiting room. That was where we found Lona.

She stood at a window looking out into the parking lot. Sunlight glared into her eyes from the chrome and glass, but it didn't seem to bother her. When Ginny said, 'Mrs Axbrewder,' she turned to face us.

I wanted her to take a step toward us, hold out her hands, do something that would give me permission to put my arms around her. But she was too much alone for that. Her pain cut her off from everything. She stood there small and brittle, with her mouth clamped shut because there was nothing she could say or even cry out that would relieve the pressure inside her. It was as clear as daylight that we'd failed her, failed Alathea. When from somewhere she found the strength or maybe the generosity to say, 'Thank you for coming,' I almost groaned out loud.

'How is she?' Ginny asked softly. She felt as much a failure as I did, I knew that. The difference was that she could keep it from interfering with more important things.

'I don't know,' Lona said. Her voice quavered, on the edge of control. 'I haven't seen the doctor since he came out to talk to me. Before I called you. He told me what he was going to do. I had to give my permission because she's under-age. But I didn't understand it. He wouldn't let me see her.

'He said' – she didn't look at us, never lifted her eyes above my chest – 'he said she's an addict. There are needle marks all over her arms.'

'It's not her fault, Lona.' What else could I say? 'Someone did it to her. She was forced into it.'

Very carefully, she said, 'I know that.'

Lona!

'How did they find her?' Ginny asked. 'What happened?' She

wanted to know if the cops had caught Thea's kidnapper. Hell, I wanted to know. But she was moving slowly, gently.

'I'm not sure. I don't understand it. I got a call. From Lieutenant Acton. He was one of Richard's friends. He said that she'd been found. He said she was wandering around somewhere. Out on Canyon Road, I think. Trying to get a ride back into town. Somebody saw that she looked sick and called the police. I don't know who it was. When they found her, she was already unconscious. In the dirt at the side of the road.'

I wanted to throw up. She was only thirteen. Things like that shouldn't happen to children.

'Did he say anything else?'

'He told me she was here. He said I should come down here right away because the doctors needed my permission to treat her.'

For a minute, I had an impulse to grab the Olds and head for Canyon Road, out toward the mountains east of the city, where only the richest of the rich people live. I wanted to bang on doors until I found wherever Alathea had come from. It was a crazy idea, of course. Maybe she hadn't been kept in that area at all. Maybe she'd just been dropped off there so that she would get killed by the traffic. But that didn't make sense. There isn't much traffic on Canyon Road. And anyway that part of town held at least a hundred houses.

Somehow I fought the impulse down.

'Is there anything we can do?' Ginny asked.

'No, thank you.' Lona's eyes didn't leave the buttons of my shirt. 'I'm all right.' If she'd been any more all right, she would've been hysterical. 'You don't have to stay if you don't want to.'

Ginny's eyes were full of tears, but she didn't let them fall. 'That's OK. We'll stick around.'

If that meant anything to Lona, she didn't show it. She turned away from us, went back to staring out the window.

Then we waited. Just waited. Which is what makes the famous Chinese water torture so unbearable. It isn't the dripping of the water – after a while, your forehead just gets numb. No, it's the waiting between drops that does it. Drives you completely bananas. Other people came into the waiting room, left again. Two angry and anxious mothers told each other what their kids had done this time. A man fumigated the room with a cigar the size of a Glock while his aged father had an ankle X-rayed. A guy and girl who'd been in a minor car wreck came in and took turns sitting around while they were checked out for whiplash. Compared to waiting, sobriety is easy.

It was almost four o'clock when a doctor finally showed up, asking for Mrs Axbrewder.

Lona whirled as if she'd been stung. Her face was so full of questions that she couldn't get them out. She just stared at the doctor and ached, dumbly begging him to take pity on her.

'She's stable physically,' he said. 'She needs care, but she should be all right. I'm having her taken up to a room. You can visit her there in a few minutes.'

Relief blurred Lona's face. She looked like she was about to give way when the doctor's tone sharpened. 'But I have to tell you, Mrs Axbrewder. We haven't been able to rouse her. She's still in a coma, and we can't reach her.'

Ginny was standing beside Lona, had an arm around her shoulders. 'How do you treat that?'

'We take care of her body and wait. Maybe she'll pull out of it tonight. Maybe tomorrow, maybe next week. Maybe – I have to say this, Mrs Axbrewder. Maybe she'll never pull out. It depends on what kind of damage has been done to her brain.

'Permanent coma is rare, but it does happen. An overdose can be like an eraser on a blackboard. It can wipe out the conscious mind. But more often only a small part of the mind is damaged, and after a while the person recovers.

'Of course, her situation is complicated by the fact that she'll be going through withdrawal. All we can do at this point is keep her body nourished and pray.'

Lona had her hands in her hair, pulling it away from her face. A woman in danger of going over the edge. Ginny gripped her hard.

'Have you ever had a case like this before, Doctor?' Ginny asked.

'Personally, no. But I've read about them. Studies say that these conditions are more likely to develop when the addict resists the drug for some reason. The mind fights the body as hard as it can for as long as it can, and then there's a backlash.'

That meant something. It was trying to tell me something. But I couldn't hear it. Pressure filled my ears. My heart. The doctor told us what room Alathea would be in. When Ginny and Lona left the waiting room, I followed them towards the elevator.

Then another question occurred to me. I turned, ran after the doctor, caught up with him at the nurses' station. 'Did you do a complete physical on her?'

He looked at me sourly. 'I don't know who you are. What's your interest?'

'My name is Axbrewder. Alathea is my niece.'

He considered for a moment, then nodded. 'I examined her. What do you want to know?'

It stuck in my throat for a second. Then I got it out. 'Is she a virgin?'

He grimaced. Disgusted at me. Or at the question. Or at the answer. 'Not by a long shot.'

I tried to swallow the acid in my mouth, but it wouldn't go down. Clenching my fists, I went to catch up with Ginny and Lona.

Ginny was holding the elevator for me. She had the same question in her eyes. I said, 'Goddamn it to hell. Yes.' When she let the door close and punched the floor button, she looked mad enough to chew steel.

Alathea's room was on the eighth floor of the east wing. We found it without any trouble. The halls are laid out square and the doors all have nice big numbers on them. But when we got to her room, another doctor stopped us from going in.

He was about as tall as Ginny, with longish red hair curling around his ears, more paunch than he needed, and bloodshot little eyes. He had freckles so bad that they looked like smallpox. His white coat was buttoned up to his neck. There was a stethoscope in one of his pockets, and his right hand gripped the handle of a black medical bag.

He smiled blandly at us. 'I'm Dr Stevens. Now that she's out of Emergency, I'm responsible for her. You can see her as soon as I'm finished. It'll just take a minute.'

Ginny nodded for Lona. We stood around in the hall while Stevens went into Alathea's room and closed the door.

He didn't take a minute, he took three. It felt like thirty, but we were in no position to complain. When he came out, he gave us his smile again. 'Don't worry,' he said. 'She'll be fine.'

With his hands in his pockets, he went down the hall away from the nurses' station.

There was something about him I didn't like. He had the look of a man who'd just told a dirty joke. But my opinion of him didn't matter. As long as he helped Thea.

We went into Alathea's room.

It was a semi-private room. Alathea lay in the bed near the door. A curtain drawn halfway across the room between the beds kept us from seeing who else was there. Past the second bed was the window. The afternoon sun slanted in through it across a long section of the floor.

Alathea looked like death. A sickly paraffin colour filled her face, and the scrubbed white of the hospital gown only made it worse. The sheets were tucked up to her armpits. From her bare arms, IV tubes ran up to bottles hanging from poles at the head of the bed. Around the slashes of adhesive tape that held the IV needles in place clustered other red marks like insect stings – tracks of them mapping the veins inside her elbows. Violation as bad as any rape.

Lona went close to her, gripped her hand, and started to cry. After that I couldn't see any more. I was blind with fury and loss.

Trying to control myself, I shambled over to the window. For a bad minute or two, I couldn't do it. But slowly my eyes started to clear. I hit my knuckles on the windowsill until I could see straight again. Then I looked around.

The room was on the west side of the building. The window hung right over the roof of the west wing, three storeys below me. That roof had been fixed up as a recreation area, with stubby trees growing out of little plots of earth, big umbrellas for shade, and plenty of wrought-iron tables and chairs. The place was full of people – nurses, patients, children, visitors. Men and women in hospital gowns walked jerkily around or sat in wheelchairs. They looked like they belonged there, catching a little sun to warm their bones.

Only Alathea didn't belong. And me. She didn't deserve it, and I hadn't earned it.

A faint breeze came in through the window. The window was double glass, insulated for the sake of the AC. But today the hospital was saving money. The air-conditioning wasn't on. Instead the window had been cranked open a crack at the top.

I turned my back on it, glanced at Alathea's neighbour. An old woman, as shrivelled as a mummy – asleep and snoring. It surprised me to find that I had pity left to spare for her. She looked like she'd outlived herself long ago.

I wiped my face with my hands and went back to Alathea's half of the room.

Lona wasn't crying any more. She sat in a chair beside the bed and held Alathea's hand as if both their lives depended on it. Ginny remained with her, standing behind her and gripping her shoulders with both hands – trying to squeeze some kind of strength into her exhausted body. I watched them for a minute or two, hunting for a way to tell them I was leaving.

I didn't get a chance. The door swung open.

Looking like a campaign poster, Stretto strode into the room.

'I came as soon as I heard.' Maybe my ears were tricking me. I could've sworn his voice echoed in the room. Somehow he got past

Ginny without actually pushing her aside. 'Mrs Axbrewder, I'm terribly sorry. All of us at the Board are just heartsick.'

He took her hands away from Alathea, held both of them himself. From where I stood, he looked like he was asking her to vote for him.

'In a way, I feel responsible. If Ms Fistoulari hadn't alerted us, we would never have known this could happen. We should have realized it ourselves months ago and taken steps to prevent it. I promise you, Mrs Axbrewder – I will use every resource at my command as chairman to make sure this kind of thing stops.'

God save me from politicians. I wanted to slug him. But Ginny was in better control of the situation. 'I'm glad to hear it, Mr Stretto.' The lash of her voice cut all his blather to pieces. 'Now I'd like to hear how you knew she was here.'

Which was a very good question.

But he was innocent the way only a politician can be. 'The police called me. Since you and I spoke yesterday, I've been doing my best to prod them into action. I even spoke to the commissioner.' He was still campaigning. 'In no uncertain terms, I told him my opinion of the way this case has been handled. Now it appears that he made my feelings clear to the officer in charge, a Detective Acton. This Acton called me earlier, no doubt trying to compensate for his former inadequacy by keeping me informed.'

Acton, huh? That name cropped up too often. I wondered just how many people he'd told about Alathea.

First things first. 'Mr Stretto,' I said, 'how many people did you tell that Alathea is here?'

He started to answer, but a knock at the door interrupted him.

I went over to it, yanked it open.

Ted Hangst stood outside.

I started to say, What the hell is this? Open house? But he caught my arm, jerked me out of the room. Or tried to anyway. People as short as he is can't actually move me around by brute force. I let him get me into the hall. After I'd closed the door behind me, I took a good look at him.

If he'd had any sleep – not to mention food – since I last saw him, it didn't show. There was fever in his eyes, and his hand on my arm trembled no matter how hard he held on to me.

'Ted,' I asked, 'what the hell's wrong?'

'Her answering service told me where you were. I've been looking for you all afternoon.'

'Looking for us? Why?'

'Why the fuck do you think?' He was more than just feverish. He was hostile and excited. 'Because you hotshots have been wrong about this thing from the beginning. That's why I gave up on you. Instead I've been talking to people.'

'So have I. I didn't get anywhere.'

'Hotshot!' he spat. He was also desperate. 'You were talking to the wrong people. You and Fistoulari never figured out why Mittie was kidnapped.'

I was in no mood to play games with him, but I didn't let it show. He was stretched to breaking point, and I didn't want to tighten him any more. He had something to tell me, something he was going to say as soon as he found a way. I gritted my teeth and didn't touch him. 'That's true.'

'You've got drugs on the brain. You're so hung up on heroin you can't see what's going on.'

'Tell me, Ted.' Softly, softly. 'What's going on?'

'Prostitution!' The word made him so mad that he turned purple. 'She wasn't kidnapped by a pusher. She was kidnapped by a pimp! He just uses drugs to control girls, make them do what he wants. What his customers want. They're all sick!'

He fell into a fit of coughing – or maybe it was sobbing – and for a long minute he couldn't go on. It wracked him pretty hard. When he got his breath back, a lot of the hostility was gone.

'It's killing me, Brew.' He sounded faint. 'There are actually men in this city who want to screw thirteen-year-old girls. They want to screw my daughter. Or worse.'

I couldn't stand it any longer. I caught hold of the front of his coat, yanked him off the ground until his face was level with mine. Through my teeth, I hissed, 'What did you find out?'

I didn't scare him. He was past being scared. And he didn't get mad, either. He was too tired. 'I'm sorry, Brew. I keep forgetting about your niece. I didn't get much. Just a description of the pimp. Or his front man. The guy who lines up the customers. He's the one you talk to if you want – want to–'

I put him down, straightened his coat. 'Tell me what he looks like, Ted.'

Dully he said, 'Tall guy. Red hair, curly. Freckles. His name's supposed to be Sven Last.'

I didn't listen to the name. Instead I concentrated on the description.

For a second it paralysed me. I stood frozen while images of a man with red hair and freckles played inside my head.

He went into Alathea's room. Dr Stevens–

Then I saw him come out of the room, walk away down the hall. There was something wrong with that picture, something I should've noticed before.

His hands–

They were in his pockets. Both of them.

Then I moved. Snatched open the door, charged into Alathea's room.

'Ginny!' I barked. 'He left his bag!'

Lona and Stretto stared at me as if I were a lunatic. I ignored them, focused on Ginny. 'That doctor was a fake. Stevens. He left his bag in here.'

It took one more second to reach her. Then she whirled, started hunting.

In an instant, she dived under Alathea's bed and came up with a black medical bag in both hands. Carefully she put it on the edge of the bed, snapped it open.

We all watched her – me, Ted, Stretto, Lona. We all saw what was in the bag.

Three sticks of dynamite and some kind of detonating mechanism. The mechanism was ticking.

Lona fainted. Stretto caught hold of the bars at the end of the bed as if he were about to join her. I ignored them both, concentrated on Ginny. The detonator didn't look familiar. In any case, I didn't know much about detonators. Neither did she.

The one thing I *did* know is that you don't try to disarm a bomb if you have no idea what you're doing.

The whole scene didn't seem real to me. I couldn't believe it. Things like this don't happen right in the middle of the afternoon.

'Ginny,' I said. Even to myself, I sounded like I was strangling. 'Tell me what to do.'

She stood up straight, closed the bag, snapped it shut. Carrying it by the handle, she walked out into the middle of the room.

'Ted,' she ordered evenly, 'go to the nurses' station. Tell them we've got a bomb in here. They have to call the cops. I'll keep in this room. Tell them to get everybody out. Start next door on either side and work away from here. I don't know how much damage this thing can do.

'Go!'

He went.

'Stretto!' She had his number now. Her voice cut into him and brought out the decisive man who'd let us see the files. 'Take Lona. As far away as you can, the opposite side of the building.'

He didn't hesitate. He scooped Lona up in his arms, started for the door. By the time he reached the hall, he was running.

'Brew, get the window open.'

The window. Great idea. Toss the bomb outside where it couldn't get Alathea. I practically threw myself at the glass.

It was built into a heavy frame, opened and closed with a crank. But the crank wasn't there.

The window was open a crack at the top. I reached up and hooked my fingers over the edge of the frame. Next I braced my feet against the sill.

Then I ripped the damn thing out of the wall.

After that I remembered the sun roof.

I turned to Ginny, panted, 'You can't. There are people down there.'

She didn't flinch. 'I don't know when this thing is going off.'

I whirled back to the opening, leaned out and yelled loud enough to tear my lungs, 'Get away! Go inside! Get off the roof!'

A couple of people looked up at me. The rest didn't seem to hear a thing.

'Brew!' Ginny snapped. 'Get Alathea out of here. Then this woman. Tell the nurses to clear out those people.'

I jumped at Alathea's bed, tried to move it. It had wheels, but they were locked. I spent precious seconds kicking off the latches. Then the bed rolled. The IV stands were built into the frame, and the bottles clinked against the poles, but the needles in her arms were safe. Heaving my weight against the bed, I guided it through the doorway and out into the hall.

A moment later Ted and Stretto came toward me. 'Take her!' I shouted at them. 'Tell the nurses to clear that goddamned sun roof!'

They caught the bed by its corners, and I turned and rushed back into the room.

Ginny knelt at the window, bent over below the level of the sill. Her right arm was hooked over the sill. Using the wall to protect herself, she held the bag out the window.

'You'll kill yourself!' I shouted.

'What do you want me to do?' Her voice was flat and fatal. 'Drop it? I'll kill everybody down there.'

I didn't argue. I went to the old woman's bed, snapped off the latches.

By the time I got her out the door, a nurse appeared beside me. She was pale with fear, but she didn't let that stop her. 'I'll take her,' she said, voice shaking. 'She's an old woman. If she wakes up with all this going on and doesn't see a familiar face, she'll be terrified.'

I gave the bed a shove for momentum and let the nurse have it. Scrambling on all fours to keep my head below the sill, I went back to Ginny.

When I reached her, I said, 'Let me do it. You're too important to waste.'

She fixed her eyes straight at me. 'Get the hell out of here. I don't want to lose you like this.'

For a moment I didn't obey. I couldn't – couldn't leave her like that. But I didn't have any choice. If we both got killed, who would nail the bastard who caused all this?

'For God's sake, Ginny,' I said. 'Use your other hand.'

I watched while she carefully shifted positions, moved the bag into her left hand. Then I started to crawl away.

I was half-way across the room when the dynamite went off.

The concussion knocked me flat. I thought my eardrums had ruptured. I couldn't hear a thing. All of a sudden the air was full of dust and sunshine and silence. Hunks of plaster dropped from the ceiling. Cracks marked the wall above and below the window. More cracks ran along the ceiling. Nevertheless everything held. I couldn't tell whether any brick had been blasted off the wall outside on to the sun roof, but I didn't hear any screaming.

Ginny lay beside me. White plaster dust covered her like a shroud. At first her eyes were open. Her lips said, 'Brew,' without making any sound. Then her head rolled to the side.

Her left hand was gone. Nothing remained of her forearm except mangled meat. But her heart went on beating. Blood pumped out of her stump on to the floor. It looked like all the blood in the world.

I couldn't think of anything else to do, so I clamped my hand around her arm just below the elbow and squeezed with all my strength until the bleeding stopped.

Hung on to her like that until help arrived.

Part Four

Friday Night / Saturday Morning

Chapter Fifteen

While the doctors took Ginny to surgery, I stayed where I was, sitting on the floor in the gutted room with my back against one wall, staring through the dusty air at nothing. The doctors had wanted to take me down to Emergency, examine me for possible concussion, shock, hearing loss, whatever. I'd refused. I was in some kind of shock, no question about it. But they couldn't do anything to help me. I didn't even want them to touch me. I sat with my back against the wall, staring at nothing. Like a drunk.

Before long the door opened and Ted came into the room. He stood close to me, but I didn't have the strength to raise my head, so all I saw of him was his old jacket and his stale shirt and his ratty tie. For a couple of minutes he just stood there. His awkward hands twitched once or twice, but he didn't say anything. Then he managed to force out a few words.

'Stretto left.'

I didn't answer. If there were an answer anywhere in the room, I didn't have it.

'Before he left' – Ted sounded like someone had gone over his vocal cords with a rasp – 'he gave me a message for you. He said he wants you and Ginny to vote for him. The next time he runs for something.'

Vote for him. Dear God in Heaven.

'Brew.' Ted was pleading with me, but I had no response to give him. 'Brew, get up. We've got to find Mittie.' He didn't seem real enough to move me. The only thing I could see in the dust and the late afternoon sunlight was the blood pumping out of Ginny's forearm.

But then I saw something else too. Thin silver streaks that fell and splashed on the floor. They made me look up.

Tears oozed from Ted's face like booze-sweat.

He had the power to move me after all.

They all had power – Stretto, Acton, Ginny, even Ted. They could all make other people feel fear or grief or respect. The bastard who did this to Alathea sure as hell had power. I was the only exception. I didn't have any of my own, so I lived off other people's. And when I couldn't get that, I accepted the most convenient substitute. Convenient and forgiving. Alcohol. Being drunk.

I didn't seem to have any choice about it. I was on my feet.

'Brew,' Ted said, 'you look terrible.' He tried to smile.

That finished the job. Despite myself, I started to function again. '*I* look terrible? How long has it been since you had anything to eat?'

He shrugged. Food was irrelevant. 'We've got to find Mittie.'

'We're going to. As soon as I know Ginny's all right. But while I'm waiting I'm going to take you down to the cafeteria and put food in you if I have to shove it down your throat.'

He attempted another smile. 'Sure, hotshot. But before you do anything you might regret, you ought to take a look at yourself.'

The mirror in the bathroom had survived the blast. When I looked in it, I saw what Ted was getting at. Plaster powder caked me so thickly that I looked like a spook. White dust made the rims of my eyes and my gums look red as fever.

I slapped at my clothes a couple of times, and spent a minute coughing. Then I ran water in the sink, washed my face and hands, dried them on some paper towels. I still looked like I'd just climbed out of a ruin, but at least I was clean enough to get by.

With Ted behind me, I left the room.

A second later I remembered something and went back. After hunting around the room for a minute, I found Ginny's purse. I fished out the keys to the Olds and took the purse with me.

After all the confusion, things in the hospital were starting to get back to normal. Cops poured in, but at the nurses' station some people had already resumed doing paperwork. I told them where I was going, and asked them to get word to me as soon as Ginny came out of surgery. Then I took Ted down to the cafeteria and bought us both supper.

Not because either of us was hungry. I had as much trouble as he did choking down whatever it was the hospital called food. But we had a long night ahead of us, and we couldn't afford to collapse. A long night – and the only part of it I was sure of was the part where I intended to knock heads with Detective-Lieutenant Acton. So I chewed away at some kind of cardboard-and-sawdust sandwich until it disintegrated in my mouth, and whenever Ted pushed his plate away I pushed it back in front of him. And all the time I couldn't help thinking that the two of us together made a pretty poor replacement for Ginny Fistoulari.

If we had any alternatives, I couldn't figure them out.

I was in the middle of repeating my threat to force-feed Ted when a man the size of a small tank appeared in the doorway, and in a voice like a bulldozer with the cutout open said, 'Axbrewder.'

Acton. When he saw me looking at him, he beckoned for me with two middle fingers of his right hand. 'I want you.'

Ted glanced back and forth between Acton and me with something like nausea in his face, but I didn't give him a chance to ask any questions. 'Stick with me,' I whispered. Then I got up and left the cafeteria.

Acton was waiting in the hall. As I came through the doors, he started to say something, but when he saw Ted following me, he changed it. 'This is private, Axbrewder.'

I stopped in front of him, looked at the dull glare in his eyes, at the way his jaws were clamped together. 'No way,' I said. 'I need a witness who can tell the judge you hit me first.'

His fists came out like pistons, caught hold of my jacket, rammed me against the wall. 'Listen, Mick,' he growled, 'I'm the law, remember? I can have you locked up so fast it'll make you piss yourself. I said this is private.'

I didn't struggle. I didn't even want to. I just stared him straight in the face. When he started to feel hesitant because I wasn't resisting, I said, 'My partner got her hand blown off. My niece is in a coma. Do you really expect me to just walk away from it?'

He held me for another ten seconds. Then he took a deep breath through his teeth and backed up.

'All right,' he said. Still deciding what to do with me. 'Tell me something. I was in the medical superintendent's office a little while ago, and this goddamn sonofabitch Stretto came in. He damn near accused me of setting that bomb myself. According to him, I'm implicated in what's happened to all these girls. Now where did he get an idea like that?'

I shrugged. Trying to stay calm. But all of a sudden my heart started to pound. Without transition I felt sure that I could get something I needed out of Acton.

'Stretto almost got killed,' I said as evenly as I could. 'Now he wants to blame somebody. You're as good a scapegoat as any.'

'How do you figure that?' He sounded like he needed a lump of granite to chew on.

'The bastard who set the bomb knew Alathea was here. Who could've told him? Five people. You, me, Stretto, Ginny, and Lona. And you're the only one who wasn't there.'

I had him now. That was the kind of argument he understood. He chewed his lip for a while. When he said, 'I didn't even know what room she was in. Who did you tell?' He wasn't challenging me any more. He was working on the case.

I said, 'Nobody,' and waited.

He chewed for another moment, then spat, 'Damn it, I did. I didn't talk to Stretto at all. He wasn't in when I called. I left a message for him with one of his secretaries.'

'Which one?'

When he finally met my eyes, he looked like he was actually angry at himself. And just like that I knew what was going on with him. He was such a belligerent cop because he didn't have any other way to let out his frustration. For almost two years now, he'd been trying to figure out what happened to these missing girls, and all he'd got was nowhere. Their deaths – and the manner of their deaths – made him sick with rage, but he hadn't accomplished a thing. So he took it out on people who made him look bad to himself. When he said, 'I didn't get her name,' I wasn't even disappointed. I was relieved. Because now I knew he would answer my questions.

'Never mind,' I said. 'We already knew it has to be somebody who works for the school board.'

His anger jumped into focus on me. 'How the hell do you know *that*?'

I took out the piece of paper that Ginny had taken from Martha Scurvey's office and handed it to him. While he checked it out, I told him where it came from.

That made a difference to him. 'Now maybe we've got something.' He put the paper away in his pocket. 'All those other sheets. We've had them analysed. We can prove they were all made by the same company – but we already knew that from the watermark. We haven't been able to prove they came from the same ream. Too many minute variations in the composition of the paper. Except for the last two. The lab-boys are ready to swear they came from the same sheet. Fiber-tear, composition, everything matches.

'If this piece comes from the same ream, we'll have some proof we can use.'

I could almost see the wheels turning in his head. Get a warrant, search the school board offices, track down the source of the paper. Embarrass Stretto as much as possible in the process. It was a good system. It might even work.

But it would take time – and I didn't have time. Mittie didn't have time. So I took hold of myself and asked, 'Acton, why did you have to scare people like the Christies? You didn't think they were pimping or pushing for their own daughters. What were you trying to do?'

He didn't look at me. But he answered.

'Ah, screw it. I was trying to make something happen. Push here, and hope the wall cracks over there. I wanted to keep it all out of the papers. Send a message to whoever was responsible. If I kept a lid on sensational stuff like that, the people who knew what was going on would know I was still after them. I wanted to make the bastards nervous.'

I almost asked him why he thought that was a good enough reason to make miserable parents feel even worse, but I was afraid he'd stop talking. Instead I said, 'It was worth a try. Tell me how you found Alathea.'

He still didn't look at me, but now it was for a different reason. 'I didn't tell Mrs Axbrewder the whole truth about that. Some guy saw her out on Canyon Road and called in. I told Mrs Axbrewder she looked sick. The fact is, she was wandering down the middle of the road buck naked. And bleeding. The guy who called said he thought she was trying to hitch a ride. When the doctor saw the cuts and scrapes on her, he said it looked like she'd crawled through a broken window or something.'

I was staring at Acton, but I didn't really see him. I was thinking, Naked. Crawled. Something I'd been trying to figure out earlier came back to me. The timing. Every one of those kidnapped girls had been missing for two or three months before turning up dead. Except Alathea. She'd only been gone for ten days. Why?

Now I knew why. Because she'd escaped. They didn't fill her up with junk and then leave her to die like the other seven. She escaped. For a while, she managed to fight off the junk. She broke a window where they were keeping her, and crawled out, and went down Canyon Road, trying to hitch a ride until it was too much for her and she passed out.

Which put her in a coma.

She'd tried to do something that nobody could do. Alone she'd struggled to climb out of a hell she hadn't chosen and couldn't refuse.

Just thinking about it made me want to scream. But I didn't. Instead I said, 'This time you'd better put a guard on her room.'

'Believe it,' Acton growled. 'Anybody who wants to get at her now will have to fight off half the department.'

I said, 'Good.'

Then I asked Ted to tell Acton everything he knew about Sven Last.

Acton had already heard that the bomb was planted by some clown pretending to be a doctor, but he didn't have the details. I made Ted spill them all. He hated doing it – hated having to say such things out loud – but I didn't leave him any choice. I wanted to cover every bet I could think of.

When Ted was done, Acton went one way to put out an APB, and I went the other. Ted followed me as if he were being sucked along in my wake.

I didn't have a very clear idea of where I was going. First I wanted to see Ginny. After that I'd try to figure out what came next.

I got lucky. I caught up with her while she was being wheeled from surgery to recovery. The aides objected, but I made them stop long enough to let me take a good look at her.

She was still unconscious – dead to the world, pale, breathing gracelessly through her mouth. The stump of her left forearm had been strapped in tight white bandages, and the rest of the arm wore a cast to keep the bones from shifting. Helpless as a kid.

I could've kissed her and she never would've known the difference.

I let her go. I was too tense to stand there. Once I'd put her purse beside her so that she'd have her .357 handy when she woke up, I found out from the aides what room she'd be in when she came out of recovery. Then I let them take her away.

With Ted still trailing behind me, I left the hospital, feeling like a murderer who just hadn't managed to find the right victim yet.

Chapter Sixteen

The sun was setting in a blood-like red wash as I drove the Olds out of the parking lot, and while Ted and I cruised down Paseo Grande toward the Murchison Building, darkness slowly thickened in the air. It was night when we parked in the basement garage and rode the elevator up to Ginny's office.

I'd taken her keys. I unlocked the door, snapped on some lights, and we went into the back room. The smell of very well-done coffee reminded me that I'd left the pot plugged in. I offered Ted a cup, then poured myself one and sat down at Ginny's desk to drink it. It tasted like burnt sweat-sock squeezings and motor oil, but I sipped at it anyway as if it were liqueur.

For a couple of different reasons, I didn't want Ted to ask me any questions. He hadn't said anything since we'd left Acton, and I didn't want him to start now. For one thing, I didn't have any answers. And questions would just interfere with what I was trying to do.

Sitting in Ginny's office, at her desk, drinking her coffee, I struggled to think like she did. I didn't have any red-hot flashes of my own, and I knew I wouldn't get any if I tried to force them. So instead I tried to look at things her way.

Six hours ago, she'd been sitting right in this chair and she'd said, *It's right here in front of me, but I can't see it.*

She'd had all the pieces she needed, she just hadn't been able to put the puzzle together. Now she was in the hospital, doped up with scopolamine or sodium pentathol, and I had to do it for her.

Which wouldn't have made sense to Ted, even if he'd been in the mood to try – which he wasn't. He stood me as long as he could. Then he said in a strained little voice, 'Let's go.'

I drank some more coffee, almost gagged. 'Exactly where?'

'After Last. He's our lead. Somebody can tell us how to find him.'

'It's too early,' I said. 'Pimps don't even *think* about business until after ten.'

'For God's sake!' he protested. 'We've got to do something. They're doing it to her right now!'

He was probably right about that. Now would be a good time for them to shoot her up if they wanted her compliant later on – say between eleven and two. But reminding me about things like that only made it harder for me to stay calm. 'Goddamn it, Ted!' I began, 'Do you think–?'

I stopped. An idea hit me – an obvious idea, something I shouldn't even have had to think about. Something Ginny would've done automatically. But for some reason it felt like more than that.

I grabbed the phone and called her answering service.

When the woman answered, I said, 'This is Axbrewder. Ginny Fistoulari is out of circulation for a while. I need to know if there are any messages for her.'

Ginny – bless her punctilious heart – had kept my name active with her answering service. In a bored voice, the woman said, 'Some man's called four times in the last two hours. Didn't leave a name. He wants her to call him back.'

She read off a phone number. I grabbed a pen, scrawled the number on Ginny's blotter. Thanked the woman and hung up.

'What is it?' Ted asked.

I was already dialling. 'Do you believe in intuition?'

'Intuition?' he rasped. 'What the hell are you talking about?'

'In that case, maybe what you ought to do is pray.' The number rang. I shut Ted out of my mind, concentrated everything I had on the secrets hidden in that phone line.

Somebody picked up the phone. A burly male voice said, 'Yeah?'

'I was told to call this number.' I held the receiver against my head so hard it felt like it was bending.

'Who'd you want?'

'I don't know. They want me. All they left was this number.'

'Your name?'

'Fistoulari.'

The man covered the mouthpiece. I heard him shouting, but I couldn't tell what he said.

A minute later another man was at the phone. 'Fistoulari?'

It wasn't much, but it was all I needed. 'No. I'm her partner. My name's Axbrewder. I was with her when you pulled your little doctor act at the hospital.'

There was a long silence. Then the voice snarled, 'Well, aren't you the clever one? How did you know it was me?'

'I'm good at voices.'

'Goodie for you.' He paused. 'Where's Fistoulari?'

'That little toy you left behind blew her in half.' I wasn't about to tell him the truth. I didn't want him to go back and take another crack at her.

'Too bad it didn't get you, too.'

'Too bad for you. Kidnapping, dealing, and prostitution isn't bad enough. Now you've got murder one. You're as good as dead, punk.'

'Yeah, well–' His voice changed, became softer and greasier. 'That's what I want to talk to you about. I heard rumours that bomb didn't do everything it was supposed to. I shouldn't have let him talk me into it in the first place. But that little whore can identify me. I want to deal.'

'Deal, hell.' I gripped the edge of the desk to keep myself from shouting. 'You killed my partner. Why should I deal with you?'

Ted stood in the light across the desk from me. He was chewing on his moustache, and his hands made fists at his sides.

'Because,' the voice said, all oil and lechery, 'I can give you the man who's responsible for all this. I'm just the errand boy. He's the one who kidnaps the girls. He's the one who gets the junk and pumps it into them until they're ready to do anything. Anything, Axbrewder. He's the one.'

I took Ginny's battered old letter opener in my free hand, bent it double, and threw it across the room hard. It took a sizable hunk out of the plaster. 'Convince me.'

'No problem. But I won't give you time to locate this number. I want to meet.'

'That sounds like a great idea. Then you can just shoot me, and there won't be any witnesses left.'

'Suit yourself,' he snapped. 'I'll be in that abandoned Ajax warehouse down at the end of Trujillo. About an hour from now. That's a good place for me, because I'll be able to tell if you bring anybody with you, like maybe the cops. If you do, you'll never find me.'

The line went dead. I was left with what felt like a perfect set of my fingerprints indented in the handle of the receiver.

Ted hadn't moved a muscle. He stared at me, dumb with pain and urgency.

I didn't want to say anything, but I forced myself for his sake. 'You got most of it. That was Last. He wants – he says he wants to deal. Trade us his boss for some kind of immunity. Either he's telling the truth, or he wants to set me up.'

Ted struggled to find his voice. 'What're you going to do?'

'What the hell can I do? I'm going to meet him.'

'He'll kill you.'

'No,' I said evenly. 'You're not going to let him.'

While he absorbed that – or tried to, anyway – I dialled the answering service again. When I got the woman, I said to her, 'Listen, this is an emergency. Call the police, get a message to Detective-Lieutenant Acton. That's A-c-t-o-n. Give him that number you just gave me. He can track it down, I can't. Tell him I just talked to Last. L-a-s-t.' I hung up before she could think of a reason not to do what I told her.

'That's going to do a lot of good,' Ted said acidly.

I shrugged. 'It's worth a try.' Got to my feet. 'I can't tell Acton where we're going. Last says he can spot it if I don't go alone. If he sets me up – or gets away from us – maybe Acton can nail him by staking out that number.'

Ted didn't answer. He looked bedraggled, as full of self-pity as wet poultry, but the dull glare in his eyes said as plain as words that Last wasn't going to get away from us.

'Come on,' I said softly. 'It'll take us a while to get down to that warehouse.'

Ted just turned on his heel and walked out of the office.

I unplugged the coffeepot, snapped off the lights, locked the door, and followed him to the elevator.

While we rode down, I said, 'It could be that he really does want to deal.' I wanted to be sure that Ted wouldn't go off half-cocked. 'He's not stupid. And he knew about Ginny and me. This partner of his must've told him we were prying. When he saw us at Alathea's room, he knew he had a chance to get us all.'

'After he sets the bomb, he gets out fast. He doesn't want to take any chances.'

The doors opened, and we headed into the basement toward the Olds.

'But then he can't find out what happened. So he starts trying to call Ginny. If somebody returns his call, he knows he's in trouble and he better find a way to get off the hook.'

I unlocked the Olds. We climbed in.

'If nobody calls back, he can figure he's in the clear. No witnesses who can tie him to the kidnappings. He can go back to pimping for his partner, and his partner will never know the difference.'

Ted paid no attention. Instead he stared out through the windshield into the night. Tears streamed down his face again. I locked my jaws to make myself shut up, and concentrated on just driving for a while.

But silence wasn't what he wanted, either. By the time we were down in the valley, working our way south along the river, he'd started to talk himself.

'She's all I have left, Brew.' He was gnawing on his moustache the way a drowning man clutches at straws. 'You probably don't know what happened to us. Things like that don't happen to hotshots like you.' He was bitter – but not at me. 'We were happy back then, she and her mother and me. Before Mittie was born, I was a cop, pounding a beat in the days before they switched to squad cars, and we had a little house over on Los Arboles, and we were happy, her mother and me.

'Except her mother didn't like me being a cop on the beat. She wanted me to be a detective. But in those days they had rules that said I was too short to be a detective. When Mittie was born, I quit the cops to work for myself. I wanted her to have a father she could be proud of.

'But it didn't work out like that. People don't hire you for what you can do. They don't know what you can do. They hire you for what you look like. You're built like a tree, and Ginny looks like a steel trap, and people just naturally go to you when they've got something important. They come to me when they've got something grubby.

'Domestic surveillance.' His bitterness was so thick it practically fogged up the windows. 'Prove that so-and-so is cheating on such-and-such. Then so-and-so can get a fat divorce settlement.

'You know something, Brew?' He chuckled sourly. 'They almost put me out of business when they first invented no-fault divorce.'

For a while he went back to staring out the window. I hoped that maybe he wasn't going to tell me any more. I was in no shape for it. But he wasn't finished. A couple of minutes later he continued.

'Her mother wasn't impressed. I wasn't doing what she thought detectives did. Solving murders, rescuing kidnapped babies, breaking up drug rings. When Mittie was three, her mother ran off with an insurance salesman.' His tears kept running, but he had a curious kind of dignity about it. It didn't make him sob or lose control. His voice didn't even shake as he said, 'I raised her myself. She's all there is.'

It took me long enough, but I finally figured out why he was so desperate. He was terrified that the pimp we were after would feel the heat and decide to go out of business. Hide under a rock somewhere.

After destroying the evidence.

As long as Alathea remained in a coma, Mittie was all the evidence there was. If the pimp knew that Alathea was still alive, he might've already killed Mittie.

I took a tighter grip on the wheel, pushed down harder on the accelerator. Because there was nothing else I could do.

Even then it took us damn near an hour to get far enough down on Trujillo to reach the vicinity of the Ajax warehouse.

I didn't rush in. When we were still half a mile away, I pulled over to the kerb and stopped.

Asked Ted if he had a gun.

He didn't.

I took out the .45 and handed it to him. While he checked it over, I flipped the switch so that the courtesy lights wouldn't come on when I opened my door. Then I said, 'Here's what we're going to do. You're going to hide down under the dash. When I get to that warehouse, I'll park in the darkest place I can find. I'll get out, leave the door open. I'll go into the warehouse wherever I can find a door.

'Give me two minutes. Then sneak out and get around the back somehow. Come in looking for me. Keeping me alive is up to you. I won't be able to do much for myself. This is his turf.'

Ted didn't say anything. He just slapped the clip back into the .45 and ducked down under the dash.

I put the Olds in gear and drove the rest of the way down Trujillo.

The city fathers don't spend much on street-lights down in that part of town. The whole place was black as a grave. But the sky still held enough light to silhouette the warehouse, and my headlights picked out the rest.

The building stood behind a steel-mesh fence, but the gates were gone. That was the only way in – which was one good reason why Last had chosen it. But that wasn't the only reason. It was a three-storey building. Battered steel siding covered the first two floors. The top floor was lined with windows on all sides. He'd probably been up there for the past half-hour, watching. If he saw anything he didn't like, he could get out of there fast.

The moon wasn't up yet. Nothing offered me a particularly dark place to park. I coasted up to the front of the building, positioned the Olds so that Ted had a good straight run to the east corner, doused the headlights, and stopped.

'At least two minutes,' I whispered. 'I'll be moving slowly.' Then I opened the door and got out.

I stood beside the car for a minute, letting Last see that I was alone. Then I moved towards the door beside the cargo entrance.

When I put my hand on the door and pushed, it squeaked bloody murder. Demonstrating my good faith, I made sure Last could hear me shut it behind me.

Inside I stood in darkness thick as stone. When I waved my hand in front of my face, I could barely sense its movement.

With the cargo entrance beside me, however, I figured that I stood in a pretty big open space. Holding my arms out just in case, I started forward. Slowly. Very slowly. My heels made an echoing sound on the concrete, but I didn't worry about it. I didn't want to surprise Last. I was counting on Ted for that.

And wishing like hell that I had Ginny covering me instead. I trusted Ted's determination, but I didn't know how much good sense he had left.

Oh, well. If he didn't have enough, that made two of us. Probably Ginny would've never let me get myself into this situation in the first place.

Then a voice barked, 'That's far enough!'

I froze.

For about a minute while I stood still, I thought I heard faint scuffling noises in the distance.

After that a light snapped on.

It just about nailed me to the floor. I was right under a powerful bulb with a reflector that focused the beam into a circle on the floor maybe fifty feet across. With me in the centre. Surrounded by a secret and dangerous darkness that my eyes couldn't penetrate.

Very neat. Last could've killed me with a slingshot.

But he didn't shoot. Apparently he had something else in mind. After a couple of minutes I heard heels on the concrete. By degrees Last materialized in front of me on the edge of the circle of light.

His right fist held an automatic with a calibre the size of a cannonball.

He came a few steps forward, no more. Not counting the automatic, his main advantage was that he could get out of the light a lot faster than I could.

I didn't even imagine moving. I didn't want to give him an excuse.

He knew how to hold a gun. It never wavered. He was grinning, and his voice sounded like margarine. 'All of a sudden, you don't look so tough, Axbrewder. How come that bomb didn't get you? I bet you wet your pants when it went off.'

Part of me wanted to just forget everything and take him. 'I came to get convinced, punk,' I said. 'Convince me.'

He glanced around. 'You alone?'

'Can't you tell? I've got two cops in my pocket. I'll get them out if you want.'

'All right.' He got down to business. 'What do you want to know?'

'Who's your partner?'

'Ah,' he grinned. 'I'm not going to tell you anything you can use. I want to deal. You get the DA to give me immunity, and then I'll give you his name.'

'We'll find him without you.'

'No, you won't.' He sounded very sure of himself. 'You're not even close.'

'You still have to convince me. I need something I can take to the DA.'

'That's why I'm here. What do you want to know?'

I took a deep breath. 'I want to know why you used a goddamn bomb. Why didn't you just needle her to death? You've done it before.'

'Not me, pal,' Last said flatly. 'He handles the junk. I never touch it. I don't even know where he stashes it.'

That got me nowhere. I wasn't thinking straight. I should've asked a better question. *Come on, Axbrewder*, I snarled at myself. *Don't blow it now.*

'All right,' I said. Holding on to myself hard. 'How many girls have you kidnapped?'

'Nine,' he said promptly. 'But I didn't have anything to do with that either. Getting them was his job. Like doping them was his job.'

'What was your job?'

'Well,' he grinned, 'The main thing was rounding up customers. Mostly I made myself available. When some john who liked his white meat young found me, I made the arrangements. Then I took him to the action.

'Other than that, I took care of them. Fed them. Got them the right kind of clothes. A lot of johns like to see a kid in fancy stuff – peek-a-boo bras, lace panties open at the cunt, stuff like that.' He was grinning so hard I could barely look at him.

I said, 'Keen. You're a nice man, Last. But I'm going to need something more solid. Tell me–'

Then I almost faltered, almost gave it away.

162

In the darkness behind Last, I saw a pale shadow, recognized Ted. Only the white of his face and hands showed.

He had the .45 in both fists, pointed straight at Last's back.

It was all I could do to go on. 'You kept each of those girls for three or four months. Then you ditched them. Why?'

Last shrugged. 'We had enough customers, but most of them are regulars, know what I mean? After a while they want fresh meat.'

'Yeah,' I growled. 'And you didn't get rid of one girl until you'd had time to break in a new one. So how come you killed Carol Christie right after you picked up Alathea Axbrewder?'

'Axbrewder,' he said, 'she some relation of yours?'

'No.'

'Yeah, well,' he said, 'that Christie chick was trouble from the word go. Something funny about her metabolism. My partner had a hell of a time getting the dose right. Either she wasn't dopey enough or she was all the way out. It was just an accident she got killed when she did.'

'An accident,' I said. 'I bet it broke your heart.'

I could see Ted's finger trembling on the trigger. Easy, Ted, I thought at him as hard as I could. Take it easy.

'What made you decide to go for two kids this time?' I asked Last. 'You never did that before.'

'Just improving the quality of our service.' Last's smirk hurt like a knife in my guts. I thought my nerves were going to snap. 'Give the customer more variety. Some johns like blonde, some like brunette. Some like a little two-on-one. And we wanted to make up for the trouble we had with Carol Christie.'

I could hardly believe it, but he actually seemed to enjoy telling me all this.

'It was a good thing we had two,' he went on. 'That Axbrewder was a feisty little bitch. We were going to have to get rid of her anyway. Some of the johns were bleeding when they got done with her.'

Well, by *God*, Alathea. Good for you!

'Hangst was another story.' I hated his grin. Right then there was nothing in the world I hated as much as his grin. 'She was just what we wanted, times two. Once she got the hang of things, she couldn't get enough.

'I'll tell you, Axbrewder.' He lowered his voice – he was about to let me in on a secret. 'Most of our johns don't like cherry meat. My partner and I used to take turns popping them. Kind of work them into shape, know what I mean? Hangst was my turn. God! she was a juicy little cunt.'

Ted was moving.

I shouted, 'No!' but I couldn't stop him.

He took one step into the light.

Fired.

The first shot hit Last like the kick of a mule. I saw the slug plough through the front of his chest.

Clenching the .45 in both hands, Ted kept pulling the trigger. I had to hit the floor. The slugs that missed Last ricocheted off the concrete and went screaming into the dark.

When I heard the slide rack empty, I raised my head, started to get up.

Ted stared at the gun. Trying to realize what he'd done.

I got my feet under me, went towards him.

Then it penetrated him. His face broke open. He dropped the .45. It landed with a clatter on the concrete.

Without a sound, he turned and ran into the darkness. Before I could even try to catch him, he was out of sight and gone.

Chapter Seventeen

chased his footsteps for a few seconds, but once I left the light I was blind. Sooner than I expected, I ran into a sheet-metal wall that rattled like thunder when I hit it. After the din died down, I couldn't hear Ted any more, anywhere.

Cursing uselessly, I went back to the corpse.

Ted had done a thorough job of it. Last was about as dead as he could get without actively being cut up into pieces. At least three rounds hit him – two in the chest – and there was a hole I could've put my fist through where his face used to be. It might've made me sick if I hadn't already been too furious to give a rusty damn. Let him rot in his own blood. I just wanted to get my hands on Ted.

I'd lost my only lead to Last's partner. The asshole who actually took the girls and shot them up. And with Last dead, that asshole wouldn't waste any time destroying all the evidence he could find.

Including Mittie.

I wanted to tear Ted Hangst into little pieces.

Unfortunately Last dead was as much of a problem as Last alive. Maybe more. Now I had a body on my hands. A body that was killed with my .45. If the cops caught me, I'd have one hell of a time explaining all this.

And explaining it would be the easy part. Getting the cops to release me would be a lot tougher. I'd probably have to sit in gaol until they identified Ted's fingerprints on the gun.

I wasn't about to take this particular rap for Hangst. And I wasn't about to let the cops lock me away, even for a few hours. That meant I couldn't afford to leave the evidence behind. So I dug out a handkerchief and used it to pick up the .45. Instead of wiping it off like

I wanted to, I carried it by the barrel while I groped my way out of the warehouse.

Out in the night, it was a relief to be able to see again. And an even bigger relief to find the Olds where I left it. In my usual brilliant fashion, I'd left the keys in the ignition. But Ted hadn't taken it. Apparently he hadn't been thinking about things like that. I was still mobile.

I still had a chance.

I got in, locked the .45 in the glove compartment, and drove out of the warehouse yard on to Trujillo without turning on my lights.

I didn't turn them on until I started to hit traffic, almost a mile back north in the direction of the city. But I still hadn't figured out where I was going.

Everything was too urgent. Mittie was in danger for her life, if she wasn't already dead. The cops would find Last's body pretty soon – I'd left the light on because I didn't know how to turn it off, and before long a patrol car would see the light and check it out. Ginny lay in the hospital with her hand blown off. Ted was running around completely bananas.

I couldn't relax, couldn't clear my head. I needed inspiration, and I as sure as hell wasn't getting it. After a while I caught myself pounding on the steering wheel with my fist.

Panting, I dropped my arm. All right, ace. You don't know what to do. What would Ginny do?

Good question. Concentration took so much effort that in five minutes the wheel was slick with sweat. Eventually, however, I dug deep enough to get hold of an idea. After which I spent a couple of miles looking for a phone booth – and wondering what I carried around in my skull instead of brains.

Last knew Alathea was in the hospital. His partner told him. How did his partner know? Through the school board somehow. Acton had called Stretto, left a message with one of the secretaries.

What *I* needed to know was basically simple. Which secretary? And who, exactly, did she tell? How many people got that particular piece of information?

Acton probably hadn't gotten that far yet. First he had to get a warrant, search the school board offices. Talk to Stretto. Maybe to Martha Scurvey. There was a good chance that I wouldn't run into him.

Finally I spotted a phone booth and pulled over. I used the directory to get Julian Kirke's address, then headed the Olds in that direction. Out toward the east side of town.

It seemed to take for ever to get there, but actually it wasn't more than forty-five minutes. He lived in one of those fancy singles apartment complexes that sits on a lot about four blocks long and has tennis courts and swimming pools as well as a 'recreation centre' for dancing and other predatory activities. This particular complex was called Encantada Square, and the apartments all had terraces and balconies with wrought-iron railings, arched entryways, redwood doors. Inside they probably had mirrors on the ceilings of the bedrooms. But the place didn't look all that expensive. The 'swinging singles' usually aren't rich.

After a little trouble, I located Kirke's apartment. It had a modest little card that said J. KIRKE in a slot above the doorbell.

When I rang the bell, I was trembling. I didn't think I could handle it if Kirke wasn't in. I needed to talk to him. If I missed him – the way I was feeling, I'd probably sit down on the floor inside his nice arched entryway and start to cry.

At the moment I had absolutely no idea how I'd managed to function at all back in the days before I met Ginny. I missed her so much I was in danger of blubbering.

Then the door opened, and Kirke stood in front of me. He kept one hand on the doorknob. In the other, he held a drink, which I identified instantaneously as scotch on the rocks. He wasn't wearing a shirt. I could see that he was a lot stronger than he looked with all his clothes on. He had the kind of muscles you get from lifting weights.

I could also see the bruises I'd made on his upper arm.

Two or three different varieties of surprise and anger twitched across his face as he looked at me. I took advantage of them by brushing past him and walking into his apartment.

His living room was designed to look nicer than it really was. Sunken floor two steps down. Soft, supposedly seductive colours. A thick cheap carpet, plastic potted plants here and there. A picture window with a clear view of the next-door neighbour's picture window. And not much in the way of furniture. Just one recliner, a stool, and a sofa big enough to sleep three or four swingers at the same time.

I paused in the centre of the room for a minute and tried to figure out how to handle Kirke. I had too many priorities – protect Alathea, get information, stay out of gaol, find Mittie alive. And nothing but terrible consequences in all directions if I failed. I was looking for some really devastating way to curse my lack of inspiration when Kirke broke the silence.

'Mr Axbrewder,' he said. 'What an unexpected pleasure.' He sounded like a beaker of sulphuric acid that he intended to throw in my face. But he hadn't done it yet. Civility and sarcasm were doing some kind of balancing act.

'Yeah.' I turned to face him.

He stood at the top of the steps, which gave him a chance to look down on me. His hand cradled his drink as if he knew what it could do to me. He'd regained his self-control – his anger and surprise were gone. He was master of the situation.

'That's the story of my life,' I said. 'One unexpected pleasure after another.'

He studied me for a moment. Then he said, 'You've had a rough day. You need a drink.' He started toward a sideboard bar behind the sofa.

'I don't need a drink,' I snapped. My nerves were in worse shape than I thought. 'I need some answers.'

He waved his glass at me. 'You sure?'

'I don't drink while I'm working.'

He shrugged and sat down side-saddle on the back of the sofa. The perfect host, showing me he didn't need to look down on me.

He sipped his scotch.

I waited.

By then you would've thought I was ready for anything, but he still managed to catch me off guard.

'I heard what happened to your partner,' he said. 'Too bad. It must be tough for you.'

'My partner?' I asked stupidly. I had the horrible feeling that I was completely out of my depth.

'Getting her hand shattered like that.' He looked thoughtfully into his glass. 'Messy. But it shows one thing, Axbrewder. You're smarter than I thought. Most of the big tall he-men I know have an irresistible compulsion to protect helpless little women. You don't have that problem. I admire that. Let them take their chances, like anybody else.

'Of course' – his civility slipped a notch – 'your partner isn't much of a woman.' He took another swallow of scotch. 'She should've been born a man.'

I must've been staring at him like a lunatic, because the next thing he said was, 'Are you sure you're all right?'

'No. Ginny is the brains of this team.' Why was I telling him that? 'Without her, I'm in lousy shape.'

I practically had to clap my hands over my mouth to make myself shut up. It was like trying to cork a bottle you're holding upside down.

'What can I do to help?' he asked.

He sounded civil again, but the sneer on his face would've turned butter rancid at fifty paces.

Suddenly everything went cold inside me, and I was calm again. Still mad enough to knock down walls with my forehead – but calm. The muscles of my face and shoulders relaxed. 'Answer a few questions,' I said evenly.

'If I can.' He was looking me straight in the eye.

'How did you know about Ginny?'

'Chairman Stretto called me this evening. He told me all about it. He wanted to brag to somebody. But bragging isn't good politics, so he used your partner as an excuse to mention his display of courage. I suspect that by now he's called most of the school board, the mayor, and half the City Council.'

I groaned dishonestly. 'Wonderful. With help like that, I'm going to need a fucking Ouija board to crack this case.'

'Why? What's the problem?' he asked. Mildly interested.

'Oh, hell,' I said. 'Why not?' I didn't look at him. I was afraid that my expression might warn him. 'This is an "information" case, Kirke. It all comes down to who knows what when. And how they found out. Like, how did Stretto know that Alathea was in the hospital in the first place?'

'That's easy. A cop called our office, a Detective Acton.'

'Did Stretto talk to him?'

'No, he wasn't in. Acton left a message with one of the secretaries.'

'Which one?'

He grinned maliciously. 'Sondra.' He liked hurting her.

Sondra. The innocent one. 'And she gave the message to Stretto?'

'No. She gave it to me. I run that office.'

'Were you alone?'

'Are you kidding?' He snorted. 'Nobody is ever alone in there. Half the office heard her.'

'Like who?'

'Let me see,' he mused. 'Mabel and Joan. Connie. I'm sure of them. There may've been a few others.'

'And what did you do with the message?'

Keep it going, Axbrewder. Don't give him time to think.

'I gave it to Chairman Stretto, of course.'

'As soon as he came back in?'

'Sure.'

'Was he alone?'

'No. Astin Greenling was with him.'

'Who did they tell?'

Kirke paused for a moment, stared at me. Then he said, 'How the hell should *I* know?'

Apparently he didn't need to time to think. He must've been as innocent as skimmed milk. Or else he was too smart for me.

I sighed. 'Yeah. Well, you see my problem. Someone on the school board is leaking information to the bastard who set that bomb. But finding out exactly who is starting to look impossible.'

He asked, 'Are you sure it's the school board?'

I went on looking out the window. The man in the next-door apartment sprawled on his sofa reading his book.

'I am,' I said. 'The cops aren't.'

He considered that for a minute. 'I know what your trouble is, Axbrewder,' he said finally. 'You're too tense. You need to relax, get your mind off it for a while.'

I turned around. 'How am I supposed to do that?'

He got to his feet. 'Change your mind. Have a drink. I have some scotch here that's to die for. It will make you kiss all your troubles goodbye.'

I glared at him. He sounded like he was making fun of me. 'I told you–' But if he knew about my drinking problem, he didn't show it. He sounded almost sincere. I made an effort to swallow my anger. 'The problem is, I'm an alcoholic. I have a hard enough time staying sober as it is.'

His jaw dropped. 'You're kidding.'

'No.'

'Oh, come on. A man like you? I don't believe it.'

Now I had the distinct impression that he was sneering at me.

'Believe it,' I growled. I was in no mood to put up with his scorn. Abruptly I started for the door.

He caught my arm. Something in his face looked too earnest to be a sneer. Too earnest – or too urgent. 'Come on. That woman you call a partner has been putting you through the wringer. Now she's convinced you that you can't even have a few drinks. You're no alcoholic. She just tells you that to keep you in line.

'Stick around. We'll put our feet up, have a few drinks, tell each other secrets. I know some things about the school board that will give you hives.'

He was making me sick. I said, 'No, thanks.' For some reason, I didn't break his hand. Instead I stepped past him towards the door.

Right then, all the decisions that I hadn't been able to make were made for me. Something in my head shifted, and I knew what I had to do.

When I reached the door, I turned to face Kirke.

He was still watching me. He held his hand out, offering me his glass. He was trying to smile.

I said, 'I had a talk with a guy named Last tonight.'

He didn't even blink. The way he said, 'Oh, yes?' you would've thought we were discussing the weather.

'He's the guy who set the bomb. Unfortunately he got shot before he could tell me anything useful.'

That made Kirke look curious. 'Did you shoot him?'

'No. But I wish I had.'

Then I left his apartment. Got out of there before my anger made me shake hard enough to stutter. When I reached the Olds, I had to lean against it and hold my head in my hands to steady my heart.

I'd done what I could for Mittie. I'd planted the information that Last was dead. If Kirke talked to anyone on the school board, anyone at all, word might get around. Then the bastard I was after might think that he didn't need to kill Ted's daughter. At least not right away.

That was the easy part. A quick gamble that might improve Mittie's chances. It wasn't why I'd started to shake.

I had the shakes because I was afraid.

Because now I knew what I had to do.

I had to talk to el Señor.

Chapter Eighteen

The idea would never have crossed my mind if old Manolo hadn't suggested it. When he'd first given me his advice, his breath smelling of anisette and secrets he couldn't or wouldn't reveal, I'd thought he was just politely telling me to go to hell. But now I knew better. Old Manolo understood things better than I did. He'd known what this case might cost me in the end.

The bare idea turned my guts to water. El Señor could sink a drunk like me without so much as making ripples. He didn't like Anglos, and he didn't like private *chotas*. All he had to do was raise one aristocratic eyebrow, and I'd find myself holding cement together in the foundation of some new building. Or bits and handfuls of Axbrewder-burger would fertilize apples up in the North Valley.

Oh, el Señor was a gentleman – sort of. He didn't bother people who didn't bother him. But off-hand I'd say the easiest way to commit suicide in Puerta del Sol is to go ask el Señor questions about his business. Some of the cops who tried it haven't been found yet.

Of course, I didn't have anything as threatening and maybe pointless as 'law-enforcement' in mind. All I wanted was to protect Alathea. Do something for Lona and Ted. Rescue Mittie. Nail the sonofabitch who was responsible.

But I was an Anglo and a private investigator. I was scared. El Señor had more reasons to kill me than talk to me.

And I was alone. That was the real crusher. I've done worse things with Ginny either backing me up or leading the way, and they weren't this bad. Because she was there. Now she wasn't. And the bastard who crippled her was going to try one of two things to protect himself – destroy the evidence, or kill the people on his trail. I was the only one left who could even take a crack at stopping him. If el Señor decided to stir me into a ton of concrete or feed me to the apples, then somebody else would die tonight, too. Somebody I cared about.

But the things that had me so scared were the same things that made me put the Olds in gear and drive away from Encantada Square. For a while, I doddered along down the road, driving like an old man – but I drove. And after a few blocks the cold air and the night helped me pull myself together. Night was something I understood. At night people did things for reasons that made sense to me. I didn't rush the drive – I needed time to recover – but I went where I had to go.

El Señor's headquarters is an old movie theatre not far from where I live. Or it used to be before he had it completely rebuilt inside. All he left was the façade, the marquee, and the ticket window. Now the place fronts as a nightclub called El Machismo. It's one of those places where people go – mostly Anglos, but certain kinds of Chicanos and Indians show up, too – when they have too much money and not enough sense to know that the man who feeds them their kicks has nothing but contempt for them.

Considering that el Señor mostly makes himself rich off the pains and weaknesses of his own people, you might think his headquarters would be down in the old part of town, an area that would help shield him from things like the law. But his location suits him. From his converted theatre he can go fishing for rich Anglos as easily as he can run numbers, extort loans, sell drugs or bodies for his own people. Puerta del Sol is full of society dudes and broads, money-punks of all flavours, who think going to El Machismo at night is 'exciting', but who wouldn't be caught dead going into the centre of town.

I parked the Olds in the lot across the street, gave the attendant a couple of bucks so that he wouldn't lose my keys, then spent a minute standing on the sidewalk. Hesitating. The marquee was lit, proclaiming 'El Machismo' in big letters the colour of cheap lipstick. On a good night, going in there was like meeting an old whore. This time I felt like I was on my way to arrange for me and a few other people to become cadavers.

But I did it anyway. Crossed the street. Paid my cover charge at the ticket window. Pulled open the black-out doors and went in.

After wading a few yards along a carpet as deep and rich as lava, I reached the club host. He looked like a matador in a tuxedo. His eyes flicked over me, and he pigeon-holed me somewhere down around not-worth-the-trouble. When he asked, 'Table for one?' he sounded so bored he was almost snoring.

'No, thanks,' I said. 'I don't want food. I want action.'

He lifted one eyebrow. 'Action?'

He was part of the screening process. He was supposed to distinguish between people who just wanted dinner and entertainment and people who were after something spicier. And he had to be able to spot *chotas*. Either way, I didn't look good to him.

But I was in no mood to argue the point. I glared down at him and said, 'I want to see el Señor.'

At that, he actually blinked. Both eyes. 'El Señor?' he asked evenly. 'Who is el Señor?'

I grimaced. 'Call the manager. I'll talk to him.'

He couldn't hold back a grin. 'As you wish.' He picked up the phone on his desk, dialled. When he got an answer, he spoke Spanish, thinking I wouldn't understand. 'With me,' he said, 'I have an Anglo who wishes to speak with el Señor. Possibly he is from the police. I think you wish to learn about him a little before you throw him out.'

He listened briefly, then hung up and turned back to me. 'One moment,' he said in English.

A moment was all it took. Then a door beyond him opened, and a man came out.

From my point of view, he wasn't tall. But he was built like an armoured car. His arms were so heavy they made his sleeves look like sausage casings, and he couldn't have buttoned his jacket across that chest with a steam winch. He didn't even make an effort to hide the gun tucked into his waistband. Under his nose, he had a hair-line moustache, and his eyes bulged like a frog's.

I recognized him by reputation. Muy Estobal. Rumour had it that he was el Señor's bodyguard.

He looked towards me. 'Will you accompany me, Señor?' He sounded like a piranha inviting me to lunch.

I shrugged and followed him.

We went through the door he'd come out of, and he led me down a long hall to a small office with a door so heavy I half expected to see a combination lock on it. When he closed it behind us, it made a permanent-sounding little *thunk*. It wasn't the only entrance to the room, but that didn't make me feel much better.

Muy Estobal didn't sit down. Didn't offer me a seat. Moving so fast that I couldn't stop him, he spun around and hit me in the stomach.

I doubled over, reeled back against the wall. For a long minute I couldn't breathe. Little suns danced around the air in front of me. My guts felt like I'd been shot with a howitzer.

While I was helpless, he checked my empty shoulder holster.

'Now, he said, 'you will tell me your name.'

With a gasp, I got my lungs working again. 'Axbrewder,' I panted. Staying doubled over.

'What are you?'

'Private. Investigator.'

'What do you wish with el Señor?'

'None of your business.'

His right fist jumped at my head like a cannonball. But this time I was ready.

I slipped his fist past my left ear and straightened up hard. With all the strength of my legs and back and shoulder, I hit him an upper-cut that flipped him over the desk behind him.

I vaulted after him, landed practically the same time he did. Before he could move, I clamped one foot down on the back of his neck. I held him that way while I helped myself to his gun, a snub-nosed Smith & Wesson .38. Then I let him up.

When he reached his feet, glaring as if he couldn't decide how to kill me first, I said, 'Now it's my turn, *pendejo*. I want to talk to el Señor. Ask him a couple of questions. I'm not here to cause trouble. No hassle, *comprende*, Estobal? I have a problem of my own, and I think he might give me a little help. One or two answers. If I don't get to talk to him, *then* I'm going to cause trouble.

'For a start, I'll break your neck.' He didn't so much as swallow. 'Are you listening, *pendejo*?'

He spat. 'Yes.'

'Good.' I took a deep breath, but I couldn't hold it. My stomach hurt too bad. I broke open his .38, took out the cylinder and dropped it in my pocket. Then I put the gun down on the desk. 'Take me to el Señor.'

Giving up the gun probably helped convince him that I didn't want to cause trouble. He picked up his .38 without taking his eyes off me, shoved it back into his waistband. Then he opened the other door to the office and stalked out.

I followed him. Close enough so that he couldn't break away, far enough back so that he couldn't turn and hit me again.

But he didn't try any tricks. He led me down another hall and out into a large room where the people approved by the host did their gambling. The air was thick with smoke, the steady clash of coins and chips, and the noises people make when they're throwing their money down a drain and calling it a good time. Roulette, craps, blackjack – all illegal as hell in this state, and every one of them nothing but a cheap shot disguised as magic, a chance to make something out of nothing.

There were house players scattered around the room – hookers, really – handsome studs and luscious broads daring the customers to believe the obvious fact that el Señor wouldn't be in this kind of business if he could ever lose. But most of these fine folks couldn't see the dare. The magic already had them by the throat. If you told them that putting their money in the toilet was gambling, you wouldn't have been able to stop them from emptying their pockets and flushing the stuff away themselves.

But that wasn't the only thing going on. Estobal moved quickly across the room, but I still had time to spot at least one man and two women who didn't have the vaguest idea that they were tossing away every cent they had. They were so stoned that you could've hit them over the head with a brick and they wouldn't have known the difference.

The really screwy thing about it all was that if you'd taken a poll in the room, most of those suckers would've told you they were more *alive* right then than under any other circumstances.

But it was none of my business, and I didn't have time to get up on my white horse about it. Estobal was holding a door open for me. When he closed it, we were in a short little hallway, maybe ten feet between doors, and there were two other goons with us. They didn't look at me, didn't wave guns, didn't even talk to Estobal. They didn't have to. We all knew what they were there for.

Estobal opened the next door, and I followed him with the two goons on my heels. Into an office that made Ginny's look like a phone booth. It sported a full bar complete with bartender, a couple of Olympic-size sofas, and a desk you could've played tennis on. The carpet was like a trampoline. I half expected to see potted sequoias in the corners.

Aside from the bartender, the only man in the room sat behind the desk. From his manicured fingertips to the ends of his Vandyke beard and moustache, he was the perfect dapper grandee. He couldn't have been more than five six. That desk should've made him look like a dwarf, but it didn't. Instead it reinforced his commanding presence, his air of possession. Somehow he fitted in that office. It was his, and he liked it the way it was.

El Señor.

Estobal marched up to the desk. Without speaking, he took his gun out of his pants and put it down on the blotter so el Señor could see that the cylinder was missing.

In Spanish el Señor asked, 'What is the explanation of this?'

I answered for him. 'I am the explanation. I am named Axbrewder. I do the work of a private investigator. I wish to speak with el Señor.'

I was hardly finished when I heard pistol hammers cocking. I didn't need mirrors to know that the goons behind me were ready to blow me in half.

'*Chota*!' Estobal spat.

Trying not to sound desperate – or even in a hurry – I said, 'I wish to speak with Hector Jesus Fria de la Sancha.'

El Señor's eyes narrowed. For a moment he studied me. Then he leaned back in his chair. 'Please to be seated, Señor Axbrewder.'

His fingers made a delicate gesture at the goons, and suddenly they were standing back against the wall. As I sat down, Estobal stamped out of the room.

After half a minute, el Señor asked quietly, 'How does it transpire that you know my name, Señor Axbrewder?'

I answered him in English. Trying to shore up my position by exerting at least that much control over the conversation. 'What difference does it make? The people who told me don't have anything against you. And I don't want to give you any trouble. I'm here for myself. Leave it at that.'

He steepled his fingers, gazed closely at the way the pink tips touched each other. 'Already you have given me trouble. You have humiliated my Estobal. Now he will be unsure of himself. Also he will be very angry. His value has been made less.'

'He'll recover,' I muttered.

'Nevertheless.' El Señor was not accustomed to being contradicted. His English had a mechanical precision more threatening than any amount of rage or screaming. 'Your presence casts doubt upon my Estobal. It casts doubt upon my personal safety. Now you say that you are here for yourself. You presume a great deal upon my benevolence, Señor Axbrewder.'

I said, 'No.' At that point I didn't really care whether I contradicted him or not. 'I'm already too familiar with your reputation for "benevolence". What I'm counting on is your reputation for honour.'

He considered me closely, then said, 'I think I do not like the tone in which you address me.'

'Señor Fria,' I hunched forward in my chair, half protecting my sore guts and half pleading with him. 'Let me tell you why I'm here. Then you'll understand my tone.'

He unsteepled his fingers, rested his arms on the arms of his chair. 'Very well. Begin.'

Begin, hell. It wasn't that easy. There were so many things I had to explain before I could get to the point. I felt a sharp urge to stand up and start pacing around the room, try to relieve the tension. But I didn't. I didn't want to make the goons nervous. For a minute I just sat there racking my brains. Then I said, 'I'll tell you what happened to my niece.'

Carefully I told him Alathea's story – her disappearance, the note, Lona's concern, her decision to hire Ginny and me, Alathea's reappearance, her condition, the bomb in the hospital. And all the time I watched el Señor's face, studying it for any kind of surprise or sympathy that would tell me where I stood with him.

But his smooth neat features didn't show a thing. When I stopped, he said, 'Some word of this bombing in the hospital has come to me. A very bad thing. What has it to do with me?'

'I told you. She's in a heroin coma. At thirteen she's been forced to become a junky and a whore, and she's in a coma.'

Abruptly he leaned forward, placed his hands flat on the desktop. 'Señor Axbrewder,' he said softly, 'I do not sell heroin to young girls.'

'I know that.' I did my best to make him believe it. My life depended on whether or not I could make him believe it.

He didn't move a muscle. 'Continue.'

'Señor Fria,' I said, 'seven young girls Alathea's age have been kidnapped in the past two years. They disappear. Their parents get phony notes. Then somehow they get hooked on heroin, and they turn into whores. And three or six months later, they end up dead. My brother's daughter was number eight. Number nine is still missing.'

'Again I ask, what has it to do with me?'

'Heroin.' I wasn't afraid any more. I was past that. My voice was as soft as his. 'Every nickel bag in this state has somebody's name on it, and you know all the names. The man who kidnaps and rapes and dopes these girls gets his junk from somewhere. You know who he is.

'I want you to tell me who he is.'

'Go to the police. Let them find him.'

'They will,' I rasped. 'But not tonight. They're not that fast. And he knows they're getting close. Tonight he's going to kill number nine and get rid of the body. Destroy the evidence.'

'I see.' Again he leaned back in his chair, considered me from a distance. Then he said, 'Perhaps I know the man. It is possible. Tell me, Señor. Why should I deliver him to you?'

Praying that old Manolo hadn't betrayed me, I answered, 'You're a man of honour. What he's doing is terrible.'

'He is Anglo. The girls are Anglo. Honour means nothing among Anglos.'

'Anglo, Chicano, it doesn't make any difference. *They're only thirteen.* Some of them are twelve.'

'You also are Anglo. You are a *chota.*'

Through my teeth, I said, 'Señor Fria, I'm her father's brother.'

Something about that reached him. He was silent for a long minute, looking at the ceiling. When he spoke again, his tone was softer. 'I myself have two daughters. If I were dead or in prison, and some evil were done to them, my own brother would pay any price to punish that evil.'

With one hand, he gestured at the bar, and two seconds later the bartender set a bottle of tequila down on the blotter. With two glasses.

'We will drink together,' el Señor said. 'Then I will give thought to this thing you ask.'

Right there, it all collapsed. I stared at the bottle while everything inside me went numb. Stared while he poured hefty jolts into both glasses. Took one himself. Pushed the other across the desk to me.

I didn't touch it.

'Drink, Señor,' he said softly.

My hand tried to move, but I didn't let it. I just sat there and stared at the glass and didn't touch it.

'Señor Axbrewder.' Soft and ugly. 'I give nothing without price. You are known to me. You are what the Anglos call "alcoholic". Also you are Anglo, and a *chota.* You have intruded upon myself and humiliated my Estobal. This is the price.'

I didn't touch it.

'Do not insult me,' he said. Soft and ugly and fatal.

I wanted to say something, appeal to him somehow, make him understand. But I didn't have any words for it. There weren't any words. If I took a drink, the name he was offering me wouldn't do me any good. Once I started to drink, I wouldn't be able to do anything. About anything.

I got to my feet. 'Sorry I bothered you,' I muttered. 'I should've known better.'

El Señor made a cutting gesture with the edge of his hand. His goons hit me before I could step away from the chair. Maybe I could've taken them if they'd given me a second to move, but they didn't.

They caught my arms, jerked me back down into the chair. One of them knotted a fist in my hair, hauled my head back. It all happened too fast. I was gasping and couldn't help myself.

El Señor came around the desk, picked up the bottle, and started pouring tequila down my throat.

Then I went blind with tears while the stuff burned its way into my guts.

Chapter Nineteen

The goons turned me over to Muy Estobal, and Estobal turned me out of El Machismo.

He was methodical about it. First he half carried me down a couple of back halls until we reached a door that took us out into a dark alley behind the place. Then he searched my pockets until he found the cylinder to his .38. Then he pounded on me.

Grinning like a barracuda.

One hit split my lips so badly that I sputtered blood every time I breathed. Another almost cracked my jaw. A couple more continued the job he'd already started on my ribs. Eventually he had to hold me up with one hand so that he could go on punching me with the other.

I suppose I should've made some effort to defend myself. I wasn't all that drunk. But everything had fallen apart on me. It was all hopeless, and I couldn't think of a good reason to exert myself. So I didn't. If Estobal wanted to beat me to death, that was his business. My brain was numb.

Numbness is a wonderful thing. I really didn't feel his fists much. Half the time I couldn't even see him.

Nevertheless I could hear him fine. He panted like a locomotive, working himself up into a terrible lather. Every time he swung, he grunted like a small explosion, a lesser bomb. After each blow came a penetrating thud, muffled and profound.

Then I heard something else. A voice – a woman's voice. It sounded dimly familiar.

It said, 'Release him.' In Spanish.

Estobal stared down the alley for a second. He braced himself to hit me again.

'I do not jest, Estobal,' the woman snapped. 'This man is known to me. I am in his debt. For his sake I will risk many things to punish you. The police will be grateful for any reason to seal you in their prison.'

Estobal pushed me away. I bounced against the wall and fell on my face. 'Do not make threats to me, girl,' he rasped. 'El Señor will be displeased.'

'Then permit him to be displeased. If he seeks to harm me, all Puerta del Sol will laugh at the man who revenges himself upon a woman.'

Estobal muttered some kind of retort, but I couldn't make it out. Then he was gone. I heard the door slam behind him.

A minute later, the woman was kneeling beside me. 'Ay, Señor Axbrewder,' she said in English. 'Are you severely hurt?'

With her help, I rolled over on to one side. My chest and face were starting to hurt, and I had to hunt a long way through pain and alcohol to find her name. 'Señorita Sanguillan,' I said. At least that's what I tried to say. 'What're you doing here?'

I heard a tearing noise. Then she began dabbing my chin and mouth with something. It felt soft, like a piece of her slip. While she tried to clean me up, she answered my question.

'I wished to speak with you. Señor Sevilla, who is known to you' – old Manolo – 'is the father of the man who married the daughter of my mother's brother. When I revealed to him my wish, he informed me that you had a great matter in your heart which compelled you to seek words with el Señor.' She kept wiping at my face while she spoke, and it hurt off and on, but I was too fuzzy to care. 'Therefore I came to this place and enquired of you. I was informed that you had been admitted to speak with Muy Estobal.' Suppressed fury rasped in the way she said his name. 'I chose to await you.'

Under her breath, she muttered, '*Pendejo.*' I knew she didn't mean me.

Groaning, I tried to crank myself into a sitting position. It wasn't easy. I wasn't absolutely sure which way was up. But she got her arms around my shoulders and helped me. With her face close to mine, she studied me anxiously.

'Is it possible for you to rise?'

I said, 'Theresa.' My mouth felt like it was full of broken glass. I could hardly mumble. 'Why did you want to talk to me?'

She hesitated, then said, 'If you rise, I will inform you.'

I shook my head. 'Just tell me.'

She sighed. 'Very well, Señor Axbrewder. But you must not think ill of me.'

I wanted to tell her not to worry, but I didn't have the strength. Or maybe what I didn't have was the moral substance.

Facing me squarely, she said, 'I have taken back the charges against the man who sought to harm me. I do not wish you to speak against him.'

That was the last straw. It was all too much for me – nothing mattered any more. I let myself fall back against the cement and closed my eyes.

'Señor!' She shook me, but she didn't weigh enough to move me much. 'You must understand. Because of this Captain Cason, I have lost my employment in the Heights. He spoke, and I was sent away without reference. He is too strong for me. He desired me to take back the charges, and I agreed so that he would permit me to find some other place of work.'

I didn't move. Why should I move? The only thing she could've offered me that would've meant anything was a bottle – and that never occurred to her. After a while she quit tugging at me. I didn't even hear her leave.

I must've blacked out. The next thing I knew, she was back. With help. Two young men – old Manolo's sons, if I understood her right. They propped their shoulders under my arms, heaved me up, and lugged me off.

I dragged along between them for a couple of minutes. But the strain hurt my chest too much, and I had to pick up some of my weight to ease the pain. Eventually old habits took over. By the time we reached her destination, I was practically walking by myself.

Her place was a ramshackle old adobe tenement maybe five blocks from El Machismo. The walls had once been painted, but now they were so chipped and weathered that the building looked diseased. Stricken by terminal futility. The young men levered me up a flight of rickety wooden stairs, and then she was home.

The one room she shared with her mother and two sisters was never going to look clean no matter how often they scrubbed it. Ordinary soap and muscle can't keep up with rats.

She sat me down in the middle of the room in the only chair. Her mother heated some water on a stinking oil stove while her sisters watched me from their blankets with frightened animal eyes. When the water was ready, the young men held my arms while Theresa scalded the cuts on my face.

The pain blinded me again. It wasn't until after my eyes cleared that I realized somebody else had come into the room.

Old Manolo.

He regarded me with a face full of sadness. But I didn't pay any attention to that. I had something else in mind.

He had a bottle of anisette in his coat pocket.

It was almost full.

As soon as his sons let go of my arms, I lunged at Manolo and got my hands on his bottle.

Putting my mouth around the mouth of the bottle tore my cuts, and the alcohol burned them like the lick of a whip. I stood it long enough to get three or four good swallows. I've never liked the taste of anisette, but right then I didn't give a shit. All I wanted was to get drunk. Drunker. Drunk enough to pass out.

I put the cap back on the bottle, stuffed it away in one of the pockets of my jacket. Then I looked old Manolo in the face. 'I took your advice,' I muttered stiff-lipped. 'Went to see el Señor. Now here I am. If you've got anything else to tell me, you'd better say it now. While I'm drunk enough to stand it.'

His old brown gaze never wavered. 'Ah, Señor Axbrewder,' he sighed, 'this night I have heard many sad tales. The daughter of your brother's widow has been found without her mind. A bomb has taken the hand of your partner. The setter of the bomb is dead, and you have come no nearer to the author of these evils. It is a deep regret to me that el Señor saw fit to withhold the knowledge you seek. Never again will I give such counsel as I gave you. I am an old man, and old men are foolish.'

His eyes held me until I couldn't stand it any more – I had to look down. I didn't want him feeling sorry for me. I was in bad enough shape without that.

'Señor Axbrewder,' he asked gently, 'what will you do?'

That was a good question. Since I didn't have an answer, I took another slug of anisette. It was starting to get to me. Some of the numbness I needed crept into my nerves.

'Will you not go to the Fistoulari woman? She has the name of a strong and clear-sighted person. Surely she will wish to know what has befallen you.'

Ginny. Just thinking about her made my heart hurt. But Manolo was a cunning old bastard, and he knew what he was doing. It was a sneaky way to give me advice, but it worked.

Ginny.

That was it, of course. Things weren't bad enough yet. They wouldn't be bad enough until I went and told Ginny that I'd screwed everything up. Then I'd be free to drink as much as I wanted. It wouldn't be my problem any more.

Everything has to be paid for. Even freedom. Humiliation is the price you pay for alcohol, one way or another.

I got to my feet, wincing at the way my ribs ground together. Shaking off the hands that tried to hold me, I went past old Manolo to the door.

I was on my way out when I recovered enough decency to turn around. Holding myself up on the door-frame, I said as clearly as I could in Spanish, 'Theresa Maria Sanguillan y Garcia, I give you thanks. I think no ill of you, but only good. When a burden is too great to be borne, it must be set aside.' Then I left.

I stumbled a couple of times on the stairs, but the railing held me somehow.

After that things got harder. Walking made my chest hurt. Also my balance wasn't good, and every time I stopped myself from falling I jarred my ribs. But I had to do it, and I did it. Went back to El Machismo's parking lot to recover the Olds.

Then I was driving. I concentrated on it hard. The last thing I needed in the world was a DWI bust. But I couldn't help making mistakes. Once I had the distinct impression I was going the wrong way down a one-way street.

I hung on to the wheel with both fists and kept moving. A couple of times when things got fuzzy, I stopped and took a swig from my bottle. Not much – just enough to hold me together. After a long time I reached University Hospital.

It didn't occur to me that there would be a problem getting in to see Ginny until after I'd parked the Olds and taken a look around. Most of the windows were dark, which reminded me of the time. Naturally the security guards and night-duty nurses weren't going to want me wandering around their hospital at this hour of the night.

But I was too drunk to let that stop me. In spite of the alcohol, I still remembered Ginny's room number.

I went into Emergency. But instead of stopping at the nurses' station, I walked straight to the waiting room as if I had some perfectly good reason for being there. Then I sneaked over to the stairwell.

The door to the stairs had a big sign on it saying, 'Emergency Exit Only.' I went in fast. Once I got past the door, the only thing I had to worry about for a while was meeting someone on the stairs.

I didn't meet anyone. If I had, I probably would've gone to pieces.

When I found the floor I wanted, I looked out through the little window in the stairwell door. I didn't see anybody. Ginny's room was just two doors down from me on the opposite side of the hall. Getting in to see her would be easy.

Too easy.

I cracked open the stairwell door a couple of inches, made extra sure that the hall was empty. Then I went across to Ginny's door. And stopped.

I didn't want to just barge in. She had strong feelings about her right to privacy. And I knew how fast she could be with her .357.

Instead of just pushing the door open and going in, I knocked.

Waited. Knocked again.

No answer.

I took the time for one more quick drink. Then I let myself into her room.

It was a semi-private room like Alathea's. The reading light over the head of Ginny's bed was on. The curtain separating the two beds had been pulled almost all the way across the room. No light came from the far side. Everything past the curtain was dark.

Ginny was sitting up in bed. The head of her bed hadn't been cranked up, and she didn't have any pillows behind her. She just sat there as if she were getting ready to answer my knock. But there was an IV hanging from a pole over her head, its tube plugged into her right arm. Which pretty well immobilized her. She couldn't have come to the door.

She looked at me.

Stared at me. Her eyes on either side of her broken nose were dark as bruises, as if she'd been mugged. Her face held a look of horror.

I didn't move. I couldn't. She paralysed me.

Her voice cut through me like the flame of a blowtorch. 'You're drunk!'

That staggered me. Rocked me back on my heels.

'You sonofabitch!' she snarled. 'How dare you?'

I blinked at her like an idiot. Ginny? She didn't understand. She didn't know what had happened to me. I hadn't expected her to react like this. I wanted to explain.

She didn't give me a chance. 'Get out of here, Mick.' The tone of her voice made my ribs grind together. 'I don't want to have anything more to do with you. Get out of my life.

'Do you hear me, *Mick*?'

186

She spat that Mick at me as if it were the worst thing she could possibly do to me without actually shooting me.

Mick. She called me Mick. Nobody calls me that. Nobody. Not since Richard – not since I killed Richard. Rick and Mick. Nobody. I nearly cried out.

'All right.' My voice shook. I couldn't control it. 'If that's the way you want it.'

Nobody! It would've been better if she'd shot me. No simple little hunk of lead would hurt like this.

But when I turned for the door, I caught a glimpse of her purse out of the corner of my eye. It lay on the floor a few feet away from her night stand.

Shot me, I thought. With her .357. Which she kept in her purse. What was it doing on the floor?

If she'd accidentally pushed it off the stand, it wouldn't have fallen that far away.

All of a sudden my skin began to crawl with intuition. A burning sensation mounted in the back of my head. Something was trying to get through to me. Reach past the stuff in my blood, make sense to me.

I struggled for it. Something–

I wanted to beat my head on the wall. I was too drunk. I couldn't think.

I had to think.

She'd called me Mick?

The pain was killing me. I couldn't stop it. I had to stop it. Had to think.

Ginny got her hand blown off because she didn't want anything to happen to me.

Think!

Her purse was too far away from the night stand. It couldn't have fallen there accidentally. Someone must've knocked it or shoved it aside.

Why?

Think.

She needed me. I had to be sober!

But I wasn't sober. I was standing there like a lush, with a bottle of anisette in my pocket and my hands clenched in front of my face. Seconds slipped away from me, and I couldn't bring them back.

Hands clenched.

Clenched the way I'd clenched them around Kirke's arm a couple of days ago.

Why had I done that?

Because Kirke said Alathea was a little whore.

I almost screamed – and everything came into focus.

We hadn't told Kirke that this case had anything to do with sex. We hadn't said a word about that to the school board.

How had he known?

Kirke!

That's why he'd tried so hard to persuade me to drink with him. He knew I was getting close. He wanted to keep me with him until he figured out some way to kill me.

Then a horror of my own landed on me so hard I almost dropped to my knees.

Kirke knew that Ginny was in the hospital. Stretto had told him what happened to her. He knew she was here.

I had no idea what to do. My intuition didn't stretch that far. I'd left the .45 in the Olds. And I was too far away–

Against the wall beside the door stood a steel armchair with a green vinyl seat. I put my hand on it to hold myself up.

Then it all came together at once – intuition, rage, fear, love. I snatched up the chair and with one sweep of my arm I threw it at the curtain near the head of her bed.

It hit something behind the curtain. I heard a muffled curse. A gun went off. The slug ploughed into the ceiling.

Ginny and I moved simultaneously. She flipped out of bed and sprawled flat on the floor, reaching for her purse. I jumped over her, dove headlong across the bed into the curtain.

The chair had torn the curtain. It came down under my weight. I landed half on the chair, half on a struggling body. It twisted frantically under me, trying to get up.

The curtain hid him. I didn't know if he still had his gun. But I didn't care. I just hammered at his veiled shape with my fists. The third time I hit something hard that must've been his head. He slumped under me, stopped moving.

I didn't stop. I heard Ginny shouting, 'Don't kill him! He knows where Mittie is!' But the pressure was too strong, and I couldn't stop.

I pounded at him with everything I had until I another gunshot crashed through the room.

Unsteadily I rolled off him. Got up.

Ginny stood beside her bed with her .357 pointed at the ceiling.

The IV tube had been ripped out of her arm. Blood dripped slowly from her elbow.

There was nobody in the other bed.

I swallowed hard, managed to ask, 'Kirke?' I hurt everywhere. My knees felt like mush, and my head floated sideways. I had to hold on to the bed frame.

Ginny nodded. Then she put her gun down on the night stand. For a second she looked like she might faint. But she fought it off. 'Oh, God, Brew,' she breathed. 'I thought he was going to kill you.'

Slowly I came back under control. Reaching down, I pulled away the curtain. Just making sure I hadn't hit him too hard.

I'd battered him pretty good, but Kirke was still breathing.

The whole room stank of anisette. One side of my jacket was soaked, and I had a pocket full of broken glass.

Chapter Twenty

Acton got an address out of Kirke. I don't know how, and I don't want to know. All I cared about was that Acton took me – and about eight other cops – with him when he went to check out that address.

It was a long way up Canyon Road towards the mountains. But Acton drove like a bat. We must've set a record getting there. The sky was turning pale, but the sun hadn't yet climbed over the mountains when we reached the house.

It sat in a little valley between two hills, completely out of sight of its neighbours. It was a rich man's place, a sprawling ranch-style house complete with everything except its own airstrip. But right then none of us felt much like admiring it. Acton broke the door down, and all ten of us went charging in.

We found Mittie alive. Hungry, strung-out, and frantic – but alive. One of the cops took her back into town to the hospital while the rest of them searched the house.

I didn't do any searching. Once I knew that Mittie was safe despite all the stupid things I'd done in the past twelve hours, a lot of the tension inside me snapped, and I had to sit down.

After a while Acton came and stood in front of me with his hands in his pockets. His fingers jiggled keys or coins or something.

I said, 'You weren't surprised to see who it was.' Which was true. When he'd reached the hospital and seen Kirke, he'd looked like he'd known it all along.

He said, 'Naw. I spent half the night talking to the school board. Scurvey and Greenling both said they got their note paper from him. He's the board secretary. He's supposed to provide things like note paper. Tearing sheets in half is an old habit of his. Didn't prove nothing, but it sure as hell made me suspicious.'

I nodded tiredly. Then I said, 'You'll have to find her father.'

'Naw,' he growled again. 'He turned himself in around 2.30 this morning. He babbled something about killing the man who set that bomb. I wanted to talk to him, but right about then we got this call' – he grinned sourly – 'about a shoot-out at the hospital. He's still sitting in the cage.'

'He used my gun,' I said. 'He didn't carry one. It's in the glove compartment of the Olds.' Then I said the only thing I could think of to help Ted Hangst. 'He was covering me. Last had a gun on me, and Ted was trying to keep me from being blown away.'

Acton nodded. I could see that he was going to accept my story without worrying about it. Another piece of tension faded, and for a few minutes there I almost went to sleep.

But then the cops started finding things. The note paper didn't give them any trouble. The desk in the den held a stack of neatly torn half-sheets. Same watermark as all the runaway notes. That and the fingerprints in the house gave the cops the kind of evidence courts love. Nine counts of kidnapping and seven of murder.

And after some more diligent searching that made the house look like it'd been used as a test site for high explosives, Acton's team found the heroin and the money. Not a particularly big cache of junk. Kirke probably had to drive down to Mexico every three or four months to stock up. But it was enough. The money came out to over a hundred thousand dollars. It was all Kirke had left after paying for housing, junk, food, clothes, and Sven Last. Obviously he kept it in cash so that it wouldn't show up in his financial records. Which explained why Smithsonian thought he was clean.

Acton rubbed his hands together. 'This bastard's going to get the gas chamber.'

A couple of cops stayed behind to keep an eye on things until the print-and-picture boys arrived. The rest of us piled into the cars and went back to Puerta del Sol.

Acton dropped me off at the hospital. The sun was up now, and all that crisp morning light made me squint. But for once in my life I was glad to see it. Nights like that last one I could do without.

It was nominally too early for visiting hours, but the hospital staff didn't make me wait. By then Ginny and I were celebrities – if that's the right word for it. The head nurse made an exception for me and took me up to Ginny's new room.

This time when she saw me Ginny smiled. It lit up her whole face.

I sat down in one of the chairs against the wall, and for a minute or two we didn't say anything. We just smiled at each other.

I didn't want to do anything else. But after a while I started to feel like I was in danger of making a fool of myself. 'All right,' I said. My voice was so husky it almost made me laugh. 'All right. I can't stand the suspense. After what I've been through, I want to know how you figured out this case.'

She looked beautiful to me. Even her broken nose was beautiful. 'What makes you think I figured anything out?'

'You were right on the edge of it.' That was something I knew for sure. 'At the time you were too tight to get it. But I'll bet you had the answer when you woke up after surgery. You probably tried to call me, but you couldn't track me down.'

She nodded. I was right, of course. Intuition didn't have anything to do with it. I just knew Ginny.

'I missed something obvious,' I went on. 'I'm going to go crazy unless you tell me what it was.'

She leaned back against her pillows, looked up at the ceiling. Fistoulari thinking. 'I missed it, too,' she said after a moment. 'It wasn't Stretto or Scurvey. We were pretty sure of that. And you were sure it wasn't Greenling. I was willing to believe you. So it had to be Kirke or one of the secretaries.'

'Finally it all came down to the way Kirke ran that office. Each of those girls was kidnapped during the day. At different times during the day. By somebody with the authority to make the girls go with him. Somebody who could supply a good excuse for himself if he got stopped. That excluded any fiancés or husbands. It had to be somebody who actually worked for the board.

'But each one of those little kidnapping operations must've taken a fair amount of time. Drive from the office to the school. Pick up the girl. Take her out to that house on Canyon Road. Run back to the office. That's what we missed.

'Kirke was the only one who could arrange so much time away from the office during the day. If one of his secretaries had disappeared for that length of time, he would've nailed her to the wall. The way he ran that place, he was the only one who could get away.'

Well, I was right about that too. I'd missed something obvious. Axbrewder the genius. Some days I'm amazed to find that I've put my clothes on straight.

Ginny was looking at me hard. I didn't understand it until she started to say, 'I'm sorry I called–'

I interrupted her. 'Forget it. I was in a fog. You had to get through to me somehow.' Then I grinned. 'And you knew Kirke didn't know my first name.'

For a minute she blinked back tears, and I couldn't think of anything to say.

There was a knock at the door. Ginny nodded, and I said, 'Come in.' It was Lona.

She wore a vaguely startled look, as if she couldn't quite believe what had happened. At first she had trouble finding her voice. Then she said, 'I wanted to tell you. I just talked to the doctor. He said' – she swallowed convulsively – 'he said Alathea is getting stronger. Her vital signs are stronger. And steadier. He said that probably means she's going to come out of it. Maybe soon. He thinks she might be all right.'

After that I couldn't see for a while. My eyes ran, and everything blurred.

Ginny said, 'I'm glad. She's a wonderful girl.'

Lona said, 'You didn't find her. You didn't save her.'

When Ginny didn't answer, I knew Lona was talking to me. Blindly I said, 'I know. She saved herself.'

For a moment Lona remained silent. Then she said, 'You caught the man who was responsible. That's what Richard would have wanted you to do.'

I had to cover my face with my hands. When I got myself back under control, Lona was gone.

Ginny smiled at me like the sun.

I got to my feet. She'd had a rough eighteen hours – she needed rest. And Ted would need me to tell the cops my side of the story. He might even need me to post bail.

But before I left there was one thing I had to do.

I walked over to Ginny and bent down. Deliberately I gave her the best kiss I had in me.

It hurt my cut mouth, but I didn't care because she wrapped her arms around my neck and kissed me back. Hard.

When we stopped, I was grinning like a crazy man. I practically floated as I turned away, started for the door.

Her voice stopped me. 'What're you going to do now?' she asked. 'Go have a drink?' She didn't sound angry or accusative. There was none of that in her tone. Just pain.

'No.' I faced her again so that she could see I was telling her the

truth. No big promises or predictions, just the truth about how I felt.
'I'm going to put that off for a while.'

THE MAN WHO
RISKED HIS PARTNER

– to *Paul Christianson* and *David Powell*
a small gesture to repay a large debt

Chapter One

Six months after that bomb took Ginny's left hand off, she still hadn't gotten over it. I didn't need a degree in psychology or a message from God to figure out what was going on. I lived with her – I could see it.

And I was living with her for all the wrong reasons. Not because she liked having me around. Not because she thought I was a particularly nice person to share a bed with. And certainly not because I was so all-fired tidy that I made the mess in her apartment stand up and salute.

No, I was living with her because she couldn't live by herself any more. She only had one hand. She needed somebody to take care of her.

If I'd said that to people who knew her, they would've laughed out loud. Sure, Axbrewder. She needs you. Tell us another one. She was Ginny Fistoulari, the boss and brains of Fistoulari Investigations. With her keen grey eyes and her attractive face and blonde hair and the way her tall lean body moved in her clothes, she could've been a society doll, the wife of some big snort who owned a country club or two, or maybe just half the first-born children in Puerta del Sol. But her nose had been broken once when some clown had clipped her with a crowbar – to which she'd replied by shooting the sucker in the face. And she'd lost her hand by holding a bomb out the window of a hospital so that it wouldn't blow up in the building or on the people below. When things got tough, she had a way of looking like her features were moulded over iron instead of bone.

As for me – at six foot five and too heavy, I was big enough that most people wouldn't ordinarily laugh at the idea that I was needed. But I was only temporarily sober. I was known to be totally fubar, 'fucked up beyond all repair,' even before that wonderful day – the highlight of my life – when in a fit of civic righteousness and alcohol I'd tried to apprehend a purse-snatcher and ended up shooting my brother instead. Like they say, anybody who can't aim a .45 better than that ought to have his brains recalled for production defects. And I was never going to get my licence back. The commission watched Ginny like a hawk because she insisted on hiring me when I didn't have a licence.

Sure, Axbrewder. She needs you. Tell us another one.

Well, in this particular case, 'temporarily sober' had been going on for six months. Almost every night, I dreamed about the special amber peace you can only find somewhere near the bottom of a bottle, and woke up grinding my teeth. Almost every day, when I wasn't braced for it, my throat ached for the lovely burn of whiskey. I still had withdrawal flashes that made me sweat and tremble and hold my head like a junkie. The simple smell of Scotch was enough to turn my guts inside out.

On bad days, when I got out of bed, I said to myself, Maybe today's the day. The day I get to take a drink. Just one. Or maybe two. Two drinks can't hurt me. I've earned two drinks.

But I didn't do it.

For a drunk like me, sobriety is like trying to push a brick wall down with your nose. Six months of it gets to be pretty painful. But I hadn't had a drink yesterday, or last week, or last month, and I wasn't going to have one today.

Because Ginny really did need me.

She wasn't actually helpless. In practice, she could've done just about anything she wanted. With her purse on a strap over her right shoulder, she could get what she needed out of it almost as fast as usual. And the doctors had fitted her with a prosthetic device – 'the claw', she called it – that looked pretty handy to me. Sure, it was made of stainless steel, which isn't exactly one of the primary flesh tones. But it strapped over her stump and worked off the muscles of her forearm, so that she could open and close the pair of hooks just by acting like she still had fingers. Down at the base, they had sharp edges that came together like scissors – which I thought was a nice touch. And they were strong enough to punch in the tops of beer cans.

She refused to wear the damn thing.

It made her feel worse.

The problem was simple. She was Ginny Fistoulari, hotshot private investigator, smart, tough, give-me-a-running-start-and-I-can-do-anything. And she was maimed. Without her hand, she felt like a cripple, ugly, undesirable, and bitter. The claw made her hate herself.

I knew exactly how she felt. I was Mick Axbrewder, the drunk who'd killed his own brother. She never would've lost her hand if I'd had the brains God gave a spaniel – if for example I'd thought of using my belt to hold that bomb.

So I took care of her.

Yes sir, we were quite a pair. Leaning on each other because neither one of us had the bare guts to stand up alone. Me, I was used to it. But I hadn't expected it to happen to her. If I hadn't been so busy being dogged and useful, I would've gone out and become a drunk again just to forget the constant misery burning like a low-grade fever in her eyes. Those eyes used to be as sharp and alive as a hunter's. Now they just hurt.

Somebody should've locked the two of us away in a nursing home somewhere so we wouldn't get into any more trouble. But maybe that wouldn't have solved the problem. And maybe trouble comes to those who need it. We sure as hell needed something.

Monday morning we slept in later than usual because we were between cases and didn't have anything better to do. I got out of bed first, used the bathroom, and went to make the coffee. While the pot was perking, I cleaned up the mess she'd made in the apartment the night before.

Her apartment was in Turtleshell, a complex near what used to be the business centre of town, before the banks moved. The building was at least middle-aged, but it was designed and furnished in the American Impersonal absence of style. She could've been living in Indianapolis. She stood it the same way she stood the clutter.

Which wasn't all that bad – her coat on the floor, clothes dropped wherever she happened to be when she took them off, coffee cups everywhere, case and tax records tossed down on the table so hard that a lot of them had splashed on to the carpet. And anyway I couldn't really object to it. I knew why she did it. It was as close as she could come to expressing her resentment.

Before she lost her hand, of course, she'd been messy out of ordinary absent-mindedness. Too many other things to think about. But now she cluttered the apartment because she knew that I was going to clean it up. She resented being dependent – so she resented me for helping her, for being the one she was dependent on – so she did little things to make my job harder.

We had a lot in common that way. I kept cleaning up after her for exactly the same reason.

In fact, we were spending more and more time playing that kind of game. When the coffee was ready, I took her a cup. But instead of drinking it, she let it get cold while she was in the shower. Then she had me pour her a fresh cup. Meanwhile I fixed her a breakfast she didn't want and could hardly choke down. If I'd been anybody else, I couldn't have made her eat breakfast by holding a gun to her head. By preference she lived on vitamin pills and coffee until at least noon.

It was a rotten way to live. If something didn't change soon, one of us was going to go off the deep end.

So after we slogged our way through another breakfast, I helped her get dressed. I buttoned her blouse – which should've been a whole lot more fun than it was – buckled her shoes, got her coat over her shoulders. I stuffed the papers she wanted into her briefcase. Then I held the door open for her, and we went out into Puerta del Sol's winter.

We hadn't had anything to say to each other for going on sixteen hours.

Puerta del Sol is far enough south so that we only get snow in alternate years. But the terrain around the city is high desert. The mountains east of us go up to 10,000 feet, which is only 5,000 higher than the Flat Valley, where Puerta del Sol sprawls on either side of the river. So the winters are about as cold as I can stand – at least when the sun isn't shining. And the sun today had a bleached-out look, like it was overworked. But Ginny and I still could've talked to each other while we walked to her office. We just didn't. Instead I huddled into my jacket, looking ridiculous the way somebody my size always does when he feels sorry for himself. And Ginny puffed at the cold while her broken nose turned red.

Her office is in the Murchison Building, on Paseo Grande. It's one of the three structures in Puerta del Sol that stand more than five storeys tall, but that turned out to be misplaced optimism on the part of the developers when all the banks moved three miles farther down Paseo Grande, away from what the real estate speculators call 'Chicano creep'. As a result, space in the Murchison Building isn't as expensive as you'd expect. That suited me. It helped Ginny stay in business. But I wouldn't go to any doctor or insurance agent who had an office there.

Unfortunately the heat wasn't working, and Fistoulari Investigations was on the wrong side for the morning sun. You could've stored cadavers in there. I picked up the mail and newspapers from the empty waiting room and carried them into the actual office. I put the mail on Ginny's desk and dropped the newspapers on the sofa I used for a chair. Then I started up the electric coffeepot. We had to have something warm to keep us going until the sun reached the picture window looking out towards the Flat Valley.

Booze would've been warmer, but I tried not to think about that.

While Ginny scanned the mail and threw it into the wastebasket, I glanced around at the only things she had hanging on her walls – her diplomas and the display copy of her licence. In this state, the commission wants private investigators to be 'professional', like doctors and lawyers. So Ginny decorates her walls with the sort of stuff that makes the commission feel good. And she has a waiting room for all the people who never come to see her. As a rule, the clients who come to see a private investigator are the ones you don't want – divorce cases and loonies. Good clients call. They expect you to go see them.

After the mail, she pulled one of the phones closer to her and started dialling. To keep myself from watching her, I picked up the papers. When I heard her ask for the manager of the Murchison Building – she was calling to complain about the heat – I stopped listening.

Amazing what you can learn from newspapers. Monday morning's edition was on top, and the headline said:

GANGSTER SLAIN
BODY FOUND IN RIVER

Under that:

Murder Mob Related, Police Say

Do tell, I said. My, my.

At 11.09 last night, according to the story, the body of Roscoe Chavez was fished out of the Flat River, down in the south part of town where the warehouses and *barrios* are. He'd been shot six times in the chest. His pockets had been filled with rolls of pennies for weight, but the body bloated up enough to float.

Somewhere in the fourth paragraph, the Puerta del Sol *Herald*'s keen-eyed and incisive reporter finally got around to using the word 'alleged'. Roscoe 'Bambino' Chavez was 'alleged' to have ties to organized crime. He was 'alleged' to be responsible for illegal numbers gambling in our fair city. The cops didn't have any particular theory about why he was killed. They were just glad he was gone.

I gave this flash the respect it deserved. Actually until this minute I hadn't believed that our fine and upstanding guardians of the law were even aware of the connection between the Bambino and Puerta del Sol's thriving numbers racket. As for why he was killed – I could've answered that with my eyes closed. He'd been killed for doing something el Señor didn't like.

Being a good citizen myself, I applauded the demise of brother Chavez. But I still wished that he'd gotten away with whatever it was el Señor didn't like. I had a small grudge against the man the *Herald*'s reporter would've called Puerta del Sol's 'crime czar' – if the cops had ever admitted that such a man existed, or if the reporter had been smart enough to figure it out. I was glad to hear that somebody had the guts to cross him.

On the other hand, there was nothing I could do to el Señor myself. He was too strong for me to mess with. And I'd never had anything to do with the Bambino. Ginny'd finished complaining about the heat. Now she was talking to her answering service. I looked to see what else was in the paper.

Near the back of the city section, an item caught my eye. I don't know why – I could just as easily have missed it. But when I started reading it, it didn't have any trouble holding my attention.

Ginny went on using the phone. Part of my mind heard her explain we didn't do that kind of work, but I wasn't really listening. I was concentrating on this news item about Pablo Santiago.

He wasn't anybody special – not like Roscoe Chavez. Just a ten-year-old kid I happened to know. Ginny and I worked for his family a couple of years ago on a protection-racket case. The Santiagos ran a grungy little *tiendita* down in the old part of town – one of those places where toothless grandmothers bought beans and tortillas at prices that were actually reasonable, and kids stocked up on Coke and licorice – until some of the local *muchachos* decided to finance their hobbies by extorting 'insurance' from small businesses. Since the *muchachos* were freelance, the Santiagos could have turned to el Señor for help. But then they would've ended up paying *him* protection money. That they didn't want, partly because they were honest, and partly because they valued their independence. So they hired Fistoulari Investigations.

Which was how I met Pablo Santiago.

According to the paper, he'd been missing since Saturday night.

I opened my mouth to say something to Ginny, but she was already in the middle of another phone call. I don't know what hit me hardest, the fact that a kid I knew was missing – another kid! Or that a Chicano kid who'd been gone for less than forty-eight hours was suddenly considered news – which wasn't exactly normal behaviour for the *Herald*. Or the sheer coincidence of it.

The combination felt like a gutful of rubbing alcohol. The last time I saw Pablo, he was running numbers. He was one of the errand boys who collected people's bets and distributed winnings.

I didn't bother telling myself that it wasn't any of my business. I have a thing about kids in trouble. And I didn't have to guess very hard to figure out why somebody as insignificant – or at least Chicano – as Pablo made the news. Because the cops were looking for him and wanted help. Because of Roscoe Chavez. On top of that, the Santiagos were good people. They deserved better than they were going to get.

I dropped the papers back on the sofa, hauled myself to my feet, and started for the door.

Before I got there, Ginny hung up the phone and demanded, 'Where do you think you're going?'

'Grocery shopping,' I muttered. Reflexive counter-punch. I didn't like her tone. When I looked at her, I saw that her resentment had moved right up to the front of her face. Not very nicely, I added, 'I'm getting tired of sitting on my hands.'

A masterstroke of tact. She loved it when I reminded her about her hand. But this time something more complicated was going on. She resented me for the same reason that she didn't snap back. Almost politely, she said, 'That can wait. This is more important.'

Always fast on my feet, I stared at her and wondered how she knew about Pablo.

But she didn't know about Pablo. 'There's a man up in the Heights,' she said. 'A Mr Haskell. I just talked to him. He wants to hire us. We need to go see him.'

If she hadn't been Ginny Fistoulari – and if I hadn't understood why she resented me – I would've said, Tell him to stuff it. But she was, and I did, so I didn't. Instead I stood there and waited for her to finish.

Her eyes wandered away while she tried to get a handle on something that looked suspiciously like panic. 'He says he needs protection. He says somebody's trying to kill him.'

Well, at least we were talking to each other.

Chapter Two

Just for practice, I took the .45 out of its shoulder holster under my left arm and checked it over. I wasn't serious. I'm not very good with a gun. And most of the time I'm too big to need one. I was just trying to get into the spirit of the occasion. Console myself for having to postpone my visit to Pablo's parents.

But Ginny wasn't playing. Her nice .357 Smith & Wesson gathered lint in the bottom of her purse, and she frowned at me in a way that said she didn't want any case that might be dangerous.

Like two people who were about to go grocery shopping, we got ready. I still wore my old raincoat over my jacket because of the cold. I helped her put on her coat. She turned off the coffeepot. I locked the doors. Then we took the elevator down to the basement garage, where she kept her Olds.

On the way, I asked, 'Did this whatsisname – Haskell – did he happen to say who's trying to kill him?'

She shook her head. Her broken nose was pale in the cold.

'Did he tell you why he thinks someone's trying to kill him?'

She shook her head again.

'And you didn't ask? Whatever happened to the famous Fistoulari curiosity?'

That got a little rise out of her. 'I thought he'd give me better answers if he had to look me in the eye.'

'You know,' I said, 'you're beautiful when you're angry.'

I thought she might express her appreciation by ramming her elbow into my stomach. Hell, I wanted her to do it. I wanted her to at least try to act like the Ginny Fistoulari I used to know. But she didn't. She just walked out of the elevator and went to her car.

I had the keys. I opened the passenger side for her and held the door while she slid into the seat. Then I walked around the car, let myself in, and fitted my bulk behind the wheel. I ground the starter until the engine caught. Then I asked, 'So where are we going?'

She stared out at the gloom of the garage. 'First Puerta del Sol National Bank,' she said distantly. 'He works at the Heights branch. Corner of Acequia and Glover.'

More to keep her going than because I was surprised, I said, 'He thinks someone's trying to kill him – and he went in to work?'

But she'd already figured that part out. 'Makes sense. He's a whole lot safer in his office in a bank than he would be at home.'

I chewed the situation over for a few minutes while I swung the Olds out of the garage and headed up Paseo Grande towards the beltway. She was right, it made sense. But sense isn't generally a dominant characteristic of people who think other people are trying to kill them. Most people don't get themselves into that kind of trouble. And when they do, they tend to panic.

Maybe Haskell wasn't surprised by what was happening to him? Or was he just that much more levelheaded than the rest of the human race?

The beltway wasn't direct, but it was quicker than plodding through umpteen dozen stoplights. Except during rush hour – and this was already the middle of the morning. In a few minutes, we were pulling up the long grade out of the Flat Valley.

Puerta del Sol sprawls. This is the Great American Southwest, and us rugged frontier-stock types don't like to live piled on top of each other. So the city spreads out. Mostly it spreads up and down the Flat Valley, where water is a little easier to come by. But it goes east, too, towards the mountains.

In that direction, it falls into roughly three sections, the Valley, the Heights – this long eight-mile grade where the city expanded when there wasn't any more room along the river – and the solid-gold real estate in the foothills of the mountains.

Overall the Heights is the newest part of the city. It's full of people like doctors and plumbers working for the day when they can move up into the foothills – or down into the old-money regions of the North Valley. I took the Olds off the beltway on Hacienda, steered my way past a strip of hamburger joints, pizza parlours, and stereo warehouses on both sides of the street, then finally got out into easier driving among the residential developments. The pale sunlight made the houses look like places where people never dreamed of trying to kill each other.

During the whole drive, Ginny didn't say a word. She didn't even comment, never mind open her mouth to give me directions, when I missed the turn on to Glover and had to go the long way around a golf course to reach Acequia. She just kept staring through the windshield with a small frown nailed between her eyebrows.

It wasn't like her to pass up a chance to give me directions. I'd been worried about her for a long time, but now something in the way I worried about her started to crystallize.

I was going to have to do something about it.

For a minute there, I considered getting drunk. I was in that kind of mood. If I got drunk, she'd be forced to dig her way out of the pit she was in – or pull the top in after her. I felt positively noble. Axbrewder bravely sacrifices his soul to booze in order to save his partner. But there wasn't anything noble about the way every cell in my body jumped up and danced at the bare suggestion of alcohol. I pushed the idea away.

When I wheeled the Olds into the parking lot, I saw that the Heights branch of the First Puerta del Sol National Bank embodied one of the new concepts in modern banking. It tried to look like a place where nothing intimidating happens – a place where your money is safe and the people are your buddies and nobody ever says no and it's all just as wholesome and American as motherhood – by disguising itself as an ice-cream parlour. It had a red pitched roof, actual peppermint stripes on the walls, frilly white curtains in the windows, wrought-iron railings for the porch, and candy cane lights on either side of the front door.

A risky way for a bank to do business. I didn't think it was going to succeed. Me, I'd rather bury my money in the ground. I could picture people walking up to the tellers and ordering a dish of tutti-frutti – right after they made their deposits and cashed their cheques somewhere else. But Puerta del Sol has a bank for about every eight people, and I suppose they have to do something to compete with each other.

Still I couldn't imagine anyone who worked in an ice-cream parlour being in danger for his life.

'Quite a place,' I commented, hoping Ginny would respond.

She got out of the Olds without saying anything and slammed the door. But when I sighed and followed her, she gave me a vaguely apologetic look. 'Whoever thought that up,' she said, pretending more sarcasm than she felt, 'ought to have his brains overhauled.'

'Shame on you,' I said. 'Didn't your mommie teach you not to say anything at all if you can't say something nice?'

She wasn't amused. But I guess she didn't like it either when we weren't talking to each other. Glaring at the bank, she said, 'My mommie taught me not to trust people who don't have better sense than this.'

Well, at least she made an effort. I happened to know that her mother died when she was four. Feeling a little better, I took a couple of quick steps to get ahead of her, then held the door open for her and ushered her into the bank.

Inside, the chairs where people had to wait for their loans to be approved or their mortgages to be foreclosed were upholstered with candy stripes, and the wallpaper had a peppermint stick pattern. Other than that, the place looked like an ordinary bank. Ginny spotted a desk with an 'Information' sign, and we headed in that direction. She had her left forearm stuffed into the pocket of her coat so that no one would know about her hand.

The woman at the Information desk wore a name tag that said, 'Eunice Wint.' She was young and pretty in a soft imprecise way, the kind of pretty that goes with baby fat. But the only thing really wrong with her was her hair. It had an indecisive style and colour that made her look like she didn't know how to make up her mind. I couldn't help noticing her engagement ring. If she'd tried to go swimming with that rock, it would've dragged her to the bottom.

She welcomed us to the Heights branch of the First Puerta del Sol National Bank and started into a bright spiel about how much she wanted to help us with our banking needs. Without actually being rude, Ginny cut in firmly, 'Thank you, Ms Wint. We have an appointment with Mr Haskell.'

'Oh.' Ms Wint blushed – which made her look about twelve years old. 'I'm sorry. How silly of me.' New at her job, I said to myself. To reassure her, I put on my Kindly Uncle Axbrewder smile. She gestured towards the offices at one end of the lobby. 'Won't you come this way?'

'Thank you,' Ginny said again.

We were both as solemn as brokers as we followed Ms Wint between the desks.

All the offices along that wall had large windows aimed at the lobby, either so that the customers could see the executives hard at work, or to let the executives keep an eye on the tellers and receptionists. The door in the corner had a neat, brass plaque:

REG HASKELL
Chief Accountant

Ms Wint didn't need to knock. The man in the office saw us coming, jumped up from behind his desk, and waved us in. But she opened the door and held it for us anyway. She was blushing again. Or still – I couldn't tell which.

'Thank you, Eunice,' he said in an easy, naturally rich voice you might expect from an actor or a preacher. As he came around the desk, he extended his hand to Ginny. 'You must be Ms Fistoulari.' Then he looked at me. 'And you?'

'Axbrewder.' I took my turn shaking his hand. He had a good grip, and his hand was dry and steady. He wore a light blue Southwest-casual banker's double-knit. 'I work for Fistoulari Investigations.' In a fit of perversity – directed at Ginny, not at him – I added, 'I do the fetch-and-carry stuff.'

Ginny gave me a glare that would've withered chickweed, but Haskell didn't seem to notice. 'Thanks for coming so promptly,' he said. 'I'm glad you're here.' Then he turned his smile on Ms Wint. 'If we need anything, Eunice, I'll let you know.'

She smiled back as if he'd made her day. But he was already on his way to the business side of his desk. Pointing out chairs for us, he said, 'Please sit down.'

He sounded perfectly natural and comfortable. In fact, he appeared perfectly natural and comfortable. He had a healthy tan and a solid, medium frame that looked like he took good care of it. Smile lines creased his cheeks. His reddish-brown hair ran back from his forehead in waves moulded to his skull. There wasn't any grey in his hair, but he was still probably about my age – around forty. His eyes were younger, however. They sparkled like a kid's. At a guess, I would've said that he wasn't in any danger at all. He was just excited about something.

On the other hand, his desk seemed too tidy for a man with a kid's excitement in his eyes. He kept all the papers in front of him as straight as numbers. Over to the left sat this morning's *Herald*, with its headlines displayed at the ceiling.

GANGSTER SLAIN
BODY FOUND IN RIVER

As we all sat down, I gestured towards the lobby and said, 'So, Mr Haskell, you're responsible for all this.' Trying the oblique approach.

'Reg,' he said. 'Call me Reg.' He pronounced it like *reg*ular instead of *reg*iment. 'I wish you were right. But I'm just the chief accountant.' He was doing wry diffidence, and he was good at it. 'Accountants don't run banks until they stop being accountants. We're like computers. We just churn out numbers. Other people make the decisions.'

'Mr Haskell,' Ginny put in with all the subtlety of a ballpeen, 'over the phone you said somebody's trying to kill you.'

This was our Mutt-and-Jeff routine. I come on all soft and friendly, Ginny goes for the bone. It's supposed to make people more honest by keeping them off balance. But Haskell didn't look particularly disconcerted.

Nevertheless he acted disconcerted. 'I'm sorry,' he said. 'This is embarrassing. I don't know why I did it.' He avoided Ginny's stare like a boy caught raiding the cookie jar. 'I guess I was just trying to make sure you would take me seriously.'

'I don't like being lied to,' she snapped. 'What made you think we wouldn't take you seriously?'

Haskell spread his hands in a rather theatrical shrug. After a quick glance at both of us, he admitted, 'You aren't the first private investigators I've called about this.'

That surprised me. There weren't that many private investigators in this town who could afford to turn down work. But I wanted a different answer first, and Ginny looked like she was about to say, Why did they turn you down? Did you lie to them, too? So I asked, 'Mr Haskell – Reg – what makes you think you need a private investigator?'

He gave me an encouraging smile. 'I'm sure they don't want to kill me. That would be an overreaction. But they would be very happy to break my legs.'

Ginny scowled formaldehyde and thumbtacks at him. 'This is fun,' she said. 'Just to keep us entertained, why don't you tell us why anybody would want to break your legs?'

He grimaced and tried to look miserable, but I got the impression that he was glowing inside. In fact, I would've taken my oath on a brand-new case of tequila that he somehow got handsomer every time Ginny poked at him.

'I was stupid,' he said. 'More stupid than usual. A week or so ago, a friend talked me into going down to El Machismo. Have you ever been there?'

I had, Ginny hadn't. We both stared at him. I didn't know what she was thinking, but my heart suddenly jumped like I'd been hit with a cattle prod.

'It's a nightclub down near the old part of town,' he explained. 'They converted an old movie theatre. But being a nightclub is just a front.' He was watching us closely now – probably looking for signs that we wanted to walk out on him. 'It's really a casino.'

'I've heard that,' Ginny said dryly. 'It's also illegal in this state.'

'I know. That's why I can't go to the police.' For a minute he seemed to lose the thread of what he was saying. Then he went on, 'But after adding numbers all day, I sometimes want a little excitement. And this friend twisted my arm.

'God, I was stupid!' His eyes were wide with amazement, like he still couldn't believe it. 'I'm not usually like that. But somehow I got' – he fumbled for the right words – 'caught up in it. You know?' He made an unabashed appeal for our sympathy. 'It was like magic. It was new and exciting and dangerous, and if you got lucky, or if you understood the odds well enough – if you were good enough – you could win.' He didn't look much like he regretted his folly. 'I lost my head.

'Also my money.' He grinned sheepishly. 'I wasn't as good as I thought. Before I realized what I was doing, I lost more money than I had with me. A lot more than I could afford.'

'Then what?' I asked. But I wasn't listening very hard. My heart still thudded around inside my chest, and I was remembering the one time I'd been to El Machismo.

'They were polite about it,' he said, 'which surprised me.' It didn't surprise me. That's how they hooked Anglo suckers. 'They gave me a loan to cover my losses, and forty-eight hours to pay it back.'

There he stopped. He didn't need to explain the rest.

Ginny said stiffly, 'The people who run El Machismo don't like welshers.' She had a tight grip on her temper. 'Why didn't you pay them back?'

Now at least he managed to look serious. 'I told you,' he said. 'I'd lost a lot more money than I could afford.' Then he shrugged again. 'And I was stupid. I underestimated them. They didn't know who I was. I thought they wouldn't be able to find me. If I never went back there, I thought I'd be safe.

'But they called me last night. I don't know how they did it, but they found me. They told me what they were going to do to me.'

'Two broken legs for one welshed bet,' I commented. 'That sounds like the going rate these days.'

Something in the back of his eyes seemed to share my sense of humour, but the rest of his face went on looking serious. 'Since then,' he concluded, 'I've been trying to hire protection.'

Sure, I thought. Anyone would feel the same way. Only he was in more trouble than he realized. None of the other private investigators he called would take the job because they didn't want any part of the trouble he was in.

Ginny didn't want any part of it either. I could see that in the way she held her head, the way her eyes seemed to have slipped slightly out of focus. She was looking for the right kind of anger to turn Haskell down. If the man who wanted Haskell's legs broken didn't get what he wanted, he'd just raise the ante until he did. Sooner or later, someone was going to end up dead. Why should she risk it? She was a cripple, wasn't she?

She sure was. I could remember the Ginny Fistoulari who never would've considered refusing a case just because it might get messy. I didn't exactly trust Haskell. Either he had a screw loose somewhere, or he wasn't telling us the whole truth. Normal honest folks get a little more upset when you threaten to break their legs. But I had my own ideas about what we needed to do. And why we had to do it.

Before Ginny could figure out how to dump him, I gave Haskell one of my smiles and said, 'You got it. Nothing's guaranteed in this business, but we'll give it our best shot.'

Chapter Three

'That's a relief.' Haskell's smile made mine look like the grin of a gargoyle. But I wasn't really watching him. Most of my attention was on Ginny.

She didn't react with any obvious outrage. The muscles at the corners of her eyes were clenched white, that's all. 'Mr Haskell,' she said, as smooth as a drill bit, 'I need a moment alone with Mr Axbrewder.'

My guts gave a sympathetic little twist, like she'd already started chewing into them.

'Of course,' Haskell replied. 'I understand.' With that boyish gleam, he seemed more charming than he had any legal right to be. 'Use my office.'

Before he got out of his chair, he reached for the phone. He dialled three digits, listened for a second, then said, 'Eunice, Ms Fistoulari and Mr Axbrewder are going to conference in my office for a few minutes. Would you bring them some coffee?' He covered the mouthpiece and asked us, 'Cream and sugar?' We shook our heads. 'Just black,' he said to Eunice Wint. 'Thanks.'

Still smiling, he made his way around the desk and out of the room.

We didn't say anything. Through the window, we could see Ms Wint coming in our direction with a Styrofoam cup in each hand.

Haskell headed towards one of the tellers, and Ms Wint seemed to be watching him more than where she was going. She nearly ran into a tall, thin man in a classy grey pinstripe. He talked softly – I couldn't hear what he was saying. But he sounded angry, and her blush looked hot enough to set her hair on fire. When he let her go and she brought us our coffee, she couldn't quite swallow all the misery in her face.

'Thank you, Ms Wint.' Ginny wasn't paying any attention. She just wanted to get rid of the girl. As soon as Ms Wint left, Ginny got up and closed the door.

I followed the receptionist with my eyes, side-tracked by her unhappiness. Ginny had to say my name to make me look at her. The way she said it, it sounded like she had a mouthful of broken glass.

I looked at her. If I'd been drowning, I would've forgotten everything and looked at her when she said my name like that.

She didn't say, I'm Fistoulari Investigations. You're just the hired help. Don't try to make my decisions for me. As soft and fierce as whip leather, she said, 'Are you out of your mind? Have you forgotten who owns El Machismo?'

Faced with that glare of hers, I crossed my hands over my stomach. 'Maybe it's the Divine Sisters of the Paraclete. What do you care? This guy's in trouble.'

'Bastard,' she lashed at me. 'It's el Señor.'

Which was why nobody else wanted Haskell's business.

Well, I remembered. But I remembered other things, too. I remembered that when Ginny was in the hospital with her hand blown off, I'd gone to el Señor because my niece was missing and I needed to know who was responsible. Instead of telling me, he had some of his muscle force-feed me a bottle of tequila. Then he let his main bodyguard, Muy Estobal, give me one of the best beatings I'd ever had. By the time he was done, I was in such terrific shape that I almost got both me and Ginny killed.

Slowly and carefully, I said, 'That's exactly why I want this case.'

She understood. She knew me well enough. But the fierceness in her face didn't change. 'Brew.' She took her stump out of the pocket of her coat and scowled hate at it. 'It's too dangerous. I'm not equipped to handle it.'

If this went on much longer, I was going to be sick. I wanted to shout at her, but I didn't. Instead, I said, 'Is that a fact? Poor little Ginny Fistoulari. Why don't you retire? Then you can spend all day every day feeling sorry for yourself.'

She was going to hit me. I knew it. Sure as hell, she was going to haul off and beat my skull open. And I was almost looking forward to it. I deserved it. Some days I was such a nice man I wanted to puke all over myself.

But she didn't hit me. She didn't even call me names. While I waited for her to tell me to get out of her life, her anger slowly changed from hot to hard, like melted iron cooling. In a voice I could've shaved with, she said, 'Mick Axbrewder, I'm going to get even with you for this.' Then she put her stump back in her coat pocket and stood up. Through the window, she signalled for Haskell.

Nobody calls me Mick. Not since my brother died. But this time I decided I'd better let it pass.

Haskell rejoined us with just the wrong hint of eagerness. Maybe he was still a kid at heart. Maybe being threatened by the bad guys was his idea of a game. That would make him hard to protect. But I didn't comment. I knew better than to interrupt Ginny now.

As soon as Haskell closed the door and sat down again, she said to him sharply, 'First things first, Mr Haskell. Are you married? Do you have a family?'

His mouth twitched, trying to grin and stay serious at the same time. 'Does that mean you're going to take the job? I didn't know whether Mr Axbrewder spoke for you or not.'

Well, he wasn't stupid, even if he did make stupid mistakes. But Ginny didn't blink. 'Are you married?' she repeated. 'Do you have children? Do you live with a girlfriend' – she must've noticed that he wasn't wearing a wedding ring – 'or your parents?'

People usually answer her when she uses that tone.

'Actually,' he said, 'I thought of that.' He was proud enough of himself to show it. 'I'm married. No children. After that phone call last night, the first thing I did was to send Sara away, out of danger. She shouldn't be hurt for my mistakes. I told her to go to a hotel. Any hotel, I didn't want to know which one. If I knew where she was, I might give her away accidentally. Maybe those thugs are listening to my phone. Or I might go to see her and be followed. I told her to call me every morning at work, and not to come home until I said so. She should be safe.'

I was mildly impressed. Sara Haskell was an obedient woman. Or Reg Haskell had more iron in him than I could see. For no particular reason, I suddenly wanted to talk to Mrs Haskell about her husband.

But Ginny just nodded and didn't pursue the question. 'Good enough,' she said. 'We'll do what we can for you. As Mr Axbrewder said, there are no guarantees. For one thing, we're human. We might screw up.' At the moment she didn't especially look like a woman who screwed up. I was feeling better all the time. 'For another, the people you cheated don't like interference. They might try to bury us, just as a matter of principle.'

He shrugged. 'If it's too dangerous—'

She cut him off. 'For this kind of work, we get seven hundred fifty dollars a day plus expenses. Fifteen hundred dollars in advance.'

I was beginning to think that nothing ever flustered Mr Reg Haskell, Chief Accountant. He glanced up at the ceiling like he was doing math in his head, then met Ginny's gaze. 'I can afford that. For a while, anyway.'

'Good. This may take a while.'

As understatements go, that was no slouch. I thought about it while Haskell wrote out a cheque and handed it to Ginny. Actually there was only one way to protect someone like Reg Haskell from someone like el Señor. El Señor couldn't afford to let welshers get away without being punished. Most of his power depended on fear, so he didn't give up easy. You had to make the punishment more trouble than it was worth. In practice, that meant you had to silence his guns, dispose of the muscle he sent out to do the job. Get the thugs arrested. Shoot one or two of them in self-defence. And even then you had to hope that el Señor kept a sense of perspective. Otherwise he might send out men indefinitely over a relatively minor bet.

I had exactly one idea about how to get started on the problem.

Ginny had the same idea. But she took a minute to get to it. She was busy covering all the bases. 'You'll be safe enough here,' she said. 'Plenty of witnesses. We'll pick you up after work. What time do you get off?'

'Four-thirty,' he said.

'In the mean time we'll try to figure out how they found you. That might give us something to go on.' Almost casually, she said, 'You went to El Machismo with a friend. What was his name?'

At that, the lines of Haskell's face shifted, and his eyes narrowed. For the first time he looked his age. Slowly he said, 'This doesn't have anything to do with him. It isn't his fault. I'd rather not involve him.'

I sat up straighter in my chair.

'I appreciate that,' Ginny said acidly. 'You want to be loyal to your friends. But you'll just have to trust us to be discreet. Right now, this friend looks like the only link between you and El Machismo. If he's any kind of regular there, they might have some hold on him. He might've told them how to find you. We have to check him out.'

Haskell studied her hard for a minute, then dropped his gaze. 'The fact is,' he said, 'he's in an even more vulnerable position than I am. If just a hint of this gets out' – he glanced towards the window and the lobby – 'it would ruin me. People who work for banks aren't allowed to be in this kind of trouble. But for him it's worse. He wouldn't be that dumb.'

Ginny snorted. She smelled the same rat I did. 'He's already been that dumb. He talked you into going down there in the first place. We have to check him out.'

Haskell didn't like her tone. 'I don't want you to do that.'

'In that case' – she rose smoothly to her feet – 'hire somebody else.' His cheque dropped from her hand and fluttered to the desk.

Right on cue, I followed her example. I wanted this case so bad it made my back teeth hurt, but it wasn't important enough to keep me from backing her up.

He surprised me by not getting angry. His eyes gleamed again. 'All right,' he said with a stagey sigh. 'All right. His name is Reston Cole. He's an executive vice-president of the bank. He works downtown in the main office.' Frowning, he muttered, 'If he gets in trouble for this, I'll shoot myself.'

Ginny didn't try to reassure him. While she had him where she wanted him, she took advantage of it. 'One more question,' she said. 'Who referred you to us?'

I was glad she asked that. Somehow I didn't think he was going to say that he got Fistoulari Investigations out of the phone book.

'I told you you weren't the first people I called,' he said candidly. He looked like he had a secret bit of spite hidden away somewhere. 'One of them gave me your name. An outfit called Lawrence Smithsonian and Associates.'

I almost whistled out loud. Lawrence Smithsonian – Ginny calls him 'fatass Smithsonian' – ran one of the few agencies in Puerta del Sol that was too successful for its own good. He was what you might call a laundry analyst. He specialized in money. How dirty money gets changed into clean money. Who does it and why. And in his spare time he hobnobbed with half the bank presidents in town.

He and Ginny hated each other. Natural antipathy – she didn't like people who got successful without keeping their hands clean, he didn't like people who were more honest than he was.

Upon mature reflection, as they say, it made sense that Haskell had called Smithsonian. A few polite questions anywhere in Puerta del Sol banking would turn up Smithsonian's name. But for Smithsonian to refer Haskell to us made no sense at all.

It wasn't for love, I was sure of that.

I probably had a blank stupid look on my face. I've never been good at poker. But Ginny didn't skip a beat. She thanked Haskell unnecessarily, reminded him that we'd pick him up at 4.30, retrieved his check, and pulled open the office door without offering to shake his hand. Not to ruin the effect of her exit, I followed as well as I could.

As we left the lobby, I glanced at Eunice Wint and waved. Sweet old Axbrewder feels sorry for everyone whose feelings get hurt. But she wasn't looking at me. She was watching Haskell's office like a woman who knew that she shouldn't hope and couldn't help it.

Ginny and I walked back to the Olds without saying anything. I unlocked the passenger door for her and went around to the driver's side. But she didn't get in. Her face was aimed in my direction, but she wasn't looking at me.

I thought it wouldn't be very good for our image if we just stood there with our brains in neutral, and in any case the sun wasn't putting out a whole lot of heat, so I asked, 'What're you thinking?'

Like her eyes, her voice was aimed somewhere else. 'He doesn't wear a wedding ring.'

'So what? A lot of men don't. You know the old line – "My wife's married. I'm not." Or maybe he just doesn't like rings.'

So much for my wit and wisdom. In the same tone, she said, 'Did you notice anything else?'

I leaned my elbows on the roof of the car and studied her hard. 'You mean besides the fact that he's just terrified in his little booties? You tell me.'

She made an effort to pull herself into focus. 'He's got that gleam. It's bound to be trouble. He's the kind of man women have trouble resisting.'

In my usual clever way, I listened to what she said instead of what she meant. 'Is that how you're going to get even with me?' I asked nicely. 'You're going to hop in the sack with him while his wife's safely hidden away in some hotel?'

'Oh shut up.' She wasn't paying enough attention to me to get mad. 'That's not the point.'

Well, I knew that. And I probably should've said so. But right then something small and maybe insignificant clicked into place in the back of my head. Pushing my weight off the car, I said, 'I'll be right back,' and headed into the bank again.

Eunice Wint sat behind the information desk again. There was no one near her. I didn't see Haskell anywhere. As unobtrusively as I could, I went and sat down in the chair beside her desk.

She'd locked most of her unhappiness away somewhere, but she still looked a little lost. 'Why, hello again, Mr–' she began with the brightness demanded by her job, then fumbled slightly because she'd forgotten my name.

217

'Axbrewder,' I supplied helpfully. I concentrated on looking like an inordinately large teddy bear – kind and warm, no threat to anybody.

'Mr Axbrewder. What can I do for you?'

'It's none of my business, of course,' I began – it's never any of my business – 'but who was that you were talking to outside Mr Haskell's office? When you were bringing us coffee?'

Somehow the question hit too close to home. She didn't do anything loud or messy, she just lost whatever capacity she may have had to tell someone as big as me to drop dead. No matter how old she was, she was too young for her circumstances.

'You mean Mr Canthorpe?' she asked. 'Jordan Canthorpe?'

I nodded. 'I couldn't help overhearing the way he snapped at you. What was he so upset about?'

'He doesn't like me to do things for Mr Haskell,' she said simply. She was too unhappy to look me in the eye. 'He says it isn't part of my job.'

'Is he your boss?' Axbrewder the teddy bear, kindly and treacherous.

She shook her head. 'He's Mr Haskell's boss. I'm in a different department.'

I acted appropriately huffy. 'Then what business is it of his who you bring coffee for?'

She was so helpless to keep her mouth shut, it made me ashamed of myself. In a soft demure miserable voice, she said, 'He's my fiancé.'

Click. And double click. Maybe it wasn't so insignificant after all. And maybe I should've paid better attention to what Ginny was trying to tell me.

'Thank you, Ms Wint,' I said. 'Don't worry, it'll all work out.' Before she could think to ask me what I thought I was doing, I heaved myself off the chair and strode away.

When I got out to the parking lot, Ginny still stood by the Olds, waiting for me. I felt like I owed her an apology – after what I'd just done, I wanted to apologize to someone – but she didn't give me a chance. Her grey gaze was fixed straight at me.

'What the hell was that all about?'

I did the best I could. 'You called it,' I said. 'He's irresistible. I'm willing to bet he's having an affair with Eunice Wint. Even though she's engaged to his boss.'

That made her raise her eyebrows. 'Axbrewder,' she said while she thought about it, 'you do have your uses.'

Then she changed gears. 'You weren't paying much attention back in the office this morning.' She was only being a little sarcastic. 'There were two calls with the answering service. The second was from Haskell.' She paused to set me up. 'The first was from Mrs Haskell.'

I stared at her. All I could remember about that call was hearing her turn somebody down.

'She wanted us to find out if her husband's unfaithful to her.'

My, my, I thought. What a coincidence. 'Do you suppose,' I asked, 'Mrs Haskell – or someone like her – hired a couple of goons to lean on good old Reg for sleeping around?'

Ginny got into the Olds. I fitted myself behind the steering wheel. She said, 'I think we'd better find out.'

On a whim, I commented, 'It does sound like our client likes to live dangerously.'

Chapter Four

But when I rolled the Olds onto the beltway again and pointed it in the direction of the new downtown, where nothing but concrete grows and all the banks have their main offices, Ginny told me that we weren't going to see Haskell's partner in crime, Reston Cole. Not yet. First she wanted to have a talk with Lawrence Smithsonian.

That suited me. It would've suited me in any case. I was as curious and maybe even as worried as she was about Smithsonian's motives. But now I had a particular reason for liking the idea. It would take time. What with Reston Cole and Mrs Haskell and some of our basic homework – like finding out whether our client had a criminal record – we had a lot to do before 4.30. We'd have to split up.

I had things I wanted to get done on my own.

So instead of driving all the way downtown I took the Olds off the beltway on Archuleta and started up into the North Valley.

By rights Puerta del Sol ought to be easy to get around in. For one thing, you can't get lost. The mountains are right over there, and it's just a question of wandering in the right direction until you hit something familiar. For another, too much of the city is new, which means it was laid out by city planners and developers. But in practice the city is more complicated.

The North Valley is complicated because the new developments and roads grew up around enclaves of old money – orchards where you least expect them, stud farms surrounded by riding trails and irrigation ditches, clusters of adobe houses and haciendas which the Spanish built any way they liked three hundred years ago. The result is a city planner's nightmare. I knew where I was going, but it still took me more than half an hour to reach the neighbourhood where Lawrence Smithsonian and Associates lived.

The place resembled a bank. Smithsonian had his own building, for God's sake, and it looked a whole lot more like a place to deposit cheques than the ice-cream parlour where Haskell worked. Naturally – at least I thought it was natural, knowing Smithsonian – the structure contrasted with the rest of the area. The neighbourhood was huge old cottonwoods, stark in the pale sunlight without their leaves, and flat-roofed houses that looked like dumps outside and mansions inside, and dogs that chased happily after everything they were sure they couldn't catch. Even the gas stations tried to fit in. But Smithsonian's building looked mostly like a cinder block with a thyroid condition.

Still, it was a fancy cinder block. And Smithsonian knew his business well enough to put his parking lot, his entrance, and even his name around back, so people felt less exposed going to see him. Even when their hearts are pure vanilla, most people don't want it known that they're talking to a private investigator.

After I parked the Olds, Ginny looked at me and asked, 'What do you suppose he's going to tell us?'

Whatever it was, I felt sure I wasn't going to like it. 'Probably not the truth.'

She considered the building morosely. 'Or he may tell us the exact truth. That's what worries me.' More vehemently than necessary, she unlatched the door and shoved it open. 'I trust him more when he lies.'

Like I say, she didn't much care for Lawrence Smithsonian.

But now she was at least thinking about our case instead of trying to come up with reasons why we couldn't handle it. That sufficed for me. I was feeling feisty enough to deal with Smithsonian as we left the car and went into his domain.

No doubt about it, he was too successful for his own good. Everything in the place that wasn't concrete was made out of glass. Inside the heavy glass doors, the heat worked, and the carpet was so thick it seemed to squish underfoot. On top of that, a by-God receptionist sat at a desk in front of a phone covered with buttons. Half the private investigators I know have trouble meeting the payments on their answering services. But Smithsonian didn't have just any receptionist. He had one who looked like the soul of discretion. In other words, she was old enough to be everyone's grandmother – and she was bored straight out of her skull.

She looked up at us discreetly as we walked in.

Ginny had the pinched white look around her crooked nose of a woman who was trying to put too much Novocain on her emotions, but she didn't hesitate. 'Is Smithsonian in?' she asked the receptionist. 'I want to talk to him.'

The woman blinked at us. Whatever she had left between her ears was calcifying fast. 'Mr Smithsonian is in conference,' she said primly. 'I can tell him you're here, but I'm afraid he won't be free for quite some time.' With an air of distaste, she added, 'You could speak with one of his associates.'

'Never mind,' I said. I'm too big to have an engaging smile, but I always try. 'We know the way.' We'd been here before. One reason Smithsonian was so successful was that even people like Ginny who hated his guts had to do business with him every once in a while. With his contacts, he knew things you couldn't learn anywhere else.

Together we headed for the hallway that led to Smithsonian's office. Behind us, the receptionist sounded vaguely apoplectic as she tried to protest. She probably had a buzzer she could push to bring the associates running, but she didn't think of it in time.

When we reached the right door, we didn't bother to knock. We just opened it and went in.

Ah, the advantages of surprise. Smithsonian wasn't in conference. He was in the chair behind his desk with his feet up on the blotter. His jacket was off, tie loose, sleeves rolled up, and his hands were propped behind his head, showing sweat stains on what should've been an immaculate shirt. His mouth was open, and he was asleep.

Obviously he needed to turn the heat down.

He woke up when I closed the door. A jerk pulled his feet off the desk, swung him upright in his chair. He gaped at us blearily, as if he didn't have one idea in the world who we were.

'Lawrence,' Ginny said, 'you look tired.' For a minute there, she was enjoying herself. 'You've been working too hard. You've got to learn to delegate. Let somebody younger do the hard jobs.'

He didn't answer right away. Slowly he got to his feet. He rolled down his sleeves and buttoned the cuffs. He straightened his tie. He put on his jacket. I had to give him credit. By the time he was done, about eight layers of film were gone from his piggy little eyes, and he looked ready.

As he buttoned his jacket over his belly, he started to smile. He wasn't really fat, he just seemed that way. Hell, he even sounded fat. In a nice plump voice, he said, 'I see you've decided to try your luck with Haskell.'

His smile was as nice and plump as a barracuda's.

222

Come to think of it, I didn't much like him either.

But Ginny just looked at him. 'How do you figure that?' she asked calmly.

Smithsonian went on smiling. 'You asked Haskell where he got your name. Even you wouldn't miss a simple thing like that. But you wouldn't need my help unless you were working for him.'

She studied him up and down. She was taller than he was, which he didn't care for, but he was too good at what he did to back off. 'You're smart, Lawrence,' she said after a moment. 'I've always said that. Haven't I, Brew?'

I gave Smithsonian a nod. 'She always says that.'

'But this time,' she went on, 'I think we can handle it by ourselves.' I was glad to hear that, even though I knew she didn't mean it. 'Thanks for offering. I was just curious. Why did you give Haskell my name?'

Smithsonian's grin got broader. He looked positively voracious. 'I didn't want the case myself. I thought it was appropriate for a female investigator with only one hand.'

I couldn't help myself – I've never been any good at holding back when anyone insults Ginny. In fact, it was a triumph of common sense that I didn't try to jump over the desk at him. Instead I slapped my hand down hard in front of him. 'Watch your mouth, fucker,' I said. 'You're going to look a hell of a lot uglier without any teeth.'

Before Smithsonian could react, Ginny said, 'Heel, Brew.' She sounded amused.

I whirled on her. I had my hands locked into fists so that I wouldn't hit her. But the way she looked stopped me. I knew that look. And it wasn't directed at me. It was aimed straight at Smithsonian.

'He has a point, Brew,' she said almost casually. 'But I don't think that's the real reason he gave us a reference.'

Well, it was worth a try. I had to admit that he wasn't likely to tell us the truth if I rearranged his face for him. Making me look ridiculous might have better luck. It might be the sort of thing he just couldn't resist.

Because I didn't have anything better to do at the moment, I crossed my arms on my chest like I was sulking and hitched my butt on to the desk with my back to Smithsonian.

'I'd have him put to sleep if I were you,' he said to Ginny. He didn't sound like he was smiling. 'If he bites you, you'll get rabies.'

All in all, I was having a wonderful time. But I went on sitting there and let her handle it.

Her mouth laughed, but her eyes didn't. Softly she said, 'Tell me the real reason, Lawrence.'

At first he didn't answer. But I guess the chance to be superior and make us both look stupid was too good to pass up. 'You figure it out.' His malice was so thick you could've spread it around with a trowel. 'If you were el Señor, and some minor punk welshed on you, would you call him up and warn him? Give him time to get out of town? Hire protection?' He snorted his contempt. 'I'm surprised you let him tell you a story like that. I know plastic flowers with more brains.'

Ginny let the insults pass. She was concentrating hard.

So was I. All of a sudden my guts twisted in fear.

Slowly she said, 'So either el Señor doesn't have anything to do with this—'

She didn't need to finish. I knew the rest.

Or else it was some kind of ritual hit. El Señor had been betrayed – his honour had been stained – and he wanted his victim to know exactly what was coming.

And a ritual hit couldn't be stopped. El Señor wouldn't care how much it cost – in time, or money, or blood. He'd bury any number of people to avenge himself.

Abruptly Smithsonian thudded me in the back. 'Get off my desk. You're wasting my time.'

I got off the desk and turned to face him. Despite the state of my stomach, I could still look fatass Smithsonian in the eye. 'So you turned Haskell down,' I said conversationally, 'because you think somebody like his wife has it in for him, and his problems are too small and messy for you. Or because you think el Señor wants him dead, and the bare idea of tangling with that kind of trouble scares you shitless. And you gave him Ginny's name because you think that no matter what happens we're going to come up manure. You're a credit to your profession, Lawrence.'

'You're wasting my time,' he repeated. At least he wasn't smiling any more. 'Leave. Or I'll have you thrown out.'

'Poor scared fatass,' Ginny said. 'Go back to sleep. We're leaving.'

I went to the door and opened it for her. We left. I even closed it politely behind me.

In the hallway, I said, 'Next time I'm going to take his heart out through his ear.'

She didn't apologize for the way she'd treated me. She just said, 'Next time I'm going to let you.'

'Are we even now?' I asked.

She didn't hesitate. 'Not by a long shot.'

Oh, well. At least we were working together. That was an improvement, anyway.

The receptionist didn't give us a glance as we walked past. She might've forgotten all about us. Apparently her job just wasn't enough to keep her mind alive.

Except for the left forearm jammed into her coat pocket, Ginny carried herself like the woman I used to know. But when we got out into the cold and the thin sunlight, she stopped. Even though she didn't look at me, I could see the fight drain out of her eyes. The way she felt about Smithsonian wasn't enough to sustain her.

'Brew,' she said, 'if he's right – if el Señor has some reason to want Haskell dead – we've got to get out. While we still can. We can't deal with this.'

Usually things like ritual hits don't seem possible while the sun is shining. They need darkness to make them real. But not this time. This time I didn't have any trouble hearing what she meant instead of what she said. She meant that she only had one hand and no self-confidence, and she was dependent on a man who might go back to drinking at any time.

I didn't try insulting her again. I tried being reasonable. 'If all that's true,' I said, 'tell me why Haskell isn't scared. For God's sake, even Smithsonian's plastic flowers would have the common sense to be scared if el Señor wanted them dead.'

'Maybe he's immune to fear.'

'Then we'd better get him locked away before he hurts himself.'

Finally she looked at me. Her grey eyes made me want to fall all over myself. 'So what's your theory?'

To keep my self-control, I took her arm and steered her towards the Olds. 'Oddly enough in this day and age,' I said, 'some people still get mad when the people they love screw around. I think someone is just threatening the irresistible Reg Haskell to make him stop whatever he's doing. And I think he knows what's going on. That's why he isn't scared. He didn't tell us the truth because he was afraid we wouldn't take him on, but what he really wants us to do is find out who's behind it. He probably hopes it'll turn out to be his wife. That way he can get himself a nice injured-party divorce. He'll be free to chase all the women he wants.'

Actually I didn't think any of that. I didn't believe it, or not believe it. I didn't have a theory. I just had a gut hunch that this case was important. I kept talking to hold my panic down – and to keep Ginny from backing out.

She knew what I was doing. After the amount of time we'd spent together, I wasn't exactly a mystery to her. But she went along with it. 'All right,' she said. 'We'll check out Reston Cole. Then we'll go see Mrs Haskell.'

That should've been fine with me, but it wasn't. I had other things on my mind. I looked at my watch. Almost noon. Trying not to sound like I expected her to yell at me, I said, 'We don't have time.'

She thought about that for a second. 'Probably not,' she agreed. 'We'll go see Mrs Haskell tomorrow.'

I took a deep breath. Very carefully I said, 'What happens if he gets knocked off tonight, and she turns out to be responsible?'

She threw a glare at me. 'You think we should split up?' She wasn't surprised, just furious. 'What a peachy idea.'

'Ginny.' I was so careful, I was practically on tiptoe. 'We're going to have to take shifts on this thing anyway. We can't both stay awake for the rest of the week. And while he's at work is our only chance to do any investigating. We might as well get started.'

She was building up a head of steam that looked strong enough to blow me away. I talked on, trying to fend her off.

'Let's go someplace where I can rent a car. Then you can go talk to Cole. You're the one with the licence.' Also the one who knew how to talk to executive banking types. 'He won't throw you out like he would me. And you'll still have time to do some of the spadework. Like talk to the cops. Find out if Haskell has any kind of background.'

Her licence gave her a legal right to certain kinds of police access, and most of the cops in Puerta del Sol didn't like me. My dead brother had been a cop.

'I'll go talk to Mrs Haskell,' I went on. 'If she gives me anything we can use, I'll follow it up. Otherwise I'll go back to the bank and see if I can spot anyone watching Haskell.'

She wanted to explode, but I made it hard for her. I was telling her exactly what she would've told me, back in the days before she got maimed. On the other hand, I would've preferred an explosion.

For a second her eyes filled with tears. Then she blinked them back. 'You know I can't drive.'

'No,' I said bluntly, 'I don't know that.' I had to be hard on her. It was either that or go step in front of a bus. 'This is an automatic transmission.' As if she didn't know. 'You've been driving it with one hand for years.'

Her mouth twisted like the beginning of a sob – or maybe the start of something obscene. Then she pulled it white and straight.

'Get out of the car.'

I stared at her.

'I said, get out of the fucking car!'

So I'm not very smart. What do you expect from a temporarily sober alcoholic? I got out of the car.

When I closed the door, she slid over into the driver's seat and cranked down the window. Rattlesnake venom would've been friendlier than the way she looked at me.

'Don't be late. If you show up at the bank drunk, I will personally feed your liver to the coyotes.'

She started the car, wrenched the shift into drive so hard that I thought it was going to come off in her hand. The only thing I could think of to say was, 'How am I supposed to find Mrs Haskell?' Even her husband didn't know where she was.

'You're the one with all the ideas about how I should run my business,' she snapped while she revved the engine. 'You figure it out.'

She took her foot off the brake, and the Olds squealed its tyres as she headed out of the parking lot.

If Smithsonian had been watching us, he would've laughed out loud. He never would've understood why I suddenly felt lightheaded and the pain in my stomach eased back a couple notches.

Ginny Fistoulari, I thought. By damn. I know that woman.

Chapter Five

Finally I kicked my head into gear and started to think about what I had to do.

For some reason, the hardest part was remembering where the nearest gas station was. But after a minute I seemed to recall seeing one a few blocks south. Hugging my coat against the cold, I began to walk.

Being abandoned by Ginny must've been good for my memory. The gas station was right where I remembered it. And my luck was good, too. The pay phone worked – and it had an intact phone book chained to the booth.

The book gave me the number of the Jiffy Cab Co. as well as the location of a convenient rent-a-relic agency. I called for a cab. Then, while I was waiting, I dialled up Ginny's answering service.

One reason she used that particular service was that they kept good records. And she had my name current with them, so when I called they treated me almost like an actual person. After fumbling around for a few seconds, they gave me the number they'd given Ginny this morning for Mrs Sara Haskell.

It was almost too easy. When I called that number, it turned out to be the Regency Hotel. Which was a little pricier than I'd been expecting. After all, Mrs Haskell was the wife of a chief accountant, not a bank president. I didn't stop to be surprised, however. I was on a roll. I asked the switchboard to connect me to Mrs Haskell's room.

She answered before the second ring. She must've been waiting by the phone, waiting for someone to tell her what was going on, waiting for something. There was a small tremble in her voice as she said, 'Yes?'

'Mrs Haskell?' I didn't like the sound of that voice. It worried me. 'Mrs Sara Haskell?'

228

'Yes?'

'My name is Axbrewder.' Plunging right in. 'I work for Fistoulari Investigations. You talked to Ginny Fistoulari earlier this morning.'

She didn't say anything. She just waited.

'Ms Fistoulari turned you down. But since then something's come up. I'd like to talk to you.'

I could almost feel the clutch of panic at the other end of the line. Then she said, 'Yes.' At least this time it wasn't a question. 'All right.'

I asked for her room number. She gave it to me. I told her I'd be there in half an hour or forty-five minutes. We hung up.

Trusting soul, I thought. Then the cynical side of me answered, Well, of course. Haskell wouldn't have married her if she weren't.

That little tremble in her voice suddenly made the whole case seem more real. Maybe irresistible Reg wasn't taking things seriously, but his wife was. I was shivering in my clothes as I waited for the Jiffy Cab Co.

They weren't exactly quick about it, but eventually they showed up. The cab took me to the rent-a-relic agency, which allowed me to drive away in a lumbering old Buick with grease-stained seats and only two hubcaps. I was just ten minutes behind schedule as I started following deer tracks and blazed trees out of the North Valley and back to the beltway.

After that I made better time. Trailing clouds of smoke in protest, the Buick cranked itself up to fifty-five or thereabouts, and we went east up the long grade towards the edge of town, where the Regency Hotel lurked in ambush for unsuspecting motorists. It looks like every highway motel you've ever seen, and you don't realize until you're already caught that it gives you twice the luxury at four times the price. But in some ways it was a logical choice for Mrs Haskell. It wasn't more than eight minutes by the mercy of the city planners from her husband's bank.

I wobbled the Buick into the parking lot around 1.00. My stomach was starting to think about food – which meant that the rest of me was starting to think about booze. Every drunk who's trying to stay sober knows the importance of food. For drunks, any kind of hunger almost magically transforms itself into the hunger for booze. But I already knew that I wouldn't have time to eat. I scanned the room numbers to orient myself, then headed around the swimming pool towards the 'private' wing at the back of the hotel.

Mrs Haskell's room was on the second floor, which was also the top floor. After the cold outside, the carpet in the halls felt as thick as quicksand and the air seemed warm enough to start fungus growing in my underwear. A drink sounded like a better idea all the time.

But I usually felt that way when Ginny wasn't with me. The trick was to keep my priorities straight. The reason Ginny wasn't with me. Mrs Haskell's voice over the phone. Get on with it, Axbrewder.

When I reached the right door, I raised my fist and knocked. I was sweating.

She answered the door the same way she'd answered the phone – right away.

She was a small blonde woman about my age, one of those attractive middle-aged women who can't seem to escape looking vaguely artificial. She had the kind of hair colour that comes from beauty salons, and the kind of tan that comes from sunlamps, and the kind of trim figure that comes from Nautilus machines. And the way she dressed only made it worse. At one in the afternoon she still wore a long chiffon nightgown with a pink satin robe over it. In one hand, she held a glass that smelled like heaven.

But the unsteadiness in her pale eyes wasn't caused by drink. 'Mr Axbrewder?' she asked. 'Has anything happened to my husband?'

For a few seconds the smell of good Scotch – J&B? – made my head swim. But I got it under control. I couldn't stand the way she looked at me. Like she'd used up all her courage just asking that one question.

'He's fine,' I said. 'May I come in?'

A moment passed while she stared at the front of my coat and blinked her eyes. Then she said, 'Excuse me. I can't see very well. I don't have my contacts in.' She stepped aside and held the door for me. 'Would you like a drink?'

I started to shake my head before I realized that she really couldn't see me that clearly. 'No, thanks,' I said as she closed the door. 'Mrs Haskell, I don't want to scare you' – not any worse than she was scared already – 'but until we get this mess cleared up it would be a good idea not to let anyone in here unless you know who they are.'

The drink in her hand wasn't the first one she'd had, and she wasn't dressed to face the day, and she hadn't even taken the trouble to put her contacts in, but she went right to the point. 'Then he really is in danger?'

I couldn't tell which answer she wanted, yes or no. 'He says he is. Until we learn anything different, we'll go on that assumption. Why would he lie?'

She sat down on the edge of the bed, still looking at me without seeing me. I took a chair from in front of the vanity. It was too small for me, but I made do with it.

The room wasn't one of the Regency's more moderate accommodations. It had flowered wallpaper that matched the bedspread and brass fixtures that matched the bedstead. The bed itself looked big enough for a game of volleyball. And the liquor cabinet was so well stocked that it made my back teeth hurt. Reg Haskell didn't pay for rooms like this on a chief accountant's salary.

His wife finished her drink, leaned one arm on the bedstead for support, and said, 'To get me out of the house.'

Sometimes it pays to be slow on the uptake. 'Is that what he told you?' I asked obtusely.

'No,' she said as if it hadn't been a stupid question. 'He told me some men want to hurt him. He told me to leave so I wouldn't be in danger – so those men wouldn't try to get at him through me.'

So far, so good. 'Did he happen to say why anyone would want to hurt him?'

She nodded. 'He said he beat those men to an investment they really wanted. They needed it to stay in business. It was too complicated to explain. But they're thugs, and until they calmed down or gave up they would want to hurt him.'

Well, well, I thought. One story for the bodyguards, another for the wife. It might not mean anything. Maybe Haskell was just ashamed to let his wife know how stupid he'd been. But it was sure as hell worth thinking about.

Not right then, however. I didn't want to lose the thread. As blandly as possible, so as not to sound threatening or judgemental, I asked, 'You don't believe him?'

She rested her chin on the arm braced on the bedstead. 'I don't know,' she said. 'I don't think I know anything about him any more.' She sighed. 'He's been making these investments for four or five years. He's good at it.' She didn't need to tell me that. All I had to do was look around. 'But nobody's ever wanted to hurt him for it.'

'Has he ever told you anything about these investments?' Carefully.

'No. I don't understand things like that.' She gave me a lonely smile. 'I don't even understand life insurance.'

I smiled back at her. 'Nobody understands life insurance.'

But she couldn't see my smile. And she obviously didn't care whether God Himself understood life insurance. I went back to my questions.

231

'The fact that he hasn't been threatened before – is that what makes you think he might not be telling the truth?'

'I don't know what I think. I used to be sure. That was why I called you. Fistoulari Investigations. He's changed so much.'

As she talked, I began to wonder just how much she'd had to drink.

'Do you think I'm attractive, Mr Axbrewder?' she asked without any warning. But I didn't have to answer. She wasn't looking at me. 'I ought to be,' she went on. 'I work at it. But he didn't change because of me. I started working at it because I saw him change and it scared me. I knew I was going to lose him.

'It had to be another woman. What else could make him so different?'

I did my level best to fade into the wallpaper. I wanted her to feel like she was just talking to herself. 'How was he different?'

'He became charming,' she said as if that explained everything.

Luckily she didn't stop. 'When we met – he was studying accounting, and I was one of the department secretaries – he was just an ordinary guy. Nice and conscientious and a little dull. I thought I was lucky to get him. Then he went to work for the bank, and he didn't set the world on fire, but it was a good job, and he was moving up slowly. If he'd had more ambition, he would've moved faster. But I didn't care about that. I liked us the way we were. It didn't seem to bother him when I gained a little weight.

'But then he had to go away for a business trip one weekend, and when he came back he was excited. More excited than I'd ever seen. He said he'd gotten involved in some kind of investment and made a lot of money. I thought that was nice. I liked seeing him excited. It made him – I don't know how to describe it. It made him sparkle. It seemed to make him handsomer. And we'd never had a lot of money.

'A few months later he took another trip and came back with even more money and he looked even more excited. He treated me like a queen, and we bought new clothes, and I could see the way other women started to look at him, and I was pleased and proud.

'But then he took another trip. And another one. And another one. And the way he glowed and laughed and teased got stronger and stronger. One day I looked at the two of us in a mirror. He looked so good it almost broke my heart – and I looked like I already had too many grandchildren.'

Abruptly she got off the bed, went to the liquor cabinet, and poured herself another glass of Scotch. I watched her with my tongue hanging out, but I didn't say anything.

'We bought a new house.' Back at the bed, she piled the pillows against the brass frame and sat there, leaning back. She probably couldn't see me at all from that distance. 'He started getting more promotions. He still treated me like a queen. I could buy anything I wanted. Do anything I wanted. He seemed to spend a lot of time courting me.

'But it wasn't any good any more. The investments were just an excuse. Why did he have to go away to do them? Why couldn't he do them at home? But he was away practically every weekend. All I had to do was look in the mirror, and I knew he was involved with another woman. He was too excited and alive for anything else. How could any other woman resist him?

'So I started to work at making myself more attractive. What else could I do? I wanted to win him back. That kept me going for a while. But I guess I'm not very smart.' Her bitterness was all for herself. None of it spilled over on to irresistible Reg. 'I finally figured out that I wouldn't know the difference even if I did win him back. There was nothing wrong with the way he treated me. It couldn't get any better. Except for the trips–

'And I couldn't ask him to give them up. I couldn't ask him if he was having an affair. If I did, he might divorce me. I couldn't stand that. Maybe I'd lost him, but at least he wasn't gone. Does that make any sense? He was still there. His eyes still sparkled when he looked at me. I didn't dare risk–

'But then he did something he'd never done before. He said some men wanted to hurt him, and he told me to get out of the house. What was I supposed to believe? I've never heard of people beating each other up over investments. I thought he wanted me out of the house so he could have that other woman visit him.

'That's why I called you. I couldn't stand it any more. I wanted to find out the truth. Without losing him. I didn't want to risk giving him a reason to divorce me.

'But Ms Fistoulari said you don't do that kind of work. And then you called and said something had come up. Suddenly I thought something had happened to him, he was telling the truth and those men hurt him and I didn't even know where he was so I could go to him. I've been distrusting him all these years for nothing.' Tears ran down her cheeks and made dark stains on the pink satin of her robe. 'I deserve to lose him. I deserve it.'

Her mouth twisted, but she didn't sob. The tears just ran and ran down her cheeks.

Right there I decided that Reg Haskell was a shit.

Unfortunately the insight didn't make my position any easier. I'd never taken seriously the idea that Sara Haskell had hired goons to lean on her husband. If that was what she had in mind, she never would've called Ginny in the first place. But I still had to do my job. And there were at least one too many coincidences running around in this case for my peace of mind.

Quietly, trying to sound natural and normal, I asked, 'Mrs Haskell, why did you call us? I mean, us personally. Why Fistoulari Investigations instead of some other agency?' I watched her closely. 'Lawrence Smithsonian and Associates, for example?'

She didn't react to the name. With an aimless shrug, she said, 'I don't know anything about detectives. I just looked in the yellow pages.' Her head lolled on the pillows behind her, but we both knew that she wasn't going to get any rest. 'Did you know,' she said, 'that Ms Fistoulari is the only woman in the yellow pages? The only woman detective. I wanted a woman. I thought she'd understand.'

But now she didn't care, that was obvious. I got to my feet. She needed help, or at least some kind of comfort, but there were too many things I couldn't say to her. I couldn't tell her that I thought her husband actually was screwing around. And I couldn't tell her that I thought he was in real danger.

But she looked so lost, I didn't have the heart for the inane reassurance I'd given Eunice Wint. Instead I just said softly, 'Thanks for your time. We'll let you know when we find out what's going on.'

In response she murmured, 'Thank you,' without seeing me and maybe without understanding what I'd said. She may not have noticed when I let myself out of the room.

She hadn't once asked me what I was doing there – what business I had asking questions about her husband. She was that lonely.

Chapter Six

On my way back to the car, I wondered if maybe Haskell hired us just to make his wife believe he wasn't cheating on her. That sounded Byzantine enough for an accountant, someone who lived by the tricks you can do with numbers. In which case, Ginny and I were completely wasting our time. But I couldn't think of any reason why Haskell needed his wife that badly. His position in the bank didn't depend on her. And she didn't have anything to do with his so-called investments.

It was too many for me. Ginny was better at sorting out things like this than I was. She was our expert on sifting the facts. I was the one who made intuitive leaps. And my intuition wasn't saying much. It had probably gone south for the winter.

So I pushed the whole mess out of my mind and got busy with other things. After I persuaded the Buick to start, I hauled it up on to the beltway and then let it slide down the long slope towards the Flat River and the Valley.

I was going to talk to Pablo Santiago's parents.

Like any normal acquaintance of the family, I hoped they would tell me that he was home safe and sound and maybe even a little bit reformed – chastened by experience, as they say. But I didn't believe it. The disappearance of a kid who ran numbers hardly a day before the numbers boss turned up dead was more coincidence than I could swallow.

The last time I'd seen Pablo, he'd been hard at work, doing what numbers runners do, travelling the streets either collecting bets or paying out winnings, depending on the day of the week. Saturday night the winners got paid. In my best Stern Uncle manner, I'd told him, *A man does not run to do the bidding of those who are themselves not men enough to do their own running.* Which was probably pretty funny, coming from me – even in Spanish. And you can't change the world by giving it stern advice. Choosing between a quick buck and the advice of an over-sized drunk, even a saint wouldn't hesitate. So kids get caught up in it. After a few quick bucks, they become loyal to el Señor and all the opportunities he offers. In Pablo's case, I felt vaguely responsible.

For that reason, I took time I should've spent doing legwork for Ginny to visit Rudolfo and Tatianna Santiago.

Their *tiendita* – the sign out front said 'Grocery' in chipped grey paint – was down in the old part of town, at least half an hour and two entirely different worlds away from the Regency Hotel. It was distinct from what Puerta del Sol calls 'Old Town', where most of the buildings aren't any older than I am, even if they are quaint as all hell, and the tourists are thick as flies on manure. Except in this case it's the manure that eats the flies. Instead the old part of town is as close as you can get to a *barrio* built out of three-hundred-year-old adobe.

A century or so ago, it was the actual centre of the city, but now it's just a warren of dirty bars and fleabag rooming houses, abandoned buildings, businesses slowly crumbling to ruin, defeated old chapels where women go in the mornings to pray that their men won't drink at night, sweat-holes where you can get into any kind of trouble your heart desires, and one cheap little park over on Tin Street.

That's just one more item on my long list of grudges against the city fathers. Everywhere you go in Puerta del Sol, the streets have names like Hidalgo and Paseo Grande and Mesa Verde – except in some of the newer developments, where the names are so cute they'll give you diabetes. But in the old part of town, streets with three hundred years of history are called Tin or Coal or Seventh. And they're crowded to the teeth with Chicanos, Mestizos, Indians, and bums of every description who grub their lives away or sell their souls for sums of money most Anglos think of as loose change.

Some days it was the only part of town I understood.

It was where I did my drinking.

The Buick made good time getting there. It liked going downhill. And I didn't have to worry about where to park it. Your average Mercedes has a street-life of half an hour in the old part of town, but the Buick looked like it belonged. I pulled up in front of the Santiagos' store and left my wheels there.

Sidewalks were few and far between here, but on this block most of the buildings had low porches that served the same function. A winter wind was blowing – not hard, but full of implied bitterness – and dust and candy wrappers and cigarette butts eddied half-heartedly past my shoes. The sky wasn't clear any more. It'd turned the dead grey-white colour of ashes. The temperature would start dropping soon.

The Santiagos' *tiendita* was one of those places that never looks clean, even when it is. The stains were too deeply ingrained, and the adobes of the floor didn't stand up well to hard use. The whole store was only a little bigger than Ginny's office, its shelves packed halfway to the ceiling. In spite of that, the merchandise was hard to see. The Santiagos kept the lights dim to save on electricity.

Both of them were there. The store needed them, and they couldn't close on a Monday. Their customers would suffer. Today probably a couple of hundred black-shawled grandmothers would come in to buy all the nickel-and-dime staples they could carry home in their old arms, to make up for Sunday's cooking. If the grocery closed on Monday, those women would have to carry twice as much on Tuesday.

Rudolfo and Tatianna were both short – at least compared to me. She was so plump that the top of the apron tied around her waist disappeared into the folds of her body. She had a round face, and her coarse black hair with its white speckles was pulled into a bun at the back of her neck. But under her fat she had the muscles of a stevedore. I'd seen how she threw cases of canned beans around the store.

By contrast, her husband was thin. You could see the bones of his forearms shift under the leathered skin when he moved his hands. His eyes were always downcast with habitual politeness. But his moustache was assertive enough to tell anyone that polite wasn't the same thing as meek. He'd used so much wax that it was in danger of catching fire every time he lit a cigarette.

They both had the kind of faces Chicanos develop in an Anglo world, sad-eyed and weary, capable of almost any amount of sorrow. Under other circumstances, they might've been glad to see me. When faces like theirs smile, it's as good as a sunrise. This time they made the effort, but they couldn't pull it off.

'Señor Axbrewder,' she said. 'After so long a time. How good to see you.'

'Señora Santiago.' My Spanish wasn't perfect, but I liked using it. 'Señor Santiago. The pleasure is mine. Are you well?'

'As well as God permits,' she replied. 'Life has many difficulties for everyone.' Her unhappiness lay in her voice like a pile of rocks, but she was too polite – and too reserved – to mention it. 'And the Señora Fistoulari? Is she well?'

I gave a shrug that wasn't anywhere near as eloquent as it should've been. 'Like yourself, as well as God permits.' The grapevine being what it was, I was sure that the Santiagos knew about Ginny's hand. 'Her injury grieves her.'

That was a bit more direct than they were used to. They stood there not looking me in the eye, politely sympathetic and just a little embarrassed. After all, I was an Anglo, even if I did have passable Spanish. They would've defended my merit with great loyalty – and high indignation if they were doubted. But everyone knows all Anglos are crazy.

To ease the situation, Santiago spoke for the first time. 'Señor Axbrewder, what we have is yours. How may we serve you?'

A good question. Now that I was here, I wasn't quite sure what I was doing. On the other hand, my feeling of responsibility didn't go away.

I should've spent ten minutes making polite conversation before I got to the point, but I didn't have either the time or the heart for it. Trying to strike the right balance between detachment and concern, I said, 'I have read in the newspaper concerning the disappearance of young Pablo.'

I was asking them if he'd come home.

Their answer was as oblique as my question. They didn't say anything.

They didn't have to.

'Señor,' I said. 'Señora.' Feeling my way. 'I have done my work for you in the past, as you know. Now I wish to do such work again. If you will permit it, I wish to seek the whereabouts of young Pablo.'

For an instant Señora Santiago's gaze flicked up to my face. Then she looked at her husband. But he didn't look at either of us.

Neither of them spoke.

Their constraint didn't seem entirely natural. My offer didn't please them, even though they had every reason to be satisfied with the work Ginny and I'd done for them.

They knew something about Pablo's disappearance that they didn't want to tell me. Or they didn't trust me.

Or they couldn't afford to hire me?

'In this matter,' I said with more bluntness than good manners, 'I do not wish payment. I have conceived a fondness for Pablo. I wish to seek him for the peace of my heart.'

She turned away and started straightening cans on a shelf beside her.

But she couldn't keep it up. With both hands, she lifted her apron to cover her face.

I didn't know what to say, so I kept my mouth shut. The silence made my stomach hurt like a bad tooth, but I forced myself to keep quiet and wait.

Santiago stared at his wife's back for a long minute. Then some combination of decency and pain made him try to explain.

'Señor Axbrewder,' he said softly, 'among our people many tales are told. Some are true, some false. Some become false in the telling. Yet no harm is intended by them. With tales our people amuse themselves, to soften the difficulties of life.'

He shifted uncomfortably. I had no idea what he was getting at.

Still watching his wife's back, he said, 'One tale concerns a large *hombre* who labours among the sufferings of others and has become devoted to strong drink.'

I almost gaped at him. So that was it. They weren't going to talk to me about Pablo because they didn't trust me. Suddenly the store seemed to become too hot, and I was sweating again.

But Santiago wasn't finished. 'I have heard another tale also.' He actually sounded like he was trying to be kind to me. 'I have heard that this same *hombre* once sought speech with that unforgiven *pendejo*' – coming from him, the obscenity sounded extravagant and bitter – 'whom the Anglos name el Señor. This the *hombre* did in his need, because of a peril to his brother's daughter and other children. But el Señor forced drink upon him and caused him to be beaten and cast him out.'

He shrugged delicately. 'I know the truth of none of these things. But the *chota capitan* has spoken to us of our son. The police seek him as they are able. You need not trouble yourself, Señor Axbrewder.'

It took me a minute to absorb what he meant. I was too mad to think straight. He was warning me. Trust didn't have anything to do with it. He was trying to tell me that a drunk el Señor didn't like had better not go around asking questions about Pablo.

But why? What did Pablo's disappearance have to do with el Señor?

All at once my instincts woke up and started jumping to conclusions in all directions. 'Señor Santiago,' I said, my voice as soft as his, 'you have spoken with el Señor.'

After a long moment he nodded.

'What has he said to you?'

Abruptly his wife whipped down her apron and swung towards me. Her eyes flared fury and grief. 'He tells us that our son will be avenged.

That Godless man speaks to us of vengeance, when the fault belongs to him and no other.'

Avenged, I thought. Oh my God. But I didn't stop. 'He is dead?' The way I said it made Santiago look at me. 'You have knowledge of this?'

'Yes, Señor,' he replied through his teeth. 'I have knowledge.'

The rational part of my mind plodded slowly along behind me, thinking, They don't know he's dead. They haven't found a body. If they found a body, the store would be closed. They'd be in mourning.

However, the rest of me had already arrived somewhere else. They knew Pablo was dead because el Señor told them. They went to him because they knew that Pablo was running numbers. They were afraid and didn't have anywhere else to turn. He told them their son was dead.

Before Santiago could recover enough of his manners and dignity to drop his eyes, I demanded, 'Did you speak to the *chotas* of this?'

Señora Santiago snapped, 'Is he a fool?' She made a gesture with her open hand that indicated her husband from head to foot. 'Would he betray his son and his life to those who care nothing by naming el Señor to them? Then both the *chotas* and that evil man would fall upon us as vultures feast upon the lost.'

I knew how she felt. Puerta del Sol's finest didn't exactly treat me with the milk of human kindness – and I wasn't even Chicano. But simple practicality, if not fairness, impelled me to say, 'Some among them are worthy of trust.'

Santiago nodded. Maybe he was just being polite to the crazy Anglo. But his wife was too angry and hurt to stop. 'This one is not. He is vile among our people.' She raged so that she wouldn't start to keen. 'It would be an ill deed to tell such a one the name of his own father. That pig.'

Well, I could think of maybe twenty detectives – and three times that many street cops – who fitted the description. 'Señora,' I asked, 'who was that man who spoke to you of your son?'

She was mad enough to answer. Her people had been dealing with Anglos for better than two hundred years, however, and her instinct for caution ran deep. Clamping her mouth shut, she looked at her husband.

Slowly he said, 'Señor Axbrewder, our Pablo is dead. He set his feet to a bad way, but he was only a child. No good or evil will restore him. If you concern yourself in this sorrow, you also may die. What purpose will be served by a naming of names?'

I didn't have an answer to that, so I made one up. 'I am Anglo. My voice is heard in places where yours is not.' Which was half true, anyway. Ginny has been known to get the DA's attention, when she wants it. 'A name may do me no harm, and yet have great power in the ears of those who merit trust.'

Santiago thought for a minute while his wife glared at the floor and knotted her hands in and out of her apron. Then his shoulders lifted in a shrug that might have been hope or despair.

'Cason,' he said. '*Capitan* Cason.'

Well, well. Captain Cason. Captain of Detectives Philip pig bastard Cason. That made sense. He was exactly the sort of man who would be assigned to investigate Roscoe Chavez' murder. The sort of man you could trust not to learn more than you wanted him to. Not where people like el Señor were concerned, anyway.

The bare idea made me sicker than I was already. I could imagine the way he'd behaved when he questioned the Santiagos.

'I know this *Capitan* Cason.' To make myself feel better, I said obscenely, 'He has the balls of a dog.'

Santiago acted like he hadn't heard me, but his wife let out one quick flashing smile.

'Yet better men stand over him,' I went on. 'If they are told what he does, they will not ignore it.'

The whole thing made me livid. 'My friends,' I said, 'I have had no drink for many months. I will do nothing that is foolish. But I swear to you that I will do all that I am able, so that those who cause the deaths of children will not continue.'

He didn't respond. He was probably afraid that he'd let me into more trouble than I could handle. But she wiped her eyes with the backs of her hands and said, '*Gracias,* Señor.'

So that I wouldn't start foaming at the mouth, I turned and walked out of the store.

I was thinking, el Señor knows Pablo is dead.

He knows Pablo was killed.

He knows why.

Chapter Seven

I didn't know why.

But I wasn't about to ask sweet old Captain Cason for an answer. I'd had a run-in with him once. Down in this neighbourhood, I'd happened on a tourist trying to rape a local woman. In an excess of zeal, as they say, I damn near put my whole fist through one of his kidneys. Cason didn't like that. In his mind, a ruptured kidney was too high a price to pay for trying to give some Mex chippy what she had coming. Since this particular 'Mex chippy' happened to be a decent and hard-working woman, he hadn't had any trouble leaning on her until she dropped the charges.

What I wanted to do with Captain Cason didn't involve asking questions.

I also wasn't going to talk to any of his superiors. Not yet – not when I didn't have anything solid to go on. And not when I couldn't imagine any man or woman stupid or reckless or even just ignorant enough to hurt one of el Señor's numbers runners. That resembled putting your entire hand in an active garbage disposal.

Like most good criminal operations, a successful numbers racket runs on trust. In other words, if you do anything to mess it up, you can trust that el Señor will cut your heart out and feed it to your loved ones with *salsa*. A kid like Pablo carrying bets or winnings is usually safer than a bank vault.

Whatever happened to Pablo, whoever did it was so out of touch with reality that it took my breath away.

No, I didn't want to talk to anyone in Cason's chain of command. The man I wanted to talk to was Sergeant Raul Encino of Missing Persons. Not because the case was on his desk, but because he was a good cop, and he might be able to tell me what was going on. He didn't really owe me any favours, but he thought he did because he cared about his work, and Ginny and I had helped him out once.

Unfortunately he was on the night shift, so I couldn't call him for a few hours yet.

That galled me. At the moment I was a hell of a lot more interested in Pablo Santiago than in threats to Reg Haskell's legs – which I wasn't sure I believed in anyway. But I didn't have much choice. Trailing cigarette butts and dust, I went back to the Buick, fired it up, and began the long drive towards Haskell's branch of the First Puerta del Sol National Bank.

I made it with fifteen minutes to spare. At 4.15, I lumbered into the ice-cream parlour parking lot and found a space near the one where Ginny sat glaring at me in the Olds.

What with winter and the cloud cover, dusk was coming early, and the air had a grey grainy quality, like amateur photography. The wind was getting sharper, and the temperature was starting to drop. The combination made my eyes water as I got out of the Buick and headed towards the Olds. By the time I got into the passenger seat where I belonged, I must've looked like I was crying.

Even that didn't work. The sight of a man my size dripping like an orphaned four-year-old has been known to make her laugh out loud, but not this time. Her face was the same colour as the air, and she didn't look at me. Her left forearm lay in her lap like a dead piece of meat, but her right kept squeezing the wheel as if she couldn't find a way to grip it hard enough.

In one of my pockets, I found a clean handkerchief. After I blew my nose, my eyes stopped watering. With as much gentleness as I could muster, I asked, 'Been here long?'

She didn't answer that. In a tone that she held deliberately flat, keeping herself under control, she said, 'Brew, I don't like fighting with you.'

I couldn't bear the way she looked. It took me through the middle like a drill bit. I folded my arms protectively over my stomach and tried not to sound too brittle as I commented, 'That's never stopped you before.'

She didn't turn her head. I had a perfect view of the way the muscles at the corner of her jaw bunched. But she remained still until she was sure of her self-command. Then she sounded soft and hard, like being tapped lightly with a truncheon.

'You're living in a dream world, Axbrewder. Face facts. We aren't equipped to handle this. It scared Smithsonian off, and he has a hell of a lot more resources than we do. If it's for real, it's too dangerous. And if it isn't, we're wasting our time.'

I absolutely couldn't bear it. 'Don't tell me.' Sonofabitch Axbrewder in full cry. 'Reston Cole refused to see you, and you let him get away with it.'

Her control scared me. It was too tight. When she broke, the explosion was going to do something terrible.

Carefully she unclosed her hand from the wheel and stared at the stress lines on her palm and fingers. 'Reston Cole,' she said, 'is on vacation. He left two days ago. His secretary says he's gone skiing in Canada. Won't be back for two weeks.

'She didn't have any reason to lie to me. She sounded too cheerful and helpful about it. And too many other people heard her.'

Oh, well. Scratch one perfectly decent source of information. It all seemed a little too convenient, but there wasn't anything I could do about it.

'What about the cops?' I asked. 'Have they got anything on irresistible Reg?'

'Not even a parking ticket.' She snorted bitterly. 'It's Monday. They didn't feel much like working. I had to sit around for an hour and a half. But they finally called back. He's cleaner than we are.'

That wasn't saying much. Most of the cons in the state pen are cleaner than I am. But I had to admit that we weren't getting anywhere.

I didn't say anything. It was my turn to talk, but I didn't volunteer. I needed Ginny to ask. To do something that would indicate some kind of decision.

Nobody ever said she was stupid. After a minute she finally looked at me. I couldn't read her face or her voice, but she gave me what I wanted.

'All right,' she said. 'I'll go along. At least for a while. What did you get from Mrs Haskell?'

I let out a private sigh of relief. Then I told her all about my conversation with Sara Haskell.

I'm good at things like that. When I was done, Ginny had the whole thing almost word for word.

While I talked, she went back to staring out the windshield. Her eyes matched the dusk. Before I finished, she began tapping her fingers on the wheel. A light touch without any rhythm – just thinking. I was so relieved that I almost kissed her.

To be honest, I was also relieved because she was thinking too hard to ask me how I'd spent the rest of the afternoon.

'I wonder what changed him,' she murmured finally. The cold outside leaked into the Olds, but she didn't seem to notice. 'How does a boring accountant turn into a lady-killer?'

'Success?' I suggested. Her mind was somewhere else, but I didn't care. 'This is America. Success is supposed to be magic.'

She shook her head. 'Risk.' For a second I thought she was answering me. Then she went on, 'There's no way to make that kind of money that fast without risk. A lot of it.'

'Not to mention breaking the law,' I muttered. I've never understood how people make money legally.

'Brew,' she said slowly, 'can you think of any kind of investment in the whole world that makes you rich over the weekend?'

That little improbability had occurred to me, but her manner made me realize that it hadn't occurred to me hard enough. For something to say, I said, 'I bet Smithsonian knows exactly what kind of investments those were.'

'Fatass,' she growled automatically. But she was thinking something else. 'Or maybe,' she said, 'he's been lying to his wife all along.'

Lying to her for five years now. 'Makes you wonder, doesn't it,' I drawled. 'What do you suppose the truth is like, if it's bad enough to make him tell his own wife lies a brick wall would have trouble believing?'

She snorted again. 'It makes me wonder about his opinion of her.'

There was an obvious point to be made about all this. So maybe Reg Haskell had been lying to his wife. So maybe he thought she had all the brains of a boiled artichoke. And maybe he was even screwing around with every woman in San Reno County. So what? None of that proved he wasn't in real danger.

If he was in danger, we had to protect him.

It was an obvious point, so I didn't make it. I didn't want Ginny thinking about el Señor and ritual hits again – and about dropping the case. Instead I pointed at the door of the ice-cream parlour. 'Let's ask him. Here he comes.'

It was 4.30 on the dot, and Haskell strode out of the bank like he didn't have an enemy or a worry within a hundred miles.

As we left the Olds, Ginny muttered, 'You ask him. I'm already too mad to be civil about it.'

Haskell waved and moved towards us, carrying his briefcase. He wore an elegant camel's hair coat, the kind that makes you think the man inside it has all the money in the world. Which reminded me for some reason that he hadn't sounded particularly rich when Ginny told him what she charged. Cash poor? I had no way of knowing. But he sure as hell wasn't cold, not in that coat. The night's chill had started to poke at me through my clothes, but he obviously didn't have that problem.

Damned if he didn't look glad to see us. Not because we were protection. Because he liked us.

But he put on his sober face when he reached us. After a discreet look around to be sure that none of the other people leaving the bank could hear him, he asked, 'Was Reston able to tell you anything?'

Something in his voice hinted at eagerness or anxiety. Or possibly humour.

Brusquely Ginny told him that Reston Cole was on vacation.

Haskell managed to look crestfallen, but I felt sure that we hadn't ruined his day. He glanced up at my face, then back to Ginny. 'So what do we do now?'

'Get your car,' she said. 'We'll follow you home.' She made no particular effort to sound congenial. 'When we get there, stay in your car. One of us will go in first. Your playmates have had all day to set up for you, if that's the way they work. Then we'll all go in and see what we can do about turning your house into a fort.'

That didn't seem to be exactly what Haskell had in mind. Maybe it wasn't enough like playing cowboys-and-Indians. But Ginny was using her nobody-argues-with-me voice, and he didn't try. With a shrug, he turned away towards a Continental the size of a yacht at the other end of the lot.

He looked too exposed for his own good. Instinctively both Ginny and I scanned the area, hoping that we wouldn't see anyone who might be classed as suspicious.

We didn't. When Haskell reached his car, unlocked it, and climbed in, Ginny let her breath out through her teeth. 'If we are honest to God going to work on this case,' she said softly, 'we'd better stop letting him walk around like that.'

I nodded. My heart beat a little funny. I was out of practice for this kind of job.

Ginny got into the Olds. I went back to the Buick.

Haskell pulled his boat out of its parking space ahead of us and sailed away like the captain of his soul, leading us further into the Heights towards the mountains.

All of a sudden I wasn't so sure that I wanted this case. The afternoon was getting dark fast. And at night everything changed. For no good reason, I believed in the danger again.

In less than a mile, the Buick's heater had me sweating. I wanted to blare my horn at the other drivers, maybe try a little demolition derby, anything to clear the road so that our private procession could reach Haskell's house before dark. I hate walking into unfamiliar houses in the dark when they might be full of goons. But thanks to Puerta del Sol's layout, half the people in the Western Hemisphere live in the Heights, and they all want to get home between 4.30 and 5.30.

Fortunately Haskell turned off the main roads after ten or twelve stoplights, and we started up into the kind of suburban development where Puerta del Sol's new money hangs out on its way to even better real estate. We didn't go all the way to the foothills, but by the time we reached Cactus Blossom Court, off Foothill Drive, we were close enough to see what we were missing.

Cactus Blossom left Foothill on the spine of a ridge and dropped almost straight back towards the city for a hundred yards before it became a cul-de-sac. From there, you could see the sunset turning the mountains pink above you. In the other direction, the whole city changed into lights and jewels.

I didn't get a very good view of the neighbourhood – just enough to see that the houses were pretty tightly crammed together, no more than six feet from each other or fifteen from the sidewalk. In this part of town, you paid for view and size, not land. Haskell's house was on the south side of the cul-de-sac at the bottom of the hill.

In fact, it was built back against a deep erosion gully called Arroyo Hombre. The arroyo used to overflow every spring when the snow on the mountains melted, until the Corps of Engineers built a flood-control project that routed all the water somewhere else. As a result, Haskell's house had an especially dramatic place to sit.

He wheeled his Continental into the driveway with considerable élan. But then he had enough sense to wait for us to catch up with him.

Ginny parked beside him. I snapped off my headlights and pulled in behind him. His lights and Ginny's shone on the doors of the double garage, but there was enough reflection to show a front yard landscaped with gravel and scrub piñon, low walls separating the properties on either side, and a recessed entryway bracketed by young cedars so well groomed that they looked like artificial Christmas trees.

Ginny ditched her lights. Haskell did the same. She and I met at the driver's window of the Continental. After the heat and frustration of driving, I felt the cold slide into my clothes like a shiv.

'Stay here,' Ginny said. Only someone who knew her as well as I did could've heard the edge of fear in her voice. Dusk hid the details of her face, but her purse hung from her right shoulder, and her hand was in her purse, gripping her .357. Neither of us could see what Haskell looked like. 'I'll be right back.'

'Don't be silly,' I replied with my usual tact. 'You got to be the hero last time. It's my turn.'

She didn't say anything. But she didn't try to stop me either.

Well, nobody ever said I was smart. I took the key from Haskell. Trying not to shiver, I went to check out the house.

When I reached the cedars, I paused to loosen my .45 in its holster, but I didn't pull it out. Instinctively I trust size and muscle more than firepower. You'd be surprised how many people are afraid to shoot at something as big as I am.

I took one more look at the last pink light gleaming from the snow on the mountains. My heart stumbled around in my chest like a drunk as I started for the door.

The door wasn't just recessed, it was downright bashful. It hid at the end of an aisle twenty feet long set into the house. Overhead hung a trellis covered with something, probably wisteria, but without leaves it let in enough light to give me some vague idea of where I was. I felt like I was walking into a shooting gallery as I went to the door as quietly as I could.

At the door, I stopped. All right, Axbrewder. Just take it easy. This is why they pay you the big bucks.

I put the key in the lock and opened the door a few inches. Then I reached my arm in through the crack, feeling along the wall for the light switches.

Luckier than I deserved. I found a panel of three or four switches. So that I wouldn't have time to panic, I flipped them all at once, pushed the door open, and started inside.

Lights came on behind me along the aisle and in the room I'd entered. The room was an off-centre atrium with a dark railed hole in the floor – actually a stairway to the lower level. A walk around the hole gave access to other rooms on this storey. No thanks to my light-footedness, I didn't make a sound. The carpet was so thick that small children could have hidden in it. The décor was new-money garish – rococo wrought-iron for the railing, gilt on the door frames, Spanish bordello light fixtures. But the stairwell in front of me looked as ominous as a cave.

No one here but us chickens. So far.

As it turned out, there was no one in the house at all. But I'd aged at least six years before I was sure. The whole place was a maze, and by the time I'd searched it all I was expecting to find the skeletons of lost explorers. One wall of the entryway aisle proved, obviously enough, to be part of the garage. However, the opposite wing was so confused with closets and bathrooms and doors in odd places that I almost didn't find the master bedroom. Fortunately the rest of the upper floor was easier. To the left of the atrium, a living room with a spectacularly tasteless wet-bar and several large windows stared out at the privacy wall. Across the stairwell, I found a study and a solarium. Opposite the living room lay a combination utility and laundry room.

The lower floor, on the other hand, was heaven for people who like to jump out at other people. Only one of the rooms was large, a den with enormous overstuffed furniture and two picture windows, one for Arroyo Hombre, the other for the lights of the city. Everything else was built into, around, or behind itself. Even the kitchen was hard to find without a compass. I kept turning left at the wrong bathroom and ending up in the room with the pool table. And I needed three tries to reach the dining room, even though it shared one wall with the den.

Eventually I was sure that the place was empty. Maybe I'd searched every room, maybe I hadn't. But I didn't believe anyone hiding in there could stand to wait that long without shooting me in the back.

Luckily I didn't get lost on my way to the front door.

Ginny and Haskell were waiting for me in the aisle. I thought that was a pretty exposed place until I saw all the light flooding the gravel yard and realized I must've turned on the lights across the front of the house when I went in. Here Ginny could at least stand between Haskell and the street and keep her eyes open.

Something about the angle of her right arm gave me the impression that she was gripping her .357 too hard. Anxiety made her skin look tight across the bones of her face.

For something to say, I muttered, 'We don't get paid enough for this kind of work.'

She took her hand out of her purse and hugged the front of her coat. 'What took you so long?' she asked unsteadily. 'We're freezing out here.'

Haskell wasn't cold. He looked pleased. 'It's a big house.'

I wanted to say, Don't be too proud of it. You'll have a lot of fun getting around here with two broken legs. But he was the client, so I kept my mouth shut.

A funny thing happened when he walked into the house. Somehow he made the furnishings look less garish. They all belonged to him, and he was at home.

While I locked the door and Ginny glanced around the atrium, trying not to let her reactions show, Haskell hung up his coat in a closet I'd missed, then walked into the study to drop off his briefcase. He came back rubbing his hands. 'Your partner has the advantage of you, Ms Fistoulari,' he said with the smile of a happy man. 'Why not let me show you around?'

'Fine,' Ginny said. 'I need to look at the locks. See how many different ways there are in here.' But she didn't do any unbending for his benefit.

Like a professional tour guide, he started right in. 'The garage is over here. Doesn't do us much good, I'm afraid.' A smile full of wry charm and self-deprecation. 'It's still full of our old furniture. We haven't gotten around to selling what we don't need.'

It's hard, I thought, to dislike a man who enjoys himself that much.

I left him to it. Back down the stairs, I went hunting for the kitchen again to see what I could do about supper. I felt like I hadn't had anything to eat for days.

At first I couldn't find anything except liquor and wine – gallons of the stuff, backup supplies for the wet-bar in the living room plus at least two other cabinets, one in the den, one in the games room. That didn't seem fair to a man with my predilections. Fortunately when I opened what I remembered as a broom closet it turned out to be the refrigerator.

Although it was big enough to be a morgue, it wasn't particularly well stocked. But I managed to locate a slab of ham and plenty of eggs and cheese. By the time Haskell had given Ginny the tour, I'd made enough omelettes to feed six people.

We ate in the dining room like formal guests. Our host tried to interest us in a bottle of wine, but Ginny said that she didn't drink while she was working, and I said I didn't drink. Then he entertained himself by telling us the exciting story of how he and Sara found and bought this house.

We didn't listen. I didn't know about Ginny, but I was straining my ears to the noises of the house. I wanted to believe that I would be able to tell the difference between the creak of contracting joists and the snap of a forced window latch.

I've said it before. At night I believe in cases like this.

Before we finished eating, Haskell ran out of one-sided conversation. Watching him obliquely, I saw the lines of his face start to sag into something that looked like creeping unhappiness. Contrast made the difference more obvious than it would've been otherwise. If he'd looked like this when I first met him, I would've assumed that his expression was normal for a chief accountant. Dull and vaguely charmless, tired of numbers. Just like the man Sara Haskell thought she'd married.

Finally he pushed his plate away, gulped the last of his wine, and asked, 'So what do we do now?'

Ginny studied him for a while. Apparently she thought that he looked more like a man should when both his legs were in danger. She'd been as stiff as sheetrock with him from the beginning, but now she eased back a bit.

'This is the boring part,' she answered. 'We sit here and wait for something to happen. We'll stay with you all night. The doors and locks look pretty sturdy. If you stay out of the den and the living room' – the only rooms with ground-level windows – 'they'll have to break in to get at you. When you go to bed, Brew and I'll take turns on guard duty. Probably in the atrium. That's the strategic centre of the house.

'If nothing happens, we'll take you in to work tomorrow.' She made an empty gesture with her hand. 'It's really that simple. The complicated part is tracking down the people who want to hurt you. We'll tackle that problem while you're at work.'

Haskell began to look a little nauseated. Maybe he hadn't thought through what he was doing when he hired us. 'You mean to tell me,' he asked slowly, 'that I have to sit here and do nothing all tonight, and all tomorrow night, and all the next night, until something happens?' His eyes were dark with unhappiness or anger. 'I'll go out of my mind.'

Despite his age, he looked for all the world like a rebellious four-year-old.

But Ginny knew how to handle that. In her punishing-parent voice, she said, 'It's up to you. All you have to do is fire us. Then we won't be in your way, and you can do anything you want.'

When she said that, I went stiff in my chair. She still wanted to get out of this case. And at the moment Haskell looked just childish or careless enough, or sufficiently convinced of his own immortality, to take her up on it.

I should've known better. Sure, she wanted out of this case. She was a responsible private investigator, however, and she took her work seriously. 'But before you make up your mind,' she said straight at Haskell, 'let me tell you something. You say you got into this mess by welshing on a bet at El Machismo.' She implied just enough disbelief to keep him on his toes. 'As it happens, El Machismo belongs to a man who runs a whole series of illegal operations in Puerta del Sol. Some people call him el Señor. Ever heard of him?'

Haskell didn't react. He just stared at her, his eyes wide.

'For people like you,' she went on like the edge of a knife, 'people who get suckered into one of those operations, he's the power in this town. The cops can throw you in gaol. El Señor can throw you in the river. And he gets that power by violence. People obey him because they know that if they don't the consequences will be worse than they can stand.

'Violence, Mr Haskell.' Her own emotions made her fierce. 'He depends on it. It holds his whole empire together. There's no chance in the world that he's going to let you off the hook, even if you are just one small sucker. At this point, he won't even let you pay him back. He can't afford to. You cheated him, and the price is blood. He'll keep after you until he gets what he wants.'

Haskell must've been crazy. While he listened, I could see that he was trying not to smile. A bit of his old gleam came back. Maybe he would get to play cowboys-and-Indians after all. Whenever anyone raised the ante, the game got better. When she was finished, he asked like a secret joke, 'Where do you want to sleep? You can use the guest bedroom.' It was hidden somewhere behind the games room. 'Or I have a cot we can set up in the atrium.'

Ginny sighed. 'We'll think of something.' She didn't know what to make of him any more than I did. And it was only 6.00. We had the whole night ahead of us yet.

'Fine.' He got up, went to the nearest liquor cabinet, and poured himself a snifter of brandy. To my hungry nerves, it smelled like VSOP. This time he didn't offer us any.

Trying to keep the initiative, Ginny asked him for copies of all his house and car keys. He got a set for each of us. Then he led us into the games room and sat down on one of the sofas like he was suddenly content to spend the rest of the evening staring at the wall.

That lasted for nearly an hour. In the mean time, my mood deteriorated by the minute. Ginny was taking the only intelligent approach to this job, but I hated it. I hated the pale tight unreachable way she sat in her chair without so much as reading a magazine, even though I knew exactly what she was doing. She was listening the same way I was listening.

Every ten minutes or so, I took a tour of the house, checked the locks on the doors and the latches on the windows, made sure the curtains were closed. Unfortunately the picture windows in the den didn't have any curtains. Every time I passed one of the liquor cabinets or the wet-bar, I felt more like murder. I wanted a drink just to prove that I deserved it.

Haskell had good timing. He waited until my tension was almost boiling. Then he looked at Ginny and me and asked out of nowhere, 'Do either of you play bridge?'

I nodded. Ginny shook her head. Surprise will do that to you.

Before I could try to unnod, he turned up the rheostat on his smile. 'You do?'

'I did. Twenty years ago, for a couple of semesters in college.' Talking to him like he was dangerously insane. 'I wasn't very good.'

'That doesn't matter. Believe me, your size alone will be good for at least one trick every board.' He was on his feet. 'Ms Fistoulari,' he said briskly, 'I belong to Jousters. It's a private bridge club here in the Heights. They have a duplicate game at seven-thirty tonight. I'd like to go. Mr Axbrewder can be my partner.'

She practically gaped at him. 'Maybe you weren't listening,' she started to say.

'I was listening.' His confidence was so strong that I could almost smell it. 'I understand the situation. But there will be a number of people at the club tonight. Jousters has good security and plenty of light.' He smiled. 'It even has valet parking. I'll be perfectly safe.

'But that's not all,' he went on, sounding like the sort of salesman who specializes in Eiffel Towers. 'I'm not suggesting this simply because I can't bear to sit still. Isn't it better to be a moving target than a stationary one? A moving target attracts attention, but it's harder to hit.'

'A moving target,' Ginny cut in roughly, 'is also harder to protect. In case you've lost count, there are only two of us on this job.'

'I understand that.' He was actively sparkling. 'But if we do this your way, and you do it well enough, it could take weeks. I can't afford that. I want to attract attention. I want to get this over with, so I can go back to leading a normal life. I don't mind taking a few chances.'

He fascinated me. I'd never met anybody brave or lunatic enough to call exposing himself to el Señor's goons 'taking a few chances'. What did he call 'leading a normal life', standing in front of freight trains to see if they could stop in time?

Naturally Ginny was less thrilled. I could see her getting ready to roast him in his socks. So I decided to share the fun. Cheerfully I said, 'That sounds like a terrible idea.'

Like a piece of steel, she said, 'It *is* a terrible idea.'

'Let's do it.'

She snapped her glare at me so hard that I almost lost an appendage. But I wasn't just being perverse. Haskell didn't make sense to me, and that made him dangerous. I wanted to find out what kind of game he was really playing.

And I felt too savage to just sit still for the rest of the night. If I did, I was going to start hurting things.

Carefully I said, 'There's one other advantage. If Haskell and I go out, whoever is out there might go after us. Or they might try to get in here.' I wanted to look at anything except the hot dismay in her eyes. Nevertheless I forced myself. This case was too important. 'If they try that, you'll be waiting for them. We'll double our chances to get what we want tonight.'

She didn't look away. I thought she might take her stump out of her pocket and wave it around to show me what was wrong with my idea. But she didn't. Bitterly she said, 'You're really enjoying this, aren't you.'

I was gripping the arm of the sofa hard. Any minute now it would come off in my hands.

'Tell you what,' Haskell said. 'We'll flip for it.' He fished a half-dollar out of his pocket. 'Heads we all stay here. Tails Axbrewder and I go play bridge.'

Ginny and I opened our mouths at him, like hooked fish. We couldn't help ourselves. He wasn't living in the real world.

He didn't wait for an answer. With a flick of his thumb, he made the coin dance and flash in the lights of the games room. It was just an ordinary coin toss, but the way he did it made it look like magic.

The half-dollar bounced on the carpet, rolled towards Ginny's feet – and came up tails.

She looked at the coin, at Haskell, at me. Softly she said, 'Oh, go to hell. Try to come back in one piece.'

I had to admire the way he'd manoeuvred us into giving him what he wanted.

Chapter Eight

'll get my coat.' Haskell left the room before I could ask him if he had any idea – any idea at all – what he was doing. As he ran up the stairs, I noticed unhappily that they didn't make a sound.

I should've gone with him. Even in his own house, I shouldn't have left him alone. But I couldn't stand to see Ginny looking like that.

'Is he out of his mind?' I asked. 'Or is he just that eager to get out of the house?'

She didn't answer – or look at me, either. I got the distinct impression that she was fighting back a desire to flay the skin off my bones.

I was too miserable and furious to think of anything better, so I said, 'You've always used that .357 with one hand. You'll be all right.'

She'd had all she could take. 'If somebody gets hurt tonight,' she said suddenly, aiming each word at me like a piece of broken glass, 'make sure it's you.'

Swearing at myself and her and everyone else I could think of, I turned my back and went after Haskell.

He was waiting in the atrium, all decked out in his camel's hair coat. He gave me a smile, but I didn't give it back. Roughly I pushed past him, went to the switch panel, and flipped them all, turning off the entryway lights outside and inside.

'I'm going first,' I muttered, 'Stay close.' Then I unlocked the front door and eased it open.

I was in no mood to be cautious, but I did it anyway. Fortunately the aisle and the streetlights on Cactus Blossom Court made it easy. All I really had to worry about was the walk from the cover of the cedars to the car.

I relocked the front door, then led Haskell to the end of the aisle.

From there, I scanned the cul-de-sac. Several cars were parked around the kerb, and the wind seemed to be getting stronger, but nothing set off any alarms in my head. I wrapped one fist around Haskell's upper arm and marched him between me and the wall of the house towards the driveway. That was my job, after all. But I didn't like it much.

When we got into the Buick, I felt safer.

'Why not take my car?' he asked.

'This clunker is harder to follow. Less recognizable.' The Buick must've liked cold and wind. It started as soon as I touched the ignition. 'And we can always hope that someone will see that showboat of yours and think you're still at home.'

I backed out of the driveway and started up the steep slope towards Foothill Drive. I didn't turn on my headlights. None of the parked cars started moving behind me. But at the intersection I had to hit the lights so that the oncoming traffic wouldn't plough into us. While my eyes adjusted, I couldn't see the road behind me. I didn't know what – if anything – was happening there as I pulled out on to Foothill and began following Haskell's directions towards his private club.

I could've stood the strain if he'd kept his mouth shut and let me concentrate. But he didn't have it in him. Halfway to the end of Foothill, he said conversationally, 'One thing bothers me, Axbrewder.' No Mr now. We were becoming buddies. 'Your partner doesn't want this job. I mean, she really doesn't want this job. I think she's afraid of it.' I heard an implied contempt in his tone. 'Why do you work for her?'

My self-control snapped. I stomped down on the brake, wrenched the Buick on to the shoulder, slapped it into park. My arm swung towards him. With my index finger, I pointed out the spot in the centre of his face where I wanted to hit him. My voice shook, but my arm and hand were steady.

'If you have any complaints, you take them to her. She's the boss. I'm perfectly capable of breaking both your legs myself.'

For a long minute, he measured me in the glow of the dashboard lights. His eyes didn't waver. I don't think he even blinked. Then, quietly, he said, 'Understood.'

Damn right. Pulling the shift back into drive, I made the Buick spit dirt like a hotrod back on to the road. Damn fucking right. If anything happened to Ginny while I was away, I'd have to do something really drastic to myself.

On the other hand, Haskell still didn't act like he was in any kind of danger. That was some consolation, anyway. I just hoped that Ginny and I weren't going out on a limb to protect a man who'd already thrown away all his marbles.

For a while I watched a pair of headlights in the rear-view mirror. But I couldn't tell if they were following us.

Jousters turned out to be on the far side of the Canyon del Oro golf course. Money being no object to the people who recreated in this part of the Heights, the course was lit all night – even in the dead of winter – and I saw several duffers beating iridescent orange balls up and down the fairways.

The club was everything Haskell said it was. It looked like a colonial mansion, and it was lit like a national monument. In Puerta del Sol, of all places. Go figure *that* out. Each blade of winter-brown grass in the lawns sweeping around it had been individually manicured. Its parking lot lay opposite the building's colonnaded portico, on the other side of the road beyond the wide arc of the driveway. It looked as safe as a bank.

Approaching the driveway, the traffic nearly stopped, blocked by cars waiting their turn for valet parking. The car behind us came right up on our bumper. Instinctively I loosened the .45 again, but nothing happened.

'By the way,' Haskell said, 'I should tell you. This is a private club. Quite a bit of money can change hands.'

It took me a minute to absorb that. 'Let me get this straight. You're planning to risk money on my bridge playing?'

He smiled.

Terrific, I muttered. That's just peachy-keen. This is going to be such fun. 'Are you out of your mind?' I asked him. 'Do you like to throw money away?'

'Don't underestimate yourself.' He chuckled. 'I anticipate a profitable evening.'

I didn't like the attitude of the car behind me. On impulse, I turned left into the parking lot instead of right up the driveway. Maybe whoever it was would do something stupid. But the car just revved angrily and roared on past. All I got out of the experience was a chance to park the Buick myself, instead of having to bother with the convenience and luxury of the valets.

Haskell had the decency not to say anything, but he looked amused.

Walking briskly in the cold, we crossed the road and hiked up the arc to the club. On the marble steps under the high span of the portico, we were greeted by a man who dressed like a butler and looked like a bouncer. He knew Haskell by name. Haskell told him who I was, and he let us through the tall white doors into the club.

Inside the place was all gilt and crystal and burgundy – and ceilings so far away you couldn't hit them with a slingshot. Another butler/bouncer type took our coats, and Haskell guided me up a long curving stairway towards the second floor. As we climbed, I murmured, 'Tell me one more time about how you can't afford to pay us very long. Membership in this place must cost half the national debt.'

He chuckled again. 'That's true. But I didn't pay for it myself. I came here once as a guest. My partner thought I wasn't very good, so he told me not to worry about winning. I bet him we would come in first. If we did, he had to buy me a membership.'

I wanted to ask him how a man who did well risking money on bridge managed to lose his head and welsh at El Machismo, but I didn't get the chance. At the top of the stairs, we went through another set of high white doors and entered the playing area.

It was a huge round room with the kind of décor you'd expect to see in a high-priced cathouse in San Francisco a hundred years ago. At least two dozen mahogany card tables were set in a wide circle around the director's table in the centre, all of them square to the points of the compass. Most of them were already occupied. A large screen to display the scores hung on one wall.

Haskell got a table assignment from the director, and I found myself sitting South opposite his North. It was a duplicate game, which meant that the same hands were played over and over again around the room. The cards were dealt into holders called boards, and for each round the boards moved counter-clockwise while the East-West teams moved clockwise. The final scoring was comparative, North-South against North-South, East-West against East-West.

After twenty years, that was just about all I remembered about bridge. The only thing I had going for me was that I made the table and most of the players look small.

Our first opponents were a white-haired man with a Colonel Coot moustache and a woman dressed like a front for a diamond-smuggling operation. They both knew Haskell. 'New partner?' the man asked him casually. 'Any good?'

Haskell was in his element. I swear to God, he looked even handsomer than he did at the bank. Shuffling the first hand of the night, he winked at me and replied, 'Let's find out.'

'Stakes?'

Haskell smiled. 'I feel lucky. How about a hundred dollars a point?'

The woman snatched up her cards like a swooping vulture. 'Luck won't do you the least bit of good,' she said severely.

For a minute I couldn't look at my cards. I was fighting too hard to hold off a coughing fit.

By the time I had my hand sorted, the bidding was over – I just passed whenever it was my turn to say anything – and Colonel Coot on my right was playing a spade slam. Disaster filled my throat, and I could hardy swallow. A hundred dollars a point! For one thing, I had to make the opening lead. For another, I only had twelve cards. I was supposed to have thirteen.

Somewhere in my hand, I located a solitary diamond and a lone king of spades, so I led the diamond. Colonel Coot won in dummy and led another diamond. I didn't know what else to do, so I ruffed with my king of spades. Then I led something else.

By the time Colonel Coot got around to drawing trump, I found my thirteenth card. The jack of spades was hiding behind the clubs. Having seen my king and drawn the obvious conclusion, Colonel Coot took a deep finesse against Haskell, and my jack won. The slam failed.

Colonel Coot muttered imprecations through his moustache. 'If you'd ruffed with your jack, I could have dropped your king.' The diamond smuggler glared at the ceiling.

Haskell didn't say anything. He didn't even smile. He just glowed like an incandescent shark.

A few hands and a couple of opponents later, I trumped one of my partner's aces and ended up blocking the declarer away from four good tricks in dummy. And a few hands later, I pulled the wrong card from my hand and accidentally end-played the woman on my right. The rest of the time, I didn't have the faintest idea what was happening. My bidding didn't bear any resemblance to the cards in my hand, and I was playing off the wall. Under my jacket, sweat soaked my shirt. We were halfway through the game before I figured out what was going on.

Haskell was using my ignorance. Counting on my mistakes. He played like he knew exactly what I would do wrong. Which gave him a tremendous advantage over our opponents. None of them knew what the hell I was doing.

Three times during the game, he offered the opposition the same bet he had with Colonel Coot and the diamond smuggler. It would've been more honest if he'd brought in a professional and not told anybody. I didn't know whether to congratulate him or call the cops.

By 11.00 the game was over. I felt like I'd spent the night in a gravel factory. When I stood up, my legs cramped, and I almost lost my balance. If someone offered me just one more hand of bridge, I was going to run screaming into the night.

But Haskell won all his bets. We didn't win the game. We were second North-South, however, and second overall. Which meant that we beat all the East-West teams.

I was dying to get out of there and hide my head under a pillow. But Haskell stood around the room for a while and graciously let people pay him his winnings.

Colonel Coot was bitter about it. He gave me a glare and muttered, 'Be watching for you next time,' then marched away to vent his spleen on some hapless subaltern.

I read the scores off the screen, did a little rough math in my head, and realized that Haskell had taken in over four thousand dollars.

He didn't smile the whole time. He didn't have to. His entire body did it for him.

On the way down the stairs, I made my brains stop rattling long enough to ask him, quietly, 'How did you do that?'

If I hadn't towered over him, he would've looked like a conquering hero. At my question, he cocked an eyebrow and thought for a few steps. Then he said, 'It's difficult to explain. I don't really play cards. I play people. You gave me a lot to work with.'

What a nice compliment, I growled to myself. I'm so proud I could just shit. But he was still the client, so I kept a civil tongue in my head.

Together we collected our coats from the butler/bouncer and went out through the portico.

Outside all the wind was gone. Behind the noises of the cars as valets brought them up the driveway and bridge players drove them away, the night was still. Poised and quiet, like your first kiss. On the other hand, it was cold as a meat-locker. I had to hug my coat to keep my bones from falling out on the ground.

People stood in knots around the columns as if they were trying to share warmth. Over on the golf course, a few hardy souls still played. What few stars shone through the lights of the city looked like chips of ice.

I gave the Buick's keys to the next valet, a kid with hopeful eyes and an unsuccessful moustache, and told him what it looked like. He sprinted away towards the parking lot, working for a good tip.

'Don't take it personally,' Haskell said. He'd already proved that he was more observant than I gave him credit for. 'I play that way because it works. It's the only way to win.'

I didn't really listen. For some reason I kept watching that kid. The way his coat flapped behind him as he ran made him look like a valiant child, too full of energy to be cold – and trying too hard to please. He reached the lot and dodged between the cars towards the back row.

'Tell the truth, now,' Haskell went on. Deep in his heart, he probably wanted me to admit how brilliant he was. 'You enjoyed yourself. Didn't you?'

'Give me a choice next time,' I said absently. Still watching the kid. 'I'd rather have my kneecaps dislocated.'

The kid reached the Buick – I could see it between two other cars. He unlocked the door and jumped into the driver's seat. Before he closed the door, he reached for the ignition.

I wasn't ready for it. In all my grubby and sometimes violent life, I've never been ready for such things. With a special crumpling noise that you never forget once you've heard it, the rear of the Buick turned into a fireball.

I should've stayed with Haskell. That was my job. I was supposed to protect him. But I didn't.

Pounding hard, I started for the parking lot.

Long legs help. And I'm fast for my size. In what felt like no more than half an hour, maximum, I reached the fire.

A couple of valets were there ahead of me. Yelling, they pointed me at their friend.

The whole Buick was burning now, but the blast had blown him clear. He lay beside the next car. Fire ate at his clothes. He wasn't moving.

The heat scorched my face, but I didn't think about it. He was only three steps away, three steps with flame whipping in all directions. The important thing was not to breathe. I ripped off my coat and ran to him. With the coat, I tried to smother his clothes. Then I picked him up and carried him out of the heat. Even though I knew it was too late.

His friends took him from me. Someone said the manager had called the fire department, the cops, everyone. With a piece of fire still burning inside me, I walked back to the club.

Haskell met me on the steps. 'I called a cab,' he said. 'It should be here in a few minutes.'

He couldn't help himself. He was grinning like a little boy after a successful raid on the cookie jar.

Chapter Nine

In an ideal world, I would've taken his head off for him, just on general principles. But he was still the client. And a second murder in less than three minutes was bound to attract a little attention, even though most of the people waiting in front of the club had gone to get a closer look at the fire. The few lazy, timid, or reasonable individuals who hadn't moved were staring in that direction. Somehow I kept all that in mind. Instead of hitting him, I knotted my fists in his fine camel's hair coat and practically carried him around behind one of the columns.

We weren't exactly invisible, but the pillar and the fire hid us pretty well. Holding him up on the tips of his toes with his back against the column, I snarled, 'You called a cab? That was quick thinking. We can just go home like none of this ever happened. What the hell are you trying to get away with?'

He wasn't smiling any more. He may even have been a little afraid of me. But he didn't flinch or look away. He watched me like an expert, measuring me. Through the bunched collar of his coat, he breathed, 'I don't want to talk to the police.'

'What makes you think you can get out of it?' The Buick was starting to burn down, but I wasn't. 'That car's rented in my name. I'm not exactly hard to recognize, and you're known here. As soon as the cops trace the car, they'll start asking questions. They'll be sitting in your office by noon tomorrow at the latest.'

Haskell shrugged inside his coat. 'Maybe – ' The cold turned his breath to puffs of steam. 'Maybe by then I can persuade you to cover for me.'

'Cover for you?' I was so mad I lifted him all the way off the ground. '*Cover* for you?'

'You can tell them this el Señor has a grudge against you. We can make up a reason why we're together. Maybe I hired you to work on a security problem at the bank. Or maybe' – he flicked up a smile, dropped it again – 'you just like to play bridge. I don't want them investigating me.'

'Fat chance,' I snarled. 'You're breaking the law. If I cover for you, I'll go to gaol. Ginny will go out of business.' I was too mad to think, but I didn't need astrophysics to figure out some of what was going on. 'That car wasn't blown up by someone who wants to break your legs. It was blown up by someone who wants you dead. I won't tell any lies for you. You've been lying to us from the beginning.'

'Of course I've been lying to you,' he wheezed. I'd made it a little hard for him to breathe. 'Don't you understand? I had to.'

I glared at him for a minute. In the lights of the club, he'd started to look slightly purple. Slowly I eased him down on to his feet. But I didn't stop leaning on him against the pillar. 'All right, Mr Haskell.' Axbrewder dripping sarcasm. 'Just for kicks, why don't you try explaining it to me?'

He took a couple of deep breaths and straightened his coat. 'Do you have any idea how many investigators I called before I called you?' He tried to sound indignant instead of defensive, but his eyes gave him away. They weren't either one. They were still measuring me. 'I tried telling them the truth. They refused to help me. When you and Ms Fistoulari walked into my office, I knew you were going to walk right out again if I told you what was really going on. So I made something up.'

'Damn straight,' I growled. 'That whole phony story about El Machismo. Including Reston Cole.' Ginny was going to be charmed.

He didn't say anything.

'Take your time,' I went on. 'I'm in no hurry. Maybe you'd like to bet on whether your cab will get here before the cops. If the cops get here first, they'll talk to the valets. They'll find out about the big crazy guy who pulled the kid out of the fire. May take them all of two minutes to come up here looking for us.'

I had to admire his nerves. I still couldn't fluster him. 'Axbrewder,' he said evenly, 'I told you I play people. It's the only way to win. And I'm good at it. I saw that you and your partner wouldn't touch the truth. I had to bet that you aren't quitters. That you don't drop things once you get involved in them. I had to hope that you would help me. Then I could tell you the truth.'

I hated that. It was too much like the way he played bridge. But we could both hear sirens in the distance. And because of the way I held him, I could see something he couldn't – a Jiffy Cab pulling up in front of the portico. I had him where I wanted him, and I wasn't about to let him go.

'You like to take chances,' I commented sourly. 'Don't stop now. Tell me the truth. See what happens.'

For a few seconds longer, he studied me and didn't say anything. Then he sighed. 'This is complicated. How much do you know about laundering money?'

Laundering money. By damn. I gave him a grin full of teeth and malice. 'Not a thing.'

I could tell that he didn't believe me. But he bowed to the inevitable, as they say.

'Suppose you have ten thousand dollars,' he began, 'but it's in marked bills. Or it's counterfeit. Or it came from a source you want to keep secret, like a bribe. What do you do? You can't spend it. You can't deposit it in your account and write cheques. You can't afford to admit that you ever saw or touched that money. So you need to launder it. In essence, you need to exchange your money for other money that can't be traced.

'There are usually two steps. First you dispose of the physical evidence, the physical money. You deposit it somewhere, change it into numbers on a ledger or in a computer. That helps, but it doesn't disguise your connection to the money. The second thing you do is confuse the numbers. Typically you put the money into a dummy account of some kind, and then transfer the numbers back to yourself through as many different stages as you can arrange – stock certificates, bearer bonds, selling your own products or belongings to yourself, whatever.

'There are many different variations, none foolproof. Often the safest thing is to work through foreign banks. But even foreign banks keep records. And they let investigators look at their records occasionally. With enough ingenuity and sweat, any laundry can be traced.'

I didn't want him to stop – he still hadn't gotten to the good part – but I was running out of time. An ambulance and two prowl cars had pulled into the Jousters parking lot. I could see a fire truck coming up the road. And the cab driver was getting restless. Any minute now, he would start calling for Haskell. Or he might get out of his cab and come up the steps to talk to one of the bouncers. Soon I would have to do some gambling of my own.

But not yet. Haskell's explanation wasn't done.

'What commonly protects most money laundries is the sheer complexity of the records involved. In retrospect, knowing what a given laundry does, the trail looks clear, even if it would be difficult to prove in court. But when you don't know that the connection exists, and can only imagine the ramifications, you could use a dozen accountants and spend thousands of hours of computer time without finding it.'

Past the edge of the column, I saw the cab driver get out of his hack. I was starting to feel the cold. Swearing to myself, I tightened my grip on Haskell. 'That's marvellous,' I growled. 'I could listen to you sing and dance all night. Get to the point.'

With perfect timing, the driver yelled, 'Haskell? Mr Haskell?'

Haskell jerked his head to the side, tried to respond. I kept him quiet by thumping him against the stone. 'The cops will be here in just about a minute,' I whispered down at him. Which was true. Two uniforms had already started across the parking lot in our direction. 'Get to the point.'

I would've given my back teeth to make him lose his self-possession. But it didn't happen. He sounded almost avuncular, as if I were a half-witted kid he couldn't help being fond of anyway, as he said, 'I know how el Señor launders some of his money.'

Well, I expected something like that. I may be a moth-eaten old drunk with no licence and less good sense, but I can smell something rotten when you stuff my head in a sack of dead fish. Nevertheless it rocked me back on my heels. Now I had the whole picture, I knew why Smithsonian had given us a recommendation and then laughed about it. No wonder no other investigator wanted this case. Haskell couldn't be protected. Not without going right to the source and putting el Señor himself out of business.

As Ginny kept telling me, she and I weren't equipped for the job.

And yet I only needed about two seconds to reach a decision.

I had an alternative. I could turn Haskell over to the cops.

I shifted my grip from his coat to his arm. 'Come on,' I muttered. 'We don't want to keep your cab waiting.'

Haskell actually laughed. Excitement danced in his eyes again. But he was pretty smart – for a lunatic, anyway. He didn't say, I knew you wouldn't let me down. If he had, I probably would've broken his arm.

Two cops came towards the club. They weren't more than twenty yards away. By rights they should've stopped us. They don't like it when people leave the scene of a crime. But they were human – and back in the parking lot the fire truck started to hose down what was left of the Buick. They turned to watch.

Haskell told the driver who he was, and we got into the back of the cab. He mentioned an address I didn't quite catch – I only heard it well enough to know that it wasn't Cactus Blossom Court. But I let that pass for the time being. Instead of asking questions, I held my breath until we were out of the cops' range.

After that I went back to work. I wasn't getting noticeably more patient with age. And every time I closed my eyes, I saw the Buick go up in flames again. I saw that poor kid lying beside the next car, his clothes on fire and him not moving at all. The cab driver could probably hear everything we said, but at the moment I didn't care.

'Dozens of accountants and thousands of hours of computer time' – not making any effort to sound calm – 'and you just happen to know how el Señor launders his money. What do you do in your spare time, walk on water?'

Now that he thought he was safe, Haskell seemed to twinkle like an elf. 'It was an accident. Somebody told me about El Machismo. It was Reston Cole, actually. He didn't say he'd ever been there. But we were having a drink, and he happened to mention that he'd heard there was an illegal gambling club in town. A few days later, I stumbled across the name again. El Machismo uses the Old Town branch of my bank.'

He mused for a minute, then said slowly, 'Axbrewder, being an accountant can be painfully boring. Every once in a while, I get so desperate for some excitement that I play little games with it.' He paused briefly. 'I don't want to go back to being as dead as I was a few years ago.' The way he said it made it sound genuine. 'When I saw that El Machismo had an account with my bank, I decided to play investigator.

'That's how I learned about laundering money.' He grinned. 'On-the-job training. My research took several months. But when I saw where the profits from that account went, I knew I'd found something.

'I learned that El Machismo is a wholly owned subsidiary of a corporation that doesn't exist. The profits go to an investment portfolio managed by our trust department. Those returns are distributed to the four people who hold all the stock in the nonexistent corporation. They also don't exist. Nevertheless two of them invest heavily in a mortgage exchange. One employs a large brokerage firm here. One backs a small, private lending company. And all four of *those* investments feed back into another portfolio managed by our trust department.'

266

He glanced at me. Then he said, 'The owner of that account does exist. It's el Señor.'

I couldn't see him very well in the back seat of the cab, but he looked almighty proud of himself.

The hack had wandered into a part of the Heights I wasn't familiar with. We definitely weren't on our way back to Haskell's house. The reasonable part of my mind wondered what new game he was playing. However, the reasonable part of my mind was pretty far away at the moment. The rest of me seethed.

Old cauldron-of-emotions Axbrewder. Being sober didn't make me calm, just bitter. I would've given a couple of fingers and any number of toes for the ability to muster the kind of information Haskell was talking about. Even Ginny would've gone way out on a limb for it. For the chance to drive at least one nail into el Señor's coffin.

But while the stars still burned and the planet still rolled, we would never, *ever* have told him what we were doing.

'Clever you,' I rasped at Haskell. 'For a smart man, you've got more stupid in you than any other three people I know.' Only the cab driver's presence restrained me from yelling at him. 'What's the matter with you? You've got some kind of death wish?'

At least he had the decency to look insulted. 'What are you talking about?'

'You found out how he launders his money,' I snapped. '*Then* what did you do? Go to the cops? The DA? The FBI? Not *you*. Not Reg Haskell, boy investigator.' I could see the whole thing. 'What blind insanity made you think trying to blackmail el Señor was a good idea?'

I was so sure I was right that I would've been surprised if he'd tried to deny it. But he didn't. He only frowned at me because he didn't like my attitude.

'Two reasons.' His voice held a hint of iron, something he usually kept hidden. 'First, I can't prove any of it. I can't prove there's anything illegal about El Machismo's money. And I certainly can't prove that those four people really don't exist.

'Second—' He shrugged. In the faint glow of the dash lights, his face looked hard and maybe even a little bit fanatical. 'I needed the money.'

'He needed the money,' I explained to the window beside me. 'I love it.' We were riding into an area of apartment complexes and condos, some of which looked inexpensive. Apparently not everyone needed money badly enough to be as well off as Haskell. 'It's going to look great on my tombstone.'

Abruptly Haskell told the driver to stop. We pulled over to the kerb in front of a place called the Territorial Apartments. Haskell got out and nearly slammed the door on me.

I told the driver to wait and went after my client.

The cold seemed to soak into my clothes like water. Without a coat, my jacket wasn't much protection. 'So what're we doing here?'

He stood in the exterior lights of an ersatz chalet-style structure, probably affordable, and glared up at me. If nothing else, he was letting me see the side of him that his wife feared. 'What do you care?' he snapped. 'A friend of mine lives here. I'll be safe for the night.'

I made a real effort to keep myself from boiling over. 'Listen to me, Haskell. It's just luck you and I aren't dead already. El Señor won't let any of us get away with this. He can't afford to. He'll send an army after you if he has to. He'll blow up your house, murder your wife, dance on your grave. Your only chance is to go to the police.' They wouldn't exactly be amused when they heard his story – but they'd want his information. 'They might be able to protect you.'

He didn't flinch or hesitate. He didn't even blink. 'It's my life,' he said. 'I'll take my chances. Just tell me whether you're in or out. Fish or cut bait, Axbrewder.'

I stared at him. For a minute there, I almost told him to blow the whole thing out his ass. Would've given me no end of satisfaction. But the plain fact was that as opportunities went he was too good to miss. Ginny might hate me for it, but I did it anyway.

'Since you ask so nicely,' I retorted, 'I'll fish. Ginny and I don't drop clients when things get tough.' Then I stepped closer to him and pointed a finger at the front of his coat, just to remind him that I could throw him across the street if I wanted to. 'But we don't like being lied to. If you aren't telling the truth this time, I'll take you apart piece by piece until I find it.'

'Fine.' Unflappable as all hell. You'd think he ate being threatened with bodily harm for breakfast. 'I have to be at work by 8.30. Pick me up here at 8.15.'

Just like that, he turned and walked away. The Territorial Apartments didn't have a security gate. He strode through the entryway out of sight like he'd been here a lot and knew exactly what he was doing.

For a while, I stood where I was, puffing vapour in the cold and thinking, He needed the money. The same man who just made four thousand dollars playing bridge.

Chapter Ten

Maybe I was losing my mind. Maybe the car that got blown up wasn't really my rented Buick. The night was too cold to hold all that fire. Maybe Haskell actually did know what he was doing. Maybe I hadn't just agreed to go on protecting a man who seemed determined to get himself killed.

And maybe Ginny would have a fit when she heard about it.

But I couldn't just stand there and let my blood freeze. I still had to function. I still had to do what I could. Feeling dissociated and crazy, I went back to the cab, got in, and told the driver to find a phone booth.

'There's one back the way we came,' he said. 'About half a mile.'

I said, 'Fine,' but I couldn't put the same decision and certainty into it that Haskell did.

At the phone booth I left the hack again, fumbled out some coins, and called Sergeant Raul Encino of Missing Persons.

Crazy people do things like that.

And God watches over crazy people. After only three or four rings, I got an answer.

'Missing Persons. Sergeant Encino.'

He sounded bored – and no one sounds as bored or indifferent or just plain world-weary as a Chicano duty officer in the middle of the night. He perked up when I identified myself, however. Deep in his heart, he was an old-world Spanish gentleman. He even resembled one, despite his uniform. Every hair and shirttail was so well behaved that it looked like he held it at gun-point. In other words, he was just a bit arrogant, with exaggerated ideas of honour and dignity. Which was why he thought he owed me a favour.

'Señor Axbrewder,' he said. 'How good of you to call.' I couldn't

269

miss his sarcasm – he was speaking Spanish for my benefit. 'I am at your service. How many lost children do you wish to discover tonight?'

I winced at that. Last time, it was seven. Nine if you counted the two who survived. 'Nice try,' I replied. In English, for his benefit. 'But this time you can't cheer me up with charm. I'm in over my head, and I need a few straight facts.'

'*Bueno*,' he said without hesitation. 'Speak.'

There was some static on the line. It sounded like fire. That poor kid hadn't even had a chance to scream. But I tried to push burning Buicks out of my mind. He couldn't have been more than a year or two older than Pablo.

'In the paper this morning,' I plunged in, 'I read about a missing kid. Pablo Santiago. I know his family. Ginny and I did some work for them a couple of years ago. So I went to see them.

'They don't think he's missing. They think he's dead.' I took a deep breath. Encino was going to love this. 'They think he's been killed.'

There was a long silence at the other end of the line. Then he said softly, 'What do you wish to know?'

From a technical point of view, he had no business knowing the answers I wanted. Hell, he wasn't even supposed to talk to me. I didn't have a licence. But I was counting on the department grapevine.

'I want to know if he's been found. If he's still alive.' My grip on myself slipped. I fought my voice back under control. 'If he's dead, I want to know how he died.'

Encino thought about that for a minute. Then he said, 'Señor, I must put you on hold.'

I heard the click as he disengaged the receiver. The fire on the line got louder.

What fun, I muttered to myself. Joy and party hats. Back in the cab, the driver kept warm by running the engine. He looked like he was taking a nap. The skin of my face felt as stiff as sandpaper, and all my joints ached. I needed to beat someone up, just to keep my blood moving. But you can never find muggers or rapists when you need them.

I tried to imagine what Encino was doing, but all I got was phone static like roasting children.

He was gone for a long time. Nevertheless I went on waiting, and eventually he came back. 'Axbrewder?' he said. 'This is a different phone.' In English. 'I can talk here.'

'And not a minute too soon.' To explain the shiver in my voice, I said, 'I'm freezing to death.' Then I asked, 'What've you got?'

The background crackle made him sound distant and unconcerned. 'For an Anglo, you aren't a bad man. Are you certain you want to involve yourself in this?'

'Ask me that some other time.' I didn't want to come unglued right there in the phone booth. 'I'm never sure. 'What've you got?'

'All right.' He really did think he owed me something. 'A boy tentatively identified as Pablo Santiago was found early Sunday morning, just a few hours after his family reported him missing.'

I couldn't help myself. I cut in, 'What do you mean, "tentatively"? Didn't you call in the family?'

He didn't answer that. 'He was found in the South Valley, on Trujillo, lying in the road. He had a broken neck. His body was extensively bruised and scraped. The medical examiner considers it an accident. "Death consistent with a fall from a moving vehicle." The boy is presumed to have been joyriding under the influence of alcohol or drugs. I will be unable to look at the autopsy report until I go off duty.'

Through my teeth, I said, 'So it was an accident. So why didn't you call in the family?' In the name of simple decency, for God's sake.

Encino chewed his end of the line for a while. I heard him tapping his fingers on the receiver. Then he said carefully, 'The detective in charge is Captain Cason.'

I already knew that. It explained everything – and nothing. Holding on to myself as hard as I could, I said, 'I know Cason. You know I know Cason. He's a bad cop. What's he got to do with Pablo Santiago?'

Encino's shrug was almost audible. 'The preliminary report is clear. The ME considers this an accident. But Cason is also investigating the death of Roscoe Chavez. He learned that Pablo ran numbers for Chavez. Perhaps the two are connected? He told the newspapers that Pablo remains missing. And he refuses to contact the family. He wishes to conceal his knowledge. He believes this secret will assist his investigation.'

That bastard. I wanted to howl, but Encino didn't deserve to be howled at. None of this was his business.

Softly I said, 'I can identify Pablo for you.'

He laughed – a short humourless bark. 'Imagine Captain Cason's delight. He will ask how you heard that Pablo had been found. You will reply that I informed you. I will be suspended. I am Chicano.' And very conscious of prejudice in the department. 'Perhaps I will be fired.'

'All right,' I said. 'It was a bad idea. When can you tell me what's in the autopsy report?'

A sigh. 'I may perhaps steal a look when I go off duty. Call me at home during the day.' Sounding especially world-weary, he gave me his home phone number.

'Thanks,' I said. Inadequate gratitude. 'Remind me that I owe you five or six favours for this.'

He didn't have to point out that I'd be doing him a favour by causing trouble for Cason. I already knew that, too. He just hung up.

I did the same and walked like an old man back to the warmth of the cab.

The driver asked me where I wanted to go. I almost told him to take me to the Santiagos' home in the old part of town. Fortunately I got my common sense back in time. Instead of doing anything rash, I gave him Haskell's address.

The ride was bearable. The heat in the cab helped my mind go blank – which was a big improvement. But when we turned down into the cul-de-sac of Cactus Blossom and I saw Haskell's house, my stomach started hurting again.

Ginny had been there alone for better than five hours now. I didn't expect that she'd had any trouble. Most people don't try to kill you a second time until they find out that the first time failed. But I was afraid she might have talked herself into a really poisonous frame of mind.

And I had to tell her what I'd learned.

One way or another, the cab driver would tell the cops where he took me. That was inevitable. But they wouldn't have any trouble tracking either me or Haskell down anyway. And there are only so many things you can worry about at any one time. I just gave him what I owed him, got out of the hack, and walked between the cedars into the black aisle towards the house.

Not knowing how else to get in without scaring Ginny and maybe getting shot, I knocked on the front door and rang the doorbell.

She took a long time answering. Long enough for me to think that maybe she was trying to tell me something. Then I heard her faintly around the edges of the frame.

'Who is it?'

The muffling made her sound far away and frightened.

I tried to pitch my voice to reach her without disturbing the neighbours. 'It's Brew. I'm alone.'

I felt the door shift slightly, like she was leaning on it. Then the locks clicked, and the door swung into the darkness of the house.

I closed it behind me, relocked it.

When I snapped on the atrium lights, I found her standing near the switch panel, her back against the wall, her right hand aimed in the direction of my belly.

But she wasn't holding her .357. She was holding a glass. The stuff in the glass looked amber and beautiful. It smelled like fine Irish whiskey.

Waiting for me all evening alone in Haskell's house had done something to her.

Her clothes were a little rumpled. Her grey eyes looked vaguely out of focus. For some reason, the lines of her face seemed slightly smeared, like a photograph with a thumbprint on the negative.

'Where is he?'

'Ginny' – my wit never fails me – 'you're drunk.'

She tried to glare at me, but couldn't quite pull it off. 'So what? Where is he?'

'What's the matter with you?' My stomach hurt so bad that I could hardly stand up straight. 'You trying to get yourself killed? What would you have done if they tried to break in here?'

She actually giggled. 'Offered them a drink.' I hated her giggle. 'They don't know we're working for him yet. Why would they kill me?' But her amusement didn't last. Like she didn't realize she was repeating herself, she asked, 'Where is he?'

For a second there I wanted to smack her. Then I thought better of it. Wrapping my fingers around her arm, I said, 'I think you need to lie down.'

That took a while to reach her through the fog. Then she wrenched her arm away. The effort nearly made her lose her balance. 'God damn you entirely to hell, Mick Axbrewder,' she pronounced, articulating each word as precisely as a piece of glass. 'I asked you a question.'

When I didn't answer, she looked for something even angrier to say. But nothing particularly scathing occurred to her. After a moment her whole body seemed to sag.

'I'm not in good shape, Brew,' she said dully. 'I wasn't in good shape before tonight, and I won't be in good shape tomorrow. I can't think straight. Nothing makes sense any more. Please don't mother me.'

It was enough to make a grown man weep. The problem was, she'd always been the strong one. The one who carried me over the rough spots. And the smell of whiskey burned in all my nerves. I didn't think I could stand it.

But people sometimes do remarkable things because they don't have any choice. Softly I said, 'He's staying with a friend. He thinks he'll be safe there.' Then, because she obviously needed more than that from me, I added, 'Let's go into the den. You can at least sit down. I'll tell you all about it.'

She didn't move. The blur in her eyes made me think that she hadn't heard me.

'Ginny, this whole mess is a lot worse than he told us.'

At that she nodded. Carrying herself as carefully as her glass, she turned and started down the stairs towards the den.

I wanted to catch up with her, keep her from falling. Deliberately I forced myself to stay a couple of steps back.

In the den, she sat on one end of the long overstuffed couch facing the picture window and the arroyo, leaning against the arm of the couch for support. I didn't turn on any lights. I didn't want anyone outside to see us. From the far end of the couch, I could only make out her silhouette in the faint glow from the atrium.

'So,' she said, a million miles away, 'how was the bridge game?'

'I had a wonderful time.' I had too much to tell her, and no idea where to start. 'He says he doesn't play games. He plays people. And he's good at it. He used me to sucker the opposition into bad bets. When it was over, he was four thousand dollars richer.'

After that, the fire came back – I could see the Buick burning in the arroyo like an *auto-da-fé* – and the rest of it was easy to tell. I just babbled. I didn't forget anything. I have a good memory for details that scare me. I described everything except Pablo and the Santiagos and Encino. That was mine. And I didn't need her to tell me that we couldn't work on two cases at once.

I only left out the part where I'd promised Haskell that we wouldn't drop him. I wanted to find out what she was thinking first.

But when I was done I couldn't tell whether she'd heard a word. She sat against the arm of the couch without moving – without even drinking – and didn't say a word. I might've been talking to myself, like a kid at a campfire telling ghost stories to explain the dark.

Finally I asked, 'Ginny, are you asleep?'

She turned her head slightly towards me. In a lifeless voice, she said, 'I searched the house while you were gone. I didn't find anything. He doesn't even keep personal financial records here. If his wife wants to know anything, she has to take his word for it.'

I sat with my arms wrapped over my stomach and waited for her to go on.

'I even checked his briefcase. It was empty. He carries a briefcase without a single scrap of paper in it.'

That surprised me, more because she seemed to think it was important than because it meant anything. 'Maybe it's just for show.'

'Sure,' she said without inflection. 'And maybe it was full when he took it in to work this morning.'

I didn't understand. 'So what?'

Abruptly she lifted her glass and drank the rest of the whiskey. Then she dropped the glass on the carpet. 'Brew' – a dying breeze sighed in her voice – 'somebody wants him dead. More people are going to get hurt. What are we going to do?'

I wanted to ask, You mean, someone besides el Señor? Do you still think Haskell's lying? But I didn't have the heart for it. Gently I asked, 'What do you want to do?'

'This is your case,' she said. 'I'm just along for the ride.' She didn't move, but she was going away. Leaving me alone. 'We've traded places. I used to be the one who went out and did things. Now I'm the one who sits around and drinks.' Slowly she pulled her legs up on to the cushions and curled herself against the arm of the couch. 'We'll do whatever you decide. I'm going to sleep.'

I waited until I was sure she meant it. Then I picked her up and carried her back upstairs to the master bedroom. Her face was wet with tears, and she went on crying while I undressed her and eased her under the sheets. But she didn't make a sound.

After that I spent what felt like the hardest night of my life. Staying awake to keep her safe, in case Haskell's enemies put in any appearance. And not drinking.

By the time dawn finally crept into the Heights, I wasn't in a very good mood. I felt old and burned out, and I'd occupied the whole night thinking about things that scared me. Just along for the ride, huh?

I was too bitter to be civil about it, so I put one foot on the bed and bounced Ginny up and down. 'Get up,' I muttered. 'The ride's about to start.'

She came awake slowly, her face puffy with sleep and too much booze. Raising her head, she looked at me. Registered the fact that she was naked under the covers in Haskell's bed while I stood in front of her with all my clothes on.

'What time is it?' Even her voice sounded blurred.

'Around seven.'

First thing in the morning, with that broken nose, not enough rest, and too much to drink the night before, maybe she wasn't the best-looking woman in the world. But she still made my back teeth hurt.

Peering at me, she asked, 'You haven't had any sleep yet?'

I turned my back on her, started out of the bedroom. 'Get up. We've got work to do.' I was an especially nice guy this morning, but there didn't seem to be anything I could do about it. Trying to calm down, I went to make some breakfast.

Showered and dressed, she joined me in the kitchen sooner than I expected. She had the decency not to want any breakfast, but she swallowed about a quart of orange juice, ate a handful of vitamins, then started on the coffee.

For a while she watched me eat. Then she said, 'Sorry about last night. I thought I told you not to mother me.'

In the privacy of my head, I replied, I'm not your mother. At the rate I'm going, I'm not even your lover. What the hell do you think you're doing to yourself? But I really didn't want to have that conversation with her. Not the way I felt. So I said, 'I'm surprised you remember even that much about last night.'

Charming as always.

She shot a glare at me. Instead of snapping, however, she said quietly, 'I remember. Try me.'

I wasn't really in the mood to eat. I had a belly full of sand, and too many things stuck in my throat. I picked up the dishes and put them in the sink. For once I left them.

'What's so important about his briefcase?'

She sighed. 'I don't know. Probably nothing. It just seems strange that the chief accountant of a bank carries a briefcase with nothing in it.'

I didn't look at her. 'What did we decide about this case?'

'We didn't decide anything.' She'd recovered a bit of acid. 'I said it was up to you. You gave me the distinct impression we're still working for him. Or why did we spend the night here?'

She studied me hard. 'Brew, what's the matter?'

I couldn't answer that, so I did the next best thing. 'When the Buick blew up.' Trying not to let my voice quiver. 'I've seen an explosion like that before. It was a gas fire.'

'Meaning what?'

'Meaning it doesn't take dynamite, or detonators, or anything fancy. All you need is enough wire and maybe a metal punch. A half-wit can do it. And it's tough to prove because the wire usually gets burned or melted too badly.'

She was still a step behind me, so she didn't say anything. I didn't like the way her silence felt.

'Whoever followed us to that bridge club saw we weren't using Haskell's car. They probably didn't need much time to find out we weren't in it.' After stewing most of the night, I still came to the same conclusion. 'They don't know he isn't here. They've had plenty of time to try again.'

She struggled for some of that famous Fistoulari self-control, but this morning it didn't sound right. 'So what's the problem? You know what to look for. Why don't you check the cars?'

That made me turn around. 'The problem,' I hissed so that I wouldn't shout at her, 'is that this time they might try something fancier. They know we've been warned. This time they might booby-trap it. All they have to do is hot-wire the cars and make a contact at the hood latch. Or set up any kind of trembler switch.'

I didn't actually know much about bombs. Just enough to be scared spitless.

'I can't risk lifting the hood. And I'm too big to fit under cars. Using a jack might be as bad as trying the hood. I'll kill myself before I even find out I'm in trouble.'

For a minute her eyes drifted out of focus. Automatically – she probably wasn't aware she was doing it – she hugged her left stump protectively under her right arm.

How do we get out of this one? Let me count the ways.

Call the cops? That would be the moral equivalent of turning Haskell in – something we'd apparently agreed we wouldn't do. And in terms of professional ethics, we were required to tell him what we had in mind first. And then quit working for him if he ordered us not to tell the cops.

Use cabs? That would leave trails that anyone with the right kind of clout could follow.

Rent more cars? Ginny's insurance company was going to be mad enough about the Buick. The kind of insurance you buy when you rent a car doesn't cover things like having the car blown up by thugs. Any more property damage, and her policy might be cancelled. The rates would sure as hell go through the roof.

I watched her think it through. By degrees, the look in her eyes grew sharper, and the end of her nose went white with anger. But she came to the same conclusion I did.

'You want me to crawl under those cars.'

I nodded dumbly.

'I already know what it's like to get blown apart. By now I ought to be used to it.'

I had reason to be in a great mood this morning. Yessir. 'If you have a better idea,' I said, trying to keep my own anger down, 'spit it out. I don't like this much myself.'

She gave me a murderous glare. 'The hell you don't.' Fiercely she snatched up her purse. 'Come on. Let's get it over with.'

Private investigators sometimes do stupid things because they don't have any choice.

She retrieved her coat, put it on. I didn't have anything except a jacket over my stale shirt and the dead weight of the .45. Following her up the stairs, light-headed with fear and lack of sleep, I could hear the sound of fire again. But now it was the Olds burning, and Ginny was stuck under it.

At the top of the stairs, I stopped to sweat for a minute. 'Some time today,' I murmured wanly, 'one of us has got to go back to the apartment for some clean clothes. I'm starting to stink.'

She didn't look at me. Her attention was aimed out towards the cars.

We made sure we had all the keys we needed. We weren't particularly cautious about the way we left the house, but that didn't bother me. At the moment we weren't in any danger of being shot.

Outside the weather felt like snow. The cold had lost its edge, and the air carried a wet smell that's rare in Puerta del Sol. Clouds the colour of lead piled over the mountains, making the morning look dull and hopeless. A perfect day for a fire-bomb. Dust and paper scraps blew like they were falling down Cactus Blossom into the cul-de-sac.

Ginny handed me her purse. Bleak as the weather, she asked, 'What do I do?'

'All right.' With my free hand, I gripped my jacket closed over my chest. 'What you're looking for is a pair of wires.' Suddenly I wasn't sure that I knew how the Buick was blown. 'They'll run from the engine somewhere back to the gas tank. They should go into the tank right at the top. Look for the breather vent or a new hole. They'll be taped close together, so that juice from the engine will make a spark in the tank.

'The safest thing to do is pull the wires out of the tank.'

She didn't move. With her head, she indicated the Olds. 'There's a flashlight in the glove compartment.'

Oh, terrific, I thought. What if the doors have been wired?

But that was one too many things to worry about. Grimly I unlocked the passenger side of the Olds. Holding my breath, I opened the door.

Nothing happened. I got out the flashlight and gave it to Ginny. The sweat felt like ice under my arms.

'Maybe you ought to stand back,' she said tightly.

Pale and cold, she hefted the flashlight as if she wanted a weapon. At the rear of the Olds, she stretched out on her back on the cement. Using her arms for leverage, she wedged herself under the car.

I couldn't watch. Lifting my face to the mountains, I stared into the wind until my eyes ran. She muttered curses while she searched. With any luck at all, I wouldn't feel the blast when it hit me.

Maybe if I died I'd go to heaven. That would be nice. In heaven, they drink good scotch. Right then, I could have used some.

Then I heard a scuffling sound as Ginny pried herself out from under the Olds. I turned around quickly and squatted to look.

She'd left a pair of wires lying on the cement behind her. They had bared ends, and they were taped close together, and they ran up towards the engine.

Breathing hard, she climbed to her feet. For a minute she leaned against me while I put my arms around her.

I wanted to stand there and hold her for a long time. But she pulled away – too angry to stand still. Panting fury, she knelt to the wires and pulled them out where we could see them. Then I unlatched the hood.

The starter made a grinding noise, and a spark snapped at the ends of the wires. The ignition had been jumped.

To be honest, I could have used a *lot* of scotch.

Trembling quietly to myself, I disconnected the extra wires under the hood of the Olds while Ginny got down on her back again and squirmed under Haskell's Continental.

This time she knew what she was looking for. She found it more quickly – another set of wires feeding into the gas tank. Another jumped ignition, another contact at the hood latch. Maybe it was the cold. I couldn't say anything. If I did, my teeth might chatter.

She rested her weight against the car, her expression half rage, half nausea. She looked tight and flushed, like a woman with a high fever. She held her left forearm clamped under her right elbow as if it hurt her.

Trying to recover a little calm, I asked, 'Are you sure you wouldn't like some breakfast now?'

Abruptly she pushed herself straight and looked at me. Her voice shook. 'I don't believe el Señor has anything to do with this. Do you hear me? I don't care what Haskell says. I don't care what evidence you think you've come up with. You can play this case any way you want, and I'll go along. But I don't *believe it*!' Her sudden shout practically rocked me back on my heels. She was right on the edge. 'It's too messy and *stupid*! It doesn't make any sense.'

'Ginny—' I didn't have anything to say. I just wanted to reach out to her somehow.

'Don't talk to me,' she snapped. 'Next time it's *your* turn to get under the fucking car.'

For a second she raised her hand to her face while her expression knotted. Then she forced herself to let out a long slow breath. When she dropped her hand, she didn't look at me.

'Let's go get Haskell,' she muttered softly. 'I want to ask him some questions.'

It's just reaction, I said to myself. That's all. She'll be fine in a few minutes. But I didn't believe it.

I believed she was falling apart. Losing whatever it was that had made her tough, clear-headed, capable. She couldn't bear the idea of el Señor. Fear and her stump eroded the conviction or self-esteem that held her together. Right in front of me, she was coming apart at the seams.

Under the circumstances, I was in no mood to go get Haskell. I had my own kind of reaction to deal with. But she was right. Even I could think of a few questions to ask him. So I made an effort to pull myself together.

We took the Continental. Let his insurance company worry about it if anything happened.

I drove. At least it's usually called driving. In spite of the crushed velour seats and the leather dashboard, the climate control and the digital clock, I felt more like I was holding a rudder while galley slaves rowed for their lives. Up Cactus Blossom to Foothill, south to the nearest useful cross street, then west towards the neighbourhood of the Territorial Apartments.

We weren't more than three minutes early when I pulled up in front of the fake chalet building. Ginny got out, opened the rear door, and climbed into the back seat. I slumped behind the wheel, feeling like a sack of dirty laundry. Since I didn't have anything bright or cheerful to say, I didn't say it.

Right on cue, Haskell emerged from the apartments. He looked scrubbed and fresh, ready to take on the world. Even though there wasn't any sunlight, and the clouds piling overhead were about as friendly as steel wool, his camel's hair coat seemed to glow with enthusiasm. He could've been a headline –

BANK EXECUTIVE CONQUERS CITY
VIRGINS SACRIFICED IN HONOUR.

Before he reached the car, Ginny leaned forward abruptly and said, 'He's wearing a clean suit.'

Just for a second, I wondered how she knew that. Then I noticed his dark brown pants. The suit he'd had on last night was light blue.

He came to my side of the car. When I rolled down the window, he said, 'As long as you're using my car, I'll drive.'

My smile felt about as charming as I did. 'As long as you're paying us to protect you,' I said, 'I'll drive.' I pointed at the passenger seat. 'Sit over there.'

I thought he was going to argue, but he didn't. With a shrug, he ambled around the Continental and let himself in.

When he'd closed the door, he turned to look at Ginny, then glanced towards me. The gleam in his eyes reminded me that I hadn't shaved. 'You two are in a good mood this morning,' he commented. 'What's the matter?'

I started the engine, pulled away from the kerb. 'Whoever blew up the Buick tried the same thing with your car.' Heading the wrong way to get to the bank. 'That always cheers us up.'

He watched me for a minute. Then he said, 'The bank is back that way.'

'Well, hush my mouth,' I said. 'So it is.'

After five blocks, I made a U-turn and returned towards the Territorial Apartments. A block before we reached them, I pulled to the kerb again and parked.

I could almost feel him trying to figure out what was going on. Finally he said, 'All right, I give up. What're you doing?'

'Waiting,' Ginny told him. 'We want to see who else comes out.'

Haskell's tan turned darker. 'Don't,' he snapped. 'This is none of your business. I'm not paying you to pry into my private life.'

'That's funny,' she murmured in a distant voice, not really paying attention to him. 'I thought it was your private life that got you into this mess.'

He gave her a look that would have split a pine board. 'You're wrong. Don't do this. Take me to work. I'll fire you.'

I smiled again. 'Fire away.' I was getting good at it. I still couldn't claim that we had him flustered, but this was as close as we'd come so far.

I didn't want him to call my bluff. Playing people was his game, not mine. He could probably get around me. But he made the mistake of looking at Ginny again.

Her eyes were hard and grey as lead shot.

He didn't fire us.

We went on waiting.

It didn't take long. After a few more minutes, a woman came out of the apartments and hurried towards her car. In spite of the weather, she was dressed like a daisy. The glow of having Reg Haskell to herself all night left her too happy for dull colours.

Eunice Wint.

Chapter Eleven

More for Haskell's benefit than anything else, I said to Ginny, 'I told you so.'

'I believed you.' Already her mind was somewhere else – probably trying to figure out how this case didn't have anything to do with el Señor. 'I always believe you when you tell me things like that.'

Haskell stopped acting angry. His skin retained its flush under his tan, but his manner changed. 'Was that Eunice? I didn't know she lives here.'

'Nice try,' I muttered as I put the Continental in gear. Smoothly the galley slaves rowed us away from the kerb. We headed in the direction of the bank.

Ginny went on thinking for a minute. Then she said, 'Mr Haskell, Brew told me what happened last night. It was a gas fire. Somebody hot-wired the ignition to make a spark in the gas tank. To be honest, that doesn't sound like el Señor's style.'

She wasn't being honest at all. El Señor hired all kinds of muscle, and they all had their own styles. But that didn't matter now. She was simply trying to soothe and unsettle him at the same time.

'It was something anybody could have done,' she continued. 'All he needed was some wire and maybe a metal punch. That's why we're prying into your private life. We have to consider the possibility that this case doesn't have anything to do with el Señor. Maybe you have a personal enemy who wants you dead.'

He turned in his seat to look at both of us. Taking us seriously again. Or acting like it, anyway. 'Why would anybody I know want to kill me?'

'We don't know that. But look at it from our point of view. Last

283

night, you told Brew you've been trying to blackmail el Señor. He'd certainly want to kill you for that. But how does he know it's you?'

'I'm sure you've done some stupid things in your life.' A touch of acid under the sweet reason. 'But I can't believe you're stupid enough to attempt this kind of scam without taking precautions. You certainly didn't walk into El Machismo and announce that you wanted to blackmail the boss. And I assume you didn't give him your name and address when you contacted him.

'Maybe,' she said, 'you'd better tell us what you *did* do.'

I approved. Despite her distress and denial, she played Haskell's own game back at him – and she did it pretty well. Now he had to give us some straight answers. Unless he wanted us to go on prying into his private life.

His eyes shifted back and forth between us. His expression was faintly speculative – measuring us again. For some reason, I remembered the way he sabotaged our opponents at the bridge club.

After a moment he let out a short laugh. 'Well, I thought I took precautions. By the time I finished tracing his laundry, I knew he wasn't kidding around. A man who went that far to protect his income wouldn't stop there.

'The file on his account gave me his address. I wrote him a letter. But first I went to the downtown post office and rented a box under an assumed name. That was my return address. Then I told the post office I would be out of town for a while. I asked them to forward my mail to my brother-in-law.' His own cleverness tickled him no end. 'As it happens, my brother-in-law's name was Reg Haskell. He had a box at the Heights branch post office.

'When I wrote to el Señor, I told him to reply to the downtown box. I thought he might be able to have that box watched, but since the mail would be forwarded to the Heights, I'd be safe.'

Then he frowned. Or at least the lower half of his face frowned. I wasn't sure about his eyes. 'Apparently I underestimated him.'

Well, I suppose if I'd been that clever I would've been tickled, too. It could've worked.

But Ginny didn't waste her time on Haskell's precautions. For a minute or two she scowled out the window. Then she looked him in the face again.

'How long ago was this?'

He turned on a wry smile. 'Actually, I just started. My first letter went out last Wednesday. I planned to give him a week. If he didn't answer, I'd send him a few photocopies to show him I meant business.

I never expected him to track me down. I certainly never expected him to do it so quickly.'

Last Wednesday? I thought. That wasn't quick, it was almost instantaneous. In Puerta del Sol, a letter mailed on Wednesday never arrives before Friday. And Saturday none of the post offices have counter service, just delivery. And yet by Sunday night Haskell was getting phone threats. If el Señor had his very own postal inspector, he still might not have been able to trace Haskell's mail that fast.

But Ginny didn't show any disbelief. She was thinking something else.

'Mr Haskell,' she said slowly, looking right at him, 'how much did you want him to pay you to keep your mouth shut?'

At that he laughed out loud. Apparently he couldn't help himself.

'I knew how much El Machismo took in every week. I thought he could spare five percent of that. Ten thousand dollars – give or take for seasonal variations.'

No wonder my stomach hurt. For a minute there, I had trouble making the Continental behave normally. 'How in hell,' I demanded, 'can you possibly need that much money?'

The humour disappeared from his face like I'd wiped it away with a sponge. The muscles at the corners of his eyes knotted. In a tone like an iron bar, he said, 'You know I can't afford that house and this car on what I earn as an accountant. I've been lucky with some investments. But recently I took some risks that turned sour on me. I have a lot to lose. Including my job. The bank doesn't smile on accountants who get in trouble with their investments. Why shouldn't el Señor solve my problems for me?'

I'd hit a nerve. I wanted to hit it again by asking him about those investments. But right then the Continental glided into the parking lot of the ice-cream parlour, and Ginny had something to say to him.

I eased the car into a landing slip. Then I sat and watched the people arriving for work while she talked.

'Mr Haskell,' she said in a detached voice, sounding slightly bored, 'it's not my job to tell you just how stupid you've been. Anybody in el Señor's position would try to have you killed. And he doesn't fail. That's how he gets away with it. It's self-perpetuating. In essence, he got his power by killing people. And his power makes it possible for him to go on killing people. Keeping you alive is going to be about as easy as changing the laws of nature.

'We need a lever. We can't match his muscle and resources. And you don't want us to go to the police. We need some way to make him back off. A threat of some kind.' Her detachment didn't make her especially persuasive. Maybe she didn't really believe what she was saying.

'We need that laundry. I want all the documentation you can get your hands on. Copies, addresses, account numbers, all of it. I want it today. First we'll show him we have the same information you do. Then we'll convince him it's protected. The cops and the DA will get it if anything happens to any of us.

'And then' – her tone remained distant, but her eyes nailed Haskell – 'we'll find out just how dependent on violence he is.'

He didn't look happy. When she was done, he shook his head. 'That won't work. I told Axbrewder I can't prove anything. It's all inferential. It wouldn't stand up in court.'

'That doesn't matter,' she replied. 'What matters is what we can make el Señor believe. As long as he thinks we can prove it, he'll have to pay attention.'

If I were Haskell, the way her mind worked would've cheered me right up. But he didn't seem to get any pleasure out of it. Maybe it wasn't enough like cowboys-and-Indians.

He stared out at the bank for a long minute. Then he said, 'I'll try.' Gleaming, irresistible Reg actually sounded morose. 'I might not be able to do it today. I don't have regular access to all those files and records.'

Ginny let the acid back into her voice. 'Give it your best shot. You're a walking dead man until we have a lever.'

'All right.' He didn't enjoy being talked to like that. 'Pick me up at 4.30.' Swinging the door open, he got out and slammed it behind him.

As he walked towardss the bank, he looked like he could feel the sky leaning down on him.

I turned around, got both arms over the back of the seat. Knotting my fists in Ginny's coat, I pulled her to me and kissed her.

She didn't know whether to kiss me back or get mad. There was too much going on. When I let her go, she leaned back against the upholstery. Tension stretched the skin of her face taut and pale. 'Someday,' she muttered, 'you're going to meet a woman who isn't scared blind by your sheer size, and she'll break her hand trying to slap you.'

I almost laughed. But I was distracted by a car pulling into the space beside the Continental. I'd seen that car before. It was driven by a woman dressed like a daisy.

'With your permission,' I said to Ginny. Mock deference. Every once in a while, I'm faster than she is. A second after Eunice Wint closed the door of her car, I got out of the Continental.

She was in a hurry – late to work – but my sudden appearance stopped her. She gave me a quick smile. 'Mr Axbrewder.' She still had the radiant look of a puppy in love. I would've felt sorry for her if I'd had the time. 'You're early. We don't open until nine.'

I met her smile with my harmless-galoot grin. 'No problem. Just one question. Mr Haskell forgot his briefcase. Left it at home. Do you think we should go get it for him?'

Poor Eunice. She never had a chance. She was too happy and young, and maybe just a little slow. Haskell seemed to like women who didn't exhibit what you might call penetrating intellect.

'Oh, no,' she said promptly. 'Don't worry about it. He doesn't need it.'

Then she realized what she was doing.

The way her skin burned was painful to watch. Even the sides of her neck blushed. Without meaning to, she told me more than I thought she knew.

Lamely she tried to cover herself by saying, 'He only takes work home over the weekends.' But it was too late for that.

I did what I could to let her off the hook. 'He's a lucky man,' I said. Trying to make my grin suggest more than one kind of envy. 'That saves us a trip. Thanks.'

With a wave for her benefit, I climbed back into the Continental.

'Someday,' I growled to Ginny, 'one of us has simply got to poke him in the eye with a sharp stick. She knows exactly why he carries an empty briefcase.'

Softly Ginny asked, 'Do you think she'll tell us?'

'You ask her. I'm sick of picking on children.'

Ginny didn't react to that. Instead she pointed across the street at a restaurant called Granny Good's Family Food. 'Let's get a cup of coffee.'

Snarling inane obscenities to myself, I started up the car and stroked over to the restaurant. This way Haskell might think we were going to leave him alone.

Inside the restaurant was identical to every other so-called 'family-style' joint in the city, with bright vinyl-covered benches, waitresses so young that they could hardly spell their own names, and a menu larded with pancakes, hamburgers, and leather steaks. I took a booth while Ginny went to use the phone. When she came back, she seemed more brittle than ever. Her nose was too pale, and her cheeks were too red, and the muscles around her eyes were tight with strain. She worked on this case because I wanted her to, but her fear hadn't diminished any.

With her left forearm stuffed protectively into the pocket of her coat, she sat down opposite me. We ordered a pot of coffee. She swallowed a few more vitamins. I stared out through the window at the bank, watching the weather congeal. The heavy clouds and the threat of snow made the ice-cream parlour look like a loony bin – the kind of place where axe murderers and Presidential assassins are locked up for their own good. It was probably the most successful bank branch in the whole city.

We didn't have to wait long. Ginny still knew how to get results over the phone. No more than five minutes after our coffee arrived, a tall thin man wearing an immaculate banker's pinstripe left the ice-cream parlour. She'd gotten his attention, all right – he wasn't even wearing a coat. Hunching his shoulders against the cold, he crossed the street in our direction.

I waved at him through the window. He came into Granny Good's and found his way to our booth.

Jordan Canthorpe, Eunice Wint's fiancé.

Up close, the prim way he carried his hands seemed about right, but his face looked too young for the suit. His hair was so blond and fine it was almost invisible, and his moustache was self-effacing to the point of nonexistence. His soft smooth skin wouldn't age well. In about ten years, people would think he was his wife's son – if he ever succeeded at getting married. On top of that, he was doing his best to age himself with worry, and it showed. His pale eyes had a harried cast.

Nevertheless he felt too much internal pressure to be easily handled. 'Ms Fistoulari?' he asked in a high voice, as tight as a wire. 'I don't like phone calls like that. I have work to do. The bank opens in eighteen minutes. Why can't you come talk to me normally in my office?'

Neither of us stood up. Ginny gave him her woman-of-steel look. 'If we did that, Reg Haskell would see us talking to you.'

I smiled and offered him a seat beside me. 'Want some coffee?'

Automatically he said, 'No, thank you.' For a moment his gaze shifted back and forth between me and Ginny. Then, abruptly, he folded himself into the booth.

'Reg Haskell is our chief accountant,' he said unsteadily. 'He does excellent work, and has for years. We're fortunate to have him. You have no business asking me questions about him. I shouldn't talk to you at all.'

It was Ginny's turn to smile. It didn't soften her gaze.

'Mr Canthorpe, Reg Haskell is in danger. He hired us to protect him. Somebody wants to kill him.'

Canthorpe stared at her. If he could've seen himself, he would've cringed at the way his mouth hung open. His voice almost cracked when he said, 'I don't believe it.'

Conversationally – and still smiling – I said, 'Last night they blew up the car we were using. This morning they tried again. I don't think they'll keep missing much longer.'

He looked at me, gulped a little air, turned a face full of distress back towards Ginny. 'I don't believe it,' he repeated. But he believed it, all right. He'd probably given more than a little thought to killing Haskell himself.

We watched him and waited while he thought himself into a sweat. A few seconds passed before he started to look horrified. Then he said, 'I don't know anything about it. Why would I?' His long clean hands hugged each other on the tabletop. 'Why do you think I know anything about it?'

Left to myself, I would've said, He's screwing your fiancé. That girl's never going to marry you now. Not after she's had a taste of irresistible Reg. Why wouldn't you want him dead? But Ginny was smoother.

'This is a complicated case, Mr Canthorpe. Mr Haskell is in serious danger, but we don't know from whom. That makes our job difficult.' Old master-of-understatement Fistoulari. 'We have to investigate every lead we can find.' As she talked, she began to let herself sound less formal. 'If we can, we want to get at his enemies before they get at him.

'What we need from you is information. There are two crucial points we have to track down. You can help us with both of them.'

Canthorpe squinted at her. He didn't seem to notice that she hadn't answered his question, but he controlled his dismay anyway. Very carefully, he said, 'Ms Fistoulari, surely you realize that the private lives of our people are just that, private. They deserve confidentiality. And I certainly can't discuss the bank's business with you.'

She didn't so much as blink. 'Before you refuse, don't you think you should hear what we have to say?'

Now he remembered that she hadn't answered his question. He took a tighter grip on himself and nodded slowly.

I leaned into the corner of the booth to watch. The seats in restaurants like Granny Good's are deliberately designed to be uncomfortable so that people will eat fast and get out, make room for other customers. Nevertheless I kept my kindly-uncle smile glued on my face and tried to be stoical.

Staring at him was part of my job. Make people nervous while Ginny talks to them. It's surprising how nervous they get when a man my size just sits there and smiles at them.

Vaguely I wondered what story she was going to tell him. She certainly couldn't tell him the truth. Professional ethics didn't countenance lapses like that.

She has more scruples than most private investigators, but she wasn't wearing them where Canthorpe could see them. 'As I say, Mr Haskell has hired us to protect him. We're licensed by the state for this kind of work. Naturally we need to know why anybody would want to kill him.

'He tells us he can only think of one reason. During the past few months, apparently, he's stumbled on to what he calls a money laundry, a way to conceal sources of illegal income. He believes one of Puerta del Sol's leading criminal figures is using your bank to process his profits from gambling, prostitution, and drugs.' She spread it on thick. 'Through a series of dummy accounts and companies, he makes his income hard to trace, disguising his involvement in criminal activities.'

She hadn't reached the point yet, but Canthorpe couldn't resist a banker's question. 'How is it done?'

She told him what Haskell had told me.

'That's quite possible.' He nodded to himself, thinking furiously. When he didn't watch what they were doing, his hands made little stroking gestures along his moustache. 'But it's highly unlikely that such a laundry would be discovered by accident.' He wasn't used to this kind of reasoning. It took him a moment to catch up. 'Hasn't Haskell gone to the police?'

Ginny shook her head. 'He says he doesn't have enough proof.'

'But if he lacks proof, and he hasn't made his findings public' – Canthorpe was getting confused – 'then this criminal can't know about them. Why would he try to kill him for knowing something he doesn't know he knows?'

She didn't waver. Making it up out of whole cloth, she said, 'Mr Haskell thinks somebody at the bank found out what he was doing and ratted on him.'

I went on smiling. In the privacy of my head, I gave her a round of applause.

Canthorpe gaped at her. 'That's preposterous!'

She put a little more bite in her voice. 'Mr Canthorpe, are you telling me that if Mr Haskell stumbled on a money laundry and began to trace it, nobody else would be aware of what he was doing? That nobody else could be aware of it?'

'Well, no.' Her tone made him retreat a step. 'I don't mean that precisely. Logs are kept. Access to files is limited or supervised. He would have to go rather far afield from his normal duties. Someone might become suspicious. Especially someone with prior knowledge of the laundry's existence.'

Apparently Canthorpe wasn't stupid. For a second there, I wondered if Ginny would be able to get around him.

Gathering indignation, he added, 'But that in itself is preposterous. No one who works for the First Puerta del Sol National Bank would ever—'

'Oh, spare me,' Ginny cut in. 'I'm sure everybody who has ever worked for any bank anywhere is pure as the driven snow. But there's only one way to be sure, isn't there?'

'To be sure?'

'Trace the laundry yourself. Find out who might've been in a position to realize what Haskell was up to.'

If I'd said that, it would've sounded like I was reading it off a cereal box. But from her it made a queer kind of sense. For him, I mean. For me, there was nothing queer about it. She was just trying to verify Haskell's story. And to set Canthorpe up for what she really wanted.

From a banker's point of view, however, her suggestion only held together by force of personality. 'That might be possible,' he said slowly. He didn't have any idea what he was getting into. On the other hand, Haskell was a subject he couldn't leave alone. 'It would be easier,' he went on, 'if you gave me a name.'

Ginny nodded fractionally and glanced at me.

Softly, so that I wouldn't sound too much like I was swearing, I said, 'Hector Jesus Fria de la Sancha.' El Señor.

Fumbling, Canthorpe pulled a note pad and a silver pen out of his breast pocket and wrote the name down.

She had him where she wanted him. When he finished writing, she said, 'That's one of the points you can help us with. The other is much easier.'

He looked at her like he was going to be sick. This was all too much for him – which was exactly what she wanted. He couldn't have walked out on us then to save his soul.

'We have to investigate every possibility,' she said. 'It's Mr Haskell's idea that somebody found out he was tracing Señor Fria's money. Personally, I consider that far-fetched.'

She could afford to admit it now. Just made her sound more plausible. Now he'd probably never figure out that he'd been lied to.

'It's more likely, I think' – her eyes were hard, but she didn't give him any warning – 'that somebody he knows, somebody he works with, wants him dead for personal reasons.'

Canthorpe's whole body went rigid. We were back to the subject that got his attention in the first place. Holding on to the edge of the table with both hands, he said, 'What personal reasons?'

It was my turn. I didn't have any trouble making my smile look sad. 'We're just trying to do our job. You know what personal reasons as well as we do. We saw Haskell leave your fiancée's apartment this morning.'

He had the opposite problem Eunice Wint did. When something hit him that hard, all the blood rushed out of him. He turned so pale that he looked like he might evaporate. For a moment he shoved the heels of his hands into his eyes. It wouldn't have surprised me if he'd started to cry.

But then he dropped his hands back to the table. They left red marks under his eyes like scars on his white skin. His voice shook, but it wasn't because he was in danger of crying.

'I'm a conservative man,' he said. 'Banking is a conservative profession. I earn a good income. I value traditional things. Honesty, family, security, fidelity. Kindness.

'Reg Haskell has no moral sense at all. He considers himself some kind of sexual buccaneer. For two or three years now, he's cut a swath through our staff of tellers and receptionists. He has them standing in line. No amount of promiscuity satisfies him, and he makes the women around him promiscuous simply by smiling at them.

'I thought Eunice would be different. She seemed too pure for him.' Even though his voice shook, he spoke with dignity. 'I had no wish to fall in love with one of his discards. A man like that has no business working in a bank.'

'A man like that,' Ginny said quietly, 'must've hurt a lot of people. Were any of them hurt badly enough to want to kill him?'

Any of them besides yourself, Mr Canthorpe?

The clarity of his anger was fading. 'That's the terrible part,' he said with more self-pity. 'His women don't act hurt. They're grateful.' Then a spasm of memory twisted his face for a second. 'Most of them.'

'Most of them?' Ginny asked.

'There was one who wasn't.' The quiver in his voice resembled disgust. 'About six months ago. She took it to heart – the way Eunice does. But I'm afraid she wasn't very stable. We had to let her go. We try not to impose our standards on the private lives of our employees, but the way she dithered around after him affected her work. One day, she made a scene in the lobby.' His face twitched again. 'We had no choice.'

'What was her name?'

'Gail Harmon.' Remembering her made him distant. He didn't seem to realize what he was implying about her. 'The other tellers called her Frail Gail. She was beautiful in such a fragile way.'

'Do you know where we can find her?'

Without thinking about it, he gave us the address, a number down on Bosque in the South Valley. Right in the middle of Puerta del Sol's *barrio*. He said it like he'd been meditating on it for hours, using it for some kind of mantra.

That surprised me. Your typical bank branch manager has better things to do with his time than sit around memorizing the addresses of people who don't work for him any more. But I thought I understood it.

Almost casually, I asked, 'Were you engaged to her, too?'

That brought him back. He sat up straighter. He didn't seem to have any blood in his whole body, but something about his eyes suddenly made him look capable of spilling some.

'I saw what Haskell did to her,' he whispered fiercely, 'and I felt sorry for her. I thought I might help her find another job, so I called the address she used when she worked for us. That was her parents' home. They told me how to locate her. I think they were sick of worrying about her.'

But he couldn't keep it going. He was in too deep. After a minute he sagged, and the truth came out.

'She took him so much to heart. I thought she might be able to explain Eunice to me. Help me understand. But I haven't called her or gone to see her. Every day I promise myself that today I'll do it. Every day I believe that I can't bear any more. But I lack the nerve.'

Then, as if it were irrelevant, he said, 'Her parents told me she's living with somebody.'

I didn't know what else to do, so I put my hand on his shoulder. 'Maybe she'll wake up,' I said. 'It's been known to happen.' Axbrewder on the verge of getting maudlin. 'Maybe she'll realize what she's doing and come back to you.'

I thought he might say, I wouldn't have her. But he just sighed. 'That would be nice.'

With her hand, Ginny pinched the bridge of her broken nose, trying to keep her priorities straight. 'Apparently, Mr Canthorpe,' she said, sounding tired and a little beaten, 'Reg Haskell isn't a nice man. He still has a right to hire protection. Murder is murder. We do this kind of work because we want to reduce the number of victims in the world.'

I hoped that he wouldn't try for a sarcastic comeback, but he just asked, 'Is that all?'

She nodded.

He said, 'Call me around four.' Then he got up and walked away. Through the window, I watched him return to the bank. He didn't look back.

After a while, I asked, 'Is Haskell really all that irresistible?'

'No.' Ginny sounded bitter and brittle, angrier than she knew what to do with. 'Canthorpe's just one of the victims. It makes him exaggerate.'

Outside the clouds looked too heavy to carry their own weight. The air was dead grey. Nothing had any colour. Mostly to myself, I said, 'Some days I love this job so much I could puke.'

Chapter Twelve

That was the wrong thing to say. She was in no mood for it. She put her one hand flat on the tabletop, her palm against the Formica. 'All this,' she said, pushing down so hard that her fingers splayed, 'was your idea, remember? You wanted this case. Don't tell me you're sick of it. I don't give a shit.'

Well, she had a point. The whole thing *was* my idea. But I hadn't exactly enjoyed it so far. 'Yes, sir, Ms Fistoulari, sir,' I muttered sourly. 'I disembowel myself in shame. Do forgive me.'

'All right.' Her voice was as white as the skin of her nose. 'All right. Go over there' – she nodded at the bank – 'and tell Haskell we quit. Then I'll drop you off at the nearest bar.'

I stared at her. Maybe she was bluffing. But I couldn't think of any way to call her on it. I couldn't risk flushing everything down the toilet. I just stared at her and held my breath and didn't make any effort to hide the hurt in my eyes.

After a minute she sighed and looked away. 'Either that,' she said, 'or go back to the apartment and get some rest. You don't look like you can hold your head up much longer.'

Slowly I scrubbed my hands over my face to pull what was left of my brains back together. I hadn't shaved, and my whiskers felt like sandpaper against my palms. When I'd rubbed some of the anguish out of the muscles of my cheeks, I dropped my hands back on to the table.

'I can't,' I said. 'The cops aren't going to sit on their butts while people blow up rented cars and kill innocent kids.' That was too much to expect, even from Puerta del Sol's finest. 'They'll get our address off the rental contract. They'll get Haskell's by asking people at his club what I was doing there. If they get mad enough about the fact I've been avoiding them, they might stake out both places.' Eventually we'd have to tell the cops what we were up to. There was no way around it. But I wanted to put it off as long as possible. 'If they catch me, they might hold me as a material witness.'

I didn't point out the obvious. If the cops held me, Ginny would have to cope with this case all by herself.

'Besides,' I added, 'I want to see Gail Harmon.'

Something about the way that came out told her more than I actually said. 'What do you mean, *you* want to see Gail Harmon? What about me? What do you expect me to do?' She looked like she wanted to take the skin off my bones. 'Spend the day the way I spent last night?'

'No.' I was too tired, and she was hitting too hard. Somehow I refrained from yelling at her, but I couldn't keep my anger down. 'I expect you to find proof that el Señor has nothing to do with this. You believe it, you prove it. Stop whining about it and *do* something.'

Then I wanted to turn my anger on myself and hack off body parts because she couldn't conceal the way she flinched. Her mouth twisted like she was going to spit at me, but her voice wasn't even sarcastic. 'I suppose that's fair.' Just dead flat. 'I'll try to disprove your theory while you tear holes in mine. What a great idea. When we took this case, I didn't realize you were so eager to get away from me.'

A sharp intake of breath pulled her lips back from her teeth. She knotted her fist. 'It's so much fun working for you. This time I don't even have a car.'

For a second there, I felt about as rotten as I deserved. Then I dug into my pocket and tossed the keys to the Continental on to the table. 'I'll take a cab back to Haskell's house and use the Olds.'

She didn't look at me. Her face was pale, and the expression in her eyes was far away, harried, and miserable. For a moment she pressed the knuckles of her fist against her forehead.

'Brew,' she said in a tight voice, 'when was the last time we actually told each other the truth?'

I hadn't told her any direct lies – and precious few indirect ones. But suddenly all the things I hadn't told her made my pulse throb in my throat. Through my teeth, I gritted, 'I am not going out to get drunk. You know me better than that.'

'No,' she muttered. 'Not any more. I don't know you at all. You pressured me into taking this case. You won't let me get out of it. But the only thing *you* do is figure out excuses to go off on your own. You want me in this case, but you don't want me with you. What kind of sense do you expect me to make of that?' Frustration and pain turned her voice as harsh as the cut of a crosscut saw. 'So far, I haven't seen any sign that you're drinking. That's true. So what? Give me another explanation.'

She sounded so fierce that I stared at her, dumbfounded. 'What do you mean, "another explanation"? I already gave you one. Weren't you listening?'

'Oh, I was listening,' she snarled back. 'I've been listening all along. You talk about the case. You insult and manipulate me. But you don't *say* anything.

'Give it a try, goddammit. Give me one reason why I shouldn't believe you and Haskell are doing this together.'

I couldn't help myself. My mouth actually hung open. *You and Haskell*. I wanted to say, Stop it. Stop this. But the words stuck in my throat.

She didn't stop. 'Or maybe,' she said, 'this is all just some clever way to get rid of me. You're tired of taking care of the angry old cripple, so you're using this case to solve the problem. Maybe get me shot by el Señor's goons. I had my hand blown off for your niece, but that isn't enough for you. You're leaving me alone so I'll be a better target.'

It was too much. The more I gaped at her, trying not to believe what I heard, the more she sounded like she was losing her mind. She looked so hurt, so abandoned, that I wanted to break my fists on the table just so that she wouldn't be alone. I'd done this to her. And I was doing it deliberately. It was too much by a long shot.

I heaved myself out of the booth. I couldn't face her accusations, even if they were justified – and completely wrong. 'By my count,' I said, 'we're just about even right now.' Then I stomped away towards the phone.

By the time I got to it, I was mad enough to rip it out of the wall.

Luckily I was housebroken at an early age. Instead of demolishing the phone, I used it to call a cab. Then I went out into the cold to wait.

Jiffy had a cab free in the neighbourhood. I only had to wait a few minutes. Nevertheless that was long enough. The wind wasn't hard, but it came down off the mountains like the edge of a knife. The clouds were heavy as lead, overdue for snow. Without a coat, I didn't have anything except my tired metabolism to hold out the cold. During those few minutes, I realized that I didn't have any idea what Ginny was going to do.

Whatever she did might be as crazy as what she said.

When the cab arrived, I pulled myself into the blast of its heater and tried to absorb as much warmth as possible while the driver took me over to Foothill in the direction of Haskell's house.

I wanted to stay in the cab for ever. Just sprawl out on the back seat and sleep in the warmth and the lulling sound of tyres on concrete until all my problems went away. Unfortunately I had my job to do. That's why they give us private investigators all that money and glory. Because we're tough as nails, true as steel – and about as intelligent as over-cooked turnips. I told the driver to stop at the corner of Foothill and Cactus Blossom, above the cul-de-sac, where I had a good view of the house. Before I paid him, I made sure that there weren't any suspicious-looking vehicles parked nearby. Then I sent him on his way and walked down the hill towards the Olds in Haskell's driveway.

Maybe I was getting sloppy in my old age. Maybe fatigue had eroded what few brains I had left. Or maybe I was just thinking too hard about not getting caught by the cops. I got into the Olds and turned the key before I remembered anything about spark wires and gas tanks.

Nothing happened. Haskell's enemies hadn't come back to check on their handiwork. I tried not to tremble or throw up while I cranked the engine. Then, devoutly careful, I backed out of the driveway and drove up out of Cactus Blossom Court.

So far, so good. I was awake, anyway, my heart stewing in useless adrenaline. And the cops hadn't caught me yet. It occurred to me that I'd gone a little crazy around the edges, but there didn't seem to be anything I could do about it.

What I really wanted to do was go back to Granny Good's and throw myself on Ginny's mercy. Dependency cut both ways. I was fundamentally lost without her. But I hung on to the wheel with a kind of religious fervour and worked the Olds down through the Heights.

When I reached the beltway, I had the wind behind me. My pulse slowed down a bit, and I began to feel better. About as stable as a bottle of gin, maybe, but less like I was about to collapse. A few flakes of snow paced me along the highway, but most of them stayed in the clouds, considering the possibilities. A cop passed me without slowing down.

I was headed for the South Valley, where the people the tourists aren't supposed to see live.

Funny how these things happen, the kind of funny that makes you question the future of human civilization. In all the history of Puerta del Sol, there was probably never a time when anyone sat down and actually decided, We're going to put all the really poor people *here* – all the dirt farmers who've lost their land, all the wetbacks who never found work, all the hippies who gooned out on drugs in the 60s and never recovered, all the Indians who left their reservations and then started drinking too much – every ruined, degraded or helpless sod in the city *here*, and then we'll build the rest of the city so that no one ever has to go where these people live. But that's the way it turned out. Pure social instinct put Puerta del Sol's *barrio* in the South Valley and then encysted it, closed it off from everywhere else. If you live in the South Valley, the only way you can even hope to find work is if you have a car – not to mention money for gas. And if you have a car and money, you probably live somewhere else.

At least they don't have organized crime in the South Valley. They're too poor to be worth el Señor's while.

From the beltway, I found Trujillo and headed south. It was a long drive. I crossed a transitional region where every trucking company in the state had at least one warehouse, followed by an area where all the warehouses were abandoned. Then I angled on to Bosque closer to the river and began boring through layers of destitution towards the hard core of the *barrio*.

At one time a lot of cottonwood, juniper, and Russian olive grew that close to the river, before the trees were cut down for firewood by people who couldn't pay their gas bills. The stumps remained, however, giving the city an excuse not to invest in sidewalks. The houses were built of cinder blocks or mud bricks – in which case only the exterior plaster kept them from washing away when it rained. At any other time of year, the bare dirt around them would have sprouted despondent little crops of tumbleweed, chamisa, and goathead. But winter and wind made the ground look like it'd been scoured down to hard clay.

The number Canthorpe gave me must've been more prosperous once, maybe fifty years ago. The house had at least three or four rooms, judging by its size, plus a pitched roof covered with actual tin instead of tarpaper shingles. The remains of a screened front porch stood along the front. But that degree of gentility hadn't meant anything for decades. The wood of the porch frame was so far gone that only its own rot and termites held it together. The door hung abjectly from its one surviving hinge, and the screen looked like it had been used for target practice by half the shotguns in Puerta del Sol.

Gail Harmon had come a long way down.

I parked the Olds in the dirt beside the road. Got out. Made sure all the doors were locked. The cold cut into me again. Surreptitiously, in

299

case I was being watched, I checked the .45. It was a pretty good bet I was being watched by someone. People who survive in *barrios* are good at looking out for trouble.

Trying to look harmless, I went up to the house. The boards of the steps and porch held my weight more out of habit than conviction. As I shifted the hanging screen door out of my way and crossed to the inner door, I made the whole front of the house shiver. It was as good as a burglar alarm.

Before I could knock on the cracked panels of the door, a man's voice from inside barked, 'Go away, *cojones*. I gave at the office.'

I could tell by the way he said it that he wasn't Mexican or Chicano.

Well, Canthorpe had warned me, even if he hadn't known what he was warning me about. Since I was being given the tough-guy approach, I took the same line myself. 'Good for you,' I said. 'Too bad that's not why I'm here. I want to see Gail Harmon.'

I heard a rustling noise from the other side of the door. People changing positions. 'Go away,' the voice repeated. Tough and getting angry. 'I don't know no Gail Harmon.'

Maybe he didn't. But two could play that game. 'Neither do I. What difference does that make? I want to talk to her.'

'You don't hear so good, asshole. I said go away. I won't tell you again.'

'Oh, come off it.' Ignoring the way the wood sagged, I leaned my shoulder on the frame of the door. 'If I go away, you'll never find out what I want to talk to her about.'

Another rustle. I figured there were at least two people on the other side of the door. The man thought about it for a minute. Then he said, 'Tell me from there.' His voice was raw with the kind of stress you sometimes hear from burnt-out cops.

I decided to chance it. Nobody ever accused me of having too much sense for my own good. A bit more softly, I replied, 'Reg Haskell.'

That got a reaction. A woman's voice started to say something. Then a pair of heavy boots thudded down on the floorboards, and the woman yelped. I heard a particular clicking sound.

'Open it slow,' the man said, 'or I'll blow you in half.' For some reason, he sounded happy.

Blow me in half, I thought. Oh, good. What fun. I'd heard that clicking sound before. In spite of the cold, my palms ran with sweat.

Nevertheless I didn't hesitate. I didn't like the idea of what was happening to the woman in there. The knob rattled loosely in my hand as I unlatched the door and eased it open.

300

It let me into a living room about the size of your average gaol cell. Tattered curtains stiff with grime covered the windows. The gas heater was working too hard, and the whole place stank like a witch doctor's brew – cigarettes and dope, spilled beer, sweat, urine, and despair. There was only one chair. The rest of the furniture consisted of pillows on the floor. Between the pillows, the boards were littered with cigarette butts, beer cans, and magazines – *Guns & Ammo*, *Argosy*, *Soldier of Fortune*.

A man sat in the chair facing me. He was as thin as a bayonet, about as tall as I am. He wore combat boots, jeans, and a black T-shirt. One sleeve of the shirt was rolled up to hold a pack of cigarettes. A cigarette hung from his thin mouth, the smoke curling into his eyes. His skin resembled stained parchment, and both his arms were blue with tattoos – a naked woman on one bicep, a dragon curving down his left forearm, a rifle lovingly etched on his right. His face looked flat and heartless and a little crazy.

With his right hand, he held an M-16 pointed at my belly, its bolt cocked and ready. His left was clenched in the hair of a young woman, gripping her so that she whimpered on her knees beside him.

'Haskell?' he said. 'Haskell? I knew Reg. I never knew Haskell. This I'm gonna love.'

The muzzle of the M-16 left my stomach in knots. But I still didn't like the way he treated the woman. Carefully I closed the door. Then I faced the woman. 'Ms Harmon? My name is Axbrewder. I'd like to talk to you about Reg Haskell.'

She couldn't react. '*Cojones!*' the man spat. He sounded more than a little disappointed. 'You're not Haskell? Fuck it.'

'If you want,' I told her quietly, 'I'll make him let go.'

'Please, Mase,' she whimpered. 'Please.'

His eyes narrowed as he raised the rifle and pointed it at my head. He looked like a snake.

I didn't make any threatening moves. 'That dragon,' I said, nodding towards his left forearm. 'Cambodia, right? Special Forces?' My brother used to talk about things like that. 'You must've earned it the hard way.'

He was at least as dangerous as a stirred-up rattler, but he wasn't any smarter than I was. Surprised by my recognition, he loosened his grip on the rifle. 'You know about that?'

'Sure.'

Still nodding, I kicked the rifle out of his hands. Instinctively he let the woman go. Before he could get his legs under him, I heaved him out of the chair by the front of his shirt, jerked him into the air, and slammed him to the floor with a jolt that rattled his bones.

Clamping one foot on the back of his neck, I pushed his face against the floorboards. For a second he struggled. Then he stopped. He must've felt how easily I could break his neck. He started frothing obscenities, but I put more weight on him until he stopped that, too.

While I was bending over him, I took a quick glance at the subscription labels on the magazines. They were all addressed to Mase Novick.

So he was a mercenary. Or had been recently. He didn't live here because he was poor. Instead he was professionally paranoid. He felt safer in the *barrio*, where people like cops, ATF cowboys, and the FBI weren't likely to come looking for him. And if he happened to shoot one of his neighbours by accident, no one would know the difference.

He was exactly the kind of man you'd hire to kill someone if you didn't have el Señor's resources.

With Novick pinned to the floor, I got my first good look at Gail Harmon. At the bank, they'd called her Frail Gail, and she looked like that more than ever now. She wore a ragged old flannel shirt with only one button to keep it closed over her breasts, jeans that probably fit her before she lost too much weight, no shoes. If she'd washed her hair any time in the past month, it didn't show. Her face was covered with freckles that would've looked perky and fresh if she'd been healthy. Behind them, however, her skin was the colour of stale dough, and the life in her eyes was being erased by dope, beer, and exhaustion.

She didn't seem to be aware that I was hurting her boyfriend. Still on her knees, she gave me a white stare and asked in a voice like a little girl's, 'Do you know Reg? Have you seen him? Does he want me back?'

She made my insides hurt worse than the M-16. I didn't need a doctor to tell me that I was out of my depth. I knew it as soon as I got a good look at her eyes and heard her voice. Inside her skull, she was already a wasteland. Before long the rest of her would end up the same way.

All of a sudden, I wanted Ginny, wanted her so badly that it closed my throat. I couldn't say anything.

When I didn't answer, Gail got to her feet. 'You said you wanted to talk about Reg. I heard you.' She was starting to sound wild. 'You said his name.'

Out of my depth, and close to drowning. Her desire to hear me say something about Haskell made her breathe harder and harder. Her eyes didn't focus anywhere. I thought she might try to hit me. To stop her, I pulled out the .45. Then I took my foot off Novick's neck.

Quickly he rolled into fighting position. But I had him covered. Directing him with the barrel of the .45, I moved him to his chair and made him sit down. Then I picked up the M-16, cleared it, and leaned it in the corner. He watched every move, his eyes blank with hate, but he didn't try to jump me.

Finally I forced the muscles of my throat to unclamp. 'Novick,' I said, and didn't care how my voice shook, 'what the hell's going on here?'

He didn't answer. He didn't move. He just fixed his hate on me and waited.

I had trouble swallowing a shout. 'Whatever it is, she doesn't know anything about it. She probably doesn't know her own name half the time. You're the one who knows. You may be strung out with drugs and paranoia, but you haven't lost your mind yet.' For a second I almost lost control. 'What the fucking hell is going on?'

A bit of a smile touched his thin lips. He liked seeing me upset. But he didn't say anything.

Gail went to him, put her hands on his shoulders. 'Mase,' she whispered softly, pleading with him, 'he said he wanted to talk to me about Reg. I heard him.' Her fingers stroked the side of his neck, the back of his head. 'Make him talk to me about Reg.'

Because I didn't have any better ideas, I said the simplest and most direct thing I could think of. 'Novick, she needs help. She needs help bad.'

At that, something I wasn't expecting came into his face. Something like a snarl of rage – or a twist of grief. 'You think I don't know that, asshole? You think I look at her and don't know that?'

'Then do something about it, for God's sake! Take her back to her parents. Take her to a doctor. Something. She isn't going to last much longer.'

'"Do something."' He laughed softly, like a splash of acid. 'You big fucker. You think you understand. You understand nothing. That Reg bastard fucker kicks her out. I take her in. I take care of her. Whatever I got, we share. What do I get? She lets me do what I want.'

Abruptly he reached into her shirt, squeezed one of her breasts. Then he knotted his hand in her hair again and pulled her down to her knees beside him. He had a virtuoso range of endearments, but she didn't react to either of them. She just kept watching me, waiting for me to say what she wanted to hear.

'But she don't want me,' Novick rasped. 'She wants Reg. She thinks Reg, sleeps Reg, smokes Reg. You think I like that?'

Without warning, he pushed her away so hard that she sprawled into the magazines and pillows. '"Do something." I'll fucking *do* something. She don't need no parents. And no doctor, either. I'll give her what she needs. I'll give her Reg Haskell's balls on a stick.'

On some important level, Gail wasn't aware of what he said, or even of what he did. She climbed out of the pillows and got to her feet, hardly strong enough to keep her balance. Her face was pale and venomous.

'You said you wanted to talk to me about Reg.' In her frail way, she hated me worse than Mase Novick did. 'You lied. You don't know him at all. If you knew him, you would have told me he wants me back.' Then she turned to Novick. 'Make him go away, Mase. I don't like him.'

He grinned at me. He didn't have all his teeth.

By then a Mongoloid idiot could've told you I'd botched the whole thing. I'd come all this way, and all I'd learned was that Gail Harmon didn't have any of her oars in the water, and Novick liked his work. If I didn't start doing better soon, I'd have to laugh myself out of Puerta del Sol. So I did something a little crazy. I said, 'Gail, someone's trying to kill Reg. I came here to find out who it is.'

At least I wasn't alone. No expression marked her face as she bent down and picked up one of the pillows. She didn't look at me, didn't see me. I had no warning when she flung the pillow at my head with all her little strength.

Faster than I thought she could move, she snatched up a beer can and threw it. Another pillow. A magazine.

While I was fending that stuff away from my face, Novick came out of his chair at me like the slam of a piston.

Surprise had rocked me back on my heels. I couldn't pull all my muscle together. But I managed to get my arm around in time. Swinging hard, I clubbed him across the shoulder, deflected him past me.

Towards the corner where I'd propped his M-16.

As he grabbed his rifle, I pivoted after him and raised the .45 so it would be the first thing he saw when he turned.

And Gail jumped on to my back. Reaching for my head, she clawed her fingernails at my eyes.

For a temporarily sober drunk, my reflexes were still pretty good.

Better than good when I didn't have time to second-guess myself. Just in time, I squeezed my eyes shut.

Her nails raked my eyebrows and cheeks. Novick brought the rifle into line on my chest and grabbed for the bolt. I opened my eyes again.

Somehow my right hand still aimed the .45 into Novick's face. With my left, I caught Gail's wrist and swung her around me, pitching her against him and the rifle.

That saved me. Before he could recover, I racked the slide of the .45 and shouted, 'Don't even think it!'

He froze. Force of habit, probably. Good mercenaries have to know when to take orders. And how to stay alive.

I felt blood on my face, but I ignored it. 'You're both insane,' I panted, out of breath more from fear than exertion. 'You're too sick to live. You should be put out of your misery.'

Saying that made me feel better. But it didn't get me out of there in one piece. They both watched me like cornered rats, waiting for their chance.

I had two choices. Drag them out of the house with me, keep them covered while I got to the Olds. Or gamble. Choosing self-respect over caution, I decided to gamble.

'Well, today you're lucky.' A drop of blood ran into my left eye, smeared my vision. I blinked it away. 'I'm not going to shoot you.' Lowering the .45, I cleared it and put it away. 'If you stop and think about it, you don't have any reason to shoot me, either.'

Which probably wasn't true, but I trusted it anyway. I gave Novick one last chance. 'Get her some help.' Then I pulled the door open and let myself on to the porch, out of the over-cooked heat into the cold.

The blood felt like sweat on my face. Closing the door behind me, I crossed the splintered porch to the bare dirt of the front yard and strode towards the Olds without looking back. I moved briskly, but I didn't run.

Which wasn't as stupid as it sounds. I'd be able to hear the door if they opened it.

They didn't. I reached the Olds, got in. For once, the engine started as soon as I touched the key. I drove a few blocks further down Bosque before I stopped to see what I could do about the state of my face.

The rear-view mirror didn't raise my opinion of myself much. Seven or eight bright weals oozing blood started in the middle of my forehead and ran down across my eyes into my cheeks. They were beginning to feel like fire. And they made my face look ghoulish, like some kind of death mask. My eyes stared wildly out at the world through streaks of pain.

I dabbed up most of the blood with a handkerchief, but I couldn't wash my wounds without soap and water. And washing them wasn't going to improve my appearance any.

Reaction set in. I felt nauseous with disgust. My hands shook, and my clothes smelled like a sweat locker. If there was any way to screw up my encounter with Gail Harmon and Mase Novick worse than I did, I couldn't think of it.

On the other hand – looking on the bright side – I wasn't sleepy any more.

Since I didn't have any better ideas, I decided to risk going back to Ginny's apartment. If the cops were there, I was shit out of luck. But if they weren't, I could shower, shave, put on some clean clothes. Pack the suitcase Ginny wanted. Take care of my face. My other priorities could wait that long.

It was a nice plan, but I was interrupted. Before I put the Olds in gear, I readjusted the rear-view mirror – and saw a tan-and-white Puerta del Sol Department of Police unit cruising down Bosque towards me.

Terrific. Just what I needed. You don't see cops in the South Valley very often. Keeping my fingers crossed, I sat where I was and waited for the car to troll on past.

It didn't. Instead it pulled to a stop in front of me, blocking the Olds. Then another car, a baby blue Dodge with a powerful exhaust and anonymous city plates, came up and parked on my rear.

Now I wasn't going anywhere without permission.

Two street cops emerged from the unit. They had their riot sticks out and ready. They came around to my door and planted themselves there, standing well back so that I couldn't surprise them. I thought I recognized one of them, but I wasn't sure. Maybe I knew him back in the days when my brother was a cop. There was something familiar and not very kindly about the way he said, 'Get out of the car, Axbrewder.'

They'd been looking for me.

At the moment, I had no idea how they'd found me.

I wanted to know. But there was something else I wanted to know a hell of a lot more.

'What's wrong, officer?' I asked, doing my best to pretend that I wasn't scratched up like a punk rocker.

Good as twins, both cops tapped their palms with their sticks. 'I said,' the familiar one repeated, 'get out of the car.'

Before I could stop myself, I replied, 'As long as we're here, do you mind if I get out of the car? I don't mean to scare you. I just want to stretch my legs.'

They swore at me with varying degrees of subtlety while I opened the door of the Olds.

Right away, they let me know I wasn't under arrest. Probably that decision hadn't been made yet. Instead of reading me my rights, or making me assume the position, or even taking away the .45, one of them jabbed me with his stick before I had both legs under me, hit me hard enough to rock me back against the side of the car. Just making sure he had me under control.

I gave them a smile that would've curdled milk, but they ignored it.

Once I was safely pinned to the side of the Olds, two more of Puerta del Sol's finest got out of the Dodge. Plainclothes detectives. One of them was a small individual with the secret harried look of a man whose wife didn't like his line of work. The other was Captain Philip Cason.

Which told me right away what I wanted to know. The story I had planned – the one Haskell suggested – wasn't going to wash.

I didn't have to connect the dots. Cason was investigating the death of Roscoe Chavez. He had an interest in Pablo's disappearance. So why would he care who blew up a car I rented? Only one reason. The cops on the scene must've tracked down Haskell's cab. And the driver must've told them what Haskell and I talked about. When el Señor's name came up, those cops just naturally passed the investigation over to Cason.

None of which explained why I wasn't being arrested. But it was a start. At least I had that much to go on when I began lying.

As he sauntered towards me, Cason grinned like the blade of a can opener. He was a fleshy man who didn't mind carrying a little fat because he already knew his own strength. He had hands like shovels, burying hands, and eyes the colour of blindness. A dapper hat perched on the back of his head, and his suit and coat looked so expensive you couldn't wrinkle them with a steamroller.

Like the street cops, he kept a safe distance. Still grinning, he scanned my damaged face. Then he said, 'Well, well.' His voice had a hoarse rasp that came from too much interrogation. 'Fistoulari do that to you? She must be one hot fuck.'

To restrain myself, I folded my arms over my chest. 'Captain Cason,'

I replied conversationally. 'Charming as ever, I see. If you weren't carrying a badge, I'd take your face off.'

He must've wanted something from me. Instead of coming down hard, he concentrated on his homicidal smile.

'I'm curious,' he remarked. 'What brings you way down here? You were always a bum, but this is low even for you.'

Not to be outdone, I countered, 'I'm curious, too. How did you find me "way down here"? I thought this part of the city scared you cops.' If I was lucky, the cold made me look like I was hugging myself to keep warm.

He didn't like my attitude. His grin faded. To compensate, he made his voice tougher. 'You figure it out, smartass.'

'All right.' Under the circumstances, an educated guess wasn't hard. 'An unmarked car watched the entrance to Cactus Blossom from Foothill. When I drove out, I was followed. Nothing obvious. All you wanted was my general direction. You told your people to report where I was headed and then leave me alone.' Even in my condition, I would've noticed a close tail. 'You didn't care where I went. You just wanted to be able to close in when you were ready.

'What I don't know is why you're wasting all this time and manpower on a two-bit case like me.'

The look of blindness in his eyes made Cason hard to read. But the way he dismissed my explanation was downright reassuring.

'One thing at a time,' he growled. 'You haven't told me what you're doing here.'

On that basis, I was reasonably sure that he hadn't already staked out Gail Harmon and Mase Novick. Novick was the sort of man who'd notice being staked out – even if he wasn't. Cason wasn't that far ahead of me.

I was tempted to retort, You figure it out. But that might make him too mad to let me go. Instead I tried to see how many lies he would swallow.

Trying to look embarrassed, I mumbled, 'Ginny and I haven't been getting along. I came to see a former girlfriend.' I made a brusque gesture towards my face. 'She wasn't amused.'

One of the street cops gave a short laugh like a pistol shot. Cason's partner studied the scuffed tops of his shoes. But I didn't care what they thought. I waited for Cason's reaction.

The idea that I came to the South Valley looking for love restored his smile. 'You always did like Mex chippies,' he rasped happily.

He was such a nice man. Nevertheless I knotted the muscles of my arms and didn't take him up on it. 'Cason,' I said, 'I don't have a coat, and I'm freezing.' Injured-pride Axbrewder. 'How much longer do you want me to stand here?'

He raised one fist, glanced with approval at the scars on his knuckles. 'Long enough to tell me why you've been on the run ever since that Buick you rented blew up in the Jousters parking lot.'

If I'd stopped to think, I wouldn't have known what to say. Did he want me to admit knowing too much about things that were none of my business? Or was he just shooting blind? But I was already in a counter-punching mood, so I kept going.

'What do you care? Did some hot-wired stoolie tell you I've got something to do with Roscoe Chavez, or are you just getting paranoid in your old age?'

His grin disappeared again. Easy come, easy go. In some states, his glare would've been classified as police brutality. 'You're cute, Axbrewder,' he chewed out. 'I didn't know what to do about you. I thought I ought to give you the benefit of the doubt. But to hell with that. I'm going to take you in for obstructing an investigation, concealing information.'

Any con will tell you that a good lie is its own reward. I snorted a laugh. 'Too bad it won't stick. I haven't concealed any information. I've already made a statement.'

His whole body seemed to swell inside his clothes. He looked like he'd invented apoplexy all by himself. 'The hell you have, you sonofabitch. I didn't hear anything about it.'

'Why, Captain,' I said maliciously, 'didn't you get a copy of the report? I guess I'm not the only one in Puerta del Sol who doesn't trust you.'

He started towards me. His fists looked hard enough to powder bricks. Then the implications of what I'd said got through to him, and he froze. Good lies are like that. His expression became as flat as his eyes. 'That's bullshit. Who took the report?'

I didn't even blink. 'Lieutenant Acton.' Acton didn't like me much. Unlike Sergeant Encino, however, he really did owe me a favour. 'I talked to him because he's an honest cop.' With a smile of my own, I added, 'Why do you suppose he didn't pass it on?' Then I finished softly, 'Talk to him, Cason. Check it out.' With any luck at all, he wouldn't believe the truth when he heard it. 'You'll be surprised by what's going on behind your back.'

To be perfectly honest, I didn't know why he swallowed that one. I didn't know why it struck such a spark when I tossed out Chavez' name. I was just glad it worked.

'Axbrewder,' he snarled, jabbing a heavy forefinger in the direction of my face, 'you're on a tightrope this time. Any minute now, you're going to lose your balance. When you do, I'm going to make damn sure there's no net.'

Abruptly he turned and stomped back to the Dodge. After a moment the small detective with the scuffed shoes followed glumly.

When they were both in the car, the small man said something. Cason started yelling, but I couldn't make out the words.

I felt like I'd turned blue in the cold, so I didn't stand on ceremony. I climbed back into the Olds and fired up the engine to get the heater working.

The Dodge pulled out, spewing dust along the wind. Trying not to look mystified, the street cops sauntered back to their unit. They took their time, but after a couple of minutes they drove off, leaving me to do whatever I wanted.

At first, I didn't do anything. I sat and shivered while the car tried to warm up. Cason hadn't told me why he was interested in me. I thought I knew the answer to that.

But I still had no idea why I hadn't been arrested.

Chapter Thirteen

For that matter, I had no idea why Haskell hadn't been arrested. Cason had even more reason to chase around after him.

The combination of Novick and Harmon and Cason and no sleep had me more strung out than I realized. A few minutes passed, and I was driving out of the South Valley on Bosque, and the heater was finally starting to do some good, when I finally realized that I didn't know whether Haskell had been arrested or not.

If Cason went to all that trouble to find out what I was doing, he must've already had men working on Haskell.

For a while I was so astonished by my own stupidity that I didn't even swear about it. Then I leaned on the gas and made the Olds rattle for acceleration as if there were something to be gained by setting a record on my way back to the bank. As if I could do any good when I got there.

By the time I got off Bosque on to Trujillo, however, I was thinking a little better. With an effort of will, I made the car and my heart slow down. Respecting the speed limits – and the haphazard way people drive in the South Valley – I headed up Trujillo and started hunting for a phone booth.

At first I couldn't find one. What with vandalism and other forms of human frustration, the phone company doesn't consider leaving its equipment in the South Valley cost-effective. But a mile or two past the abandoned warehouses, I spotted what I needed – a seedy-looking Muchoburger joint with a pay phone.

I parked the Olds, went inside, and changed a dollar bill. Then I looked up the number for the First Puerta del Sol National ice-cream parlour and dialled it. When the bank came on the line, I recognized

Eunice Wint, so I pitched my voice up a couple of notches and asked her in Spanish if I could speak to Señor Haskell.

She didn't speak Spanish, but she caught the name. 'Mr Haskell? Do you wish to speak to Mr Haskell?'

'Si, Señorita.'

'Just a moment, please.'

I heard the clicking while she connected me. Then Haskell's phone rang.

He picked it up right away. Since I didn't say anything, he asked if he could help me, who was I, what the hell was going on. When I was dead sure it was him, I hung up.

So he hadn't been arrested either. Not yet, anyway. Probably for the same reason that Cason had left me running around loose – whatever that was.

Relief left me exhausted all of a sudden. And the smell of greasy hamburgers made me look at my watch. It was already a little after noon. You could lose your whole life just driving in and out of the South Valley. I still had things to do, but in my condition food was probably the better part of valour. I bought a couple of hamburgers and about a quart of strong coffee. Then I sat down and tried to pull myself together while I ate.

Why hadn't Cason hauled Haskell if not me in to find out what the hell we thought we were doing? All that coffee and any amount of heartburn later, I still had no idea.

Since I wasn't making any progress, I gave up on it. I didn't have to pick up our client until 4.30 – which meant that I had four entire hours, minus driving time, to get some sleep. Or to work on what had happened to Pablo Santiago.

After stuffing my trash in a can that hadn't been emptied for a while, I went back to the phone.

For a second my brain refused to cooperate. Then I kicked it, and it coughed up Raul Encino's home phone number.

It rang a dozen times or so with no answer. That didn't cheer me up, but I hung on. After all, what do night-shift cops do during the day? They sleep, that's what. And maybe his family – if he had one – was out. In school, grocery shopping, something. I let the phone ring.

Finally the line opened. A fatigue-numb voice said, 'Encino.'

'Axbrewder.' For some reason I wasn't relieved. I was scared. Those hamburgers felt like buckshot in my stomach. 'Sorry about this. Tell me about Pablo Santiago's autopsy, and I'll get out of your life.'

'Axbrewder.' I heard the distinct thunk of the receiver landing on a hard surface.

The phone didn't pick up any breathing, or even any movement. When he came back, he didn't sound asleep any more. He sounded like he had a gun in one hand and a riot stick in the other.

'Axbrewder?'

'I'm still here.'

'Are you sure you wish to stick your nose in this?' The stiffness of his English contrasted ominously with his fluid Spanish. 'For an Anglo, you have some decency. Consider what will happen if you hinder Captain Cason's investigation. Anything you do will make enemies. To find the killer of a man like Roscoe Chavez – even a bad cop will jump for the chance. Consider what will happen if they find I leaked this autopsy to you.'

I understood him, and it made tiredness swim around in my head. Oh damn it all. His poor parents. They could probably stand it if he was just dead.

'In other words,' I said from some distance away, 'he was killed. It wasn't an accident. He was killed, and it has something to do with running numbers.'

'Listen to me,' Encino said sharply. 'Cason is not a man to be laughed at or dismissed. Leave it for him.'

'No, you listen,' I retorted. Somehow I made myself sound like my mind wasn't out there flapping in the wind. 'I know Pablo's parents. They have a stake in this, and I seem to be the only one who cares. I'm just a crazy Anglo – what harm can I do? *I'll* never tell where I got my information. And if I haven't got enough sense to cover my own ass, that's not your fault. What does the autopsy say?'

There was a long silence. Then Encino sighed. 'Pablo Santiago died of a broken neck.'

I waited. When he didn't go on, I said, 'I already knew that. You told me.'

'I told you,' he replied with old-world asperity, 'he died of a broken neck, bruises, and injuries consistent with an accidental fall from a moving vehicle. That remains true. However, the ME is now sure the neck was broken before the fall. Partially crushed windpipe and other internal damage to the throat indicate strangulation.'

Now it was my turn not to say anything. Encino spelled it out for me. 'Someone killed the boy' – as if I needed it spelled out – 'and then threw him from a car to make it appear accidental.'

'Shit,' I muttered profoundly. 'Shit on everything.'

I could almost hear him shrug over the phone.

My head was going in eight directions at once. 'Has anyone told the family yet?'

'Would I be informed?' In his own way, he was about as pleased as I was. 'This case is not mine.'

'All right,' I said. 'All right.' I needed to get off the phone. 'Thanks. I owe you. Remember that.'

'Go away,' he replied. 'I consider it even.'

I didn't thank him again. I just hung up.

My reaction probably would've been pretty entertaining to watch. There's this huge clown with raked eyes in a Muchoburger joint, of all places. First he puts the receiver back in its cradle like it was a snake that just bit him. Then he goes outside, flapping his arms wildly at the doors and the cold. He kicks one of the tyres of his car as hard as he can, damn near breaks a bone in his foot, and almost falls down. Finally he fumbles the door open, stumbles into the seat, and tries to tear the steering wheel apart. What fun. I couldn't have been happier if I'd fallen into a cement mixer.

I didn't just want a drink, I wanted Ever-Clear. The closest thing I could get to intravenous alcohol. What had happened to Pablo made me sick enough. But what really made me rage was that the cops had found his body more than two days ago – and still hadn't bothered to tell the family.

Steaming like a beaker of acid, I pointed the Olds in the direction of the old part of town.

There was still a lot of lunch-time traffic – and no good roads between me and where I was headed. But after I did a few stupid things and nearly got hit once, I managed to recapture some of my grasp on reality. After all, I was in over my head – and I was used to taking orders – and I didn't have Ginny with me. On top of which, I was slaphappy from lack of sleep. Being reminded of all that helped me realize I had to be more careful. By the time I reached the narrow streets of the old part of town, I was at least a loose approximation of a responsible citizen.

When I pulled the Olds to a stop in front of the Santiagos' *tiendita*, I saw right away that it was closed.

Closed. On Tuesday. At 1.20 in the afternoon. While I stared at the door, an old woman with a basket on one arm rattled the knob with a kind of forlorn desperation, then wandered away muttering toothlessly to herself.

By then, I'd felt sick for so long that it was becoming metaphysical.

314

Trying not to hunch over, I got out of the Olds and walked into the alley that led to the back of the building.

A small flurry went past me, but the clouds still held on to most of the snow. The wind felt like it left my clothes in ribbons. Fortunately I didn't have far to go.

Behind the store, beside the small delivery dock, a weathered old stair led up to the apartment where the Santiagos lived. It didn't look like it could carry my weight, but I trusted it anyway. I thumped my way up the treads and knocked on the door as soon as I reached the landing.

For a while, there was no answer. Then Rudolfo Santiago unlocked the door, opened it a crack, and peered out at me. When he saw who I was, he closed the door again.

Faintly through the wood, I heard him call to his wife, 'Señor Axbrewder comes to speak to us concerning our Pablo.'

After that he pulled the door open all the way. 'Señor Axbrewder.' His sad eyes flicked to my face, then settled on the middle of my chest, too polite to stare at or react to the way my mug had been redecorated. 'Enter. Enter.'

'*Gracias.*' As I went in, I added in Spanish, 'Such cold chills my heart.'

Señora Santiago was there to greet me. While her husband closed the door, she gave me a frank anxious scrutiny before she remembered her manners and lowered her gaze. 'Señor Axbrewder,' she said, 'be welcome. Come to the fire. Will you drink coffee with us?'

Even in her home, she wore an apron knotted around her waist. But that fitted – she was a woman who worked. The small living room showed the effects of attention and love instead of money. It was spotlessly clean. There were no rugs on the floor, but the boards had been cleaned and waxed so often they'd acquired an antique glow. She'd even dusted the vigas holding up the latia-and-plaster ceiling.

A massive frame couch and a similar chair piled with old pillows instead of upholstery filled the space in front of the beehive fireplace in one corner. I could smell piñon from the fire. A few *santos* presided over the room from niches cut into the adobe walls. The ceiling was uncomfortably low for me, but still the whole place tugged at my heart. It felt like a home.

As cold as I was, I couldn't resist the fire. But that was all the hospitality I could stomach. 'My thanks, Señora,' I said. I didn't like the way my voice sounded in that room. 'Please pardon my rudeness. I have not come for courtesy.'

The weight of what they wanted to know oppressed the air. But they were too polite – and too reserved – to say it out loud. Instead Santiago seconded his wife. 'A little coffee, surely? To ease the cold?' At the same time, with a gesture that betrayed his tension, he offered me a cigarette.

I shook my head. 'Again my thanks. I have no claim upon your kindness.'

Señora Santiago knew what to say to that. 'A man who has served us so well in the past, and who now wishes to aid us in our sorrow, he has no claim? What we have is yours. Some coffee at least you must have.'

She started out of the room, bustling in a way that suggested she'd already cooked six meals and cleaned the apartment twice today. Holding back grief by keeping herself busy.

Her husband stopped her. 'My wife, Señor Axbrewder has another matter in his heart. He wishes only to speak of that.'

Ignoring the slight tremor in his hands, he inserted a cigarette under his moustache and struck a match. Then he moved closer to the fireplace so that he could flick his ash into the hearth.

'Señor Axbrewder,' he said quietly, 'say what brings you to us.'

For a second there, in the warmth of the fire and the hominess of the room, I almost lost the handle. I wanted to say, I found someone who saw Pablo. Two days ago. Alive. On a bus. Heading south. For Mexico. He'll be all right. I should never have come here – I didn't have the right.

But lies weren't an option here. Pablo's parents had already closed the store. They weren't going to believe any phony consolations.

'Señor,' I asked, 'Señora, why do you not work in your store today?'

Her face twisted. Abruptly he threw his cigarette into the fire. At first I thought they weren't going to answer. Then I saw that he was waiting to regain his self-control.

In a voice as flat as a board, he said, 'That one who is named el Señor considers it unseemly that we labour in our store when our son has died. Has he not spoken to us of Pablo's death? At his word, we must grieve. Tomorrow a funeral will be held, though we know nothing of our son's end. For this' – traces of bitterness spilled past his restraint – 'el Señor pays from his own pocket.'

I suppose I should've expected that. I already knew that el Señor knew why Pablo was killed. And he ruled the old part of town like a private fiefdom. When he told his people that their sons were dead, he expected them to by God *grieve*. He could even afford to be magnanimous about it. After all, he wouldn't notice the cost of the vigil and the prayers, the funeral and the candles. I probably could've afforded them myself.

But it still hurt. The arrogance of that bastard made me want to go back to kicking tyres. I couldn't hold down my bitterness anywhere near as well as Santiago did.

'In this,' I said, hating myself and everything I had to say, 'he speaks truth. Pardon me that I must bring such news to you. I have learned that the *chotas* have found the body of Pablo. A broken neck caused his death. They seek the one who did this evil, but they do not find him.'

Me they believed. I had that one advantage over el Señor. Until I spoke, some kind of hope had kept them going. I took it away.

For a moment Tatiana Santiago's eyes went wide as if she were having a stroke. Then she cried out sharply, 'Ayyy!' and snatched up her apron to cover her face. Her whole body clenched, and she didn't seem to be breathing any more.

Her husband closed his eyes. Slowly he sank down to sit on the hearth. Neither of them moved.

It felt like my doing. But I wasn't done. I had something else to say.

'Your pardon.' How could I stop apologizing to them? The effort to contain what she felt left her rigid. He couldn't seem to bear to open his eyes on the world. 'I must speak of this. I beg of you that you do not go to the *chotas* and demand the return of your son's body.'

At that, she whipped down her apron. Her face was livid – it seemed to hold about three hundred years of outrage. '*Not*? You say that we must *not*? He is my son. My son! His neck has been broken, and the *chotas* hold him from us, and they say nothing to us, having no decency and no heart and no honour, and you suggest that we must not demand his return? Have you become such as they are? Have you resumed drinking?'

'My wife,' her husband said softly. 'My wife.'

But she couldn't stop. 'It is my right! To hold the son of my body in my arms and to mourn him as he should be mourned, *it is my right*! Of what use is his death, if he is not mourned?'

'Señora, hear me.' It hurt to defend what the cops were doing, but I owed that to Encino. And to the Santiagos. They would get into terrible trouble if they did anything rash. 'For what they do, the *chotas* have reason. They wish to conceal from Pablo's killer that his crime is known. Considering himself safe, he will be careless, and more easily snared. This they believe. Therefore they have withheld your son from you.

'You must permit them to work as they will.'

I didn't say the rest. I didn't tell her that el Señor might have another reason for insisting on a funeral. It might be a deliberate effort to sabotage the cops. To clear the field for himself. All I wanted was to persuade the Santiagos to be passive, so that they wouldn't stick their heads on the block by defying either el Señor or Cason.

But Señora Santiago wasn't interested. 'A great and worthy purpose,' she shot back. The force of her outrage made me feel crude and ugly. 'For this a mother and father are denied their grief? For a secret which is known even to you?'

'Señora.' In simple self-defence, I put some bite into my voice. 'He who revealed this secret to me will suffer greatly if what he has done becomes known to *Capitan* Cason.'

She stopped. She didn't acknowledge my point or make any promises, but she didn't aim any more of her pain at me. For a minute I feared that her face would fall apart. Somehow she held it together in front of me. After all, I was little better than a stranger. Dignity counts for something.

She turned to her husband. In a thin strained voice, she asked him to invite me to Pablo's vigil. Then, slowly, as if she knew how fragile she'd become, she left the room.

He didn't respond. His eyes were squeezed tight, but the rest of his body sagged, slack and useless. Moving like they had minds of their own, his hands took out his cigarettes, stuck one between his lips. He didn't light it.

I wanted to apologize again, but there wasn't much point. I gave him a moment to say anything he might want me to hear. Then, torn between rage and misery, I crossed the room towards the door.

'Señor Axbrewder.' His voice sounded like dust settling.

I paused at the door, waited for him to go on.

'When you discover the killer of my son,' he said after a while, 'I wish to assist you.'

Wondering what he had in mind, I said as gently as I could, 'Leave the *chotas* to their work, Señor Santiago.'

'I spit on the *chotas*,' he replied without inflection, without energy. 'When you discover the killer of my son, I wish to assist you.'

I couldn't promise that, so I opened the door and let myself back out into Puerta del Sol's leaden and threatening winter.

Chapter Fourteen

From the old part of town, I went back to Ginny's apartment. Funny how I still thought of it as her apartment, even though I'd been living there for six months – and taking care of it. I didn't find any cops staking out the place, so I let myself in.

Its impersonal tidiness felt safe to me, made me want to go to bed and not wake up again for about six weeks. But I fought that off. Instead I took a shower. Ran water as hot as I could stand on to my face until the marks of Gail Harmon's nails burned like stigmata and the bones of my skull felt like cracked glass. Then, trying for a little self-respect, I shaved and put on clean clothes.

After that I packed a suitcase for Ginny and me. Since I wasn't thinking very clearly, I had to go through it like a catechism several times before I could believe that I had everything we were likely to need for a couple of days. Her prosthetic hand I left where it was. At the time, it didn't seem like my responsibility.

By a little after 3.00, I was ready to leave. I couldn't come up with anything useful to get done in the time I had left, so I decided to go to the bank and wait for Haskell.

Left entirely to myself, my personal approach to this case wouldn't have involved trying to solve it myself. Instead I would've asked someone else for the answer. Somewhere in Puerta del Sol – if you knew where to look for him, and how to talk to him – lived some old Mestizo or Chicano drunk with a grizzled face, cirrhosis of the liver, and no experience at all with personal hygiene, who knew exactly why Pablo was killed. He also knew what Roscoe Chavez had done to get himself thrown in the river. He might even know who wanted Reg Haskell dead. And he might sell that information, if he trusted me – and if I offered him the right price.

I knew how to find men like that. And I'd spent enough time lying in my own puke with them to be trusted. Unfortunately they only came out at night.

Since I didn't seem capable of solving the case by reason or intuition, I spent the drive wondering why it wasn't snowing yet when the weather looked as angry as a high sea and the wind coming down off the mountains made the Olds rock like a rowboat. That kept me awake until I got up into the Heights and reached the ice-cream parlour.

The Continental wasn't there – which didn't exactly surprise my socks off. The fact that I had no idea what Ginny might be doing made a small worm of fear crawl across my stomach, but I figured I didn't have the right to complain. I could stand a little fear for the sake of recovering my partner.

Unfortunately when I'd parked the Olds I still had almost an hour to kill. Saying to myself that I would sit there and wait was easy. Doing it wasn't. Without quite meaning to, I slumped further and further down in the seat. Before long I was asleep.

Which was a mistake. I knew it was a mistake as soon as it happened, because I found myself standing alone in the parking lot with all the cars gone – except for my rented Buick, which was down at the far end. Without warning, I heard an explosion. When it hit, the car filled up with fire. I could see the kid inside, clawing at the door, trying to scream.

At the same time, all the lot's concrete powdered and turned into snowflakes. Snow blew into my face from all sides. I could hardly see the Buick.

When I headed towards it, someone started shooting.

I turned. I saw muzzle flashes and a dark shape behind them, but the snow hid the shooter. Whoever it was, however, wasn't shooting at me. The shots were aimed at the Buick.

Suddenly I understood. Ginny was pinned down behind the Buick. The shots were meant to trap her there until the car exploded.

I couldn't figure out why she wasn't shooting back.

I ran to help her. Now the bullets came after me, tugging through my clothes like snow. But I didn't feel them.

I ran for a while. Then I reached the Buick and dodged around behind it.

Ginny knelt there near the car. Her .357 lay on the ground beside her.

'Pick it up!' I shouted. 'Shoot back!'

She gave me a look like a lash of hate and shoved her arms in my direction. Both arms.

Her hands were gone. Both of them. Blood pumped desperately from the stumps.

'This is your fault,' she said like the snow in the air and the fire in the car. 'You did this to me.'

Then something grabbed at my shoulder, and I think I yelled.

When I got my eyes open, the snow was gone. I lay sprawled in the Olds, one hip wedged under the wheel. The door stood open, letting cold blow into my bones.

Haskell bent over me in his rich man's coat, one hand on the door, the other just leaving my shoulder. Past him, I saw people from the bank on the way to their cars. They were hurrying, hunched into their coats and scarves against the weather.

Haskell looked angry enough to start shooting himself.

Oh good, I thought. Just what I need.

'What happened to you?' he demanded. 'Is that how you do your job? You go around brawling?'

It took me a few seconds to realize that he was talking about the marks on my face.

I couldn't resist. 'Actually,' I rasped, pulling myself up in the seat, 'it was a former girlfriend of yours. Remember Gail Harmon?'

'Damn it!' he snapped back, 'I didn't hire you to dig up my life.' I knew the signs. I could tell he wasn't afraid of me. 'First you browbeat Eunice. Then you drag Gail into this. God only knows why. I've had enough. You're fired. Hear me? You and Fistoulari don't work for me any more.' That was the trouble with him – he didn't seem to be afraid of anyone.

I didn't care. I'd had all I could stand. 'Do tell,' I growled. 'What do you suppose your wife's going to say when we tell her you fired us because we found out about your girlfriends?'

Inside his coat, he became as still as a poised snake. Like the edge of a straight razor, he said, 'Don't tell me you've talked to my wife.'

Maybe he was as good at playing people as he said. His tone made me ashamed of myself. 'What are you afraid of?' I retorted angrily. 'She's bound to find out about them sooner or later. What difference does it make if we get to them first? We're still trying to save your life.'

'No, you're not.' He was so good at outraged innocence you'd think he practised in front of a mirror. 'You've been fired. Leave my wife out of this.'

The cold made the raw skin around my eyes hurt worse. Parts of my brain were still muzzy with sleep and nightmares. I didn't know how to argue with him. 'Oh, come off it,' I said intelligently. 'You can't fire me.'

'It's already done.'

'You can't,' I repeated. For some reason I didn't shout at him. 'I'm just the hired help. You can only fire Ginny.' A snarl came out of him, but I cut through it. 'Until she tells me we're fired, you can't get rid of me.'

The wind ruffled his hair, giving him an unexpected look of wildness. 'Fuck you,' he said. 'I don't need you.'

'Of course you don't.' Suddenly I wasn't angry at him any more. Anyone who could make a statement like *I don't need you* and believe it needed all the help he could get. 'But in the mean time, how are you going to get home? Ginny has your car. You're stuck with me for a while anyway. You might as well let me give you a ride.'

He chewed on that for a minute. His face was red with cold and tight with anger, but something about his stare reminded me of playing bridge. Abruptly he nodded. 'All right. I'll take it up with Fistoulari.' He walked around the hood, pulled open the passenger door, and got in. Preserving his air of righteous indignation, he didn't look at me. 'Let's go.'

With a mental shrug, I closed my door and started the engine. The Olds coughed a few times – sympathy pains for the way I felt.

Haskell sneered at the dashboard, which didn't make me or the car any more cheerful.

I made a special effort to be on my good behaviour while I drove. But I couldn't stand the silence. That nightmare repeated itself across the back of my mind, and I needed distraction. After a few blocks I said as conversationally as I could, 'Explain something. I've met your wife. I don't think I told her anything you wouldn't want her to hear. But I talked to her long enough to know how she feels about you. I don't understand why you involve yourself with all these other women.'

He cocked an eyebrow. Apparently my naivety amused him. 'Wouldn't you? Don't you want to sleep with every attractive woman you see?'

Driving carefully, I answered, 'I'm not that predatory.'

He snorted. 'You mean you're afraid of the consequences.' His tone suggested disdain for consequences of all kinds. 'Let me tell you something, Axbrewder. I love my wife. I know how loyal and trusting she is. She gives me exactly what I want in a wife. But that isn't all I want.

'I want everything.' The way he said it made it sound special rather than unreasonable, as if the sheer size of his desires were a virtue. 'All of life. I want to make love to every woman. I want to have the best of everything. I want to stretch myself right to the limit and prove I can do anything.' He watched me sidelong to see how I took it. 'Accounting doesn't provide many opportunities for that.'

'So you play bridge.'

That observation didn't raise his opinion of me. 'I told you. I don't play games. I play people.'

Trying to get even, I asked, 'What does that have to do with those investments you're having trouble with?'

His attitude curdled 'Forget it,' he retorted. 'You're off this case as soon as I talk to Fistoulari. Stop prying.'

Well, at least he still had that raw nerve. Maliciously I said, 'I'll tell you what I really don't understand. You talk a good game, but any moron can see that you wouldn't want to fire Ginny and me unless you're afraid of what we might find out. You're so determined to protect your secrets, you'd rather risk being killed.'

In reaction, he swung towards me on the seat. 'Listen, Axbrewder,' he said like the wind thumping against the side of the Olds. 'Pay attention. I'm going to say this so that even you can follow it. I'm not afraid of you. I don't have anything hidden. I just don't like what you're doing.

'I live the life I want, and I'm not going to permit two airhead detectives to mess it up. If you were actually trying to protect me, that would be fine. But you act like I'm the enemy. I can't think of one good reason why I should put up with that.

'The only thing el Señor can do to me is kill me. At the rate you're going, you're going to wreck my life. Any moron can see that I'm better off without you.'

Coming from him, that was quite a speech. I didn't care whether he meant it or not. 'Too bad,' I replied acidly. 'You're really not as smart as you think. Instead of bitching so much, you should ask what we've uncovered.' I wanted to make him ask. But I was afraid he wouldn't, so I spelled it out. 'Maybe el Señor wants you dead, maybe he doesn't. But Gail Harmon has a boyfriend who wants to kill you so bad it keeps him awake at night. And he's a Special Forces vet. He's perfectly capable of doing it.'

Haskell didn't respond. Instead he turned away in his seat, his face expressionless. But that was all I needed. While he stared out through the windshield, I couldn't restrain a smile.

By then we were on Foothill, nearing the turn down into Cactus Blossom Court. Instinctively I slowed down. Just for the exercise, I drove past Cactus Blossom to look for signs of a stake-out. Parked cars with people in them, that sort of thing. But I didn't spot any. Cason had apparently given up his interest in us. So I turned around in a driveway, went back to Cactus Blossom, and nosed the Olds over the hill.

As we started down the slope, I saw the Continental parked in Haskell's driveway.

Other cars occupied other driveways around the Court. Only one sat at the kerb, a black Cadillac the size of a hearse. It was parked facing downhill above Haskell's house and across the road.

When I looked at it more closely, I saw exhaust thick with cold wisping away from the Caddy's tailpipe – and the silhouette of a driver behind the wheel.

Fuck. Without transition, sweat filled my palms, making them slick and uncertain.

Coasting slowly down the hill, I muttered to Haskell, 'Don't get out. If anything happens, hide under the dash.'

He snapped a look at me. 'Why? What's going on?'

Maybe I was wrong. Maybe the Cadillac was just waiting for passengers. Any second now people would come out of the nearest house, and I could relax.

I didn't take the chance.

Carefully I pulled in behind the Caddy. Left the engine running. The driver looked short and wide through his rear window, and he wasn't wearing a hat, but I couldn't tell anything else about him. He may've been watching me in his mirrors – I couldn't tell that, either.

I checked the .45 for reassurance. Then I opened my door. Pretending to be a good neighbour, I intended to ask the man in the hearse if I could help him. At least see who he was.

But as soon as I stuck my head and shoulders out of the Olds, the Caddy started to roar. Tyres screaming, it burst away from the kerb, accelerating wildly down into the cul-de-sac.

Just for a second, I watched him go – not so much surprised as simply wondering whether he might plough between a couple of houses and end up in someone's back yard or maybe the arroyo. Then I saw him begin to turn.

He made the kind of squealing, fish-tailing turn you see in the movies, tyres tearing their hearts out on the pavement, and came clawing back up the hill at us.

324

What looked like the barrel of a shotgun protruded from the driver's open window.

Fortunately I was still half in the Olds. With my right hand on the wheel, I wrenched myself back into my seat.

The Caddy closed on us fast. It would pass right by me. The driver would fire at point-blank range, blow me halfway to next Saturday. I didn't even have time to close the door.

I didn't try. Jamming the gearshift into drive, I stomped down on the gas pedal.

My heart beat once while I sat there thinking that the Olds was going to stall. I couldn't see the man's face, but I could sure as hell see the shotgun.

Then the Olds moved. It sounded asthmatic and miserable, but it did its best to match the Caddy's haul-ass lunge down into the cul-de-sac. Momentum slammed my door for me.

By guess or by God, my timing was perfect. The shotgun seemed to go off right in my ear, but the blast missed me. Some shot licked the trunk of the Olds. The rest tore a huge clump of dry pampas grass in the nearest yard to shreds.

Haskell clung to his door and the edge of his seat – scared or excited, I couldn't tell which.

Careening down the hill, I snatched a look in the mirror and saw the Caddy smoke into reverse. The driver began backing up after us.

I stood on the brakes. While the Olds tried to stop, screeching like tortured steel, I twitched the wheel to the right. Damn near flipped us, but I got what I wanted. Now we looked like we were trying to turn in that direction. And we hit the kerb almost hard enough to burst a tyre, which helped the illusion I was trying to create.

Immediately the Caddy angled over to that side to cut us off.

This time, I got the timing right all by myself. With the Caddy hammering down towardss us, I fisted the Olds into reverse, floored the accelerator again – and stopped before we went twenty feet. Now I was ready. Out of the Caddy's path. And positioned to ram it if it didn't crush its rims when it slammed the kerb.

It had good brakes. It came down the hill like a cart of bricks, but somehow it slowed enough so that it didn't lose a wheel when it hit the kerb.

For a few seconds we stayed where we were and looked at each other. The goon in the Caddy had his shotgun aimed at us. But he was on the wrong side now. His passenger window was closed. And he could see what I was about to do to him.

He made up his mind without hesitation. Gunning his engine for all it was worth, he did his best to get back up the hill before I could run into him.

I let him go. The Olds was never going to catch him, anyway. And I didn't particularly want to shoot it out with him right there in the street. Already Haskell's neighbours were emerging from their houses to see what the commotion was about.

Instead of trying to be a hero, I got the Olds moving again and rolled it into Haskell's driveway.

'Come on,' I ordered him. My voice sounded tight and breakable, but I couldn't help it. 'Let's get inside before someone comes over to ask us what the hell we're doing.'

The sonofabitch didn't even have the decency to look scared. His eyes shone with a tension I couldn't read – it could've been adrenaline or stroke. Without a word, he got out of the car and started towards the house.

I followed him, feeling stiff and cramped, and cursing because I hadn't managed to see the goon's face.

Haskell was passing the cedars into the aisle towards his front door before I regained enough composure to wonder why Ginny hadn't come out to investigate all that caterwauling of tyres.

Faster than I could think it through, I jumped after Haskell, caught him by the arm. Surely by now –

'What is it?' Haskell demanded. 'What's the matter?' I couldn't see his face clearly in the relative dusk of the aisle, but he sounded like a man with a fever.

Blocking him against the wall to keep him out of my way, I pulled out the .45.

I was too scared to make sense. Maybe two bad days and no sleep had left me paranoid. But if she was all right, where *was* she? I could've used her a couple of minutes ago –

'Axbrewder–'

'Don't ask,' I hissed. 'Shut up. Stay here.'

As quietly as I could with my muscles stiff and my kneecaps quivering, I moved towards the door.

When I touched the knob, a voice snapped, 'If you open that door, I'll blow you in half.'

Her voice twisted a knife under my ribcage. She sounded too demented to be the woman I knew.

'Ginny.' What was happening to her? 'It's Brew. I've got Haskell with me. We're all right.'

She didn't answer.

'Ginny, we're coming in.'

Despite the way my hands shook, I holstered the .45, got out the keys, and unlocked the door.

When I eased it open, I saw her leaning against the wall near the light switches. None of the lights were on – I couldn't make out her face. But the .357 hung like a dead weight from the end of her right arm. She could hardly keep her grip on it.

The stump of her left forearm she held clamped over her heart.

Acid filled my throat. I couldn't swallow it. She looked like she'd gone over the edge. Like fear and incapacity had finally pushed her further than she could bear.

Like she'd learned something that made this case worse than she could possibly stand.

I wanted to put my arms around her, hold her as hard as I could, just so that my bones would stop shaking. But Haskell shoved his way into the house between us.

I closed the door behind him, relocked it. He reached past her to snap on the lights. In the sudden glare, her battered expression and her tight face went through me like a cry.

Haskell considered her, his back to me. His scrutiny reminded me that he'd never seen her stump before. Until now, she'd kept her left forearm hidden in a pocket.

I bunched my fists. If he said anything I didn't like, anything at all, I was going to deck him. At the moment I didn't care whether he survived the experience or not.

But he didn't comment on her appearance. Or her hand. He didn't even mention firing us. Softly, kindly, as if he were a friend of hers, he said, 'I need a drink. You want one?'

She couldn't meet his eyes. Dumbly she shook her head.

He shrugged. With a spring in his steps, he turned and went down the stairs, leaving us alone.

'Ginny.' I didn't know how to say it. I needed you out there. How did it get this bad? 'What happened?'

'I heard the cars,' she said dully. 'I'm getting to be like you. Intuitive. Somehow I knew you were in trouble. I grabbed my gun and ran up here.' She was too ashamed to look at me. 'But when I reached the door, I couldn't– I just couldn't–'

Abruptly she threw her .357 at the floor. It bounced once, but the carpet absorbed the impact. Tears spilled from her eyes as she looked at her empty hand and her stump.

'You know, it's funny,' she said past the knot in her throat. 'I didn't want this case. But until today I never really believed el Señor had anything to do with it. It didn't make sense. For God's sake, Haskell's just an accountant. How could he possibly be involved with a thug like el Señor?'

Almost holding my breath, I asked, 'What changed your mind?'

She looked at me then. With all her fear and pain and disgust, her eyes still had room for a flash of wild anger.

'Haskell has been lying to us all along. I know why el Señor wants him dead.'

Chapter Fifteen

A minute later, she said, 'Brew, what happened to your face?'
I dismissed that. 'I'll tell you later.' But then I didn't say anything. I stood there like a dummy and stared at her.

I was confused. Not by her announcement – I can understand plain English, if you enunciate clearly and don't use big words. No, I was confused by how I felt about it. Normally I would've been at least relieved. She thought she knew the answer. And she was usually right. No matter how bad the answer was, just having something solid to work with helped.

But I didn't feel relieved. The way she looked left my insides in a knot.

She studied me for some kind of reaction, practically hanging on to me with her eyes. She was counting on me for something.

I couldn't afford to let her down. But I needed time to think, so I went to the head of the stairs and listened for some indication of what Haskell was doing. I thought I heard the clink of a glass – he was fixing himself a drink. With any luck, he might stay down there for a few minutes.

Turning back to Ginny, I said quietly, 'Don't let him hear you. When I picked him up, he said he was going to fire us. He doesn't like us prying into his personal life.'

She still leaned against the wall as if she couldn't hold up her own weight. But her brain kept functioning, and she was making an effort to cope. 'Has he changed his mind?'

'I don't know.'

I moved back across the atrium to stand in front of her. I wanted to be close enough to put my arms around her if I got the chance. But I knew that wasn't what she needed – even if she thought it was. She needed to find her way back to the woman she used to be. Take-no-prisoners Fistoulari.

'Maybe that little demolition derby out there made him reconsider,' I went on. 'But we might be better off if he doesn't know how much we know.'

She nodded. What she was thinking brought the misery back into her eyes, but she forced herself to say it. 'Did you see who it was?' She indicated the street with a jerk of her head. She hadn't had a shower for two days, and her hair looked stringy and unloved.

The phone rang. I waited until Haskell picked up an extension downstairs. His voice came vaguely up from below. He sounded like he was telling a neighbour that car chases and shooting on Cactus Blossom Court were nothing to worry about.

'No.' I couldn't hide my anger. 'Every time I looked at him, he had a shotgun pointed at me.'

However, the man in the Cadillac hadn't looked much like Mase Novick.

Unfortunately Ginny was in no shape to consider that I might be disgusted at myself. She took my tone as a comment on her failure to come to my rescue. 'Brew,' she said softly, 'please don't.' Her face was pale with need and anguish. 'I've already got more than I can stand.'

I understood. Folding my arms over my chest to keep them out of the way, I murmured, 'Don't worry about it. If you count the three or four thousand times I've let you down, I don't really have much to complain about.'

She took a deep breath, held it. Running her fingers through her hair, she straightened it a bit. Slowly she got herself under control. Her broken nose, and the slight flaring of wildness in her eyes, kept her from looking calm. But she did everything she could to turn off her desperation.

'So tell me,' she said, trying to sound normal. 'How was your day?'

I shook my head. Watching her struggle with herself was going to be the death of me. 'You first. I want to hear about it before Haskell gets curious.'

She tried to produce a sour smile. Apparently her day hadn't turned bad right away. 'I'm not like you,' she said almost steadily. 'I can't live on hunches and instinct. I have to rely on old-fashioned investigating.

'Sara Haskell said her husband made his money with investments during business trips, *weekend* business trips. I asked myself how that was possible. I mean, try to think of an investment where you can buy in, make money, and cash out again over the weekend. I had a theory, so I came back here, picked up a few family pictures of our client' – she'd recovered herself enough to drip sarcasm on Haskell – 'and drove out to the airport.'

Staring at her, I asked, 'Why?'

'A lot of people fly in and out of Puerta del Sol. There are seven airlines and who knows how many counter personnel. But I thought that if a man made a lot of trips, and always went to the same place, and always used the same airline, he might get himself remembered. Especially if he tried to make every female employee he met go weak at the knees.'

I knew from the way she was telling it that she'd found what she was looking for. I made an effort to listen for Haskell while I concentrated on her voice.

'Brew,' she said, her voice so soft she was almost whispering, 'where do you suppose he goes to invest his money over the weekend?'

I didn't say anything. I wanted her to lay it out for me.

'He goes,' she said, 'to Las Vegas.'

That surprised me in several different ways at once. But the first thing out of my mouth was, 'And he wins?'

'Not necessarily. I think he did at first. I think that's how he got into this. But either way, I can prove he's been to Vegas at least thirty times in the past few years. One of the ticket clerks for Southair recognized his picture. And I'm sure at least two other women there know him. They just didn't want to admit it. So I leaned on the station manager a bit, and he finally let me look at their passenger manifests. Southair has more direct flights to Vegas than anybody else, and his name turned up on a lot of them. Out on Friday evening, home on Sunday.'

'He didn't bother to use a different name?'

'Why should he? It's not exactly illegal to go to Vegas over the weekend.'

I digested that for a moment – and kicked myself for not thinking of it. It wasn't quite what you might expect from the chief accountant of a bank, but in other ways it fitted. It explained where he got his money, explained his 'investments'. And poker was even better than bridge for a man who liked to play people, especially if he could get into a private game where he didn't have to face the house odds. Come to think of it, Vegas was the perfect place for the man who wanted to have everything – including excitement.

And Haskell admitted that some of his 'investments' had gone bad recently. If he'd gotten himself into a game with some pros, they might've given him quite a bit of line before reeling him in.

For a second, I caught a flash of the implications. A few years ago, a friend, an acquaintance, or maybe just a brochure in full colour persuaded him to break out of the boredom of being an accountant, go to Vegas for some thrills. And while he was there, he did well because he didn't make the mistake of playing the cards. He played the people. He had power. He had control. He was alive. It was like magic.

So he went back. Again. And again. And started getting used to it. Counting on winning. Spending more and more money at home. He began to feel like he could do anything, which made him look like he could do anything, which helped him succeed.

And then, ever so slowly, the pros pulled the rug out from under him. All that power, control, magic – slipping away. Of course, he didn't believe it. He was Reg Haskell. Nobody outplays Reg Haskell. So he turned to other kinds of games to get the money he wasn't winning in Vegas any more. And that led –

But I was ahead of myself. With an effort, I pulled back. Ginny still had things to tell me. 'All right,' I murmured. 'So he went to Vegas a lot. That doesn't prove he's been lying about el Señor.'

'No,' she said, 'it doesn't.'

'In fact, it fits. After he began thinking he could outplay the big boys – and maybe even got addicted to it – he started to lose. A bit at a time, until he was in deep shit. So when he stumbled on that money laundry, he decided to try el Señor himself. That way he gets the money he needs, and he restores his belief that he can do anything.'

'Slow down,' she said impatiently. 'It sounds good, but it doesn't hold up. I'm not finished.'

Fine. I was just saying the same thing myself. Tightening my grip on myself, I waited for her to go on.

'When I was done at the airport,' she explained, 'I finally got around to calling the answering service. They said Canthorpe had been trying to get in touch with me all morning. When I called him back, he was in a lather. He said the cops had paid him a visit. In fact, it was your old friend Cason. He asked Canthorpe the same questions we did about that money laundry.'

'They tracked down the cab driver,' I put in.

She nodded. 'I figured that. Anyway, Canthorpe says he gave Cason the same answer he was going to give me.

'There *is* no money laundry. Haskell made the whole thing up.'

'He did *what?*' No doubt about it, I was bright today. Even though she'd warned me. And I really should've been expecting it. 'How did Canthorpe find that out so fast?'

She looked at me hard. 'It was easy. Nobody in his right mind banks under a name like "el Señor". And Hector Jesus Fria de la Sancha doesn't have an account anywhere with the First Puerta del Sol National Bank.'

It was that simple. Haskell's story couldn't be true.

When I thought back, I realized that Ginny and I had no reason to believe Haskell even knew el Señor's real name.

The sheer audacity of his latest lie dazzled me. No wonder he didn't want us to pry any more.

At least now I knew why Cason hadn't arrested anyone. In effect, Canthorpe told him that this case didn't have anything to do with the one he was working on. Cason probably rousted me just to double-check – or maybe to warn me out of his way.

If Haskell wasn't curious yet about what we were doing, he wasn't a well man. But as long as he left us alone, I intended to discuss him.

'Did Cason talk to Haskell?'

She shrugged. 'I asked Canthorpe that.' She was waiting for me to get to the important stuff. 'He said no.'

'Did Canthorpe mention to Cason that we asked him the same questions?'

'I asked that too. Same answer.'

'No?' I didn't know what that meant. Canthorpe might have any number of reasons for giving the cops as little information as possible. Some of them I didn't like much. But I let it go for the time being and did my best to face the issues Ginny had in mind.

'Well, at least now we know why Haskell wanted to fire us. He must've seen Cason talk to Canthorpe, so he jumped to the obvious conclusion. We called the cops on him. But he can't admit that's why he wants to fire us without also admitting he's done something illegal.' I was spinning more inferences than I could keep track of all at once. I had one other idea I wanted to pursue, but it could wait. 'What's he trying to hide with all these lies?'

'His ego,' she snapped. 'He wants us to think he's a big deal, and he isn't. He's just a petty philanderer who's gotten in over his head and can't give up his delusions of grandeur.'

Well, maybe. I didn't know what she was getting at. 'You said you've finally started to believe that el Señor wants Haskell dead. But if the money laundry doesn't exist, Haskell can't threaten him. Why try to kill someone who can't threaten you?'

'I know,' she sighed. 'It doesn't sound like it makes sense. But that's the way it hit me.'

For some reason, she stopped watching my face. When she dropped her eyes, she saw her .357 lying on the carpet. Grimacing to herself, she bent down and picked it up. Then she didn't know what to do with it, so she let it dangle loosely from her hand.

'Haskell goes to Las Vegas,' she said. 'For a while he wins. Long enough to get hooked. Then he starts to lose. He's a small fish with sharks on his tail, and the nice life he's bought for himself is going to disappear. What does he do for money?

'Brew.' Slowly her eyes came back up to mine. 'I don't know whether it's true. But it's the kind of story I can understand.' Pain and fear filled her gaze. A little thing like that – a story she could understand – took the heart out of her. It made what she was up against seem real. 'Where can he get that kind of money? Loan sharks, that's where. From el Señor.'

'And since he keeps losing,' I finished for her, 'he doesn't pay the money back. El Señor's finally gotten tired of it, and he wants his pound of flesh.'

She nodded. 'And Haskell doesn't tell the truth because he doesn't want to admit that he's gotten himself into something that grubby and useless. It doesn't fit his glamorous image of himself. And he likes to live dangerously.'

It made sense. I had to give her that. And it resolved some nagging questions, like how el Señor possibly could've tracked Haskell down so fast. Nevertheless I couldn't shake the sensation that there was something wrong with it. A sore place in my gut told me over and over again that we'd underestimated someone. Who, I didn't know – just someone.

My personal candidate was Jordan Canthorpe, but I didn't get a chance to say so. Before I could tell Ginny not to jump to any conclusions until she heard about my day, feet-on-carpet sounds from the stairs stopped me. We shut up and watched as Haskell's head showed past the rim. He paused there for a second, then came up the rest of the way towards us.

'Am I interrupting something?' His sharp eyes watched us warily. Somehow he consistently conveyed the impression that he was taller than he was. He wore a casual khaki suit I hadn't seen before, and his hair was damp – he'd been in the shower. 'It's my life you two insist on investigating. And I heard one of you mention danger. I think I have a right to know what's going on.'

His audacity was wonderful. Brass balls polished to a shine.

334

Apparently he hadn't told us one true thing in two days except his name, and yet he acted like we were abusing his trust.

But Ginny didn't bother to admire the show. For no particular reason, she tightened her grip on the .357. Facing him, she said in a voice like a scalpel, 'Brew tells me you want to fire us, Mr Haskell.'

She made the statement into an attack, but he met it without any trouble. In fact, he looked like he might be sneering quietly to himself. 'I've changed my mind.'

'Why is that?'

Almost smiling, he said, 'I was wrong to question the way you're handling this case. I think I'm a pretty good judge of people. I can see now that I don't need to worry about what you're doing.'

There was more than one way to take that, and I thought I knew which way he meant it. I was just getting ready to yell at him when Ginny stopped me.

'In that case' – her tone would've made Genghis Khan sit up and take notice – 'you can leave us alone to finish our conversation. We'll let you know when we've reached a decision.'

He carried it off better than I would have. He didn't try to argue, protest, fight back. He didn't say anything else about his rights. He didn't even ask what kind of decision it was we had to make. On the other hand, he didn't look the least bit ruffled or unhappy either. 'I'll be in the den,' he said with just a touch of what you might call hauteur. Then he turned on his heel and went back down the stairs.

When I figured he was out of earshot, I murmured, 'I wonder how long it's been since that man told anyone the truth about anything.'

'I'm not sure,' Ginny said distantly. 'I think he just told me the truth about myself.'

I looked at her. Suddenly I was mad at her, too. 'The hell he did.'

I would've gone on, but she made a gesture that cut me off. 'We really can't spend the rest of the night standing here.' Back to being reasonable. 'We've got to get to work. Maybe you'd better tell me about those scratches.'

Good point. That's exactly what I wanted to do. Her theory fit well enough, but it didn't seem particularly inevitable. We didn't have anything as handy as evidence to go on, so we couldn't afford to rule out other possibilities. Like one or two of the inferences I'd been in the middle of a few minutes earlier.

But when I started to talk, my emotions confused me. What I really wanted to tell her about was Pablo and the Santiagos, not Gail Harmon and Mase Novick. On top of that, she had no business looking so damn breakable. By the time I'd said two sentences, I was talking such gibberish that I had to go back and start over.

Squeezing down hard on my brain to make it behave, I described my run-in with Frail Gail and her head-hunter boyfriend. Also my little chat with Captain of Detectives Philip Cason. To make sense out of it for her, I had to give her some news she'd missed about Bambino Chavez and Cason's investigation. When I was done, however, she let that side of the question go. It became irrelevant because we knew Haskell had lied about the money laundry. Instead she concentrated on the obvious implications of my story and tried not to look relieved.

'That's quite a coincidence,' she commented. I was giving her exactly what she wanted most – a reason not to believe that we stood in the way of a ritual hit. 'There's a man in Puerta del Sol who dreams about wasting our client – and Jordan Canthorpe just happens to have his address memorized.' But she didn't say it. She didn't want to hope that hard. 'What's your theory?'

I shrugged. 'As far as Canthorpe is concerned, it's simple. Haskell has been screwing around with his fiancée. Looking for a little consolation, Canthorpe goes to a former girlfriend and meets Novick. Next thing you know, he's pointing Novick like a loaded gun at Haskell's head. Too good an opportunity to pass up.

'On Haskell's side, it's more complicated. Stop and think about it. Having el Señor after you isn't something you can be wrong about. Either he is or he isn't. And if he is, there are plenty of intermediate steps. You don't pay the loan shark, the loan shark gets mad, you get threats, harassment, nasty phone calls. When the goons come after you, you know why.

'No matter what he tells us, Haskell would know it if el Señor were after him. And all we really know about him is that he's a bullshit artist.

'If I had to guess, I'd say that he's using us to solve two different problems at once. He wants us to protect him from Novick. At the same time, he *is* in trouble with el Señor. He's into the sharks for more than he can cover, and they're starting to get mean. So he lies to us, makes us concentrate on el Señor, with the idea that any defence we come up with against the sharks will ward off Novick as well.'

Then I stopped. Once I'd said all that, I didn't believe it any more. No particular reason. I just didn't like the relief that rushed into Ginny's face.

Nevertheless I still didn't tell her that the Caddy's driver hadn't looked much like Mase Novick.

At least she played fair. It cost her an effort, but after a minute she said, 'Haskell is probably capable of anything, but why would Canthorpe tell the cops Haskell lied about the money laundry? It was a perfect chance to misdirect everybody, cover whatever Novick did.

Instead he let Haskell off the hook.'

Since she was playing fair, I had to do the same. 'That's simple. Haskell's story was too easy to check. As soon as the cops brought in their own accountant, they'd uncover the truth. Which could get Canthorpe in trouble.

'In any case, he didn't want Haskell taken into protective custody where Novick couldn't get at him.'

'All right,' she said. Her forehead knotted while she concentrated on not jumping to conclusions. 'That works so far. But if Canthorpe is really that smart, why did he give us Novick's address? Why try to get Haskell killed and then tell us what we need to know to protect him?'

I spread my hands. It was just a theory. 'Maybe he panicked. You sure as hell took him by surprise this morning.'

She shook her head. I tried to do better.

'Or maybe he's even smarter than that. Maybe he's smart enough to know that Novick is an unguided missile. He might do anything, go off anywhere. Once you launch something like that, you'd best dig yourself a hole, climb in, and pull the hole in after you. Maybe that's what Canthorpe is doing. Making himself look as innocent as possible.'

That was what she wanted to hear. Seeing how much she needed to believe it gave me a quicksand feeling in the pit of my stomach. From the look of things, I was doing her a favour. I was making what we were up against small enough for her to handle. But I knew better. The woman I loved was getting further and further away, and I couldn't do anything about it.

So I didn't respond when she straightened her back, shook the slack out of her muscles, made an attempt to smile at me. I didn't respond when she stepped closer to me and looked at my scratches again.

'After we nail Novick,' she said softly, 'I think I'll go find Frail Gail Harmon and break her fingers.'

Now she wanted me to act like nothing had changed between us.

I couldn't do it. Instead I replied, 'That'll be fine. What're we going to do in the mean time?'

My lack of enthusiasm hurt her. Frowning, she peered into my face. Then she drew back. Whatever she saw in my eyes made her stop looking at me.

She waggled her .357 aimlessly in front of her. 'First I'm going to go get my purse. Put this thing away. After that–' Her struggle to pull herself together, be as strong as she remembered being, made me want to wail. 'I'll go have a talk with Sara Haskell. Before it gets dark and late enough for Novick to try again. I want her permission to look at lover-boy's bank accounts and financial records. They might tell us a lot – if we hire somebody to interpret them for us. I know she's probably too loyal to do it, but it's worth a try.

'What about you?'

By that time the misery was back in her face. And it was my doing – which naturally made me as proud as horseshit. What would it have cost me to comfort her a little, even if I hardly knew who she was any more? But I was still furious inside, fuming mad and barely able to keep a lid on it. I'd gotten us into this case to recover the Ginny Fistoulari I used to know, and it wasn't working.

Until she asked, I hadn't thought about what I might do. Right away, however, several ideas occurred to me. They must've been percolating in the back of my head, waiting for me to feel as savage as they did. I picked the one she wasn't likely to argue with and said, 'I think I'll take Haskell to visit Ms Wint.' Eunice didn't deserve that, but she wasn't my client. 'Maybe she can tell us something useful about her fiancé.'

Ginny nodded. She still couldn't look at me. 'Good luck.'

All alone, she went downstairs to get her purse and her coat.

Chapter Sixteen

But I didn't go see Eunice Wint. Not right away. I waited until Ginny left the house. Then I went downstairs myself.

Haskell was in the den on the couch, turning a drink around and around between his palms. For some reason, he was able to look more relaxed when he was moving than he could when he was sitting still. His tension showed in the way he turned his head as I walked into the room.

'That took long enough,' he remarked. 'I thought I'd have to sit here while you two negotiated world peace.' Then he noticed my expression. Adjusting his tone, he said, 'Fistoulari didn't tell me anything. What have you decided?'

'Come on,' I said. The pain of my scratches seemed to come and go. At the moment they felt like I'd been raked by a tiger. 'Let's take a ride.'

He didn't get up. 'I have a better idea. It's been a long day. You look like you could use some rest. Why don't we stay home and unwind for a while? Have a drink.' He waved his glass. 'Put your feet up. Do you play poker? We could try a few hands. It'll make you feel better. Take your mind off your troubles. Loser pays for dinner.'

'You're going to pay for it anyway.' Even at my best, I'm not exactly a scintillating conversationalist. 'It's a business expense, part of the bill. Come on.'

'What's the hurry?' Apparently he didn't want to move. 'It's only' – he glanced at his watch – 'five-thirty. The trouble with you is that you never give yourself a break. We're safe here. What can happen? The door is locked isn't it?' He nodded towards the picture window. 'Nobody is going to shoot at us from the arroyo.'

That was true – for a while. The light was still in our favour. But it wouldn't last. Dusk gathered quickly, and the weather looked like maybe it had finally made up its mind to snow.

'So relax,' he said. 'Have a drink. I'm serious.

'I'll tell you what. If you'll unbend enough to join me, I'll entertain you for a few minutes. I'll bet you' – he dug into his pocket, pulled out his half-dollar – 'you can't flip a coin ten times and have it come up heads more than three or less than seven times. What would you say the odds are?'

Haskell was doing a little research, trying to find out where he stood. But I didn't care. 'The odds are,' I said, 'if you don't come with me, I'm going to drag you.'

He stared into his glass and swirled the amber from side to side. 'You still haven't told me what you've decided.'

'That's true.' I didn't particularly want to muscle him, but I'd do it if I had to. 'You still haven't told us what happened to the records on that money laundry. You were supposed to get us documentation so that we'd have something to fight with. Where is it?'

He looked at me – a long, hard look steady as a steel probe. Then he said, 'I left them at the bank. Where they'll be safe. If I brought them here, anything could happen to them while you and Fistoulari were out "investigating" my private life.'

He was good, no question about it. I almost believed him, even though I knew he was bluffing. He could tell me my mother was a cocker spaniel, and I'd be tempted to believe him.

He required an answer. But if I told him what I had in mind, he'd never go along with it. Holding his gaze, I said, 'We don't like to leave things unfinished. We'll keep working until we find out what's going on here.' I wanted him nervous. 'Until we take care of whoever is after you.

'In the mean time, I've got errands to run. I can't leave you alone, so you're coming with me. If you don't like the way I "investigate", this is your chance for a little damage control.'

I wasn't as good as he was. But I was a hell of a lot more sincere.

He kept me waiting while he finished his drink. Then he got to his feet and gave me a smile that made my scalp itch. 'You're in luck,' he said brightly. 'I didn't have any other plans.'

I resisted the temptation to poke him in the stomach, just to remind him of his mortality. Instead I told him to get his coat.

When we left the house – carefully leaving the lights on and locking the door – we found that Ginny had taken the Olds. We were stuck with Haskell's showboat Continental. Considering our destination, that didn't cheer me up. Still, it was better than walking. Haskell wanted to drive, as usual, but I wasn't that dumb. Once I'd talked him into the passenger seat, I fired up the Continental – which was like turning on your own private hydroelectric power station. Then I drove out of Cactus Blossom Court in the direction of the beltway.

Even the luxurious suspension felt the wind. Heading west on the exposed surface of the beltway, the car made small lurching movements in the gusts. I had the unsteady feeling that we were about to spin out of control. Outside the range of the headlights, all we could see was the thickening dusk, as if the wind were slowly turning black.

Haskell rode in silence for a while, watching the day go out. However, he wasn't any good at sitting still. He had his half-dollar in his hands, turning it back and forth between his fingers. Every now and then he flipped it gently. Then, abruptly, he stuffed the coin back into his pocket.

'You're an unusual man, Axbrewder.' He made it sound like he was continuing an earlier conversation. 'I don't know what to expect from you. You have a relatively grubby job, but you act like you've never forgiven yourself for not being a saint. You're big and tough, you carry a gun, you throw your weight around, and yet you're as touchy as a cat.

'Tell me something. Why don't you drink?'

That's why he was good at playing people. His accuracy was frightening. I think he did it with radar. I wanted to spit a nasty retort, but I stopped myself in time. Practising self-mortification, I told him the truth.

'I'm an alcoholic.'

'Ah,' he breathed. For a second there, I could've tricked myself into thinking he sympathized. But then he laughed. 'That's perfect. Somebody wants to kill me, and who do I get for protection? A drunk and a cripple. If I were counting on luck to keep me alive, I'd be as good as dead.'

I almost ran off the road. 'Ginny isn't a cripple. She's just lost her left hand.'

'I'm not talking about her hand,' he explained. 'She's going to pieces in front of you. If you can't see that, you're in worse trouble than I thought.'

I measured the distance between us, wondering if I could hit him hard enough to do some damage without losing control of the car. Then I had a better idea. I let out a loony sound that resembled a laugh.

'Oh, come off it, Haskell. You're just upset because she doesn't find you irresistible. Every now and then, people make the mistake of underestimating her. Some of them are dead.'

'Is that a fact?' His tone made his opinion clear. But he didn't say anything else for a while.

Rush-hour traffic thinned out as I turned off the beltway and pointed the Continental south on Trujillo. The headlights didn't expose the way the city changed around us, but I could feel the difference. Down in the South Valley, people were starting to huddle together so that they wouldn't freeze to death.

Eventually Haskell asked me where we were going. I told him to wait and see. After that he forced himself to keep his mouth shut.

I found Bosque easily enough, but in the dark I almost missed Gail Harmon's house. I spotted it as I was going past. Lights showed at the windows.

Feeling as savage as I did, I intended to stir up quite a bit of trouble. But I didn't want to be stupid about it, so I drove by without stopping. After a bit of confusion on the unfamiliar streets, I managed to work my way around and back in the other direction until I hit Bosque again. Then I turned off all my lights, eased the Continental down the road, and parked in front of the house beside the one I wanted.

'Are you sure you know what you're doing?' Haskell asked. 'If you want to pry into my life, you've come to the wrong place. I've never been down here. I'm not sure I know anybody who has ever been in this part of town.'

You'd be surprised. It's amazing what pain and loss do to people. But I didn't answer him. I had better things to do.

I took out the .45, checked the clip just to be on the safe side. Then I looked at Haskell. 'Stay quiet. Don't get out of the car. I'll be back in a few minutes. If anything happens, try not to be seen.'

He opened his mouth, closed it again. He must've noticed that I was already ignoring him.

I found the switch for the courtesy lights and turned them off. Easing the door open, I got out. Left the door partway open so that I could get back in quickly. The cold went through my clothes as if I stood there naked.

The .45 clamped in my fist, I moved cautiously towards the side of the house to look in one of the windows.

In my place, a smarter – or maybe just saner – man would've been looking for Novick. I'd arrived at the right time of night, the time when a man with killing on his mind might be at home getting ready. No doubt a smarter man would've staked out his house until he left, then followed him to find out what he meant to do. If he went to Haskell's house, he'd get nailed.

But that wasn't why I was there. Just the opposite. As I peeked in the window, I prayed I wouldn't see him.

I didn't. The window showed me a bedroom lit by a dim red bulb hanging from the ceiling and decorated with beer cans and gun magazines. No one was in the room. But a shadow moving past the doorway told me that the house wasn't empty.

Not wanting to put my weight on the front porch, I moved around to the back of the house.

There Novick and Harmon had collected enough garbage to start their own landfill. I needed both hands for caution and balance, so I put the .45 away. Somehow I had to navigate the piles of cans and stacks of broken furniture and pools of slop without crashing into anything or breaking a leg.

Eventually I managed it. But I was never going to get my Boy Scout skulking badge. By the time I reached the back door, I heard Gail's voice.

'Is that you, Mase?'

She sounded small and vulnerable, but not especially scared.

Before I could react, she opened the door and looked out at me.

The steps up to the door put her slightly above me. The light in the kitchen behind her let her see me a lot better than I could see her. But that was all right – as long as Novick wasn't home.

She'd taken me by surprise, but I didn't let that slow me down. 'Hi,' I said like I did this kind of thing every day. 'Remember me? I'm the man who wanted to talk to you about Reg Haskell.'

She didn't say anything. Her silhouette didn't move. But at least she didn't close the door.

'I couldn't talk this morning,' I said, 'not with Mase here. I couldn't let him hear me. He wants to kill Reg.'

'So do I,' she murmured. She sounded far away, made tiny by distance. 'I love him.'

I resisted an urge to ask her which one. Neither of them was what I would've called a logical response.

'You said you wanted to talk about Reg' – a note of bitterness came into her voice – 'but you didn't. You just wanted to hurt Mase.'

'No,' I countered. 'I work for Reg. I don't want Mase to hurt him. That's why I couldn't talk while Mase was there.' Since she didn't seem likely to panic at the moment, I decided to take a chance. 'Where is Mase?'

Slowly she turned to look behind her. Then she peered out at me again. Everything she did was slow. 'He went out,' she said. 'I thought he came back, but it was you.'

I could hear the ruin of her life in the way she spoke. That and the cold made it hard for me to sound calm. 'Gail, let me tell you why Reg sent me.'

She considered that. She was in a different mind than she'd been this morning. 'If you do,' she said finally, 'Mase'll kill you, too.'

You mean, I thought, me in addition to Haskell? Or me in addition to you? But I couldn't sort it out. 'No, he won't,' I said. 'I want you to come with me. That's why I'm here. I want to take you to Reg.'

Her outline stiffened against the light. 'To Reg?'

'He's waiting for you. We want to take you to a place where you'll be safe.'

Also I wanted to poke a stick into the hornet's nest of Novick's mind. Stir up trouble, as they say. The quick way to find out who your enemies are. Ugly, brutal – and efficient.

'Will you come with me?'

'To Reg?' she repeated. She seemed to be breathing hard. 'You'll take me to Reg?'

I nodded. 'Yes.'

'Just a minute.' Moving like a figure in a dream, she shut the door on me.

While I hesitated, I heard what sounded like a drawer opening, closing. Then she swung the door open again and came down the steps to me. 'I'm ready.'

I could see her better now without the light behind her. She wore the same clothes I'd seen her in earlier – a ratty flannel shirt with only one button, jeans that made her look anorexic, no shoes. If I'd had any confidence at all in what I was doing, I would've taken her back inside to get a coat. As it was, however, I wrapped one hand around her thin arm so that she wouldn't get away and used the light to help me negotiate the trash towards the car.

Some of the stuff she stepped on must've hurt her feet, but she didn't seem to feel it.

I felt it for her. I felt the cold for her, too. But mostly I made her hurry because I was afraid that Haskell would drive away if he saw us coming.

Fortunately the dark shielded us. We reached the Continental. I jerked open the rear door, steered Gail into the back seat, then strode around to the door I'd left open.

By the time I got in and shut the door, Gail had her arms around Haskell's neck over the back of the seat. She made muffled noises, crying into his ear.

Without light, I couldn't see Haskell's face. But his hands strained on Gail's arms to keep her from strangling him.

'Axbrewder, you bastard,' he gasped, 'you bastard.'

Grinning maliciously, I snapped on the dashboard lights.

Her crying changed into words. 'Oh, Reg, I love you, I love you, Reg, I love you.' The grip of her arms looked frantic.

Haskell braced himself. He was about to do something violent to make her let go.

'Listen to me, Haskell,' I said, putting all the conviction I could muster into my voice. 'You helped create this mess, and you're going to help clean it up. She's killing herself with malnutrition, booze, and dope, and she hasn't got enough mental balance left to know it. The clown she lives with would love to put us all in the morgue, and she doesn't seem to understand that, either. Your name is the only thing I can say to her that she'll pay attention to.'

Haskell managed to loosen Gail's grip so that he could breathe and turn his head. 'You bastard,' he repeated softly, 'I didn't cause this. I'm not responsible for her.'

I ignored that. 'She needs professional care. I want to take her to a hospital. But I can't persuade her to go with me. And nobody can force her to sign herself in for treatment. She has to do that herself.' I faced him like a set of brass knuckles. 'You're going to talk her into it.'

In the faint glow of the lights, he looked dark, menacing, his face covered with shadows. 'How?'

'I don't care. Tell her you love her. Tell her she'll save your life. Tell her any damn lie you want. Just talk her into it.'

She murmured his name over and over again, desperately pleading for a response.

He said, 'I can't. I got tired of her months ago.'

'Fake it!' I snapped. 'You like playing people. Play her.'

For a minute longer, he stared at me with pieces of murder lurking in the shadows on his face. Then he turned around, reached his arms towards Gail. One hand stroked her hair, the other hugged her shoulder, while he met her feverish kissing.

'Gail,' he croaked, 'I'm sorry. I was wrong. I'm sorry.'

She clung to him for her life.

I started the Continental, hit the lights, and headed back up Bosque towards Trujillo. In the direction of San Reno County Public Hospital.

While I drove, I concentrated on not hearing the way Haskell and Gail mooned at each other. She was out of her mind, and he was too good at it. I would've gagged in revulsion, except for the simple fact that I'd forced him into this. After a while his endearments began to fray around the edges. I gritted my teeth and kept going.

Fortunately San Reno County Public Hospital – affectionately known as *SaRCoPH*, short for *sarcophagus* – is in the South Valley, in the marginal area where the respectable part of Puerta del Sol dwindles towards the *barrio*. The drive seemed to take a week or ten days, but we actually arrived around 7.00.

SaRCoPH isn't the best hospital in the city, but it isn't the worst, either, even though it looks like a cross between a steel foundry and a vivisectionist's lab. And it's the only one where they don't look at you cross-eyed if you've got no visible means of support. Once we got there, however, the tricky part started.

I didn't have much trouble with the starched personage on the other side of the emergency admitting desk. She could see that Gail needed help, so she accepted my explanation – that Gail Harmon was spacey with dope and neglect and needed treatment for malnutrition, in addition to psychiatric evaluation – and ignored the information that Haskell and I were friends who had found her half-comatose in her apartment. Probably the nurse considered us a couple of good-time bozos who had picked Gail up, realized she was in worse shape than we thought, and now wanted to get out with as little involvement as possible. Instead of making me feel like a bad liar, she simply filled out the required forms and passed them over for Gail's signature.

That was the problem. Gail didn't seem to have the first idea where she was or why, but in some dim corner of her mind she'd figured out that we were going to abandon her. She kept one arm curled like a C-clamp around Haskell's right arm. With the other, she pulled at his neck, trying to bring his head down for more kisses.

'No, don't leave me here, don't, please, take me with you, Reg,' she begged softly, 'don't leave me again.' Her eyes somehow failed to focus on his face, giving her a vacant look. The tone of her voice already sounded lost.

Haskell was near the end of his rope. He didn't look at her. Instead he faced me with a gleam of desperate fury in his eyes.

I cocked my fists on my hips and glared back.

The woman in the starched uniform rustled her papers. 'We need your signature on these forms, Miss Harmon,' she said. 'We can't help you without your permission.'

'Sign them, Gail,' Haskell snapped. The gentleness, the fake affection, was gone. He still didn't look at her. 'I want you to sign those forms.'

'No,' she pleaded. 'You're going to leave me again. Why are you going to leave me? What've I done? I don't understand. Please tell me what I've done. I won't do it again, I promise, I swear. Please don't leave me.'

I couldn't watch. Hours ago I'd passed into the kind of grim helpless rage that keeps some people swimming long after they should've drowned. 'Get on with it,' I rasped at him. 'We haven't got all night.'

At that his face went blank. But I didn't stop.

'You're the expert on getting women to do what you want. You're the one who wants to prove he can do anything. So *prove* it.'

With no expression at all, he glanced down into Gail's urgent face. Nothing about him gave me any warning.

Suddenly he swung the arm she hugged, wrenched it away from her so hard that she almost fell. 'Stop clinging!' he shouted like the door of a furnace opening. 'All you ever do is *cling*! You suck all the life out of me. You beg and wheedle and whine! You demand everything! You're going to cling me to *death*!'

As full of righteousness and fire as the Wrath of God, he roared, 'Sign those papers!'

Her whole body seemed to cry out to him in chagrin, remorse, contrition. But her face didn't. It was empty, deserted. Her eyes didn't focus on anything.

'Yes, Reg,' she said. 'Of course.'

She went to the desk. The nurse handed her a pen. She signed her name somewhere on the nearest piece of paper.

Haskell turned his back on her. 'You lousy bastard,' he hissed at me. 'You're going to pay for this.'

For maybe the first time since I'd met him, I felt like I was seeing the real Reg Haskell instead of one of his lies or bluffs or manipulations.

But I didn't pay any attention. Gail left the desk, moving towards him – ignoring the starched woman who tried to call her in the other direction – and something started to hum in the back of my mind like a wire in a high wind. At the back door of her house –

I couldn't talk this morning, I'd said, *not with Mase here. He wants to kill Reg.*

So do I, she'd said.

I'd heard a drawer in the kitchen open, close.

She didn't hurry, but she was so close to him I was almost too late. Somehow I shouldered him aside and caught her wrist as she drove a paring knife at the small of his back.

As soon as I stopped her, she went wild. Screaming like a demented cat, she tried to repeat what she'd done to my face earlier. I should've been able to hold her, but she seemed to have more arms and legs than I could keep track of. Fortunately the nurse had enough presence of mind to call for help fast, and a couple of orderlies came running. They got Gail off me with my clothes and most of my skin intact.

Haskell didn't say anything. I didn't say anything. I wanted to hit him so bad that my arms felt like they were going to fall off. And I couldn't bear to look at Gail Harmon's betrayed face as the orderlies wrestled her away. The woman in the starched uniform was the only person nearby who didn't resemble an accusation, so I talked to her.

'I know none of this makes sense.' I gave her one of Ginny's business cards. 'Call us in the morning. We'll tell you everything we can. By then we should be able to put you in touch with her parents.'

The nurse just nodded. No doubt she'd seen people crazier than me in her time. She dismissed me by going back to her paperwork. I turned away.

One hornet's nest stirred up. One more to go – a subtler one. I closed a fist around Haskell's arm so that I wouldn't take a swing at him and steered him out into the cold towards the car.

I felt him watching me sidelong while we walked, gauging me. After a minute he demanded, 'Say something, Axbrewder. I did what you told me. I got her to sign.'

Maybe he was proud of himself. For some reason I didn't think so. I thought he was trying to cover up the fact that he'd lost control for a moment.

When I didn't respond, he started to sneer. 'I hope you like the results. I imagine this is how you assuage your guilt. You put on your Good Samaritan suit and "help" people who are too far gone to stop you. Well, congratulations. You've just cost her what was left of her sanity.'

Without quite meaning to, I ground my fingers into his arm until he gasped. 'Just remember this, Haskell. You're the one she tried to kill. At this point, your life is just a list of people who want you dead.'

He didn't answer. Maybe he didn't have an answer. Or maybe his arm was about to snap. Gritting my teeth to take up the slack, I forced myself to relax my fingers.

A thin sigh leaked up out of his chest. Other than that, he kept his composure.

We got back into the Continental. It started so easily that I didn't trust it. Such instant ignition made me think of sparks and gas tanks. Haskell was right. I hadn't done Gail Harmon any real favours. Fortunately he'd exhausted his reserves of social conversation. Slumping a bit more than usual, he tried to rub his arm without letting me see him do it while I took the beltway up into the Heights towards the Territorial Apartments.

He didn't question our destination. He must've assumed we were on our way back to his house.

Gusts of wind hit us head-on as we climbed the long grade, making the car shudder slightly like it was too well bred to work this hard. Bits of snow came crazily down the tunnel of the headlights. Cars going the other way lit the almost horizontal slash of the flakes. The snowfall looked thicker than it was, however. I had trouble seeing through the reflection, but I didn't need to turn on the wipers.

And off the beltway the visibility improved. Buildings broke up the straight blast of the wind. There wasn't much traffic. The sane daytime population of the Heights had apparently decided that this was a good night to stay home. I found the way to Eunice Wint's apartment easily enough.

Before we got there, Haskell realized where we were headed. He straightened up in his seat. The faint light of the dash made his face look stiff as a mask.

When I parked in front of the Territorial Apartments, he turned to look at me. Like his face, his voice didn't have any expression I could read. 'Your last stop was a roaring success,' he said. 'What do you have in mind this time? Do you think Eunice is working with el Señor? If you loan me a gun, we could go in shooting. We might catch them red-handed.'

I bit back an impulse to ask him what el Señor's name was. Ginny and I weren't ready to spring that on him yet. Shrugging his sarcasm aside, I gave him as much of an answer as I could stomach.

'I want to ask her a few questions about Jordan Canthorpe. You aren't any good at keeping your infidelities secret. She's terrible. The people you work with know exactly what's going on. And jealous fiancés have been known to carry things to extremes.

'Canthorpe has motive, opportunity, and means. But Ginny and I don't know if he's the kind of man who would go that far.'

That didn't ruffle Haskell, but at least it made him stop splashing acid on me. In a steady tone, he asked, 'So why bother Eunice? She's really just a kid. Ask me. I can probably tell you more about Jordan's character than he knows himself.'

'Because you might be wrong. It's been known to happen.'

Buttoning my jacket to create at least the illusion that I was dressed for the weather, I climbed out of the Continental.

I didn't stop him from joining me. If I left him alone, he might drive off. He could easily have another set of keys. And I didn't have any idea which Territorial Apartment Eunice Wint lived in. So I let him go with me. In fact, I let him lead the way.

The building was a standard apartment complex, square cinder-block construction behind the ersatz chalet style. The entryway led to a central courtyard with an untended swimming pool, its scum freezing in the cold. The apartments were ranked around the pool in two layers, like a cross between Alcatraz and *Better Homes and Gardens*. The management had spent enough on lights to keep strangers from falling into the pool, but not enough to make the place look habitable.

Haskell took me up some chipped cement stairs to a door on the upper level. The light made the door look badly faded, vaguely destitute. It rattled on its hinges when he knocked.

Trusting and innocent as usual, Eunice didn't even ask who was there. She just undid the lock and swung the door open. At the sight of her lover, her face lit up like a touch of sunlight. Then she noticed me, and her pleasure turned to embarrassment.

'May we come in, Eunice?' he asked non-committally. 'Mr Axbrewder wants to ask you a few questions.'

Just like that, as smooth as oil, he took control of the situation, left me gaping in the doorway as if he and Eunice were going to humour me because it was Be Kind to Dumb Animals Week. Just by being there, he seemed to take possession of the room. The way he slipped his arm around her and kissed her was proprietary and protective.

I closed the door behind us, wondering what she knew about him that he wanted to hide.

She was wearing a worn terry-cloth bathrobe as threadbare as the carpet. It looked like it had attended too many high-school slumber parties. An elastic band held her hair back from her face. A manicure set on an end table beside the dispirited couch suggested that we'd interrupted her in the process of beautifying herself for the night. Which in turn made me think that she'd been hoping for a visit from Haskell later on.

She made an obvious effort to rise to the occasion, but her surprise and uncertainty got in the way. Intending something polite and appropriate, she opened her mouth and asked me, 'What happened to your face?'

Haskell laughed contentment and malice. 'Axbrewder has a part-time job at night. He puts on make-up and scares children into obeying their parents. He's a professional bogeyman.'

Eunice tittered nervously. She didn't know what else to do.

Neither did I. In less than a minute, Haskell had made my questions impossible. I felt like an idiot. Obviously I never should've let him into the apartment ahead of me.

But I couldn't just stand there until smoke started coming out my ears. I had to do something. So I faked an avuncular expression to hide my disgust, and blundered ahead.

'Mr Haskell likes to kid around, Ms Wint. Unfortunately my business is a little more serious than that.

'Do you know Gail Harmon?'

Haskell's relaxed posture and superior smile didn't change. Nevertheless I saw the small muscles around his eyes go tight.

Eunice considered the name for a moment. Then she shook her head.

I believed her. If she'd tried to lie to me, she would've blushed for three days.

'She used to have a job where you work,' I explained. 'I wanted to ask her the same questions I'd like to ask you. She's the one who scratched my face.'

That confused her. She didn't know which end to tackle first. 'Why did she—? What questions—?'

'She used to know Mr Haskell fairly well,' I told her. That took me pretty close to the edge of professional ethics – the part where it says you keep your client's dirt to yourself – but I didn't much care. Still, I made an effort to watch my step. 'I'm talking to all kinds of people about him. Perhaps he hasn't told you what I'm doing here.'

She shook her head again. He hadn't explained anything about me.

'I'm his bodyguard, Ms Wint. I'm trying to protect him. I asked Gail Harmon if she knew anyone who might want him killed.'

'Killed?' Her hands fluttered to her face in alarm. 'Reg?' She cast a horrified look at him. 'You didn't tell me—' Back to me. 'Is somebody trying to kill him?'

'I'm afraid so.'

'Oh my God.' Instead of her usual blush, she turned pale. For a second I thought she was going to faint. But she lowered herself to the couch and stayed there, her eyes staring at something I couldn't see. 'Oh my God.'

'Nice going, Axbrewder,' Haskell rasped. Angry or amused, I couldn't tell which. 'You have all the finesse of a bulldozer, do you know that? What good do you think you're doing?'

I gave him a glare that would have chipped paint, but I didn't let him deflect me. 'Ms Wint,' I said – gambling a little, but what the hell – 'forgive me if I seem callous. I'm just trying to do my job. For some reason, women who know Reg Haskell don't react normally when I tell them he's in danger. Gail Harmon tried to tear my face off. And you – you believed me right away, didn't you. As soon as I said it, you knew it was true. And you haven't asked me why.'

Haskell tried to interrupt, but I stopped him by grabbing his bruised arm and digging in a bit.

'You know what I think, Ms Wint? I think you know someone who would like to see him dead. And I think you know why. Who is it?'

She didn't look up. Images and possibilities unreeling in her head transfixed her.

'Ms Wint.' Quietly, but with an edge in my voice. 'I need your help. I'm trying to protect him.'

Her lips moved. Her eyes lifted to my face and dropped again. She seemed to be trying to pull her thoughts together from a dozen different directions at once.

'Is it Jordan Canthorpe? Your fiancé?'

Without knowing how, I'd touched something deep in her – some loyalty to her own choices and mistakes, some kind of dignity. A bit of her colour came back, and she looked at me straight.

'Mr Axbrewder, I think every other man in the world must want Reg dead. He's the only one who's really alive. The rest of you are just going through the motions.'

That was it. I couldn't ask her any more questions. If anyone else – even Sara Haskell – had offered me that load of horseshit, I would've laughed at it. But from Eunice Wint I accepted it. She was only an innocent bystander, after all. She had the right. And I'd pushed my own meanness as far as I could stand it. The idea of jumping up and down on a girl who had fallen in love with someone other than her fiancé sickened me.

And maybe she was right. I sure as hell didn't have anything to match the gleam of Haskell's grin.

So I let go of his arm. I said, 'Thank you, Ms Wint.' I gestured for him to follow me, and I let myself out of the apartment, making a special effort not to pull the door off its hinges.

He caught up with me at the bottom of the stairs. Ready for anything in his nice, warm coat. He didn't make the mistake of smiling at me, but he couldn't keep the bounce out of his stride, couldn't hide his eagerness. Someone was trying to kill him. It was even more fun than bridge.

From where I stood, the temperature felt like it had actually gone up a couple of degrees. Poised for some serious snow.

As we walked out to the car, he said, 'Now tell me, Axbrewder. When have I ever been wrong?'

Reg Haskell, old buddy, old pal. You were wrong when you hired Ginny and me. You should've been enough of a man to face your problems yourself.

Chapter Seventeen

osing the Continental off Foothill over the crest into Cactus Blossom Court, I saw Ginny's Olds parked in Haskell's driveway. All the exterior lights of the house were on.

A car I didn't recognize sat beside the Olds.

A little abruptly, I pulled over to the kerb. The car was a late-model beige Mercury sedan, and I had the feeling that I'd seen it before. Probably there weren't more than five hundred cars just like it in Puerta del Sol.

Maybe it belonged to Sara Haskell? That was a dizzying prospect, as they say.

I turned to Haskell. 'You recognize that car?'

He shrugged. 'It looks like Jordan Canthorpe's.'

Muttering curses to myself, I jerked the Continental into reverse, backed into the nearest driveway, and headed in the opposite direction.

Haskell watched me like I was an amusing and slightly dangerous lunatic. 'Don't tell me,' he said, 'let me guess. You think it's a trap. You think the branch manager of the First Puerta del Sol National Bank has your partner at gun-point, waiting to shoot me when we walk in. You're paranoid, Axbrewder. You should've asked me whether Jordan's capable of that.'

I didn't answer. I was thinking, Canthorpe. Or Canthorpe and Novick. Or Novick alone. I couldn't afford to take the chance. Reacting intelligently, for a change of pace, I drove a mile back down Foothill to a gas station and used the pay phone to call Haskell's house.

Ginny answered after the fourth ring. 'Hello?' The way her voice twitched on the word scared me. Suddenly all the things I feared didn't seem paranoid at all.

I braced myself inside the phone booth, clamped the receiver to the side of my head. 'Ginny. You all right?'

'Brew.' Relief and exasperation – and a small stretched tremor like a hint of hysteria. 'Where are you?'

'Are you all right?' Please, Ginny, tell me you're not in trouble. Make me believe it.

'Of course I'm all right. Or I was until I had to spend half my life waiting for you. What are you doing? Where the hell are you?'

She didn't sound all right. She sounded ragged and overwrought, close to craziness. But she wouldn't have talked that way if she'd been in danger.

I let a sigh slip through my teeth. 'There's a car parked next to yours. I don't know who it belongs to, so I decided to check before I barged into the house.'

'That's Canthorpe.' She didn't seem particularly interested in how smart and cautious I was being. 'Get over here. You're going to love this.'

I said, 'Five minutes,' but she didn't hear me. She'd already hung up.

I'm fine, I thought. Thanks for asking. Actually, my evening has been pretty entertaining. I'll be glad to tell you about it. Since you're so interested.

I put the receiver back in its cradle – gently, Axbrewder, gently – and returned to the car, trying to believe that what I felt didn't matter.

As I got into the Continental, Haskell gave me a quizzical look. His air of superiority wasn't what I needed at the moment. When I didn't say anything, he murmured, 'Don't keep me in suspense. What's going on? Is Fistoulari being held hostage? Are we going to storm the house?'

Damn him, anyway. 'Better than that,' I muttered as I wrenched the car away from the gas station and aimed it back up Foothill. Snowflakes did crazy little dances in the headlights as we rushed through them. 'You're a bridge player. We're going to table the dummy. That's you. We're going to put your cards down where everybody can look at them.'

He replied with a moment of frozen silence. Then, slowly, he shook his head. 'It's amazing,' he mused. 'I don't know how you stay in business. Do you treat all your clients like this?'

No. Just the ones who lie a lot.

Gritting my teeth, I wheeled the Continental down Cactus Blossom.

There weren't any cars except Ginny's and Canthorpe's outside. The rest of the neighbourhood had already put its cars away. I parked the

Continental, and we got out. Without any particular caution, we walked into the aisle leading to the front door. I used my key to let us in.

When I got the door open, I heard Ginny call from downstairs, 'Is that you, Brew?' She sounded the way a knife looks after you use its edge to turn screws for a while. 'We're in the den.'

I answered to reassure her. Smiling slightly, Haskell took off his coat, hung it up in the closet. Behind the smile, he wore his sober, serious face. But the shine in his eyes made him look like a kid playing some keen game he thought he was going to win. When I'd relocked the door, I gestured him ahead of me, and we went down the stairs.

In the den, its picture-window blind against the darkness of the arroyo, we found Ginny and Canthorpe on their feet waiting for us.

Canthorpe's pinstripe had lost its immaculate line. For all I knew, he'd been wrestling in it. And his self-effacing moustache seemed even thinner than before. Stress and anger showed in his pale eyes.

In contrast, Ginny's eyes looked sunken and hollow. The skin of her broken nose was white against the high hot patch of colour on each cheek. She made no effort to conceal her stump.

'Jordan,' Haskell said amiably, 'what brings you here?'

Canthorpe didn't respond. His fingers twitched at his sides.

'Would you like a drink?' Haskell went on. Polite and amused, on top of his game. 'I need one. Ms Fistoulari? Axbrewder, you deserve a drink by now.'

'Mr Haskell,' Ginny said carefully, 'this isn't a social occasion.'

'I know that.' Not ruffled at all. 'Somebody is trying to kill me, and I hired you to protect me, but all you've done is dig into my life and attack me with what you find. This will be more of the same. But we can still be courteous about it.'

He repeated his offer of drinks. None of us accepted. He shrugged to say it was our loss, not his, and left the room. When he returned a minute later, he carried a tall glass full of liquor and ice cubes. For an irrational moment, I hated him because I needed that drink more than he did and I couldn't have it.

'Now,' he said, glancing casually around at us, 'what is it this time?'

I think he was having fun.

But Ginny was in no mood for it. Internal pressure put a lash like a lick of venom in her voice. 'Mr Haskell' – soft and poisonous – 'before you accuse us of unprofessional conduct, I want to say just once that we did not tell Mr Canthorpe your half-assed story about el Señor's money laundry. We talked to him because we thought he could help us figure out how el Señor found you so fast.' And because he still has reason to want you dead, Reg Haskell, even though you aren't worried about that at all. 'We did not bring him into this in order to attack you.'

Haskell couldn't argue. He couldn't claim that the question of how he'd been discovered wasn't crucial. Instead he sat down on the couch facing the window, made himself comfortable, sipped his drink, and waited for her to go on.

'When I called him this afternoon to see if he'd made any progress,' she said, 'he informed me that your entire story is a fabrication. There is no money laundry. You've been stringing us along from the beginning.'

Haskell widened his eyes. Lowered his glass to his knee. Looked at Canthorpe. 'That's cheap, Jordan,' he said softly.

Then he faced Ginny. 'I told you from the start that I couldn't prove anything. That doesn't mean I'm lying. It just means the connections are tenuous. And there is no way that he could have checked my research in just one morning. Not without asking me for details to put him on the right track.' It was a good performance. He did righteousness well. 'Before you take his word over mine, you ought to consider his reasons for wanting to hurt me.'

'Damn you, Haskell,' Canthorpe snapped. 'Not everybody in the world is as unscrupulous as you are. I wouldn't stoop to lies because of you. And let me tell you something. I know—'

Ginny cut him off. 'As it happens,' she said sharply, 'I don't need to take anybody's word for anything. We've talked about el Señor all day' – straight at Haskell – 'but we've never mentioned his name. Obviously he must bank under his own name. Otherwise you wouldn't know it was him.

'Mr Haskell, why don't you tell us el Señor's real name? Just to prove you know what it is.'

He met her glare without blinking. As a precaution, I shifted positions slowly, moving around behind the couch to grab at him if he tried anything stupid. For a long minute, he didn't respond. Apparently the fact he'd been caught lying again was a matter of intellectual rather than personal interest.

When he spoke, he didn't sound worried, just curious and thoughtful. 'That's clever. You told Jordan the name, and he checked the account computer. He found out that nobody by that name banks with us.'

'That's right,' she said. 'But there's more.'

He raised an eyebrow. 'Really? I would have thought you had enough by now to keep you entertained.'

In response, she raised her left forearm like she'd forgotten it didn't have a fist any more. Maybe she didn't realize what she was doing. She was too tense, too close to the edge.

'This isn't entertainment,' she gritted. 'It's my job. I believe in doing it right. But for that I need the truth. All you've given us is lies. Not because you have any reason to lie. If you did – if we were dangerous to you in some way – you wouldn't have hired us in the first place. No, you tell lies because you think it's fun. Part of the game. You get your jollies by manipulating people, jerking them around. You've been playing with us from the start. Well, grow up, Reg.'

She turned his name into a snarl. 'The game's over. When I got back this evening, Mr Canthorpe was here waiting for me. Your lies about a money laundry made him suspicious, so he did some checking of his own. We know where you get your money, Reg.'

'My money?' he asked innocently. 'You mean my investments?' But he didn't look particularly guilty. Just interested. Curious about what was coming next.

'Investments, shit,' Canthorpe put in. From him the obscenity sounded quaint. But his face was pale with vehemence, and his hands clenched at his sides. 'You've been using the bank's money to finance your gambling habit.'

'Wait a minute,' Haskell retorted. 'Hold it right there.' Oddly enough, his protest sounded more genuine this time. 'I do not have a gambling habit.'

But if he thought he could stop Canthorpe that way, he'd misjudged his boss. 'I don't care what you call it,' Canthorpe snapped. Anger quavered in his boyish voice. 'You've risked the bank's money for personal gain. I've seen the records.

'This Friday, when the books were closed at three-thirty, you had exactly one hundred and twelve dollars, eighty-two cents in your account. But you have overdraft protection on your bank credit card. You stayed a little late, and you persuaded Eunice' – he stumbled over the name – 'Eunice Wint to cash a cheque for you. For five thousand dollars.

'You knew, of course, that your withdrawal wouldn't go on to the books until Monday morning. And when it did, it would show up as exceeding the limit on your card instead of as passing a bad cheque. So you would have a few days' grace to pay it back.

'But this time you didn't need grace, not the way you have in the past. This time you came in early Monday morning with twenty thousand dollars in cash and deposited it to cover your cheque.

'You haven't always been that lucky. I haven't had time to check the whole history of your account, but I've been over the records for the past six months. You've pulled this stunt fifteen times. Nearly two weekends out of three. The average balance in your account has gone from something over ten thousand dollars to just exactly one hundred and twelve dollars, eighty-two cents, and last month your credit card carried you for three weeks before you repaid the money.

'You've been pouring your own money down the drain. And you've risked the bank's money along with it. On top of that' – he looked like his collar was choking him – 'you've implicated my fiancée in some kind of gambling scam.

'What's the matter with you, Haskell?' he demanded with more force than I thought he had in him. 'How sick are you?'

Canthorpe's revelation came as a jolt. No wonder Ginny looked like she'd gone too far out on the wire and was losing her balance. His information punctured a lot of theories. For instance, it left us with absolutely no reason to believe that Haskell had ever had anything to do with el Señor. Not even indirectly, through loan sharks.

At the same time, it made Canthorpe look innocent. If he'd already put Novick on to Haskell, why would he come here and act righteous over a few thousand dollars of the bank's money? That exposed too many of his private emotions. It didn't make sense.

In other words, we no longer had any explanation for what we were up against. We only had two hard facts to go on. Haskell had lied to us. Steadily and repeatedly. And somebody was trying to kill him. No wonder Smithsonian had sneered at us when we took this case. We were in deep shit.

At least now we knew why Haskell carried an empty briefcase. Friday morning he took it in to work empty. Friday evening he came home with a briefcase full of money. On Monday he reversed the process.

I suppose I should've been grateful for small favours.

But Haskell didn't swallow Canthorpe's accusation. Looking bright-eyed and bushy-tailed, he watched Canthorpe until the branch manager stopped. Then he shrugged and took a pull at his drink. His insouciance was perfect.

'Jordan,' he said almost kindly when he lowered his glass, 'you're just upset. None of that proves I've been gambling.'

I must've looked as blank and amazed as Canthorpe did. Haskell's reply was like defending yourself against a murder rap by claiming you hadn't had anything to drink. The bank didn't care what he *did* with the money, it cared that he *took* it. He must've been losing what was left of his grasp on reality.

Or this case had dimensions we didn't know about yet.

But Ginny didn't seem surprised or baffled by Haskell's attitude. One way or another, it apparently made sense to her.

'That's true,' she said harshly. 'None of that proves you've been gambling. But while Mr Canthorpe was researching your account, I did some checking of my own.'

Slowly he turned his head to look at her like he wasn't sure she merited his attention.

'I spent this morning at the airport,' she informed him. 'And this evening I had a talk with your wife.'

He stiffened just enough to make a difference. 'You know' – his voice was soft and dangerous – 'I could have sworn I told you to leave her out of this.'

'Just for the record,' I murmured, 'no, you didn't.' But no one took any notice of me.

Ginny smiled like the edge of a hacksaw. 'Just doing my job.' Before he could interrupt, she went on, 'At first, I thought she might not be able to tell me anything. All by herself in that hotel, alone hour after hour with no idea what in hell's going on, she's going crazy. You've kept so much secret from her, and she wants to trust you so badly, she's practically paralysed. The only thing she can do is talk to total strangers about you, asking them for reassurance because she thinks you're getting ready to dump her. She really doesn't know a thing about what you do with your time when you're not with her.'

Canthorpe had moved back a few steps to lean against the wall beside the window, studying his fiancée's lover while he waited for his chance to talk again.

'But finally I asked the right question. A simple, practical question.' Ginny watched Haskell sharply. 'She told me who your travel agent is.

'After that, it was easy. I went to your travel agent. Flashed my licence around, offered to get a few subpoenas. They let me look at their records. I know which flights you took to Las Vegas, on which weekends. I know the hotel you stayed in. If you push me that far, I can go there, show people your picture, and find out exactly what you did – what game you played in, how much money you lost, the whole thing.

'I'll do that, Haskell.' She chewed the words at him. 'I'll uncover so much dirt about you that you'll never get another accounting job in this state.

'Unless you start telling us the truth.'

I couldn't see his face any more – I'd moved completely behind him – but he didn't seem particularly upset. His hand was steady as he raised his glass and finished his drink.

After a moment he said evenly, 'It looks like I underestimated you.' The idea didn't exactly fill him with chagrin. 'I hadn't realized you consider investigating your clients more important than protecting them. I wanted to avoid telling you how much trouble I'm really in. I didn't want to take that chance. I knew I would lose my job if anybody at the bank found out what I'd been doing.'

He shrugged. 'But I've lost it anyway. You've cost me that. If you don't do your job now, you're going to cost me my life. So I'll tell you the truth.' He put rat poison in his voice. 'That way you won't have any more excuses.'

Then he stopped, however. Instead of continuing, he stared out at the cold black night and thought until Ginny said in exasperation, 'Get on with it, Haskell. I've had all I can stand.'

'Do you people read the paper?' he asked with obvious sarcasm. 'Do you know who Roscoe Chavez is?'

That went through me like the stroke of a knife. 'Front-page news yesterday,' I said simply to help myself handle the shock. 'Bambino Chavez was one of el Señor's lieutenants. He turned up dead on Sunday.'

I had to stop. If I went on babbling, I might say something about Pablo.

'That's right,' Haskell commented dryly. 'If you check back far enough, you'll learn that Roscoe Chavez and I went to high school together.' He snorted a laugh. 'He and I were on the soccer team together. In fact, an assist from me let him score the winning goal in the conference championship. It would've surprised me if he ever forgot who I was.

'I started going to Vegas a while back. I wanted some relief. Being an accountant was going to bore me into an early grave. I had to spice it up somehow. Vegas gave me a chance to feel alive for the first time in years. It practically resurrected me. And I made a lot of money.

'About a year ago, I ran into Roscoe there. We were staying at the same hotel. We had an old soccer pals reunion, commemorating his moment of glory. We took in a show, played some poker, had a lot to drink. It was fun. One thing I'll say for him. Roscoe knew how to have a good time.

'If you still think I'm lying' – poison again – 'do the research. It can't be hard to learn who I spent my time with. It was always the same. First Roscoe and I got together whenever we were there. Then we started planning our trips together. He had an interesting life, and he liked to talk about it, especially to his old soccer buddy. He wasn't the brightest man I ever met, but he was exciting company.

'Then, about six months ago, we both hit a streak of bad luck. We were playing poker with a group of regulars at the hotel, and we'd been taking them to the cleaners for months. But when our luck shifted we started to lose a bit. I mean *I* lost a bit. Roscoe lost a lot. He shovelled money out of his pockets with both hands. In fact' – now his tone held a smile – 'my few winnings came from him.

'After a few months, he began to get desperate. He'd used up his reserves. He needed a stake to win his money back. But I couldn't help him. I didn't have anything to spare myself.

'We spent a while commiserating. Then he suggested that maybe I could help him after all. He knew how he could get his hands on some money by ripping off his boss. El Señor.'

Oh God. I had to brace my hands on the back of the couch to keep myself on my feet.

'And you bought it?' Ginny snapped. 'He offered you a scam to rip off el Señor, and you *bought* it? What do you use for brains? Oatmeal?'

'I didn't see anything wrong with it,' Haskell shot back angrily. 'I needed money myself, you know. What better place to get it? And his scheme looked good. He ran el Señor's numbers racket. He knew the whole operation inside out. All he needed was a secret partner, somebody that nobody in Puerta del Sol could connect to him. Then it was simple. He would give his partner the winning number a few days in advance. His partner would bet that number and collect the winnings. They would split the take. What could go wrong?'

As he talked, he recovered his equanimity. Maybe it was the sound of his own voice that steadied him. 'I assume you noticed I didn't go to Vegas last weekend.'

Ginny nodded stiffly. Canthorpe watched Haskell with a kind of fascinated nausea.

'Friday evening,' Haskell explained, 'I used my bank card to borrow five thousand dollars, and I placed the bet. We had to be cautious because I wasn't one of their regulars, so we didn't get greedy. I didn't

362

put all the money on the right number. I spread it around, small sums, a lot of separate bets with different runners.

'The hundred bucks I put on the right number paid forty-to-one.'

He spread his hands. 'I picked up my winnings Saturday night. Sunday I gave Roscoe his half. I thought we were all set.' The memory seemed to sadden him. 'Sunday night I got the phone call I told you about. Monday morning I read in the paper that Roscoe was dead.

'I guess his boss must've found out what he was doing.'

Must've found out. Christ on a crutch! For once we had a story that seemed to cover everything. It was a terrible story. I couldn't keep my kneecaps from trembling.

'Who did you place your bets with?' I tried to sound nonchalant, but I didn't come close.

'Huh?' Haskell craned his neck to look up at me behind him. 'What do you mean?'

Ginny went on staring at him. Something in her eyes looked vague and lost. Her worst fears were landing like vultures on her shoulders.

'I'm talking English, aren't I?' I returned. 'It's a simple question.' I may very well have been losing my mind, but I couldn't stop. 'Who did you place your bets with?'

'I told you, I spread my money around.' He didn't like peering up at me, so he lowered his head. 'I went wherever Roscoe told me to go. I must've seen twenty different runners.'

'Haskell.' I had a little trouble breathing. 'I know how the numbers work in this city.' Don't try lying to me. 'I know some of the runners. Where did you go?'

He may have been cocky, but he wasn't stupid. He didn't miss my point. 'The old part of town,' he said warily. 'Phone booths. Bars. Alleys. I can't tell you addresses or names. But if you go with me, I can take you every place I went.'

'The runners,' I said. 'Describe some of them.'

'Come off it, Axbrewder.' Heavy disdain. 'I was down there at night. They're all Chicano kids. They all look alike to me. I wouldn't recognize one of them if I saw him again.'

Damn him. Damn everything. I wanted to take him by the throat and shake him until he learned a few decent lessons about fear. It was just possible that he was responsible for Pablo's death. If Pablo had figured out or stumbled on to what the Bambino and Haskell were up to, Chavez could easily have broken his neck and dumped him out of a fast car in self-defence. And if el Señor found out, that would explain his attitude towards the Santiagos – his insistence on an honourable funeral, his promise that he would avenge Pablo's killing.

Pure speculation, nothing but moonshine. But it fitted. It fitted well enough to hurt.

El Señor wanted Haskell dead for the same reasons that Roscoe Chavez had been killed. A ritual hit.

We were supposed to protect him.

Feeling desperate, I ached to ask Ginny what she was thinking. I hadn't told her anything about Pablo. Whatever troubled her was something else entirely.

And she didn't know how to deal with it. Her face was pale, and her eyes had lost focus. Abruptly she announced, 'I need a drink after all.' She didn't look at me or anyone else as she left the den as if she were fleeing.

I almost went after her. I'd never seen her like this before, and it appalled me.

But before I could turn away, Haskell said to Canthorpe, 'I hope you're satisfied.'

His tone held me. It was too quiet. I could hear venom.

'You'll be able to fire me now. You've endangered my marriage. Sara won't know what to think about all this. And you may even get me killed. I hired Fistoulari and Axbrewder to protect me, but you've compromised them for me. You must've waited a long time for a chance to do something like this to me. I wonder' – he looked casually at his fingernails – 'what I'll do to get even.'

Canthorpe came off the wall like he'd been hit with a cattle prod. A couple of steps later, however, he snatched himself back under control. Framed by the blackness of the window, his boyish face looked as fierce as it could. But his eyes weren't stupid, or weak either, and bone lay behind every line of his face. He was a better enemy than he probably realized. Maybe he was better than I'd imagined.

Deliberately he straightened his jacket and his tie. In a cold voice, he said, 'You simply don't understand, do you? You're in every conceivable kind of trouble, and all you can do about it is threaten me. Well, your threats don't frighten me. They're asinine. You may be charming and talented, but you're an empty hull instead of a man. It shouldn't surprise me that you don't understand. You have a goat's conception of love.'

Haskell started to laugh. 'Ah, the injured pride of the impotent man. You shouldn't let yourself be vindictive, Jordan. It makes you ridiculous.'

364

'*Listen* for a minute,' Canthorpe snapped back. 'I'll add it up for you.'

Ginny had come back into the den. She stood beside me, a glass in her hand. Straight Scotch, I knew it by smell. Her grip was white, like a mute call for help.

'You can't threaten me,' Canthorpe went on, 'because you've already cost me what I care about most. There is no significant harm left that you can do to me. The best you can hope for is to minimize your own losses.

'Keeping you alive is none of my business. I couldn't help with that if I wanted to. But the bank *is* my business. You've made dishonest use of the bank's money. I could have you fired in a heartbeat.

'However' – some of his vehemence faded – 'the bank doesn't appear to have lost any money.' He nailed his gaze to Haskell's face. 'I could let it pass. I could keep what you've done to myself. On one condition.' Unexpected colour came into his cheeks. The labour of his heart made his voice throb. 'Leave Eunice alone. Stop seeing her. Tell her it's finished, you don't love her, you don't want her any more.' His mouth quivered involuntarily. 'Give me a chance to win her back.'

At that, Haskell began laughing.

'A chance?' He could hardly get the words out. 'To win her back?' He laughed so hard that I thought he was going to pop something. Or I was going to pop it for him. 'You're dreaming.'

Gradually he subsided. With obvious malice, he told Canthorpe, 'Some people are content to eat cardboard all their lives. But not after they've tasted steak. You can't go back. Nobody can go back.'

'You bastard,' Canthorpe panted. 'You bastard.' Sudden tears covered his face. 'I hope they cut your heart out.' Turning with a jerk, he walked unsteadily towards the end of the room.

Now he no longer stood between Haskell and the picture window.

That was all the warning we had. It wasn't much.

As soon as Canthorpe cleared the way, a brick came through the glass. It seemed to appear out of nowhere, a piece of night that suddenly turned hard and heavy enough to shatter panes. The window burst into splinters. A spray of glass followed the brick.

Straight at Haskell.

Double-glazed insulation panes absorbed most of the brick's force. It thudded to the carpet a good ten feet from Haskell's shoes. Chips and splinters carried further, but they didn't reach him either. Bits of snow swirled in out of the dark.

Which was the whole point, of course. You couldn't tell how thick the glass was unless you looked at it up close in good light. Some energy-conscious homes have triple- and even quadruple-glazed windows. That much glass can deflect even a high-powered rifle bullet – and you would only get one shot because it would make the entire window crazy with cracks.

In fact, you probably wouldn't use a rifle at all. There were four of us in the room, and you would want to take us all out at once. And that would make it even more important to get the glass out of the way first.

While we stared like paralytics at the brick, and shards of cold made moaning noises past the ragged edges of the window, a hand grenade took a casual flip through the opening, hit the carpet, and rolled to a stop in front of Haskell.

We could all see as plain as the glass glittering in the nap of the carpet that the pin and the handle were gone.

An old army surplus grenade, the kind you can order with a coupon from *Soldier of Fortune*. Despite its age, however, it would be powerful enough to gut the room. And that many screaming steel fragments would do a nice job on the four of us.

Ginny recovered first. She barked, 'Move!' in a voice that went through all my muscles like a jolt of electricity.

I moved.

Like we'd been practising it for months, she bent down and shoved her forearms under the edge of the couch while I reached for Haskell.

My part was easy. Under the circumstances, he didn't feel particularly heavy. In one motion, I latched on to his shoulders and heaved him over the back of the couch.

He hit the wall pretty hard, but I didn't waste time worrying about that.

Ginny had a tougher assignment. And apparently she'd forgotten that she only had one hand. She didn't brace herself right for the leverage she needed. With both forearms under the edge of the couch, she jerked upward – and her right arm slipped free. She lost her balance, stumbled backward. Hit the wall about the same time Haskell did, and almost as hard.

Those old grenades give you seven seconds before they tear you to pieces. I didn't know how much time I had left, and I didn't care. What difference would it make? I still had to take my best shot, beat the detonation if I could.

Jamming my hands under the couch, I pitched it forward, shoved it upside down on top of the grenade.

The grenade went off.

366

It made a muffled crumpling noise like popping a paper bag underwater. The couch burst stuffing at the ceiling. I felt the shock of the explosion and did my best to fall backwards, away from it. Wood and cloth went to shreds. Metal springs twanged like tortured rebar. The walls spit chips everywhere.

But the couch absorbed enough of the blast.

As I landed on the floor, silence clapped back through the room. The innards of the couch seemed to geyser everywhere, obscuring the hole in the window so that I couldn't see out – and whoever was out there couldn't see in.

Haskell lay against the wall, his eyes wide. Across the room, Canthorpe gaped at the couch like he was about to throw up. He was the only one of us on his feet.

Ginny knelt near me, bracing herself with her good arm. She didn't seem aware of anything around her. As hard as she could, she slammed her stump against the wall.

Again. And again.

'Damn this thing,' she panted. 'Damn it. Damn it.'

First things first.

'Canthorpe,' I said. A lunatic calm possessed me. My voice was quiet and conversational, crazy in the aftermath of the grenade. 'Get the lights.'

Something in my tone got his attention. He moved towards the switches. His path kept him out of the field of fire.

I turned to Ginny. 'Stop it. I need you. Get your gun.'

The stuffing settled like snow in the centre of the room. When Canthorpe reached the switches, the lights went out.

Ginny stopped.

'Don't move,' I breathed to Haskell and Canthorpe. 'Don't say anything. He knows this is a trap.'

Ditching the lights was a gamble. It warned whoever was out there. But it also evened the odds. I got up on my knees, snatched the .45.

'But he might come in after us anyway.'

Ginny crawled past me in the dark, then paused.

I thought I heard someone start up the hill in the narrow lane between the privacy wall and the side of the house.

That made sense. Circle around, take us from behind. I headed for the stairs, hoping to cut him off.

Behind me, Ginny whispered hoarsely, 'Brew! Wait for me.'

She reached the stairs a few steps after I did.

We'd left the atrium and entryway lights on. I didn't even think about turning them off. I didn't want the man outside to know where we were.

Near the top of the stairs, I tightened my grip on the .45 and stopped. If I were him, I might try to break in through the living-room window, on ground level before the hill sloped down towards the arroyo. It wasn't exposed to the outside lights of the house and the street. And the atrium lit the doorway to the living room but left the window dark. He could watch for us – and we would have a hard time surprising him.

Avoiding the line of the light, so that my shadow didn't touch the doorway into the living room, I left the stairs and moved to stand beside the door-frame.

Ginny followed, her face as pale as bone. A smear of blood oozed from abrasions on her stump. Behind her clenched teeth, she looked like she was hyperventilating.

I waited for the sound of breaking glass. We'd left all the windows locked. The goon would knock in one pane to reach the latch. Or he would just crash through the window.

He didn't. I heard nothing. Nothing at all. Not even a car out on the street.

I was wrong. He wasn't coming in this way. Then where? Where were the other windows on this level?

'Shit,' I sighed to Ginny through my teeth. 'The bedroom.'

Just to be on the safe side, I jumped in front of the doorway to the living room, leading with the .45 – reassuring myself that the window was closed and intact.

It wasn't. Nothing was broken. But it was wide open.

Before I could react, he came out at me. While I turned towards him, he hammered me in the chest with the butt of his rifle. I went down like I'd been kicked by a horse.

No way to defend myself. My lungs felt like they'd been nailed to the floor. Somewhere on the other side of a wall of pain, my arm struggled to do something with the .45. But my muscles might as well have been cut. I couldn't even raise my hand. All I could do was watch him raise the M-16 to swing it again. This time it would crush my skull.

'Don't do it!' Ginny yelled. She sounded wild.

So wild that Novick froze in mid-swing.

Her .357 jutted right into his face. From that range, the muzzle must've looked like the snout of a howitzer.

His hands made twitching movements towards his belt. Maybe he wanted the knife sheathed on his left hip, maybe one of the grenades clipped on the other side.

She rasped, 'I mean it. I've killed people this way before.'

Somewhere under the dope or fever in his eyes, his instinct for survival still functioned. Slowly he pulled his hands back until his weapons were out of reach.

Somehow I took a breath. After a minute or so, I figured out how to move again.

Chapter Eighteen

By the time I got to my feet, I was starting to think maybe Novick had cracked a couple of ribs, and Haskell and Canthorpe stood near the head of the stairs, staring. For different reasons, they both looked like kids – Canthorpe because he had that kind of face, Haskell because this was probably as close as he'd ever been to a real live game of cops-and-robbers. Just judging by appearances, neither of them could've possibly had anything to do with Mase Novick, with his tattoos and his murderous cornered-animal expression. Or with Ginny either, for that matter, who looked like a whiskey bottle with the bottom broken out of it, ready to slash in any direction.

'Who is he?' Canthorpe asked softly.

'Cover him,' she panted at me. She was breathing hard – too hard. Her aim at Novick wobbled perilously.

Despite the stress on my chest, I pulled up the .45. Directing the muzzle at Novick's guts, I said tightly, 'I hope you try something.' My voice sounded like it had to squeeze its way through a pile of rocks. 'I'd love to get even.'

Ginny sagged a bit. But she didn't lower her gun. 'Haskell,' she said as if she were fighting suffocation, 'get some rope.'

He nodded. Glad to participate.

As soon as Haskell crossed the atrium and entered the garage, she turned her .357 on Jordan Canthorpe.

'Don't move.' She was practically gasping. 'Don't talk. Don't think. You've already had your chance.'

His face went wide. His mouth gaped open. All the colour ran out of his skin. Completely innocent. Or surprised as hell to get caught.

Two things went through my head like ricochets. Either she was wrong. Or Haskell had lied to us again.

Wait a minute, I wanted to say. Let's think this through. But Ginny was in no condition to hear me. Her teeth clenched at the air as if that were all that kept her from passing out. The lines of her face looked too sharp. I forced myself to concentrate on Novick.

In a tone of demented detachment, I advised him to lie down with his nose in the carpet. Canthorpe tried to find his voice, but Ginny's white grip on the .357 stopped him. By the time I had Novick stretched out the way I wanted him, Haskell came back with a coil of clothesline.

When he saw what was going on, he stopped. 'Jordan?' Then he wheeled on Ginny. 'Fistoulari, what the hell are you doing?'

Keeping the .45 aimed at Novick's spine, I went over to Haskell and took the rope. 'If I were you, Reg' – a bit of friendly advice – 'I would keep my mouth shut for a while. No one here gives a flying fuck at the moon for your opinion.' Then I went back to Novick.

With one knee, I pinned him while I lashed his wrists together. '*Cojones*,' he rasped at me. 'Motherfucker.' A lick on the side of the head with the .45 shut him up. Just to be on the safe side, I tied his wrists to his ankles, bowing his back until his shoulders looked like they might separate.

'Now him,' Ginny panted. The barrel of the .357 indicated Canthorpe.

Oh, good. If you have to go off the deep end, you might as well go all the way.

'Ms Fistoulari, I don't know what you think I've done' – Canthorpe sounded steadier than I expected – 'but you're wrong. I don't even know who this man is.'

'Now him,' she repeated through her teeth. 'Come on, Brew.'

I didn't argue. I wasn't ready. My chest hurt, and cold air from the windows only made it worse. In some sense, I was responsible for what had happened. I was the one who stirred up Novick's beehive brain. So I did what she told me.

Canthorpe gave me a glare of outrage and appeal, but he didn't resist. Soon I had him trussed up too – like Novick, but not as hard.

That gave Ginny a respite of some kind. She lowered her gun. Taking a deep breath, she held it until she could stop panting. With her sore stump, she wiped her face. Sweat streaked the hair on either side of her face. Her eyes were out of focus – relieved and lost.

I knew what was coming, but I didn't know how to deal with it. Trying to postpone it, I went into the living room and snapped on the lights to see how Novick had gotten in.

The window was open all the way. The damage around the latch suggested that the window had been forced with the blade of a knife. A heavy-duty knife, like the one Novick carried.

That should've made enough noise to warn me. Therefore Novick must've reached the house ahead of Ginny and Canthorpe. Maybe they arrived just when he'd started to break in. Interrupted him. But then they went down to the den. Presumably he followed to keep an eye on them, leaving the window open in case he needed it.

Ginny had been so close to the edge – not to mention fixed on what Canthorpe was saying – that she'd never thought to check the house.

When I returned to the atrium, I found her sitting on the floor, her gun in front of her. Haskell watched her as if he expected her to begin singing Christmas carols. Canthorpe muttered over and over again, 'You are out of your mind, Ms Fistoulari. You are out of your mind.' She didn't look at either of them.

As soon as I rejoined her, she said, 'Call the police, Brew.'

She didn't look at me, either.

'Ginny.' There was no good way to say it. 'Maybe we should go over this once or twice. I'm not sure we've got it right.'

'I said, call the police.' Her voice was acid. 'This bastard almost broke you in half. He threw a hand grenade at us. How innocent do you think he's likely to be?'

'More than you do, anyway,' I retorted. I wasn't primarily interested in Novick. Nevertheless the whole situation hinged on him.

'I don't care.' Her hand curled into a fist. 'I'm not going to tell you again. Call the police.'

That probably wasn't a bad idea as far as it went. And it might leave me time to talk her out of giving Canthorpe grounds to sue us. I said, 'You're the boss,' and went back into the living room to use the phone.

I called Detective-Lieutenant Acton. By now I'd stretched the favour he owed us pretty thin, but I thought I could count on him to hear what we had to say before he jumped to any conclusions. Maybe he'd even forgive me for getting him in trouble with Cason.

He had a voice like the exhaust of a Peterbilt, and when he got on the line he tried to tear my ear off with it. I let the first couple of blasts go by, then told him enough to get his attention. Finally he snarled, 'All right, all right. I'm on my way. Give me half an hour.

'But when I get there, you damn well better be ready to tell me the whole story. You hear me, Axbrewder? The whole story.'

I said, 'Sure,' and hung up.

While I was on the phone, I heard Canthorpe and Haskell talking to

Ginny, but they stopped when I reappeared. Haskell had moved closer to her. The excitement was gone from his face – he looked unnaturally serious. Canthorpe had squirmed himself into a position that let him keep an eye on her.

Novick lay where he was, muttering to himself. Ginny still sat on the floor, her back against the wall beside the doorway to the living room. She kept running her fingers through her hair, trying to pull it back from her face.

Softly I said, 'Acton's on the way.'

She ignored that. 'Want to hear something crazy, Brew? Our client wants us to believe Canthorpe is innocent. Novick just tried to kill him, and Canthorpe knew about Novick and Harmon, and he has the only real motive in this whole mess, and our client still wants us to believe his boss didn't sick Novick on him.'

'It's true,' Canthorpe protested. 'I swear it.' Her attitude scared him worse than being tied up.

But she dismissed him with a humourless snort. 'Our client,' she went on, 'just can't bear it that we've caught him lying again. All that bullshit about being involved with Roscoe Chavez. He's just been trying to make himself feel important. As if anybody other than a jilted fiancé would consider him worth threatening. As I remember, our client didn't even know the name "el Señor" until he heard it from us. He probably got "Roscoe Chavez" out of the newspaper.'

'Damn it, Fistoulari.' Haskell was angry now – or faking it well. 'I'm not that stupid. *Nobody* is dumb enough to invent trouble like this. I'm good at games, but that's all they are, games. I wouldn't lie about something this serious.

'Until tonight I wanted to manipulate you. I admit it. But I didn't know how much I could trust you. I didn't want to tell you what I'd done. I was afraid you might turn me in. But now I've told you the truth. You're looking in the wrong direction. El Señor is trying to kill me. Because Roscoe and I ripped him off.

'I don't care about motive. Jordan is not the kind of man who would try to have anybody killed, for any reason.'

She ignored him. 'I'll tell you something, Brew.' She sounded like she wanted to laugh and couldn't pull it off. 'I've had enough. I'm getting out of this business. As soon as the cops get here, this case is closed. I'm going to quit. Find some other line of work.' Maybe instead of laughing what she wanted to do was cry. 'I can't take any more of this shit.'

'Ginny.' I had to stop her somehow. She was going to break my heart. 'We've got to think this through. Before Acton gets here. It isn't as simple as it looks.'

She didn't even glance up at me. For a long moment she didn't say anything. Then her voice came past the edge of her hair like a flick of hate. 'Mick Axbrewder, what in hell are you talking about?'

Sweet Christ on a stick. This was going to be such fun.

As steadily as I could, I said, 'I haven't had a chance to tell you about my evening yet.'

'What's to tell?' She really didn't want to hear it. 'You went to talk to Eunice Wint. You took your precious time, but it didn't get you anywhere. You blew it somehow. If you'd pushed her, she would've told you enough to convict her fiancé. But she's pretty and stupid, so you felt sorry for her. You don't have to tell me about it. I'm not interested.'

'I can see that,' I snarled. I'd lost my unbalanced calm. Now I was just unbalanced. 'But you ought to be. You ought to know by now that it doesn't take all evening for a girl like Eunice to make me feel sorry for her. What do you suppose I did with the rest of the time?'

Bitterly she said, 'I'm afraid to ask.'

I bent over Novick and turned him so that I could see his face. I was rougher than I meant to be. When I was done, pain glared in his eyes. '*Pendejo*,' he hissed. 'You're tearing my arms out.' But I ignored his distress. I just wanted to be able to watch his expression.

'Before Haskell and I talked to Eunice,' I said to Ginny, 'we went to Novick's house. The house he shares with Gail Harmon. We took her and checked her into a hospital.'

That didn't hit Novick for a second or two. Pain and craziness made him slow. Then a spasm of fury convulsed his face. 'Bastard!' he coughed. 'Fucker!' All his muscles corded, trying to break the clothesline. 'Cocksucker! You took my woman? *My woman*? I'll kill you. I swear I'll kill you.' I thought he was going to froth at the mouth.

Which answered one question. He wasn't here because of what I'd done. He must've already been on his way when Haskell and I went to his house. That gave me a queer useless sense of relief.

Unfortunately Ginny didn't miss the other implications. 'Don't tell me,' she retorted fiercely. 'Let me guess. You were going to say the only reason he came here and tried to kill us all was because you snatched his girlfriend. He was just an innocent bystander until you made him mad. By the way, that was brilliant, Axbrewder. Real genius. Sawdust is smarter. But never mind. It isn't true. He didn't know you took his girlfriend until you told him.'

Now it was my turn not to look at her. I couldn't stand it. Instead I concentrated on Novick. Both Canthorpe and Haskell watched me with varying degrees of alarm and hope, but I ignored them.

'Novick,' I said through his cursing, 'listen for a minute. Bite your tongue and listen. This is your life we're talking about. Years of hard time for attempted murder. Listen.'

'Go fuck yourself, *pendejo*. I'm so scared I shit my pants.'

'I know. You're as tough as a Glock. Listen anyway. Someone has been trying to kill Haskell for two days now. Three attempts so far. Obviously it was you the third time. But what about the other two? Should we pin those on you as well?'

From my point of view, that was the crucial question. I thought I knew the answer. But I couldn't risk putting words in his mouth. And if he refused to say it – if he decided to play belligerent all the way to the state pen – then I was stuck.

But apparently he didn't like being blamed for things he didn't do. 'Yeah, *cojones*,' he spat. 'I can think of a reason. I didn't know his fucking name before you told me. Gail called him Reg. She never told me who he was. She didn't want him killed. *You* told me Haskell.' Triumph glittered in his wild eyes. 'I looked him up in the phone book.'

But Ginny wasn't having any. 'That's a crock. He's lying. Why not? What's he got to lose?'

Somehow I forced myself to face the fever of her alarm. She looked like she was being eaten alive from the inside.

'It's true,' I insisted dully. 'I told him Haskell's name. I didn't know – but as soon as I said it, I could see that I'd made a mistake.'

'He couldn't have booby-trapped the Buick last night. And he wasn't–'

She cut me off. 'I'm not going to argue with you. You're out of your head. You need professional help. Novick tried to kill us, and we caught him. With a little research, the cops can prove Canthorpe hired him. We've done our job. It's over. I don't care how many dumb mistakes you've made, or how responsible you feel. It's over. As soon as the cops get here–'

'Ginny–'

'–this case is closed.'

I opened my mouth, but she didn't let me speak.

'Shut up, Brew. You've said enough. I don't want to hear any more. You had better sense when you were a drunk.'

Abruptly she wrenched herself to her feet, scooping her .357 off the carpet as she stood up. Maybe without realizing it, she pointed the gun at my stomach.

To Haskell she said, 'You'll get my bill in the morning.'

He threw up his hands. 'I should've fired you this afternoon while I was thinking about it,' he muttered angrily. 'I changed my mind because I thought I could trust you. I thought you were too stupid to stumble on to the truth. And I thought you were honest enough to stick with me. I was wrong both times.'

'Ginny.' I had to lock both fists to keep myself from howling. 'God *damn* it, it wasn't Novick in the car that tried to nail us this afternoon.'

She actually tightened her grip on the .357. 'You bastard.' Her voice shook. 'What makes you so sure?'

'I was there, remember?' I couldn't help it, I was shouting at her. 'He's too tall, too thin! And he's in love with that fucking M-16. The goon in the car had a shotgun.'

'He probably *has* a shotgun,' she fired back. 'He probably has one of every gun known to man. And he was in a car. Aiming a shotgun at you. You couldn't tell how tall or thin he was.'

I wanted to hit myself in the head, just to make her stop. 'I *saw* him. It wasn't Novick.'

'What kind of car does Novick drive?' Haskell asked. 'Maybe it wasn't the same car.'

Ginny ignored him. 'You saw him,' she said, like she was threatening me. 'Sure you saw him. I bet you couldn't even tell whether it was a man or a woman.'

I just stared at her for a second. Then I said, 'You know better than that.'

'I *do*?' Something inside her seemed to snap, and all at once she sounded almost cheerful. Completely out of her skull. 'Let's go outside.' She waggled her gun at my stomach. 'I'll prove it to you.' A wild smile lit her face. 'I'll prove you couldn't tell whether it was a man or a woman from ten feet away.'

Suddenly my throat felt too dry to talk, and my heart knocked against my rib cage. Ginny, I thought. Oh my God.

Her cheerfulness only lasted a few seconds. When I didn't respond, her expression turned savage. Before I could defend myself, she stepped forward and poked my stomach with the muzzle of her gun. 'I said, let's go outside.'

The way I saw it, I only had two choices. I could take the .357 away and hit her until she got her sanity back. Or I could do what she told me.

376

I did what she told me. With a shrug, I crossed the atrium to the front door. Unlocked it. Opened it.

All the outside lights were on. I could see everything.

Alerted by the noise of the door, and the sound of my shoes on the cement walk, a man came out of the snow around one of the cedars into the other end of the aisle.

I recognized him right away.

Short and squat, roughly the size and shape of an Abrams tank. Muscle bulging on him everywhere made him look like he'd been packed into his coat at a sausage plant. A hair-line moustache under his nose tried to humanize his face, but his protruding eyes insisted that he was actually a reptile.

I'd had a run-in with him once. It still gave me nightmares.

El Señor's bodyguard. Muy Estobal.

He looked surprised. He hadn't expected me. But he didn't let that stop him.

Immediately his right hand emerged from the pocket of his overcoat, holding a snub-nosed Smith & Wesson .38. The lights lit the snow behind him so that he stood against a background of swirling white bits as if the world were going to pieces.

While I struggled to claw the .45 out of its holster, he started shooting.

Something that felt like a cannonball punched through my belly, slammed me off my feet. The jolt when I hit turned all my bones to powder.

I heard Ginny yell behind me. Then she began to lay down fire in the aisle as if she'd lost her mind.

Chapter Nineteen

For what seemed like a long time, or maybe it was short, I was in no condition to keep an eye on my watch, I thought I was conscious when I really wasn't. I must've been unconscious because I missed all the transitions.

When I landed on the walkway, it turned out to be a hospital gurney in a hurry, and Ginny and Muy Estobal had transformed themselves into people wearing green robes and caps. Except the gurney was a big bed with high railings all around it, and curtains hanging from runners in the ceiling to surround the bed replaced the white corridor walls. The people in green holding me down by both arms looked suspiciously like IV stands with tubes that disappeared into layers of tape around my forearms.

But it didn't feel like being unconscious. It felt like walking wide-awake and terrified on to the business end of a harpoon, and then standing there helpless while someone stirred my guts to soup with the blade.

At first it was nothing except red-grey pain combined with one long scream driven like a spike through the centre of the world. My only problem was I needed stomach muscles to scream, and I didn't have any. Eventually, however, I became more lucid. Lucid enough to count every single nerve cell torn apart by Estobal's bullet. The pain was impossibly precise.

Nevertheless I lost track after a while. By degrees I came to understand that I hadn't been shot at all. Oh, no – nothing that tidy and manageable. I'd been blown up. Like my rented Buick. With that poor innocent kid inside. It was always the innocent who got roasted. And it was always people like me who saw the danger too late to save them.

No question about it, I was having all kinds of fun.

But what I knew most clearly – knew with the utter certainty and conviction that only comes to you when you're drunk or crazy, all the way off your rocker with booze or grief – was that I didn't have time for this.

The night held only so many hours, and they were getting away from me. There were people I needed to talk to. Information dealers. Two old men drinking together in an odd and half-unreconciled partnership because they were too old and too tired to compete with each other. Until 2 a.m. when the dives in the old part of town which welcomed and even honoured grizzled *muchachos* like themselves closed, they would follow their exact and unpredictable circuit from place to place, receiving and dispensing knowledge in their relatively humble area of expertise, earning themselves bottles of indifferent mescal with what they knew or could deduce. After that, for maybe an hour or two – or less, considering the snow – they would go to that cheap little park on Tin Street and finish their last bottle together. The same place where I used to spend the nights and wait for Ginny. And then they would be gone. They would evaporate into the dwindling night, disappear so completely that you would never be able to prove they even existed.

I needed to talk to them. I needed to reach the old part of town and find them and talk to them before time ran out. I couldn't afford to lie around like a side of beef in an abattoir and let the night get away from me.

When I finally pried my eyes open and saw Ginny near the head of the bed, I tried to explain. But my mouth and throat were so dry I couldn't dredge up anything more than a croak. That held me back long enough to realize that I couldn't say anything to her. If I did, she would refuse to help me. Simply because I'd been hurt, she would refuse.

In my condition, I didn't have the strength to tell her why she was wrong.

When she heard the strangling noises I made instead of conversation, she leaned over the bed. Her fingers stroked my face, running gently around the marks Gail Harmon had made on my cheeks. 'Mick Axbrewder,' she said, even though no one calls me Mick, not even her, 'you look awful.' I couldn't focus my eyes on her face, but her voice had a damp blurred sound, like tears. 'I did this to you.'

That didn't make sense. With an effort, I twisted my croaking until it sounded a bit more like words.

'Where am I?'

'Don't worry about it.' She tried to be comforting. Maybe she even tried to smile. 'You've done enough for one night. Everything is taken care of. Just relax and get some rest.'

I persisted. What else could I do? 'What time is it?'

'Late. You got out of surgery half an hour ago. You were lucky again. Anybody else would be dead by now. Or have their internal organs seriously damaged. Not you. That slug just tore up your guts a bit.'

She sounded brittle and lonely, like a woman standing on the edge of a wasteland. But she fought to put a good face on it.

'The doctor told me more than I wanted to know. Somehow the slug missed your lungs, your kidneys, and your liver. And it didn't hit bone going in, so it didn't mushroom. You're in surprisingly good shape. You'll hurt like hell for a while. Then you'll be all right.'

Damn woman. She couldn't possibly know what I was thinking about, but she still wouldn't give me a straight answer. For a minute there frustration and pain made me so mad that I wept.

She leaned on the rail of the bed, holding one of my forearms with her good hand. 'Brew,' she said softly, 'I'm so sorry. This is my fault. I was so fucking determined to prove you were wrong about the driver of that Cadillac. I needed to believe Haskell was still lying. I couldn't think about anything else. So I set you up to get shot at point-blank range.'

Her voice bit in like the edge of a saw, ripping across the grain of her self-respect. Luckily I still couldn't focus on her face clearly. God knows how bad she looked.

'When I saw Estobal there and he started shooting – when you went down –'

'We should never have taken this case.'

Well, maybe. But it didn't matter. I was running out of time. And I didn't know how to get through to her. And one of those IVs fed stuff into my veins that made me want to sleep for three or four weeks. So far the pain was all that kept me awake – and that had started to fade.

I tried again. 'Where am I?'

She didn't seem to hear me. 'I used to think I was tough,' she murmured, far away with hurt. 'Mentally, not physically. I used to think my mind could stand anything. I never knew I was so dependent on my hands. When I finally understood I was never going to get my hand back, and the best I could hope for was a *prosthetic device* that made me look like I was only half human, not a person at all, never mind how I looked as a woman–'

She caught herself, the words like barbs in her throat. 'Something went out of me. Whatever it was that held me together. And I discovered I wasn't tough at all. I've been using you to carry me ever since.' Softly she swore at herself – vicious, down-to-the-marrow curses, swearing to hold back the grief. 'We never should've taken this case.'

I wanted to scream at her. Silly of me. I didn't have the stomach for it. The whole situation was getting away from me. Hell, even consciousness was getting away from me. I could hardly remember what was so important to me.

As clearly as I could, I croaked, 'I don't care about that. What time is it?'

Her reaction sent a quiver through the bed. Pieces of something wet landed on my face, trickled down my cheeks. 'Fuck you, Axbrewder,' she said stiffly. But then she softened. She stroked my face again, spreading the wet around. 'Ah, hell. They've got you so doped up, you probably can't understand a word I say. We'll talk about it later.'

That was a lie, and I knew it. The loss in her voice made it obvious. She would never talk about this again.

'In the mean time, you're not going anywhere.' Now she was trying to be kind. 'This one' – she pointed at the IV on my left, a large plastic packet full of red stuff – 'replaces the blood you lost. That one' – the other IV – 'is your medication – antibiotics to fight off peritonitis, dope for the pain, sedatives, nourishment. You're going to spend a lot of time asleep.'

I was going to *scream*, pain or no pain. But at last she took pity on me.

'But if it will help you rest,' she sighed, 'you're in recovery at University Hospital. It's a little after ten-thirty. The nurses will check on you in an hour or so. If you're stable, they'll transfer you to a room. You'll have a private room. All those hospitalization premiums I've been paying have got to be good for something.'

Involuntarily I groaned. University Hospital was too far from the old part of town. I couldn't possibly walk –

'I'm sorry, Brew,' she said contritely. 'The doctor warned me not to keep you awake. I'll leave now. If you need me, I'll be in the waiting room. I'll see you again after they transfer you to your room.'

She seemed to be receding. Or maybe it was me. Wandering away from consciousness to find the real source of my pain. The bed had a distinct tendency to float. But I couldn't just let go. That would be too easy. Easier than anything. Even the road to hell.

'Ginny,' I croaked like the damned. 'Wait.'

She didn't exactly come back into range, but at least she stopped receding.

'What happened to Haskell?'

She wanted to treat me kindly, but our client wasn't a subject that brought out her gentle side. 'He got lucky,' she rasped. 'If you hadn't been bleeding like a geyser, I would've redesigned his vital organs for him. If he'd told us the truth from the beginning–' She stopped herself. 'As it was, I was too busy. And Acton got there before the ambulance did. I turned the whole mess over to him – Haskell, Canthorpe, Novick, everything. We're out of it. You don't have to worry about it any more.'

Wait a minute, I wanted to say. It isn't that simple. Haskell's story about Chavez changed everything. As soon as it got around, Haskell's case would be turned over to Cason. Which would be like flushing the whole thing down the toilet.

Ginny had never flushed a case down the toilet in her life.

My lucidity was amazing, especially when you consider that Ginny – in fact, the whole room – had disappeared. I must've been three-quarters unconscious while I watched ideas and possibilities walk back and forth in front of me, as primed for violence as assassins or rapists. But somehow I forced my eyes open again. Somehow I shoved my left arm across my chest and used those thick fumbling fingers to pull the IV needle out of my right forearm.

I couldn't afford to screw up now. Absolutely not.

Concentrating fiercely, I slipped the needle back under the bandages so that it looked like it was still plugged into my veins. If a nurse glanced at those bandages, saw what I'd done –

The exertion took everything I had left. When I was done, the bed tipped over and pitched me out into the black middle of the night.

But it worked. Sweet Christ, my stomach, oh the pain it worked. I wasn't getting any more painkillers or sedatives, and the unintentional jostling when the nurses and aides eased me out of the ICU bed on to a gurney roused me in a sweat of agony. This definitely wasn't sane. Nevertheless after the first groan I managed to keep myself quiet and limp. My guts hung out in shreds, but if I couldn't fake being relaxed and practically asleep the nurses would wonder why I was in so much pain and check the IV.

I was never going to have the courage to pull that same stupid stunt twice in one night.

Fortunately – or unfortunately, depending on your point of view –

nurses and aides are human, too, and they've been known to get tired and maybe even a little careless in the middle of the night. None of them noticed that my IV oozed into my bandages instead of dripping into my veins. Instead they gave me an elevator ride for three or four hundred floors, wheeled me along a few miles of corridor, and finally shunted me into a room.

Lifting me by the sheet under me, they heaved me off the gurney into bed while I did my utter best to pretend that I wasn't being crucified. I feared passing out again, but this time I wasn't that lucky.

Then I heard a young woman whisper in surprise, 'Did you see this?' Opening my eyes a slit, I saw an aide show my .45 to the nurses. 'Is he a cop?'

'I don't know,' one of them replied. 'But he has a licence for it in his wallet. Put it back.'

With a shrug, the aide dropped the .45 into a grocery sack on top of the bureau. Apparently my clothes were in that sack as well. Soaked with blood. By now, the blood would be dry – crusted and harsh. The clean, tidy part of me wanted to throw up. The rest vetoed the idea. I should be glad I had any clothes at all. Now all I needed –

But I couldn't think of what I needed. The state of my gut crippled me. I tried again.

Now all I needed – was some way to reach the old part of town. Bravo. Good for me.

Well, lessee. Put your mind to it, Axbrewder. Some way to get from here to there.

I couldn't walk. I'd have to drive.

Good again. Doing fine. Keep it up.

I couldn't drive. I'd have to get a ride.

Go on.

I couldn't call a taxi. No cab driver in his right mind would drive a gut-shot man *away* from a hospital.

So who could I call? Who would be willing to drive me all over town while I bled to death? Who did I know who might conceivably be that desperate?

I waited until the nurses and aides left, and the door swung shut, and the only light in the room came faintly through the window from the city. Then I pulled the IV away from my right arm.

Slowly, carefully, hurting like Satan and all his demons, I rolled out of bed to the left and got my feet to the floor, then rested there trying not to breathe because breathing tore at my guts like a heavy-duty sailfish lure.

Braced myself.

Stood up.

You can do it, I told myself. Just use the pain. Make it help you.

For a while the room swirled like a sink draining all the life out of me. But pain hung at the centre of everything, and it didn't let me go. Eventually I got my hands on the side table at the head of the bed, held on there until the walls slowed down. Then I fumbled for the reading lamp.

When I snapped it on, the light hurt my eyes. But once the pain shifted from my eyeballs back into my skull, I was able to see.

The phone was on the table right in front of me.

Good. Fine. Keep it up. One thing at a time.

The other IV still restricted my left arm. But I could move it some, so I used that hand to lift the receiver. Almost randomly, I stabbed at the buttons until I finally got through to Information.

Information listed six Rudolfo Santiagos.

Six! I couldn't call them all. I couldn't stand that long. When the operator's mechanical voice started reading the addresses, however, I recognized one of them. Somehow I managed enough sanity to ask the operator to connect me.

The phone rang for ever. Three or four times at least. Then a man's voice answered in Spanish. My mouth and throat felt like I'd been living on a diet of wool socks. In fact, my whole body was stretched and urgent with thirst. My IV was practically empty. How much blood had I lost? The voice on the other end of the line demanded an answer three times before I figured out how to say something.

'Señor Santiago?' I croaked.

'*Si?*' A question, suspicious and bitter.

One thing at a time. Swallow. Clear your throat. Come on, Axbrewder.

'I must speak with Señor Santiago.'

'Ay, Señor Axbrewder.' Thank God he recognized me. 'What transpires? You do not come to the vigil of our son? A curse upon all telephones. Your voice does not sound well. Have you been harmed?'

He paused to let me respond. But I couldn't pull myself together. In a whisper, he asked, 'Have you discovered the killer of my son?'

Ah, God. Everything hurt, and I didn't know what to do about it. Had I discovered the killer of his son? Of course not. I couldn't bear it.

But there had to be some reason why I stood there holding on to the phone when I should've been horizontal and unconscious, pumped to the gills with medication. Eventually I remembered what it was.

384

'Señor Santiago,' I said, 'I am injured. I must have someone to drive for me. Will you come?'

'I?' Shock showed in his voice. 'You desire that I should *drive* for you? My son has been slain. Even now we hold vigil for him' – his shock turned quickly to outrage – 'although his body is denied to us, and all we are given for our grief is an empty coffin and fifty dollars of candles. Also the time is beyond one in the morning. I do not–'

'Rudolfo,' I heard in the background, his wife's voice, 'do not shout. It is unseemly. Some respect we must have, for those who watch with us at least.'

Intensely he whispered at me across the dark city, 'Have you discovered the killer of my son?'

With elaborate care, as if I were responding directly to his anger and sorrow and incomprehension, I said in English, 'I'm in University Hospital. Meet me outside Emergency. As soon as you can. Bring me an overcoat.' Then I remembered something else. 'And a pint of mescal.'

For a moment he didn't say anything. When he spoke, his voice shook with the effort he made to keep it quiet.

'Señor Axbrewder' – he sneered the words – 'I will not leave the vigil of my son so that I may run errands for a gringo whose heart is set on drink. Doubtless you are "injured" by the excess of your drinking. For such as you I feel no pity.'

Through the line, I could feel the force of his yearning to slam down the receiver, the pressure of his desire to shout, You promised to find the killer of my son!

His vehemence sent a sting of panic through me. I fought the pain out of the way. 'I don't know who killed your son.' I stayed with English because I didn't have the strength for Spanish. 'But I know how to find out. There are two men who might know the answer. If I can reach them tonight.'

The silence at the other end of the line changed. Trying not to sound like a wild man, I kept going.

'They won't talk to the cops. They wouldn't even talk to you. But they might talk to me.' If I found them before they disappeared for the night. And if I looked and talked and smelled like the Mick Axbrewder they remembered, Axbrewder the drunk, tanked to the scalp with mescal and tired self-contempt. 'I can't get to them if you don't give me a ride.'

He didn't answer right away. I could hear him breathing, thinking. Fighting his way through his tangled emotions. I was an Anglo and a drunk. And I wasn't just asking him to trust me. I was asking for his faith.

Abruptly he said, 'I will come.' Then he hung up.

For some reason I didn't put the phone down. 'Don't forget the mescal,' I said. I could get by without the overcoat. Freezing to death didn't worry me. But I had to have that bottle of mescal.

After a while, however, I noticed that I had a dial tone clamped to the side of my head. Moving my arm with a jerk, I clattered the receiver back into its cradle.

Now all I had to do was get dressed and sneak out of the hospital before Ginny came to check on me again. That was all. A mere bag of towels, as some clown I once knew used to say. Child's play.

Well, so was the Spanish Inquisition, if you just thought about it from the right point of view. But I didn't think I could bear being caught and stopped. The idea appalled me.

So I propped myself against the bed while I untaped the other IV and pulled it out of my arm. Then I inched my way across the room towards the bureau.

Sneaking out of the hospital wouldn't be the hard part. Putting on my clothes would.

It promised to be a pure gold immaculate and absolute sonofabitch.

Concentrate on something else. A few weeks after leaving the bed, I arrived at the bureau. All my clothes and possessions were in the paper sack. It should've been easy to think about thirst. My mouth and throat felt like I'd eaten a pound of alum. When I'd shrugged my hospital pyjamas to the floor, I got my first look at the bandages on my stomach. They were marked with small red stains like stigmata. Involuntarily I stared at them in a kind of fascinated horror.

But Ginny might show up any minute. By twisting my shoulders into positions that gave me cramps, I managed to slip my shirt on. The fabric was stiff with dried blood, and it had nice neat holes over the bandages, front and back. I buttoned it approximately and tackled my pants.

Putting them on was hell. Double-dipped fire-and-brimstone with chocolate sauce and peanuts. But I did it anyway. The pain made me mad, too angry to give up. Then, instead of passing out, I pushed my feet into my shoes and slipped my jacket over my shoulders. The holster for the .45 I left behind. I didn't have the heart for it.

With the dead weight of the gun in my jacket pocket, I fixed my attention on the door of the room and started towards it.

With my luck, I thought, Ginny would arrive right then. Sure. Why not? But she didn't. I reached the door, and no one was there. I couldn't hear anything except the way I whimpered when I breathed.

When I'd mustered my courage – not to mention what you might laughingly call my strength – I opened the door a few inches and scanned the corridor. Nobody there at all.

Halfway down the hall, I saw the red-lit 'Exit' sign and the door labelled 'Emergency Exit Only.' I didn't hesitate. Couldn't afford to. From the room I limped towards the exit as if I knew what I was doing.

Unfortunately each ordeal led to another one, and what came next looked worse than everything else combined.

Stairs. Lots of them. At least three or four flights.

That sort of thing could be the life of the party. Hey, gang, I've got an idea! Let's all shoot ourselves in the belly and walk down stairs! Even hanging on to the rail with both hands, I felt every step shred my guts. It would've been a whole lot easier to just fall and roll to the bottom. Only the simple logic of the situation kept me going. I was doing it, wasn't I? And if I was doing it, it must've been possible.

The last flight, I lured myself with promises of water. When I reached the bottom, I'd find a drinking fountain and have all I wanted. But I didn't keep that promise any better than all the others I'd made. Instead I went into one of those curious lapses of awareness where your body keeps on moving but you can't remember anything about it afterwards.

Presumably I was in the surgical wing of University Hospital. Therefore I must've come out of the stairwell opposite the Emergency waiting room. I must've gone straight out through Emergency to the parking lot. And the nurses and security guards must've been too busy to notice me.

As far as I could remember, I lost track of things somewhere in the stairwell and came back to myself in the snow outside. The night and the clouds had closed down hard over the city, leaving everything black and thick, beyond redemption. But the Emergency and parking-lot lights reflected off the snow, creating quaint pockets of visibility in the darkness. The snow fell almost straight down, gently, without any wind behind it. For some reason I didn't feel cold.

Cocooned in pain, my shoelaces untied and no socks on, I shuffled through the accumulating slush and tried to look conspicuous so that Rudolfo Santiago would find me.

When a set of headlights slapped at me through the snowfall, they almost knocked me down. They were aimed right at me – I must've been standing like a derelict in the middle of the right-of-way. Knives of light cut through my eyes and did things to the inside of my head. Then they stopped moving. A car door opened.

'Señor Axbrewder,' he said. 'I am come.'

I didn't have the strength to move. Now that he was here, I had trouble remembering what I was supposed to do about it. But he had a front-row view of the bloodstains on my jacket and shirt. After a moment I heard him cursing.

He got out and came over to me. In the headlights, he looked like someone had poured acid into the wrinkles of his face, making them deep and dark. 'Ay, Señor Axbrewder,' he murmured, squinting concern at me, 'this is madness. You are indeed sorely injured. You must return to the hospital for your life.'

A vagrant eddy of wind swirled snow across my face, and I almost fell. I shut my eyes, put one hand on his shoulder for support. 'It's not as bad as it looks,' I said thinly. I owed him Spanish, but I didn't have it in me. 'I'm just a little weak. This will only take a couple of hours. Then you can bring me back.'

He wasn't persuaded. 'Haste will not restore Pablo to life. I desire that the killer of my son be repaid for his evil. Yes, assuredly. But one day or two or a week will change nothing. Is it necessary that you suffer?'

If I'd had any muscles left in my belly, I might've laughed. Sure. Why not? If nothing else, suffering was sure as hell educational. And sometimes it was the only thing I could do to pay my debts.

But this was no time to discuss religion. 'I don't call it suffering,' I said. 'I call it doing my job.'

He hesitated a minute longer. Then I felt him shrug. 'As you wish. I will assist you.'

He let me lean more of my weight on his shoulders and slowly guided me around to the passenger side of his car.

The car was so old that it no longer seemed to have any specific make or model – it was just a generic clunker. But the engine ran. The doors opened. One of the windshield wipers worked.

Trying to keep the stress off my torso, I eased into the car. But there was no way to sit that didn't put pressure on my guts.

Santiago closed my door, walked around to his side of the car, and got in. 'Now, Señor Axbrewder,' he said. 'Where does one go to speak with these two men who may have knowledge of my son's killer?'

'The old part of town.' I was definitely on my way out. 'The little park on Tin Street.' There didn't seem to be any way I could hold

myself together. 'Get as close as you can.' It was going to
humiliating if I started to cry in front of him. 'But st
reach the park.' On the other hand, if I passed out, I mi
consciousness for weeks. 'Don't let them see you brin

Judging by his silence, he hadn't understood a word. I
put the car in gear. All Anglos are crazy. With exag......
unaccustomed to snow – he crept out of the parking lot.

As it happened, I didn't start crying. And I didn't go the way of the
gooney bird. Pain has more imagination than you might expect from a
mere sensation. Or maybe it's the way the brain reacts to pain. In any
case, I hadn't exhausted the possibilities – not by a long shot. This time
the way I hurt was like the snow, blown against the windshield and set
dancing by the movement of the car. Rendered as blind as a wall by the
reflected light. Delicate and impenetrable. Hypnotic. I stared into the
snowfall until it seemed that the whole world contained nothing but
misery.

And eventually it came to an end. Santiago nosed his car to the kerb
just around the corner from the Tin Street park.

When we weren't moving, the snow swirled less, and I could see
better. I recognized the place with an ache of familiarity. I'd spent a lot
of time there, drunk out of my mind. But not just drunk. Desperate,
too. This park was where I used to go when my self-revulsion finally
grew too strong to be ignored. Here I waited like I was praying for
Ginny to come along and rescue me, call me back to work. When the
bars closed, I came here with drunks and bums like myself, whoever
happened to be in the neighbourhood that night, and we shared
whatever was left of the booze we'd scrounged against the long lonely
dark. Then the others wandered off to their private hovels, *barrios*, or
beds. But I stayed where I was, lying curled up on a bench with my
arms and knees hugged over my stomach and waiting with the passivity
of the damned for Ginny to come. The sight of the old place sent a lick
of panic along my nerves, and my head cleared a bit.

The blunt edge of an adobe building blocked our view of the park.
Santiago ditched his headlights, killed the engine. Abruptly our
enclosed little world turned quiet. When my ears adjusted, I could hear
the faint wet sound of snow on the hood and roof.

Santiago struck a match to light a cigarette, and the yellow flare
showed his face for a second. He looked old and tired, but his eyes
caught the light like bits of glass.

Sucking on the coal of his cigarette, he reached into one of his
pockets and brought out a flat pint bottle.

My hands shook when I took it. He watched me hard while I pushed the pain out of my way and forced my fingers to screw off the cap. Right away I smelled mescal, strong as a shout. Thirst clenched my throat. It was just possible that if I took a good long drink I wouldn't hurt any more.

Covering most of the mouth of the bottle with my thumb, I splashed mescal on to my clothes. Quite a bit of it. To hide the stink of blood. Then I unlatched the door and opened it a few inches so that I could pour about a quarter of the bottle on to the street. Finally I replaced the cap and dropped the bottle into my other jacket pocket, opposite the .45.

Santiago still didn't say anything. Reaching into the back seat, he produced an overcoat. Its old fabric was greasy and smelled like mildew.

I had to get going. No time like the present. Apprehension and the scent of mescal made me urgent. I nodded towards the park. 'You can wait in the car. Or watch from the corner. Just don't be seen. Otherwise they won't talk.'

He nodded stoically.

Pain burning in every muscle, I levered myself out of the car and stood up. I couldn't raise my arms, so I just pulled the overcoat on to my shoulders and let it hang. Now I felt the cold. The overcoat didn't make any difference. But at least I could hold it closed so that the bloodstains wouldn't show.

Softly Santiago murmured, '*Vaya con Dios.*'

Stiff-legged, slow, and awkward, I started forward to try my fate.

The snow fell without interference now, soft and silent, covering everything. We weren't more than five blocks from the Santiagos' store. But in the old part of town the night belonged to Puerta del Sol's other population, its midnight denizens. In winter the park was nothing more than three scruffy cottonwoods and a few loose-jointed benches marked by patches of bare dirt in the dry brown untended grass. But the snow gave the place a blanket of beauty and innocence.

A few streetlamps erratically installed and randomly vandalized around the area shed a filtered light. As I approached the park, I saw two hunched figures sitting together on one of the benches.

I didn't have to pretend I was under the influence. The way my gut hurt was enough. I lumbered ahead slowly, my shoes full of snow. When I reached the edge of the park, I stopped, pulled out my bottle, took off the cap, corked the mouth with my thumb, and went through the motions of drinking. Then I put the bottle away and moved closer to the two men on the bench.

I didn't deserve to be so blessed. Oh, I'd earned the right to know their habits. I'd paid for that knowledge. But it was months and months old, a long time in the life of a drunk. Anything could have changed. I didn't deserve to find them there, right where I'd left them.

Yet there they were, Luis and Jaime, not quite looking at me in the same way that I didn't quite look at them. They'd soaked themselves in alcohol for so long that the rest of their names, along with most of their past, had dissolved out of them. Twenty years ago, they were both powers in Puerta del Sol, purveyors of fine secrets and competitors for the leverage secrets could buy. But the world got away from them. The city's population boom produced a geometric increase in the number, complexity, and value of whispers. Younger men, more cunning men, specialists came along, reducing Jaime and Luis to the status of amateurs. To survive, they began specializing themselves. The heart had gone out of them, however, so naturally they gravitated to the subject with the least competition because it was the least interesting and violent – numbers gambling. With what they knew, their ability to advise and forewarn, to sift rumours or start them, they kept themselves in tortillas and mescal. And after enough mescal the past was mostly forgotten.

Jaime claimed – for no obvious reason – that he was a good decade older than Luis. He looked like a shrunken version of me, his clothes stained in front and rotting under his arms, his cheeks grizzled, most of his teeth gone. He had a constant open-mouthed smile that made him look like an idiot. In contrast, Luis would've appeared almost dapper if all his clothes hadn't been at least fifteen years old. Somehow he contrived to remain clean-shaven, barbered, even manicured. He had the face of a grandee, and he frowned at the world with disapproval and dignity.

But behind their differences they were closer to each other than brothers. No kinship of blood could compete with the mescal they'd shared.

They greeted me by lowering their eyes and not speaking. At one time, I was a true companion. The amount I drank with them made up for the fact that I was Anglo, and although I was too big for decency, I had good and honourable Spanish. But I'd been away, reputedly sober. Nothing would forfeit their tolerance, never mind their trust, like being sober.

And if they didn't trust me, I was lost. They wouldn't answer my questions. And they would sure as hell let el Señor know I was asking those questions. And el Señor wouldn't take the news in a forgiving mood. Not after my previous offences. What I was doing now was probably more dangerous than going to talk to him in person.

Jaime and Luis waited, courteous and non-committal, for me to begin.

I didn't look at them directly either. I was too far gone to really grasp the danger. But I needed answers. After a minute of mutual politeness, I took out my bottle again and offered it to them.

Jaime grinned into the snow. Luis gave me a nod like a bow, accepted the bottle gravely, and sampled it. Then he passed it to Jaime. Like his companion, Jaime drank precisely the right amount for good manners – enough to compliment the mescal, not enough to seriously lower the level in the bottle. Still grinning, he handed it back to me.

I screwed the cap on to the bottle. But I didn't put it away.

Their eyes on the mescal, Jaime and Luis shifted over, making room for me on the bench.

'*Gracias.*' The screaming chainsaw in my stomach made the word come out blurred and thick. Carefully I eased myself down and tried to make my involuntary whimpering sound like a sigh. I felt like I was going to faint. 'Are you well?'

'Very well,' Luis replied. He had a bottle of his own propped between his thighs. That explained his and Jaime's presence. They hadn't finished their bottle. But it was nearly empty. I'd caught them just in time.

'Luis is heartless,' Jaime put in at once. 'Very well, he says. *He* is very well. Assuredly so. He does not suffer as I do. He has no piles to make his life a torment.' His tone was as amiable as his smile. His complaints were so ingrained that they'd become a gesture of friendship. 'He has been spared the canker which eats in the gums, causing the teeth to fall out. Unkindly he says that he is well while my pain grows extreme.'

That was a hint. 'I, too, suffer,' I said. 'Providentially there is solace.' I uncapped my bottle and handed it to Luis.

He took a swig and gave the bottle to Jaime. While Jaime drank, Luis said to me, 'This one lacks all fortitude. Others feel pain also, but they do not speak of it unceasingly.'

'Truly.' I needed a way to make the conversation do what I wanted. But my feet were freezing, and thirst and pain muddled my mind. 'However, fortitude and honour are alike. Not all possess them equally.' While part of my brain tried to concentrate, the rest yearned for drink. 'As one man varies from another, so one people varies from another.'

Jaime nodded, passing the bottle back to Luis. 'It is so. Lacking my pain, you do not understand my fortitude.'

Luis looked at him. 'Without question it is true that your fortitude is either greater or less than any other. But that is as Señor Axbrewder has said. Not all possess fortitude and honour equally.'

A step in the right direction. Luis used my name, admitted he knew me. And while Luis drank from my bottle, Jaime aimed what was left of his teeth at me companionably.

'And also one people varies from another,' he agreed. 'It is said that the Anglos know as little of courage and dignity as of courtesy.' He seemed to be insulting me, but there was no insult in his tone. 'Yet behold Señor Axbrewder. He acknowledges his suffering, yet he does not speak of it. And his politeness is well known.' In demonstration, he took my bottle from Luis. 'It becomes necessary to think better of Anglos.'

He was asking me obliquely to account for myself.

I felt too weak to respond. In front of me, the edges of the world seemed to bleed away. Snow made everything muzzy. But I'd already come this far. It was silly not to say something.

'Ah, it is nothing. I suffer loneliness only. It shames one to speak of it.'

Luis cocked an aristocratic eyebrow. 'The woman,' he asked delicately, 'the private *chota* who gave you employment? A man must have a woman. Does she not ease your loneliness?'

'That one,' I murmured, hoping that my pain sounded like disgust and sorrow. 'At one time I took great gladness in her. But since the loss of her hand' – it was a safe bet that Luis and Jaime knew the story of Ginny's injury – 'she has become shrewish. She permits me no rest. She demands my service in every way.

'It is not enough that I must do her work. I must drive her car. I must clean. I must cook. I am a servant to her.'

If I'd said that to anyone else, I would've been met with embarrassment and male shame, men wondering how I could let myself be so humiliated. But Jaime and Luis were drunks. Like me, intimately familiar with humiliation. My version of events didn't do Ginny's reputation any favours, but at the moment I didn't care. I needed to provide a reason why I'd gone away – and why I'd come back.

'*Compadres*, it is unbelievable. She requires me to kneel before her to place her shoes upon her feet.

'Also,' I said, 'she denies me a man's right of strong drink.'

Luis understood implicitly. He handed me my bottle.

While I cradled it in my hands and wondered how to get rid of it, Jaime took the bait I dangled in front of him.

'Plainly,' he said, 'she is a woman of no fortitude.'

And Luis added, 'All women are harridans. But the saints know that no woman of our people would behave thus to a man. To require that he kneel before her!'

'Your pardon. It is not my place to complain.' Deferentially I passed the bottle back. 'But it becomes a man to be philosophical. I wish to understand the differences of our women. To me, it appears that all Anglo women are as mine, lacking fortitude and courage, and holding a great contempt for their men. Yet the women of your people are such as Señora Santiago, bearing herself with dignity and reserve even when her son is slain.'

I'd started to rush. With an effort, I stopped and held my breath while my heart thudded.

Luis took a long drink and gave the bottle to Jaime. I couldn't see any change in Jaime, but Luis's face seemed sharper, harder. The snow muffled everything around us. The only sounds we heard were our own voices and breathing. I could feel blood seeping from my bandages down into my pants.

Luis asked evenly, 'Are you acquainted with Señora Santiago?'

'*Si*, surely.' Nonchalance was beyond me. I had to do without it. 'Señor and Señora Santiago hired my service some years ago. They honoured me with their respect. I grieve for Pablo with them.'

Then I couldn't stop. I was out of my depth – and out of strength. Harshly I demanded, 'What manner of man kills the son of such parents as Señor and Señora Santiago?'

Luis still watched me like he'd caught a whiff of something he didn't like. But Jaime lowered the bottle – empty now – and grinned like a banshee.

'A gringo.'

I wanted to pass out. A gringo? Not Chavez? *Not?* I gave an involuntary twitch of surprise, and the pain almost tore a yell past my teeth. 'Ah, then it is simple,' I said, trying to defuse my improper intensity. 'Pablo was slain by a gringo. Therefore the matter is one of money.'

'Assuredly.' Jaime sounded almost happy. 'The night was Saturday.

394

Pablo bore with him the winnings for his numbers.' Rendered simple by alcohol, he seemed proud of his knowledge for its own sake. 'Twenty thousands of dollars.'

That was it. The whole thing. Just, *A gringo*. And, *Twenty thousands of dollars*. It proved exactly nothing. Nothing of any kind. And yet it gave me almost the entire story.

Almost. There was one detail I might be wrong about. One bit of information that might change everything.

But I couldn't ask for it. Luis's eyes had gone hard. Whatever it was that he didn't like had become clear to him. Even though he and Jaime were drunk, I was no match for either of them. And if they believed that I was manipulating them, using them for some Anglo reason, they would need no more than ten minutes, tops, to contact el Señor.

'Señor Axbrewder,' Luis observed softly, 'you do not drink with us.' He reached for the bottle Jaime held, but it was empty. He tossed it into the snow and lifted his own. It still held an inch of mescal. 'You have shared generously with us. Permit me to share with you.'

He extended the bottle towards me.

Just like that, I was trapped. With the radar of the drunk, he'd realized that there was something wrong with me. This was the test. If I refused to drink, I might find myself installed in a storm drain before morning.

I wanted to drink. I was dying of thirst anyway. And I'd created this whole mess. I hadn't told Ginny about Pablo. I wanted to drink myself out of my skull, and to hell with it.

But I wanted something else more. I wanted to *get* that bastard. Nail him to the wall for what he'd done.

If I was right about him.

I reached for the bottle.

And fumbled it.

A quick lurch to try to catch it pulled a cry out of my chest, and I fell off the bench, face down into the snow.

On top of the bottle.

For a minute agony held me there. Then Luis and Jaime lifted me by my arms. At first they weren't gentle. But then they saw the bloodstains on my shirt. Their surprise changed everything.

'Mother of God,' Jaime breathed. 'Shot. This is madness, Señor Axbrewder. Whose bullet have you caught?'

Panting hard and shallow, I fought for balance, strength, anything to keep me going. 'Muy Estobal.'

'*Pendejo!*' Jaime dropped my arm roughly. 'You are truly mad. Do you believe that I also wish to be shot?'

Turning and cursing, he hurried away into the snowfall. I lost sight of him almost at once.

I should've fallen. But Luis didn't let me. When I swung my head around to look at him, he seemed to be smiling.

'You have fortitude, Señor Axbrewder,' he said. 'Also *cojones*. I honour that.'

'Please.' Spanish failed me. I was nearly gone. That fall did something terrible to me. 'Tell me why Chavez was killed.'

Luis gave a snort that might have been laughter. 'El Señor came upon the Bambino making the beast of two backs with his daughter.'

That fitted. It all fitted. I was going down. But Luis held me up until Santiago came out of the snow to take me away.

Chapter Twenty

For a while the whole world was snow. It fell everywhere in silence, the way dead men grieve. But then I felt something warmer against the welts around my eyes. And my posture put pressure on my guts, sharpening the hurt. I was sitting down. In the passenger seat of Santiago's car, apparently. The heater blew at me, melting the snow in my hair, warming it away from my face. I'd lost my overcoat in the park.

'Now hear me, Señor Axbrewder.' Emotion and uncertainty congested Santiago's voice. 'You are seriously unwell. If you do not speak to me, I must return you to the hospital.'

Well, that made sense. He had to take my word for my condition. If I couldn't talk, he had every reason to assume the worst.

But I didn't want to go to the hospital. I didn't have any evidence. In a hospital bed I could lie there and tell people what I thought to my heart's content, but no one would do anything about it. Not as long as I couldn't produce one measly scrap of sane or at least concrete evidence to back me up.

And there was something else. Something itching at the back of my brain. Only I couldn't remember what it was. I was fine as long as I let the pain do my thinking for me. But when I tried to impose what I wanted on the process –

Not Luis. But Jaime. Jaime for sure. He would pass word to el Señor that I was walking around the Tin Street park with a bullet hole in my belly, asking questions about Pablo.

That wasn't it. But it was important enough to get my attention. With an effort that made me want to puke, I lifted my head from the back of the seat.

397

'I hear you,' I breathed thinly. 'I'll be all right. Just need a little rest. Don't take me back. Not yet.'

He studied me closely. After a moment he demanded softly, 'Have you learned who killed my son?'

'*Sí*.' I answered in Spanish to make him believe me. 'I know him.'

For an instant his eyes widened. Then his face closed. All the pity that made him take care of me was gone.

'Let us go. He must be made to pay for what he has done.'

I agreed. It sounded simple enough, when you put it that way. Leaning my head on the seat back again like I couldn't lift the weight of my thoughts, I gave him Reg Haskell's address and told him how to get there.

In response he jerked his old clunker into gear and started so hard that we went around the corner out of control and almost broke a tie-rod on the opposite kerb. Which reminded him that he didn't know how to drive on snow. He tried again, slowly this time. We eased out on to the road and headed north-east through the old part of town, aiming for the Heights.

Of course Haskell wouldn't be there. I mused on that instead of watching where we were going. Ginny had turned him over to the cops. To Acton, who was at least honest. But that was just as well. I couldn't deal with Haskell in my condition. All I wanted was to tear his house apart until I found something, anything, that might pass for evidence. So that he wouldn't be able to lie his way out of trouble again.

Now I remembered.

Ginny had turned Haskell over to Acton. In the process, she was bound to mention Muy Estobal. Which implied el Señor.

As soon as el Señor's name came up, the case would go over to Cason.

Bingo. Captain Cason. He'd rousted me for concealing evidence of a crime – and then hadn't bothered to do anything about it. Purportedly he'd been after me because the cab driver had overheard Haskell and me talking about el Señor. But Canthorpe had demonstrated that Haskell was lying. Therefore Cason had lost interest in both of us.

Now, for the first time in what seemed like for ever, I wondered whether that made any sense.

Cason was investigating the long-overdue demise of Roscoe Chavez. A rented car got blown up, and neither the renter nor his passenger waited around to be questioned, and the cab driver who took them home reported that they spent the drive talking about an el Señor money laundry. Naturally the matter was passed to Cason. It might connect with his investigation. Pursuing a possible lead, he identified Axbrewder and Haskell, and went to all the trouble to tail and roust Axbrewder.

And then he learned that Haskell's story was a fake. So he forgot the whole thing.

Oh, really?

I didn't have anything better to do, and loss of blood was making me light-headed anyway, so I tried to think about that. Attempting to consider the situation from Cason's point of view, I asked myself what kind of man tries to give himself an alibi by inventing lies about el Señor. Then I asked myself how many Anglos in Puerta del Sol, *especially* bank accountants, even know el Señor exists? If I were Cason – who hated my guts – wouldn't I be just the teeniest bit curious about what the hell was going on?

Sure I would.

Cason wasn't. Or he had some other reason for letting us go.

I didn't much like the sound of that.

Most of the painkiller had probably been flushed out of my system by now. A damp sensation under my shirt indicated blood. On the other hand, my head really did seem to be getting clearer.

I'd begun to understand just how lunatic my intentions were.

Also I wondered how Ginny would react when she found my room empty. Whatever she did, it wasn't likely to be gentle. For either of us.

I'd almost talked myself into covering my ass by stopping at a phone booth to call the hospital, talk to Ginny or leave a message, when Santiago's relic brought us up Foothill to the top of Cactus Blossom Court.

Snow still fell. It was at least a couple of inches thick on the road. Santiago approached the slope carefully so that he wouldn't start into a skid. I had plenty of time to see that Ginny had left all of Haskell's lights on.

I could also see his Continental in the driveway.

That didn't mean anything, I told myself. After hearing Ginny's story, Acton wasn't likely to let Haskell drive himself downtown. Nevertheless the sight of his car reminded me of all the times I'd been wrong – and of how easily I could get into trouble just by walking into Haskell's house.

Worried now, I told Santiago to stop.

Still near the top of the hill, he slid the car to a halt against the kerb. Some instinct prompted him to turn off the headlights and cut the engine. Darkness seemed to swallow us while my eyes adjusted, but soon I could see Haskell's house clearly through the snow.

Santiago eyed the house, then looked at me. Automatically he stuck a cigarette in his mouth. But he didn't light it.

'This Anglo who killed my son – this "Reg Haskell" – he lives there?'

I nodded.

He turned towards the house again. Roughly he asked, 'What is your intent?'

I was desperate to keep him out of danger. I didn't want him to pay for any of my mistakes. 'I'm going down there.' I tried to sound like I knew what I was doing, but the pain made me sound too harsh. 'You're going to wait here.'

His stare told me I had to do better than that. I tried again.

'He isn't home. The *chotas* have him. But they don't know he killed Pablo. They might keep him in protective custody for a while. Or they might let him go.

'I want to search his house. For evidence. To prove what he did. But if the *chotas* let him go – or if they come to search his house themselves – or if Muy Estobal returns – I won't find any evidence. I'll end up back in the hospital, and no one will believe you when you say he killed your son. They'll want proof.

'I need you to stay here and watch. Warn me if any one comes. Honk your horn. Twice, short and quick. But don't honk until you're sure they're coming to the house. And make sure they don't see you. I don't want them to know where the sound came from.' That way you won't be in as much danger.

Santiago didn't like it. But this was all new to him, and he didn't know how to argue with me.

'You are certain this killer is not in his house?'

'No,' I said in Spanish. 'But I believe it. Yet because of the hazard I cannot go to search for evidence unless you consent to keep watch for me.'

The end of his cigarette bobbed up and down as his jaw muscles knotted. This wasn't exactly his idea of revenge.

'Señor Santiago,' I said softly, 'Pablo was your son. But we have no evidence. Without evidence it is possible to be mistaken. Any man may accuse another, out of malice or error. For that reason there is law. If you wish to commit murder yourself, return me to the hospital and go your own way.'

He was a good man – angry as hell, hurt and bitter, hungry for violence or relief, but a good man. After a long minute, he sighed and let his weight sag into the seat. 'I will keep watch. Did not I myself attempt to teach my son the importance of law? Him I failed. I will not fail you.'

I wanted to thank him, but I didn't know how.

Fearing that I might change my mind or lose my nerve, I creaked open the door, put my feet into the snow, and lifted my torn guts out of the car.

Snow filled the light from the streetlamps. Flakes drifted heavily into my face. I closed the door with my hip and leaned against it, trying to call up reserves of strength or at least stubbornness that had been exhausted days ago. Then I hunched over the pain, folded my arms protectively across my stomach, and started down towards the house.

Slowly. Carefully. The footing was bad, and if I slipped the fall would rip what was left of my insides apart. Somehow I made it. The snow covered my footsteps. It covered the blood I'd left on the walkway. I didn't make a sound as I crossed the gravel.

Here the light cut through the snowfall, bright as accusation. Fortunately I didn't need stealth. I couldn't have managed it. Fumbling for the keys, I passed the cedars and went straight down the aisle to the door.

Except I *did* need stealth. If the snow hadn't muffled me so well, God knows what he would've done. Under the circumstances, however, the twist of my key in the lock only gave him a few seconds' warning. Then I got the door open and found myself standing right in front of him.

Our client, Reg Haskell.

For a while we stared at each other. His eyes seemed to go blank at first. But then they got brighter and sharper as if he'd turned up a rheostat of adrenaline or excitement.

'By God, Axbrewder,' he said, 'if you weren't right here I would have sworn nobody could walk around with a bullet in his stomach. You're astonishing. How do you do it?'

He stood at the top of the stairs. He hadn't changed his clothes since the last time I saw him, but there was a suitcase on the floor on either side of him.

I closed the door. Conserving my strength, I didn't relock it. Then I took a few steps towards him, carrying the pain as well as I could. My right hand slipped into the pocket of my jacket and wrapped around the butt of the .45.

A detached part of my mind wondered how far he intended to go. Did he mean to skip town completely, leave the state and maybe even the country? And if so, would he take his wife? Or did he just want to hide from el Señor for a while?

But I didn't ask those questions out loud. I was still too surprised.

I stopped moving, and he looked at me more closely. Concern that might conceivably have been genuine crossed his face. 'Axbrewder, you look terrible. What are you doing to yourself? You're a wreck.'

Panic and thirst closed my throat. I was in no condition to deal with him, no condition at all. I had to force my voice through miles of cotton, as if it were wrapped in bandages.

'Cason let you go.'

He ignored me. 'Can I get you something? I mean it. You look terrible. You ought to lie down. How about a glass of water?'

A glass of water would've been heaven. I had to glare at him until my skull throbbed in order to concentrate.

'Why? Why did he let you go?'

Haskell shrugged. 'I told him the truth. He didn't have any reason to hold me.'

'What was the truth? I've never heard it. All I've heard is lies.' I wanted to flay him somehow, lay him bare. But I didn't have the strength. I sounded like I'd swallowed a bucket of sand. 'That's how you play people. You don't really care about cards or dice or coins. The kind of gambling you're addicted to is manipulating people.'

Then I stopped. I wasn't getting anywhere. He just stood there and looked at me like I'd gone out of my mind.

I changed directions. 'Never mind. I already know what you told him.' Actually I had no idea, but that didn't matter at the moment. 'Tell me something else. Why did you hire us in the first place? You must've known you were taking a risk. You talked to Smithsonian about us. He's an asshole, but he's not stupid. Why buy that kind of trouble for yourself?'

'Come on, Axbrewder.' Haskell didn't show even a flicker of uncertainty or fear. 'You know why. I needed protection. Somebody honest and tough enough to face el Señor. I could see Smithsonian didn't fit that description. And he has resources you lack. Money, personnel, intelligence.' Reg didn't mind calling a space a spade. 'He might mess with things I wanted left alone. You and Fistoulari looked like exactly what I had in mind.

'You scared me for a while,' he admitted. 'I thought I'd made a mistake – and I don't make very many. You insisted on prying into my life instead of nailing the people who want me dead. I said I was going to fire you, and I meant it. But then I saw Fistoulari coming unglued.' His contempt was plain in his voice. 'Just thinking about el Señor made her panic. After that I knew I didn't have to worry about her. And you were still too stubborn to stop protecting me.'

Abruptly he shrugged. 'Now I don't need you any more. Cason is going to take care of el Señor for me. Your job is finished.' Then he resumed looking concerned. 'Let me call an ambulance for you. You should get back to the hospital.'

He made me so mad that I wanted to pull out the .45 and blow his face off. But I didn't. Instead I nodded at his suitcases. 'Cason is going to take care of el Señor for you. Is that why you're on the run?'

At first he affected surprise. 'On the run?' Then he gave me one of his laughs. I hated his laughs. 'You have brain fever, Axbrewder. I'm not running anywhere. I'm going to join Sara. I'll check into her hotel, and we'll have a kind of mini-honeymoon. Celebrate the end of my problems. Cason already has the room number, in case he needs us for anything.'

He said it so well that I almost wanted to believe him. On one of my good days, I might've found the logical flaw in his lies. Or I might've devised some way to trick the truth out of him. But I'd almost come to the end of myself, and I wasn't done yet. I just had to trust my intuitions and do what came naturally.

'If Cason let you go,' I said, 'you must not have told him the whole truth. You must not have told him that you killed Pablo Santiago.'

At least I got his attention. His eyes went wide and his mouth opened. 'Who?'

Then for the first time it occurred to me that he might not know Pablo's name.

'Pablo Santiago.' The last of my endurance was oozing out of me, and I didn't have anything that even resembled evidence. 'That kid you killed. The numbers runner.

'All that crap about Roscoe Chavez. You got his name out of the newspaper. You never had anything to do with him. You just used him to give us a reason why el Señor is after you. Like that crock about the money laundry. Or the one about welshing on a bet. The truth is, he wants you dead because you murdered one of his runners.'

Haskell looked shaken. Maybe he really was shaken. 'Axbrewder,' he muttered. 'What in hell–? You must be out of your mind. Where did you *get* an idea like that?'

'From you.' Small dark spots started to swim across my vision. My throat burned for something to drink. 'You can't get your priorities straight. You hire us to protect you, and then you handcuff us with lies to keep us from doing our job. Innocent clients don't act like that.

'Here's the truth. You've had trouble with your "investments". Gambling is like that. You got hooked on the excitement and the fancy living, and you kept digging yourself in deeper. Like any other kind of addict.' I knew all about it. 'Finally things got too bad to handle any other way, so you decided to try to clean up playing the numbers. Friday night you goosed your bank out of five thousand dollars and went down to the old part of town for more "investing".

'But Saturday night when you went to pick up your winnings there weren't any. Imagine that. The runner had packets of money stuffed all over his body, twenty thousand dollars, but none of it was for you.

'Unfortunately he didn't realize that you're such a hotshot no one can beat you and you're willing to take on *any* odds just to prove how virile and fucking *alive* you are.' Between anger and pain, I'd nearly passed out. 'He probably didn't even resist when you took hold of him and broke his neck and piled him into your car. Or piled him into your car and then broke his neck. Then, when you had all the money, you pitched him out on Trujillo. You wanted the cops to think he was killed by the fall while he and his buddies were out joy-riding.

'It was all so easy. Probably made you feel like a real man. You only made about half a dozen mistakes.'

'Mistakes?' He looked like he'd never heard the word before.

'You didn't stop to think that el Señor's runners might be supervised. Watched. And whoever does that job has to know all the bettors. If the runner quits, or gets fired or promoted, or dies, el Señor doesn't want to start from scratch.

'Also the supervisor sets up the runner's schedule. You had to use an identifying word or name to place your bets. He got all that, along with your description. And you were so clever, you went to a bunch of runners and placed a whole series of bets. When the supervisor heard about one man placing all those bets, he naturally got suspicious. He probably had Pablo tailed. There was probably an eyewitness when you killed him. That's how el Señor found you so fast. The witness followed you home.

'On top of that, on Monday morning you deposited exactly the same amount of money el Señor lost when Pablo was killed.'

I was near the end, but I had to finish. 'And you made the mistake of killing a kid I knew and liked. His parents deserved a whole lot better than what you did to them.'

For a minute Haskell just stood there and stared at me. Then he chuckled softly. I couldn't even guess what was going on inside him.

'You know,' he said, 'you have a hell of an imagination. If Roscoe were alive, he'd laugh himself silly. He and I were willing to try a scam. But not murder!'

'No,' I said. 'That one won't work either. Chavez was killed because he got caught fucking el Señor's daughter. It didn't have anything to do with business.'

'Really?' The thought fascinated him. 'Then maybe we could have gotten away with it after all. Maybe I could have—' But abruptly he shook his head, made a dismissive gesture. 'That doesn't matter right now. You need help. I can't let you die in front of me like this. First I'll get you some water. Then I'll call an ambulance.' He showed no hesitation as he started for the living room. 'Come on. You can sit down in here.'

Decisively he entered the room and headed towards the wet bar.

I tightened my grip on the .45 and went after him. What else could I do? He was right – I needed water and an ambulance, in that order. Almost immediately. My whole head felt flamed with thirst, and the dampness at my waist was getting worse.

Vaguely I noticed that the living room was cold. For a second or two I couldn't figure out why. Then I realized that the window was still open. He hadn't bothered to close it. Snow collected on the sill and the carpet.

Which meant – come on, Axbrewder. What does it mean?

He was in a hurry. That was it. Such a hurry to get out that he hadn't even bothered to close the window.

The analytical mind at work. A veritable steel trap.

He'd gone behind the wet bar. Stupid of me to let him do that. Now I couldn't see his hands. I tried to secure my grip on the .45, but my arm seemed to be losing sensation, all the blood draining out of it. Fortunately I heard liquid being poured. Then he came out from behind the bar, carrying a full highball glass.

He pushed it at me. 'Here. Drink this. I don't care if you think you're God Himself. You can't last much longer.'

How did he know I was so thirsty?

My vision went grey at the edges. All my senses contracted around the glass in his hand, shutting out everything else. After all, I'd lost a lot of blood. I needed fluids.

Still clutching the .45 with my right hand, I took the glass in my left. Haskell smiled like a cherub while I dragged the glass up to my face and drank.

But he hadn't put water in the glass. He'd filled it with vodka.

Reflexively I swallowed a couple of times before I recognized the truth. Then I started to gag and sputter, tearing up my stomach. The glass fell somewhere, vodka sprayed at Haskell. He ducked, backed away. I tugged out the .45 – and alcohol bit into my guts like the business edge of a bandsaw.

I didn't scream. Not me. It was the whole room that screamed. The floor shrieked under my feet and the walls howled agony at each other and the dark wooden bellow of the wet bar hit me like a club. The lights exploded in my head, bits of glass and anguish squalling back and forth until my brain ripped to tatters. Some goon with a crane and a meat hook caught me by the belly and yanked me off my feet, but I never saw him.

I couldn't see anything at all except Haskell. He was all that remained of the world, and he straddled me like a conquering hero. He had the .45 in both hands. Pointed into my face.

'Actually' – he sounded like he was screaming too, but that couldn't be right, he must've been gloating – 'it *does* make me feel fucking *alive*. You're tough, I'll give you that. But you've never been a match for me. Don't you know you can't drink anything when you have a hole in your stomach?'

No. I didn't know. No one ever told me.

Maybe I'd gone all the way out of my head. Behind the way the room seemed to yowl and screech, I could've sworn I heard a car horn. Two quick cries in the distance, like a wail with its throat cut.

Apparently I was wrong. Haskell didn't react.

'But you're worth what you get paid,' he smirked. 'You've finally saved me. Now I don't have to run. Instead I'll simply wait until el Señor sends somebody after me again. I'll shoot him with your gun. Just to be safe, I'll shoot you with his gun. That will buy me enough time to figure out my next move.'

No, I wasn't out of my head. I should've been, but I wasn't. He heard the same thing I did.

A key in the lock of the front door.

It's always the trivial details that kill you. If Ginny had known that I'd left the door unlocked, she could've walked right in and nailed Haskell. Or if I'd locked the door after me, one turn of the key would've unlocked it and she still might've been quick enough. But her first twist locked the door. Then she spent a couple of seconds rattling the knob before she tried turning the key the other way.

Quickly Haskell crept into the atrium.

He wanted to shoot one of el Señor's men. But none of them had a key to his front door. He couldn't risk killing someone else with my gun.

Her key still in her hand, Ginny pushed the door open. She was in a hurry – too much of a hurry to be careful. Her eyes scanned the atrium. Then she saw me through the doorway. Simple horror seemed to make my vision as clear as sunlight.

She wore her claw. Its stainless steel hooks caught the light and leered like a grin in double vision.

I tried to shout, tried with all my heart. But I couldn't. Spasms of pain clenched every muscle in my chest. Faint with anoxia, I gaped in her direction like a stranded fish, but nothing came out of my mouth.

Then it was too late. Haskell hit her on the back of the neck with the butt of the .45, and she dived face first into the carpet.

When he saw that she wasn't moving, he smiled as if he could hardly keep his laughter to himself.

With the side of his foot, he pushed the door shut, but he didn't take his eyes off Ginny and me. 'Better and better,' he chortled softly. 'I told you I don't need luck. Skill makes its own luck.' He was having the time of his life.

But he didn't forget to be cautious. He kept Ginny covered while he retrieved her purse and helped himself to her .357. Then he disappeared into the bedroom while I gagged and retched up blood and tried to move and couldn't. When he returned, he had a thick roll of white bandage tape.

Deftly, like he'd been practising for years, he taped Ginny's wrists behind her. Still grinning, he dragged her by the shoulders of her coat into the living room and dropped her beside me. Paralysed with pain, I couldn't even twitch when he pushed me on to my front, tugged my arms behind me, and secured my wrists, too. Then – just to keep me from getting bored – he hooked a shoe under my rib cage and levered me on to my side.

Did I scream that time? Not old man-of-steel Axbrewder. My mind went blank with transcendental agony, and I lay still, trying to be dead.

'This will be quite a shoot-out,' he said. He had a gun in each hand, for all the world like a kid playing the best game of cowboys-and-Indians. 'I'll be able to take care of all my enemies at once. One of you will kill el Señor's hit-man. Not her.' Enjoying his own contempt, he kicked Ginny's artificial hand. 'She doesn't deserve it. I'll give you that honour. Do wonders for your reputation. Unfortunately you won't survive to take credit. And el Señor won't be able to threaten me again for a while. He'll be too busy defending himself against a double murder charge. Even if the cops can't prove anything on him, I'll still be innocent. I'll walk away with twenty thousand dollars and a fresh start.'

Abruptly he seemed to remember he still had things to do. He put the guns in his pockets, moved to the wall switch, and snapped off the living-room lights.

'Don't worry,' he said over his shoulder. 'I doubt you'll have to stay in the dark for long. With the lights off, el Señor's thug will think I'm going to bed. He'll come after me soon.'

Then he left the room. In the atrium, he hit the switches for all the entryway and exterior lights. A glow from the lower level lit his way down the stairs. After that I couldn't see him any more. When he reached the bottom, he flipped more switches, and the last glow vanished. Night rushed into the room through the open window, as cold as the snow.

In the dark, I could hear Ginny breathing raggedly. She sounded like Haskell had broken her skull.

When I tried to say her name, nothing came out.

Everything else was silent, muffled by snow and pain – the night outside, Haskell's movements downstairs, my internal bleeding – everything except the raw faint rasp of air in and out of Ginny's lungs. I tried again.

But I didn't make a sound.

Dear God, what if he *had* broken her skull?

'Ginny.'

Ginny Ginny Ginny, like an echo down into the bottom of an abyss. No answer.

Ginny Ginny – stop that, I told myself. Forget the pain. So it hurts. So what? Push it out of the way. Try again.

'Ginny.' For God's sake. 'Wake up.'

From so far away that the distance wrenched my heart, I heard her breathing catch. She took in a muffled gasp, let out a groan.

'God,' she exhaled. 'Damn that sonofabitch.' A slurred murmur. 'Who in hell–?'

Through the dark, I felt her stiffen. 'What happened? Brew?' Her voice started to rise. 'Brew?'

'Quiet,' I sighed at her. I felt like I was whispering blood. 'He'll hear you.'

'Who? Where are you?' She made scuffling sounds. Her head knocked against my shoulder. 'Mick Axbrewder,' she hissed furiously, 'what in *hell* are you doing here?'

'Haskell is here.' My voice was a wisp. It sounded even further away than she did. 'He's going to kill us.'

She froze. I felt her listening to the dark. After a moment she breathed carefully, 'Why?'

Working at it practically one word at a time, I gave her all the explanation I had strength for. 'He stole that twenty thousand. From one of el Señor's runners. Broke the kid's neck.'

My memory played tricks on me. I saw the parking lot attendant burn horribly. I saw Señora Santiago cover her face with her apron. I thought I heard Ginny hit her stump against the wall of the den.

'Pablo Santiago.' I should've told her when I first read it in the paper. But I'd needed it for myself. To help me bear the grief of losing her. 'That's why el Señor–'

'Why el Señor wants him dead,' she finished for me. 'Damn right.' Then she faltered. 'Pablo?' She'd known his parents as well as I had.

'Yes.' I felt like I was weeping.

She sighed. 'I wish I'd known. It might've made a difference.'

Of course it would've made a difference. She would've understood what I was doing.

But that wasn't the difference she had in mind. Her voice hardened. 'When I went to your room and saw you weren't there, I almost threw a fit. And I would have, too, but I knew I didn't have time. I had to catch you before you got out of the hospital.

'One of the ER nurses remembered seeing you in the parking lot. And one of the security guards thought you were picked up by a man in an old clunker. They didn't stop you because it never occurred to them you might be a patient.

'That left me with nothing. You were gone.' She choked on the word momentarily. 'I couldn't imagine what craziness you had in mind. All I knew was, you had a bullet hole in your guts and were probably bleeding like a stuck pig.

'So I went to see el Señor.'

'What?' Somehow she surprised me enough to penetrate the pain. 'You went–?'

'Sure. What did you expect? I had to assume that was where you were going. Nothing else made any sense. So I tried to get there ahead of you.

'I didn't see Estobal around El Machismo. When I finally talked my way into el Señor's office, I told him to call off his dogs. We'd turned Haskell over to the cops. That was the end of the case as far as we were concerned. He didn't have any reason to hurt you again. In fact, he was ahead of the game. You took a bullet in the gut, Estobal didn't have a scratch. I told him to leave us alone.'

I tried to imagine any one in Puerta del Sol telling el Señor what to do. But I couldn't.

'He just laughed at me. When he laughs at people—' She shuddered. 'He told me the cops had already released Haskell. Surely I must've know. Why else would I go to el Señor with such a childish trick? Nothing I did or said would save his life. Or the life of anybody who got in the way. Then I was escorted out.

'I wanted to ask him how he knew what the cops had done with Haskell. But I didn't get the chance.

'With Haskell on the loose, I assumed Estobal was on his way here. And maybe you'd come here, too. Maybe you'd figured everything out. I had to move fast. First I went back to the apartment, got the claw. I hate it, but it's better than nothing. Then I came here.'

Musing blood, I filled in the rest. Now I knew what was going to happen. I knew what she would do.

I couldn't bear it. The mere thought made me want to puke. No one in their right mind would take that kind of risk. But I had no choice. Neither of us did. There wasn't any other way to get back the woman.

'Haskell knows Estobal's coming,' I said. 'It's a trap. He intends to shoot Estobal with our guns. Frame all of us for killing each other.'

For a few seconds she went still. Then, grimly, she whispered, 'Roll over, Brew. Give me your wrists.'

The command in her voice was familiar, like an old friend. That was my only consolation.

Alcohol had turned my guts to jelly and anguish. I could hardly twitch. Nevertheless I did it somehow. Rolled over. Shrieks yammered against the back of my teeth, but I didn't let them out.

Almost immediately she grappled for my forearms. With her hand, she felt her way to the tape. Then, fumbling with uncertainty and desperation, she pushed one hook of the claw between my wrists under the tape.

Down at the base, the edges of the hooks were like a pair of shears.

Bunching the muscles of her forearm to make her artificial hand open and close, she cut the tape.

I nearly wailed. For a couple of seconds, I feared that she would sever the tendons in my wrists. But it worked. My hands twisted loose.

With my arms free, I could shift positions more easily.

At first I lay there gasping while my head spun and my chest hurt. Now was my chance to be a hero. Right now. Everything so far had been preparation. Sabre-rattling and fanfares. Now I had to prove myself. To myself.

The crucial point was to leave Ginny's wrists strapped so that she couldn't stop me. The rest was simple. Creep downstairs into the maze of Haskell's house. Spring his trap on him. Then come back upstairs in time to deal with Estobal. Just like in the movies. Then Ginny would realize how much I loved her. She'd go all soft and feminine, and I'd be big and strong, and we'd live happily ever after.

Neat, huh?

I didn't even try it. Instead I levered myself around until I could reach her wrists. Blinded by darkness, I located the tape and dug my knife out of my pocket. But my fingers were numb. I could barely open the knife. Cutting at the tape felt like slitting her wrists.

At first I couldn't do it. Somewhere in the background, I thought I heard myself sob. But when I tried again more gently, I managed the slip the blade under the tape.

The tape parted with a tearing sound like a wail.

'All right,' she breathed. 'All right.' She sounded ready and fatal, like a stick of dynamite with a lit fuse. Quickly she crouched beside me. 'Now we're in business.

'I'm going after that bastard. Wait for me in the atrium. You can watch my back. If you see or hear anything, throw something down the stairs. I'll know what to do.'

Even though she couldn't see it, I nodded.

I didn't hear her go. The carpet muffled every sound. But I felt her moving away, evaporating into the dark. Soon the house swallowed her.

Haskell's house. He knew his way around better than both of us put together. And he was armed. And he expected someone to come after him. What chance did she have?

Bleeding quietly to myself, I got up on to my hands and knees. The pain in my stomach filled the room, and as it expanded my life stretched thinner and thinner. I was nearly gone. Without light, I couldn't get my bearings. But then I made out a faint glow reflecting from the streetlamps through the open window. I crawled in that direction.

When I reached the window, I found a snowdrift melting into the carpet. Snow piled nearly three inches deep on the sill. It seemed to flow into my face, cooling the sting of my scratches – offering to cool the hot damage in my guts. Ginny needed me. I propped my hands on the sill, wedged my legs under me, and tumbled out through the window.

The impact when I hit the ground turned everything to the soft thick falling blankness of snow.

I didn't know how long I lay there, cradled by the cold. Probably not very long. If a significant amount of time had passed, I would've been beyond reach, my mind and my blood both drained out of me and no way to get them back. I wouldn't have been able to hear the horn.

A car horn. Two quick blasts.

Someone was coming.

That's why I was out here. In case someone came. To take them by surprise instead of being trapped in the house.

Like Ginny.

I had to make myself move again.

For a while I thought I might actually pull it off. I couldn't stand at all. When I tried my feet seemed to spread out through the snow, and my knees refused to straighten. But I could crawl. A few inches at a time. Towards the front of the house.

But the snow accumulated in front of me. It fell on my back, weighed me down. It was soft and kind, it wanted me to rest, and it was too heavy to refuse. The cold made my bleeding hurt less. I got as far as the corner. If I'd looked around it, I could've seen the cedars guarding the entryway. Seen Haskell's Continental. But I didn't look. I couldn't go any further.

By now I was too late. The horn had tried to warn me, but el Señor's emissary was already in the house. Estobal, no doubt. There was nothing I could do about it. Some things you just have to forgive yourself for.

Lying on my face, I let everything get away.

For a while I slept. I needed the rest. All my problems left me, and I felt peace approaching. It was right around the corner. Coming this way. The only time in my life that I'd ever had any peace was stone drunk. And it never lasted. First it was amber and bliss, the pure blessing of alcohol. Then it changed into something else. Maybe anger. Maybe grief. Maybe nightmares and the howling spook of the DTs.

Or maybe voices.

Two men rasping at each other.

I recognized Rudolfo Santiago, hissing curses and pain. Then I made out the other voice.

Muy Estobal.

'Silence, *pendejo*,' he snarled in Spanish, 'or I will crush your arms. You sought to warn the house of my approach. Now you will make recompense. You will shield me from bullets, serving as hostage, or I swear by the Mother of God that I will leave you with no bone intact.'

'Butcher,' Santiago croaked. 'Son of a whore.' But he couldn't match Estobal's strength. By degrees I heard him fail.

It was worth one last try. I'd been given another chance. If I waited, I'd be too late. And Ginny would be caught.

Come on. Just once more.

I raised my head. Shoved my arms under me. Levered my weight on to my legs.

Lumbering drunkenly, I rounded the corner and headed for the aisle of the entryway.

The snow covered me. It was good as stealth. I made no sound.

Past the cedars, I almost fell. But a few steps down the aisle, I crashed into Estobal from behind.

That saved me.

My momentum carried us a few more steps. He lost his grip on Santiago. My arms wrapped around his neck.

He spat a curse. Recovering his balance, he tried to twist away from me.

I had no strength like his. Nevertheless I caught my right forearm under his chin and hung on.

His hands clawed at my arm. He yanked me from side to side as if I weighed nothing. Heaving himself backwards, he slammed me against the wall. His bulk sledgehammered at my torn guts.

As if he thought that he could make me let him go kill Ginny.

Noises like shots went off in the distance.

I gripped my right wrist with my left hand so that I could pull with both arms. My forearm ground into his throat. I held on.

Santiago crowded into the struggle.

He was too close. He would get hurt.

A second later he reeled away like he'd been kicked.

He had Estobal's .38.

Estobal battered me around in the aisle like a rag doll. Must've been an entertaining sight – Axbrewder being flapped in the breeze like so

413

much wet laundry. With a little advance notice, you could've sold tickets. But I didn't feel any of it except the one sharp absolute scream where my stomach used to be. And as long as that scream lasted I held on.

I didn't hear his larynx snap. Some time later we folded together to the cement. I didn't notice much difference.

When the light came on in the aisle, however, it snagged what was left of my mind. I turned my head in time to see the front door jerk open and Ginny appear, her .357 ready in her fist.

Quickly she scanned the aisle. Seeing Santiago surprised her, but she didn't falter. As soon as he lowered the .38, she pointed her claw at Estobal.

'Is he alone?' she demanded. 'I've taken care of Haskell.' Her eyes, and the whetted lines of her face, burned with an alert grey fire. 'He's dead.'

'Good for you,' I sighed while I started to pass out. 'Help me. I'm bleeding.'

Chapter Twenty-one

Not being exactly what you might call on top of things at the time, I didn't see how the rest of the night turned out. But I heard about it later.

Cason showed up with about six squad cars and made a big deal out of storming the house. When he found that there was no one left to shoot at, much less arrest, he tried to give Ginny bloody hell for ruining his case against el Señor. He'd let Haskell go to bait a trap. He said. He wanted to catch Estobal in the act of attempting to kill Haskell. He said. *I* say that he and his troops arrived a little late to be convincing.

Anyway, Ginny took his hide off for him. In front of his men. But she didn't tell me that part. Santiago did.

At least now I could assume that I didn't have to worry about el Señor sending anybody after me. Not for a while. True, I'd killed his bodyguard. But he had too many other problems to deal with – like, why one of his employees was so eager to shoot people. I might be safe for a long time.

The next day I regained consciousness. And the day after that I could talk again. Another miracle of modern medicine. It's amazing what transfusions and antibiotics can do for you. During visiting hours Ginny and I finally got a good look at each other.

She stood beside my bed looking like she'd put on her best clothes just for me. Her hair shone, and she wore exactly the right amount of make-up. The only thing that kept her from being beautiful was the uncertainty in her eyes. Her broken nose didn't count. I'd always liked her nose. And her claw didn't bother me.

I felt grungy as hell in comparison. The baths they give you in hospital beds aren't ever the same as being clean. And I hadn't shaved since I could remember.

Nevertheless I smiled up at her as well as I could. 'Hi,' I said. A conversational masterstroke. My pleasure at seeing her was genuine. I just wasn't any more sure of myself than she was.

She gave me back a crooked smile. 'Hi, yourself.' Then she nodded at my IVs. 'They wanted to tie you in bed this time. I told them not to bother. Nobody pulls a stunt like that twice.

'On the other hand' – she shrugged, grimacing wryly – 'most people don't even do it once. I wish I knew what in hell possessed you to be such a hero.'

That was an indirect reference to the source of her uncertainty. She didn't want to come right out and name it, so she tried to sneak up on it instead.

Maybe I knew better. Or maybe I was still muzzy-headed with drugs and convalescence. Whatever the reason, I didn't fall into the trap.

'Me?' I protested, taking a stab at humorous sarcasm. 'You're the one who went to see el Señor. When I tried that, it almost killed me. And you're the one who went after Haskell. In that house, in the dark, without even a gun.'

Later she told me how she did it. She made it sound simple. She went downstairs as quietly as she could, but when she reached the kitchen she made just enough noise to help him find her. She opened the refrigerator, helped herself to a carton of milk, and hid behind one of the counters, using the fridge light to watch the room. When Haskell finally came to investigate, she hit him with the milk. That didn't keep him from shooting, but it threw him off balance, let her get close. Then she punched his throat out with her claw.

'You've got some nerve,' I went on, 'accusing *me* of being a hero.'

She smiled a little. But she wasn't deflected. 'I mean it, Brew. I want to know. Why did you do it?'

She was dangerously close to what she really wanted from me. That made me nervous. On the other hand, it was an opportunity for me as well.

'I'll trade you,' I countered quietly. 'You tell me why you decided to put on your claw.'

We must've looked pretty silly, dancing around each other like this when both of us knew exactly what was going on and refused to say it. But it had to be that way. After a fashion, we were protecting each other.

416

She nodded, accepting the trade. 'Talking to el Señor did it. I felt so helpless. You've been there. You know what he's like. I wasn't in his league.

'That changed the way I thought about' – she glanced down at her artificial hand – 'about things. Until then, a hand and a claw felt like so much less than two hands. Too much less. I just felt crippled. But then I realized that a hand and a claw is still a hell of a lot more than a hand and a stump. And I needed all the help I could get.'

Carefully she avoided saying what she didn't want me to hear. *I did it for you.* As long as she didn't say it, I couldn't be sure it was true.

And as long as I could think that she did it for herself, that she accepted the claw because she was willing to live with it, I had reason to hope.

So I answered her question the same way.

'Mostly I think I was feeling useless. I wanted to work on Pablo's murder for myself. Prove I was still good for something. But I didn't get anywhere. I needed to talk to people who might know why he was killed. Leaving the hospital, getting a ride from Santiago – that was my only chance. If I waited until I healed, the case would be closed. Or cold.

'Santiago must've told you the rest. When I realized Haskell killed Pablo, I had to go looking for evidence.'

'He told me,' she agreed. 'Knowing you, it even makes a weird kind of sense. But after you'd done all that – after I finally got there, and we were free, and you didn't have to worry about it any more – Brew, what in God's name made you decide to climb out the window? You might've haemorrhaged to death.'

I shook my head. 'It's my turn.' If I'd been more alert, I could've enjoyed this little game. 'First you tell me what in God's name made you decide to go after Haskell without so much as a weapon. You didn't have to do that. We could've both climbed out the window.'

She let out a snort of disgust. 'You're right. That was stupid. But I was too pissed off to do anything else. That bastard lied and lied to us, and then he planned to kill us. I couldn't stand to think he might get away with it. If I'd had any sense, I would've called the cops and let them handle it.'

I wanted to applaud. This was getting to be fun. 'You worry me, Fistoulari. Next to you, I'm the personification of logic and sweet reason. Jumping out the window was the best idea I had all night. Haskell believed that Estobal would come after him, so I figured I could count on it. But if Estobal caught me in the house, I was a goner. My only chance was to get behind him.'

It was working. The anxiety in her eyes began to fade.

I hardly missed a beat. 'Speaking of Rudolfo Santiago,' I went on, shamelessly changing the subject, 'what do you hear from him? How are he and Tatianna doing?'

That made her frown a little. My answers didn't satisfy her. But I put on an I'm-an-invalid-so-you-ought-to-humour-me look, and she relented.

'I went to see them yesterday. They're still grieving, but I don't think they're as bitter about it as they were. He's secretly proud of himself. He believes he saved your life by taking Estobal's gun. Which is probably true, by the way. And I got the impression that she's relieved it was an outsider who killed her son, an Anglo, not someone who's part of her community. All Anglos are crazy. That makes her feel better.'

'Good.' Since I couldn't get out of bed anyway, I was grateful for everything I didn't have to worry about. 'I presume Canthorpe's off the hook?'

She nodded.

Good again. 'I'd be surprised if there was anything we could do for Eunice Wint. What about Sara Haskell?'

Ginny's frown narrowed into a black scowl. But it was a special scowl, one I fell in love with years ago. It said, I'm Ginny by God Fistoulari, and I'll be damned if I'm going to laugh at this.

Her voice hard with control, she said, 'They served the papers this morning. Mrs Reginald Haskell is suing us for "wrongful death". She thinks we used excessive force on her poor husband. Also we were incompetent. My licence is suspended until the board can schedule a hearing.'

I would've at least chuckled for her, but my stomach still hurt too much. 'How long will that be?' We were safe on this one. The board gets pretty snooty sometimes, but when they heard the evidence they would throw out Mrs Haskell's case. Politely, of course.

She shrugged. 'Ten days? Two weeks?'

'That's OK. A little vacation won't hurt you. And I won't be on my feet for a while. You wouldn't want to work without me.'

I'd given distraction my best shot, but she refused to give up what she wanted to know. Instead she rephrased it.

'Brew,' she asked intently, 'why did we take that case? What made it so important? What did we go through all that for?'

418

It was the same question she'd been asking all along. And she wanted an honest answer. But I didn't let the earnest grey of her gaze lure me into a mistake.

Distinctly I told her, 'Because Haskell wanted protection against el Señor. That time I went to see him, I was desperate. Your life was in danger. It wouldn't have cost him anything to help me. But he refused.' Instead he'd forced me to drink when her life had depended on my sobriety. 'I knew this case was dangerous, Ginny. I just wanted revenge.'

She understood. Both sides of it – what I said, and what I didn't. It seemed to make her face soft and sad and relieved all at the same time. 'You know something, Axbrewder?' she murmured. 'Sometimes you're almost a nice man.'

Bending down, she rested a kiss on my forehead.

My guts still hurt, and I had IVs plugged into both elbows, but I didn't care. I put my arms around her and welcomed her back.

THE MAN WHO
TRIED TO GET AWAY

– To Real and Muff Musgrave,
friends to treasure

Chapter One

Of course, I lost weight. People do that after they've been shot in the gut. But I could afford a little weight. Cooking for Ginny had given me more pounds than it did her. My real problem was movement.

Muy Estobal's bullet had torn me up pretty good inside, even if it did leave my vital organs alone. And I hadn't done myself any favours with all that hiking around the night after I got shot. The doctor told me that if I walked to the bathroom with my IVs nailed to my arms every hour or so until he started hearing 'bowel sounds', he would maybe consider removing my catheter. As a special reward for being such a good patient.

That was easy for him to say. El Señor didn't want him dead. It wasn't his problem I might die because of the simple fact that I couldn't get out of bed.

I needed to move. To escape from the hospital. Before el Señor sent Estobal's replacement after me.

So far I'd only been stuck here for forty-eight hours, and it was already driving me crackers. If they hadn't given me so many pills, I wouldn't have been able to sleep at night. I would've stayed awake the whole time, watching the door. Expecting to see some goon with at least an Uzi come in to blow me away.

Ginny hadn't been much help. She kept telling me that there wasn't any danger, there was too much heat on el Señor, he couldn't afford to risk having me hit so soon. Which should've been true, I suppose. And I should've believed her. I'd believed her when she first said it.

Hadn't I?

But after that, unfortunately, I got a phone call.

It came during the day, when the hospital switchboard was on automatic, and the winter sunlight and the blue sky outside my window made everything I could see look safe. But I must not have been feeling particularly safe, because I believed my caller right away.

When the phone rang, I picked it up and said, 'Huh' because that's easier than 'hello' when your whole torso is strapped with bandages and you don't feel much like breathing deeply anyway.

A voice I almost knew said, 'Get out of there. He wants you. You're a sitting duck.'

Then the line went dead.

Cheered me right up, that did.

When I told Ginny about it, she looked just for a second like she believed it, too. Her grey eyes sharpened, and the lines around her broken nose went tight. But after that she grinned. 'Probably somebody's idea of a joke.'

Oh, sure. I'd killed Muy Estobal, el Señor's favourite muscle. Together, Ginny and I had disrupted el Señor's revenge on a man who'd ripped him off and murdered one of his people. Everyone around him probably laughed out loud whenever my name came up.

But my caller wasn't finished.

The next day, the doctor heard gurgling in my guts – bowel function struggling back to life – and took out the catheter. I got the thrill of starting to feed myself hospital gruel, which tasted like puréed dogfood. And I was encouraged to get out of bed and actually stand until pain made my head ring like a gong and my famous bowels hurt like they'd been shredded.

I was horizontal again, holding on to the bed and doing my best not to gasp, when the phone rang.

This time my caller said, 'I mean it. You haven't got much time. He wants you dead.'

I felt like I was inches away from recognizing that voice, but I couldn't pull it in. Gremlins in spiked boots raced up and down my intestines, distracting me.

'Who?' I asked. At the moment I didn't care how much it hurt to breathe so hard. 'Who wants me dead? Who are you? Why are you warning me?'

The line switched to a dial tone.

So when Ginny stopped by for her daily visit, I made her get the .45 out of my locker and leave it where I could reach it.

'You're taking this too seriously.' She sounded bored. 'El Señor is practically paralysed right now. The cops are watching everything he does. Even crooked cops are going to be honest for a while, with this much heat on. The commissioner is talking about "wiping out organized crime in Puerta del Sol". The newspapers are jumping up and down. I get interviewed at least once a day. Fistoulari Investigations never had so much publicity. I'm actually having to turn clients away.

'Brew, you're safe. Just relax. Get well.'

Just relax. Why didn't I think of that? 'If this is supposed to be a joke,' I muttered past my bandages, 'I'd hate to meet whoever's doing it when he's in a bad mood.'

'You sure you can't identify the voice?'

I shrugged. It wasn't very comfortable, but it was better than arguing.

'I'll check with the switchboard on my way out.' Now she was humouring me. 'Maybe they can take your line out of the automatic circuit. If we screen your calls, maybe we'll find out who's calling.'

I wanted to say, Don't screen my calls. Get me out of here. But I didn't. I let her go. She and I had too many problems, and the worst of them was that we were afraid of each other. We hadn't had a straight conversation in months because we were both too busy trying to control each other's reactions. She was afraid that if she said or did the wrong thing I'd go get drunk and never be sober again. And I feared that I might push her back into being the lost woman she'd become after she lost her hand.

She wore her 'prosthetic device' now, the mechanical claw that took the place of her left hand. Which was an improvement. But she still wore it like a handicap instead of something familiar, something she trusted. I figured that the only reason she wore it was to appease me. She was afraid of what I might do if she didn't. She had it on to protect me. Or to protect herself against me.

I loved her. I used to think she loved me. But it didn't show. Everything was twisted. We might as well have been chained together by our various fears. So I didn't tell that her I was too scared to stay in the hospital by myself. I didn't want to add to her worries.

Unfortunately the switchboard couldn't take just one line off automatic. The next day, I got another call.

By then I'd spent twenty-four hours expecting it. I was just a touch jumpy when I reached for the phone. Ol' nerves-of-steel Axbrewder. Weak as spaghetti in that damn bed, I fumbled the receiver on to the floor and had to pull it up by the cord to answer it.

'Sorry,' I said.

'Don't hang up,' I said.

'Tell me what's going on,' I said.

Impressive, no?

The silence on the line sounded like snickering.

'How did you get my number?'

'Hospital information,' the voice I almost knew replied. 'Anybody in Puerta del Sol can find out what room you're in just by asking. You're a dead man.'

Leaving me with that cheery thought, my caller put down the phone.

A couple of hours later, Ginny showed up. I told her about the call, but she didn't seem particularly interested. Instead she studied me as if I were exhibiting strange side effects to a new medication. 'This has really got you going,' she commented. Observant as all hell.

'Think about it,' I snarled as well as I could. 'How many people hate me enough to consider this kind of joke funny?'

But my vehemence didn't ruffle her. 'Think about it yourself, Brew,' she replied calmly. 'How many people love you enough to give you this kind of warning?'

That stopped me. Who would know that el Señor actively wanted me dead? Only someone close to him. And who in that group would give a good goddamn what happened to me? Which one of his people would risk warning me?

No one fitted that description.

I made an effort to look more relaxed. 'I guess you're right. It must be a practical joke. Some minor sociopath dialled the number and liked my reaction. Maybe he even dialled it at random.' I was trying to play along with her. Defuse anxiety. But the idea that I wasn't worried was pure bullshit and moonshine, and I couldn't keep it going. 'It's just a coincidence that I've actually got enemies.'

'No, you don't,' she retorted, grinning. Maybe she found it funny when I sounded so pitiful. Or maybe she was just keeping her guard up. 'That's what I keep trying to tell you. El Señor is paralysed. There isn't anybody else.'

I liked her grin, no matter what it meant. But it didn't cheer me up. Things like immobility and helplessness put too much pressure on my morale.

I was recovering too slowly. Where the hell were my recuperative powers when I needed them? Movement is life. I was running out of time.

I waited until Ginny left. Then I climbed vertical and practised lugging the tight lump of fire I called my stomach around the room.

Unfortunately that just aggravated my discouragement. About the time that pain and exhaustion got bad enough to make me sob, I decided to lie down and just let el Señor kill me.

Teach her a lesson, that would.

Self-pity may not be my most attractive quality, but I'm damn good at it.

So she took me completely by surprise when she came in early the next morning, before any phone calls, and asked, 'Can you walk out of here?'

I stared at her.

'Well, can you?'

I stared at her some more.

She sighed. 'If you can get out of bed,' she explained with elaborate patience, 'put your clothes on, and walk out of here, we're leaving. I've got a job for us.'

That early in the morning, I was still muzzy with sleeping pills. Nevertheless a few dopey synapses in my head went click. Before I could question them, I said, 'You believe those phone calls.'

She nodded sharply.

'I can't talk the cops into protective custody, but hospital security is watching your room most of the time. And the nurses here remember you.' She gestured with her left arm, and her claw gave me a flash of stainless steel. She'd lost her hand to a bomb in this hospital. 'They're doing what they can to keep an eye on you.'

She didn't let me interrupt. 'It isn't enough. If you don't get out of here today, I'm going to move in with you.'

I shook my head without realizing it. 'Why didn't you tell me? Why did you try to make me think you were laughing at me?'

'I didn't want you to worry,' she snapped. 'You're supposed to be recuperating, not lying there in a muck sweat.'

'Aye, aye, Captain Fistoulari, ma'am, sir,' I muttered.

In a fine display of moral fortitude and physical courage, I closed my eyes.

'Brew.' Her patience slipped a notch. 'I'm serious.'

'So am I,' I said through a haze of drugs and fear. 'Go away. This stinks.'

'What's the matter? Those calls obviously bother you. Don't you want to get away from them?'

'Yes,' I admitted. 'But not like this.' In fact the whole idea made me cringe. I was tired of being protected. Not to mention being protected against. 'If it's a real job, the last thing you need is a half-ambulatory cripple on your hands. And if it's a nursemaid exercise for my benefit, just to keep me out of trouble, I don't want it.' For a few months now I'd believed in myself enough to stop drinking – but that, as they say, was tenuous at best. The last thing I needed was one less reason for self-respect. 'You said you're turning clients away. Pick a job you can do by yourself. Leave me alone.'

Unfortunately that shut her up. She didn't say anything for so long that I finally had to open my eyes to see if she was still in the room.

She was.

She stood at the window with her back to me, hiding her face against the morning. Something about the line of her back, the way she held her shoulders, told me that I'd hurt her.

'Ginny–' I wanted to explain somehow, if I could just think of the words. But nothing came out of my mouth.

After a while she asked the glass, 'Why is this so hard?'

'I don't know.' My usual frightened contribution to our relationship. 'Everything we do to each other matters too much.'

She turned.

With the sunlight behind her, I almost missed the fighting light in her eyes. Wearing the conservative suits she preferred, her respected-private-investigator clothes, her blonde hair tidy around her fine face and her mouth under control, she looked like nothing so much as an up-and-coming businesswoman, lean and ready. Except for her broken nose, and that light in her eyes, and her claw. The punk who broke her nose was long dead. She'd shot him more than once, just in case he missed the point the first time.

'It's a nursemaid job,' she said straight at me, 'a piece of cake. You may remember the commission suspended my licence.' Her tone dripped pure acid. 'It's temporary, but for the time being there are only certain kinds of jobs I'm allowed to take. And the fee is real. You know I can't afford to ignore that. And it's out of town. Up in the mountains, where el Señor isn't likely to find you. It'll give you a week where you don't have to do anything worse than walk around.'

I did my best to shake my head in a way that would make her believe me. 'I don't care about that. I–'

She cut me off.

'*Listen.* Just once, listen to me. I suppose I could take what money I've got and borrow the rest and just buy you a plane ticket. You could disappear. Make it hard for el Señor to find you.

'But that won't work. We've tried it before, and it never works. You end up drunk somewhere, and eventually I have to come get you.

'Or I could go with you. I could sit around watching you until we both went wall-eyed or my money ran out. That won't work either. You know it won't.

'The only thing that ever does you any good is a *job*. As far as I can tell, you only stay away from alcohol when you've got people depending on you.

'Well, this job isn't exactly hard. We can't take on anything difficult with you in this condition. But it's still a *job*. It'll give you something to do, people to take care of. I don't have anything else to offer.

'I don't care whether you want it or not. We're going to accept that job if you can just *stand*.'

For a second there I felt so sick that I wanted to throw up. Absolutely puke my life away. I had an existential knife in my guts. She was protecting me again. Protecting against me again.

But then, all of a sudden, it occurred to me that knives cut both ways. Whether she intended it or not, she was offering me a chance to take care of myself. A chance to get up on my feet and make some of my own decisions.

So I relented. I wasn't exactly gracious about it. In fact, I was angry as hornets. But I said, 'I don't know why I bother arguing with you. I don't like nursemaid operations. I don't like being nursemaided. But I haven't got any better ideas. In any case, you're going to take care of me no matter what I do. I don't have the strength or the will power to stop you. This way I can at least try to return the favour.'

Ginny glared at me. The flash of her claw in the light reminded me that she had her own reasons to hate being taken care of. She'd been dependent on me for six months after she lost her hand – and she was only just now starting to get over it. Sounding bitter, she rasped, 'Is it the sleeping pills, or are you always this perceptive?'

I ignored her irritation. The pain in my stomach lost its metaphysical significance. A job. Something to *do*. I wanted that, no question about it. As soon as I agreed to go back to work, I forgot that knives do only one thing, and it isn't called healing.

Helping myself up with both hands, I got out of bed.

Chapter Two

I remembered getting dressed. I'd done it once before, when the hole in my gut was more recent. But that time I'd been too full of drugs and panic to have much rational grasp on what I did to myself. This time I knew where every single suture inside me was, and I could feel it pulling.

One thing you've got to say for us private investigators. We know how to have a good time.

Technically, of course, Ginny is the private investigator. She's Fistoulari Investigations. I'm just the hired help. I haven't had a licence for this kind of work for years – not since I tried to help a cop who happened to be my brother apprehend a purse-snatcher and accidentally shot him. Under the influence of alcohol. Amazing how the things we love best are the things that hurt us most. I couldn't remember the last time I had one entire day where the idea of a drink didn't sound like heaven.

But I didn't drink when I was working. In fact, I hadn't had a drink since the day I figured out that Ginny needed me as badly as I needed her – since the day she lost her hand. But that was starting to change. She wore her claw now, did things for herself. Every time I saw her, she was more the woman I used to know, the Ginny Fistoulari who could go after Satan Himself and not take any prisoners.

Which was a good thing, as far as it went. The only problem was, it left me with fewer ways to protect her. Or to protect myself against her.

On the other hand, getting dressed was *work*, no question about it. And we had a job to do. That was at least useful as a distraction.

She watched me have fun with my shirt for a minute or two. Then she said, 'Why don't I go get your paperwork done? That way we won't have to wait around for discharge.' She knew how I felt about having an audience while I suffered.

I shook my head. I wanted her to go away, that was a fact. But I also wanted her to watch me struggle into my clothes. I wanted her to have no illusions about my physical condition. And if she stayed, she could talk to me. Help me through the peculiar ordeal of putting on my underpants.

For no particularly good reason, I said, 'That doctor's going to have a spasm when he hears about this.'

'No, he won't.' She was sure. 'I talked to him earlier. If you're well enough to get dressed, you're well enough to go home. All we have to do is keep an eye on you – take your temperature, watch for infection, that sort of thing. I already have your pills.' Gazing innocently at the ceiling, she finished, 'I didn't tell him about the job.'

Well enough to get dressed. At the moment, that was debatable. Also trivial. She'd obviously spent some time getting ready for this case. That held my interest.

'Tell me about the job,' I asked to keep her talking. 'Who are we nursemaiding besides me?'

'You'll love it.' She made a studious effort not to wince every time my face twisted. 'For once I've got us something easy. Might as well be a vacation.

'Does the name, Murder On Cue, Inc. mean anything to you?'

I shook my head again. If Murder On Cue, Inc. was a company that arranged assassinations, I planned to send them after the bastard who invented underpants.

'It's a small outfit, only two people as far as I can tell. Unless they have a secretary hidden away somewhere. Roderick Altar and his wife. They run what they call "mystery camps". They get people who like to try to solve crimes, play at being Sherlock Holmes for a few days. Then they hire actors and plan a scenario and take the whole crowd to some secluded place where the real world won't get in their way, and they stage a murder or two for these people to puzzle over. Nobody except Altar and his wife knows the difference between the actors and the guests. Whoever solves the murder wins.'

'Be the first kid on your block to catch a killer,' I muttered. With my underpants on, I had to rest for a while. I couldn't look at Ginny. I didn't want to see whatever was in her eyes. 'Don't these people have anything better to do?'

'Apparently not.' As a matter of policy, Fistoulari Investigations doesn't sneer at people with money. They tend to pay better than

431

people without. But I could tell that Ginny shared my visceral reaction to Murder On Cue, Inc.

'So what do they need us for?' I asked to deflect myself from my socks. 'Don't they want to catch their own killers?'

'Security,' she answered.

She didn't elaborate.

At last I had to look up at her. 'What the hell do people who think killing is some kind of game need "security" for?'

She shrugged. She was studying me intently, trying to see into my wounds – trying to understand them. 'According to Altar, he's just the organizer, the guy who pulls the practical details together, like where these people stay, how they get there, what they eat, who feeds them. His wife's the murder enthusiast. She hires the actors, plans the scenario. She even screens the guests. I guess Murder On Cue is her hobby.

'He says he wants security for the insurance. Supplying protection for his guests and their belongings, he gets better rates. But his wife has different ideas – he says. She wants security because – how did he put it? – "the presence of private investigators makes the ambience more credible." And it gives the guests some extra competition. Solve the crime before the professionals do.'

My brain must've been in worse shape than I realized. I actually got both socks on before I thought to ask, 'You mean she isn't going to tell us who the actors are? What the scenario is? We're supposed to play the same game they're playing?'

Ginny gave me a tight little smile. 'Playing *along* is part of the job. Mrs Altar won't tell the guests who we are, and we aren't supposed to either. The only thing they'll know is that two of them are investigators. But we don't really have to try to solve the crime. In fact, we don't really have to do much of anything.

'Our main job is just to keep an eye on the general safety of the situation. Apply a little common sense. Keep the guests from getting carried away. According to Altar, they've never had any trouble. He doesn't want to start now.'

Maybe I'd finally grown accustomed to the pain. I closed my eyes, lifted one foot into my pants – and was amazed to discover that I'd survived the experience. I still felt like I was performing an appendectomy on myself with an apple corer, but aside from the usual lightheadedness and agony I was doing fine.

Trying not to pant – trying to prove that I really did have a wit or two inside my skull – I produced another question. 'What do you know about this Altar? And his wife.'

'Do you want help?'

She meant with my pants.

I ignored her offer. After a moment she pretended that she hadn't said anything.

'Roderick and Sue-Rose Altar. I haven't met her. He's in his early fifties. Not exactly fat, but he likes food more than exercise. Used to be a venture capitalist, until he made too much money to justify working. Now he manages his investments. And takes care of Sue-Rose and her enthusiasms.

'I don't have your talent for snap judgments' – a reference to my ingrained preference for intuition over reason – 'but if you pushed me I'd say he's just a bit bored with Sue-Rose and her enthusiasms and his whole life.'

That settled it. A nursemaid job if ever there was one. If Murder On Cue had ever put on a mystery camp where anything actually happened, Roderick Altar probably wouldn't have been bored. I should've gone back to rejecting the whole idea. Unfortunately I'd thought of another reason why I couldn't do that. Ginny wouldn't abandon me – and the harder I made it for her to protect me, the more likely she was to get hurt herself. So I kept my opinion of useless work to myself.

Almost like I'd done this sort of thing before, I put my other foot into my pants and pulled them up.

Someone should've applauded, but my audience didn't bother.

Get off the bed. Tuck in my shirt. Thread a belt through the loops. Buckle it. Keep your breathing shallow and act like you aren't about to fall on your face. A dazzling performance, Axbrewder. So maybe it was just a nursemaid job. If it required me to stand and walk and possibly even shake hands, it was going to be as much as I could manage.

'What about your coat?' Ginny asked. 'You want help with that?'

I wavered and wobbled in front of her. For some reason, she looked taller than I was – which should've been impossible, considering that I'm six five and she isn't. Maybe it was *déjà vu*, a reminder of all the times she'd come looking for me, looking for a way to rescue me from myself, and I'd stood there unsteady with drink and let her pretend that she needed me. Whatever the explanation, I didn't like it. So I asked the kind of question that usually got me in trouble.

'Why us?'

I'd caught her with her mind somewhere else. Probably still trying to guess how far I'd be able to walk. 'Why us what?'

'Why does Roderick Altar want Fistoulari Investigations?' Speaking distinctly was as close as I could get to sarcasm. 'You don't usually do this kind of work.'

'I asked him that.' She still wasn't thinking about my question. A frown knotted the bridge of her nose, and her eyes kept flicking away from me as if she didn't enjoy what she saw. 'He said he must've heard my name somewhere. Or read it in the paper. I told you I've been doing interviews.'

Which finally struck me as odd. She ordinarily didn't have much patience for the media. So I put in, 'Why?'

'Trying to keep a high profile,' she explained absently. 'As long as we're news, we'll be harder to hit. But I don't think he actually cares who we are, or whether we're any good. He isn't that interested.'

What she said made perfect sense, of course. But I still hated it. I suppose the truth was that I'd been angry at her for a long time. She should've let me drink myself into my grave, instead of rescuing me over and over again. And she should've been stronger when she lost her hand, instead of putting the burden on me – refusing to wear her claw, requiring me to take care of her for six months because she felt so crippled, so much less than a human being, not to mention less than a woman, that she didn't have the courage to do anything except hurt.

Now that she'd returned to being herself – put on her claw and taken control of the situation – I was even madder. Her vulnerability had been my only defence against my own weaknesses. It had compelled me when nothing else worked. The less she needed me, the more helpless I felt.

Our feelings for each other had gotten pretty twisted over the years.

If there was one true clear thing hidden away inside me anywhere, it was that I wanted to get those feelings untwisted. And as far as I could see, work was my only way to untwist them. A nursemaid operation was a lousy opportunity, but I didn't have any others at the moment.

I stuck to the point of my questions.

'You still haven't answered me. Didn't you tell me Murder On Cue has been doing mystery camps for a while now?'

Ginny made an effort to come back from wherever her head was. 'So?'

'So Roderick Altar has hired security before, too, and it wasn't us. So what went wrong? Why wasn't he satisfied with whoever it was? Or has he really had some trouble he isn't telling us about?

434

'Why have we got a nice safe job like this right now, just when we happen to need it, and it's the only thing the commission will let us handle?'

I had her attention now. 'Are you serious?' she asked, staring at me. 'Is this really the way your mind works? Axbrewder, you're sick. Or they're giving you too much medication. Coincidences do happen, you know. Every event in life isn't aimed at you.'

But that wasn't my point. 'In other words,' I countered, 'you didn't ask him. You let him offer you this job, and you didn't even ask him why.'

The tip of her nose had gone white, which usually happens when she's furious. Ominously quiet, she said, 'All right, Brew. Spit it out. What's your problem now?'

Luckily I knew her well enough not to take this anger personally. She wasn't mad at me. She was mad because I'd touched a nerve.

I looked at her straight. 'You don't usually miss that kind of question. You aren't thinking hard enough about this job. You're thinking too much about me.'

'It's a nursemaid operation,' she snapped back. 'How much thought do you think it requires?'

I didn't try to answer. I didn't have to. As soon as she heard what came out of her mouth, she caught herself, and her eyes dropped. 'All right,' she said again. 'I get the message. I do worry about you too much. There's no job so simple it can't get messy if you don't pay attention to it.

'Put on your coat. Call a nurse when you're ready to go.' Without waiting for my opinion, she headed towards the door. 'I'll meet you at the discharge exit.'

In some way I'd shaken her self-confidence. Maybe I'd just reminded her that she had as many reasons to be angry as I did. Or maybe she was still more vulnerable than she liked. Disgusted at herself, afraid for me, and more desirable than any other woman I knew, she left me to figure out the pain in my gut for myself.

Chapter Three

The coat was too much for me. Ginny had unearthed a thick and somewhat ratty three-quarter-length sheepskin from my closet – a relic of more prosperous times – and I couldn't face hauling it up my arms and over my shoulders. Instead I pushed the buzzer to call a nurse. Then, while I waited, I retrieved the .45 and hid it in one of the pockets of the coat. The coat was pretty heavy anyway. Maybe no one would notice the extra weight.

The hospital staff must've had orders to get rid of me as soon as possible. A nurse arrived with a wheelchair almost right away. Without any discernible sense of loss over my departure, she put my coat on for me, helped me sit down, and gave me a ride to the discharge exit. By then Ginny had finished swearing on her soul to pay every conceivable penny of my bill. She and the nurse manoeuvred me into the passenger seat of her creaky Olds. The nurse slammed the door.

Ginny fired up the Olds. To distract myself from the many pleasures of sitting in this position with miles of tape strapped around my ribs and every suture straining, I asked, 'Now what?'

Spinning the wheel one-handed, Ginny took us out of the parking lot. Instead of looking at me, she watched the traffic for ambushes or tails. Her purse lay open beside her so that she could reach her .357. Just in case.

'The camp doesn't start until tomorrow,' she said, 'but today we have an appointment with Mrs Altar. Look the place over, find out what she wants us to do. I told you it's up in the mountains. I gather Murder On Cue is renting an entire hunting lodge for the week, complete with staff. A place called Deerskin Lodge.' She tried not to sneer when she said the name, but she couldn't help herself. Then she added in a different tone, 'It's a good three-hour drive. Can you stand it?'

I didn't answer that. I was too busy showing off my he-man private investigator stoicism. 'The Altars like isolation.'

Ginny nodded. 'Adds to the appeal of the situation. Makes the guests feel like they really do have to solve the crime, or else they might get killed themselves. Also prevents intrusion from the real world.'

Leaning on the accelerator, she took the Olds up the access ramp on to the freeway and began the long climb out of the valley where Puerta del Sol sprawls along the Flat River. The sky was grey with winter, and a temperature inversion trapped a pall of wood smoke and exhaust fumes over us. Nevertheless the San Reno Mountains reared up ahead like they didn't give a damn about such things, filling the whole eastern horizon of the city.

'According to Roderick Altar,' Ginny concluded, 'they've used this lodge several times now, very successfully. The setting is perfect, and the staff know what to do.'

'Duck,' I snorted cryptically.

'Huh?'

'The staff know what to do. Which is duck. They don't want to get hit by flying bullets when all those amateur sleuths start apprehending each other.'

'My, my.' Ginny Fistoulari making polite social conversation. 'You're in a good mood this morning.'

With an effort, I swallowed more sarcasm. Her comment had the effect of making me realize that I had one more reason to dread this job, one I hadn't admitted yet. I hated nursemaiding and being nursemaided. I hated the things she and I did to each other. And I also – this came as a surprise – didn't want to make a fool of myself in front of eight or ten crime buffs. After all, 'detection' and 'investigation' aren't the same thing. The guests probably knew a hell of a lot more about 'detection' than I did. 'Mystery' camp was their game, and I wasn't likely to be good at it.

What fun.

Hunkered down into my pain, I concentrated on surviving the drive up to Deerskin Lodge.

The freeway ran through Pico Canyon and across the high plains to the east of the San Renos, but we turned off while we were still in the mountains. For half an hour or forty-five minutes, we had good clear road. It went in the direction of Puerta del Sol's ski resorts, and no one is more willing to invest in good clear roads than ski resorts. After the resort turnoff, however, the driving conditions deteriorated. We'd had an unusual amount of snow Tuesday night, and today was the next

Monday. At this elevation, at this time of year, the temperature extremes chew hell out of the roads.

We slogged up into thick pine forests and unexpected meadows, but I was in no condition to appreciate your basic winter wonderland scenery, sunshine glistening everywhere, white draped over the trees, nothing on the ground except snow and game-tracks. I was too busy hurting every time the Olds lurched into a pothole or skidded over a patch of glaze.

But eventually I got tired of stoicism. 'Why do they start on Tuesday?' I asked Ginny, just to break the silence.

By now she must've been sure we weren't being followed. Instead of watching the rear-view mirror, she concentrated with a kind of aimless ferocity on her driving. 'A group of hunters left the lodge yesterday. The staff won't be ready for more guests until tomorrow.'

'And how long does our job run?'

'Seven days, counting today. Everybody's supposed to go home Sunday night.'

How nice. A week of keeping amateur Sherlocks from shooting each other. There was just one problem. 'What do we do after that?'

Obviously she wasn't on my wavelength. 'After what?'

'After this week. El Señor won't give up on me that fast. We'll still have the problem this job is supposed to solve.'

Ginny flicked a glance at me, then turned her eyes back to the road. Carefully she ruddered the Olds around a shiny curve. 'By then you should be stronger. According to your doctor. The more you move around, the faster you'll recover – as long as you don't do anything crazy. And the commission probably won't keep me suspended much longer. We can find a job that'll get us out of town. We won't be restricted to hand-holding operations.'

I didn't like the sound of that. I didn't want to spend the rest of my life hiding. But there was no point in complaining about it. The rational vestiges of my mind understood that Ginny was just trying to keep me safe. One job at a time, one decision at a time. That was all anyone could do.

At the moment, however, I didn't feel equal to it. I wanted to get away and never come back. Some problems you can't do anything with except run.

I made Ginny stop the car and help me into the back seat. Getting in was tough, but once I'd stretched out on my back my insides hurt less. As long as I didn't get car-sick, I'd probably survive the rest of the trip.

'Take a nap,' Ginny said over her shoulder. 'I'll wake you up before we get there.'

'Fine,' I murmured as if I had that much common sense. But I didn't sleep. I spent the time trying to figure out what was wrong between us.

I didn't regret the bodyguard job that ended up with Muy Estobal's bullet in my gut and Estobal himself dead and el Señor angry at me. We'd needed that job. Without it, Ginny might not have recovered her essential self-esteem, her ability to function. Now she'd resumed being the woman I liked and desired and trusted.

So what was wrong? Why did I get the impression that we didn't love each other any more? Why were we still afraid of each other, angry at each other?

Actually, her feelings weren't hard to understand. She was angry at me because I'd pushed her into opposing el Señor. I'd forced her into the position of having to wear her claw or quit altogether. And because after all this time I still wanted a drink. I'd been a drunk for too long, and I wanted a drink for the same reason every drunk wants one. To prove I deserved it. Confirm my world-view, as they say. Reassure myself with the certainty of my own unworth. Which didn't exactly make me an easy man to trust.

But why was I angry at her? Was it simply because she kept me away from alcohol? Was it because nothing she did ever solved any of my problems?

On some level, I knew that being angry at her and being angry at myself were the same thing. But at the moment I couldn't pin down why.

She didn't break the silence until she stopped. Then she said, 'Time to shift. I told Altar you're injured, but I don't want anybody to think you're incapacitated.'

Oh, well. I was about as ready as I was likely to get. While she opened the door, I rolled off the seat to get my arms and legs under me. Then I crawled backwards out into the snow and stood up.

Sort of. My posture wasn't notably upright. But at least I could breathe the sharp winter and look around.

The air tasted cold and clean, like someone had just invented it for the first time. On the other hand, the wood smoke over the lodge reminded me that there was usually nothing new or even particularly clean about the things people did indoors.

Nevertheless I had to admit that Deerskin Lodge was a good place for a mystery camp – isolated, self-contained, and beautiful. We stood on a rise at the front gate, with the lodge and its outbuildings below us

439

at the end of a driveway at least a hundred yards long, in the bottom of a hollow with mountains on three sides, a barbed-wire fence around the whole spread, and the next phone a good hour or so away by car. The real world sure as hell wasn't going to intrude here – which, when I thought about it, struck me as a mixed blessing.

Most of the hollow had been cleared, but the people who built the camp had obviously tried to preserve as many of the original trees as possible. In fact, the middle of the lodge roof had a particularly patriarchal long-needle pine growing out of it. And a dozen or so evergreens still occupied the hollow, most of them down near the buildings.

Aside from the lodge itself, I counted six outbuildings. Most of them looked like cottages, and I jumped to the brilliant conclusion that they housed the staff. I couldn't tell how many of them were occupied, but two had smoke whispering from their chimneys and vehicles parked outside, a battered old sedan, a stretch pickup truck, and a Land Rover.

At a guess, the lodge looked big enough to feed, shelter, and recreate twenty people or so, with room left over for plenty of closets, complete with skeletons. It had been built in a haphazard – i.e. rustic – way around its central tree, but one wing plainly included a kitchen, and the others probably held bedrooms. Unlike the trees, the pitched roofs had shed the snow, baring their shingles. Small vent windows under the eaves let air in and out of the attics.

Out front stood a van that could've carried ten people and their living-room furniture. If that was Sue-Rose Altar's idea of transportation, you had to admit she at least knew how to take her hobbies seriously.

Ginny studied the terrain with a wistful look on her face. After a minute she murmured, 'Kind of makes you wish we really were on vacation, doesn't it. This would be a good place to relax.'

For absolutely no good reason at all, I suddenly wanted to burst into tears. The joys of convalescence. I would've been willing to sacrifice actual body-parts to make our relationship into one where we could take vacations together.

The expression on my face must've revealed more than I wanted. Holding me with her grey stare, she asked carefully, 'You all right?'

I wasn't equal to answering that question. Instead I told her one of my usual lies. 'I don't like feeling this weak, that's all. Don't worry about it.'

440

Like the rest of my lies, this one wasn't a lie because it was untrue. It was a lie because it wasn't enough.

She went on studying me. 'We'll have to spend some time with Mrs Altar. Hang on as long as you can. But if you need a break, let me know. I'll arrange something.'

Still taking care of me.

When I nodded, we got back into the Olds. With pain throbbing in my chest, and my skull full of something that felt like grief, I concentrated on the road while she drove us down to the lodge.

Sue-Rose Altar must've seen us coming. She emerged on to the porch, a wide wooden structure that covered the front of the building, and waved at us while Ginny parked beside the van.

She was a tidy little woman, older than she appeared at first glance, with perfectly waved grey hair and a sparkle of child-like enthusiasm in her eyes. She wore a sable fur coat so lustrous that it may still have been alive, and her boots were clearly designed for feeling pretty indoors instead of for sloshing around in the slush.

For Ginny's sake, I took a deep breath and tried to get out of the Olds as if I did that kind of thing every day.

Mrs Altar greeted us delightedly. 'Ms Fistoulari. Mr Axbrewder. How wonderful.' I noticed right away, however, that she didn't risk her boots in the snow. Nothing gets past the hardened private investigator.

Leaning over the rail of the porch, she continued, 'Did you have any trouble finding this place? I hope so. I love being so isolated. It's just perfect. I get so excited before one of my mysteries, Rock can hardly stand me. Come up, come inside. Let's get to know each other.'

Ginny gave me a look, just checking that I was still ambulatory. Then she put on her professional smile and led the way up half a dozen steps to the porch.

'Mrs Altar.' She didn't make any effort to hide her claw as she shook Sue-Rose's hand. 'Pleased to meet you. I'm Ginny Fistoulari. This is Mick Axbrewder.'

I lagged behind, doing my utter damnedest to pretend that I knew how to get up steps.

'Your husband,' Ginny added, 'said you would help us get oriented, let us know what to expect, that sort of thing.'

'Buffy,' Mrs Altar burbled. 'Call me Buffy. Rock is so formal, but I don't let him get away with it.' She didn't seem to be aware that I hadn't caught up with Ginny yet. 'I'll call you Ginny and Mick. We'll all be on a first-name basis by supper-time tomorrow. It's going to be great fun.'

That did it. Nobody calls me Mick. My friends have better sense, and my enemies don't like the results. Before Sue-Rose 'Buffy' Altar could go on, I surged up the stairs and said almost politely, 'Call me Brew. I prefer Brew.'

Just for a second everything seemed to stop. Mrs Altar blinked at me uncertainly. Ginny ignored me in a way that suggested she'd done this on purpose for some reason. I stood motionless with pain thudding in my guts and sweat creeping past my hair-line despite the cold.

Then Mrs Altar recovered her composure. 'Well, of course. Brew. How nice. Rock told me you've been hurt. I think it's very brave of you to come out and work for us so soon after your injury. But this will be just like a vacation. We'll all have loads of fun. Come inside, and I'll show you around.'

Her fur positively gleamed as she turned and moved briskly towards the door.

I gave Ginny my usual look of blood-curdling happiness. She continued retailing her professional smile, no discounts for personal friends. Softly, as if she weren't sure I could follow the conversation, she murmured, ' "Rock" must be her husband.'

'Oh,' I said intelligently.

She went after Mrs Altar. I shambled along behind her as well as I could.

Inside the air was warmer – but not as much warmer as I'd expected. Apparently Deerskin Lodge relied on fireplaces for a lot of its heat. The large room we entered had three of them, but they weren't lit.

Built around the tree trunk, the room itself was a high-ceilinged lounge with waxed wooden floors, knotty pine panelling, rough-cut beams, any number of stuffed animal heads for décor, and sturdy furniture sprawling everywhere. The atmosphere had a faint tang of ashes, the kind of smell you get when a chimney isn't working right and the fireplace has a minor back-draft.

'This is the den,' Mrs Altar announced. I wasn't sure she'd ever stopped talking. 'This is where we gather to reveal how we solved the crime. If we solved it. That's my favourite part of the whole week. Don't you just love those scenes in books, where the famous detective explains his reasoning and takes everyone by surprise? I like to see how people react to the mysteries I've cooked up for them.

'This time we have eight guests. That makes fourteen people altogether, eight of them, me and Rock, you two, and our two actors. But remember, I want you to act like guests as much as you can. That's part of the fun, not knowing who the real detectives are. You can make up any cover you want, I don't mind, I like surprises.'

'What can you tell us about the guests?' Ginny put in when Mrs Altar paused for breath. 'The more we know, the better we'll do our job. And the better cover we can figure out.'

Buffy gave her an arch glance. 'I'm sure that Rock told you we don't want to reveal who the actors are – or what the mystery is. That's part of the fun, too. We'll all be on the same footing.' All of us, of course, except Rock and Buffy. 'But I'll be glad to give you the names.'

'Please,' Ginny replied with just a hint of asperity.

'Well, let's see.' Mrs Altar made a show of consulting her memory. 'There's Mac Westward and Constance Bebb. They're famous – they're "Thornton Foal", the novelist. They like to come to camps like this for ideas and atmosphere. Then there's Houston Mile and Maryanne Green. Houston has been to two of my camps before, but I've never met Maryanne. He always brings a different woman with him.

'There's Joseph Hardhouse and his wife, Lara – and Sam Drayton and *his* wife, Queenie. One of them is a doctor. Sam, I think. Yes, that's right. Joseph owns a chain of restaurants. Oh, and Catherine Reverie and Simon Abel. They're from back east. They want to try running a mystery camp of their own, and they're coming to see what it's like – see how Rock and I do it.'

Yep, that was it. Counting on my fingers, I got up to ten. Eight guests and two actors. Just enough suspects to be a challenge. Not enough to be realistic. I thought it would be a good idea to sit down, but I couldn't find an excuse, so I stayed on my feet and tried not to sway too much.

'Why do the rest of them come?' Ginny asked. She meant, Why do grown people waste time on something like this? 'You explained Mac Westward and Constance Bebb, Simon Abel and Catherine Reverie. What about the others?'

'Why, for the same reason I'm here,' Mrs Altar replied with polite astonishment. 'They love mysteries. They like to be involved.'

Oh, naturally. Why didn't I think of that?

I could tell from the shape of Ginny's smile and the tightness around her eyes that she shared my reaction. She wanted a better explanation.

The truth probably had something to do with liking excitement and safety at the same time. Thrills without risk. Like riding the roller-coaster in an amusement park instead of, say, tackling white-water rapids in an open canoe.

No doubt about it. I was going to have a wonderful time.

'Come on,' Mrs Altar continued. 'Let me show you around.'

As we crossed the den, I was vaguely surprised that the floorboards didn't creak. Wooden floors usually don't like me much. But Deerskin Lodge had been built to last.

The next big room was the dining room. It had a fireplace at either end, massive wrought-iron lighting fixtures, and one long table of polished pine, with enough heavy chairs to seat at least fourteen people. But I ignored details like that. Instead I focused on the fact that the walls were decorated mainly in gun cabinets.

Rifles on one wall. Shotguns on the other. Handguns interspersed here and there. I recognized a Winchester 30–30 carbine, a Purdy that looked powerful enough to buckle plate steel, even a General Patton Commemorative six-shooter. They were all mounted for show instead of use, all closed behind glass doors. But when I touched the latch on the nearest door, I found that it wasn't locked.

Under each of the cabinets were rows of drawers. Mrs Altar had already moved out of the room, still talking, but Ginny paused to watch while I pulled a drawer open.

It was full of ammunition. In this case, rounds for the .30–06 Remington mounted level with my nose.

I checked three or four drawers. Each held ammunition for the guns in the cabinet above it.

Murder On Cue might as well hold its mystery camps in an arsenal. Rock and Buffy had enough firepower at their disposal to slaughter an entire regiment of paying guests.

Ginny wheeled away from me and cut into our guide's monologue. 'Mrs Altar.'

Sue-Rose stopped. 'Please, call me Buffy. I mean it. I really can't abide formality.'

'Mrs Altar.' Ginny put a snap in the name. 'I want all these guns taken down and locked away. Somewhere where your guests can't get at them.'

Mrs Altar positively gaped in surprise. 'Whatever for?'

'You've hired Fistoulari Investigations for security. Those guns are a security risk. Your guests could shoot up half the county before we realized they have that little common sense.'

'Oh, really.' Mrs Altar frowned in vexation. 'You can't be serious. What kind of people do you think come to my mystery camps? Rapists? Child molesters? This is recreation, fun. Our guests have always been responsible members of society. We've never had the least trouble.

'We only need security for the insurance. Rock must have explained that to you. You don't have anything vital to do. The job you're really being paid for is to play along with our mystery, help us enjoy it.'

'I don't know anything about that,' Ginny retorted, 'and I don't care.' She wasn't actually angry. She just sounded angry to make her point. 'You hired me for security, and I mean to take it seriously. That includes routine safety precautions. Locking those guns away is definitely a routine safety precaution.'

Of course, she could've suggesting locking up the ammunition instead. But that idea had a couple of problems. For one thing, it made her look like the kind of woman who backed down – which could make her job a lot harder later on. And for another, she knew as well as I did that a gun without ammunition is more dangerous than ammunition without a gun. If nothing else, people can hit each other with guns. They don't usually throw ammunition at each other.

But Mrs Altar didn't care about things like that. Unlike Ginny, she *was* angry. 'I've never heard anything so ridiculous. What good is a hunting lodge full of empty gun cabinets? What kind of atmosphere is that?' If she kept this up, she'd scorch the hair on her coat. 'If we expected trouble, any trouble at all, do you think we would have hired *you?*'

When she heard what she said, however, she had the good grace to look a bit embarrassed. 'I mean, Brew just got out of the hospital. Knowing you aren't at your best, we would never have hired you if we weren't sure there would be no trouble.'

'I appreciate that, Buffy,' I put in. 'But guns are dangerous anyway. People want to touch them. You say your guests aren't the kind of people who shoot each other. That makes the situation even more dangerous. People who don't know much about guns are the ones who have accidents.

'We aren't criticizing anyone. We aren't even complaining.' Axbrewder's best imitation of sweet reason. Sometimes when Ginny acts fierce I back her up by acting soft. 'The whole point of a precaution is to prevent trouble, not cause it.'

'Humour me on this one,' Ginny put in, sarcastic now instead of angry. 'I'm the only security you've got. If I walk out, you won't have time to hire anybody else. Locking up the guns won't ruin your mystery. But without two professionals to play against, your guests might not have anywhere near as much fun.'

Obviously Mrs Altar was accustomed to getting her own way. On the other hand, she must've been able to see that Ginny wasn't bluffing. Frowning her irritation, she said, 'Oh, very well. You can talk to Art about it. He should be around here somewhere. But Rock will be very displeased by your uncooperative attitude.'

Still fuming to herself, she led us out of the dining room towards the kitchen wing.

Ginny cocked an eyebrow at me.

'Makes you wonder,' I whispered, getting even with her for encouraging Buffy to call me *Mick*, 'who used to do security for them.'

She snorted. 'All right,' she whispered back. 'I admit it. I should've found out more about how we got this job. I should've asked who used to do it, and why they aren't doing it now. You satisfied?'

I wanted to say something about just how satisfied I was, but we were already entering the kitchen, and Mrs Altar had stopped to introduce us to the two people there.

Speaking as someone who probably should've spent his life being a short-order cook instead of prying into other people's misery, I was impressed by the kitchen. Deerskin Lodge had the equipment to take first-class care of its guests. The room was nearly as spacious as the den, with gleaming stainless steel food lockers built into the walls, massive conventional, convection, and microwave ovens, plus two huge gas cook tops and more appliances than I could count on short notice – can openers, coffee mills, Cuisinarts, blenders, knife sharpeners, the lot. Not to mention utensils and pots and pans, most of them hanging from racks bolted to the beams. Also a Hobart dishwasher big enough to double as a car-wash.

With a kitchen like that, Christ wouldn't have needed a miracle to feed the five thousand. I could've done it myself, if I were healthy.

Both people in the kitchen were working. The woman sorted what looked like a few hundred bags of groceries – supplies for Murder On Cue, Inc. She was exceptionally pretty in an exceptionally pale sort of way. Her long wavy hair was so blonde it was almost white, and her skin seemed outright translucent, letting all the light around her shine in to her bones. Somehow her eyes managed to appear deep without having any colour. She didn't wear rings or bracelets, but from her neck a small silver crucifix hung on a fine chain.

She met Mrs Altar's greeting soberly, without a smile. The depth of her eyes and the lines of her face gave the impression that she was a woman who never smiled at anyone.

446

'Brew, Ginny,' Mrs Altar said, still sounding miffed, 'this is Faith Jerrick. She's the cook for the Lodge.'

Instinctively I distrusted Faith Jerrick's cooking. She was too thin to have much appreciation for food.

'That's Art over there,' Mrs Altar continued, pointing at the man. 'Arthur Reeson. He's the manager.'

At first all we could see of Reeson were his legs. The rest of him was buried under one of the cook tops. The noises he made suggested that he was repairing the stove's innards. But when he heard his name mentioned, he disimmured himself and stood up.

His dark good looks contrasted strangely with Faith Jerrick's paleness – black eyes, black hair, swarthy skin made even darker by a premature five-o'clock shadow, grease stains, and pipe-dope. He was nearly as tall as I am, and his tight work-shirt betrayed an indecent amount of muscle. Like the cook, he didn't smile, but his expression only resembled a glower because his skin and brows were so dark. It was nothing personal.

'Art,' said Mrs Altar, 'this is Ginny Fistoulari and Mick Axbrewder. They'll be with us for the rest of the week.' Deliberately disavowing us, she added, 'Ginny wants to ask you something.'

When he heard our names, Reeson's eyebrows went up. But they didn't stay up. Instead he showed us his stains to apologize for not shaking hands. Then he nodded unnecessarily at the cook top.

'Pilot-less ignitions are a great idea.' His voice sounded permanently hoarse, as if he'd done too much shouting in his life. 'If you get a gas leak, they don't blow up the kitchen. But they're a sonofabitch to fix. What did you want?'

As a general rule, Ginny wasn't what you could call reluctant to assert herself with strangers. But she knew how to be civil about it. 'Mr Reeson,' she replied evenly, 'Mr Axbrewder and I are private investigators. Mr Altar hired us to keep an eye on the safety and security of his guests for the next week. I'm concerned about the guns in the dining room. They're a hazard, especially around inexperienced people. I'd like them locked up somewhere. I don't care where, as long as you can keep the key to yourself.'

Art Reeson's eyebrows went up again. Maybe they were on automatic, went up and down by themselves. 'That's unusual,' he said, almost croaking. 'I've never been asked to do that before. What's changed?'

'I can't answer that,' Ginny said without a flicker. 'I don't know who did security for Murder On Cue in the past. I have no idea why they didn't object to the accessibility of those guns. But *I* object, Mr Reeson. I'd object in the same way if Deerskin Lodge kept cases of gelignite lying around.'

Reeson didn't exactly avoid her eyes, but he didn't precisely meet them, either. 'I'll have to ask the owners. They make the rules around here. I can't touch the guns myself without permission.'

In a tone that didn't invite discussion, Ginny said, 'Please. As soon as possible.'

Brightly Mrs Altar remarked, 'Well, that's taken care of, then,' as if a particularly thorny dispute had been successfully negotiated. At once she started talking to Faith Jerrick.

'Now, Faith, I hope you have some truly special meals planned for my guests. You've done wonderful things for us in the past. I expect you to surpass yourself.'

'Yes, ma'am,' the cook replied distantly.

Mrs Altar looked Faith up and down, and sighed. 'And please call me Buffy. You know I prefer that.'

'Yes, ma'am,' Faith repeated. Unlike Reeson, she had the gift of avoiding people's eyes without making a point of it. Apparently she was a woman who didn't argue much – and didn't pay much attention to arguments.

With a sable shrug, Mrs Altar turned back to Ginny and me. 'I don't know why I bother,' she admitted. 'I've never been able to get her to use my name. Shall we go?' She gestured us out of the kitchen. As soon as we reached the relative privacy of the hall, she added, 'In fact, I don't think I've heard her say more than four words. Yes, no, ma'am, and sir. I think she isn't, you know' – Buffy tapped her forehead – 'all there.'

Inspired by my usual instinct to come all over manly and protective in the presence of frail women, I muttered, 'Maybe she just doesn't have anything she wants to say.' But Mrs Altar ignored me, and Ginny had the decency not to laugh out loud.

All this moving around had just about finished me. At the moment I wasn't especially conscious of pain. My guts had taken on a generalized throbbing that felt bearable simply because it was diffuse. But the strain of convalescence and movement and concentration had used up my strength. And I couldn't imagine what contribution I was making. Nobody would miss me if I took a little rest somewhere.

I managed to catch Mrs Altar before she launched another monologue. 'Buffy, is there a phone I can use? I should check in with our office.' Which was patent bullshit, but maybe Mrs Altar wouldn't know that. 'You can show Ginny the rest of the lodge while I'm on the phone.'

Fortunately Ginny could take a hint when she's in the mood. 'That's right,' she said promptly. 'Your husband gave me the impression that Deerskin Lodge has more staff than just Faith and Art. You can introduce me to them and finish showing me around while Brew makes his calls.'

'All right.' Unlike the matter of the guns, this request didn't trouble Mrs Altar. 'There's only one phone. Our guests aren't supposed to spend their time talking to the rest of the world. But naturally a phone is a necessity. It's in the manager's office. This way.'

She steered us down a hall away from the den. In a moment she stopped in front of a door with a mail-slot. 'Of course,' she was saying, 'the lodge doesn't need a formal manager. The owners have an office back in Puerta del Sol. And the staff has been here for a long time. They know what to do. But Art uses this room to do his paperwork – bills and files, registrations, reservations, I don't know what all.'

The door wasn't locked, so she had no trouble letting us in.

It was an office, all right. I recognized it right away by the filing cabinets and desk, the adding machine and phone. Everything possible was made of wood – rustic as all hell – but the oak of the desk and chairs didn't quite match the blond pine panelling and floorboards. Which probably didn't matter because the lodge's paying guests weren't expected to come in here.

Ginny stayed outside. After a quick glance around the room, she told me, 'We'll come back for you when we're done,' and set Mrs Altar into motion again with a touch on her arm. Together they receded down the hall.

I heard Mrs Altar say, 'There are only two other people here. Petruchio and Amalia Carbone. Truchi and Ama. He works with Art and takes care of the grounds. She's the housekeeper. They'll be around somewhere, but they'll be busy. I don't think I've ever seen either of them when they weren't busy.'

Left to myself, I went into the office and closed the door.

I wanted to lie down, but the room lacked a couch, and I didn't think I could come up with a decent excuse for sprawling on the floor, so I sat in the chair behind the desk. It was the biggest one in the room, and it had solid armrests. Also it tilted, so that I could adjust my guts into a somewhat more comfortable position. All I wanted was to hurt less and go to sleep for a while.

But there's something about sitting at someone else's desk that makes you feel like looking in the drawers. I resisted the impulse briefly. Then I decided what the hell. I was a private investigator. Poking my nose in where it didn't belong came with the territory.

Of course, I didn't find anything interesting. The drawers held perfectly ordinary files and supplies – grocery receipts, boxes of paper clips, stuff like that. But my knees didn't quite fit the desk, and my position while I looked through the drawers shoved them high up under the writing surface.

One knee bumped something.

Probably one of the supports. So what? And this was my first day out of bed. I had no business hunching forward and twisting the sin out of my stomach to look under the desk.

I did it anyway.

I found a pistol in a holster glued to the wood where the person at the desk could reach it easily. I unsnapped the holster, pulled out the gun.

It was a Smith & Wesson .44 with a long, underlugged barrel, the kind of gun you use when you want to hit something small and far away and make sure it stays dead.

For no special reason except I'm an intuitive fool and can't resist the impulse to jump to conclusions in all directions, I suddenly felt sure that Art Reeson liked guns. The owners didn't use this desk, he did. He liked being surrounded by weaponry.

He probably didn't want to do what Ginny had asked him.

I hesitated. Apparently he'd worked for Deerskin Lodge for a long time – and the owners certainly wouldn't keep a manager who made a regular practice of waving guns around. Murder On Cue had never had any trouble. Maybe he was just indulging an innocent fetish.

Nevertheless where I come from people who like guns that much are always trouble. No exceptions.

Sometimes being intuitive helps. And sometimes it makes you look like an idiot. But I was too tired and sore and possibly even feverish to be reasonable, so I made a snap decision. Swinging open the cylinder, I poured out the shells and dropped them into the bottom of one of the drawers. Then I put the .44 back where I found it.

After that, like a man with a job well done, I leaned back in the chair, closed my eyes, and napped the nap of the just.

Chapter Four

Ginny came back for me without Mrs Altar in attendance.

I didn't know how she managed that, and I didn't ask. I was just glad Buffy wasn't there to see how thorough my incapacitation had become.

From somewhere, Ginny produced a glass of water and any number of pills. My antibiotics, she said, and one or two things to help manage the pain, but I knew her well enough to be suspicious. I was morally certain some of those pills were vitamins. She believes in vitamins, the more the merrier.

After the pills, she led me to the dining room, where Faith Jerrick put some soup on the table for us. Chicken noodle, of course. It tasted like she'd made it all by herself, fresh from a can. Compared to hospital suet, however, it didn't taste too bad.

Eventually I felt good or at least stable enough to ask about Mrs Altar.

'Gone back to the city.' Ginny watched me for indications I might someday recover my health. 'I gather she wants a final rehearsal with her actors. She'll pick us up with the rest of her guests early tomorrow afternoon.'

'What're we supposed to do in the mean time?'

Ginny shrugged. 'Finish here. Get you as much rest as possible.' She considered for a moment, then added, 'I don't want to go back to the apartment. El Señor's goons might find us. We'll check into a motel.' Nothing about the process seemed to interest her much. She lacked the mothering instincts to be a good nursemaid. On the other hand, she stuck by her own decisions. 'I packed our suitcases this morning,' she concluded. 'They're in the Olds.'

Without warning, I felt sorry for myself again. For the next week, at least, I wouldn't even be able to choose my own clothes.

Obviously a nap hadn't improved my mood. But I still had a job to do, so I did it. I told her about the gun I'd found.

I didn't mention emptying it. Probably too embarrassed.

She did her best to look involved. 'So what does the famous Axbrewder intuition tell you about Art Reeson?'

It was my turn to shrug.

She drank down the rest of her soup. Then she said, 'My sentiments exactly.'

When we were done, we drove back to Puerta del Sol. We checked into a motel. She helped me wash up because I couldn't handle that job by myself yet. I ate more soup. Then I got as much sleep as I could.

Several times during the night, I looked over at her. She was sitting up in bed, staring at the ceiling like a woman who wanted badly to be somewhere else. Her claw lay dead on the night-stand beside her.

When I saw her like that, she scared me. I would've said something, but I didn't trust myself. If I pushed her in the wrong direction – towards giving up on me – I'd be lost. Under other circumstances, I would've at least stayed awake with her. As it was, I couldn't even do that.

But the next morning I felt better.

A misleading statement. The truth was, I felt like I'd spent the night wrestling with the Angel of the Lord, and all I'd gained from the experience was a whole new collection of aches and pains. And yet I did feel better. The nature of my hurts had changed. They felt less like I'd committed seppuku recently, more like the consequences of wild overexertion. Easier to live with.

So I ate my antibiotics and vitamins. I let Ginny take my temperature. I practised dressing myself. I experimented with motel restaurant cream of wheat – which wasn't a success, unless you happen to like lumpy Elmer's glue. Then Ginny and I spent a bit of time deciding on our 'cover' so that we'd know what to tell Murder On Cue's guests.

The whole time she looked miserable. I suppose she might've told me what was going on if I'd asked her a direct question. But I didn't have the nerve.

At last it was time to go. We were supposed to meet Roderick and Sue-Rose Altar in the parking lot of the Camelot Hotel a little before 1.00. According to Ginny, Rock and Buffy chose the Camelot because that's where their out-of-town guests stayed.

We arrived a few minutes early, but the van beat us anyway. Somehow it managed to look even bigger than it did up in the mountains. I've lived in apartments that were smaller.

The sliding door stood open, and a man in a suit waited beside it, looking bored. For winter in Puerta del Sol, the day was warm – he didn't need an overcoat. For that matter, I didn't need my sheepskin. But I didn't have anywhere else to keep the .45.

'That,' said Ginny as she wheeled the Olds to a stop near the van, 'is Roderick Altar. Sue-Rose must be getting the rest of her group together.'

When we climbed out of the Olds, the man glanced at us and nodded. If he was surprised to see Ginny carrying our suitcases, he didn't show it. Instead he murmured, 'Ms Fistoulari.' Then he asked, 'Mr Axbrewder?'

He didn't offer to shake hands, so I didn't either.

He was about his wife's height, pudgy and going bald. The remains of his hair were plastered across his scalp to disguise a patchwork of liver-spots. The tight merino wool of his suit expressed money, but his face only conveyed a lack of interest. He looked like a man who used to get excited, years ago – before the extra flesh on his cheeks and jowls sagged, dragging him down. Only a woman who called herself Buffy would've called him Rock.

'My wife's inside.' He indicated the hotel unnecessarily. 'She should be out in a few minutes.' Then he said, 'Before she gets here, I want to talk to you.'

That was fine with me. I wanted to talk to him, too.

Ginny and I paused in front of him, waiting for the dullness to fade from his eyes.

It didn't. In a flat tone, he said, 'My wife tells me you objected to all those guns.'

'That's right.' Ginny didn't offer to justify herself.

Altar nodded. 'It's about time someone did. I don't like guns. In fact, I don't like hunters. They're a hazard.'

Well, well. That was a surprise. Buffy Altar had apparently overestimated her husband's passion for the ambience of Deerskin Lodge.

He'd given me an opening for the questions I wanted to ask. Unfortunately Ginny had questions of her own, and they weren't the same. Before I could go ahead, she said, 'I gather you don't share your wife's enthusiasm for these mystery camps. Why is that, Mr Altar?'

He looked towards the hotel. Obviously he didn't want Buffy to hear his response. When he'd satisfied himself that she wasn't about to materialize from the asphalt, he replied, 'I just told you. I don't like hunters. "Solving the crime" is hunting in another guise, that's all. It's an unequal contest. Even if our murderers were real – and armed – they wouldn't stand a chance. We have them outnumbered. Secrecy is their only hope. As soon as they make a mistake, we can overpower them. The exercise is trivial by nature.'

Ginny smiled sharply. Altar may not have been interested in what he was doing, but all of a sudden she was. 'I'm not sure I understand,' she commented. 'Most people wouldn't draw that parallel between game animals and murderers.'

Rock didn't take offence – but he also didn't take fire. 'I'm not saying I approve of murder. I'm just explaining why hunting doesn't appeal to me.'

'But aren't you what they call a venture capitalist?' Ginny was a hunter herself, born and bred. 'Isn't that "hunting in another guise"? Hunting for the right people and the right opportunities to make money?'

For the first time Altar's fleshy features lifted, and his eyes showed a hint of energy. '"Hunting" is the wrong word. Or it's hunting for the opposite reason. The whole point of venture capitalism is to find valuable underdogs, the victims of unequal contests, and help them overcome bad odds, beat systems which are organized to defeat them. It's like hunting in order to help the game escape.'

'Or,' I put in, 'like hunting for murderers to help them get away.'

Just for a second, I thought Altar might laugh. He actually did smile. 'Well, I wouldn't want to go that far.' This time he made an overt show of verifying Buffy's absence. Then he told us in a conspiratorial whisper, 'But I've been known to disturb a few clues, just for the fun of it. Make the crime a little harder to solve.'

Ginny's smile had a different quality altogether. 'You devil,' she said distinctly. 'I can see we're going to have to keep an eye on you.'

At once he hooded his expression. 'You'll never catch me,' he murmured. 'I'm too good at it.'

Well, at least now we knew why he was willing to work with Sue-Rose on Murder On Cue, Inc. He wanted to sabotage her hobby. I didn't know whether to laugh or snarl.

But I didn't waste time deciding which. While he was still in the mood for revelations, I said, 'Tell me, Mr Altar. How did you happen to choose Fistoulari Investigations for this job?'

That subject clearly didn't interest him at all. 'Oh, I heard about you somewhere,' he said with a shrug. 'Someone told me you do good work. I had my doubts when Ms Fistoulari said you were in the hospital recently. You've been injured? But I took your reputation into account. And the job isn't challenging.'

And, I added for him, if one of the hunters you don't like isn't at his best, so much the better. But I kept that to myself.

'I gather you've been doing this for a while,' I continued. 'We aren't the first security you've hired. Who had the job before we did?'

Unfortunately Rock Altar wasn't listening. Even Ginny had stopped paying attention. Instead they both watched a souped-up blue Camaro roar into the parking lot as if the driver had blood on his mind.

Automatically Ginny braced herself. Her hand found its way into her purse. But I didn't react. The sun was shining, and the sky was as clear as a dream. And the parking lot was too public. No one in his right mind would try to shoot me here. Besides, the Camaro had its windows up. When goons with guns drive by to blow you away, they always have their windows rolled down.

So much for my chance to ask Altar how we got this job.

The car skidded into a nearby parking space. The doors burst open. A woman jumped out of the passenger seat. A man stood up from the driver's side.

'You're a menace!' the woman shouted. 'You nearly got us killed! I've never been so scared.'

She laughed happily as she protested.

'Hey, I got us here,' the man retorted. 'And we aren't late. You said you didn't want to be late.'

He was laughing, too.

They ran into each other behind the Camaro. She made a pretence of trying to slap him. He hugged her so hard that her feet left the ground. They laughed some more.

'Dr Drayton,' Altar murmured without too much disapproval. 'Mrs Drayton. Glad you could make it.'

I remembered their names. Sam and Queenie Drayton. Apparently they were local – a conclusion I jumped to because they hadn't spent the night at the Camelot. But I didn't care where they were from. I didn't even care why he considered it a good idea to drive like a drunken kid. What I wanted to know was, Where did she get a name like Queenie?

She subsided while her husband turned to size us up. He wore a tweed jacket and good slacks that didn't match the scarf flung carelessly around his neck. With his strong jaw and wavy hair and perfect teeth, he looked more like a movie star than a doctor. In fact, his face betrayed altogether too much pleasure for a doctor. Maybe he had some kind of low-stress specialty, like Facial Blemishes of the Rich. Or maybe he was one of Buffy's stooges.

On the other hand, it was easy to understand why any man would be happy in Mrs Drayton's company. She wasn't beautiful – maybe she wasn't even pretty. But her hazel eyes looked straight at the world, afraid of nothing, and her wide mouth seemed to fill up with joy when she smiled. She had a slim, athletic, endearing body. Her coat hung open, and the way her breasts moved under her cashmere sweater gave the impression that she didn't wear much support. Or need it.

Down, Fang, I said to myself.

Fang didn't pay any attention.

'Mr Altar?' Drayton asked, looking at me.

'I'm Roderick Altar,' Rock answered. He didn't offer to shake hands with Sam Drayton either. 'This is Mr Axbrewder and Ms Fistoulari. My wife is inside.' He nodded towards the hotel. 'We should be ready to go in a minute or two.'

Drayton didn't seem to mind not shaking hands. He gave his wife a squeeze, then let go of her. 'I'll get our bags.'

Fishing out his keys, he unlocked the Camaro's trunk and produced two large suitcases and a black medical bag. For an actor's prop, his bag looked unusually authentic. Used and familiar.

Altar opened the back of the van. Drayton heaved his suitcases and the bag inside. Then, since our suitcases were handy, he put Ginny's and mine beside his. Ginny thanked him with a nod. I thanked him by making a studious effort not to grin at Queenie.

Sue-Rose chose that moment to emerge from the Camelot with the rest of her guests in tow, followed by a bellhop pushing a luggage cart the size of New Hampshire.

Eight of them, by actual count. I reviewed their names to myself, but across the parking lot I couldn't guess which name went with which person.

Buffy beamed at all of us. As soon as she was close enough to be heard, she said, 'I'm so glad you could all make it. This is going to be wonderful. Let's load up and go. I can't wait to get started. We'll introduce ourselves when we're on our way.'

Sam and Queenie shared a look and a shrug to contain their laughter. Ginny and I didn't have any last-minute messages for each other, so we just nodded. Altar stood at the van's sliding door like a butler who didn't care whether he got fired, and all the rest of us piled in while the bellhop filled up the back.

Unfortunately piling in didn't come easily. It necessitated too much stooping, which put too much pressure on my guts. By the time I reached a seat, I thought I was going to pass out.

I found myself in what would've been called steerage on an ocean liner, the bench seat across the rear of the van. Other passengers had better accommodations, individual 'captain's chairs' with armrests and ruffled upholstery. The Altars sat up front. She took the driver's seat, obviously in charge. He slumped beside her, slowly sinking from view. Behind them, Ginny had the seat closest to the door. She'd already begun talking to the man across from her, but I couldn't tell anything about him except that he had broad shoulders and the slickest hair I'd seen since Brylcreem went out of fashion.

Next came a man about the size and general shape of a mushy dirigible, possessively holding hands with his companion, a small flushed creature who, like Rock, looked like she was being consumed by her chair. Then two men, one of them handsome, the other not. Then two women matching the opposite descriptions. I occupied one of the corners, with Sam Drayton beside me, Queenie beside him, and the last woman beside her.

I didn't know what to make of the fact that this woman had already taken notice of me. Ordinarily I'm used to being noticed – too big to ignore. But she didn't seem struck by my size. Which should've pleased me, I suppose. She had dark brown wavy hair swept back from her face with elegant casualness, and her make-up emphasized her beauty artlessly. Gloss or moisture glistened on her parted lips. Her wide brown eyes were soft and intent.

Us virile-type males are supposed to jump right up and salute when attractive women look at us like that. But for some reason I wasn't pleased. In fact, I didn't like it at all. Intuition again. I suspected her of looking at me like that because she knew I was in pain.

Buffy fired up the van. She was talking to Rock – in a moment she would address the rest of us. Before that happened, however, the woman beside Queenie Drayton reached her hand towards me and said softly, 'We should introduce ourselves. I'm Lara Hardhouse.'

Somehow I twisted my torso enough to get my arm free. As I shook her hand, I noticed that her fingers were cool, caressing. I tried to keep my pain from showing, but it made me sweat helplessly as I muttered, 'Axbrewder. Call me Brew.'

To distract everyone from the spectacle of my obvious discomfort, I introduced Sam and Queenie. The three of them shook hands. But they didn't pay much attention to each other. As soon as he finished with Lara Hardhouse's fingers, Drayton leaned over and put his mouth close to my ear.

'I don't like the way you move,' he whispered. 'What's the problem?'

So much for my theory that he wasn't really a doctor.

'Abdominal injury.' I didn't bother to whisper. Ginny and I'd decided to use my limitations as part of our cover. 'I've only been out of bed for a couple of days. A vacation is supposed to help me heal.'

Drayton glanced at my belly. Then he nodded towards the front of the van. 'You should sit in one of those seats. More comfortable.'

'I *should* do a lot of things.' All this courtesy wore on me. 'Taking my pills. Getting more exercise. Improving my personality. Unfortunately I just get cranky when people tell me what I *should* do.'

The doctor smiled as if he understood perfectly. 'Convalescent blues,' he pronounced. 'That's a good sign. It means you're finally well enough to realize just how lousy you feel. Don't worry, it doesn't last.'

He turned away, wrapped his hands around Queenie's, and proceeded to ignore me.

Too bad Lara Hardhouse didn't do the same. Instead she kept her gaze on me, her eyes moist with sympathy.

Mrs Altar didn't make any announcements until she had the van rolling in the direction of the freeway. But after that she couldn't contain herself.

'Well, this is wonderful.' We could all hear her. The van was as quiet as a mausoleum. 'I get so excited before one of my mysteries. Rock keeps telling me that Murder On Cue is a business, but I can't think of it that way. I just love it. We've done everything we can imagine to give you a crime you'll enjoy. Haven't we, Rock?'

Rock's reaction – whatever it was – remained hidden by his seat back.

'Now,' Buffy went on as if we were all about to start singing campfire songs, 'it's time for introductions. I'm Buffy, most of you know that, and this is my husband, Rock. You'll all probably start from the assumption that he and I didn't "do it", but that's precisely why you shouldn't be too sure we're innocent. Let's work towards the back. Tell us who you are and what you do and why you're here.'

She paused expectantly.

The man beside Ginny looked over to her, giving me a glimpse of his profile. His face had aggressive lines – sharp brows, a nose you could've used to open cans, a chin like clenched knuckles – softened by a wide flexible mouth. His jet black hair lay slicked back from his forehead like a streak of grease. Ginny murmured something I couldn't hear – she may've told him to go first – and he nodded.

Turning further to scan the rest of us, he said, 'I'm Joseph Hardhouse.' Like his mouth, his voice was flexible, capable of all kinds of inflections. 'I own Granny Good's.' Granny Good's was a chain of family-style restaurants based in Denver. 'We make a lot of money, but the work is almost as boring as the food.' He smiled humorously. 'I take vacations like this to get away from worrying about the price of hash browns, or cooks who don't wash their hands enough.'

Sam and Queenie Drayton chuckled. I didn't hear any other reactions.

'Murder fascinates me,' Hardhouse continued, 'the whole question of why people kill each other. To be fair, I should warn you that I think I know the answer. If I'm right, that gives me an advantage this week.' His tone concealed whether or not he was joking. 'But I don't like to lose, so if I'm wrong I'll never admit that I said anything like this. You'll only find out what my answer is if I win.'

'That isn't fair!' Buffy protested in good-natured reproach.

'Neither is murder,' Hardhouse countered. 'That's part of what makes it interesting.'

Still smiling, he passed the introductions to Ginny.

She studied him briefly with an expression I hadn't seen on her face for a long time. Then she announced calmly, 'Ginny Fistoulari. Mick Axbrewder and I run a construction company in town.' She did it again, set me up for people to call me *Mick*. There was nothing I could do to stop her. 'Last week he didn't watch where he was going and nearly impaled himself on a bundle of rebar. But I can't make him rest unless I stand over him, and then I don't get any work done myself, so I signed us up for this. At least he'll be away from heavy equipment. And if the mystery gives him enough to think about, he might not drive both of us crazy.'

I should've been angry. She knows I don't let anybody call me Mick. But as I listened I realized what she was doing. That Mick and her joshing tone dissociated us from each other. It disguised our relationship. Which might conceivably make our job easier.

I didn't like it. But I decided to let her get away with it, at least temporarily.

Obliquely I noticed that we were on the freeway now, picking up speed. The van ran almost silently, and I couldn't feel any vibrations from the road. For some reason, that made me nervous, as if we'd lost contact with reality.

The dirigible heaved himself around to look up and down the aisle. His smile was like too much butter icing on a cake, so rich that I could feel my cholesterol level rise. Maybe it explained his bad teeth. Still holding hands with his companion, he said, 'Ah'm Houston Mile, and this here pretty little filly is Maryanne Green.' His accent was so thick you could've used it to stucco houses. 'We're from the great state of Texas, where Ah've got a few little ol' oil wells and just a bitty stud farm.'

'Now don't you be too modest, Houston,' his 'filly' put in, her voice as sweet as his smile. 'You raise the finest Arabians in the state, and you know it. Why, just last year,' she informed us, making sure we understood Houston Mile's finer qualities, 'place and show at the Kentucky Derby were sired on Houston's farm.'

From where I sat, I could see dimples and devotion, but not much else.

'Well, Ah am a mite proud of them long-legged heart-breakers,' Houston responded, 'if Ah do say so mahself. But not too proud to exercise mah brains ever once in a while. Ol' Buffy and Rock do put on a fine mystery. Stumped me ever' time so far, and that's a fact.'

At that Buffy laughed happily, and Houston Mile licked his fat lips as if he wished he were licking Maryanne Green.

I could tell right away that I had a lot in common with both of them.

The handsome man behind Maryanne was next. He actually stood up, offering all of us to get a good look at him, but he didn't smile. He had one of those faces that was too young for itself, as if it hadn't made up its mind what it would be when it grew up. He must've been at least thirty-five, but he looked about nineteen. Now that I could see him clearly, I wondered why I'd thought him handsome. His features were too soft for that, almost malleable.

'I'm Simon Abel,' he said seriously. I seemed to hear a hint of Boston in his voice. 'I'm here with Cat Reverie.' He indicated the woman sitting in front of me, and she stood up, too. 'This is a working vacation for us. I used to be a house painter. She ran a hairdressing salon. But we saved up, and now we want to go into business for ourselves. We want to run our own mystery camps. We came to see how Rock and Buffy do it.'

A house painter? Simon Abel looked about as much like a house painter as Sam Drayton did like a doctor. I decided to reserve judgment until I got a better look at his hands.

Cat – Catherine? – Reverie, on the other hand, looked exactly like a woman who ran a hairdressing salon. Her lush auburn hair swept down on to her shoulders as if you were supposed to write a poem about it. Her bulky sweater and long skirt concealed her figure in a way that made you think you'd find it stunning if you got a glimpse of it. She was pretty in a professional fashion, as if she were just an advertisement for herself, not a real woman.

Her smile was the exact opposite of Simon Abel's. 'Of course,' she beamed, 'the reason we want to run a mystery camp is because we love mysteries. Miss Marple, Nero Wolfe, Marlowe, they've always been my favourite books.'

With an air of studied naturalness, she smoothed her skirt under her and sat back down.

Until Abel folded himself into his chair again, I didn't realize that he hadn't actually looked at anyone except Cat Reverie while he stood.

That left two people who needed no introduction, mostly because they were the only ones left who stood a reasonable chance of being Constance Bebb and Mac Westward, the famous novelist. For their sakes, I hoped they really were famous. To me, they looked like the sort of writer you've never heard of. The woman wasn't more than middle-aged, but she had the prim graceless air of a worn-out schoolteacher. Despite his corduroy jacket and turtleneck shirt, the man made me think of mashed potatoes that someone forgot to put in the refrigerator a few days ago.

He remained in his seat and didn't say anything. She rose to do the talking for both of them. 'I'm Constance Bebb,' she said as if she weren't sure we'd done our homework, 'Connie, and this is Mac Westward. We're collaborators. Together we write the Thornton Foal novels.'

There she paused like she expected a round of applause.

Somewhat to my surprise, she got it. *I'd* never heard of Thornton Foal – and I was still looking for Buffy's shills. But Maryanne Green and Cat Reverie clapped enthusiastically, Simon Abel breathed, 'Wow!' and Joseph Hardhouse arched his black eyebrows. Queenie Drayton shifted forward as if she recognized the name happily.

Now that she had her applause, however, Constance Bebb didn't seem particularly interested in it. 'Thank you,' she said dryly. 'It's nice to know that some people still read.

'We like attending mystery camps,' she continued in the same tone.

'They give us ideas. The experience of thinking about someone else's puzzles is invaluable. And guessing who did it in books is too easy. A reader doesn't have all the distractions that make real crimes so difficult to solve. Camps like this help us make our own books convincing.'

Mac Westward nodded like a man drifting into senility.

Constance Bebb sat down. Lara Hardhouse, Sam and Queenie Drayton, and I introduced ourselves. Hoping it would do some good, I stressed *Brew*. Then Buffy Altar took over again.

'You're a wonderful group. I think this camp will be the best we've ever had.'

The way she drove showed that she knew what she was doing, but I had to keep reminding myself. The tone of her enthusiasm didn't inspire confidence. I didn't trust people who had such a pleasant relationship with their own lives.

'You all know what we'll be doing, so I don't need to explain too many things. We'll be at Deerskin Lodge for a vacation. It's as simple as that. All we have to do is relax and enjoy ourselves – until the mystery starts.

'But there are a few points I want to emphasize.' A few of which she was especially proud. 'Four of the people in this van are professionals. Two of you are actors, and two of you are private investigators. For you, there's one absolute rule. You can't reveal who you really are. All the rest of us are counting on you to keep your real reasons for being here secret.

'With everyone's cooperation, we can make our mystery really unique. For instance, one of our actors is probably here to be the murderer – unless it's me or Rock – but that doesn't mean the other will be the victim. The victim could be any of you. But that doesn't mean you're out of the game. You'll be informed that you've been killed, and we do ask that you play along, but you'll be informed in a way that doesn't reveal who killed you. After that, you can continue to try to solve the crime yourself. The only restriction – since you're dead – is that you won't be allowed to ask any questions. You'll only be able to listen and observe.

'Doing it this way has tremendous advantages. Because the victim doesn't have to be one of the actors, we can have more than one victim. We can have a whole series of murders. In fact, that's one of the ways the murderer can win. He can win, of course – or she – by not getting caught. Or he can win by killing us all.

'And since the victim doesn't have to be one of the actors, we can't guess the murderer simply by knowing who the victim came with.

That's partly why it's so important for the actors and the private investigators to keep their identities secret.

'Now.' Buffy's speech was like her driving – her enthusiasm concealed her expertise. 'How will you be informed that you've been murdered? We used to use notes, little pieces of paper that said something like, "There's an adder in your bed. As soon as you pull back the covers, you're dead." But that made life too easy for the murderer. He could leave his notes anywhere. There was too little connection to the crime. And the notes always gave you the chance to argue that you didn't pull back the covers of your bed, so you weren't dead.

'Instead we now use blue marbles. The murderer has a supply. If you find one in your purse or your pocket, you're dead. If you pull back the covers and see a blue marble in your bed, you aren't dead, but if you find the marble after you're in bed, you are. Of course, if you don't find the marble at all, the attempt on your life failed. To kill you the murderer has to put it where you'll be sure to find it.'

At this point Joseph Hardhouse made a show of turning out his pockets.

'No,' Mrs Altar laughed. She'd seen him in the rear-view mirror. 'Nobody's been killed yet. Our murderer doesn't want to take the chance that we might stop and call the police. In fact, nobody will be killed for at least a day. That will give us all the time to become familiar with Deerskin Lodge, to get to know each other a bit – and give the murderer time to figure out the best way to start killing us.'

My pain had one advantage. It gave me an excuse for the way I looked. My companions weren't likely to realize that most of what showed on my face was disgust. The idea that fourteen grown men and women would spend the next six days hunting for blue marbles should've been funny, but I was in no mood for it.

Luckily for me, the speech was almost over. 'Oh, just one more thing,' Buffy said after pausing long enough to make me think she'd finished. 'The weather forecast. You'll all be delighted to hear that we have a big winter storm coming in. We should get it some time tomorrow, or the next day. The mountains are supposed to get at least a foot of snow. We'll be practically snowbound – I hope.'

Oh, good. More ambience.

For the first time in twenty-four hours, it occurred to me to wonder whether those guns had actually been locked away.

The rest of the guests seemed appropriately excited by Mrs Altar's announcement, but Mac Westward chose this occasion to emerge from his silence. In a cold lumpy voice, he asked, 'Will we be safe?'

Apparently the surprise of hearing Westward speak acted as a catalyst on Rock. As soon as Buffy answered, 'Oh, of course,' her husband pulled up his head and faced the back of the van.

'Deerskin Lodge,' he said firmly, 'is fully supplied and equipped for the worst winter weather. If necessary we can live there comfortably for weeks. There is a phone. We can call for help if we need it. And if the line goes down, the manager, Arthur Reeson, has a snowmobile he can use to reach the nearest town. I think we can all count on our safety, Mr Westward.'

In response the male half of Thornton Foal folded his arms over his chest and subsided.

Now that Buffy was done, the guests started talking to each other. Most of them seemed genuinely excited about this vacation. Almost simultaneously, Simon Abel and Catherine Reverie leaned across their respective aisles to tell Mac Westward and Constance Bebb how thrilled they were to meet one of their favourite writers. Joseph Hardhouse acted like he was eager to resume a conversation with Ginny, but Houston Mile interrupted him. Despite his accent, Mile knew how to enunciate clearly when it came to money, and his voice carried – I heard him ask Hardhouse how much profit could be made in the restaurant business. Maryanne Green listened as if she were entranced.

To distract myself from the particular smile Ginny focused on Hardhouse, I turned to Sam Drayton and asked the first brilliant, insightful question I could think of.

'What's your specialty, Dr Drayton?'

He looked at me, grinning like a movie star. Just for a second, he hesitated. Then he said privately, so that the women in the next row wouldn't hear him, 'Rebar accidents. You know what I mean – puncture wounds with blunt rods, slow poisoning, that sort of thing. Amazing how busy it keeps me.'

He took me by surprise. 'In other words,' I muttered, keeping my voice as quiet as his, 'you don't believe me.'

He nodded. 'Just getting poked in the stomach wouldn't do enough damage. Having one of those rods rammed right through you would do too much. You wouldn't even think about a vacation like this.'

Too bad the other people on the bench seat were listening. Queenie Drayton I could tolerate – I already had an almost adolescent crush on her. But Lara Hardhouse was another matter. She took everything we said too seriously.

However, I couldn't do anything about Lara or Queenie, so I

464

concentrated on Drayton. 'You think I'm faking it. You think I'm one of the actors.'

Still grinning, he mouthed the word, *no*. 'You're no actor. The pain is real. I just don't buy your explanation.'

As if she'd been holding her breath, Lara said in a little bursting whisper, 'Mr Axbrewder is a private investigator.'

'Good God.' She startled me, which helped me sound convincing. 'What makes you think *that?*'

Both Sam and Queenie stared at her, but she didn't hesitate. 'You aren't just *in* pain,' she explained. 'You *know* about pain. All about it. I can see it in your face. You work with it all the time, you live with it. You aren't the kind of man who takes this kind of vacation.'

Well, shit. So much for my cover. But I couldn't just give up on it. Constance Bebb and Cat Reverie might've overheard what we were saying. And I wanted to do whatever I could to make Lara less interested in me.

'You're wrong,' I said straight at her. 'I just look like this because I'm an alcoholic.'

That was a mistake. Sam Drayton nodded to himself, and Queenie looked away as if she were embarrassed. Their reactions were about what I expected. But Mrs Hardhouse suddenly became so interested in me that her whole face burned with it.

At least I didn't have to put up with any more conversation for a while.

Chapter Five

Instead of probing me, Murder On Cue's guests talked to each other. I suppose I should've been listening – you never know when a 'clue' will crop up. But between them Sam Drayton and Lara Hardhouse had given me a scare. And that made me want to go to sleep. It was like having a hole in my moral guts as well as in my stomach. Leaning my head against the wall of the van, I closed my eyes and tuned out my fellow travellers.

Ginny wouldn't be amused if the people around me already believed I was a private investigator.

Buffy would be livid.

I was in pretty sad shape if I couldn't even get through the first hour of a nursemaid job without screwing up.

I wanted a nap, but I didn't really expect to get one, not under these conditions. So I was surprised when I jerked open my eyes, blinked my vision into focus, and found that we were already high in the mountains. It must've been the deterioration of the road that woke me up. Sunlight glittered on the leftover snow, still clean and mostly unmarked, and the trees arranged themselves against the hillsides and the sky like they were posing for a travel poster. For a minute there I felt completely disoriented, as if someone had changed the world around me and all the rules were different.

I hoped I hadn't been snoring.

During my nap, some of the guests had traded seats. Cat Reverie now sat opposite Simon Abel, talking with Ginny and Joseph Hardhouse. Lara Hardhouse had moved across from Mac Westward, where apparently she'd actually succeeded at engaging him in conversation. Sam and Queenie Drayton listened quietly. I had Houston Mile beside me, with Maryanne Green beside him and

Constance Bebb in the other corner. Maryanne was quizzing Connie about Thornton Foal while Mile supervised. He smelled like petroleum oozing through an inadequate buffer of breath mints.

When he noticed that I was awake, he showed me how bad his teeth were. 'Feelin' better, son?'

Well, no. I felt disoriented and bitter – not to mention bloated, as if my guts were filling up with blood. So I nodded and gave him a smile as convincing as his.

'Like Ah say,' he continued, 'Ah've done this before. Crime is intriguin', and ol' Rock and Buffy put on a fine show. It do challenge a man to keep up.' Then he paused and peered at me expectantly.

A moment or two passed before I realized that this remark was intended as a question.

I didn't want to encourage him. 'Not me,' I muttered. 'This is Ginny's idea. She's the boss. I'm just here because bed-rest makes me crazy.'

In response he chuckled and leered. 'Ah know what you mean, son. Bed ain't good for but one thing, and rest don't come into it.'

With one hand, he stroked Maryanne's upper thigh.

Luckily for me, touching Maryanne distracted him. He turned to lean over her and left me alone.

Eventually we reached the gate and the long driveway that led down to Deerskin Lodge. Buffy stopped to announce our destination and let everyone take a look. Then she drove down into the hollow and parked in front of the lodge.

One by one, we off-loaded ourselves into the mud and slush. I was the last one out.

By the time I'd dragged my sore carcass between the seats and through the door, a man had emerged from the lodge to deal with the luggage. He had a peculiarly old-world face, with creased sallow skin, a drooping off-white walrus moustache, and bland innocent eyes – the kind of face you'd expect to see on some mafia don's simple-minded cousin. He wore a battered old pea coat which concealed his frame, but the way he handled the suitcases convinced me that he was strong.

He must've been Petruchio Carbone, Truchi. He and his wife, Amalia, were the only members of the staff I hadn't met.

I half expected Art Reeson to put in an appearance. Welcome the guests as Deerskin Lodge's official representative. But he didn't show.

Mrs Altar had already reached the steps to the porch, keeping her contact with mire and muck to a minimum, but the rest of us stood around near the van and studied the mountains and trees and buildings, the absolute sky. Getting used to being here. Ginny had joined a little cluster that included Joseph Hardhouse and Cat Reverie. I edged closer to her, looking for some hint to help me interpret the way she dissociated herself from me. But her glance in my direction was studiously impersonal.

Under the circumstances, however, I couldn't help noticing that her entire face had changed since the parking lot of the Camelot. Now she looked fascinated rather than disinterested. The lines of her jaw and nose were keen, and her eyes shone like glass after you clean away a film of dust and oil.

I also couldn't help noticing that she seemed to have lost the self-consciousness – or the shame – that used to make her hide her claw. Now she treated her stainless steel hand as if it were as much a part of her as anything else.

And, on top of all that, I positively and entirely couldn't help noticing that her attention and keenness were focused on Hardhouse. She actually reached out to him a couple of times, touched his arm gently, like a girl hoping to be asked out on a date. His pleasure, which shone like his hair, was divided sort of equally between her and Catherine Reverie, but she ignored Cat to concentrate on him.

That hit me hard. Harder than it should've, probably, but I wasn't exactly at my best. I'd known Ginny for years, loved her for years, but I hadn't seen her look at me like that since I could remember.

All of a sudden, I knew what introducing me as 'Mick' meant. She was leaving me on my own – abandoning me, as they say, to my own devices. She'd done what she could for me by bringing me here, putting me in a safe place. That was enough. Now she intended to pursue her own interests.

At the moment those interests had nothing to do with me. Instead they revolved around Joseph Hardhouse.

The insight left me numb with shock. Instinctively I tried to retreat.

When I turned away, I found myself blinking dumbly into the face of Lara Hardhouse.

She stood close to Mac Westward. Something about the way she accompanied him conveyed the impression that she'd appropriated him, probably without his being aware of it. But the ache in her eyes was aimed at me, and it was so intense that it practically stopped my heart.

She regarded me like she understood what had just happened.

Because I was numb with shock and couldn't afford to think, I pushed that possibility away. Instead I decided – on no basis

468

whatsoever – that I knew what troubled her. Her husband was a philanderer, and it was killing her. She worked to make herself beautiful and share his recreations, trying to win him back, but nothing could make him love her the way she wanted. She needed help. She didn't look at me like that because she pitied me. She just thought we had something in common.

We did. But I didn't want to think about it. All I wanted was distance from my own dismay.

By then Buffy had started talking again, making a speech of welcome. I came in on the part where she said, 'Truchi will take care of your bags. Unless they don't have tags on them.' Pleased with her own humour. 'In that case, you'll have to sort them out for yourselves.

'Come inside, and I'll show you where your rooms are. Once you've had a chance to settle in and fresh up, you can get oriented and do a bit of exploring before dinner.'

I didn't know what else to do with myself, so I lurched along behind the group towards the stairs and the porch.

'This is the den,' Buffy announced as she led us into the big lounge with the tree trunk and the stuffed heads. The room was considerably warmer than yesterday, heated by fires crackling in all three fireplaces – which solved the back-draft problem. 'The dining room and kitchen are that way.' She pointed in their direction. 'The bedrooms are along these other two halls. There are more rooms than we need, but we'll be scattered to give you all' – she smiled a mystery lover's smile – 'as much privacy as possible.'

As if she were heading up a regatta, she steered us towards our quarters.

Sam and Queenie Drayton shared a room, of course. So did Houston Mile and Maryanne. And Rock and Buffy. I wasn't surprised that Connie, Mac, Simon Abel, and Cat all had separate rooms. But I was a little taken aback by the fact that Joseph and Lara Hardhouse weren't together.

Neither were Ginny and I. Her room was down the other hall from mine.

On top of that, I didn't much care for my room. Sure, it had a bathroom and a bed, which were about the only things I absolutely required. But the bed looked to be about a foot too short, and the chairs were delicate. Chintz and doilies mostly decorated the room, and on the walls hung sepia prints of hunters standing over dead beasts. It was the sort of room where you'd expect vacant women to sit and knit while they waited for their menfolk to come home from putting holes in animals. Or people.

I sneered at it in an attempt to distance myself.

I needed as many ways as I could find, so I was glad when I heard a knock on my door, and Petruchio Carbone came in with my suitcase.

He tilted his head to ask me where I wanted him to put my stuff. 'On the bed.' I didn't have any better ideas. 'I'll take care of it later.'

With a shrug, Carbone flipped my suitcase on to the coverlet like it weighed practically nothing – which it probably did. Then he moved towards the door.

I wasn't eager to be left alone. To stop him, I asked, 'Have you worked here long, Mr Carbone?'

He paused, looked at me with an air of impersonal sorrow, scratched his head as if the question were more complex than I realized. After a moment he said uncertainly, 'Ten years?'

'So you know Mr and Mrs Altar? You've seen their mystery camps before?'

His shrug was eloquent without actually shedding any light on the subject.

'What are they like?' I didn't care. I was just trying to survive. 'How do the camps go? What do you think of all this?'

He fixed me with his simple-minded-cousin gaze. Under his moustache, his mouth looked like he'd never smiled in his life. 'Since I'm working here,' he said distinctly, 'everybody who comes is crazy. I pay no attention.'

He left to finish distributing luggage among the guests.

Crazy. Sure. Including me. I slipped off my sheepskin and draped it over my suitcase. Then I lowered my pains into a particularly flimsy rocker and tried to imagine how I could endure being here for an entire week. Cut off from Ginny. Left alone to watch her while she looked for love or at least excitement elsewhere.

Fortunately I was still numb enough to function when she knocked on my door and walked into the room. Her eyes held a fighting gleam, and she didn't bother to ask how I was doing. Before I could muster what courage or anger I had left, she said sharply, 'Come on, Brew. I want to show you something.'

When she issues orders like that, I obey. No matter what. Trying to conserve my physical resources, I got up slowly – but I got up.

She strode out of the room. I followed.

Ahead of me and pulling away, she went down the hall to the den, then veered off towards the dining room.

When I caught up with her, she was standing in front of the gun cases.

All the guns were still there.

For some reason, my eye caught on a .22 rim fire Winchester with a pump action that looked like a brand-new design pretending to be old. And over on the other wall hung a by-God varmint pistol, one of the best – a Kimber Predator with bolt-action and a scope sight.

More for completeness than to satisfy my curiosity, I touched the latches on the cases again. Still open. The drawers under the cases still held ammunition, neatly arranged so that the loads for each weapon were directly below it.

After a moment I realized that I was whistling softly through my teeth. I didn't really care about the danger. I was just grateful for the distraction.

Ginny didn't look at me. 'What do you think?' she asked quietly.

'I think,' I replied profoundly, 'one of us is going to have to have a talk with Rock. Or Buffy.' I kept my voice down as well. 'Or both.'

'I know that, you idiot,' she rasped. 'I meant, what do you think we should do about the guns? Take them ourselves? Make Reeson lock the cases and give us the keys? How far should we push this?'

'That's what I meant, too.' I didn't like being called an idiot, but I was in no mood to object. 'Whatever happens, it has to come from the Altars. And Reeson has to do it. If we intervene ourselves, we'll blow our cover. Which will make dear sweet Buffy furious. She'll fire us. Then we won't have anywhere to go except back into town.'

Into el Señor's range of fire.

Now Ginny looked at me. She was furious herself, but when I didn't drop my eyes she twisted her mouth into something that might've been intended as a smile. Leaning close to me, she whispered, 'God, I hate it when you're right.'

With a flash of her skirt, she stalked away in search of Mr or Mrs Altar.

Again I followed her.

She damn near collided with Buffy as Mrs Altar came through one of the doorways with Sam and Queenie Drayton, Joseph Hardhouse, and Catherine Reverie.

'Ah, Ginny, Brew.' Buffy wore a smile so bright you could've used it to read by. 'We were just going to take a walk around the grounds – the "policies" of the lodge, as they say in those wonderful old British novels. Will you join us?'

'Can you wait a minute?' Ginny countered. The change in her voice astonished me. I'd expected assertiveness – take-charge-Fistoulari in full cry. Her professional integrity was at issue. But instead she sounded positively amiable. 'Brew and I have a problem. We need to talk to you.'

'Oh, not right now,' Buffy protested with a girlish pout. 'We had our hearts set on a walk. Freshen our appetites for dinner. Isn't that right?' she asked her companions.

None of them contradicted her, although Sam muttered something that could've meant anything, and Queenie seemed to be stifling a secret laugh.

'Tell you what,' Buffy rushed on. 'Rock and I'll make time for a quiet chat after dinner. I'm sure we'll be able to straighten everything out.'

Which indicated that she knew what Ginny wanted to talk to her about.

Ginny acquiesced gracefully. Another surprise. 'That'll be fine,' she said with no hint of irritation. 'Maybe I'll come on that walk with you after all.'

Queenie looked up at me. Under other circumstances, I could've drowned in her dark eyes. Her voice was like music as she asked, 'What about you, Brew?'

But I was already floundering. I shook my head stupidly.

She smiled and shrugged, and Buffy led her party towards the front door. Cat Reverie clung to Hardhouse's arm. The way she tucked her hip against his thigh gave me the impression that walking wasn't her preferred form of exercise.

Ginny accompanied them outside contentedly, as if she'd never been angry in her life.

Calling, 'Wait for me,' Simon Abel hurried past to catch up with them. Then they were gone.

I stared after Ginny's back for a long time after the door closed. What was going on here? Who was that woman? The Ginny Fistoulari I knew wouldn't have taken no for an answer from a Sherman tank. Not where her job was concerned. She would've insisted on a private conversation. What made her so easy to get along with all of a sudden?

Hardhouse, that was the answer. She'd swallowed her irritation and assertiveness for his sake. No, worse than that. Her determination had evaporated as soon as she saw him.

She was gone. Just like that.

I needed a drink.

It would probably make me sick, but at the moment I didn't care. Now I had a hole in my heart as well as my stomach, and this numbness wasn't going to last much longer. When it wore off, I would be in serious trouble.

Unfortunately – or fortunately, depending on your point of view – I didn't get a drink. On my way towards the dining room to locate a liquor cabinet, I met up with Roderick Altar.

He appeared especially vague, blurred by his lack of interest in his own thoughts. But he didn't hesitate when he saw me. 'Mr Axbrewder,' he said as if I were what he'd just been thinking about, 'I need to talk to you. Is Ms Fistoulari around? Can you come to the office for a moment?'

A session with Rock wasn't what I'd had in mind, but I didn't dismiss the opportunity. When you're floundering, you'll grab hold of anything – which in my case happened to be my job. The client wants talk? The private investigator gives talk. Especially when he also has things to discuss.

'She's out,' I explained, 'but I'm here. In fact, I was looking for you.' Some lies are easy. 'We have a problem.'

I thought I caught a glimpse of relief on his features. Maybe he didn't want to face Ginny with what he had to say. 'This way,' he muttered with his usual lack of ceremony and walked off in the direction of the office.

Since yesterday a new stack of papers had appeared on the desk. Guest registration forms, all filled out – probably by Rock. He made himself at home in the big chair behind the desk. I envied him his assurance, but I didn't argue. Hardship puts grit in your soul. Bracing my stomach in one of the less comfortable chairs, I waited for him to begin. The dullness of his gaze made it hard to think of him as a venture capitalist – or as any other life-form that liked risk.

But at least he didn't beat around the bush. Without any of his wife's social shuck-and-jive, he said, 'You noticed the guns.' His eyes didn't quite meet mine.

I nodded. 'We weren't amused.'

Rock sighed. 'I wasn't either. I've just had a talk with Art Reeson. Did you meet him yesterday?'

I nodded again.

'He spoke to the owners of the lodge yesterday afternoon. I gather this was after you and Ms Fistoulari told him you wanted the guns locked away. Apparently they refused permission. They say they accumulated their collection at considerable expense, and they're proud of it. It's part of the *appeal* of Deerskin Lodge.

'They take the position that we knew the guns were here. We could have objected to them before we hired the lodge. In addition, we've hired the lodge in the past without objection. Therefore they're unwilling to ask Reeson to take on the extra effort and inconvenience of easing Ms Fistoulari's mind.

'And yours, of course,' he added as an afterthought.

'I see,' I said. I wasn't sure I liked being an afterthought. 'And how do you feel about that, Mr Altar?'

He shrugged without shifting his eyes, which were focused on the middle of my shirt. 'As I told you, I don't like guns. They're an unnecessary opportunity for accidents, even a temptation. On the other hand, we've never had any trouble. Our guests come here to *play* at crime, Mr Axbrewder. Most of them would be horrified to encounter the real thing.' After a moment's hesitation, he said, 'I'll go further than that. I think most of our guests play at crime in order to defuse their horror of the real thing. They're afraid of being victimized. Safe danger, safe hunting create the illusion of invulnerability.'

Then he spread his hands. 'I would prefer to let the matter drop.'

I was tempted to let myself get involved in a discussion about motivation. But my personal danger seemed too real. I needed to stick to business. So I asked, 'What if we don't?'

Rock frowned as if he didn't understand the question.

'What if Ginny and I don't agree to let the matter drop? What happens then?'

That at least brought his gaze up to mine. When he met my eyes, I saw the toughness that had been missing until now – the toughness that had been atrophying from disuse ever since he'd become Buffy's partner in Murder On Cue, Inc.

'Then,' he said slowly, 'you'll look like a fool. Whatever you do, the guns will remain where they are. And your identities will be exposed to no purpose. That will significantly reduce your value to us. I doubt that your fees will be worth paying solely for the sake of lowering our insurance rates.'

'I see,' I said again. 'Leave the guns alone or get fired.'

Rock faced me without blinking. He didn't like guns. He didn't even like Murder On Cue. But on this subject he was prepared to back his wife as far as necessary. He couldn't possibly know that Ginny and I couldn't afford to be fired right now. As far as he knew, we might take a stand and refuse to budge. He accepted that risk.

Like it or not, I had to respect him.

So I tried a different tack. 'Mr Altar, do you have any idea how much trouble Ginny and I'll be in if those guns are involved in an accident, or even a crime, and the commission holds an inquiry? We'll be held responsible. We could lose our licence.' That is to say, Ginny could lose her licence. 'We *know* better than to leave guns like that just sitting around.'

He shook his head. 'I think not. You were hired at the last minute. The circumstances here weren't under your control.' The way he lowered his eyes suggested that he was trying to negotiate. 'If necessary, I'll testify that you did your best to have the guns locked away.'

That was slim. The commission already disapproved of Ginny for keeping me on the payroll. We were both under investigation for our run-in with el Señor. Altar's testimony wasn't likely to improve our credibility much.

Nevertheless his offer at least made it possible for us to avoid getting fired. And it gave me something else I wanted.

An opening.

While he thought we were still dickering, I asked for the second time, 'Tell me, Mr Altar. How did you happen to choose us for this job?'

That took him by surprise. He glared up at me. 'I've already explained that. I–'

I interrupted him. 'You didn't finish. You didn't tell me who had the job before we did.'

He obviously wanted to ask what this had to do with the question of the guns. But he swallowed his curiosity, at least for the moment.

With a perfectly straight face, he said, 'Lawrence Smithsonian and Associates.'

When he mentioned that name, the bottom fell out.

'In fact, I've known Lawrence for years, at least by reputation. You must know him, too – he's highly regarded in banking circles around Puerta del Sol. And Murder On Cue has always had a good relationship with his company. We would have used his people as a matter of course, but just two days ago he was forced to pull out. Some sort of professional emergency, he couldn't tell me the details, but he needed all his people.

'He gave me your names.'

Altar said all this blandly, easily. He had no idea what he was doing to me. 'Now that I think about it, that's where I first heard of Fistoulari Investigations. Lawrence assured me that you would be perfect for the job. I trusted his judgement, of course.'

Lawrence Smithsonian. Ginny called him 'fatass Smithsonian'. He was the one who got us into trouble with el Señor in the first place.

Another recommendation. He'd sent us a client who'd killed one of el Señor's numbers runners. Which was about as charitable as helping us step in front of a locomotive.

And now we were here because of him? What the hell was going on?

Suddenly the whole game had changed. If Smithsonian got us this job, we could be sure of one thing. He did it out of malice.

And he knew something about it that we didn't.

My throat had gone dry. I had to fight to make my voice work. 'Did Smithsonian—' I choked, stopped, tried again. 'Did your friend Lawrence happen to say *why* he thought we'd be perfect for this job?'

'Well, I wouldn't call him a friend.' My reaction clearly baffled Rock. 'He's only an acquaintance. But no.' He consulted his memory. 'He didn't explain. However, he did imply we would be doing him a favour if we took you on. I had the impression he owed you a debt and wanted us to help him repay it.'

A debt. Oh, right. Absolutely. Smithsonian didn't owe us a debt. He owed us blood.

I got to my feet. That nice protective numbness was gone. My head reeled, and a hum filled my ears. For some reason, however, problems like that didn't seem to affect my balance. I went towards the door almost steadily.

'Mr Axbrewder.' Altar must've called on resources he hadn't used for a long time. His voice snapped after me, but softly, softly, just a threat of the whip, not an actual blow. For the first time, he sounded like his nickname was more than a whim of Buffy's. 'What about the guns?'

I wanted to laugh, but if I'd tried it would've come out falsetto with panic. 'Don't worry about the guns. It's too late now.'

He wasn't satisfied. 'Will Ms Fistoulari agree?'

'It's too late for both of us.' That was all I cared about. But it wasn't the answer he wanted. I stopped with my hand on the doorknob and grinned back at him like a banshee. 'She'll leave the guns alone. That's the least of your problems.'

Back in my room, I spent the rest of the time before dinner cleaning my .45.

This was going to be a hell of a vacation.

Chapter Six

My gun was a .45 Glock with enough stopping power to maim an automobile, but it didn't do me any good. The only actual use I'd ever gotten out of a firearm was shooting my brother. On the other hand, I didn't spend all that time cleaning it in order to use it. I did it to calm myself down. Basically I'm a tidy soul. I like to clean things. Back in Puerta del Sol, I would've scoured Ginny's apartment. Here I cleaned my .45.

By the time I was done, I'd reached a decision. I wasn't going to tell Ginny about Smithsonian.

It scared me spitless, but I was too stubborn to back down.

After all, why was I here? Not to get away from el Señor – that was Ginny's reason for bringing me, not my reason for coming. I was here to protect *her* from el Señor. And to start taking care of myself. So that I wouldn't be so vulnerable to her.

Joseph Hardhouse gave me an immediate, tangible reason to desire less vulnerability. As far as I could figure out, the only glue holding me and Ginny together these days was the chemical reaction between her protective instincts and my weakness. Now that she'd put me somewhere safe, at least for a week, the glue had already begun to break down. What did I have to lose by facing Rock's information on my own?

As of now, Lawrence Smithsonian was *my* problem. If Ginny wanted problems, let her think about what she was getting into with Lara's husband.

Unfortunately reasoning my way through the puzzle Smithsonian represented wasn't easy. I had nothing to go on except intuition.

Well, start from the facts. Lawrence Smithsonian, bless his piggy little heart, had sent us the job that led to Ginny killing our client and me killing Muy Estobal. So what? He wasn't exactly one of the world's sweethearts, but he could not have premeditated the whole thing. Even if he'd actively wanted to get us into trouble with el Señor – which by itself was plausible, considering his dislike for Ginny – how could he have known we would take the case? How could he have known how it would turn out? Fatass Smithsonian was just nasty, not prescient.

So why was I scared now? What was the danger? He knew something about this job we didn't. What, for instance? I had no way to figure that out. Assuming that Ginny and I'd just gotten ourselves into another disaster of his devising – well, what exactly *was* the disaster? How did I arrive at the conclusion that this camp was anything more than a nursemaid operation? What did I use for evidence?

Intuition. That's all.

And something else. Something that nagged at me and refused to come clear.

But I was in no mood – and no condition – to suffer over it. The back of my brain would talk to me when it damn well felt like it, not one heartbeat before. And I had other agendas . . .

I still meant to have a drink. If Ginny wanted to get burned playing with Joseph Hardhouse, that was *her* business. I had an entirely different fire in mind.

By the time I finished cleaning my weapon, I heard chimes out in the hall. When I opened the door, I saw a woman walking away from me, beating rather aimlessly on a small xylophone. From the back, she looked like a cross between everyone's favourite grandmother and the Pillsbury doughboy. Amalia Carbone, the housekeeper, announcing dinner.

Until Cat Reverie emerged from the room across from mine and smiled at me, I didn't realize that I hadn't heard Buffy's companions return from their walk. No banging doors, no creaking floorboards, no talk, nothing. The rooms had better insulation than I'd expected.

A couple of things surprised me about Cat's appearance. She'd changed her clothes. Now she wore a drop-dead gown, black and slinky, which showed enough cleavage to reanimate a corpse. And she seemed glad to see me.

'Brew.' She beamed up at me. 'Good timing.' Slipping her arm through mine, she hugged my biceps. 'You can escort me to dinner.'

I'd seen her walk with Hardhouse, so I was braced for the way she tucked her hip against my leg. Immediately I noticed that her posture had one particular advantage. It made her look like her breasts might come out of her dress at any moment.

But I wasn't interested in her. She wasn't Ginny. She wasn't even Queenie Drayton. I didn't pull my arm away – but I also didn't smile. With my usual charm, I asked, 'What's all this about? I thought you were after Hardhouse.'

Just for a second, her smile flicked away. Nevertheless she recovered quickly. 'I am,' she admitted in a tone that contained a world of possibilities. 'But you could persuade me to change my mind. I like men.

'No,' she amended at once, 'that's not quite right. I like strength. I like muscle and toughness. Unless I'm losing my touch' – she chuckled as she squeezed my arm – 'you have both.

'Take me to dinner,' she commanded before I could respond. 'Maybe later I'll find out whether I'm right.'

While I groped for a snappy retort, I was interrupted.

A door slammed behind me. A hand came down on my shoulder. Simon Abel.

He glared at me, lines pinched around his mouth. Unfortunately anger didn't suit his too-young face. Instead of lending him force, it only made him look like a petulant kid.

'If you don't mind,' he snapped, 'she's with me.'

He gave me a problem. Nobody touches me – not like that. No matter how weak or wounded I am. But Cat's face wore a laughing expression for my benefit, and I didn't like that either. I didn't want to take sides between them.

So I pulled my arm out of her grasp and caught him by the wrist. Holding him hard enough to make him wince, I put his hand on her shoulder for him.

'Take her,' I said with a malicious grin. 'She's yours.'

Then I strode ahead of them towards the dining room. For a few paces, anyway, adrenalin helped me walk like a normal person.

God, I wanted a drink. More and more, I couldn't think of any other way to stand being myself.

Most of the crew had already assembled in the dining room when I arrived. And most of them had changed for dinner. Ginny and Mac Westward were the only exceptions. Hardhouse had produced an actual dinner jacket, and Lara's gown rivalled Cat's. Houston Mile and Rock had on suits, Buffy and Maryanne Green wore dresses which would've done justice to an Easter service, and even Constance Bebb gave the impression that she'd donned her best tweed. As for the

Draytons, Sam looked merely elegant and movie-actorish in a sports coat and cream scarf, but something about Queenie's silk blouse and flowing skirt almost broke my heart.

Feeling more than ever like the ugly duckling, I hunched into the room and glowered democratically at everybody.

Cat and Simon followed a moment later. They were both flushed, but for different reasons, and they didn't touch each other. Cat headed towards Hardhouse. Abel stood in the doorway, looking baffled by his own anger.

'Ah, here we are at last,' Buffy announced happily. She may've been immune to awkward situations. 'Please don't think dinner is a formal occasion. Some of us just like to dress up. It makes us feel that we're taking part in an Agatha Christie novel.

'Why don't we sit down?'

Smoothly she assigned seats. No haphazard arrangements for Sue-Rose Altar. After a bit of shuffling, we were all in our places, Rock and Buffy at the ends of the long table, Maryanne, Westward, Lara Hardhouse, Drayton, Ginny, and Simon along one side, Joseph, Cat, and me, then Connie, Mile, and Queenie down the other. Everywhere we looked, gun cases loomed behind us. Either the guns didn't belong there, or we didn't, I couldn't decide which.

When we were seated, Buffy rang a little bell, and Amalia Carbone appeared. I hadn't seen her face before. More than anything, she looked like someone you could trust to make spaghetti sauce.

Faith Jerrick trailed behind her. A demure net contained Faith's fine, almost white hair. She wore her crucifix outside her blouse. She didn't look at any of us.

Both she and Ama carried bottles of wine. From opposite ends of the table, they started offering wine to the guests.

I was never much of a wine-drinker, but I knew the difference between white and red. Suddenly my pulse began to clamour in my head, and my throat felt too tight to breathe. I'd arrived without expecting it at a crisis. The mere idea of alcohol made my whole body constrict with eagerness. I stood on the brink of something irrevocable – a choice more important than I could measure. I deserved a drink, didn't I? Wasn't that the one true thing I could say about myself? I was an alcoholic, and alcoholics drink because they deserve to drink. Being sober was just a smoke-screen, a way of hiding the truth – of pretending to be something I wasn't.

And Ginny didn't give a shit. Obviously. She didn't look at me. She'd already cut me off. She sat too far away from Hardhouse to focus her attention on him, so she talked to Sam Drayton. Even he held more interest for her than I did.

Self-pity is a wonderful thing. It justifies whatever you want. I couldn't think of one reason why I shouldn't get stone drunk as fast as possible. When Faith brought the red wine to my place, I nodded, and she filled my glass.

Looking at it, I realized for maybe the first time in my life that wine can be as lovely and seductive as rubies. It lacked whiskey's tranquil amber promise, but its attractions were still powerful. The lights in the dining room made my glass seem deep enough to drown in.

'Let me propose a toast.' Buffy raised her glass. She was in her element. Her smile sparkled like her earrings, and her skin appeared to glow. When she looked that happy, I could understand why Rock went along with her hobby.

We raised our glasses. She paused dramatically, as if she knew what this moment meant to me, then said in a clear voice, 'To a beautiful murder and an elegant solution.'

Ginny gave me a glance like a sneer, but she didn't watch while I brought my glass to my mouth.

Lara watched. Her own wine forgotten, she stared at me intently, almost avidly, as if she were hungry for the implications of my drinking. Her lips were parted and moist, unmistakably ready to be kissed, and a dusky smoulder filled her eyes. All of a sudden, she was the loveliest woman in the room, and every ounce of her was aimed at me.

Her intensity went through me like a kind of panic. Abruptly – too abruptly for grace, never mind discretion – I put the wine down untasted and picked up my glass of water. Conspicuously late, I joined the toast.

Everyone at the table seemed to stare at me. Ginny's face had an odd congested look, like conflicted fright. I couldn't read Lara's reaction, but Sam gave me an unabashed grin, and Queenie murmured almost too softly to be heard, 'Good for you.'

As if in acknowledgement, Hardhouse proposed another toast. 'May we all get what we want most this week.' His voice grated on my nerves, but I drank with the group anyway.

His toast made his wife blush. Maybe it had something to do with infidelity.

Then Houston Mile started to chuckle. 'Son,' he said down the table at Hardhouse, 'if Ah required an opportunity such as this to get what Ah want most, Ah wouldn't bother. Ah'd purely lie down and die.'

'You must have simple wants, Houston,' Hardhouse replied. 'Perhaps you aren't very ambitious.'

'Oh, Houston is ambitious,' Maryanne Green put in, sounding rather breathless. 'He's amazing, really. He can do anything. No one ever beats him – no one ever says no to him.'

That I doubted. There were people right here who were perfectly capable of saying *no* to Houston Mile. But accuracy wasn't the point – not to Maryanne, anyway. Her words seemed to inflate Mile, take up some of the slack in his appearance. Somehow she made him look less bloated, more like he fitted inside his skin.

He gave an aw-shucks grin. 'How that woman do talk,' he said expansively. 'Ah'm just a good ol' boy from down home, if Ah do say it mahself. But I got no qualms about mah taste in horseflesh. Or womanflesh.'

Now it was Maryanne's turn to blush.

'Don't let Mr Mile mislead you,' Rock put in unexpectedly. His air of vague disinterest may have been a disguise, concealing the man who liked to tamper with clues. Without looking at any of us, he explained, 'He's been to two of our mystery camps. At the first, he was the first to solve the crime. At the second, he was the only one to solve it.'

Buffy clucked disapprovingly. 'Now, Rock, you shouldn't tell them things like that. You'll embarrass Houston. And you'll intimidate everyone else.'

Embarrass Houston Mile? No chance. In fact, he said as much himself. 'Ah'm not embarrassed, Buffy. Ah got mah reputation to maintain. Tell you what,' he said to the rest of the table. 'Ah'll lay you a small wager, whatever you like, Ah already know Buffy's actors. Ah got 'em figured. *And* Ah know which of us is supposed to be detectives.'

Faith and Ama had brought out food. Cream of broccoli soup, I think it was. But eating didn't prevent us from listening hard.

'Fascinating,' Queenie Drayton breathed. 'Are you really sure?' When Mile nodded, she went on, 'I'll bet with you. I think I have it figured out as well. What shall we bet?'

At once Mile flapped his fat hands in protest. 'Miz Drayton, a gentleman don't wager with a lady.'

'Oh, come on,' Cat Reverie chimed in eagerly. 'In this day and age? Don't you have women's liberation down there in Texas? Go on, bet with her. I want to know what you both guess. Maybe you aren't as good at this as you think.'

Her challenge didn't ruffle Mile. He acceded easily. 'Miz Drayton, if you insist Ah'll wager the princely sum of ten dollars that mah figurin' is righter than yours.'

'Done,' Queenie said without hesitation.

'So tell us,' Cat demanded. 'Start with the actors. Who do you think they are?'

Simon had his face buried in his food. Ginny was smiling unaccountably at Hardhouse. From where I sat, it looked like she was wasting her time. While she spoke, Cat Reverie kept one hand clamped to Hardhouse's thigh. However, everyone else paid close attention to Queenie and Mile.

Everyone except Mac Westward. He paid no attention to anything except his wine.

'No!' Buffy insisted before either Mile or Queenie could answer. 'If you're right, you'll ruin the fun for the rest of us. And if you're wrong, you'll help us eliminate possibilities.

'I'll tell you what. Write your guesses on a piece of paper. Give them to me. When the camp is over, I'll read what you wrote. Then the rest of us can judge who wins the bet.'

I had to give her credit. Sue-Rose Altar knew how to run a mystery camp.

Cat pouted, but both Queenie and Mile accepted Buffy's terms. For the moment, anyway, they kept their faces studiously blank, bluffing each other like mad.

As if he'd been ready for this since the beginning of time, Rock produced a sheaf of paper. He passed a sheet to Queenie, a sheet to Mile. Then he supplied pencils.

Queenie and Mile wrote briefly. She chewed the end of her pencil between names and glanced up and down the table, apparently suppressing a giggle. Mile approached the exercise more laboriously.

When they were done, they both folded their lists and handed them to Buffy. She unfolded the papers and read them solemnly, as if this were a momentous occasion. I waited for the background music to swell, playing the 'suspense' theme from *The Deerskin Lodge Murders*.

She couldn't keep it up, however. When she read Mile's list, she burst out laughing. 'Houston Mile, you should be ashamed of yourself.' But then she put both papers away in her purse.

Mile favoured us with an oleaginous grin, exposing his bad teeth.

I turned towards Cat to catch her reaction.

Apparently she'd already lost interest in guessing games. Instead she leaned towards Hardhouse. Now she had both hands on his leg under the table.

Mac Westward cleared his throat. He was gazing up at the ceiling as if it had a message written on it. After squinting upward for a minute, he read it to us.

'Mystery Camp of Fools. Good title.'

For the first time, Connie Bebb spoke. 'Do you think we could get away with it? It may not be original enough.'

Westward didn't answer. His attention returned to his wine.

Faith and Ama brought the next course – prime rib with sweet potatoes and homemade dressing. Unfortunately the soup was already as much food as I could handle. I tasted enough of the meal to raise my opinion of Faith Jerrick. After that I concentrated on water to keep myself from thinking about wine.

Gradually the conversation became general. Ginny and Sam Drayton began discussing ozone depletion in the troposphere, of all things. Cat was consumed – the perfect word for it – with Joseph Hardhouse. Beside me, Connie dipped at her food like a recent graduate of Miss Manner's school for 'excruciatingly correct behaviour'.

Buffy kindly kept Simon Abel off the conversational streets. At the other end of the table, Maryanne Green worked so hard to strike some kind of spark from Rock that I feared she might do herself an injury. But I could hardly make out what either pair said. That left me with the disturbing prospect of Lara Hardhouse.

Nominally, at any rate, she was talking to Westward. In fact, she'd actually succeeded at getting him to listen to her. He tilted towards her with his elbow propped on the arm of his chair and his chin braced on his palm. While she spoke, he stared abysmally at her food, as if he found it depressing.

She kept her eyes on me, however. Her gaze held an appeal, a need almost strong enough to be called supplication. She might've been asking – begging? – me to rescue her from something.

Whatever it was, it couldn't have been Westward. If she'd left him alone, he might've fallen asleep. But instead she was telling him what she thought was wrong with most mystery novels.

'It's the puzzle,' she explained. 'How did the murderer get into the locked room. Why isn't there any blood. Who could have switched glasses with the victim. It all gets in the way. It's only an intellectual game, like a crossword puzzle – it prevents you from caring about what happens. It's just curiosity, not suspense. Real suspense is emotional, not intellectual. It has to do with liking one of the characters and not knowing whether he'll be the next victim. It has to do with hating the murderer and wanting him to get caught – or liking him and not wanting him to get caught.

'I don't care whether Mr X must've killed her because he's the only one who knows how to remove wine corks with an ice pick. I care that he did it because he was in love with her and couldn't stand seeing her sleep with anyone else.'

There Lara paused as if she were waiting, not for Westward's reaction, but for mine.

I was mildly surprised to see that he did react. Without shifting his stare – or his posture – he mumbled, 'You're right. But you're also wrong.'

Lara and I both gave him time to go on. He didn't. Instead he drank more wine.

'Mac's being cryptic,' Connie announced primly. 'He's had too much to drink.' If Westward felt the effect of her jibe, he didn't show it. 'The subject happens to be one we feel strongly about.'

She didn't raise her naturally soft voice. Nevertheless its firmness took over the table. Everyone stopped talking to hear her. Buffy in particular watched and listened as if she were studying at the feet of a priestess. But even Cat Reverie and Houston Mile stopped whatever they were doing to pay attention.

'Mac means,' Connie said, 'that you're right about intellectual puzzles, but you're wrong about suspense.

'The problem with building a mystery novel on an intellectual puzzle is the implicit assumption that anyone is capable of anything. This is debatable in itself, but the puzzle goes one step further. It implies that everyone is *equally* capable of anything. Therefore the only way to distinguish between equal possibilities is to focus on *how* the crime was committed rather than on *why*.

'But surely this is nonsense. Everyone is *not* equally capable of anything.

'If we reject that assumption, the "mystery" becomes, who *is* capable of this particular crime? Which one of the characters has the capacity for it? But even if we accept that anyone is capable of anything, we still have to recognize that different people – being different, *unequal* – require different kinds of stress to bring out their latent capabilities. The "mystery" becomes, what kind of stress would make a given individual capable of this particular crime? Is that kind of stress present?'

Buffy was too excited to sit still. 'But surely,' she said, unconsciously echoing Connie, 'one of the capabilities you're talking about is the ability to commit the crime in a way that will conceal or confuse who did it. That's an intellectual ability. Whether a murderer gets caught doesn't depend on what kind of person he is. It depends on how smart he is.'

Constance Bebb, however, was at least one half of Thornton Foal, the famous novelist. She didn't suffer interruption gladly. In an austere tone, she replied, 'We wouldn't be interested in these crimes if they weren't committed by people who were smart or desperate or unscrupulous enough to try to avoid the consequences of their own actions.

'Nevertheless the true function of the mystery novel is not to construct the physical or intellectual puzzles you complain about, Mrs Hardhouse' – Connie didn't pretend that she wasn't snubbing Buffy – 'but rather to search and analyse character, to probe emotional puzzles, to define the resources and restrictions which make one individual incontestably him – or herself and no one else. The true detective identifies "who did it" by understanding that only one unique person could have committed this particular crime under these particular conditions of stress.'

By then Cat had apparently had all the edification she could tolerate. As Faith and Ama began to clear the plates, she announced brusquely, 'I want some port. Do you have any port?'

But Connie was determined to finish her speech. While Faith returned to the kitchen, Connie went on talking.

'So you see, the suspense of the novel does rest on a puzzle. But it is an emotional puzzle, a psychological puzzle. And the better the construction of the puzzle, the more suspense it generates. Why do you like a certain character? Why do you care what happens to him or her? Is it because you understand them, or because you don't? Is it because you believe they are capable of the crime, or because you believe they are not? And how accurate are your beliefs? The best mystery novels – like the best crimes – search and analyse the reader, the observer, by the very process of searching and analysing the participants. Ultimately the suspense of the story arises from the fact that we ourselves are being tested by it.'

When she finished, Mac Westward raised his glass like a salute and drank a silent toast to his collaborator.

I couldn't help myself. She made me look at her in a new way. Softly I murmured, 'You're starting to make me wish I'd read more mystery novels.'

486

'You should,' she replied like a stern aunt. 'There is no more profound question than the question of murder.'

I doubted that. From my perspective, the question of suicide went deeper. I didn't have too much trouble thinking about what made people decide to kill each other – or not. But self-murder was more like alcoholism. It was fascinating, almost compulsory, but I couldn't get my mind around it.

On the other hand, I had no intention whatsoever of mentioning a subject like that in front of a group like this.

In any case, I didn't get the chance. 'You're very persuasive, Ms Bebb,' Hardhouse put in with an amiable chuckle, 'but I think that last assertion was a little too sweeping.

'Murder is only murder – you want somebody dead, so you do something about it. We all feel that way sometimes. And, as you say, under the right provocation we'd all act on it. A man comes home from work and finds his wife in bed with another man, so he shoots them both. We can all sympathize. But there's no mystery in it. It doesn't really "search" us.

'I think Buffy is right. What makes a murder interesting – what makes it profound – is the desire to conceal it. To *benefit* from it. Crimes of passion are just that, passionate, emotional. They don't mean anything except that one person got upset, so another person ended up dead. Deliberate, premeditated, *concealed* crimes, on the other hand' – he smiled like the blade of a table saw – 'have interesting implications.'

They sure did – at least from my point of view. Especially if you were the intended victim. But I kept my mouth shut. Now was no time to mention el Señor. And I was busy watching Ginny.

Her eyes practically glowed at Hardhouse. She seemed to find him more desirable by the minute. When she spoke, she sounded like she was challenging him – but she didn't look that way.

'Does this have something to do with your theory about why people kill each other?'

He flashed an avid smile at her. 'I can see,' he admitted, 'it was a mistake to bring that up. I've made myself more obvious than I realized. If you want to play fair,' he added humorously, 'you should try to forget I said any of this.'

Right.

Several of the guests may've wanted to pursue the subject, but at that moment the port arrived. Faith set an elaborate crystal decanter down in front of Cat, and Hardhouse immediately busied himself filling her glass. Then he offered port to the rest of the table. By the time everyone had turned him down, new conversations were underway.

I had to do something about the way I felt before it got out of hand. Also I couldn't stomach the sweet sick smell of port. More by luck than skill, I managed to catch Ginny's eye. After that I stood up and excused myself.

Queenie looked at me mischievously. 'Do you play bridge, Brew? If this were a Christie novel, we'd all spend the rest of the evening playing bridge. We need some way to pretend we don't know one of us is going to be killed.'

If she'd asked me that earlier, I might've said yes. Any excuse to spend some time in her company. But now I was too strung out.

'Sorry,' I said – and tried not to wince at the sound of loss in my voice. 'I only play bridge when I drink.'

Walking roughly to hurt my guts – I needed the distraction – I went to my room.

Ginny took for ever to arrive. At least twenty minutes. She'd left my pills and vitamins on an especially delicate end table. I considered flushing them down the toilet. I considered smashing the end table. Finally I took some of whatever was in the bottles. Maybe if I tried to stay healthy, she'd give me another chance.

When she knocked, I told her to come in. She stuck her head past the door, but didn't accept my invitation. 'I'm going to go corner Rock and Buffy,' she said in a vaguely impersonal tone. 'You want to come? Don't if you're too tired. I can handle it.'

I beckoned her in. 'That's what I want to talk to you about,' I lied. I needed some way to insist, and this was as good as any. 'I've already cornered Rock.'

'Oh?' At least I had her attention now. She moved into the room and closed the door behind her. Her claw resembled a surgical implement in the lamplight. 'How did that come about?'

I was sitting on the bed. In a better world, I would've faced her standing, but I didn't trust my legs to hold me. In a far better world, I would've met her gaze.

'After you went on that walk' – I did my best to sound non-committal – 'he came looking for us.'

I paused. After a moment Ginny asked, 'What did he want?'

'Apparently the owners of the lodge told Reeson not to lock up the guns.' I had a talent for reporting conversations, so I repeated what Altar had said almost word for word.

She didn't like it, but she didn't get mad. Frowning hard, she muttered, 'Well, I can't say I'm surprised. Just disgusted. Common sense must be an anti-survival trait. If too many people had it, we'd collapse from over-population.' Then she asked, 'What did you tell him?'

I was tempted – just tempted – to get mad myself. If she cared about stuff like that, she shouldn't have left me to talk to him alone. But that would just give her an excuse to turn her back and walk out. Which was about the last thing I wanted.

So I said, 'I told him we'd let the matter drop.'

She nodded slowly. 'That's probably what I would've done. Approximately. I don't want to get fired. I can't risk going back to town with you in this condition.'

My condition. No question about it, I was really starting to hate my condition.

I could tell she wanted to leave, but the expression on my face must've stopped her. Looking at me a little harder, she asked, 'Was there something else we need to talk about?'

Something else? Surely you jest. What else could there be? El Señor wants me dead, and Lawrence Smithsonian went out of his way to get us this job, and I'm losing you. I've got a hole inside me you could drive a truck through. No, there's nothing else we need to talk about.

'Brew?' Her tone betrayed her concern. I still had the capacity to worry her. 'What's going on?'

I had to do better than this. Too much was at stake.

Touching the bed with my palms, I said almost like I wasn't begging, 'Stay with me tonight.'

Her eyebrows went up. Her eyes flicked to the bed, then back to my face. 'You just got out of the hospital,' she observed with studious neutrality. 'Are you that well?'

I shook my head. The truth, Axbrewder. Tell her the truth. Just this once.

'I'm that lonely.'

She moved closer, leaning over me so that I had to look straight into her eyes. For a long moment her grey gaze seemed to search me all the way to the back of my brain. Instinctively I held my breath. She didn't smile or glare or do anything else to reveal what she felt.

Abruptly she pulled away and went back to the door. As if it were the last thing she would ever say to me, she replied, 'God loves you. Sit on your hands.'

Then she left.

It's an old joke. This guy takes a girl he doesn't like to the prom.

She's miserable, she wants romance. Trying to get him to be nice to her, she complains, Nobody loves me, and my hands are cold. He says, God loves you, sit on your hands.

In other words, Take care of yourself. For a change.

I couldn't stay awake. One advantage of convalescence. Since I had nothing better to do, I went to bed.

Chapter Seven

When I got up the next morning – later than usual for me – there didn't seem to be any victims. Not yet, anyway. No strangled hilarious screams during the night. No blue marbles reported anywhere. As Buffy had promised. I didn't exactly distrust her – but I didn't exactly trust her, either. Or Deerskin Lodge. Or Murder On Cue, Inc. Just to be sure, I checked the roll.

Listening shamelessly outside one of the bedrooms, I heard Houston Mile and Maryanne Green giggling. At least he was giggling. She may've been whimpering.

Sam and Queenie Drayton were on their way to their room as if they wanted to do some giggling of their own.

Off to one corner of the den, Rock and Westward sat smoking cigars at each other, engaged in a silent fumigation contest.

Near one of the fireplaces, Buffy, Connie, Simon, and Ginny – of all people – sat at a card table, apparently playing canasta. I hadn't realized that Ginny knew how to play canasta. In fact, I hadn't realized that she knew how to hold cards with her claw. But she did both without any obvious strain.

That left Joseph and Lara Hardhouse unaccounted for. And Cat Reverie. Maybe they were still asleep.

My stomach hurt almost as bad as my soul, and anyway I hate the whole world until I've had some coffee. Ignoring various greetings, I shambled towards the kitchen in search of caffeine.

In the dining room I found a breakfast buffet, complete with sweet rolls, scrambled eggs congealing over a can of sterno, orange juice, and – yes – coffee.

I also found Lara. She sat at the table, pushing her food back and forth on her plate.

Just my luck. The perfect breakfast companion. I had to admit that she looked as beautiful as ever, but the darkness in her eyes announced a restless night as plainly as a billboard. Whatever ate at her had become hungrier.

I wasn't what you could call grateful that she'd kept me away from the wine at dinner. Frightened was more like it. Something about the nature of her attention scared me.

Hoping she'd leave me alone, I poured myself some coffee. But as soon as she realized that I didn't mean to say anything, she started to talk.

'That was a brave thing you did last night.' Her voice was like a caress. 'Ginny doesn't treat you very well. It would have been easy to have a few drinks, to drown your sorrows.' She made the cliché sound more poignant than I would've believed possible. 'I admire courage like yours.'

Involuntarily I stared at her. Courage? Are you kidding?

Slowly she turned her coffee cup around and around in its saucer, but her eyes ignored her hands. 'I wonder,' she murmured, 'if you realize how attractive your courage makes you. Some women believe a perfect body and a healthy libido are what they want in a man, but I like courage' – she moistened her lips – 'and pain. They give me hope.'

I faced her with my mouth practically hanging open. No question about it, she was too many for me. There was more going on here than I could guess. And my famous intuition didn't come to my rescue. It needed caffeine, just like I did.

Fortunately we were interrupted. Hardhouse and Cat Reverie came into the dining room, so absorbed in each other that they actually held hands.

When they saw Lara, neither of them blushed. Neither of them even had the grace to look flustered. They let go of each other, however – that was something. With an empty laugh, Cat headed for the coffee pot. Hardhouse faced his wife as if the lines of his pugnacious features and the slickness of his hair held a message only she could read.

The way I felt about Joseph Hardhouse had one advantage. Seeing him had the effect of kick-starting my brain. All of a sudden, the sheer shamelessness of his attitude, and Cat's, seemed too blatant to be real. I recovered my ability to jump to conclusions.

'Don't tell me. Let me guess,' I said almost pleasantly. 'You actors have all the fun. Tonight you'll switch partners and go through the same charade again. Is this Buffy's idea of a murder scenario?'

In unison, like they'd been practising it for weeks, Hardhouse, Lara, and Cat turned to gape at me.

Then Lara protested, 'Oh, Brew! How could you think–?' Her voice was practically a moan. Turning her face away, she blundered up from the table and fled the room.

Cat broke into a smile that made my skin crawl.

Hardhouse took a step towards me. His eyes looked as hard as his jaw, his forehead. With the index finger of his right hand, he tapped me gently over the heart. 'Nobody here is an actor,' he articulated. 'I play for blood, not sport.'

Cat aimed her smile at him as if she understood.

'But even if we're all actors,' he continued, 'it's no business of yours. You have your own wounds, and they're about as much as you can handle. You don't need any more trouble.'

I had to say something, so I rasped, 'Actually, trouble is what I'm best at. Wounds just sharpen my concentration.'

Listen to me, Hardhouse. Don't mess with Ginny.

I waited until he dropped his hand. Then I took my coffee out to the kitchen.

I didn't have any particular reason to be there. I just needed to leave the dining room – and I didn't want to face Ginny in the den. For the first time, it occurred to me that I wasn't the only one who stood to get hurt in this situation. Axbrewder at his unselfish finest. If Ginny was attracted to Hardhouse, so attracted that she couldn't stay away, he might do her real damage. She might end up looking at me the way his wife did.

On the other hand, she wasn't what you could call helpless. If he wanted to mess with her, he might wake up one morning with a stainless steel prosthetic device installed in his chest.

He was right about one thing, anyway. It was none of my business. Even though the thought of them together made me want to scream my heart out.

Thinking about Ginny reminded me of my pills. They hadn't done me any good last night, so I decided to ignore them. Instead I started on the coffee.

The kitchen was deserted. Faith Jerrick must've been busy elsewhere. For a second I thought I caught a faint whiff of gas. Maybe Reeson wasn't done working on the stove. Maybe he just hadn't done a very good job. Or maybe I was wrong. The smell faded when I tried to verify it.

After a while I noticed a hard rhythmic thunking sound in the distance. It seemed to come from outside the lodge.

Sipping my coffee, I wandered over to one of the windows.

The day was overcast, and it looked cold. Wind fussed through the branches of the evergreens like it was in a bad mood. Apparently the snowstorm Buffy had promised us was on its way.

Not far from the cottages and the rear of the kitchen, Art Reeson stood chopping firewood.

He was good at it. The axe rose and fell like an extension of his arms. He didn't put any apparent effort into it, but chips flew from every cut. The logs almost seemed to fall into sections by themselves. He'd taken his jacket and shirt off, despite the cold, and his back steamed delicately.

Well, if he could stand the weather, so could I. My coat was back in my room, but I had on a heavy sweater to conceal the bulk of my bandages. After I finished my coffee, I limped out through the kitchen and down the steps.

I didn't have anything particular in mind. He and I could discuss the guns again, but that was just an excuse. All I really wanted was to get away from Murder On Cue for a while.

He saw me coming and stopped. The overcast sky made his black hair and dark skin look less stark, more natural – more like a way of blending into the generalized grey. If the clouds got any thicker, he might be completely invisible. Maybe night was his natural element. He scowled at me, but he didn't seem angry. For all I knew, that scowl was his version of a smile.

'What's the matter, Mr Axbrewder?' he asked. His voice still sounded like it'd been hoarse for years. 'You walk funny.'

I scowled back. Two could play that game. 'Old war wound.'

He looked me up and down. Then he shrugged. 'You're a bad liar.' It was definitely possible that his scowl was a way of smiling. Or of concealing a smile.

'Really?' I drawled. 'Most people think I'm pretty good.'

'Most people,' he pronounced with the same assurance he had when he swung his axe, 'don't know anything about liars.'

'And you do?'

'We're all liars, Mr Axbrewder. Most people don't know anything about themselves.'

'And you do, Mr Reeson?' I repeated.

Now he smiled. If his scowl was a smile, his smile must've been a glare of anger. 'Call me Art. We don't really need all this firewood. But

494

I didn't have anything better to do this morning. Faith and the Carbones do all the real work around here. Come have a cup of coffee with me.'

I gave him a grimace, just to remind him that he hadn't answered my question, but I didn't hesitate. 'Sure.' The cold was worse than I'd expected. I'd already started to shiver.

'Good.' He sank his axe into the stump he used for a splitting-block. From a tree branch nearby, he retrieved his shirt and wool jacket. While he pushed his arms into the sleeves of his shirt, he led me towards one of the cottages.

Smoke gusted from its chimney and a Land Rover sat out front. Ama and Truchi Carbone probably lived next door – that house was obviously occupied as well. So where did Faith Jerrick live?

I learned the answer as soon as Reeson took me inside. She lived with him. We found her in the immaculate little living room, sorting laundry. Her method for folding towels and sheets made them look starched and ironed, permanently creased, and her stacks were as precise as the arrangement of the furniture, as clean as the floorboards and walls and curtains. If she'd met my gaze – just once – I might've considered her the ideal woman. My whole life, I've wanted to meet a woman as tidy as I am. And she had profound eyes.

But she didn't meet my gaze. She didn't look at Reeson either. She glanced up when we came in, but she didn't actually appear to focus on us.

'I offered Mr Axbrewder a cup of coffee.' Reeson's tone eased in her presence. 'He's going to tell me about an old war wound.' If he was laughing at me, it didn't show.

'Call me Brew,' I put in. Then, rather awkwardly, I added, 'Don't go to any trouble.'

I said that because her reserve made me uncomfortable. As if I were intruding somehow.

But apparently she didn't mind the intrusion. Setting her laundry aside, she said, 'Please sit down, Mr Axbrewder. You're welcome here, in God's name.'

Still without actually facing either of us, she left the room. Through the doorway, I heard her making kitchen noises.

I raised my eyebrows at Reeson. '"In God's name"?'

His shrug didn't commit him to anything. 'She's religious,' he murmured. 'More than religious. Ecstatic. God talks to her. She prophesies. Some time ago, I guess she decided I agree with her. I used

495

to try to argue with her, but now I leave her alone. Let her think what she wants about me.

'She's a good woman.' Which sounded like an odd thing to say in that non-committal fashion. 'We all have our ghouls and beasties, Axbrewder. And we all have ways to keep them at bay. Religion is hers, that's all.'

And mine was alcohol, I suppose. Which explained why I was in such bad shape without it.

'What's yours?' I asked.

He smiled again. 'I try not to let people lie to me. I get scared when I think I'm not hearing the truth.'

That wasn't quite what I expected to hear. I thought he would make some reference to guns.

'Your "old war wound", for instance,' he continued. 'I get nervous when I hear things like that.'

I was developing a distinct preference for his scowl.

On the other hand, he didn't have any obvious weaponry nearby. Maybe he could've hidden a derringer in one of the seat cushions, but I doubted it.

We were still on our feet. For some reason I wanted to stay that way, so I forced myself to sit down. 'What difference does it make?'

He sat down too. Like his axe-work, all his movements were natural, relaxed. 'I'm the manager here.' His voice stayed husky. 'I'm responsible for what happens. You and Fistoulari are security for Murder On Cue. I can understand why you wanted the collection locked away. What I can't understand is why somebody who can hardly walk takes on a job like this.

'The Altars would hire a blind man if he helped jazz up their mysteries.' Reeson clearly had no great opinion of Buffy and Rock. 'But why do you want the job? If anything goes wrong, you'll be useless. That makes me think you're playing some other kind of game. It makes me nervous. Tell me about your "old war wound", Axbrewder.'

Faith came back into the room, carrying a tray with two melmac mugs, a creamer and sugar bowl, and a steaming pot. 'Mr Axbrewder.' She offered me a mug. I declined cream and sugar. 'Art.' He took a mug and a bit of sugar. She put the tray down, then poured coffee for both of us. After that she went to stand behind his chair. Still not quite looking at me, she rested her fingertips on his shoulders.

He reached up gently to stroke her fingers, but he kept his attention on me.

'I got shot,' I said bluntly. 'About a week ago.'

496

'Guns,' Faith breathed. Just for a second I received the full depth of her gaze. Then she slipped out of focus again. 'They are evil, and all things done with them. God is love. He has no use for guns.'

Which probably explained why Reeson didn't have any in sight.

But he wasn't deflected. His scowl intensified. 'Who shot you?'

Again I asked, 'What difference does it make?'

'You were shot' – in spite of its hoarseness, his voice had force – 'but you're still alive. Maybe you're on the run. Maybe you're hiding out here. Maybe whoever shot you is coming after you.'

That was a little too shrewd for my taste. I didn't mind sitting in his living room sparring with him about how grown men keep the ghouls and beasties at bay, but I didn't like where this conversation was going.

'He isn't,' I said with a grin of my own, as humourless and bloody as I could make it. 'I broke his neck.'

Take that and be warned.

Distinctly Faith said, 'I will pray for your immortal soul, Mr Axbrewder.'

I wanted to laugh out loud. Humourless and bloody with a vengeance. 'Pray for *his*, Ms Jerrick. Three other people might've died if I hadn't gotten him first.' Ginny among them. 'He was a professional killer, and I couldn't stop him any other way.'

Gravely she replied, 'I pray for all who are lost to the Lord.'

By this time Reeson's scowl looked positively joyous. 'You must be made of iron, Axbrewder. But you still haven't told me why you took on a job like this when you can hardly walk.'

I took a slug of coffee to hide my bitterness. It was still hot enough to scald my tongue. 'I'm not on a job like this. Ginny is. Murder On Cue only needs one of us. I'm just here so that she can make sure I take my pills while I recuperate.'

I'm a better liar than he thought. This time he believed me. Or he acted like he did, anyway. Abruptly he slapped his thighs and rose to his feet, as smooth as a piston. But when I started to get up, he stopped me. 'Axbrewder, I sympathize. Let me know if there's anything I can do to make it easier. Those people over there' – he meant the guests – 'would drive me crazy. They're all spinning lies as fast as they can. That's the whole point of these mystery camps. Give them a chance to practise their illusions. Come over here any time you feel the need to get away. We'll do our best to tell each other the truth. You two stay and talk to each other. I need a shower.'

Scowling heavily, he kissed Faith.

Maybe she was as religious as she sounded. Maybe she spent so much time communing with God she didn't need to look anyone else in the eye. But there was nothing spiritual about the way she kissed Reeson back. Her whole body concentrated on it.

Fascinating. She may've been the perfect woman after all. But I didn't let that distract me. 'Before you go, Reeson,' I put in, 'answer a question for me. Do you know who did security for Murder On Cue the last time they were here?'

His eyebrows did a little jump on his forehead, but he hardly hesitated. 'Sure. I don't remember the guy's name, but I remember who he worked for. Until now, they did all the security for the Altars. Lawrence Smithsonian and Associates. Do you need to know who specifically? I could look it up.'

'No. I'm just curious. Do you happen to know why he didn't object to those guns?'

'I told you. The Altars would hire a blind man if they thought he'd add to the fun. That guy was just f–' he glanced at Faith sharply, caught himself, 'just kidding around. The life of the party. For him it was a vacation. You and Fistoulari are the first security they've had who take the job seriously.'

'Thanks.' I was done, so I let him go.

When he left the room, Faith moved to sit in the chair he'd vacated. Apparently she'd taken his suggestion as a commandment. But she didn't offer me any small talk.

Studying her made me rethink my position. Maybe I didn't really like perfection. Ten minutes with a woman who never looked me in the eye, and I'd spend the rest of my life drunk.

Since Faith refused to look at me straight, I didn't have anything to restrain me, so I asked one of my less tactful questions. 'You're a devout woman, Ms Jerrick,' and you sure as hell know how to kiss, 'but you aren't married. Why do you live with Art?'

Maybe she didn't look at people, but she sure as hell heard what they said. From her scalp to the skin of her arms, she blushed. She was so pale normally that I hadn't realized she had so much blood in her.

Nevertheless she didn't evade the issue. 'Art and I are married in the sight of God,' she answered firmly.

Her assertion was open, as they say, to more than one interpretation. A cynic could've had a field day with it. Unfortunately – or fortunately, depending on your point of view – it doesn't take much to make me ashamed of myself. Her blush was enough. Back-pedalling furiously, I said, 'I'm the kind of man who jumps to conclusions. Right now, I'm jumping to the conclusion that he's the reason you work here.

Wouldn't you rather live closer to your church – closer to people you can worship with?'

That put her on more secure ground. 'Mr Axbrewder, I don't choose my life.' As fast as it came, the red faded from her skin. 'Choosing belongs to the Lord. It is in His hands. My task is not to choose, but to serve. It is a wife's responsibility and joy to serve her husband, just as it is the soul's responsibility and joy to serve God. Art lives here. He works here. What else would you have me do?'

'Don't you get lonely?'

'Lonely?' She seemed genuinely surprised. 'How could I be lonely? Art is with me. The Lord is with me in all things, rising and sleeping.' Her tone began to hint at the ecstasy Reeson had mentioned. 'My soul is a guest at God's great feast. Only the lost are lonely, Mr Axbrewder.'

Damn her, anyway. She was right. Only the lost are lonely. But I didn't enjoy hearing it from her. I was more than a bit lonely myself.

My back-pedalling had become a rout. The Lord had made her mighty against His enemies. Mostly trying to cover up my disarray while I looked for an escape, I asked, 'What about Art? Why does he work here? He seems like a man' – as soon as I said this, I realized that it was true – 'who could do anything he wanted.'

The lines of her face gave me the impression that she was mildly disappointed. She didn't want to answer practical questions, she wanted opportunities to witness for the Lord. But apparently her concept of service included answering practical questions.

'He likes the isolation. He likes the balance between office work and physical exertion. And his job is very flexible, Mr Axbrewder. He sets his own hours, he works when he chooses, he takes vacations whenever the mood strikes him. The owners trust him completely.' She was proud of this. 'They leave the lodge entirely in his hands.'

What, entirely? Something about that sounded wrong to me. 'But surely he checks in with them on a regular basis? He calls them when decisions need to be made?'

He called them about the guns?

'How should I know?' She was serene in her ignorance. 'It's not my place to watch how he serves his employers. But why should he call? He has worked here for years, he has proven his faithfulness. Good service is rewarded with trust.'

You mean he *didn't* call about the guns?

No, I was wrong, I had no business jumping to a conclusion like that. Under Faith Jerrick's influence, my intuitive instincts were starting to blow fuses. Or maybe in some obscure way I was being seduced.

'Speaking of good service, I'd better go see how my partner is doing.' I reached my feet with an ungainly heave. 'Like Art, she doesn't really need anyone to check on her. But when I don't do it, I feel like I'm goofing off.'

Faith stood up gracefully, gave me a polite nod. I left in a hurry.

Outside, the wind slapped my face, and the cold jolted into my lungs. Which had the effect of restoring my rationality. Very therapeutic. The weather was deteriorating. Clouds heavy with snow boiled across the tree-tops. Dimness filled the air like dusk. If I stayed out here long enough, I might recover active sanity. Or freeze to death.

Or maybe they came to the same thing.

In the mean time, however, I didn't know what to do with what I was thinking. Reeson never called the owners about the guns? That made no sense. He'd been the manager here – the *trusted* manager – for years. No matter how much he liked guns, he knew how to be responsible. And Faith loved him – Faith, who hated guns. I was losing touch with reality, no question about it.

And yet I couldn't stop wondering if he really was a man who used telling the truth to keep the ghouls and beasties away.

Chapter Eight

My sweater didn't protect me from the cold. You'd think all those bandages would be good for insulation, but they weren't. My guts felt like they were being gnawed on by wind and chill. Unsteady as a drunk, I shambled back to the lodge.

Through the kitchen to the dining room. Not a Hardhouse in sight, blessed be the Name of the Lord. On general principles, I stayed there long enough to eat a piece of dry toast. I needed time to get warm. Also time to brace myself to face the crew in the den.

Ama Carbone went through the room, carrying an armload of sheets and towels to the laundry. Like Faith, she kept busy trying to make the world clean.

I should've helped her. Laundry is something I understand.

Instead I braved the den.

Murder On Cue's guests had rearranged themselves in my absence. The canasta game was finished. Apparently the Hardhouses had gone to ground somewhere. So had Ginny. Which I took as a bad sign. But what the hell, in my condition I took everything as a bad sign. Houston Mile, Maryanne Green, and Cat had joined the rest of the group. Rock and Westward had given up their smoking contest.

Mile was telling a story. Everybody else listened.

He stood beside one of the fireplaces, leaning a pudgy arm on the mantel in the relaxed shit-kicker pose of a good ol' boy raconteur – what my brother used to call a 'raccoon-tuner'. His timing was good, I had to admit that. I hadn't heard the first half of his story, but everything he said sounded by-God funny, and most of his audience laughed harder and harder as he went along. It had something to do with a half-naked girl and a hoe – a hoe-er. A whore, get it?

Hearing his story promised to be more fun than I could stomach, so I headed for my room.

As I left, I saw him glare in my direction. He didn't like it when people walked out while he was the centre of attention.

Well, good. Now I knew how to insult him. If I ever needed it.

After that, however, my luck improved. In the hall outside my room I met Queenie Drayton. Without Sam.

'Hello, Brew.' Her voice might as well have been music.

Involuntarily I stopped in front of her. Or maybe we stopped in front of each other.

'Sam,' she explained in a tone of affectionate disgust, 'has a talent for falling asleep at the most awkward times. It comes with being a doctor, I suppose.'

I couldn't tell whether it was all that life in her eyes or the way her breasts stroked the inside of her flannel shirt that made me want to propose marriage.

'What's everyone else doing?' she finished. 'Is anything going on?'

I hadn't had a crush this bad since high school. Maybe I should've been embarrassed. But she didn't seem to need it. I muttered something incoherent about Houston Mile and stories. Then I pulled myself together.

'Come to my room,' I suggested. 'I'd like to talk to you.' Lamely I added, 'And you'll miss the punch line.'

Laughter carried down the hall. She cocked her head to it for a moment – which reminded me that she liked to laugh herself. Then she gave me a smile like a gift.

'I think I should warn you, Brew. When a man invites me to his room, he almost always ends up telling me the story of his life.'

I snorted to disguise my pleasure. 'I'll try not to be that boring.'

Before she could change her mind, I steered her to my door.

Amalia had already cleaned my room. The bed was made, and I had fresh towels. Like Faith, she got her job done.

I ushered Queenie inside, closed the door, seated her in one of the chairs, settled my bulk on the bed. Quickly, so that I wouldn't lose the opportunity, I said, 'Tell me something. How did a real honest-to-God, human person like yourself come by a name like Queenie?'

She responded with a chuckle deep in her throat. 'You're trying to turn the tables on me.'

'Sure,' I admitted. 'Why not? I already know the story of *my* life. Believe me, you can live without it.'

'But you can't live without mine.' She was teasing me.

I made an effort to match her. 'It's all I have left.'

Unfortunately that almost came out like I meant it. My interest was genuine, but I didn't want to sound pitiful about it.

Her eyes never shifted from my face – a stunning contrast to Faith Jerrick. In her gaze I seemed to see shadows pass across the background of her mind, hints of understanding, glimpses of empathy. At the same time she went on trying to heal me with the warmth of her smile.

'Well, for one thing,' she said, 'it's not a nickname. It's my real name. I wish I could say it's a family tradition. I used to tell people that in college, when I was feeling especially self-conscious. "My mother's name was Princess, so I'm Queenie." But you know, in a funny way that's almost the truth.

'It was my father's idea. Princess was his pet name for my mother. They had a houseful of sons, and when I finally came along he was so delighted he lost his common sense. I guess he always wanted a daughter. And he doted on my mother. He thought she hung the moon.

'My mother tried to warn him. Queenie isn't the kind of name you give a child if you want her to have a comfortable social life. But I guess he couldn't imagine the whole world wouldn't feel the same way he did about me.'

I concentrated on her like a puppy. When she stopped, I murmured, 'They loved you. They loved you down to the ground.'

She chuckled again. 'It wasn't fair, really. They gave me a terrible handicap with my peers. At least when I was a teenager. I don't mean the name. They deprived me of the definitive adolescent experience – thinking my parents didn't love me. Believing they didn't understand me.

'I could hardly talk to my friends for years. We didn't have anything in common. Their parents were all mean and hateful and petty – just like the parents of teenagers are supposed to be. Sometimes,' she concluded happily, 'I felt so left out I could hardly stand it.'

'Poor you,' I agreed. 'You've suffered awfully.'

'Does it show?'

'I'm afraid so.' If she kept this up, I might start feeling better – and then I'd be in real trouble.

She pursed her lips. Which made me think about kissing her. With just a hint of seriousness, she said, 'Maybe that's why men tell me the stories of their lives. They're all so unhappy, and they know I'm a kindred spirit.'

'No.' The temptation to be serious was more than I could bear. 'It's because you're real and happy, and you've got room in your heart for the things you hear.'

Also because she was profoundly beautiful. Not pretty or glamorous – something more. But I didn't let myself say that.

She went on gazing into my eyes, the lines of her expression as clear as words. They said, I've got room for you, too. If you want to talk.

Which was exactly *not* what I wanted.

'So tell me,' I said, changing subjects with all the delicacy of a bulldozer, 'what names did you write down for Buffy?'

Just for a second, Queenie looked startled. She probably thought she knew what this conversation was about, and I took her by surprise. In a musing tone she said, 'Brew, there's more to you than meets the eye.'

I shrugged. 'That's the bandages. If I took them off, you could see everything.'

With an odd air of chagrin, she caught her lower lip between her teeth, held it. But she never looked away, never flinched. 'In other words,' she murmured slowly, 'the truth about you is in the wound. Not in the man who was wounded.

'I don't think Buffy wants us to talk about our guesses.' She didn't miss a beat. If I needed the subject changed, it was changed. 'She'd love it if we were wrong. But she doesn't want to take the chance we might be right. She wants us to work it all out for ourselves. Alone.'

Too true. On the other hand, I didn't give a flying fuck at the moon what Sue-Rose 'Buffy' Altar wanted. Except she was my client, so I had to make at least a token effort to keep my job. 'I'll make it easier,' I responded. 'Just tell me who the actors are.'

'Why does it matter?' she countered. Doing a little probing of her own. After all, she loved mysteries.

'Come off it, Queenie,' I retorted. 'You know why it matters.'

By which I intended her to think I meant, You know I'm a private investigator. What I really meant, however, was, It matters because of Ginny. I need the truth about Joseph Hardhouse.

'All right.' Her smile took on a suggestion of glee. 'I think the actors are Houston and Maryanne.'

I couldn't keep my face from twitching. 'Why them?'

She didn't hesitate. 'I don't think he deserves his reputation as the resident hotshot. He isn't that bright. And he's too slimy to live. Do you know, he actually tried to put his hand up my dress at dinner last night? He's got to be faking it. Or else he doesn't like his "little filly" as much as he claims.

'As for her – if she isn't an actress, she'll set women's liberation back fifty years. No self-respecting woman would treat that man that way unless she was acting.'

Well, I had to agree. No self-respecting woman would. The key word, however, was 'self-respecting'. Maryanne was acting, all right. But it wasn't because Buffy paid her.

'Thanks,' I said, lying through my teeth, 'that helps.'

'In other words,' she observed acutely, 'you don't believe me. You think Houston Mile really is as slimy as he seems.'

Considering the noises I'd heard from Mile's bedroom this morning, I replied, 'No. I think he's even slimier.'

Queenie studied this idea. 'And Maryanne puts up with it. She *feeds* it.' She shivered. 'That's disgusting.'

Almost at once, however, she recovered her good humour. 'OK. I can live with that.' She didn't mind being contradicted. She was playing a game she enjoyed. 'I've been wrong before. Now it's your turn. Who do *you* think the actors are?'

I shrugged again. 'Joseph and Lara Hardhouse?'

Her eyes widened. She closed her mouth. Then she actually looked away from me, *looked away*. She was like me, too good at jumping to conclusions. And this time she'd jumped to a conclusion full of pain.

'Brew,' she said softly, as if she wanted to warn me or comfort me somehow, 'I can only tell you one thing about Joseph. He isn't acting. That isn't an act.'

Oh, good. Just what I wanted to hear.

'So what you're saying is' – when her gaze came back to me, I looked away, I couldn't face her honesty any more – 'I might as well kiss Ginny goodbye.'

Since I wasn't looking, I didn't see Queenie get to her feet. The next thing I knew, she stood at the door. But she paused with her hand on the doorknob.

Carefully she said, 'Talk to Sam.'

I glared at her. 'Why?'

Her smile was another gift, better than the last one. 'Because he's worth talking to.'

A beat or two later, she added, 'Don't forget, you still owe me the story of your life.'

She didn't wait around for my reaction. Shutting the door gently behind her, she walked off.

I needed a drink, I told myself. I needed to get drunk. But I didn't believe it. Somehow alcohol had lost its allure. What I really needed was to punch someone's lights out. Break a few bones. Rearrange the world I lived in.

After a while I began to think that even Mile's stories would be an improvement over my own company, so I followed Queenie out of the room.

The hallway was turning into a great place to meet people, make new friends, have interesting conversations. Before I'd taken two steps, Simon Abel appeared.

'Brew,' he asked immediately, 'have you got a minute? I'd like to talk to you.'

Unless I was going deaf in my old age, he sounded anxious about something.

Well, talking to people was my job, whether I understood what they had in mind or not. On top of that – as soon as I heard his tone, I realized that I wanted something from him.

'Sure,' I said, 'I've got minutes coming out my ears,' and led the way back into my room. He knew Cat Reverie better than anyone else here. That made him a potential source of information about Joseph Hardhouse.

I offered him a chair, but he shook his head – he was too tense to sit. I, on the other hand, needed more rest. Even though I was in the mood for violence, all this exertion wore me out. I lowered my pain on to the bed again.

He shoved his hands into his pockets, took them out again. Looked around the room. His soft features worked to assume a shape that didn't fit them. On a hunch, I decided not to give him too much help. He conveyed the impression he was just a kid, despite his chronological age – and kids usually aren't good liars. Unless you help them.

'Brew,' he announced after a certain amount of obvious dithering, 'I owe you an apology.'

'Huh,' I replied intelligently.

'I was wrong last night. Before dinner. I shouldn't have jumped on you like that.'

'Huh,' I said again.

'Cat isn't your problem,' he explained. 'It isn't your fault she likes to flirt.'

Fixing him with my best blank stare, I asked, 'You call that flirting?'

'Oh, yes.' Once he got started, he was in a hurry to have his say. 'I know she talks like she wants to screw every man she's ever met who isn't dead between the legs. And when you look like she does, you don't have any trouble getting a response. But she doesn't mean it.'

I had trouble keeping my stare blank. Who did he think he was kidding?

'It's like a knee-jerk reaction with her,' he continued. 'She does it to everybody. She doesn't believe how beautiful she is. She doesn't believe men would be attracted to her no matter what she did. She doesn't really believe she can be loved. She has to go looking for it. She has to prove to herself over and over again that she can get a reaction.

'It isn't really sex she wants. She wants to believe in herself. But you can't prove love. Nobody can make you believe they love you. *Sex* you can prove. Flirting is as close as she can get to proving she can be loved.'

He astonished me. Not because I thought he was right – or wrong – about Cat Reverie, but because I hadn't expected him to reveal so much of himself so quickly.

'So why are you doing it?' I asked bluntly.

Apparently he had the innocent man's ability to miss the point of what he'd just said. 'Doing what?'

'Still trying to prove you love her. You just told me you know it can't work.'

He had an answer ready. 'Because I *do* love her.

'Brew, I think of her as a woman who's lame. Emotionally lame. And it breaks my heart to see her so – so unsteady on her feet. Unable to believe in herself. So I keep trying. When she flirts with someone like you, and I act jealous, it does her good. It *sustains* her. It doesn't cure her self-doubt, it can't, but at least it contradicts her preconceptions. It contradicts the idea that she can't be loved.'

This speech had a practised sound. He knew it too well. But I still suspected that he was telling me the truth about himself.

'Bullshit,' I remarked politely.

Which was obviously not the reaction he'd expected. He stared back at me. A flush of anger or embarrassment crept into his face.

'Do you think–?' he began.

'Listen.' I had no business acting so superior, but sometimes it's a useful technique. 'It can't work. I'll tell you why. You want her to believe she's lovable. You're trying to prove it the only way you can – by showing it. But your way of showing it just demonstrates that she has the power to hurt you. She flirts. You get jealous. Fear and pain. So what are you really showing her? That she's a woman who hurts people. She even hurts people who love her. How much self-esteem do you expect her to learn from lessons like that?'

He didn't take his own life lying down, I had to give him that. I could see confusion, rage, hurt, shame, all written in red across his features. Unfortunately for him, he had to choose one before he could answer. That took him a moment, and the delay made him look foolish. The real secret of life, as all us wise men understand, is to keep moving like you know what you're doing, instead of standing still while you sort it out.

Finally he was ready. Trying to pretend that he hadn't already missed his chance, he protested, 'What the hell gives *you* the right to criticize *me*? Who the hell are *you*? Aren't you the one who wanders around with a constant wince, soaked in self-pity, putting yourself down, showing everybody how much you hurt?'

His voice rose. He knew how to shout – something else he'd practised. 'Aren't you trying to demonstrate to all of us how rotten Ginny is, just because she has the hots for Joseph and doesn't care about you any more? Aren't you trying to persuade *her* she's rotten?

You think I want to teach Cat she's unlovable? What about *you*, Axbrewder? *What about you?*

I smiled at him. I'm belligerent when I'm cornered, and I don't take the truth gracefully. On the other hand, I didn't have the actual strength to bounce up off the bed and remove his head for him. So I said, 'Nice speech, Abel. There's the door. If you don't make your exit now, you'll ruin the effect.'

For his own obscure reasons, he didn't continue raging. He also didn't leave – at least not immediately. Instead he stood where he was and gaped at me, blushing like I'd caught him with his pants down.

Poor guy. He probably didn't deserve to look so silly. I made an effort to contain my anger. 'I didn't mean to be critical.' Wincing again, but what the hell. 'You're right, I was out of line. What you and Cat do with each other is none of my business.'

All his reactions seemed odd. Now I'd reassured him somehow. Practically smiling, he muttered, 'Damn straight,' like he hadn't really learned to swear yet. Then he walked out of the room while I groped to understand him.

As soon as the door closed, however, my anger came back in a rush. *Aren't you trying to persuade her she's rotten?* He'd turned the tables on me. Instead of telling me about himself, he'd exposed me. *Persuade her she's rotten.* Was it that bad? Was that the real point of all my wounds and helplessnesses, my drinking and guilt? To convince her that she didn't deserve anything better? So that she wouldn't walk away from me?

Christ, Axbrewder. You're a prince.

No question about it. I definitely needed to do something violent.

I also needed an answer about Joseph Hardhouse. Unless that and violence came to the same thing. Almost desperately, I left my room to look for Lara.

That may not have been one of my more sensible decisions, but it was the best I could come up with on short notice.

Unfortunately looking for her meant that I had to deal with the people in the den.

Fortunately Houston Mile no longer held the stage. He must've done enough raccoon-tuning to content him for a while. Now he sat with Mac Westward and Maryanne Green under a moose-head with a rather mouldy set of antlers. In fact, he seemed to have Westward trapped. He spoke quietly, but his voice carried. Everyone in the room heard him describe some of the more pleasurable aspects of greenmail. Maryanne sat beside him, palpating his knee from time to time – hanging on every word.

Westward, however, didn't look trapped. Behind his usual cold lumpy expression, he looked like a novelist considering new motives for murder.

On the other side of the big tree, Ginny and Constance Bebb shared a private discussion. I knew Ginny well enough to see that Connie had her full attention, and she didn't want to be interrupted. Which was fine with me. I didn't know what to say to her anyway.

Buffy and Rock sat with Simon Abel and Cat as far as they could get from everyone else. Just because I'm the kind of guy who thinks things like that, I thought they all looked furtive.

The Draytons and the Hardhouses weren't present.

I wandered over to the front door and went out on to the porch. Pretending that I wanted to check on the weather.

Outside, conditions had deteriorated. The wind had died down, apparently because the air had grown so grey and thick that it was hard to shift. As a result, the cold seemed less bitter than before. A few flakes rode the breeze like advance-men, testing opportunities for the snow behind them. The idea that Deerskin Lodge's position in the bottom of this hollow would provide shelter was an illusion. The hillsides and the surrounding mountains made the wind swirl. More snow would probably fall here than anywhere else.

I scanned what I could see from the porch. If I were more diligent, I would've taken my coat and gone for a walk, just to get a better picture of my situation. How many doors did the lodge actually have? Where were they? What were the best ways to get from one place to another?

I didn't do it. At the moment I didn't give a shit about being diligent. What I really wanted was to learn something horrible and dangerous about Joseph Hardhouse. Then I wouldn't have to feel so wrong towards Ginny. I could justify my reactions.

I succeeded. In a manner of speaking.

Avoiding observation from the den, I moved down the porch, away from the windows. And when I reached the corner, I spotted Hardhouse and his wife.

To all appearances, they were taking a stroll together among the trees. I only saw them in glimpses between the dark trunks. But they were unmistakably holding hands.

While I watched, they stopped. Hardhouse put his back against a tree. They wrapped their arms around each other and kissed like they meant business.

Chapter Nine

When Ama called us to lunch, Buffy and all her guests responded with excitement. Lunch marked the passage of time, the heightening of suspense. The moment approached when someone would be killed.

The only one not excited was me. My convalescence didn't seem to be going especially well. I felt vaguely feverish, slightly giddy, and the pain in my guts had taken on a new, rather watery dimension. On top of that, I was so sleepy you could've sold me over the counter as a soporific.

In spite of my condition, however, I noticed that Cat Reverie and Hardhouse had lost interest in each other. Instead Ginny had turned up the rheostat of her focus on him. Meanwhile Lara was being even more attentive to Mac Westward. And Sam and Queenie Drayton seemed almost insufferably fond of each other.

But I didn't care. After lunch I went back to my room and climbed into bed.

I wanted to sleep for the rest of the week. Unfortunately I started dreaming about snow. And Muy Estobal. And Lawrence Smithsonian. Snow was pain, and I crawled through it for ever until I found myself with my arms locked around Estobal's neck and no way to let go. He was too strong for me, he broke me apart piece by piece, and I couldn't defend myself because I was full of tequila, *tequila*, of all things, but I hadn't drunk it, no, that was el Señor's doing, he'd forced it into me, and Smithsonian watched me cling to Estobal and die, grinning like a self-righteous moray eel.

Which wasn't the way it actually happened, of course. Smithsonian hadn't been there when I killed Estobal. And I hadn't been full of tequila. Nevertheless my dream seemed inevitable, truer than reality. I felt almost grateful when a knock on my door woke me up.

'Come in,' I croaked like I was dying.

Whoever was outside tried to come in. Apparently I'd locked the door.

When did I start locking my door? I could sort of remember having done it, but I couldn't remember why. To keep Ginny out? Or Lara Hardhouse?

Trying to scrub the incoherence off my face, I stumbled out of bed.

When I got the door open, I found Mac Westward there.

Blinking at me as if he couldn't believe his senses without corroborative testimony, he asked, 'Were you asleep?'

I shook my head. 'I had to get up to answer the door anyway.'

The situation didn't seem to require courtesy – or even intelligence – so I left the door open and got back into bed.

Westward stood in the doorway for a while. Eventually, however, he reasoned his way to the conclusion that I'd invited him in. He entered the room and closed the door.

Sounding more than ever like an inedible vegetable, he observed, 'You're hurt worse than I thought.'

I couldn't get Smithsonian out of my head. 'Everything is worse than I thought,' I remarked profoundly. 'Did you come to watch?'

'It's tempting. The Altars outdid themselves with you. You would be the perfect victim.'

Until he said that, I hadn't realized that he was capable of sarcasm.

'Westward,' – I lacked the energy to look at him, so I kept my eyes closed – 'you came to see me. I didn't invite you. It's *your* job to make sense, not mine. What do you mean, "The Altars outdid themselves"?'

He paused. Maybe he was searching for a comfortable chair. But I didn't have to wait long before he began to explain.

'Two of us are actors. Two are private detectives. There are twelve candidates. But I can eliminate Connie and me. You may not know who we are, but too many other people do. And I can eliminate the Draytons. No actor – or detective – would choose medicine as a cover. His ignorance would be too easily exposed.

'We're left with eight possibilities.

'Mr Axbrewder,' – his voice took on a pedantic tone – 'I'm morally certain that if Joseph and Lara Hardhouse were hired to be here, they were hired as actors rather than as detectives. That leaves only six people who could conceivably be detectives.

'Whom would you suspect? Houston Mile and Maryanne Green?

Impossible. No one could trust a man like that – except possibly another Texan. What about Simon Abel and Catherine Reverie? Improbable. In my view, they both lack substance.

'Only you and Ms Fistoulari remain.

'I grant that you, too, are an improbable candidate. You were born to be murdered, not to prevent murders. But Ms Fistoulari is entirely credible. And if she is a detective, you must be also.'

All right, already. So Mac Westward was more awake than I'd realized. So what? As far as I was concerned, he could announce the murderer right now and take a bow. Buffy would be furious, of course – but the rest of us could go home.

'Mr Westward,' I said in the general direction of the ceiling, 'you didn't come here just to persuade me that I'm a detective. Why don't you cut out the rest of the lecture and tell me why you *did* come?'

He thought about that briefly. Then he asked, 'Do you mind if I smoke?'

'Yes,' I said. 'Cigars make me puke.'

Hell, it was my room, wasn't it?

His silence conveyed a shrug. 'I notice,' he commented after a moment, 'that you didn't ask me why I'm sure the Hardhouses aren't detectives.'

I kept my mouth shut. I didn't want to think about anything that involved Joseph and Lara.

He ignored my silence. 'It's because they take the initiative. An actor might do that in a situation of this kind. A detective, never. If a detective has his own agenda when he's on a case, he's useless. His job is to react to circumstances, not create them.'

Oh, good. Just what I needed, another sermon. Why did everyone in this fucking place think I required their wisdom?

'Get to the point, Westward.'

'The point? You really are a belligerent and unhelpful man. Perhaps I should reconsider my assumptions. It may be that your relationship to Ms Fistoulari isn't professional. You may not be a detective – you may simply have the misfortune to be her lover. That would explain your attitude.'

I do believe I'd hurt his feelings. Whatever brought him to me was something he cared about more than he liked to admit.

'However,' he went on, 'you're still the only one who can advise me. For my needs, your attitude may actually be a benefit rather than a handicap.'

That was too many for me. I opened my eyes. In fact, I sat up and dropped my legs over the edge of the bed.

'*Advise* you?' I demanded. 'Me?'

'Why not?' He didn't meet my gaze. Instead he stared at one of his cigars, watching the way he rolled it back and forth between his fingers, crinkling the wrapper. 'You're the only one here who may be able to understand my predicament.'

'Which is?'

He took a deep breath, let it out with a sigh. As if he were reading the words off the cigar band, he said, 'I think Lara Hardhouse wants to have an affair with me.'

Oh, my. In fact, My goodness. What have we here?

Mac Westward, you're scared. You're scared of that woman.

'And what makes you think I'll understand?'

He still didn't look at me. 'I also think she wants to have an affair with you.' For a moment he fell silent. Then he added, 'If you want to know the truth, I think she wants you more than me. But she can't have you. You're invulnerable. You're too full of self-pity to care what anybody else wants.' The male half of Thornton Foal was actually sneering at me. 'She's picked me to be your replacement.'

'Westward,' – for his sake as well as my own, I made an effort to pull myself together – 'maybe I'm as full as self-pity as you think. Maybe that even makes me invulnerable. But I'm not stupid. It doesn't matter what Lara Hardhouse wants. No one in his right mind would want her. That woman is trouble.'

When I said that, he stiffened. 'She's *in* trouble. It's not the same thing.'

Oh, well. With a sigh of my own, I asked, 'What kind of trouble?'

'Her husband,' Westward said promptly. 'He has affairs himself – he has so many that his women have to stand in line. First Catherine Reverie. Then your Ginny. Queenie Drayton will be next. And he treats Lara like dirt. She needs someone to value her, someone to cherish her. She needs to believe that she doesn't deserve what he does to her.'

Bullshit, I thought. Crap and bovine droppings. But I didn't say that out loud. After talking to Simon Abel, I didn't feel righteous enough. Instead I tried a different approach.

'Let me see if I understand,' I said in my best Sardonic Uncle Axbrewder tone. 'You didn't really come here for advice. You came because you want a clear field. You want me to promise that I won't try to get into Lara's bed ahead of you.'

Westward was an interesting fellow. I was morally certain, to use his term, that he was spitting mad. But he didn't glare at me, or raise his voice. He didn't even turn red. On the other hand, he did peel the wrapper off his cigar. Then he stuck the cigar in his teeth and lit it. Even though his hands shook.

'Mr Axbrewder,' he articulated, 'what do you think the life of a "famous author" is like? Autographings? Fans? Glamour and groupies? Nothing could be further from the truth.

'The average mystery novel sells less than five thousand copies in hardcover. And less than forty thousand in paperback. *If* it's published in paperback. *Nobody* reads mystery novels. Even the people here who recognize the name Thornton Foal don't actually *read* his books. I know that from listening to their conversations. Connie and I don't attend mystery camps because we like them. We attend because without the tax write-off we can't afford vacations. Neither of us owns a home. No bank will loan us money.'

For a moment he hung fire. Then he mustered his courage and got to the point.

'I don't get very many chances with women.'

Which explained why he thought that I would understand. And why he feared that I would get in his way.

His honesty deserved an honest response. Cutting right to the heart of the matter, I replied, 'You say you want advice. Here it is. Watch your back.'

'Thanks,' he snorted bitterly. Puffing a cloud of smoke in my direction, he stood up and stomped out.

Damn cigar. The room smelled full of smoke and loneliness. But that didn't stop me from lying back down in bed and pulling the covers up to my ears.

I slept longer than I expected – which should've done me good, I suppose. When I woke up, however, the sensation of fever in my head had intensified, and my intestines felt like they were sloshing around inside my belly. Oh, well.

Unfortunately my health didn't seem like a good enough excuse to stay in bed for the rest of my life, so I got up. I did my best to hide my wounds under a clean shirt and sweater. Then I went out to face the world.

I found Connie alone in the den. She sat at the card table, playing a kind of solitaire I'd never seen before. Apparently everyone else had found something else to do.

When I entered, she looked up and said, 'Good afternoon, Mr

Axbrewder,' without quite smiling. Maybe she would've welcomed a chat, but her manner didn't actually encourage it, and anyway my head was too fog-bound for small talk. Instead of joining her, I went to a window to look out at the weather.

A premature gloom had taken over the world, but I couldn't see anything else. The heat of the fireplaces and the cold outside blanked the glass with mist. But I heard voices, so I moved to the door and stepped out on to the porch.

Buffy must've been ecstatic. She was getting all the ambience she could decently want. It came down as thick as rain, so thick that the gusts and swirls of wind hardly registered. At a guess, we already had six inches on the ground, and the depth of the early dusk promised more. For most practical purposes, Deerskin Lodge would be as isolated as she could wish.

I had a different reaction. Snow reminded me of Smithsonian. And Smithsonian made me think of people getting shot.

The people outside didn't share my memories – or my mood. All this ambience filled them with glee. Laughing like schoolkids, Sam and Queenie had tackled Cat and Simon in a snowball fight, and Maryanne pranced through the middle of the battle like a cheerleader. As soon as they saw me, however, all five of them scooped up snow and flung it in my direction.

Waving my hands to ward off attacks, I retreated into the lodge.

But then I didn't know what to do with myself. Indecisively I stopped to watch Connie's game. Like almost everything else I'd seen since we arrived, her version of solitaire made no sense to me. After a minute I gave up trying to follow it.

'Tell me,' I asked, 'are mystery camps usually this boring?'

She raised her head, studied me gravely. 'Usually,' she replied, 'they're worse.'

For some reason, this failed to improve my humour.

Before long the combatants came inside, laughing with each other, scattering snow. When they'd warmed themselves at the fires, they dispersed to dress for dinner. That and Ama Carbone's performance on the xylophone brought me to the belated realization that I'd slept most of the afternoon away.

What this unaccustomed capacity for sleep meant I had no idea. Was I recovering? Slipping into peritonitis? Did I care? Not especially. When Murder On Cue's guests had gathered, I accompanied them into the dining room.

We sat in the same arrangement as last night, with artillery and

516

wrought-iron fixtures impending over us. Faith and Amalia served a dinner generically indistinguishable from the previous one – perfectly acceptable and maybe even tasty food, if your stomach could handle it. Cat Reverie demanded port again, and when the decanter arrived she commandeered it possessively, as if she wanted to prevent anyone – but especially Hardhouse – from sharing it. Other than that, none of us admitted that we might be less than happy with each other. The general mood was one of barely contained eagerness.

Mile bared his rotten teeth like a pouncing predator. Westward had an unexpected spot of colour on each cheek, and he drank less than last night. Excitement seemed to ease Lara's troubles somehow. She fixed her deep dark eyes on me repeatedly, but behind her somber expression she seemed less aggrieved, more at rest. Maryanne burbled like a kid. Drayton smiled at everything – except during those brief moments when he noticed that I wasn't eating. And Buffy positively bristled with anticipation. Even Ginny had a glow that I hadn't seen for a long time, at once satisfied and hungry, as if she'd found something to nurture her and intended to have more of it.

The sight felt like a knife in my wounded guts. I tried to distract myself by thinking about Lara. Unfortunately she resembled Connie's card game. I needed someone to tell me the rules. Did she feel better because she'd had a reconciliation with her husband, or because she knew that she could use Westward to get even with him?

I had no trouble staying away from the wine. Fever was good for me, apparently.

As a group, we tried to act normal for a while. But at last Queenie couldn't stand it. With a deliberate shiver, she burst out, 'Someone say it. Tonight one of us will probably be murdered.'

'Isn't it wonderful?' Buffy chimed in. 'Don't you just feel like you've never been more alive in your whole life?'

Both Hardhouse and his wife nodded sagaciously. Westward nodded, too, but I was sure that he had no interest in murder.

'Well, Buffy,' Mile drawled, 'Ah wouldn't purely agree with them sentiments. Life is where you find it. If you've never stood there and seen a bitty ol' oil well turn gusher – why, Ah'd say there's all kinds of ways of feelin' alive. Give a man a pretty little filly and let him teach her to run' – on cue, Maryanne produced a schoolgirl blush – 'and you'll learn somethin' about feelin' alive.

'But a situation like this one here, now, it do have its advantages. Knowin' Ah might be killed, knowin' Ah got to outsmart me a killer or die – why, it purely makes me feel like a gusher mahself.'

The leer he aimed at Maryanne wasn't easy to misinterpret.

'Why?' I hadn't intended to say anything, but Mile brought out the contentious side of my personality. 'No one will actually die. Why do you care who it is? Why do you care if it's you? We're all safe. There aren't any' – just for a second, I fumbled through my fever for the word I wanted – 'any consequences.'

Ginny gave me an unreadable look. Rock nodded vaguely.

Buffy wanted to protest, that was obvious, but Sam forestalled her. As if he were practising his bedside manner, he said, 'You're right, of course. This isn't the real world. In the real world, crimes have consequences. There you have to care about them. Here you don't.

'But none of us are confused about this, Brew. We know it isn't the real world. It's a vacation. And,' he added seriously, 'it only works because we've all agreed to make it fun for each other.'

All except me, I thought. But maybe I was wrong. Some of the other guests may've made entirely different agreements.

Nevertheless I felt actively betrayed when Ginny put in, a bit too intensely, 'Sam's right, Brew. You should make an effort to get into the spirit of the occasion. It might speed up your recovery.'

I heard what she said. I even heard what she meant. Getting into the spirit of the occasion worked for *her*. She was recovering just fine. Without me.

There was nothing I could say to that, so I shut my mouth.

General conversation. Food. Anticipation. Some of the other guests viewed the world through a haze of wine. Personally I viewed it through a haze of fever. Dessert. Coffee. I didn't have any coffee. It might reduce the haze – and I needed the haze. It was my only protection.

When dinner ended, we went into the den and sat around the fireplaces and tried to pretend that we had something in common. Somehow I found myself cornered by Drayton. He must've made it happen on his own because I sure as hell didn't have a hand in it.

'Are you all right, Brew?' he asked seriously. 'You don't look good.'

I smiled like one of Reeson's ghouls and beasties. Oh, sure. Absolutely. Of course. I feel great. 'The truth is,' I admitted for the second time, 'I got shot. I think my entire life has a hole in it.'

He ignored the metaphysical implications. 'Shall I take a look?'

I shook my head. 'You're on vacation, doctor.'

For a moment he studied me soberly. 'You know, Brew,' he said after a while, 'I can think of worse things than practising a little medicine on my vacation.'

518

I considered my options. Queenie had told me to talk to him, but I doubted that she'd had a medical consultation in mind. For no clear reason, I trusted both of them. Maybe I trusted him because he was married to her. That in itself was a significant recommendation. Or maybe I was just sentimentally vulnerable to people who knew how to love each other. But whatever the explanation, I didn't want to talk to him in my present condition.

'I'll let you know,' I answered as well as I could. 'I've got enough pills to stock a drugstore. They're bound to do me some good eventually.' Then I added, 'Thanks for the offer.'

He frowned like he thought I was making a mistake, but he shrugged and left me alone.

Some time later, I noticed Cat Reverie trying to catch my eye. When I finally met her gaze, she gave me what they call a 'meaningful look'. Then she moved away in the direction of the dining room.

I had no intention of following her. None whatsoever. Completely out of the question. On the other hand, however, Ginny had told me to *get into the spirit of the occasion*. And avoiding how I felt about that was probably the most important thing in my life at the moment. The spirit of the occasion, sure.

Making no effort to be inconspicuous, I lurched after Simon Abel's girlfriend.

I caught up with her in the dining room. She'd acquired the decanter of port and two glasses. Faith and Ama had cleared away the dinner dishes. I could hear the Hobart running in the kitchen. It sounded the way my stomach felt.

Cat treated me to her best imitation of arch allure. 'Come into the parlour,' she said. Like the spider to the fly.

'The parlour?' I hadn't known that the lodge had a parlour.

'It's this way.'

The spirit of the occasion. I followed her some more.

Clearly I should've done some exploring. Then I would've known about the parlour, a medium-sized room complete with a thick Persian rug, a fireplace, a couple of windows, a wet bar, two deep armchairs, a loveseat, and altogether too many doilies. The fire burned like the mouth of hell. Truchi or Reeson sure kept busy stoking all these blazes.

Cat closed the door behind me. 'Have some port?' She waggled the decanter.

Well, I could make an effort to get into the spirit of the occasion, but I didn't want to be ridiculous about it. Sighing, I shook my head.

She shrugged, poured herself a glass. Then she put the decanter and the extra glass down on the wet bar. Outside the windows the world had gone black. If I stood close to the panes, the light behind me showed snow still coming down as if the Heavens themselves had broken. A foot of it so far? – more than that? But past the short reach of the light everything disappeared, swallowed by dark and cold.

Slowly Cat ambled to the other side of the fireplace. We faced each other across the front of the hearth. She stood with her hips cocked so that the tight sheath of her dress stretched over her breasts. Her nipples hardened against the fabric, as alluring as the look in her eyes – and just as premeditated.

'I get the impression,' she said, 'that you don't like me.'

Opening gambit. Now it was my move. 'I get the impression,' I countered, 'that we've already had this conversation. What happened to Hardhouse? Did he decide to go back to his wife?'

Apparently my brand of seduction didn't trouble her. She chuckled deep in her throat. 'Back to his wife? Not Joseph. A man like that never goes back.'

'Then what went wrong? You can't expect me to believe that he got tired of you in just one night.'

Now she laughed out loud. 'Well, thanks for that, anyway. I'll take it as a compliment.' Hints of firelight caught in her eyes, cast a shade of unnatural red on her cheek. 'I didn't get tired of him, either. He has' – she grinned salaciously – 'a lot on the ball. But I like variety. I like strong men.'

She hadn't tasted her port yet. Still carrying her glass as if it made her more desirable, she started towards me. Her hips pulled against the sides of her dress. 'As many as I can get.'

Well, this was fun. If she had her way, I was about to become another notch on her garter-belt.

Smiling nauseously, I said, 'That's interesting. Simon says you do it because you have a self-esteem problem. You're trying to prove that you can be loved because deep down inside you don't really believe it.'

Just for an instant, she faltered. Maybe Abel meant something to her after all. But her Avid Temptress pose met the challenge. She reached me. Her empty hand stroked the front of my sweater. Softly she pronounced, 'Simon is a wimp.'

I wanted to croak out a laugh – or a cry for help. 'And you think I'm not?'

Languorously – I think that's the right word – she raised the hand with the glass and rested her wrist on my shoulder. Her free hand slipped to the back of my neck, drawing us closer. Her belly rubbed against my lower abdomen. Her breasts brushed my bandages.

'You're hurt, sure,' she breathed up at me. Firelight filled her eyes. 'But under all that pain you're made of iron. I can see it.

'Kiss me. Hurt me if you want to. I love strength. I love strong men. I want to be kissed hard.'

For some reason I thought I heard a shot.

At exactly the same instant, a tidy little circle appeared in one of the window panes.

Poor Catherine Reverie, determined and doomed.

I wasn't holding her. My arms still hung at my sides. She had no one to catch her. She thrashed like a convulsive and went down, splashing blood and bone and grey meat from an appalling hole in the side of her head. In the process, she spilled her port all over me. It soaked into my sweater, rich and cloying, and it made me stink. The glass rolled off into a corner somewhere and broke.

The spirit of the occasion. Sweet Christ.

This was going to be one *hell* of a vacation.

Chapter Ten

Ignoring the pressure on my guts, I dropped to my knees and lifted her in my arms as if I thought I could make a difference. But Catherine Reverie was the deadest looking body I'd seen in a long time, all the grace and desire and confusion blown out of her. Her blood added its stain to the port on my sweater. The rug was definitely ruined.

After a while I realized that I wasn't accomplishing anything. There were things I ought to do. If I could just figure out what they were.

Ginny would know.

I lowered Cat back to the rug – lowered her gently, not because she cared, but because I did. Heaved myself upright. Lurched to the door and opened it.

'Ginny,' I panted. 'Come here.'

She would never hear me if I didn't do better than that.

'*Ginny!*'

She emerged from a room just a few doors away, flashing her grey eyes and her claw. The room must've been Joseph Hardhouse's. Why else would he appear right behind her as she strode into the hall? On the other hand, they both had all their clothes on. They didn't even look rumpled. Her right hand clutched her purse.

Relief twisted along the pain and the sloshing wetness in my guts.

'Brew?' Ginny snapped. Her attention focused on me, sharp, capable, and complete. It steadied me almost immediately. 'What is it? What's happened?'

Other people heard me shout as well. They came into the hall from the den, Drayton first with Mile and Maryanne behind him and others trailing. But Ginny arrived first. I pointed her into the parlour. Then I shifted my bulk to block the doorway.

Hardhouse glared at me, his face dark with irritation. His hair formed a carnivorous streak across his skull. But I didn't let him pass.

Chewing unladylike obscenities, Ginny scanned the parlour, Cat's body, the windows. Quickly, carefully, she jumped over Cat to the fireplace, then reached around to the windows one at a time and pulled down the blinds. Which should've occurred to me. If a sniper wanted to kill one of us, why not all of us? Maybe he'd only left me alive because I'd knelt down beside the body, out of the line of fire. I wasn't doing my *job*.

As soon as she'd covered the windows, Ginny wheeled towards me.

'What happened?' she demanded. 'Did you see anything? Were you,' she continued as if the smell of port filled her attention and no other question mattered, 'drinking with her?'

She jerked me off balance as effectively as a magician doing misdirection. I gaped at her and did nothing to prevent the guests from pushing past me into the parlour.

Drayton and Hardhouse stooped beside the corpse. Hardhouse's anger had shifted. Now he looked both furious and ecstatic. In contrast, Sam concentrated too hard to show any reaction.

'Shee-it. Shee-it.' That was Houston Mile. His face had gone pasty, like rancid cooking oil.

When Maryanne saw Cat, she gave a little squeal and tried to throw herself into Mile's arms. He shoved her away so hard that she sprawled on the loveseat. Warding off panic with both hands, he backed towards the corner and wedged himself in as if he were trying to hide.

Just for a second, Maryanne stared pure hate at him. Then she began to bring great wrenching sobs all the way up from the pit of her stomach. They shook her whole body, but they didn't make a sound. She was as quiet as Cat.

Buffy, Rock, and Connie all seemed to appear at the same time. Buffy arrived bright with anticipation. Presumably she believed that one of her murders had been committed. She went right up to the body like she meant to congratulate Cat for an outstanding performance.

Then she broke into screams.

She had a throaty yowl, full of harmonics and horror – it went right into my bones. And she didn't stop. She screamed and screamed.

'Rock!' Ginny yelled. 'Make her shut up!'

He didn't do it. Cat's body fixed his attention as if it were the only thing left in the world.

A lot of people react that way to violent death. They can't integrate something so far outside their range of experience. It changes the meaning of everything they know.

From the floor, Sam muttered through his teeth, 'What did she do to deserve this?'

Buffy went on screaming.

Like a schoolmarm with a young bully to discipline, Connie stepped forward and smacked Buffy twice across the face, hard.

Shocked, Buffy covered her stinging cheeks with her hands and sobbed into her palms.

By then Lara and Mac Westward had arrived, holding hands demurely, like kids on their first date. But the sight of Cat changed his entire face. His usual congealed expression vanished, and his eyes burned sharply. He shoved past me and actively shouldered Hardhouse out of his way so that he could kneel beside Cat as if he wanted to study her – as if after years of writing about murder he wanted to see what it really looked like.

Hardhouse surged to his feet, glaring dark emotions in all directions.

'Brew!' Ginny barked through the confusion. 'Who's missing?'

'*Joseph.*' The sheer intensity of Lara's whisper made her voice carry. '*What have you done?*'

So softly that I almost didn't hear him, he hissed back, 'Nothing. I didn't do it.'

'Queenie Drayton,' I answered Ginny. I still had a job to do. 'Simon Abel.'

But Queenie wasn't missing. She appeared as I said her name. She paused in the doorway to assess the situation. If she were shocked or frightened, she didn't let that deter her. As soon as she saw where she was most needed, she went to the loveseat and put her arms around Maryanne.

Maryanne buried her face in Queenie's neck and continued sobbing.

Ginny cut through the crowd towards me. Her purse lay on the floor under one of the windows. Her fist gripped her .357, and her claw moved like a threat.

'Joseph!' she cracked out, as convincing as a whip, 'Sam! all of you! No one leaves this room until we find Simon!

'Rock, you're supposed to be in charge here. Go to the office, use the phone. Call the nearest cops. Do it *now.*'

Her voice lashed him into motion. He left the parlour like a frightened sleep-walker.

'Come on, Brew,' Ginny commanded.

I followed her out into the hall and swept the door shut.

524

She knew where Simon's room was. She'd been paying attention when Buffy handed out living assignments. Faster than I could move, she headed into the den and down the other hall. I was a good ten steps behind her when she reached Abel's door.

She didn't wait for me. Before I got there, she turned the knob and threw the door open.

Ginny! She should've waited, she needed me to back her up. Pulling out the .45, I lurched into a run.

The room was empty.

'Damn it,' I panted thinly, hardly able to breathe, 'don't *do* that. You know better.'

She ignored me.

As soon as I stopped swearing at her, I noticed the cold.

Abel had left his window open.

Snow had fallen on the sill, on the floor inside the window. Not a lot, maybe no more than an inch. Just enough to make it obvious that the snow hadn't simply settled there. It had been disturbed on the floor and the sill. As if Abel had gone out that way.

Ginny pulled the blind down. Then she checked the bathroom. I checked the closet. Nobody there either.

Haste and panic made pain throb in my abdomen. My guts seemed to flop around loose inside me. A minute passed before I realized what *was* in the closet.

'He's still outside,' she said.

And, 'He won't get far.'

And, 'We need to get all the blinds down. Maybe Cat isn't his only target.'

'Ginny,' I said like a choked fish.

On the floor of the closet, I could see a bit of snow. It looked like the remains of a footprint.

A rifle stood poorly concealed in the corner.

Ginny looked at it. She studied the snow. Using one of Abel's shirts so that she wouldn't ruin too many fingerprints, she picked up the rifle and sniffed the muzzle. Then she showed it to me.

I recognized it from the collection in the dining room – a Winchester .30-.30 carbine. Its muzzle gave off the unmistakable smell of cordite and burned oil.

I put the .45 away.

'Why,' I asked the cold and the fever, 'didn't he close the window? Did he think we wouldn't check his room?'

'Maybe he isn't very smart.' Ginny gave me the Winchester to carry. 'Let's check the cases, see if anything else is missing.'

I nodded. Maybe I was being stupid. I simply couldn't imagine Simon Abel blowing that hole in Cat's head.

We moved more slowly now. We had more reason to be cautious. From the hall we reached the den. We couldn't hear Buffy sobbing. We couldn't hear voices at all. Like the rest of the rooms, the parlour was too well insulated.

Don't be stupid, I told myself. Not now. Maybe he didn't mean to kill her. You can't judge the intent by the wound it makes.

We encountered no one in the den. Or in the hall between the den and the dining room. Or in the dining room. The Hobart in the kitchen had finished running. For a second I assumed that the kitchen was empty, too. Then I heard noises that sounded like flatware and plates being stacked.

'Sonofabitch,' Ginny gritted under her breath.

At least half a dozen guns were missing.

I remembered some of them. The Purdy shotgun. A Ruger .357 Magnum. And, of all things, the General Patton Commemorative.

The rest could've been anything.

Reeson was bound to have an inventory. He could tell us what kind of firepower we were up against.

But it didn't make sense. Anyone who needed that Purdy or the Ruger would have no use for a Commemorative six-shooter.

Unless he – or she – knew nothing about guns.

'Looks like we're in for a siege,' I commented, feverishly casual.

'Sonofabitch,' Ginny repeated.

She led the way into the kitchen.

We found Faith Jerrick there alone, taking dishes from the Hobart and piling them neatly on one of the counter tops. She raised her head when we came in. I'd never seen her look anyone in the eye, but she sure as hell looked at Ginny's revolver. As she stared at it, she turned so pale that I seemed to see the pure colour of her bones through her skin. One hand crept up to the fine chain around her neck and clutched at her crucifix.

At first Ginny and I didn't say anything. We concentrated on making sure that Faith didn't have company.

I carried the Winchester like a club – which I guess made it obvious that I wasn't about to do any shooting. Faith kept her attention on Ginny. Voice shaking, she prayed, 'May God forgive you for what you do.'

526

Just for an instant, Ginny flinched in surprise. Then she glanced at her .357 and made a disgusted gesture. 'There's been a murder,' she rasped. 'The killer is outside. He may want to shoot someone else.' Then she jumped to a decision. 'But you should be safe. If anybody wanted to kill you, they could've done it long ago. And they wouldn't have shot one of the guests. We need Reeson. Can you go get him? I could send Brew, but I want him with me.'

She wouldn't be in danger. Unless she accidentally encountered Cat's killer.

I should've gone. That was my job. But I didn't have the strength for it. And Ginny she was in charge.

Faith jerked a nod. Like a woman who would've panicked and run if such things hadn't been forbidden by her religion, she turned for the back door. In this case, however, her religion probably had more to do with Reeson than God.

We had to keep moving, search the rest of the lodge. We couldn't just stand around waiting for Reeson. But before we could start, we heard something that sounded exactly like the front door of the den opening. We heard boots stamping the floor.

Ginny headed in that direction fast. Changing my grip on the .30-.30 as I stumbled along, I did my best to keep up. I wasn't more than five steps behind her when she charged into the den.

Simon Abel blinked at us. He wore a heavy winter coat and cap, but I couldn't make out the details. They were caked in snow. Snow clung in clots to his legs and feet. He looked like he'd been out making snow-angels.

Ginny barked, 'Freeze!' in a voice that threatened to crack the floorboards. Her .357 lined up straight on his face.

He didn't freeze. Maybe he was too scared. He wheeled away as if she'd already fired.

Inadvertently he blundered against the door and knocked himself down. Snow blew across him from the porch. Eighteen inches of it had accumulated outside, and it was still falling.

Ginny rushed forward, crouched nearly on top of him. Then she corked the muzzle of her gun on his nose.

Eyes white with alarm, he gasped out, 'Don't shoot! I killed her! I confess! Don't shoot me!'

I stopped. Ginny didn't need me. Not now. Maybe she never did. I could afford to take a few moments, try to get my breath back. Find some answer to the pain.

Altar came into the den. Presumably he'd just left the office. He moved slowly, almost aimlessly, like a man who couldn't remember why he was here.

He didn't seem to notice Ginny or Simon. When his eyes managed to focus on me, he said in a blank voice, 'The phone is dead. The snow must have pulled down the line.'

I've always tried to be a responsible member of society. Still holding the Winchester, I went around Ginny and Abel to close the door.

Chapter Eleven

It was just as well I shut the door. Snow had already started to drift in from the porch. Outside it blanketed everything, as thick and terminal as volcanic ash. I suppose the phone lines could've come down under that kind of weight.

Now that Ginny had Simon on the floor, she didn't quite know what to do with him. He'd confessed too fast for his own good. Which probably didn't make her feel like trusting him. Reaching down, she clamped her claw in his coat to haul him upright.

'Mr Altar!' Abel gabbled, 'Rock, I only did what you told me, I was only doing my job, tell her, don't let her shoot me!'

Something about the particular tone of Simon's hysteria penetrated Altar's fog. For the first time, he shifted his attention towards Simon and Ginny. Slowly a flush spread across his face. In a moment he looked almost crimson, on the verge of a heart attack. Bunching his fists, he hissed, '*You fool!* You weren't supposed to *do* it!'

In our respective fashions, Ginny, Simon, and I all gaped at him.

When he realized that we were staring at him, Altar's rage paled out. He blinked at us. 'He's an actor,' he muttered as if he were apologizing. 'He was supposed to be acting. He wasn't supposed to *do* it.'

'It's a little late for that,' Ginny panted as she pulled on Abel's coat.

He tried to untangle his feet so that he could cooperate. 'No, wait.' He was as confused as the rest of us. Or he was good at acting confused. 'What are you talking about? What's going on?'

Before anyone could answer, an idea as terrible as Ginny's .357 struck him, and he jumped away from her so fast that her claw lost its grip. The fingers came together with a metallic snap.

'Cat?' he asked. '*Cat?*'

I suppose I should've grappled for him, helped Ginny keep him under control. But I felt feverish and unloved, and too much snow had fallen, and Simon Abel was an actor who'd been hired to do a job. On top of that, Ginny didn't want my support. Instead of exerting myself, I said, 'The parlour,' and pointed him in the right direction.

He turned and ran.

Ginny gave me a glare that would've curdled blood and went after him.

He headed straight for the parlour, threw open the door, rushed into the room.

The atmosphere was tense, as if half the people there had just stopped shouting at each other. You could almost hear Mile sweat.

From behind I couldn't watch Abel's face. But I saw everyone else flinch away from him. Even Sam Drayton. Even Hardhouse.

He ignored them. Maybe at the moment he didn't know that he had an audience. He went rigid with shock. Then he let out a howl, broken off when he flung himself down beside Cat's corpse, scrambling to take her up in his arms.

Ginny kept her gun on Abel, mostly to show the rest of the group that she was still in charge. I set myself in the doorway and took a quick inventory of the guests. I had an active desire to avoid any more surprises – to be sure that no one could come at my back, except maybe Rock.

Queenie must've been good at comforting people. Maryanne was stable now, if not exactly calm. She acted frightened at the sight of Simon – or at the sight of Ginny's gun – but she didn't start crying again. Queenie faced us all with her arm around Maryanne and waited to find out what was going on.

Connie approached comforting Buffy in a completely different way. Her manner was stern, authoritative, and her mouth kept a tight inflexible line, like it was held in place by C-clamps. Her eyes watched everyone with impartial suspicion.

I couldn't tell whether Buffy felt comforted. Mostly she just looked catatonic.

Joseph and Lara stood close to each other, as close as they could get without actually touching. His jaw jutted aggressively. A strange intensity that might've been eagerness or dread glittered in her eyes.

The sight of them together made me shiver.

Mile had recovered from his initial panic. Now he tried to bluster – or he did until Simon came into the room. Then he shut up. I could almost see anxiety ooze from his pores.

Sam Drayton and Westward didn't seem to be doing anything in particular, except ignoring Mile. Sam was accustomed to crises and death. We could count on him. In contrast, Mac's detachment and curiosity struck me as loony, essentially unreliable.

No question about it, I was getting feverish. Another shiver went through me. Sounding positively amiable, I commented to the group, 'Doesn't look much like a murderer, does he.'

Sam, Mac, and Joseph turned to stare at me.

I waggled the rifle. 'This is probably what he used. He won't be shooting anyone else for a while.'

While Simon rocked Cat and hugged her like he was trying to squeeze the death out of her, Ginny attempted to get Buffy's attention.

'Buffy. *Mrs Altar.*'

But Buffy, as they say in hospitals, was unreactive.

'Brew, where's Rock?'

I glanced down the empty hallway, then looked back at Ginny and shook my head.

'I want to know what the Altars hired Simon to do,' she demanded as if she expected the rest of us to come up with the answer. 'I want to know what went wrong.'

Simon surprised me by hearing her. He lifted his face out of Cat's hair. In the kind of voice you sometimes get from junkies and drunks, people who have had too many neurons blasted, he said, 'They hired me to kill her.'

Buffy didn't react to this, either. But Drayton had other ideas. He turned on Simon.

'Why would they do that? They've been running mystery camps for a long time. Why would they suddenly decide they want someone dead?' He pointed at Cat. 'And why *her*?'

'She was unfaithful,' Simon answered in the same voice. Maybe he hadn't noticed the blood on his clothes. 'I loved her. I did everything I could to take care of her, make her happy. That's what men are supposed to do, isn't it? Take care of women who need them? But she didn't care. She wanted other men. She wanted sex – sex with everybody. Except me. They hired me to kill her. The jealous lover.'

Sam wanted to protest. Probably we all wanted to protest. But Ginny objected first.

'No, Simon. That isn't quite right.' She spoke softly now, almost gently, like she didn't want him to feel threatened. 'You're an actor. The Altars hired you to *pretend* to kill her. She's an actor, too. They hired her to *pretend* to be the victim. That was the scenario. A jealous lover and his wanton girl friend. They didn't want you to really kill her.'

'No, of course not,' Simon agreed. He was nearly as unreactive as Buffy. 'I wouldn't do that. I love her.'

'You just did,' Hardhouse pronounced, each word as harsh as a blow. 'You shot her through the window.' He flicked a glance at me that could've meant anything. 'Unless it was Brew you wanted to kill, presumably because he was fooling around with her, and you hit her by mistake.'

In unison, Sam, Queenie, and Mac opened their mouths. Like me, they hadn't considered this possibility before.

It had never occurred to me that Ginny might've had a better reason than lack of trust for not sending me out after Reeson.

'No, of course not,' Simon repeated. Obviously he hadn't understood Hardhouse. But a few seconds later it hit him. 'Wait a minute.' His face changed radically. He was too young for himself – or his personality had too many unintegrated pieces. Nothing looked natural on him. His dismay as he put Ginny's .357 and Cat's corpse and the rifle together seemed artificial, manufactured in some way. 'You think I *killed* her? You think *I* killed her?'

No one responded.

Abruptly he dropped Cat, let her head thud back to the rug. Then he jumped to his feet and started shouting.

'Weren't you listening? I love her! I've loved her for years! I wouldn't kill her!'

'You confessed, boy,' Mile put in, apparently trying to create the illusion that he'd regained his self-possession. 'We heard you. We got us enough witnesses to hang you.'

'No, you don't understand!' Simon shot back. 'I was confused. I thought you were talking about the *camp* – about the *mystery*. The reason we're all here.

'I'm an actor. Cat and I were hired to put on a mystery for you. She was supposed to act as promiscuous as she could, and I was supposed to "kill" her for it. With one of those blue marbles. Then you could try to figure out who did it.

'When' – he faced Ginny with a gulp – 'when you waved that gun at me and yelled, I panicked. I thought you were taking the camp too seriously. Right from the start, I thought you were a little crazy. I didn't know you were talking about a *real* murder.'

The blank stare he got back for this speech wasn't lost on him.

Whatever else you said about him, you probably had to admit that he was an experienced actor. He knew he was "dying".

'*Look*.' He pulled his coat open and shoved one hand into his pocket so suddenly that Ginny automatically tightened her grip on the .357. Maryanne winced. Connie's mouth clenched disapprovingly. But what he brought out wasn't a weapon. It was small collection of blue marbles. '*I was hired to pretend to kill her*. They wanted me to "kill" as many of you as I could before you caught me.'

'*You* heard Rock in the den.' Simon turned his appeal on me. 'He hired me. He admitted it.'

I ignored him. His reactions, and Ginny's, and the fever made me feel that I'd lost contact with reality.

'That's true,' Ginny answered Simon in a leaden voice. 'I'm sure almost everything you say is true. You're an actor. You were hired. But that doesn't prove anything. It doesn't mean you didn't kill her.'

He was working himself up into a frenzy of protest. 'Why would I do that? I loved her!'

'For the same reason you were supposed to kill her,' Hardhouse retorted. He seemed to be enjoying himself. 'She screwed around. You loved her, and she didn't love you back. You couldn't stand watching her get into every bed except yours.

'You must have planned this from the beginning, as soon as Rock and Buffy offered you the job. You figured that pretending to kill her would be the perfect cover for really killing her.'

'That's insane!'

Simon wanted to sound hot and indignant and righteous, command the stage in a way that would make all of us believe him. I could see that. Unfortunately a sob burst out of him, ruining the effect. 'I didn't do it,' he insisted as hard as he could. 'I didn't kill her.' But he only managed to look pathetic.

'Miz Fistoulari,' Mile drawled, getting to be more like himself by the minute, 'you have purely done us a service. Ah confess, Ah was a mite worried we was all likely to get shot. But you got him, and we're safe. Ah always knew there was somethin' fishy about him.'

He spread his arms to Maryanne. 'Commere, you pore lil' filly,' he said like he actually thought he could soothe her. 'We're safe now. No sense cryin' about it.'

The Lord works in mysterious ways, His wonders to perform. Maryanne got up from the loveseat and went into Mile's hug like a kid who needed her daddy.

Just for a second, Queenie's face twisted as if she wanted to puke. But she didn't say anything.

'We *are* safe, now, aren't we, Ginny?' Connie asked sternly. 'He must have shot her. Who else could have done it? And you have his rifle. Surely we can tie him or lock him up somewhere until the police are able to get through this storm.'

Ginny hesitated. She looked at me, frowning. She hadn't had much time to think – but she was already a good distance ahead of me. 'If I were you,' she said slowly, 'I wouldn't jump to that conclusion.'

The room started to tilt. I had to put my hand on the door-frame to hold it steady. Her warning was aimed at me more than Connie and the rest of the guests. Fortunately no one else saw me lose my balance. They all concentrated like mad on Ginny.

'What do you mean?' Connie demanded in her best irate school-marm manner. 'Why do you think we aren't safe?'

'Miz Bebb's right,' put in Mile. He'd wrapped himself around Maryanne like melting margarine. 'We can't be in danger. Who else could have shot her?'

Abel insisted again, 'I didn't do it,' but no one listened.

'I don't know.' Ginny kept looking at me as if she could see fever radiate from my skin. 'But a couple of details worry me. Rock says the phone is out. We can't call the police. We'll have to wait until morning and then see whether Reeson or Carbone has a vehicle that can drive in this kind of snow.'

'Buffy mentioned a snowmobile,' Maryanne put in. 'Or Rock did. I'm sure of it.'

Ginny nodded. 'The second point is that more guns are missing.' Steadily, as if she didn't notice the sting of apprehension around her, she added, 'If Simon took them, he didn't put them the same place he put the rifle.'

Alarm, protest, panic – voices all going at once.

'Guns.'

'Where did you put them?'

'How many of us were you planning to kill?'

'What's happening to us?'

For a minute I lost contact with the room. As it tilted, my brain slipped a few cogs. As if I wanted to change the line of reasoning that made me so sick, I ran backwards to the question of the snow on Abel's windowsill.

'Calm down!' Ginny demanded over the noise.

At once the whole group collapsed into silence.

'You're intelligent people,' she went on. 'Brew and I are professionals. Reeson has at least a four-wheel-drive, as well as the snowmobile. We'll figure out what to do. There's no immediate danger. Just don't stop using your heads.'

Use my head. Sure. I lifted my weight off the door-frame and moved precariously towards Simon.

He looked at me like I might club him with the Winchester. Probably he was under too much stress to realize that I didn't mean him any harm. I took him by the arm and pulled him towards a corner of the parlour, out of the way.

Ginny gave me another glance, then decided to leave me alone. 'Sam,' I heard her say, 'go find Rock. He's wandering around the lodge somewhere. But if you can't track him down in a couple of minutes, come back here. I sent Faith after Art Reeson. At the time, I thought she'd be safe. Now I'm not so sure. If they don't show up soon, we'll have to organize a search.'

'Right.' Sam paused to give Queenie a quick kiss. Just in case. Then he left.

'Simon,' I said, shivering as if I could feel the draft in his room, 'tell me something. Are you a fresh-air nut?'

He didn't need to be a good actor to peer at me like I'd lost my mind.

'Do you always leave your windows open?'

His soft features twisted into a laborious squint, as if he thought his life depended on his ability to distract me. 'Brew, help me,' he whispered. 'I didn't kill her. You know that. They're going to turn me over to the cops. I'll be convicted if somebody here doesn't believe me.'

'Relax.' I smiled like I'd just escaped from an institution. 'The cops aren't that good at convicting people these days. Tell me why you left your window open.'

If he kept scrunching up his face so hard, he'd break something. 'Is this a gag?' His voice jerked above a whisper. He forced it down again. 'I didn't kill her. Why are you talking about windows?'

I really didn't have the strength to argue. And I wasn't going to explain – I didn't want to plant ideas in his head. Which left me without a lot of alternatives. But I still had some muscle, and I still had a grip on his arm. I started to squeeze, grinding my fingers into his biceps.

'Simon,' I said softly, 'just answer the question.'

The pain made him gasp almost immediately. 'I didn't.'

'Didn't what?'

'Leave my window open. I never leave my window open.' Speaking faster and faster to stay ahead of the pain. 'I keep it locked. I live in LA. Cat did, too. We just said we were from back east for cover. If you don't lock your windows, everything you own is gone when you come home.'

I eased my grip. 'For some reason,' I remarked distantly, 'I'm not surprised.'

I'm sure he would've liked to rub his arm, but I hadn't actually let go of him yet. 'What has my window got to do with this?' he asked. 'What difference does it make?'

'If you're telling the truth, it probably makes a lot of difference.' Although at the moment I couldn't have explained how or what to save my soul. I was just trying to do my job – just trying to account for the facts. 'If you're lying, it doesn't make any difference at all.'

Feeling light-headed, I shifted my attention back to Ginny.

She was saying, 'On the drive up here, Rock told us we had nothing to worry about if we got isolated. That's still true – as far as it goes. We can keep Simon under control. We only have a problem if he isn't the one who killed Cat.'

'Why do you keep saying "if"?' Hardhouse asked. Maybe it was my imagination, but he sounded almost seductive. 'What makes you think Simon didn't do it?'

Ginny smiled humourlessly. 'Professional scepticism. When you look at a picture, and one detail doesn't fit, sometimes the whole picture is wrong. Why did he take all those guns? Where did he put them? What did he plan to do with them? Until he answers questions like that, I'm going to keep saying "if".'

'She's dead,' Buffy murmured for no apparent reason. 'It's my fault.' She wasn't talking to any of us. 'We're stuck here. We're going to die. It's all my fault.'

'Nonsense,' Connie put in, quietly but firmly. 'You couldn't have known this would happen. And you had the good sense to hire Ginny and Brew. We'll all be fine.'

'I didn't take "all those guns",' Abel insisted. He sounded tired, as if I'd worn him out. 'I don't know what you're talking about. I don't know anything about guns. I didn't shoot Cat.'

With his usual charm, Mile told Simon to shut up.

When I noticed Art Reeson in the doorway, I couldn't decide whether to feel relieved or worried. Rock and Sam stood right behind him. He and Rock wore a certain amount of snow, but most of it was on him. His coat shed cakes of the stuff, he had snow in his hair, even snow in his eyebrows, snow packed on his legs. For a moment he didn't say anything. He just looked at Cat and me and Ginny like he wondered how much trouble we might give him.

In a lame voice, Rock explained, 'I couldn't think of anything else, so I went to find Art. But he was already on his way. Then Sam found us.'

'Mr Altar says the phone's dead.' Reeson sounded more than ever like he'd done too much shouting, and his hoarse rasp made what was left of my stomach twist. For some reason I felt sure that I wouldn't like what came next. 'That shouldn't have happened,' he continued. 'We have snow up here all the time. It never pulls down the phone lines.'

The liver spots on Rock's head gave him a diseased appearance. He said, 'Art checked the cars.'

'We've never had trouble with the phones,' Reeson insisted. 'That made me nervous. I wanted to be sure we've still got a way out of here.'

He stopped.

'Don't drag it out,' Ginny drawled. 'Tell us the good news.'

Reeson shrugged. He didn't have any trouble looking at her straight. 'Nothing works. The van, Truchi's truck, my four-wheel-drive – even the snowmobile. They've been immobilized. Somebody took the rotors out of all the distributors.

'We can't leave. We can't get help. We're stuck.'

Probably Maryanne whimpered or groaned. Probably Mile swore. Probably Queenie said something like, 'Oh, no!' But I couldn't be sure. Mac Westward was laughing too loud.

Chapter Twelve

Apparently Reeson didn't know whether to take offence or not. He ignored everyone who tried to question him – Hardhouse, Drayton, even Ginny. 'What's so funny, Mr Westward?'

Mac stopped laughing like someone had flipped a switch and turned the sound off. 'Nothing. Nothing at all. This is just perfect. It's just like in all the novels.'

'Don't say that, Mac,' Queenie murmured as if she knew she couldn't stop him. 'Don't say it.'

He said it without pausing. 'A group of people get together for something they think is innocent. But it isn't innocent at all. They're cut off, isolated. Then the murders start. They try to figure out who's doing it before they all die, but they can't. Finally there are only two people left. One is the murderer. The other isn't. But the reader doesn't know which is which. The classic murder mystery. Thornton Foal wrote a book just like it several years ago.'

Then he started to laugh again, cackling like a gooney-bird.

'*Mac!*' Connie's command was like the way she'd slapped Buffy, sharp and to the point. '*Pull yourself together.*'

Westward stopped again. Without transition he went all red and puffy around the eyes, like he was allergic to laughter.

'This is crazy!' Houston Mile protested at Reeson. He could've used authority lessons from Connie, but he did his best. 'Ah won't *have* it. You are *incompetent*, boy, and Deerskin Lodge will be liable!' I hadn't realized that he knew such big words. 'How could you allow this to happen?'

Reeson fixed Mile with the sort of glare I've always wished I could produce – the sort that makes people turn pale. He hardly raised his voice, but we all heard him.

538

'Did you call me "boy"?'

Mile probably wanted to yell some more, but the words didn't come out. Instead he gaped like he had something nasty stuck in his throat.

'I must have misheard you,' Reeson commented without a trace of humour.

'All right,' Ginny put in quickly, 'that's enough. Both of you *boys* can show off your macho to each other later. We have a problem. We need to make some decisions. If we stay cooped up in this room, we'll start hitting each other. Let's go to the den. Brew, Art – make sure the windows are covered.' She didn't want anyone to take potshots at us.

Sam nodded sharply. 'Good idea.'

'Who?' Maryanne quavered. 'Who's left? Why would anybody want to shoot at us?'

No one took any notice of her.

'I'll go with you,' Hardhouse said to Reeson and me. Offering to share the heroics.

Reeson didn't thank him. Neither did I.

Lara made no effort to hold him back.

'If you don't mind,' Connie said firmly to Ginny, 'I'll take Buffy to her room and stay with her. She doesn't have anything to contribute at the moment. And she's in no condition to be left alone. If you can't make decisions without me, let me know.'

As an idea, that one stank. We should all have stayed together. Nevertheless Ginny gave her permission with a nod.

I didn't argue the point. Reeson, Hardhouse, and I returned to the den.

We weren't particularly nervous about shutting the blinds and closing the curtains. Reeson and Hardhouse probably believed that Simon qualified for the role of Cat's murderer. And I was half giddy with the smell of port and blood, not to mention the hot liquid sensation burbling in my guts. When we were done, Reeson stoked up the fires while Hardhouse went back to the parlour to let Ginny know. Soon everyone except Connie and Buffy was in the den.

Ginny kept Abel covered, although he didn't make any threatening moves. Probably thinking too hard to actually do anything. Holding hands, the Draytons sat down on one of the couches. Mile sat down, too, collapsed fatly into a heavy armchair, but Maryanne stayed on her feet, behind his chair with her hands on his shoulders. The balance between them had shifted subtly. They were both scared, but now she was the one doing the comforting.

In contrast the Hardhouses had resumed acting like an estranged couple. More changes. Still participating in the heroics, he placed himself on guard duty at the entrance to the hallway that led to Buffy's room. She came over to me.

'Brew.' She reached out, but my expression must've warned her against touching me. Her hands faltered in front of my chest, fluttered back to her sides. 'Are you all right? You look awful.' Fortunately she kept her voice low. 'What did she do to you? What was that woman doing to you?'

It took me a moment to realize that her question had something to do with sex or alcohol.

I shook my head. Assuming that I wanted to talk to her at all, now wasn't the time.

If Westward noticed Lara's attitude, he didn't show it. He had other things on his mind. Whatever had started him laughing earlier was gone. Now he looked almost as lost as Rock. The bafflement in his eyes made me wonder whether he even knew who he was without the other half of Thornton Foal.

I stayed on my feet, ostensibly guarding the front door.

Ginny had Simon sit down. She pointed out seats to Lara and Mac. Then she took a chair herself, sitting where she could see everyone. Reeson she left squatting by the nearest hearth, tinkering with the coals. Deliberately she put her .357 down on an end table by her right hand.

'Art,' she began before anyone could get the impression that she wasn't in charge, 'what about Faith and the Carbones? They're stuck in this with us. Shouldn't they be here?'

'Faith didn't shoot anybody,' he said flatly, like he'd missed the point of the question. 'I told her to stay home with the doors locked. If you want to get at her, you'll have to go through me.'

But he hadn't missed the point. 'The Carbones need to know,' he went on. 'They have a right. But they didn't shoot anybody either. They've been here longer than I have. They like the job and the hours and the place. As far as I'm concerned, you're all better suspects.'

I accepted that. So did Ginny. 'All right,' she said, sounding as steady and uncompromising as he did. 'That's good enough for now. You talk to them when you get the chance.'

Reeson nodded at the flames.

'We have several things to consider,' she continued to the back of his head. 'We need you for all of them. You're the manager here – you know what our resources are, what we can do. Like it or not, we're dependent on you.'

540

He nodded again. The firelight in his eyes gave him a look of sharp concentration.

Ginny raised three fingers and touched them one at a time with the tips of her claw. 'First, we need some way to get a message out of here, call for help. We can't wait around for a thaw – or for one of us to find those rotors. Second, we need to keep Simon out of trouble' – she smiled bleakly – 'until the cops get here.' Simon winced at this, but she ignored him. 'Third, we need the rest of those guns locked up. We can't let anyone else appropriate any artillery.'

Before Reeson could respond, Maryanne protested in a wobbly voice, 'You still sound like you think Simon didn't do it. Like you think we're still in danger. I don't understand.'

'That can wait.' Ginny was in no mood for interruptions. 'Right now, we need to figure out what we're going to do.'

Sam released Queenie's hand, shifted forward in his seat. 'I don't think so, Ginny. I'm sure you're right about the practical situation. But we also have an emotional problem. We're all scared. A woman has been murdered. We need to know who did it. I don't mean that the things you listed aren't important, but we need this first. If Simon *didn't* do it, this is a life-or-death issue for all of us. The cops can't help us. Locking Simon up won't help us. And we may need those guns.

'What do you know that we don't, Ginny?'

Mile and Mac muttered their agreement. Maryanne nodded eagerly. Queenie put her hand on Sam's shoulder, a touch of approval. Hardhouse stuck out his jaw and watched Ginny with his eyes smouldering. Off in his own world, Rock mumbled something that sounded like, 'How did he get them?'

Ginny pulled in a deep breath and scanned the room. Then she gave in.

Facing Simon, she said, 'I'll go first. After that it's your turn.'

While his eyes widened, she turned to the rest of us. 'I won't bore you with the standard lecture about circumstantial evidence. I won't talk about how "things are never what they seem" – except you'd be amazed how often that turns out to be true. I'll keep it simple.

'I know Joseph didn't do it. I was with him in his room. I know Brew didn't do it. She wasn't shot at close range. What about the rest of you? What alibis have you got?'

'We were in the den,' Sam returned promptly.

'All of you?'

He thought for a second. 'No. Houston and I. Maryanne.' He looked around. 'That's all.'

'Queenie?' Ginny asked.

Queenie didn't hesitate. 'I was in our room. Alone.'

'Lara?'

Lara raised her hands to her face as if she were hiding a blush. 'Mac and I were out on the porch,' she said awkwardly. 'Talking. Isn't that right, Mac? We came inside when we looked in the window and saw the den was empty.'

'Yes!' Mac confirmed almost assertively. 'We were together. Neither of us did it. This is crazy.'

'Unless you did it together,' Ginny retorted, smiling like a Venus flytrap. 'Team murder is dangerous. You never know how far you can trust your partner. But it's an efficient way to kill somebody and not get caught.

'What about you, Rock?'

'How did he get all of them?' Rock muttered. He hadn't heard a word Ginny said. 'That's what I don't understand.'

Ginny shrugged. 'What about Connie? What about Buffy? Anybody know where they were?'

No one answered.

'You see the problem. Only nine of us have alibis. Only seven of them look good on paper. 'How many of you are willing to swear Connie or Buffy or Rock or Mac or Lara or Queenie isn't capable of murder?'

'Well, speaking for myself—' Queenie put in.

Ginny overrode her. She had no intention of wasting time on a general discussion. 'Your turn, Simon,' she announced. 'Give it your best shot.'

He was readier now than he'd been earlier – he knew his role. Just for a second, he faced her sincerely and said, 'Thanks.' Then he got started.

'I know I'm the obvious suspect.' He tried to control his tension by clenching his fists. 'I'm the one who came inside all covered with snow right after—' He swallowed hard. 'I can't prove I was just taking a walk because I didn't like what she was doing with Brew. Joseph was bad enough. Two men in two days was more than I could stomach. I can't prove I'm innocent.

'But look at what you're accusing me of. *Think* about it. I stole some guns – how many?' He glanced at me. 'I don't even know how many are missing. But I stole them. I hid the rest, took that rifle, and went outside. I disabled all the vehicles, just to make sure I couldn't escape.

Did I mention I've got a death-wish? I've been planning to get caught all along.

'Anyway, then I shot Cat.

'How did you find the rifle?' he asked Ginny.

'You left your window open,' she answered. 'You climbed in through the window, hid the rifle in your closet, then went out again to come in innocently through the front door.'

'*Right*, of course, how could I forget. I went back to my room through the window and ditched the rifle in the most obvious place I could think of, just to prove I knew what I was doing when I hid the rest of those guns.' He rolled his eyes, spread his hands at the ceiling. 'Then I went outside again and came in at exactly the right moment to make you all believe I shot the woman I love. And of course the first thing I did when Ginny caught me was *confess*.'

His hands slapped down on to his thighs.

'How *stupid* do you think I *am*?'

He silenced the group. He had no talent for righteous indignation – we weren't bowled over by the power of his performance. Nevertheless his simple logic silenced us. When you added it up the way he did, it really did sound stupid.

After a minute Ginny repeated, 'You see the problem.'

'Since you put it that way' – Hardhouse grinned wolfishly – 'I have to admit you've got a point. I don't think I've ever hired a *busboy* that dumb.'

Mac steepled his fingers judiciously. 'Unless he's being clever instead.' The professional novelist speaking. 'He may be trying to conceal his guilt by making it appear stupidly obvious.'

'Oh, come on!' Simon protested. 'Damn it, what do you people use for brains? If I wanted to kill her, this is the *worst* place to do it – and the worst conditions. Here we know one of us did it. I was sure to get caught. Why didn't I do it back in LA, where I could dump the body and nobody would ever know she was even missing? Do you think this is the first time she's ever cheated on me? Do you think–'

Ginny cut him off. 'That's enough. The point's been made. You're the only suspect we've got, but that doesn't mean you're the only suspect there is.' To the rest of us, she added, 'Use your heads. If we want to stay alive, we need to make sure Simon can't shoot anybody else. And we have to assume he didn't shoot anybody at all. We have to plan for the possibility there's still a killer loose around here.'

Reeson had turned away from the fire to watch Ginny closely.

When she stopped, he said softly, 'You know, you're good at this. That makes it interesting.'

In a plaintive tone, like he was tired of waiting, Rock asked, 'How did he get all those rotors? Weren't any of the cars locked? Didn't you have the snowmobile in a shed somewhere? Wasn't the shed locked?'

Ginny's grasp on the situation had apparently improved Reeson's humour. Cheerfully he scowled. 'Did you lock your van, Mr Altar?'

Rock blinked blankly. 'No.'

Reeson shrugged. 'Why should you? Why should Faith or Truchi or I lock any of our vehicles? Nobody steals cars up here. Or snowmobiles either. And nobody immobilizes them. We depend on them too much.

'Most of the time,' he concluded, 'we don't even take the keys out of the ignition.'

'Good,' Hardhouse commented. 'I like it. You're right – this makes it interesting.' He sounded sarcastic, but I detected relish. 'It's looking like more fun all the time.'

'At any rate,' Sam rasped, 'it looks like more fun than convincing the cooks to keep their hair out of the soup. Right?'

I got the distinct impression that he'd decided he didn't like Joseph Hardhouse.

Hardhouse grinned. 'You should try it. After six months in the restaurant business, you'll think having your teeth extracted is more fun.'

'Too bad it makes so much money,' Sam retorted. 'Otherwise you could quit with a clear conscience.'

Hardhouse didn't have to grope for a comeback. 'Maybe if I quit and became a doctor,' he said, 'I wouldn't have such trouble keeping my conscience clear.'

'Listen.' Ginny snapped her claw to get their attention. 'Bicker on your own time. We've got more important things to worry about right now.'

Sam held up his hands to show that he was finished.

From my point of view, the smile Hardhouse aimed at Ginny looked positively voracious.

'If I've made myself clear,' she went on, 'we're back where I started. We have decisions to make.'

'Not really.' As smooth as a hydraulic lift, Reeson rose to his feet. 'As you pointed out, I'm the manager here. And as *he* pointed out' – with a jerk of his head, he indicated Mile – 'the lodge doesn't want any liability suits. That makes the situation my responsibility. I'll take care of it. I don't mean I'm going to catch your killer for you. But I can solve some of the other problems.

'Over the years, I've done a fair amount of winter camping. I have the gear and the experience to cope with this weather. In the morning, I'll hike out of here. If conditions aren't so bad outside the valley, I can probably reach a phone by the end of the day. Otherwise it may take me two days. But the Carbones and Faith can handle everything here while I'm away.'

'You should take one of us with you,' Ginny remarked. 'Winter camping isn't exactly safe alone.'

'I should,' he agreed, 'but I won't. I don't have two sets of gear. And my tent only sleeps one. I'll be all right.

'Before I go,' he continued, 'I'll tell Truchi to hide the guns somewhere. He won't let any of you know where they are. That way' – his glare conveyed a secret humour – 'none of you will be tempted to declare yourselves vigilantes and shoot up the lodge.'

'Wait a minute,' Mile protested. 'Wait a goddamn minute.' Reeson had touched a sore point in him – a point sore enough to push him past his fear. 'We need them guns. If Ginny's right – and Ah don't say she is – we got to defend ourself. We got the *right* to defend ourself. How're we goin' to do that with no guns?'

'Well, I don't rightly know, Mr Mile,' Reeson drawled back, aping Mile's accent. 'Maybe you folks is just goin' to have to place your trust in God – and Miz Fistoulari.'

Mile flushed. Obviously he wasn't accustomed to mere employees who talked that way. But he also wasn't accustomed to facing down men with Reeson's talent for toughness. Probably hoping that only Maryanne could hear him, he muttered, 'Sonofabitch,' and lapsed back in his chair.

'Guns aren't for amateurs, Houston,' Ginny said harshly. 'I'd rather have one killer on my hands than a roomful of armed amateurs trying to defend themselves.'

Tired of feeling useless, parked by the front door and forgotten, I tried to make a contribution. 'Even experts miss sometimes,' I said through my fever. 'The goon who shot me did. But the really amazing thing is, amateurs never do. They always hit *some*thing.'

Ginny nodded and turned back to Reeson. 'What about Simon?'

'That's harder,' he admitted. 'The lodge doesn't have any rooms you can't get out of if you're locked in. And I suppose you don't want to do anything as "inhumane" as tying him to a chair for the next three or four days. I don't know what else to suggest.' Then he thought of something. 'Except the wine cellar.'

'Wine cellar?'

'It isn't really a cellar,' he explained, 'just a room off the kitchen. Only one door, no windows. There's a padlock on the outside. I think Ama has the key.

'It's insulated so it stays cool, but it doesn't get cold. We can put an electric heater in there. And it has room for a cot and a chair, maybe even a table. We have plenty of card tables.

'You could use it.'

'No!' Simon said.

'Good,' Ginny said.

'You don't understand,' Simon protested. 'I get claustrophobia. I'll go crazy in there.'

Right away I didn't believe him. He sounded like he was acting again.

Ginny didn't believe him, either. 'On the other hand,' she answered with an edge in her tone, 'once you're locked in the wine cellar, we'll all know you're innocent if somebody else gets killed. And you can be reasonably sure you won't be the next victim.'

In other words, she wasn't willing to take the risk that he really was Cat's killer. Personally I was glad I didn't have to make the decision. Since I didn't think he had anything to do with the murder, I probably wouldn't have had the heart to lock him up. And when I turned out to be wrong, I'd have real trouble living with myself.

Ginny got to her feet, holding the .357 again. Her movements lacked Reeson's oiled precision, but she looked ready and dangerous in her own way. 'Anybody got any problems?' she asked the room. 'Anything else you want to discuss?'

Maryanne bent down and murmured something in Mile's ear. He nodded without speaking. Somewhere under his fat, he'd probably clenched his jaws, but it didn't show.

Sam and Queenie looked at each other. Then she said for both of them, 'Tell us what you want us to do.'

I liked her so much it made my back teeth hurt.

Mac studied Lara. He was slowly returning to normal – only the specificity of his concentration on her betrayed the state of his emotions. Apparently the shock of Cat's murder had already become secondary to him. His loneliness ran so deep that what Lara represented was more important.

As for her, she returned his attention like he had the power to make her insides melt.

In contrast, Rock now seemed like he was actually present in the room. He'd finally caught up with the rest of us. He met Ginny's question by raising his head and doing his best to look decisive. 'This is what we hired you for. Although God knows we didn't want this to happen. You're in charge.'

Joseph Hardhouse echoed Rock. 'We'll do whatever you say.' But he added a vibration to the words, a second or third harmonic that echoed painfully in the core of my heart.

Ginny approved with a sharp nod. 'I have handcuffs in my purse,' she told Simon. 'I'm going to put them on you while Art rousts out the Carbones. Once Ama makes the wine cellar comfortable, I won't keep you cuffed.

'Joseph,' she asked, 'will you get my purse? I left it in the parlour.'

He nodded and went.

I still had nothing useful to do. Ginny was too good at this sort of thing.

'Before Art leaves,' she continued, scanning the room, 'maybe he and Truchi can do something with Cat's body so it doesn't' – she was deliberately harsh – 'start stinking up the lodge. In the mean time, the rest of us should search for those missing guns.'

So that's what we did. Or rather, that's what they did. Leaving Simon cuffed to one of the armchairs, Ginny split the guests into teams and put them to work. Judging by her choices, she trusted no one except the Draytons. She let them work together – alone. But she paired Mac with Rock, and sent Lara to keep an eye on Mile and Maryanne. Hardhouse she kept to herself. Each team she assigned a wing of the lodge.

She didn't need a degree in medicine, however, to see that I was in no condition to do any searching. Instead she told me to take Connie's place with Buffy so that Connie could join the hunt.

That made sense, of course. I couldn't stay on my feet much longer. Nevertheless it felt *wrong*. I was her partner. I should've done this job with her. To hell with the fact that my head no longer felt successfully attached to my neck. She still needed a partner.

But I didn't argue the point. Instead I told myself that she knew what she was doing. If I didn't lie down soon, I was going to fall down. And I wanted to get away from Hardhouse.

Tossing the Winchester to Reeson, I went to relieve Connie.

In the Altars' room I found Buffy asleep on one of the twin beds.

Shock and unconsciousness had wiped the camp-activities-director look off her face, the deliberate cheeriness and competence. Now she seemed both older and younger, the way some people do when they're scared – worn-out and vulnerable.

Connie sat in a rocking chair beside Buffy's bed, watching over her, as prim and austere as one of the fates.

'Well, Mr Axbrewder,' she asked me, 'what's been decided? What's being done?'

She required an answer, but I'd lost the ability to concentrate. Ginny needed a partner. People were searching the lodge. I should've been one of them. As if this were the crux of the whole situation, I said, 'You're supposed to call me "Brew".'

'That,' she retorted with some asperity, 'was when we were all guests together at a mystery camp. Now there's been a murder. You and Ms Fistoulari are the professionals in charge until the police arrive.' Apparently she could tell that I had no idea what her point might be. 'To be effective,' she explained, 'you must have authority. I intend to grant you that authority.'

'Oh, good,' I said. I didn't want authority. I wanted to lie down.

Restraining impatience, Connie repeated, '*Mr* Axbrewder, what's been decided? What's being done?'

She had a right to know. Somehow I told her.

She spent a moment absorbing the information. Then she pronounced, 'You shouldn't have any trouble with Mrs Altar. I expect she'll sleep for quite a while. Use the other bed and get some sleep yourself. I'm sure Mr Altar won't object.'

Mutely I obeyed. As if she were the one with all the authority, I went to the bed and eased my guts into prone.

I must've been in worse shape than I realized. An entire swimming pool sloshed around inside me, but that didn't prevent me from becoming one with the mattress almost immediately.

Maybe because she understood how Buffy and I felt, Connie didn't switch the light off. That turned out to be a good thing. It helped me identify where I was when Buffy's crying woke me up.

Softly she sobbed into her pillow, clamping it over her face like she wanted to suffocate herself.

The swimming pool sensation in my gut was worse than ever. I had difficulty heaving all that water upright. But I got myself over to her bed somehow. Sitting beside her, I pried one of her hands loose so that I could hold it.

'Buffy.' I sounded like a rusty bandsaw, but that was the best I could

548

do. 'Buffy, it's all right. Don't worry. It's going to be all right.' Pure bullshit, but I didn't even notice. 'We'll take care of everything.'

Clinging hard to my hand, she pulled her face out of the pillow. Her hair was a fright, and the skin around her eyes looked like one of those plastic surgeries where the patient goes into collagen rejection.

'She wasn't supposed to die,' she gulped between sobs. 'I never wanted her to die. I didn't want anybody hurt. It was just supposed to be fun.

'Now she's dead and it's my fault. It's all my fault.'

'No, it's not.' I comforted her like she was a sick kid. 'Don't be silly. It's not your fault. No one blames you.'

That must've been what she wanted to hear. It seemed to help her stop sobbing. Nevertheless she had to protest against it, probably because she wanted it so badly.

'We're here because of me. Because I wanted to do this. Murder On Cue is mine. Rock doesn't care about it. He only helps out because he's my husband. I put us in this situation. I made it happen. Cat wouldn't be dead if I hadn't.'

I repeated myself like a half-wit. 'Don't be silly.' Fortunately as my voice limbered up I sounded a bit more soothing. 'That's like blaming the guy who built the lodge for making a place where someone might be shot. It's not your fault.'

Gradually she relaxed. Her breathing still shuddered and caught going in and out, but the pressure to sob grew less inside her. Her damaged eyes searched my face as if I were someone she could believe, someone who told the truth.

'I've never seen a dead body,' she said in a small voice. 'Nobody I care about has ever died. Even my parents are still alive. My favourite teacher from high school is still alive. I never knew my grandparents. When I saw her there in all that blood–' Her mouth quivered pitifully. 'I keep thinking this is going to ruin my life.'

Most days, I think that people who let the presence of blood and pain in the world ruin their lives deserve to have their lives ruined. But this time, for some reason, her concern just reminded me that I didn't smell so good. I needed clean clothes and a shower and a fresh outlook on life.

So I didn't dismiss her self-pity. Instead I said, 'Maybe it won't. It's too soon to know.' Then I tried a distraction. 'Tell me more about Rock. What does he get out of doing this?'

'I used to worry about that,' Buffy admitted. She was too stunned or vulnerable to question what I asked her. Hell, she hadn't even questioned my presence in her room. 'He doesn't like mysteries. I thought he would. He's usually good at puzzles. But there's something about this kind of puzzle he doesn't like. I don't know what it is. I used to worry that if he helped me with something he wasn't interested in, he'd lose interest in me.'

She paused. I didn't hurry her.

'But then I found out,' she went on. 'Why he does it. How he stays interested. What he does to stay interested.' She was thinking in pieces – but at least she was thinking. 'Houston told me. The first time he came to one of our camps. You mustn't underestimate Houston, Brew,' she insisted. She wanted me to believe whatever it was that Mile had told her. 'A lot of people don't like him.'

With unexpected acid in her voice, she commented, 'I think most of the women he brings with him don't like him.' Then she resumed, 'But he's devious. That makes him good at mysteries.'

She took a deep breath, and a quiver ran through her. Faltering as if she feared my reaction, she revealed, 'He told me Rock tampers with the clues. He makes it harder for us to figure out who did it. That's how he stays interested.'

So she knew. I couldn't decide whether to be relieved or amazed. From the beginning, it had nagged at me that Rock was willing to sabotage his wife's beloved hobby. But if she knew . . .

'You don't sound upset,' I said. 'Doesn't it bother you?'

'Oh, no,' she replied quickly. Too quickly? 'Do you know what it's like when you're getting older and bit by bit your husband starts to look like he's dying of boredom? It takes the heart out of you. There's nothing you can do about it. You try to look good. You work at it. But you can't make yourself younger. So you try to catch his mind instead – since you can't catch his eye any more. But Rock doesn't like mysteries.'

She let an old sigh out of the bottom of her lungs. 'I want him to stay interested. I'm glad he's found a way to do it. And now that I know about it, I can enjoy it. I don't know what he'll do, of course. But just knowing he'll do something makes the mystery better. It puts more pressure on everyone, even the actors. It's become a game he and I play with each other.'

She smiled in a wan attempt to convince me that she was content. 'Almost a way of courting each other. If you know what I mean.'

Actually I thought I did. In a perverse sort of way, it even seemed reasonable.

But I didn't buy it. It was too damn convenient.

After all, Roderick Altar didn't like hunters. He wasn't just uninterested in Buffy's game, he disapproved of it. And he'd talked me out of taking a stand about those guns. If they'd been locked up originally, Cat might still be alive.

Where did he draw the line? How serious did the game have to get before he played it honestly? The last thing Ginny and I needed to worry about right now was a man who couldn't or wouldn't make the distinction between killing people with blue marbles and killing them with actual bullets.

When the door opened, however, and Rock and Ginny came into the room, my immediate concern evaporated. He didn't look like a man who meddled with murders. He looked like a man who needed sleep. He'd gone grey with fatigue, the colour of lead and strain. Most of his body seemed to slump on his bones. The sight of him reminded me that he'd freely admitted tampering with Buffy's clues. That odd piece of honesty made him appear less dangerous now.

Instead of mentioning my worries, I asked, 'Did you find anything?'

Rock didn't respond. Dumbly he shuffled across the room, sat down on the edge of his bed, and stared morosely into his empty hands. It was Ginny who said, 'Not a thing. If you don't count Mile's collection of pornographic paraphernalia.'

She sounded distant rather than tired or disappointed, as if the waste of the search had no real importance. Or less importance than other things.

'Come on, Brew.' She surprised me by resting her claw gently on my shoulder. 'We've done all we can for tonight. The sun'll be up in a few hours. I want to see you in bed before I collapse myself.'

She'd stopped trusting me. She'd stopped using me. But she hadn't stopped taking care of me.

I could see that she was in no danger of collapsing.

I sighed and struggled to my feet.

We left Rock and Buffy sitting on the edges of their respective beds. The only obvious difference between them was that she looked at him but he still didn't look at her.

Probably I should've confronted Ginny then. The halls were empty, no one else was around. I wasn't likely to get a better chance. I should've said, I'm your partner. Stop treating me like an invalid. Stop charging into rooms without me to back you up. Stop telling other people to do my job.

But I funked it. I told myself that I didn't have the strength. The truth was that I didn't have the courage. The simple effort of walking to my room exhausted the last of my resolve. If she hadn't stood over me and made me do it, I wouldn't have taken off my clothes before I crawled into bed.

After all, I *was* an invalid. I couldn't change that just by hating it.

Instead of saying what I needed to say, I murmured, 'Simon's window bothers me. It doesn't fit.'

Ginny looked at me as if her brain were somewhere else entirely. 'What do you mean?'

'He didn't have to make himself look so guilty. He could've shot Cat and stashed the rifle, then closed the window and joined us through the lodge. Even if he had a reason to come in through the front door, he could've closed his window first. By the time we searched his room, the snow would've melted. You wouldn't know the window was ever open.'

'You don't think he did it.' She still wasn't paying attention.

'No, I don't.' I couldn't be honest for myself, but I could do it for Simon.

She shook her head. 'Joseph says the same thing. According to him, Simon doesn't have the right kind of motive. That's part of his theory about murder, I guess. Jealousy is too primal. If Simon killed Cat, he'd want her to know it was him. He'd do it face-to-face. He wouldn't attempt a charade as elaborate as this one looks.

'It doesn't matter whether I agree or not. Locking Simon up is still a good idea. It protects the rest of us. Since he can't kill anybody else, whoever wants us to think he's guilty won't risk destroying the illusion.'

She was way ahead of me. As usual. For once, I found that reassuring. She didn't love me any more, and she couldn't treat me like a real partner, but she was still Ginny Fistoulari. She knew what she was doing.

Before she left my room, I rolled over and sank back down into the depths of the pool.

Chapter Thirteen

When I woke up, I found sunshine splashed brilliantly across the rugs in my room, and the doilies looked positively luminous, and I was in a completely different world of fever. I felt as clear as crystal – and as empty as glass. Like a computer with no software to run it. Precise and useless.

Obviously I'd slept too long.

I blinked at the ceiling for a couple of minutes without once wondering why my curtains were open. The snowstorm had blown past, that was the important thing. Reeson could get out of here. Maybe we could even count on him.

Apparently the sun had been up and doing its job for a while now. Piously setting a good example for the rest of us. No doubt I'd missed Reeson's departure. But I felt too clear and empty to be disturbed by the mere fact that I lay abed like a debutante after a ball when theoretically I was 50 per cent in charge of keeping everyone else alive. Fever seemed to be the solution to all my usual emotional difficulties.

On that philosophical note, I got out of bed.

I needed a shower badly. I could still smell blood and port on my skin. On top of that, a distinct whiff of something rancid rose from the general vicinity of my bandages. But of course the bandages prevented me from taking a shower. And I was probably too weak for so much exertion. I didn't bother with it. I didn't bother with shaving. I knew I was supposed to take my pills, but I didn't bother with them, either. What good did being clear and empty do me, if I couldn't make my own decisions like a grownup?

On the other hand, I drew the line at wearing my dirty clothes again. Axbrewder the cleanliness freak. I dragged a heavy cotton sweater over my head, hauled up a pair of pants. The only thing I put in my pockets was my .45.

My feet seemed incredibly far away, almost impossible to reach. Finally I dismissed the problem of socks. Instead I pushed my toes into a pair of loafers Ginny had packed for me. Then, feeling better than I had for days, I went out to face the world.

It was a good thing that my head was so clear. Otherwise I might not have been able to keep my balance. My legs had different amounts of strength, and I listed to one side as if the freight inside me had shifted.

I didn't find anyone in the den. They were all outside, standing on the porch or up to their knees in the snow. When I joined them, none of them paid me much attention. Reeson must've gotten a late start. They were all watching him go – watching their hope trudge out of sight over the white horizon. I could see his tracks in the snow, running up the driveway to the gate at the rim of the valley.

I spotted him in time to see that he didn't turn or wave. He just plodded away, a small black figure disappearing into the background of white snow and dark trees.

Despite the end of the storm, the air hadn't become significantly warmer. And a steady wind blew. Reeson's trail had already started to fill in and fade, erased by powder. In an hour or two all sign of his passing would be gone. The snow wouldn't hold a trail until the sun or the air made it wet enough to stick.

'Mr Axbrewder.' Connie Bebb had noticed me at last. 'I'm glad you got some sleep. You needed it.'

Then Lara Hardhouse turned. Even though she stood at Mac Westward's shoulder, she flashed me a smile that would've looked friendly if it hadn't held such unmitigated desire.

She and Mac had kept to the porch, along with the Altars and Connie, Houston Mile and Maryanne Green. Of that group, only Lara and Mac didn't seem the worse for wear. Connie looked wan and thin, stretched too tight. A quick frightened little twitch worked the corner of Maryanne's mouth, as if she feared being hit. She tried to control it by compressing her lips. For his part, Mile had the sluggish self-absorbed air of a reptile about to moult.

Rock and Buffy now resembled each other the way old married couples sometimes do. From him she'd picked up a grey tone, the leaded weight of defeat. From her he'd acquired puffy eyes and a frenetic glance. If he'd had any hair, it would've stuck up in all directions.

Apparently Simon Abel still occupied the wine cellar. But Faith Jerrick stood on the porch, too, along with Amalia Carbone. Amalia's husband, Petruchio, had joined Sam and Queenie Drayton, Joseph Hardhouse, and Ginny out in the snow. They'd clustered together like the official farewell committee, supervising Reeson's departure.

When Connie said my name, Ginny and Hardhouse looked at me in unison, as if they'd achieved a new partnership during the night.

The sunlight reflecting off all that clean snow made them squint, but it didn't trouble me. I was clear and empty, and the brightness passed through me without leaving a mark.

Sam and Queenie faced in my direction as well. I had no idea how well they could see me.

In my vacant fashion, I was surprised to see that Faith didn't have a coat – or even a sweater. Nothing more than a long apron warmed her blouse and skirt. As pale as she was, I would've expected her to be susceptible to chill, one of those delicate creatures whose feet are always ice. But she didn't look cold. Folding her arms under her breasts, she stared up at the spot where Reeson had disappeared as if she could still see him – as if she'd burned his image into her retinas. Maybe that was why she never looked at other people directly. She couldn't actually see anyone except him.

'Does he really know what he's doing?' I asked her. Since my life probably depended on him, I had a personal interest.

I couldn't be sure that she'd heard me until she said, 'Oh, yes.' Naturally she didn't so much as glance in my direction. 'Art always knows what he's doing.'

Does he? I thought. He must be impossible to live with. But I didn't say that out loud.

As if my arrival were a signal, the people out in the snow started moving. Truchi strode off towards one of the cottages, unhampered by anything as minor as eighteen inches of snow. Ginny and Hardhouse approached the porch, with Sam and Queenie behind them.

As she came up the steps, Ginny blinked the glare out of her eyes to look at me more closely. Now I didn't need intuition to tell me that something was happening to her, something important. I could see it in the muscles around her eyes and mouth. They must've been clenched for so long I'd gotten used to seeing them that way. Otherwise the change when they relaxed wouldn't have seemed so dramatic.

'I came to your room,' she said almost casually. 'Before Art left. I was going to wake you up. But when I saw how hard you slept, I decided to leave you alone.' She almost smiled. 'But I opened your curtains, just in case you wanted to wake up.'

She was gone. Lost to me. Like people, relationships die. They can even be killed. The only problem when that happens is that you have to go on living.

Fortunately the fever protected me. Instead of pissing and moaning and generally feeling sorry for myself, I shrugged a bit and said, 'Thanks.'

She didn't trust my reaction. Frowning now, she asked, 'Are you all right? You don't look good.' A moment later she demanded, 'Have you been taking your pills?'

Hardhouse slipped his hand under her arm like he wanted to get her away from me. 'Brew's a big boy,' he said. 'He's old enough to take his own pills.'

Briefly she did me the courtesy of ignoring him. 'Isn't that right?' Ginny murmured to me. 'I'm supposed to stop taking care of you? That's what you want?'

But Hardhouse didn't mean to be ignored. 'You're too good at it,' he commented helpfully. 'He needs to learn the truth about himself. He can't do that when you cover for him.'

She glanced at him quickly, as if this perception had the power to change her life.

Obviously the two of them had spent some time talking about me. Somehow I got the impression that his idea of 'the truth' wasn't very flattering.

I opened my mouth and pretended to laugh, but nothing came out.

With him somehow indefinably in charge, he and Ginny led the way back into the den. The Altars, Mile and Maryanne, even Connie followed like sheep. Ama Carbone did the same, but not from any herd instinct. She just had work to do.

Faith Jerrick remained on the porch, watching the point of Reeson's departure as if the simple intensity of her yearning could ensure that he came back.

Sam and Queenie stopped in front of me. Concern filled their faces.

'Don't say it,' I said, groping for the right note of amiable lunacy. '"You don't look good." If I hear that one more time, I might believe it.'

The Draytons were holding hands, gripping each other hard. With my new clarity, I didn't have any trouble noticing the whiteness of their knuckles. Softly, speaking personally to Sam despite the fact that I could hear her, Queenie observed, 'You could help him whether he wants it or not. I don't think he has the strength left to stop you.'

He scowled, not at her, but at what she said. 'I don't like doing that. I'm not sure it's ethical. And it doesn't usually work. As soon as he recovers a bit, he'll just go back to trying to kill himself.'

'That's not your problem,' she countered. 'You've helped people before when they were too sick or hurt to ask for it.'

'Sure. But this is a different situation. In the hospital, or my office, I can always assume that people want my help, even if they're too far gone to ask. I'm entitled to assume that under the circumstances. I don't think I can assume it here.'

She conceded with a sigh. 'I just don't like feeling so helpless.'

'May I say something,' I put in, 'or is this a private discussion?'

Both Sam and Queenie faced me.

'Sam is right,' I told her. 'It's none of your business.'

Without quite meaning to, I hit a nerve. Her eyes filled with tears. His face went hard, as if I'd just lost his friendship.

'Faith,' he said steadily, 'Brew hasn't had any breakfast. Take him inside. See if you can get him to eat something. If he won't go with you, I'll drag him.'

'Yes, Dr Drayton.' Being given something to do seemed to release Faith from her trance. Not glancing at any of us, she moved to the door and held it open.

Queenie's tears had more effect on me than Sam's anger. The fever only defended me from my own pain, not hers. But I couldn't think of anything useful to say, so I turned away and let Faith escort me back into the lodge.

Following her, I shuffled into the kitchen. Along the way I noticed that the guns were gone from the cases in the dining room. Truchi, at least, was doing his job.

In the kitchen, Faith pointed me at a stool at one of the counters, then moved to a refrigerator and began pulling out food.

I sat down and watched her.

I probably should've told her not to bother, but my mind was elsewhere. The empty cases had reminded me of Art Reeson and Cat Reverie and how helpless we all were. Or maybe I just wanted a distraction from Ginny and Hardhouse – and Sam and Queenie. So I asked Faith, 'Is this what he does on his vacations? Go camping in the dead of winter?'

Apparently she didn't consider my question unexpected. In her condition, no reference to Reeson was unexpected.

'Sometimes.'

There's nothing like a one-word answer to inspire the imagination. 'Do you mean he sometimes goes camping on his vacations? Or he sometimes goes camping in the dead of winter?'

She thought about this while she put a plate of cold toast and bacon in front of me, along with a pot of strawberry jam. 'Would you like something hot? I can warm up the bacon. Or scramble some eggs.'

Instead of gagging, I waited for her to get around to my question. I felt sure that she wasn't being evasive. She simply lived in a mental world very different from mine.

After a moment she said, 'Both.'

'Do you go with him?' I was trying to evaluate Reeson's ability to get through the snow and save us.

'No,' she answered without hesitation or rancour. 'Why should I?'

I shrugged. 'Keep him company?'

She stood across the counter from me, her arms folded over her midriff again. If she cared that I hadn't touched the food, she didn't show it.

'I would if he asked me, of course,' she explained as if the subject were somehow profound. Her manner was more subdued than the last time I talked to her. If anything, that made her more convincing. 'But I have no reason to go, expect to please him. I don't need to go anywhere. God is with me wherever I am. That's all I need.'

'I see.' I didn't see at all. 'Sometimes he goes camping in the winter. Sometimes in the summer. And sometimes he doesn't go camping. If he wants a vacation, he does something else. And you don't go with him.'

She nodded gravely.

'Where does he go when he doesn't go camping?'

'You'll have to ask him, Mr Axbrewder.' I hadn't offended her. I'd just touched something outside her chosen world. 'He doesn't take me with him, so I don't know where he goes.'

'You mean, even when he does something besides camping for his vacation, he doesn't take you with him?'

'Why should he?' Her calm was perfect. 'While he's away, I have God for company. And after he goes away, he comes back.'

She said this as if it accounted for everything.

Not to me, it didn't. 'But why doesn't he tell you where he goes?' I pursued. 'Doesn't he even leave phone numbers, in case you need to get in touch with him? What about emergencies?'

Clearly I lacked the capacity to ruffle her. 'What emergencies do you imagine I'm afraid of, Mr Axbrewder? Truchi and Ama are here.' Almost as if she were looking at me, she went on, '*God* is here. If you could believe in Him, you would know there is truly nothing to be afraid of.'

'I'm trying,' I muttered. Bafflement seemed to breathe a fog across the blank glass of my emotions. 'It just doesn't make sense.' For a second there, confronted by her immaculate and irreducible self-absorption, I felt something surge behind the clarity and the emptiness and the fever – something that tasted and smelled and even hurt like utter rage. *Nothing to be afraid of.* No question about it, I would've been better off with her religion, all my questions answered and no more need to think.

Where else did she get so much *trust*?

I had to get away from her before I lost my balance entirely. At that moment I didn't give a shit whether she thought I was rude or not. I got up and lurched out of the kitchen.

When I reached the den – which seemed unusually far away, like I'd taken a wrong turn somewhere – I found it practically empty. Maryanne Green sat alone in front of the embers of one of the fires, as if she'd been left behind. A deer's head with glassy death in its eyes leaned over her. She looked up when she heard me shuffling over the floorboards. Something in her expression warned me not to join her.

Too bad. I needed help – I needed to escape Faith emotionally as well as physically – and Maryanne was the only resource available. I sat down beside her and asked the first question that came into my head. 'Where's everyone else?'

'Most of us were up all night.' She didn't turn her head – and she didn't try to sound anything except bitter. 'We couldn't find the guns. But Simon is in the wine cellar. We're supposed to be safe now. Ginny said she wanted to get some sleep. Everybody else thought that was a good idea.'

Her tone did what I wanted – it hooked my attention. 'But not you.'

For maybe the first time, I looked at her closely and noticed that she wasn't young. Until then I'd assumed that she was practically a kid. She had a fresh face, and I felt sure that Mile preferred girls to women. But the skin around her eyes had too many fine lines, and her cheeks weren't resilient enough.

'Houston didn't want sleep,' she answered. 'He's scared, I guess. When he's scared, he does things to me. It reassures him. Maybe he isn't on top of the world. Maybe he can't do everything he wants. But at least he can do what he wants to me.

'But I'm scared, too. He doesn't understand that. Ginny scared me. If she had just let me think Simon did it, I might have been able to stand it. I might have been brave enough. But now I'm scared. I've never been so scared. And what he does hurts. It hurts a lot. Sometimes I think it's going to be more than I can bear.'

Her voice trailed away, dying like the coals in the fire.

I could guess what happened. 'So you told him no.'

She nodded dumbly.

'And he threw you out.'

She nodded again. 'He says he won't even pay my way home.' Then, before I could come up with a reply, she added, 'I could kill Ginny for this.'

She sounded perfectly sincere.

Suddenly my balance failed. Like Faith, Maryanne touched something in me that I didn't understand and couldn't use, a mad blank anger. 'Oh, come on,' I rasped. 'What do you want her to do? Ignore the chance that Simon is innocent? If he didn't kill Cat, someone else did. And if it's someone else, we don't know what his motive is.' Or hers. 'Which means we can't predict what'll happen next. Maybe we'll all get shot at. Ginny is just doing her job.'

Maryanne didn't try to answer me directly. I'd missed the point. She had a completely different grievance. Glaring at me like I'd just crawled out from under a rock, she countered, 'But she isn't much of a woman, is she.'

Oh, boy.

'I don't know what you see in her. Or Joseph sees. It isn't fair. She wants to be a man. She throws her weight around and tells everyone what to do and swears like a man. She humiliates you. And you lap it up. You ought to hate her, but instead you follow her around like a puppy. She's castrated you, and you think you like it. And Joseph can't wait to get his hands on her. He ought to know better – a man like that. *He* ought to know better. Do you know where they are right now?'

No, don't tell me that. Do *not* tell me that. More than anything else, I didn't want to know where Ginny and Hardhouse were right now. Otherwise I would burst with fever and fury.

'It's none of my business,' I said as quickly as I could, trying to stop her.

I didn't stop her. But at least I deflected her.

'Cat was someone I could understand,' she went on. 'I can't figure out why you didn't like her. She wanted you to be *male*. She wanted to revel in your maleness. That made her a woman, a real woman. And Lara's a real woman, in her own way. I don't know how she manages to see anything *male* about Mac, but at least she wants Joseph to be himself. She likes him the way he is.'

As an interpretation of Lara, this stunned me. But I didn't interrupt.

'Even Queenie is a woman.' Maryanne concentrated on the coals as if she thought that she could make them blaze by scowling at them. 'She has too many opinions, and she wants everyone to take them seriously. But she doesn't get in Sam's way. She knows he's a man. She wants him to be a man. Not Ginny.'

Maryanne actually shuddered, a hard quiver of revulsion. 'She doesn't want you to be a man. If you tried, she'd try to prevent you. She wants to make us all *afraid*. Why does she do it? What does she get out of it?'

'I have a better question.' I was full of panic, terrified of my own emotions, and I couldn't afford to think about Ginny. 'Why do *you* do it?'

Poor woman, she knew exactly what I meant. I'd asked her real question for her, the question that made everything else hurt. She turned a gaze like hate at me, and her bitterness came up from the bottom of her heart.

'What makes you think I have a choice?'

I spread my hands helplessly.

'Look at me,' she demanded. 'Do you see anything that makes you think I have a choice? I'm not young. I've never been able to get a husband. There aren't any jobs I know how to do. I guess it isn't considered a good thing any more to be a woman, but that's what I am. That's all I am. And I'm not beautiful like Cat. I don't have Lara's talent for looking mysterious and passionate. I don't even have breasts like Queenie. Mine sag, and they have stretch-marks, and my hips are puffy.' She may have wanted to weep, but her bitterness didn't allow her anything that direct and simple. 'I don't have a choice.'

'Then,' I said softly, like it was my job to break her heart, 'you better go back to Houston.'

She gave me a look of pure black murder – but she didn't hesitate. Jerking to her feet, she knotted her hands in the front of her blouse and wrenched at it so one of the seams tore and a few of the buttons popped. They clicked to the floor and rolled away, whispering across the wood.

'I'll tell him you attacked me,' she said in a dead voice that didn't match her eyes at all. 'That'll get him excited.' But an instant later she thought better of it. 'No, he'll never believe it. He has your number – he knows what you're capable of. I'll tell him it was Joseph. He'll believe that.'

Looking more attacked than any woman I could remember, she turned and strode out of the den. Only the defiant flounce of her skirt showed that she knew she was really her own victim.

So much for clarity and emptiness. Maryanne seemed to sweep all that away in her wake, leaving me frantic. Now my head felt like it was being pumped up with confusion, inflated like a balloon, and emotions I didn't want to recognize expanded in me.

Am I really like that? Have I got it as bad as she does?

Have I made myself such a cripple with Ginny that I no longer have any choice?

I must've been sicker than I realized. I'd lost the centre of myself, and I couldn't contain the fever. Without being entirely aware of it, I slumped forward like I was fainting and thudded to my hands and knees on the floor.

Luckily that jolted me out of my tailspin. The pain was therapeutic. I was too old to abase myself like this, begging the fireplace and the empty den to take pity on me. And I didn't want to look ridiculous, even to myself. So I took a few deep breaths, then got my legs under me and stood up.

Just to prove that I could do it, I hunched over to the hearth and tossed two or three fresh logs on to the fire. After that I retreated to the chair and collapsed.

All that exertion made my head explode. Fortunately it didn't hurt. I simply lost consciousness with a burst like a popping bubble.

I had no sense of time, so I didn't know how long I was out. And as far as I could tell I didn't dream. I didn't have that excuse for being so disoriented. Nevertheless my confusion went right to the bone.

I felt hands on my shoulder, but I didn't know what they were. They shook me, shook me so hard that my head lolled around like my neck was broken, but they had no meaning. Then I heard someone coughing – coughing violently enough to bring up their shoes. A voice knotted with strain choked out, 'Mr Axbrewder! Mr Axbrewder! Wake up!' Male or female, I couldn't tell.

And I didn't care about any of it. I didn't consider it worth waking up for until a spasm took hold of my lungs and ripped me open from the top of my head to the pit of my stomach.

I tried to lurch upright, but I'd begun coughing too hard to get my legs under me. When I opened my eyes I could see smoke. Smoke as thick as acid filled my eyes and chest. Spasms pulled claws through my ruined abdomen.

'Wake up!' the voice wailed thinly, like the small cry of a newborn. Then it frayed into retching.

The lodge was on fire? I couldn't tell.

Scrubbing at my tears, I cleared my vision enough to see oily grey-white smoke as it erupted from the fireplace in great billows, swelled outward like the end of the world.

The lodge wasn't on fire. But this was no ordinary smoke. No wood in all the world burned like this, even with fresh logs on the fire and the chimney plugged.

I made another effort to get up.

Amalia Carbone had me by the shoulder. I couldn't make out details, but I recognized her general shape. She strove to haul me to my feet, save me somehow, but she didn't have the muscle.

It helped that I wasn't alone. Old reflexes kicked in. She wanted to rescue me. If I didn't move, we might both die.

The smoke made me gag as if my lungs were full of blood, but I reached one hand to Ama's head and pulled her ear down to my mouth so that she could hear me.

'The doors,' I gasped. Despite my desperation, I could scarcely force out a whisper. 'Inside. Close them.' So that everyone else doesn't asphyxiate. 'Then get help.'

Then I braced myself on the arms of the chair and climbed upright.

When she saw that I could stand, Ama let go of me and disappeared into the smoke.

My vision swam with tears, and I couldn't straighten my spine. Coughing clenched my guts. But I didn't make a sound, that was the odd thing. I couldn't even hear myself gag. Ama moved in shrouded silence. But then I heard doors slam. One. Two three. The two bedroom wings and the hall to the dining room.

Hunched over nearly to my knees, I blundered towards the front door.

For a while I couldn't find the knob. And for a while after that I couldn't get the door open because I was leaning against it, holding it shut. I'd stopped coughing, overtaken by a spasm that locked up all my muscles until my head whirled for air and I felt like I would never breathe again.

Then I wrenched the door past my bulk and stumbled outside.

I couldn't stop. Trailing an outrush of smoke, still in spasm, I pitched down the steps and fell on my face.

After a minute or two I started spitting blood into the white pure drifted snow.

Chapter Fourteen

For a while I lay there and retched, bringing up bile and blood. The absence of pain astonished me. Apparently the circuit in my brain which acknowledged pain had gone into overload and shut down. I hadn't had much air recently, and fire filled my lungs, but I hardly noticed. For the moment, anyway, that stuff had no personal impact.

I didn't start to think again until sweet clean cold oxygen finally cleared my wits. Then I raised my head and saw the impression my face had made in the snow.

It was red and dark, as dark as blood from the heart. Not a lot of blood, but enough to get my attention.

I'd torn open some of my sutures.

Someone had just tried to kill me.

From my perspective, lying there in the snow while my body cooled and spasms trembled through me, the evidence seemed irrefutable. I'd been alone in the den. Asleep. God knows how long. And wood didn't burn like that, not like *that*. So someone must've put something in the hearth, something to produce all that acid violent smoke. And blocked the chimney so that the smoke wouldn't escape. The easy way to do it would've been from the roof. Drop the stuff down the chimney and then pack it with snow.

Whoever did that must've done it because I was alone in the den asleep.

Simple.

Unfortunately what came next wasn't simple at all.

Simon Abel hadn't just tried to kill me. He'd been locked in the wine cellar all night –

And Cat –

565

For some reason I remembered a voice.

It said, *Get out of there. He wants you. You're a sitting duck.*

Sweet Christ.

At least my mental circuits were still out. Even the implications of that memory didn't hurt.

But I had to move. Snow was soaking into my clothes. And lives depended on me. This mess revolved around me somehow. I had to prevent as much of it as I could from spilling over on to innocent bystanders.

Which meant that I needed Ginny.

Which meant that I had to move.

Oh, shit. This was going to be such fun.

The temporary stay of pain I'd been granted helped. All I had to deal with was my weakness. God, I felt *weak*! My entire body hardly contained one useful muscle. Just holding my head up tested me to my limits.

Too bad, Axbrewder. Weakness was just an excuse, another way of trying to evade my responsibilities. Like booze. And self-pity.

So move, already.

Somehow I climbed to my feet.

Around me the lodge and the snow and the dark trees veered unconscionably from side to side, and I couldn't get anything into focus. But I fought to keep my balance. Eventually I found myself blinking in bright sunlight at the driveway out of the valley.

The wind had erased all sign of Reeson's departure. As far as I could tell, he'd never left.

When I turned and let my head tilt back, I was able to see the roof of the den. Sure enough, the snow all around the chimney had been trampled down, shoved aside.

And the roof was probably easy to reach from the attic.

That made sense, anyway.

A step at a time, I forced myself up on to the porch.

That close to the front door, however, I realized that I couldn't go back in through the den. Harsh smoke still poured outward, looking for me. If Ama had gone for help – if she'd made it out of the room all right – the help hadn't come yet. In fact, there was a good chance that no one knew what had happened. Too many closed doors stood between the bedrooms and the den.

I didn't mind. I didn't want to talk to anyone except Ginny.

Shuffling like a cripple, I tottered back down the steps and around the lodge to the nearest door, the outside entrance to one of the bedroom wings.

The wrong one, of course – the wing with my room, not Ginny's. But I couldn't afford to let minor frustrations upset me. If I did, I might lie down and never move again.

Creeping down the hall as if I actually wanted to catch people by surprise, I went to Joseph Hardhouse's door.

That was reasonable, wasn't it? Ginny had been spending a lot of time in his company. It was more efficient to check every possibility along my way, instead of going to her room and being forced to double back. Wasn't it?

Apparently I was in no mood to be honest with myself.

But Hardhouse might be taking a nap. If so, I didn't mean to wake him up. At least that's what I told myself. For all practical purposes, I looked like a wounded abominable snowman. If I woke him up, he'd ask questions. I didn't want to deal with that.

So I turned the knob quietly and eased the door open. In near-perfect silence I peeked inside.

Oh, well. People who sneak around deserve what they get. Life has a way of insisting on honesty, whether you have the courage for it or not. Hardhouse lay on the bed. So did Ginny. They were both naked. He thrust his hips between her legs, hard as a ram. She clung to him and made small groaning sounds I hadn't heard for a long time – sounds I used to love.

She wore her claw.

For some reason that was what hurt – that small detail closed the circuit, restored me to pain. She wore her claw. After everything she'd lost, he made her feel like a woman again. No, more than that. He made her feel so much like a woman that the claw didn't matter, it couldn't stifle her desirability.

It was too much. Entirely too much. I closed the door – gently, gently, so that she wouldn't see me – and did my best to walk away.

I didn't get far. Doors stretched along the walls, but I couldn't tell which one was mine. Tears filled my eyes, and I couldn't see through the blur. Clutching at the nearest doorknob, I turned it and fell like an axed tree into the room.

The rug caught me. I made almost no noise.

Providentially, as you might say, it was the Draytons' room.

They, too, were in bed together, with their arms around each other, naked. But they heard me come in. When I toppled, they jerked up like I had them on strings.

'Brew!' Queenie gasped.

I hardly saw either of them. Sam seemed to arrive beside me without going through the middle stages of getting out of bed and standing up. With no apparent effort, he rolled me on to my back. Checked my pulse, my skin, my respiration. At the same time he snapped, 'Get my bag.'

Queenie obeyed. She didn't step back to pull a robe around herself until he had what he needed.

With a pair of scissors he cut my sweater open. Then I heard him say, 'Christ, Brew. What have you done to yourself?' But I couldn't get his face into focus, so I had no idea whether he expected an answer. Maybe he was just making conversation.

More work with the scissors. Somewhere past the pain I felt the pressure on my stomach ease. He must've cut off my bandages. After a moment he said, 'Well, that's not too bad.' Then he demanded, 'Haven't you been taking your antibiotics? This is a serious infection.'

Like the last one, that question may've been rhetorical. He didn't wait for an answer. Instead he checked my face, wiped my mouth, stuck a finger in around my teeth. 'You're bringing up blood,' he announced. 'That's bad, but I can't tell how bad yet. The infection may make your sutures leak. Or you may have torn them open. If you're just leaking, I can probably help you. If the sutures are torn' – for some reason he sounded angry – 'you need emergency surgery.'

'Can you do it here?' Queenie asked.

'I don't know. I'll have to think about it. We'll see how he responds.' Sam wrapped something around my arm and pumped it tight. Slowly he let it loosen. 'He's lost blood, but his BP is strong. That's good. He hasn't been bleeding long. Or he hasn't bled much.'

On the principle that I should be grateful for small blessings, I tried to smile. But my heart wasn't in it.

'Get a glass of water,' he instructed crisply. 'Maybe we can locate some more good news.'

Apparently I'd stopped crying. Why, I didn't know. But my vision finally improved. When Queenie came back from the bathroom with a glass, I was able to focus on her.

'Brew,' Sam said firmly, 'Queenie will hold your head up for you. Don't try to help her – keep your abdomen relaxed. But drink as much water as you can.'

I nodded incrementally. He adjusted his stethoscope. Kneeling beside me, Queenie wedged an arm under my neck and tilted my head off the rug. Then she put the glass to my mouth.

When she did that, incandescent memories burned through me.

I was out of bed, where I had no business being, no business at all because I'd only been shot a few hours ago, but I needed to catch a killer and maybe rescue Ginny from el Señor, that was my only justification. And the killer handed me a glass of water. Smiling. *Axbrewder, you look terrible. What are you doing to yourself? How about a glass of water? Drink this. You can't last much longer.* So I drank it. But it wasn't water, oh, no, he was a killer, all right, and he knew what he was doing.

He gave me vodka.

Involuntarily I gagged and thrashed against Queenie's arm, twisted my head away, fought a recollection of pain as hot as a magnesium flare. Alcohol, my favourite stuff on God's earth, had nearly eviscerated me.

'Brew, relax!' Sam commanded. 'Let Queenie hold your head! We're trying to help you!'

Wildly I looked at him, at her, as if I needed some other kind of help, anything to get me away from that glass of water. But this was a bedroom in Deerskin Lodge, and the other room where I'd swallowed vodka and nearly died was days and miles away, although the snow remained the same. I had no idea who'd killed Cat – and tried to kill me. If I couldn't trust the Draytons right now, I was a goner anyway.

I didn't relax very well. But I raised one hand and helped Queenie steer the glass to my mouth.

Sam put his stethoscope on my stomach and listened while I drank. The water tasted like the air outside, sweet, clean and cold, and once I got started I gulped at it until it was gone.

Sam listened hard for a minute, then looked at me. 'Well, I think we can say your bowels haven't gone into shock. You're luckier than you deserve. Since I'm the only doctor here and it's up to me, I'm going to guess you haven't torn any sutures.' He nodded to Queenie, and she lowered my head back to the floor. 'I'll clean you up and apply a clean dressing. But first I'll give you an injection.'

He returned to his bag. I let him take his time. I had places to go, things to do. But for the life of me I couldn't imagine how I would bear them.

'This,' he announced when he was ready, 'is the thermonuclear device of antibiotics.' He swabbed my arm vigorously with something that smelled like betadyne. 'I'll give you regular injections while my supply lasts.' Then he poked a needle into my skin. 'If you go back on your pills right away and take them *religiously*, you may be able to fight off this infection.'

After he pulled the needle out, he withdrew. Maybe he'd gotten tired of working on me naked. When he returned he was wearing a sweater and slacks.

'I'll start on your bandages in a couple of minutes,' he said. 'Maybe by then you'll be strong enough to stand. In the mean time, why don't you tell us what in hell you think you're doing?'

Tough ol' Axbrewder, as hard as plate steel and twice as remorseless. As soon as I heard the question, I started crying again.

'Brew,' Queenie breathed, 'oh, Brew, what's happened? What's going on?'

I would've cried a lot harder, but I couldn't make my stomach muscles cooperate.

'All right.' Sam studied me without flinching. 'Don't try to talk right now. Take it easy. That's what you should be doing anyway. You're safe here. You can rest as long as you want. Believe it or not, even this will pass.' Apparently he knew how much comfort that thought would be. Frowning, he added, 'Eventually.'

No. Positively not. I refused. Despite the fact that I whimpered like a baby, I absolutely declined to lie here and rest while Cat's murderer wandered around loose. Not when she'd been killed for me.

'I can't.'

'The hell you can't,' Sam retorted harshly. 'I'm your doctor. If I tell you to lie there and rest, by God, you're going to lie there and *rest*.'

'No.' I shook my head, rolled it weakly from side to side. 'No.' I needed to articulate one of the first principles of my life, but all I managed was the small sound like a beaten child. 'I can't.'

'Why not?' Queenie put in. 'Why not? Talk to us, Brew. Tell us what's going on.'

I couldn't argue with her. I needed help. Without the Draytons, I might not even be able to stand.

'Ginny and Hardhouse are having an affair.' I went on crying. 'I caught them.'

Sam and Queenie looked at each other. Maybe they were dismayed. Or maybe they just felt sorry for me. Probably everyone here already knew about Ginny and Hardhouse.

'You can't do anything about that.' Sam's roughness had shifted to another pitch. 'You've spent too much time lying to each other. You can't undo the past.'

'You don't understand.' I had to do better, had to get through to him somehow. 'I need her. Simon didn't shoot Cat. The killer was aiming at me.'

Queenie pulled a sharp hiss of surprise through her teeth.

'Oh, shit,' Sam said fervently.

They both stared at me, frozen with shock.

'He just tried again,' I said because I had nothing left.

They believed me. I could see it on their faces. Maybe my damaged condition convinced them.

'How—?' she began in a small voice. 'Why—?'

'Later.' He swallowed hard to make his throat work. 'I don't think Brew has time to explain right now.'

No question about it, he was good at emergencies. With a shudder, he threw off his shock. Before I could do anything more than nod, he dug back into his bag and came out with another needle and syringe.

'All right,' he said for the second time. 'This will help you manage the pain, and it won't put you to sleep. Once we get you on your feet, you'll be able to stay there for a while. That's as much as I can do.' He swabbed at my arm again. 'But you'll have to pay for it.'

Before I could ask him what he meant, he stuck the needle in and said, 'You can start by taking some advice.'

I blinked at him. Advice?

'I'm not your doctor now,' he continued. 'This is too important. I'm your friend. You can believe that. Queenie and I are your friends. Too many people here have something to gain from your weakness. The killer certainly does. Joseph and Lara do. Perhaps even Ginny does. And everyone else has something to lose. So listen to me. *Listen.*'

Lara had something to gain? Ginny did?

I didn't ask. I listened.

'You need Ginny. The two of you need to trust each other. Our lives may depend on that. The time has come for you to start telling the truth. I'm sure you think you're honest. You're certainly honest about your opinion of yourself. If I put you on the evening news, you would tell the whole country what a shit you are. But that isn't good enough. You have to tell the truth about what you feel. What you want. Nobody will ever trust you until you trust yourself. And truth is the only trust that counts. Do you hear me?'

Unlike the first injection, this one got my attention. It hurt with glow that spread out from my arm into the rest of my body, lighting my sore nerves with warmth, comforting my torn and abused tissues. It resembled the amber peace drunks live for, the state of grace which sometimes comes in the still space between not enough alcohol and too much. There was a difference, however. This glow didn't protect me. I felt several distinct pains at once, and none of them faded. The shot simply warmed away their ability to paralyse me.

'I said, do you hear me?'

Oh, I heard him. I may've been damn near crazy, but I knew when I was being cared for. I looked at him straight and took hold of his arm.

'Help me up.'

He and Queenie shared a searching glance. Then she braced me on one side, and he supported me on the other, and they eased me to my feet.

The effort made my head swirl. My guts throbbed in the distance, like drums announcing disaster. When Sam pulled away, I could hardly stand without him. But Queenie kept me upright until he came back with rolls of bandages and more betadyne swabs.

'This will hurt,' he said calmly, 'but you may not notice any difference.'

Tearing open the swabs, he began to scrub at my belly.

It hurt, all right. So what? When he strapped me into a new dressing, it put so much pressure on my guts that I had trouble breathing. I didn't care. He was making it possible for me to do what I had to do.

After he finished, he studied me for a while – took my pulse again, stroked the muck sweat off my forehead, peered into my pupils. Then he told Queenie to let go of me.

She obeyed.

I stayed on my feet.

'Good.' He nodded brusquely. 'We'll be here if you need us.'

'Just a minute,' she said. From a bureau she produced a bulky sweater, one of his. It was a bit too small, not enough to cause any problems. They helped me get my head and arms into it. She tugged it down over my bandages.

I had no time to thank them. As soon as she stepped back, I started putting one foot in front of the other towards the door.

Sam held it open. I went out into the hall.

Headed for Joseph Hardhouse's room.

This time I made no effort to be quiet. Assuming that I could've done it, I had no reason to try. For a moment I held the doorknob as if it were the last support I would ever get. Then I turned it and pushed the door open and lurched into the room.

They were done, at least for the time being. They sat in bed against the headboard, propped by pillows. Her neck rested on his arm. The tips of his fingers stroked the tip of her breast.

She went stiff when she saw me, blank and rigid – expressionless with surprise or anger. He jerked his head up, glowered furiously. Neither of them said anything.

I faced him because I couldn't bear to see her naked in his embrace. But I spoke to her.

'Tell him to get out.'

'It's my room,' he retorted. After the initial jolt, his glare looked happy, practically victorious. He liked to flaunt his conquests. '*You* get out.'

I concentrated on Ginny. 'Tell him. I need to talk to you.'

His laugh sounded like bricks grinding together. But she pushed him away, swung herself out of bed, and began putting her clothes on. Jeans, a cotton chamois shirt. Her eyes never left me. They were grey and hard and blank, unreadable.

After a moment Hardhouse shrugged and followed her example.

When he was dressed, he came over to me.

He could've knocked me down with one hand. But I had a grip on the .45 in my pocket. If he touched me, I was going to do my damnedest to shoot him before he got away. However, he intended a different kind of violence.

With a grin that bared his teeth, he nodded towards Ginny and said, 'That claw's the sexiest thing I've ever seen.'

Then he left. The door clicked shut behind him.

Just for a second after he was gone, she gaped at the door as if he'd stunned her. But then she regained her focus. Grimly she strode towards me.

In her claw, she held her purse by the strap, ready for anything. Her crooked nose had gone white. The lines between her brows seemed deep enough to be part of her skull, and her grey eyes glinted at me. Her face betrayed nothing. Sounding almost neutral, almost willing to forgive me, she said, 'This had better be good.'

You have to tell the truth.

How? That smoke had nearly killed me. An infection raged in my guts. Lies were my only defence.

Carefully, so that I wouldn't make a mistake, I unknotted my fingers from the .45 and took my hand out of my pocket.

Then, with all the strength I could summon through the fever in my head and the glowing stimulant in my veins, I hit her.

The blow rocked her back on her heels. Her cheek went pale, then flamed red.

That was the best I could do.

So fast that I didn't see it happen, her .357 came out of her purse. The barrel lined up on my face. She'd shot a man in the face once, after he'd broken her nose. She'd already thumbed back the hammer. Her knuckles were white on the grip.

'Do that again,' she rasped, a low snarl from the core of her bones. 'Do it.'

Tell the truth.

I could still feel the impact of hitting her like a tremor in my belly. The muzzle of her gun looked big enough to blast me out of existence. But I was full of hurt and loss and old rage, and we were finished with each other anyway. There was nothing worse that she could do to me.

I tried to hit her again.

My second blow was weaker than the first, and she saw it coming from miles away. She slipped it aside by twitching her head. With nightmare slowness, the .357 came back into line.

But she didn't shoot me. Instead she used her claw to jab at my stomach.

Red blossoms of pain burst behind my eyes. Gasping, I crumpled to my knees.

I couldn't move or think. Involuntarily I clamped my arms over my belly. They didn't do me any good. If Sam's new bandages hadn't protected me, I would've been torn open.

On the other hand, I didn't start to cry again. I was spared that indignity. I was too mad for tears.

Past flowers and explosions, I saw the .357 drop to the rug, saw Ginny fall to her knees. She took hold of my sweater, closed her fingers and her claw in the soft material. 'Brew,' she breathed, panting softly, 'Brew, what're you doing? What the hell do you think you're doing?'

Telling the truth. 'Giving you an excuse to ditch me.' Pain and rage had left me half dead. I had no idea why I could still speak. 'I won't put up with the way you treat me any more.'

'*Brew.*' Red bloomed on her face, in her eyes. 'What in *hell* are you talking about?'

'I'm your partner.' That was the truth as well. I could say it because I had nothing left to lose. 'Your partner. I won't let you ignore me.

'Cat was killed by accident. It should've been me.'

I thought she would shout at me, but she didn't. 'What do you mean? Brew, make sense.'

'I love you. I've always gone about it wrong, but I love you.'

She shook her head. 'Not that. What about Cat? Why should it have been you?'

I didn't insist. I still needed her for this.

'He just tried again. In the den. He must've been trying to kill me when he shot Cat. He hit her by accident.'

Her hand and her claw pulled at my sweater. 'Who?'

'I don't know. Not Simon. He's locked up.'

'Why?'

The truth.

I said it. 'He works for el Señor.'

'What?' Her demand for understanding was profound and passionate. '*What?*'

'Ginny.' I said her name and looked into her eyes to anchor me against a rising flood of anger. Oh, Ginny, please. 'You never found out how we got this job.'

Abruptly she shut up. Despite the white heat of her attention, she knew that she didn't need to question me. She knew that I would tell her the whole story.

'You never asked Rock or even Buffy how we got this job.'

I remembered a voice. A voice that said, *Get out of there. He wants you. You're a sitting duck.*

'You never asked who had it before. You never asked where Rock heard about us. It wasn't a coincidence. It didn't just happen.'

A voice that sounded muffled and familiar.

'It was Smithsonian. Lawrence Smithsonian.'

Ginny opened her mouth, closed it again. Her eyes and her hand and her claw clung to me.

'He always did security for Murder On Cue. This time he pulled out at the last minute. Some kind of emergency, he said. But he gave Rock your name. He recommended you. And he was the one who called me. In the hospital. Threatening me. I knew the voice was familiar, but I couldn't place it. He was giving you a reason to take the job when Rock offered it. He set us up. Someone at this camp works for el Señor. He's a professional killer.'

Ginny absorbed what I said as if she took it in through her pores. She didn't protest against it or argue with it or try to reinterpret it. She simply accepted it.

She trusted me that much, at least.

Slowly she said, 'We used to think Smithsonian did business with that reptile. Now we know.'

Then she was ready.

'What happened in the den? How did he try to kill you?'

I told her.

'How did you get out?'

I told her.

'Then what did you do?'

That was hard, but I told her.

The information should've pissed her off, but she didn't let it deflect her. 'Does anybody else know about this?'

'They should by now. I told Ama to get help.'

Without warning she let go of me and surged to her feet. I nearly fell on my face, but she didn't notice. 'We'll check on Simon,' she announced. 'Maybe whoever was on the roof left a trail. This damn snow has to be good for something. Then we'll get everybody together and warn them.'

'Tell them' – I couldn't raise my head to look at her – 'it's because of me. Cat's dead because of me. They're all in danger because of me. I brought it with me.'

That hit a nerve. 'God *damn* it, Brew!' Sometimes she was so strong it astonished me. Fiercely she reached down, grabbed hold of me, heaved me to my feet. As livid as a shout, she snapped, 'Did you know that was Smithsonian's voice when we took this job?'

I shook my head weakly.

'Did you put it together when you found out how we got this job?' No.

'How long ago did you recognize his voice?'

Rage and panic threatened to choke me. 'A few minutes.'

'Then,' she said like the cut of a bucksaw, 'stop blaming yourself. I'm *sick* of it. You aren't accountable for things you didn't know. *You* didn't kill Cat. And you sure as hell aren't the reason we're snowbound. We haven't got time for one of your culpability jags.'

'Ginny.' I could swallow my fear. Sam's injection helped with that, the same way it helped with the pain. But I couldn't force down my anger. She was right, we didn't have time, the situation was urgent. Nevertheless I needed an answer. If I had to, I'd hit her until she gave me one. 'Why are you fucking Joseph Hardhouse?'

She may've been on the verge of saying, We haven't got time for *that* either. But something stopped her. Maybe it was the memory of his parting shot – of the surprise she'd felt when he said her claw was sexy.

Or maybe it was just the extremity on my face. Maybe she could see that I'd come to the end of myself. Whatever the explanation, she didn't refuse me.

'You want to talk about whose fault this is?' The intensity of her outrage made her gulp for air. 'Of course you do. You love it. It gives you an excuse to drink. Well, *I'm* responsible for getting you shot. That bullet in your stomach is *my* fault.

'You remember how it happened? You tried to warn me. You tried to tell me the truth. But I couldn't face it. I didn't listen. Instead I forced you to walk straight into Estobal's line of fire.'

Well, in a manner of speaking. If you just assume that I hadn't moved my own feet – hadn't ignored my own judgement in order to do what she told me. But that was bullshit. On some level, I'd known that Estobal might come after us. I'd recognized the danger. I simply hadn't trusted myself enough to deny her.

Her anger didn't let her see the situation in those terms, however. 'How do you expect me to feel now?' she went on. Except for the place where I'd hit her, her whole face was white and savage. 'Do you think I *enjoy* seeing you limp around with all that pain on your face? I took this job to try to save your life, but the way you behave, you never let me forget I gave you this problem in the first place. And now you tell me I've helped set you up by not paying attention to my job.

'Christ, Brew, what am I supposed to do for self-respect? How am I supposed to start liking myself again? I'm a *cripple*. And I don't mean *this*.' She jerked her claw past my face. 'I'm so twisted inside I can't even pay attention to my *job*.

'I *hate* that.

'I need some reason to believe I'm worth having around. All I ever get from you is misery. Joseph is the only man I've met who acts like being crippled doesn't get in the way. He likes me the way I am. He *wants* me the way I am. Who he is doesn't even matter. I don't care if he's a shit, or cheats on his wife, or buggers his busboys. He makes me think my whole life doesn't have to be as twisted as my relationship with you.

'You say you're my partner.' She had no time for transitions. 'Are you coming, or do I have to deal with Cat's killer on my own?'

She didn't wait for an answer. Retrieving her .357, she shoved it back into her purse. Without so much as a pause in the doorway, she stormed out of Hardhouse's room and left me alone with my astonishment.

Her explanation wasn't what astonished me. It didn't exactly comfort me, but it made sense. I knew how she felt. No, the astonishing thing was that we weren't finished with each other. She still expected me to back her up.

I stayed where I was for a moment or two, swaying gently to myself, letting go of my grievances. Then I followed her.

Chapter Fifteen

The hall seemed long. What the hell, everything seemed long to me. But Sam's injection did its job. I was still ambulatory. I caught up with Ginny in the den.

Ama and Truchi had already gone to work. They'd opened the front door and several windows, and one of them, probably Truchi, had set up a big space fan to blow smoke out of the room. Smoke still curled out of the fireplace, but a bucket and puddles of water on the hearth indicated that the fire itself had been doused pretty thoroughly. I could smell a tang of acid, enough to make me think about gagging. The fan worked well, however, and the air was mostly breathable.

Judging by appearances, Ama hadn't suffered too much damage. Her eyes were red and puffy, but she looked solid on her feet, ready to do whatever was needed. Of course, smoke inhalation can kill anyone, but she probably hadn't been in as much danger as I was. She wasn't likely to bleed to death when she coughed.

Frowning slightly above his off-white moustache, Ama's husband tended the fan and watched the wisps from the fireplace with a gaze that managed to look innocent and doubtful at the same time. If he had an opinion about the situation, he kept it to himself.

'Do you know what caused this?' Ginny asked.

Petruchio shrugged. 'Snow,' he pronounced succinctly. 'Chimney.'

'I mean the smoke.' Ginny's tone hinted at exasperation. 'Wood doesn't make that kind of smoke.'

My only encounter with Truchi, the first day of the camp, had been cryptic. I guess I didn't expect him to have much grasp on practical reality. So I was surprised when he pointed at the fireplace and said without hesitation, 'Ratsbane.'

Ratsbane? I thought.

'Ratsbane?' Ginny demanded.

Ama shrugged. As laconic as her husband, she pronounced. 'Rat poison.'

Ginny nodded once, sharp with recognition. 'Trioxide of arsenic. That's what they make rat poison out of. Or they used to. It's been a long time since I looked it up.'

Arsenic, I mused. Terrific.

She moved to the fireplace and peered inside. I did the same thing, except more slowly.

Back against the firewall, we saw the remains of a cardboard box big enough to hold a case of beer. Blackened powder spilled out of it. Powder had probably covered most of the wood, but water had washed it down into the ash.

'That,' she commented, 'is a hell of a lot of rat poison.'

I thought Amalia would answer, but it was Truchi who said, 'We got a hell of a lot of rats. Every year a new supply. We kill them every spring, and every spring they come back.'

That made sense, I suppose. Deerskin Lodge must've been the best source of food in twenty miles.

But Ginny stuck to the point – which had nothing to do with the feeding habits of rats. 'Where do you keep the stuff?'

Now Ama replied, 'In the wine cellar. So we can lock the door.'

I turned away from the fireplace so abruptly that I almost fell down.

The wine cellar. Shit.

Ginny had the same idea, only faster. Striding towards the kitchen, she told the Carbones in passing, 'Get everybody together. Everybody. I don't care if you have to wake them up. If they can't stand the smoke, use the parlour. We'll be back in a couple of minutes.'

'You need the key,' Ama responded.

Ginny slapped her purse. 'Art gave it to me.'

Nearly running, she left the den.

I stumbled along behind her as best I could.

I didn't know where the wine cellar was – I'd missed the ritual of locking Simon up last night. But Reeson had called it 'just a room off the kitchen,' and that's what it was, easy to find. All I had to locate was a door with a padlock.

It stood between the drying-pan of the Hobart and one of the walk-in refrigerators. Sharing a wall with appliances like that, the room had to be well insulated. They put out too much heat for wine.

Ginny fished the key from her purse. With characteristic ease, she found what she wanted in there without hunting for it. But she still had to clamp the lock steady with her claw so that she could insert the key. That gave me time to come up behind her and at least pretend that I was guarding her back.

Leaving the key in the padlock when it snikked open, she jerked out her .357, hooked her claw on the knob, and swung the door aside.

Over her shoulder, I saw that Simon had left the light on – a shaded bulb hanging on its wire to about the height of my forehead. But we didn't need its illumination.

Sunshine and cold poured in through a hole in the far wall.

Past the open space which held the card table and the chair and the cot stood four racks nearly as tall as I am – maybe two hundred bottles of wine. The room's interior insulation had simply been nailed to the studs in 4 × 4 sheets of dirty white asbestos or some related material. Apparently whoever had decided to convert this room to a wine cellar only cared about the wine itself, not about the décor.

One of the insulation sheets had been pulled down. It lay under the cot. And the exterior boards between the studs had been knocked or broken or pried out, leaving a gap to the outside. Ginny could've squirmed through it, even if I couldn't.

Simon certainly could have.

He must have. His sleeping bag was twisted on the cot. A half-eaten sandwich occupied a plate on the table. But he was gone. In the snow outside, we could see his trail. It headed away from the buildings up into the trees.

Ginny didn't bother swearing. The situation swore for itself.

Just trying to cushion the shock for myself, I muttered inanely, 'I suppose you're sure this is the right room.'

She nodded. 'And I'm sure if we trace that trail we'll find where he got up and down from the roof.

'Also' – she hesitated, flashed a glance at me – 'I'm sure that if we don't follow him right now we'll never catch him. The wind will blow his trail out. He'll be as good as vanished.'

Sure. I understood. Parts of my brain had caught up with the circumstances. In fact, I understood too much. Panic crowded my throat. I had to force down bile to say, 'Don't look at me. I'm in no condition to go hiking.'

'I know,' she replied softly. 'I'll go.' She hesitated again, longer this time. But she didn't look away. 'You'll have to take charge here. Make sure nothing else happens.'

I nodded. It was my job to keep the guests alive. Which meant that I'd have to let them know what the real dangers were.

'That,' I said in a voice like a saw-blade with broken teeth, 'is why they pay me the big bucks.'

For a second I saw a gleam of appreciation in her eyes. 'Do it,' she said. 'I need boots and a coat. Then I'm gone.'

Good luck, I might've responded. But I was already alone. I could hear her heels on the kitchen tile, running.

Pure craziness, of course. I had a high fever and damaged sutures. She had no business leaving me in charge. I had no business accepting the responsibility.

But it was my *job*, and I knew how to do it. I sure as hell had the background for it. A little while ago, I'd accused Ginny of professional sloppiness. The time had come for me to put up or shut up.

The bare idea left me so weak that I could hardly move without leaning against the walls and counter tops. Nevertheless I propped myself across the kitchen and through the dining room back to the den.

Everyone was there except Faith Jerrick and Sue-Rose Altar.

Truchi had turned off the fan, closed the den again. I could still smell arsenic smoke. I'd probably be able to smell it for days. But I couldn't do anything about that.

While the door and windows were open, the room had gone cold. Looking for warmth, Murder On Cue's guests had pulled their chairs and a couch or two close to one of the other fireplaces. Truchi knelt there under the trophies, stoking a few small flames.

Mac Westward and Lara Hardhouse sat together. Although they didn't look at each other, they held hands grimly, almost desperately, as if that were their only comfort. They both seemed oblivious to the dark and strangely fond way her husband regarded them.

Constance Bebb had a seat beside Hardhouse. Apparently she wanted to distract him from Lara's flagrant behaviour – which I thought was unusually courageous of her. But she didn't have much success.

Somehow Maryanne had enticed Mile into a reconciliation. She sat practically in his lap, her arms entwined in his fat. No doubt because his fingers were cold, he kept one hand inside her blouse.

With their chairs so close together, Rock, Queenie, and Sam seemed to be keeping each other company. Rock ignored his companions, however. His eyes were fixed on Truchi, but he didn't really see the handyman. Instead he seemed to be watching his life curdle.

Sam and Queenie, of course, didn't need company. Nevertheless they were the most alert people in the room. They noticed me as soon as I appeared.

'Brew!' Sam jumped up and came over to me. 'Where's Ginny? What's going on?' That may not have been exactly what he meant.

I ignored him for a moment. I didn't have much energy to spare, and I needed all my concentration.

Amalia stood against one of the walls nearby with her strong forearms folded over her apron. As she faced in my direction, I asked as if I had the right to make demands, 'Where's Faith?'

Her eyes looked less puffy, but they remained red, and they leaked at the corners. She turned her head towards Truchi.

Without shifting his gaze from the fire, he answered, 'I forgot.'

'Where's Buffy?' I asked Sam.

He studied me carefully. 'She isn't handling the shock well. I gave her a sedative this morning. She won't wake up for a while yet.'

Which presented an interesting problem. I had no reason to assume that Simon would try to get away. More likely he'd stopped under cover of the trees to watch the lodge, see what happened after he plugged the chimney. If so, he'd known for a while now that I was still alive. *And he could see Ginny coming, he could pick her off whenever he wanted, he still had plenty of guns*, no, don't think about that, you can't do anything about it. He might double back, come after me again. And Faith and Buffy were alone. If he wanted hostages – or just more victims . . .

I didn't have much choice. I had to trust one or two people and take my chances.

In order, as you might say, to establish my credentials, I took the .45 out of my pocket, worked the slide with a vehement clack, held it up in front of me. Then I started talking.

'They aren't safe. Simon broke out of the wine cellar.' Several people gasped at this announcement, but I ignored them. 'We have to assume that he still has those missing guns. Truchi, go find Faith. Bring her here. If she won't come, stay with her. He probably isn't after her. But he might want a hostage.'

Without argument, Truchi rose to his feet and left.

I didn't watch him go. I had other things to think about.

'Sam, can you lift Buffy?'

His eyes wide, he nodded.

'Go get her. Bring her here. She can sleep on a couch for a while.'

Queenie rose to help him. He stopped her with a glare and strode out of the den.

Biting her lower lip, she sat down again.

Inadvertently she steadied me. She was troubled, deeply concerned, but she wasn't terrified. She could still do what she was told. I needed that.

'Now.' I waggled the .45, more to remind myself why I was here than to keep anyone's attention. 'I'll tell you what I know.' My weakness hadn't receded any. Looking for support, I lumbered over to the fireplace and braced myself on the hearth. 'It isn't much, but you're entitled to it.' The stonework hadn't had time to heat up yet, so I wasn't uncomfortable. And I could put the .45 down on the mantel in easy reach. That way I wouldn't have to waste strength holding a gun.

Everyone stared at me – even Rock. I didn't particularly enjoy being the centre of so much fixed horror, but there was nothing I could do about that. I tried to tune it out.

'Simon broke out of the wine cellar,' I began. 'Right through the wall. I have no idea how. That isn't critical right now.' Actually it might very well be critical, but at the moment I didn't have time to think about it. 'What matters is that he's gone. Ginny went after him. She'll stop him if she can. If she can't' – I mustered an awkward shrug – 'she'll do her best to slow him down.'

The rest of the idea I left hanging.

Knees bent under the weight, Sam returned with Buffy. He was breathing hard, but he kept the strain to himself. I waited until he set her gently down on a couch beside the tree trunk and took his seat with Queenie. Then I went on.

'We think we know what he wants.' The medication in my veins and the support of the hearth helped me say it. 'He's after me.'

'Oh, Brew,' Queenie breathed.

Sure, everyone stared at me – but not the way Joseph and Lara did. They concentrated as if their eyes were on fire.

'Cat was an accident. He wanted to hit me, but we were standing too close together. That's why he came back. I'm still alive. Maybe he didn't realize how guilty he would look. After all, he couldn't know how many of us might have alibis. Or maybe he just didn't expect us to lock him up. Maybe he thought he could bluff his way past us. The point is that he *did* come back, and he got locked up.'

Truchi re-entered the den with Faith Jerrick. Neither of them made a sound. I felt a lunatic desire to congratulate the man who laid the floorboards. They didn't squeak for anyone.

At least now I could stop worrying about hostages.

I went on.

'So this morning he broke out and climbed up on the roof, lugging a box of rat poison which he found in the wine cellar. While the rest of you were in your rooms, I fell asleep here. Alone. He dropped his box down the chimney, packed it with snow. Then he headed out of the valley. His trail is pretty obvious.

'I don't think he went far. If it were me, I'd stop up among the trees and watch for results. Rat poison is arsenic – or something worse. That smoke could have killed me easily enough. But he'd want to be sure nothing went wrong. He probably stopped.

'And something did go wrong. Ama rescued me.' I nodded in her direction. 'I escaped outside. If he was watching, he knows I'm still alive.

'I figure being an actor is just cover. He's a professional killer. He won't leave until he gets me. And he won't care how many of you he has to eliminate in the process.

'It's too bad he shot Cat,' I concluded, mostly to myself. 'She probably knew enough about Simon to help us out. At least she could've answered some questions.'

No one said anything. They were all too shocked. Maryanne looked as pale as an extension of Mile's fat. Houston himself was so upset that he took his hand out of her blouse. Connie concentrated fiercely on my face. Mac and Lara clung to each other.

But then Queenie found her voice. '*Why* does he want to kill you?'

I did my best to face it. 'Ginny and I were working on a case. The one where I got shot. I killed a man named Muy Estobal. He was a bodyguard for what you might consider a "crime lord" in Puerta del Sol. People call him "el Señor". Now el Señor wants me dead. He has his reputation to protect. Not to mention the people who work for him. He can't afford to let them be knocked off with impunity.' I shrugged. 'But he doesn't do his own killing. He hires pros for that.'

'How do you know this, Mr Axbrewder?' Connie put in. 'How do you know Simon is working for this el Señor? You made no mention of it last night. What have you learned since then?'

Now for the hard part. My vision had gone grey around the edges, which made me think that Sam's injection wouldn't last much longer. I was weak and sick, and I'd spent my life loathing helplessness. Which was why I liked alcohol. It gave me something to blame my helplessness on.

But Ginny knew all that, and she'd still left me to deal with the situation here while she went after Abel. No matter how helpless I felt, I was still her partner.

'There's a private investigator in Puerta del Sol,' I answered harshly. 'Ginny and I think he works for el Señor. And we know he hates us. We think he set us up.

'When I was in the hospital, he called me several times, threatened me. But he disguised his voice. I didn't recognize it. He was giving us a reason to get out of town for a while. At the same time, he arranged for the Altars to hire us, so that we'd have a convenient place to go. Somewhere isolated enough to suit a hit man.'

Rock's lips moved. Despite the jolt I'd given him, his brain still functioned. Softly he said, 'Lawrence Smithsonian.'

Several other guests tried to ask questions. I didn't give them a chance. 'He always did security for Murder On Cue. Isn't that right, Rock?' A rhetorical question. 'But this time he pulled out at the last minute. And he gave Rock Ginny's name. He persuaded Rock to hire us, in spite of the fact that I can scarcely stay on my feet. He set us up.'

Unfortunately that wasn't enough. I had to say it all. 'Cat is dead,' I pronounced as if someone really should've been swinging a scourge at me, 'because I made an irresponsible decision. When Rock told me how we got this job, I still hadn't figured out that it was Smithsonian who called me in the hospital. I didn't recognize his voice until a little while ago. So I decided not to tell Ginny what Rock told me.

'If I'd told her, she would've known there was something wrong here. She could've done everything differently. Made you all be more careful. Insisted on locking up the guns earlier. Cat might still be alive.'

'Jesus, Axbrewder!' Hardhouse swore. 'That was bright. What do you use for brains?'

Talking at the same time, Mile made a reference to 'criminal negligence'.

I didn't listen to them. I was listening to Queenie.

'In God's name, why, Brew?' she protested. 'Why didn't you tell her?'

Momentum is a wonderful thing. Since I'd already started, I found it almost easy to keep going.

'I was angry.' A pitiful excuse, but there it was. 'I was tired of being treated like the team cripple – like the only difference between being shot and being drunk was how much blood I lost. And,' I insisted, 'I hadn't recognized Smithsonian's voice yet. I didn't realize' – a small understatement – 'the scale of the problem. I thought I could take care of it myself.'

Hardhouse sniggered quietly.

'Do you hear me, Axbrewder?' Mile shouted. His face had gone an apoplectic red. 'Ah'll break you for this! Ah'll have you up on charges, criminal charges! You'll lose your licence. Ah'll make sure you never work again, goddamn sure!'

'If you get out of this alive, you're welcome to try.' After what I'd just been through, I could face down a slob like him any day of the week. 'But I should probably tell you that I haven't had a licence for years.' Deliberately I picked up the .45. 'I killed one too many people.

'Until Ginny gets back' – if she got back – 'I won't take any grief from you. You're going to do what I tell you. Exactly what I tell you. And you're going to keep that fat lump you call a mouth shut. I'm wounded and sick, and I haven't exactly covered myself with glory so far. But I'm a pro. Like Abel. I've been shot at, and I've killed people. I'm *familiar* with it.

'That makes me the best hope you've got.'

To my astonishment, Westward spoke first. 'You don't need the gun, Axbrewder.' The way Lara held his hand seemed to give him confidence. 'Just tell us what you want. We'll do it.'

I scanned the group. No one argued. Faith didn't raise her eyes, but she nodded as if she were thinking about something else.

So I told them.

Chapter Sixteen

What I told them wasn't anything special. Stay together. Lock your door if you absolutely have to be alone. Keep your windows covered and latched. If you see Simon, call for help. If he grabs you, don't resist. Dead hostages aren't worth much, so he won't hurt you unless you force him to.

Survive until Reeson gets back with help.

The one thing I didn't mention was weaponry, self-defence.

Mile noticed the omission right away. As soon as I stopped talking, he demanded, 'What about them guns? We got to have 'em. We got to protect ourselves.'

I let out a thin sigh. Some problems never go away. They just keep coming back, stupider each time.

'If by "protect ourselves" you mean we've got to start shooting at everythin' that moves, you're wrong. That's my job. I wouldn't give you a gun even if Simon wanted you personally. I don't trust you.'

I guess circumstances had finally pushed him past the point of cowardice – or point of discretion, anyway. He bounced out of his chair and stood in front of me, jowls aquiver.

'Now you listen to me, Axbrewder. You've gone too far. Ah don't forget we're in this mess on account of you. Ah don't forget your negligence has already got one of us killed. There just ain't nothin' Ah can do about that right now. But if you think Ah'm goin' to sit here on mah hams and let you risk us some more, you best think again. It's your job to protect us? Fine. *Ah* don't trust *you*. You got a drinkin' problem, and a hole in your guts, and you admit bein' irresponsible. You ain't no protection at all.

'Ah mean to get me a gun, Axbrewder. *You* get it for me, or Ah'll get it mahself.'

I shook my head. 'No, you won't.'

'Why not?' He did his best to bristle at me, which made him look like indignant jello.

'Because if you do' – slowly I aimed the .45 at his face – 'I'll blow your fucking head off. It's *me* Simon wants, and I'll be goddamned if I'm going to let a chickenshit like you do his work for him.'

Mile's features wobbled on their bones, and his skin went pale. Involuntarily he brought up his hands to ward me off. A step at a time, he retreated to his chair.

I held the .45 so that everyone could see me release the slide. 'We're all scared.' To myself, I sounded positively reasonable. 'That's natural enough. But scared people are trigger-happy. Leave the guns to Ginny and me.'

Assuming, of course, that we'd ever see Ginny again.

No doubt sensing that I needed the support, Sam got to his feet. 'I'm willing,' he said to the group. 'Brew has made some mistakes, but he's still a professional. I'm ready to trust him.'

'As I am,' Connie seconded promptly. And Mac displayed his new initiative by agreeing with her.

Since no one else put in an objection, I was elected trustworthy by default.

That was a relief of sorts, but I didn't dwell on it. 'All right,' I said, doing the best Ginny Fistoulari imitation I could muster. 'Life goes on. That means we need lunch.' I had no idea what time it was, and I didn't care. I just wanted to inject a note of normalcy into the situation. 'Faith, how soon can you get us something to eat?'

Apparently Reeson's absence was the only fact that had any personal impact on her. 'Half an hour,' she murmured, just distinctly enough to be heard.

'Good.' I put the .45 away. 'In the mean time, let's make sure our windows are covered and latched. Truchi, I want the outside doors locked. No one goes out,' I told the group. 'You might not be able to get back in. And you don't want to risk being exposed.'

Westward gave me a humourless smile. 'That's what they do in all the novels. They turn the lodge into a fortress. Then they discover that they've locked the real killer in with them.'

I was too tired to argue with him. Fortunately I didn't have to. 'This isn't a novel,' Hardhouse put in. 'Right now, a fortress sounds like a good idea to me.'

Maryanne, Sam, and Lara shared his opinion. Mile probably did, too, but he had guns on the brain and couldn't think about anything else.

I shrugged. Faith, Truchi, and Amalia left the den. Murder On Cue's guests stood up, too nervous to remained seated. Unexpectedly helpful, Hardhouse offered to carry Buffy back to her bed.

Sam and Queenie came over to me. In an undertone, he asked, 'How are you doing?'

'Who knows? I'm relying on you to keep me on my feet.'

'I'll do what I can. But I don't want to help you overdo it. That could turn into a perverse form of suicide.' Then he asked, 'Did you take your pills?'

'I've been busy.'

'Queenie,' Sam ordered like he was back in surgery, 'go get Brew's pills.'

His tone didn't bother her. 'Where are they?'

'You'll find them,' I said. The truth was that I couldn't remember where I'd left them.

When she walked away, Sam and I were alone – except for Rock. Everyone else had gone to check on their windows.

Rock moved closer. Obviously he wanted to talk to me. I looked at him wanly. 'Yes?'

As if he feared eavesdroppers, he breathed, 'I didn't want to say this in front of the group. But I think you're wrong.'

Sam went rigid with attention. I didn't have the strength.

'What about?' I asked.

'About Simon.'

Oh, good. Just what I needed.

But Rock didn't go on. I had to prod him. 'Don't make me guess. I'm in no mood for it.'

'It's the timing.' He stared hard at my feet. 'When did you kill this Muy Estobal?'

For some reason, I was vague on the details. 'Last week.'

'Is that the only reason el Señor wants you dead?'

'Far as I know.'

'Then–' Rock hesitated, not as if he were unsure, but as if he wished he had the will to look me in the face. 'It isn't Simon.'

I held my breath.

'I signed a contract with him – Murder On Cue hired him and Cat – over a month ago.'

Well, shit. Shit on everything.

I felt a sudden, overwhelming desire to sit down.

Simon, I'm sorry.

'In other words,' Sam said in case I needed the explanation, 'it would be an absolutely staggering coincidence if a professional killer who works for el Señor just happened to accept an acting job from you over a month ago and then turned out to be in the right place at the right time to attack Brew.'

Rock nodded rather helplessly.

'Why didn't you want anybody else to know?' Sam pursued.

'Because it doesn't mean there isn't a killer after Brew. It just means the killer isn't Simon. Or any of us. Everyone here signed up weeks ago. You and Queenie were the last, and you sent in your money two weeks ago. Only Brew and Ginny got involved at the last minute.

'I don't know Lawrence Smithsonian well. We're acquainted, that's all. And I thought he had a good reputation. He always took our camps' – Rock swallowed – 'about as seriously as I did. I have no way of knowing whether he works for el Señor.

'But Simon isn't the killer.'

Sam accepted this. 'That makes sense.' He definitely liked mysteries.

'Come on.' I lacked the courage to explain what I had in mind, but I knew what to do. 'I don't want to go outside alone.'

Before either of them could ask any questions, I lumbered off in the direction of the kitchen.

Faith Jerrick was there, stirring a pot of something. I ignored her. She'd locked the back door, but the dead-bolt didn't need a key from the inside. I turned it and went out.

'Don't lock the door,' Sam told Faith as he and Rock followed.

Outside. Down the steps. Around the corner of the building to the wall of the wine cellar.

The wind was blowing harder, but it hadn't completely filled in the marks outside the lodge – or Ginny's trail towards the trees. It still hadn't covered up the broken boards of the hole that let Simon out. I didn't have to dig for them.

'Brew,' Sam kept asking, 'what're you doing?'

I ignored him, too.

The stains of oil and weather made it easy to piece together the way the boards used to fit in the wall. And when I did that, what had happened became obvious.

Pressure-notches marked the outer edges of the boards – the kind of notches you get when you break boards out of a wall with a crowbar.

Simon hadn't escaped by himself. This hole had been made for him.

Wind curled around me, into my clothes, into my heart. I felt as bleak as the winter, chilled to the bone, dying for spring. Sam said something. Rock said something. I didn't hear them. I was exposed out here, an easy target, but I didn't care. Pieces of things that I should've thought of earlier fitted together like the boards, and they told the same story.

Sam took my arm, shook me to get my attention. 'Brew?'

Like the wind, I said, 'Simon is dead.'

Then I said, 'He was framed.'

So that we wouldn't recognize the danger in time. And maybe so that Ginny could be lured away.

Sam forced me to hear him. 'How do you know?'

I showed him the boards. 'Someone broke into the wine cellar from the outside.'

'Maybe he has an accomplice.' The mystery-lover talking.

'No. For the same reason we know he didn't do it.'

And I could prove it.

How did I manage to be so goddamn *stupid*?

'You're all innocent. None of you came in at the last minute. He was framed.'

Unless –

My head reeled. I wouldn't be able to keep my balance much longer. For some reason I had the .45 in my hand again. Maybe that was why Sam held on to my arm. I jerked out of his grasp and jabbed the muzzle up under Rock's chin.

Sam could've stopped me. He was strong enough. But apparently he'd reached a decision about me days ago. He held back now for the same reason that he'd helped me earlier.

Despite the cold and the wind, Rock's face turned as white and grey as stale dough. He tried to back up, but I had my fist in the front of his shirt.

'No–' he gurgled.

'Listen to me, Rock.' I dug into him with the sight of the .45. 'This is your last chance to tell the truth and get away with it. After this, it's going to cost blood.

'You like messing up mysteries. You told me that yourself. You like helping the killer get away. If you're doing that now, say so. Before anyone else gets hurt.' Even though it was too late for Ginny, far too late. 'If you're lying about Simon – if you helped him escape – and I find out about it the hard way, I'll make *damn* sure some of the blood that gets spilled is yours.'

'No. No.' His voice cracked. 'Are you crazy? I wouldn't do that. I mess up Buffy's mysteries. I change the clues. Yes. Those are *games*. The people who come to our camps are just *playing*. Nobody ever gets *hurt*. I wouldn't have anything to do with a real killer.

'Take me inside.' He shivered with cold and urgency. 'I have all the registrations and contracts in my briefcase. I'll show you when they were signed. Ask Buffy. She knows when I hired Simon. She interviewed him.'

So much for that theory. I let him go. I hadn't actually believed that he was involved. But the alternatives were worse.

Much worse.

'"Mess up Buffy's mysteries"?' Sam asked in a strained tone. '"Change the clues"? What kind of camp is this?'

Rock wheeled on him. Appalled or angry, he yelled, 'I don't like mysteries!' Almost immediately, however, his passion collapsed into chagrin. 'Anyway, Buffy knows about it,' he said like a shamefaced kid. 'Houston told her.'

I flapped a hand at him – I wanted them both to shut up.

Rock stumbled past Sam and leaned against the side of the lodge as if his heart were going bad on him. Sam moved towards me. I stared out along what was left of Ginny's trail. The trees looked too black to allow survival. If I were him – whoever he was – I wouldn't shoot her until she reached the trees. Then I could leave her body where it fell without being seen.

'You can't go after her,' Sam said abruptly. 'You aren't strong enough.'

As if we were talking about the same thing, I replied, 'He was framed. We locked him in that little room and left him to die.'

'You can't stay out here,' he added. 'You're too visible. With the right rifle, he can pick you off whenever he wants.'

'He didn't even have to follow us,' I went on. 'He knew we'd come here.' A hit man I wouldn't recognize if he walked right up to me. 'Smithsonian told him. For all we know, he was already here when we arrived.'

'That doesn't change anything.' Sam put as much bite as he could into his voice. 'We still have a professional killer to worry about. We still need to take care of ourselves. If we want to stay alive.'

'Cat is dead because I was irresponsible. Simon is dead because I was stupid.'

At least that got his attention. 'What? You mean you could have figured out he was in danger? You had some way of knowing he didn't shoot Cat?'

I sat down in the snow. I'd lost my balance anyway, and I needed rest. My whole body felt like it was on fire. Fever or guilt, I couldn't tell the difference. Sam hunkered in front of me, deliberately blocking the line of fire from the trees. I handed him the .45. Then I scooped up snow in both hands and rubbed it over my face.

Snow.

It wasn't cold enough, but it helped.

That was it. Snow. The snow on Simon's windowsill.

'Yes,' I murmured to Sam. 'It was right there in his room, but I didn't see it.'

He'd said that he always kept his window latched.

'When we went into his room, we found the rifle in his closet. Which doesn't make sense in the first place. It's too obvious. But there was something else. His window was open. There was snow on the sill. Snow on the floor. But not a lot. An inch, maybe. And it was messed up. It showed that someone went in or out. Or both.'

'So?' Sam asked.

'Let's go inside,' Rock pleaded from the wall. 'I'm freezing.'

'So it doesn't fit. Suppose he unlatched his window before he went for his walk. He'd have to leave it open at least a bit, or else he wouldn't be able to raise it from the outside. So he went out. Then he came back in through the window, got the rifle, and went out again. He located me and Cat in the parlour. He shot her. Then he returned through the window.

'At that point he was in a hurry. But once he'd ditched the rifle he had plenty of time. He could've closed the window behind him when he left again. The snow might melt before we checked his room. Assuming he wanted to make us think he'd left the window open all along for fresh air, he should've closed it down to a crack. Then there would've been less snow. And he wouldn't have denied leaving the window open.'

Sam nodded intently.

'But what if he was telling the truth?' I went on. 'Then it fits.'

'I'm going inside,' Rock said in a miserable tone. I heard him slog away.

Wet cold soaked into my pants, but I didn't care. It helped me cool down.

'The killer was watching the lodge. He already had the rifle with him – he'd already taken the guns. He saw me and Cat in the parlour. He saw Simon go out. He went inside. In a hurry, so that he wouldn't miss his chance. He threw open Simon's window and jumped out. Ran

594

around the lodge and shot Cat. Then he rushed back into Simon's room, ditched the rifle, and went out through the window again. Leaving the window open because he was still in a hurry. And because he wanted to draw attention to Simon. Now there's an inch or so of snow on the sill and floor, and it's messed up.'

'Brew,' Sam said. He sounded calm the way a doctor does when he doesn't want to scare you. 'That's pretty thin.'

I looked at him while water trickled through my whiskers.

'I think I understand what you're saying,' he explained, 'but it requires too many inferences. The amount of snow depends on how long *and* how wide the window was open. There are too many variables. You're jumping to conclusions you can't trust. The evidence is too ambiguous. You can't blame yourself for what's happened to Simon.'

'That's not the point.'

He watched me steadily. 'Then what is?'

I did my best to be clear. 'The point is that we had good reason to question Simon's guilt. But I didn't think it through. I ignored some of the possibilities. I didn't figure out that if he didn't do it someone else did it to him. And if someone else did it to him, he was in danger. The real killer wouldn't want to take the chance that Simon might be able to prove his innocence somehow. I should've realized that if Simon didn't kill Cat he'd be a target himself.'

'You did,' Sam retorted. 'You locked him in the wine cellar. By rights, that should have been the safest place in the lodge.'

True enough. Ginny probably would've told me the same thing. In fact, she'd probably thought of all that last night and just hadn't mentioned it. But she wasn't the issue here. I was. I was supposed to keep all these people alive, and I hadn't even figured out that Simon might be in danger.

There in the snow, with Sam studying me and cold everywhere, I decided to *get* the sonofabitch who did this. Just holding the fort until Ginny came back wasn't enough for me any more. Somehow I intended to *get* the bastard.

As if I'd accepted Sam's reasoning, I said, 'We can't stay out here. Let's go inside.'

He approved. 'Good idea. You're not due for another injection, but you could use some rest.'

Something still bothered me, another detail I'd missed, like the evidence that Simon might be in danger. It had to do with this hole in the wall. But I decided not to nag at it. I had plenty of other things to think about. And it might come clear faster if I left it alone.

In any case, what I really wanted to do was go to my room and shave. I hated feeling this scruffy. It messed up my brain, and I couldn't afford that. If I wanted to catch Cat's killer, I needed to be able to *think*.

Chapter Seventeen

Standing up was easier said than done, but Sam helped me. No one shot at us. He gave me the .45, and we returned to the kitchen.

The Carbones had joined Faith. With an air of impersonal weariness, as if his fatigue were metaphysical rather than practical, Truchi watched Ama help Faith with lunch.

Queenie and Rock stood there as well. As Sam and I clumped into the kitchen, shedding clots of snow, she approached us with a handful of pills and a glass of water.

Behind her, Rock wandered away like a man who had no idea where he was headed.

Sam let go of me. I braced myself on a counter top while he hugged Queenie.

'What's happening?' Her voice was softly intense. 'I asked Rock, but he didn't make much sense.'

With a tilt of his head, Sam referred the question to me.

'Sam's taking me to my room,' I replied as if that were an answer. 'I want to shave.'

Queenie frowned. However, Sam's expression persuaded her to contain herself. 'First your pills,' he ordered me. 'As long as you need a nurse as well as a doctor, you'd better do what we tell you.'

She handed me the pills and the glass of water.

I took them. Then I let Sam and Queenie help me in the direction of my room.

Truchi observed our departure as if he wondered whether pain had any spiritual justification.

Maybe Sam's injection was wearing off. I reached my room too tired to do anything as energetic as shaving. Ignoring my wet pants, I sat down on the bed, took as much air as I could into my cramped lungs, and tried to remember what strength felt like.

With an odd sense of dislocation, I noticed that I hadn't covered my window. In fact, I hadn't latched it. I'd told everyone else what to do, but I hadn't done it myself.

Brilliant, Axbrewder. I was off to a great start.

Fortunately Queenie had the presence of mind to latch and blind the window for me. At once the whole room went as dim as the inside of my head.

'All right,' she said firmly. 'Tell me.'

Again Sam looked at me.

I nodded.

He told her.

She gnawed on the information for a minute or two. Then she asked, 'Are you going to tell this to everybody else?'

I said flatly, 'No.'

'Why not?'

'Three reasons.' It's amazing how clear you can be when you don't mean it. I was just stalling for time. 'First, we can't be sure we're right. We haven't got enough facts. Second, nothing has changed. What we need to do until Reeson gets back,' never mind Ginny, 'remains the same, no matter who the killer is. Third, these people are scared enough already. If we start telling them stories about a faceless hit man, they may panic. That will make the situation even harder to control.'

Fourth, my brain still didn't function worth a damn. I couldn't find the flaw in my own reasoning, the small detail I'd missed.

Queenie opened her mouth to ask another question, but the sound of Ama's chimes in the hallway interrupted her.

I didn't know which impressed me more − the lunacy of playing lunch chimes or the determination to behave normally at a time like this.

Both Sam and Queenie considered me. I said, 'You go ahead. I'll be along.' To ease their obvious doubt, I added, 'I have to learn to walk on my own some time.'

The way they consulted each other without speaking made them seem like the most married couple I knew. After a moment Sam gave me a nod. 'But if you don't show up in ten minutes, I'm coming back.'

I agreed. I was in no mood for an argument.

When they'd left, I spent a while mustering my resources. Then I got up off the bed. In the bathroom, I washed my face. Grimly I ground my electric razor over my whiskers like I wanted to eradicate my essential mortality, clean away the part of me that felt too grubby and human to cope.

In an effort to efface the clinging smell of port and blood and smoke, I slapped on so much aftershave that I reeked like a brothel. Mostly to prove that I could do it, I put on dry pants. Trying to warm my frozen feet, I put on socks. Somehow I remembered to transfer the .45 to my pocket.

At the same time I tried to decide how to do my job.

From my perspective, that implied not trusting anything I'd come up with so far. I'd already demonstrated that my brain was ripe for a factory recall. And I had at least one nagging inarticulate intuitive reason to believe that there was more to this mess than met the eye.

So I had several options. I could reverse my field like a running back and tell everyone my latest theory. That might elicit some interesting responses. Or I could play the mystery-lover's detective and go around probing people like mad, seeing what came out.

Or I could make a concerted effort to convert my crippling disadvantages into strengths. I could use my weakness as a kind of camouflage to conceal what I really had in mind.

I liked that idea.

Before Sam had a chance to come back for me, I went to lunch.

When I'd succeeded at tottering to the dining room, I found everyone there ahead of me. Buffy and Rock sat at the ends of the table where they belonged, but they looked gloomy and beaten, like they'd been dispossessed. The guests had seated themselves in their proper pairs – Joseph and Lara, Mac and Connie, Houston and Maryanne, Sam and Queenie. Faith and Ama had just started to clear away bowls of vegetable stew.

They all stared at me. Except Faith, of course. And Amalia, who concentrated on her work.

For a moment I didn't sit down. Instead I blinked back at the group – mostly at the Hardhouses. The belligerent shape of his face never relaxed, but his flexible smile seemed almost affectionate. If I didn't know better, I would've thought that he was glad to see me. And the dark intensity in her eyes only made her beauty more poignant.

I couldn't figure them out. Why were they still together? Why did they look so much like they'd achieved a reconciliation after each time one or both of them got into bed with someone else?

Oh, well. My instincts told me nothing, and I had no other clues. Shrugging to myself, I sat down.

Like magic Faith appeared beside me with a bowl of stew. I sipped at it as if everyone weren't watching me.

By accident I sat across from Mac Westward and Constance Bebb. Over my spoon, I noticed that Mac had a bottle of wine at his place. He was the only one drinking, but he didn't let that slow him down. Every now and then, he aimed an oblique glance at Joseph or Lara. When he did that, he gaze conveyed an astonishing depth of venom and helplessness.

At his side, Connie was stiff with disapproval.

Maryanne's face gave a whole new meaning to *paleness*. This wasn't Faith's devout translucence. It was the kind of pale you get when you drain all the blood out of the heart. She looked like the victim of a vampire.

As for Mile, he kept chewing something even though he didn't have any food in front of him. The malice in his little eyes gave the impression that he'd acquired a taste for violent fantasies.

Of all the people at the table, only Sam and Queenie seemed to have kept their emotional balance.

Ama passed around a platter of bacon, lettuce, and tomato sandwiches. I waved them away – stew was as much as I could stomach. So did Buffy and Lara. But Hardhouse and Mile stocked up as if the prospect of murder made them ravenous.

By degrees the group stopped watching me so hard. On the other hand, no one had any conversation to offer. At intervals someone glanced up at the empty gun cases, then looked away.

Abruptly Hardhouse threw his napkin into the air. 'You people,' he said in a tone of humorous disgust, 'act like we're all doomed. Don't you have any ideas? Can't you think of anything to say?'

Maryanne actively flinched. Sam raised his eyebrows.

Like soft acid, Connie articulated, 'Perhaps you can, Mr Hardhouse.'

'Perhaps I can,' he admitted. Rubbing his hands together, he scanned the table. 'For example, here's an idea. Houston and Queenie had a bet, remember? They were trying to guess who the actors are – and the detectives.' His grin included me. 'They wrote down some names so that they couldn't cheat later by changing their minds.

'Let's settle the bet.'

Both Buffy and Rock gaped at him like he'd suggested a gang rape. Sam started to object, but Mile got there first.

'Shee-it, boy,' he snarled fatly. 'You out of your mind? We got us a real killer on our hands, and about the only thing standin' between us and murder is Axbrewder's opinion of hisself.' A subtle reference to my position on gun control. 'This ain't no vacation. It stopped bein' a vacation when Cat Reverie took that slug in her head. I ain't got time to play vacation games so you can be entertained.'

Mile's outburst didn't daunt Hardhouse. 'Shee-it, yourself, Houston,' he drawled. 'What I had in mind isn't a game. We know who the actors and detectives are. Nobody cares whether you win or lose that bet – although I would guess from your attitude that you were wrong on all four names.

'What interests me,' he went on, 'is your ability to think. You're right, we're not on vacation now. We're trying to survive. And we're up against a professional – a man who kills for money and gets away with it. As far as I can see, our best chance to survive is to play the mystery game for real. If you have it in you. If you can stop feeling sorry for yourself long enough to think.'

'If that's what you want to know,' Queenie put in without hesitation, 'why didn't you just say so?' She sounded curious rather than irritated. 'Why bring up that bet at all?'

Hardhouse shrugged. 'It's a place to start. As I say, nobody cares what your guesses were – but I'm quite interested in your reasoning. From there, we might be able to work our way to an understanding of our situation. And that might save us.'

'I don't have the papers,' Buffy said unexpectedly. I'd thought that she was too shell-shocked to follow the conversation. 'But I remember what they said.'

'Houston said the detectives were Ginny and Brew. But he said he didn't think we'd hired any actors this time. He said Rock and I were going to do the crime ourselves.'

'Shee-it,' Mile repeated, ladling out disgust like rancid lard.

Buffy didn't stop. Maybe she didn't hear him.

'Queenie named Ginny and Brew, too. But she thought the actors were Houston and Maryanne.'

At this Maryanne let out a little laugh like a glimpse of hysteria.

All the rest of us sat still with our brains going numb.

'In any case,' Hardhouse concluded as if he hadn't been interrupted, 'I doubt that we have anything better to do.'

'But what is there to understand?' Maryanne asked. Her voice sounded like her pallor – like she'd used up all her courage a while ago. 'Simon killed Cat. We know that because he's gone. He wants to kill Brew. We know that' – for a moment she seemed to lose the handle –

'we know that because of Lawrence Smithsonian. What is there to understand?'

'Oh, I don't know,' Hardhouse mused. 'I'm just not sure the situation is that simple.' He paused briefly. Then he explained, 'For example, I'm not sure Simon shot Cat.'

'Why not?' Connie interjected. The gleam in her eyes looked hard and irreconciled, like a threat.

He met her gaze and smiled. 'His speech last night impressed me. One thing I think we can be sure of. When he shot at Brew and hit Cat, he knew he'd missed. He must have been able to see the wrong person go down. He knew he hadn't finished his job.'

'So?' pursued Connie.

'So he knew he might need that rifle again. And we know he's a professional. So why did he hide the rifle in his own closet and then re-enter the lodge in a way that forced us to suspect him? That doesn't sound very professional to me.'

Westward burped up some wine. 'He wanted to look so foolish that we wouldn't believe in his guilt.'

Hardhouse was enjoying himself. 'I doubt that. He couldn't be sure how we would react. For all he knew, we might do exactly what we did do – lock him up so that he couldn't kill anybody else. We forced him to reveal himself at a time when he needed to keep himself and his intentions secret.

'I don't know about you,' he said to the rest of us, 'but I find it easier to believe the killer is someone else.'

Rock squirmed in his seat. He opened his mouth to say something, closed it again, looked at me.

Sam and Queenie looked at me as well.

What the hell. As long as Hardhouse wanted to do my thinking for me, I didn't see any reason to stand in his way. Indirectly he was helping me keep a low profile.

'Tell them,' I muttered.

Apparently Sam approved of my change of tactics. Without hesitation, he explained my theory about the killer and Simon.

'Christ Almighty!' Mile was so angry that he spattered saliva on the tablecloth. 'Do you mean to say there's two of us dead now, *two of us dead*, and you want us to practise our *reasonin*?' Ignoring Hardhouse, he aimed his ire at me. 'You knew about this, you and Rock and them two' – he swung a hand at the Draytons – 'but you wasn't goin' to tell the rest of us. You wasn't goin' to tell me because you *know* Ah won't put up with it! By God, Ah'm goin' to keep mahself alive if I got to kill ever' one of you to do it!'

Slamming down his napkin, he bounded to his feet. His chair clattered against the wall behind him. So hard that he nearly made the floorboards complain, he stamped out of the room.

Just for a second, the rest of us sat with our eyes wide and our mouths open, as if we actually believed him.

Then Hardhouse glanced at the ceiling. 'For a fat guy, ol' Houston sure is temperamental.'

Before she could stop herself, Maryanne let out another burst of laughter.

'But if you don't count him,' Sam put in, making sure everyone knew that I still had his support, 'nothing has changed. Our problem remains the same.' He nodded at Hardhouse. 'If we want to survive, we need to think.'

Connie nodded as well. Even Maryanne nodded, doing her best not to laugh – or wail. Mac took a long drink and refilled his glass. Lara studied me with her eyes on fire, as if I'd suddenly become wonderful.

Which was as good a reason as any for me to get out of there. After all, I had my own pose to maintain. 'Speak for yourself,' I muttered, levering my weight off my chair. 'If I want to survive, I've got to get some rest.'

'Good idea,' Sam said. 'I'll check on you in a few minutes.'

No one took exception to the fact that I proposed to be alone, even though I was the killer's target – and in no shape to defend myself. Presumably we'd locked him out. Certainly we'd covered and latched our windows. The group let me go like it never crossed anyone's mind that I wasn't being sensible.

My withdrawal wasn't entirely a pose, however. My insides were having a strange reaction to the stew – 'digestion' possibly – and I feared that if I didn't lie down soon I would puke. With my guts gurgling like a worn-out sump, I returned to my room.

But I wasn't really sleepy, so I didn't take off my clothes. Instead I stretched out on the coverlet and let the room's dim quiet filter through my head. For a while I succeeded at what I needed most, which was to not think about Ginny. If I did, I might panic – which wouldn't do any of us any good.

Nevertheless when I heard a hand on my doorknob I thought it might be her. My heart jumped like I'd been poked with a cattle-prod. I was half off the bed by the time Sam and Queenie entered.

'Brew?' Sam asked when he saw the distress on my face, 'are you all right?'

I groaned vaguely and sagged back down.

He had his medical bag with him. At once he started to examine me. Took my pulse and temperature, listened to my stomach, checked my pupils. When he was done, he nodded approval.

'Considering how badly you care for yourself, you're pretty lucky. Your temperature is coming down, your bowels work, and your blood pressure is almost normal – for someone in your condition. I'm starting to believe that you haven't torn any sutures. If you stay right where you are for forty-eight hours, you'll be almost as healthy as you were when this camp started.'

That good, huh?

Dully I said, 'You know I can't do that.'

He repacked his bag. 'I know. Under the circumstances, you can only hope that you don't get any worse. I hate to say this, Brew, but you need to do some thinking ahead.'

I frowned at him.

'Assuming you survive until Reeson brings help, you can't go back to Puerta del Sol like this. You won't be able to defend yourself. You'll have to go somewhere else. You'd better decide where while you can.'

'Don't tell me,' I muttered, 'let me guess. The medical profession has determined that the best cure for a gunshot stomach is profound depression, and you're trying to help me recover. You want to make me as miserable as possible.'

Sam didn't smile, but his eyes held a humorous glint. 'You know, Axbrewder' – he snapped his bag shut – 'you're a cantankerous sonofabitch. That's a good sign.'

Queenie came to stand beside him. 'There's something I want you to know,' she told me. Her straight brave gaze raised my temperature at least a couple of degrees. 'I think Rock made a better choice than he realized when he hired you and Ginny. I don't blame you for the danger. You couldn't possibly have known this would happen. But since it *is* happening, I'm glad you're here. I might not trust somebody else.'

Sam put his arm around her waist and gave her a squeeze.

Sudden tears burned the backs of my eyes. Which made me feel incredibly foolish. Charming as ever, I said, 'Get out of here. I'm supposed to rest, remember?'

Sam nodded. 'Come on,' he murmured to his wife. Apparently he knew when to leave his patients alone with their emotions.

604

Before she let him draw her away, however, Queenie bent over me quickly and kissed my forehead.

With their arms around each other, they headed towards the door – and nearly ran into Lara Hardhouse.

'I'm sorry,' she breathed softly, seeming flustered by the encounter. 'I knocked, but I guess you didn't hear me.

'How is he?'

'At the moment,' Sam answered, sizing her up, 'he's doing as well as can be expected. If he gets lots of sleep and plenty of antibiotics, he'll be all right.'

'Good.' Her hands made awkward little gestures, fluttered like a bird with a broken wing. 'I'm glad. I've been worried about him.' Then, as if she were summoning reserves of courage, she added unexpectedly, 'He shouldn't be alone.'

'He needs rest–' Sam began.

Lara broke in. 'But he's in danger. More than the rest of us. How can he rest? If he sleeps, he'll be helpless.' She took a deep breath. The mixture of determination and fear in her eyes made her extraordinarily beautiful. 'I'll stay with him.'

Studiously non-committal, Sam referred the question to me.

What I thought was, No! Get that woman away from me.

What I said was, 'I don't mind.'

If anything, the nameless panic Lara inspired in me had intensified. But that didn't seem like an adequate reason to avoid her. If I intended to turn my weakness to my own advantage, I couldn't afford to ignore the opportunities it created.

Sam shrugged and left with his wife.

Lara closed the door behind them – and quietly turned the lock.

Then she walked towards me like a hungry woman approaching her first and maybe her only chance for food.

As if I were helpless, I stared at her while she came to the bed and sat down and leaned over me. Her hair fell like abandonment on either side of her face as she kissed my mouth.

Her lips clung to mine, the kiss of a woman ready soul and body to be ravished by love. Despite its gentleness, she put everything she had into it. Her mouth held mine as if she fed on me.

I'd never been kissed like that. Not once in my whole life. Ginny wasn't a woman who let herself go that way.

For a moment I forgot my weakness. As she kissed me, something that might as well have been strength filled my veins, and I ached to put my arms around her, wrap her into my heart until my loneliness burned away.

Which was probably why she scared me so badly.

So I didn't put my arms around her. After the first rush, I didn't kiss her back. Instead I lay there like I'd never had any use for love and waited for her to pull away.

Finally she did. 'Oh, Brew, Brew.' Trouble darkened her eyes, and she was unquestionably the most beautiful woman I'd ever seen. 'What's the matter? What's wrong?'

I shrugged as well as I could while her hair hung over me and her beauty leaned so close to my face. A desire to weep choked my throat. Thickly I said, 'I don't know why you're doing this.'

'Isn't it obvious?'

'Not to me.' The struggle to force words past my grief made me fierce. 'You're married. Cat told me,' poor Cat, all her loveliness and grace blown out of her, 'your husband is pretty impressive in bed. You've already had one affair since you got here. Mac would kill for a woman like you.' An unfortunate choice of words, but what the hell. 'And I'm so damaged I can hardly stand. You don't need me. If you're looking for a way to get your husband's attention, use somebody else.'

'Oh, Brew.' If she kept saying my name like that, she'd break my heart. 'You don't know. You don't understand.

'You're wrong about Joseph. Believe me, he isn't what you think. He doesn't want me. He wants' – she hunted for words – 'women like Cat. Broken women. If he could break me, it would be different. But I can't let him do that. Can I? I have to keep myself from being broken somehow.

'Mac is sweet, but he doesn't mean anything to me. He's just' – she let me see all the pain in her eyes – 'just a distraction. A way to protect myself because you won't let me near you. If you let me, I would sell my soul for you.'

Which didn't make any sense, of course. What, sell her soul for a gut-shot and unreliable private investigator she hardly knew? Bullshit. Yet somehow she made me believe it. Just for a moment or two, she inspired me to believe that her passion ran so deep. Her eyes were moist, luminous with her particular vulnerability.

And I wanted to respond. I've always been a sucker for vulnerability.

Putting one hand on her shoulder, I moved her aside so that I could sit up. In response, she slid her arm across my shoulders as if she thought I wanted that. I lacked the will to resist, but I didn't encourage her, either.

606

Roughly I said, 'You'll have to do better than that.'

She avoided my gaze. Instead she watched my mouth, wanting it. Her lips parted. Gloss or moisture made them shine.

'What do you mean?'

'Look at me.' My fierceness changed slowly, growing purer. 'What do you see? I've been shot. A killer is after me. I brought him here because I couldn't get my brain out of the fog enough to recognize a voice over the phone. My life is a daily struggle with booze. If it weren't for Sam and his bag of tricks, I wouldn't even be able to sit up. What kind of woman wants a man like that?'

'Brew. Oh, Brew.' She did it again. 'You're wrong about yourself. You only think that way because you're surrounded by people who sneer at you. Your partner isn't any better than you are, but she acts like she is. Really, she's worse. She doesn't even know she's crippled. But it's false, Brew. It's false. Don't you know what you are?'

I held her gaze as if I wanted to fall into her eyes and drown.

'You're a *man*. Compared to you, Joseph is only male. And Mac isn't even that. You're the only *man* here. You know everything there is to know about pain. Terrible things have happened to you, and you've been so hurt, so hurt – you've been lost in alcohol. Your partner doesn't care about you. You've been shot by a professional killer. Your enemies have torn at you until you can barely stay on your feet. But you aren't broken.

'That's what being a man *is*,' she said as if she'd built her life on it. 'You endure everything there is to endure, but you don't break.

'I don't know how any woman can look at you and not want you, not want to take every part of you inside herself, for comfort and healing and passion. If she did that – if you let her – she would be whole again.'

Well, she was wrong about one thing, anyway. I didn't know everything there was to know about pain. She'd already taught me something new. I didn't know how to face it.

But I did. We can all be brave if we need courage badly enough.

I'd lost my ferocity. The naked heat of her confusion had burned away my anger. Gently, almost tenderly, as if she were a sore child I wanted to soothe, I said, 'That has got to be one of the worst reasons for sex I've ever heard.'

At last I'd succeeded at hurting her. Good for me. Her arm dropped from my shoulders, and her eyes seemed to go blank, almost opaque, as if she'd slammed the doors behind them shut. A hot spot of crimson appeared on her cheek.

'Maybe I was wrong,' she retorted. 'Maybe you *are* broken.' Her tone held so much concentrated acid that I actually winced. 'Broken in so many pieces that you can't tell you've been shattered. Maybe those bandages' – she poked a finger at my ribs, eliciting another wince – 'are all that holds you together.'

Before I could think of anything to say, we heard a scream.

More of a howl, really, a full-throated yell of rage and frustration and loss. A woman's howl, but doors and walls muffled it, I couldn't identify the voice. Nevertheless it had enough power to cut into me like the bite of a drill.

She screamed twice and then stopped.

My mind went blank with shock. But I'd already reached the door. I had the .45 in my fist.

The door refused to open. Lara had locked it.

Frantic to get out, I twisted the lock, hauled open the door, lurched into the hall.

I couldn't tell where the scream had came from. But Sam Drayton ran past me. I followed him.

Down the hall just a few doors. To Mac Westward's room.

By the time I got there, Lara and Queenie were right behind me. We found Connie standing beside the bed, Sam opposite her. She gasped for air in hard desperate chunks, the flush of her screams still on her face. She looked wild-eyed and extravagant, like a schoolteacher gone feral.

Sam examined Mac. But I didn't need a doctor to tell me that he was dead. People who lie with their heads at that angle are always dead. He must've been sleeping the sleep of the drunk when someone walked in and snapped his cervical vertebrae.

Queenie gave a little wail and hurried over to Connie. But Connie didn't react. She didn't want comfort. She stood rigid, panting hoarsely, like a woman who wanted blood.

The intensity of Lara's expression surpassed my capacity to interpret it.

We were the only ones in the room. No one else appeared. The other guests must've heard Connie's screams, but they didn't come to investigate. Apparently they'd already reached the same conclusion I did.

The killer wasn't outside where Ginny could hunt him down. He was in the lodge with us.

Chapter Eighteen

It didn't make any sense. I couldn't think. I could only stare at Mac. The angle of his neck made me want to throw up. Somehow I'd never clearly recognized the vulnerability of drunks.

And the insoluble simplicity of the problem appalled me. Anyone could've come into this room and done that to him, anyone. It didn't take strength. All it required was a working knowledge of how necks break. The killer could be anyone.

But what staggered me most, made my whole moral world stand on its head, was the certainty that Mac hadn't been killed by accident. Not like Cat.

Which implied –

I couldn't think.

Sam stood in front of me, glaring, his eyes hard – too hard. In a brittle voice, he said, 'This changes everything, doesn't it.' For the first time he sounded breakable. There were limits to what he could bear.

Like an echo in an empty room, I said, 'Everything.'

And Connie said, 'Everything,' contemplating murder.

'Any one of us,' Sam went on, 'could be next.'

Come on, Axbrewder. *Think*, for God's sake!

'You found him like this?' Queenie asked Connie. 'Did you scream right away? How long ago did this happen? Did you see anything? Why were you here?'

See, Axbrewder? *She's* thinking. Doing what people need to do when their lives are in danger – trying to get a grip on the problem.

Do it, you sonofabitch. Mac was dead. Killed deliberately, not by accident, killed for reasons that belonged to him and no one else. Which implied –

'Brew,' Lara asked softly, urgently, 'what're we going to do?'

Well, look on the bright side, I told myself. Simon might still be alive. The killer was here in the lodge, one of us. And none of us could possibly have killed him, lugged his corpse up into the hills, and then come back before the rest of us realized the danger. Ginny might well be safe. She was hunting a panic-stricken actor, not a professional hit man.

But that didn't matter, not to us, not now. I had a more immediate problem. The killer was *here*, and I was supposed to deal with him – and I had no idea what was going on.

'What're we going to do?' Lara repeated.

'Survive.' My voice shook. Hell, my entire body shook. 'Which means that we're going to stay together. The whole group, everyone, in the same room. That way, whoever did this can't kill anyone else.'

'Right!' San snapped. Somehow I'd said what he needed to hear. 'I'll get them into the den. We can talk there.'

He hurried out the door.

'Brew' – Queenie left Connie, came over to me – 'is that safe? Should I go after him?'

Everything had happened too quickly. I couldn't think fast enough. She was right, I shouldn't have let Sam go alone. He might be the killer himself. Or the next victim. I should've sent Queenie and even Lara with him. But he'd left before I could get my brain in gear and my mouth open.

'No.' I refused to risk Queenie too. 'He'll be all right. It's too soon for another murder.' To keep her from arguing, I said, 'Take Connie to the den. Stay with her. I'll be along in a minute.'

Like her husband, she needed to move, to do something. She turned back to Connie.

Connie didn't budge. Rigid with strain and fury, she demanded, 'Mr Axbrewder, how are you going to catch Mac's killer?'

I wanted to yell at her, I don't know! Catching killers is Ginny's job! Don't you understand? I'm just the hired help! But that didn't seem particularly useful, so I swallowed it. Instead I faced her straight.

'I'll start by questioning you.' Pay attention. This is a threat. 'As far as I can tell, only two people here have a reason to want him dead, and you're one of them.'

Queenie raised her hand to her mouth in shock, but she didn't interrupt. Lara studied me intensely, as if every nerve in her body were on fire.

Connie didn't flinch. She didn't even protest. But her face twisted and went pale, like I'd punched her in the stomach.

Well, I knew how that felt, but I didn't apologize. None of this made sense. That *was* Smithsonian's voice on the phone, I was sure now, and the shot that killed Cat could've been aimed at me, and someone had definitely tried to suffocate me with rat poison. No one except el Señor actively wanted me dead. But in that case Mac should still be alive. Mainly so that I wouldn't start to whimper in frustration, I ordered Queenie and Lara to get Connie out of the room.

They obeyed.

Connie didn't resist. I'd knocked the fury out of her. She walked with her arms folded over her stomach, protecting her pain.

Unfortunately I didn't have the vaguest notion what to do next.

Search for clues. Sure. What did I expect to find? Would I recognize a clue if I saw it? The only thing in the whole room – or the whole lodge – that mattered was the angle of Mac's neck. He hadn't been given a chance to defend himself. To understand his plight, or fear it. A useless death. As soon as he'd started pouring wine into himself at lunch, he was a goner.

He didn't deserve it.

Unless you believed that he deserved to die for screwing around with Lara Hardhouse.

I wanted to scream, but I didn't. Instead I studied the room for a while, trying to convince myself that I'd notice anything out of place, anything significant. I checked his windows. Behind their blinds, they remained latched. I checked his bathroom. The sink held a strand or two of hair that might've been Lara's. However, I wasn't really looking for clues. I just wanted time to calm my nerves.

Without this hole in my guts, I might've vacuumed the rug and dusted the chintz in an effort to restore my sense of moral order. But my wounds refused to go away.

As soon as I stopped shaking, I headed for the den.

Most of the group had assembled ahead of me. Comfortable fires had raised the room's temperature and cleared the last arsenic reek from the air. Nevertheless Murder On Cue's guests huddled in front of the hearths as if shock or fear had chilled them. But they didn't huddle together. Schisms of distrust separated them. Only Sam and Queenie clung to each other. Maryanne and Connie sat as far away from each other as possible on the same couch. Rock and Buffy had claimed opposite armchairs, facing different fires. And Joseph and Lara Hardhouse seemed to confront their marriage from either side of the tree trunk like a couple who couldn't choose between loathing and passion.

As self-effacing as ever in their distinct fashions, Amalia Carbone and Faith Jerrick stood back against the walls, out of the way. Of all the people there, only Faith didn't look suspicious of anyone. Even Ama glowered frankly at us all from her withdrawn position. But Faith had a friend in God, and that sufficed.

Which left –

I twisted against my bandages to scan the room. 'Where's Mile?' I asked Maryanne. Facing Ama, I asked, 'Where's Truchi?'

Maryanne gave a wan grimace. In a small forlorn voice, she said, 'He didn't tell me. When we heard what happened – when Sam came and got us – Houston just left. He didn't say anything.'

Ama was a good housekeeper. She knew her place. But she was also furious. In Italian she muttered something that sounded remarkably like, 'That son of a goat-fucker.' Then she answered in bitter English, 'He abuses my husband.'

Somehow I knew exactly what that meant.

Riding the remains of my adrenalin, I headed out of the den. On my way, I commanded, 'Wait here,' as if I could take everyone's obedience for granted.

I found Mile and Petruchio Carbone in the kitchen. Which was a good thing, because otherwise I wouldn't have known where to look for them. Mile had his back to me, he didn't hear me coming. One fat fist gripped the front of Truchi's shirt. The other brandished a wad of bills. Must've been several hundred dollars.

'It's yours,' he was saying. His voice sounded like what happens when you step on a stick of margarine. 'It's all Ah have on me, but you'll get more. A lot more. No questions asked. All Ah want is a gun. The biggest cannon you got hidden. And ammunition. Ah mean to blow me away a killer.'

Truchi didn't betray my arrival with any shift of his head or flick of his gaze. Under the droop of his moustache, lines of sadness shaped his mouth, and his eyes seemed to regard Mile with profound fatigue. Apparently his reaction didn't require words. He said nothing.

His silence didn't bring out the best in Mile's temper. Mile knew how to get what he wanted, and the name of that how was *money*. When money didn't work, he turned frantic. Or vicious. This time, it was vicious.

'You wop shit.' He waved bills in Truchi's face like a club. 'You listen to me, boy. You think you can say no to me, you got that wrong. Try it and you're dead meat. The minute Ah get to a phone, Ah'll buy me this lodge and everythin' on it. Then your job is mine. Your *ass* is

612

mine, fucker. Ah'll make piss-sure you never work again. You and that thick slut you call your wife are goin' to be in the crapper 'til you *starve*. Where Ah come from, we eat you spick and wop bastards for breakfast. You get me a gun or you're *dead*.'

Truchi looked all this in the eye without a flicker. Considering his strength, he probably could've beaten Mile to jello with one elbow stuck in his ear. But maybe he figured that the owners of Deerskin Lodge wouldn't approve if he pounded the by-products out of a guest. Or maybe he was just impervious to abuse and had no use for violence. Either way, he didn't respond.

I had a different reaction.

Someone had already tried to kill me. Twice, maybe. I faced a series of crimes that I couldn't understand and didn't know how to handle. Ginny was gone, and the infection in my guts put up a good fight against the antibiotics, and too many things were my fault. On top of that, I smelled an insidious little reek of gas. Reeson hadn't done a particularly good job on the stove.

The odour reminded me of smoke and arsenic.

I picked my spot. I measured the distance.

Then I hit Mile in the back hard enough to rattle my teeth.

Afterwards my pulse hammered like it was about to split open my skull. But I didn't care. There's no substitute for job satisfaction.

Mile slammed against Truchi and flopped to the floor like a bowl of overturned oatmeal. The way he arched his back and tried to crawl away from the pain worried me for a second. Maybe I'd broken something for him, or sent him into kidney shock. But I didn't worry much.

Truchi glanced down at Mile briefly. Then he looked at me and gave a sad shake of his head. No doubt Mile and I had confirmed his belief that everyone who ever came to the Lodge was crazy.

I didn't worry about that, either. Stiffly I said, 'Bring him,' and turned away.

By the time I got to the den, I could feel the floorboards wobble under me, and my head hurt as if someone had buried an axe in my brain. Everyone watched me enter. Even Faith turned her head in my direction. But I didn't say anything at first. Instead I went to the nearest hearth to prop myself in my familiar position against the mantel. I took the .45, the symbol of my authority, out of my pocket and set it handy. While my head pounded, I glared around the room.

'If anyone else wants to argue with me, do it now. You've got one minute.' Anger and blood-loss left me giddy. 'If you give me any more grief after that, I'll turn my gun over to Mile and let the lot of you fend for yourselves.'

They all stared at me.

As if on cue, Truchi came into the den with a coughing and defeated Houston Mile over his shoulder. He dropped Mile on the couch between Maryanne and Connie, then retreated to stand beside his wife. Mile's colour suggested apoplexy or infarction. He didn't try to talk.

After that no one said anything. No one dared. Maryanne studied Mile as if he nauseated her. She made no effort to comfort him.

'All right.' Time to do my job. Now or never. 'Sam probably told you what happened, but we're going to take it from the top anyway. This is just like playing mystery camp, except now everyone's life is on the line. Not just mine. You first, Connie.'

'What?' Connie stared at me like I'd frightened her out of her outrage. Maybe I'd been too hard on her. I wanted information from her. And I wanted access to her professional expertise, the knowledge that she'd acquired being half of Thornton Foal.

But I didn't go easy. 'Start with right after lunch.' I didn't plan to go easy on any of them. 'Tell us what you did. Why you did it. Don't leave anything out. Then tell us why we shouldn't think you killed him.'

At any rate, she wasn't in shock. And she wasn't the kind of woman who stayed frightened. She had too much fury in her.

'Mr Axbrewder,' she said in a congested voice, 'you're treating me like a fool. I'm the one who discovered Mac's body. I'm the one who screamed. Any murderer with an ounce of sense would make absolutely certain she was somewhere else when the body was found.

'This is a small group, Mr Axbrewder. For the most part, what we do here' – her gaze held my face – 'is painfully transparent. I knew Mac was in trouble. How could I help it? For one thing, he doesn't drink like that. Not at lunch. Not in the middle of a mystery. And for another, he doesn't have affairs with married women.'

In the background, Lara flushed. But no one made any comment.

'As far as I know,' Connie continued, 'he doesn't have affairs at all.' She seemed unaware that she referred to Westward in the present tense. 'He's an inward man, a writer, not an actor. What he does is *create*. And he is good at it.' Outrage crowded her throat. 'Our society doesn't take the mystery novel seriously as literature, but Mac should be taken seriously. His gifts–'

She gulped down emotion, tightened her grip on herself. The not

614

focus of her eyes made them look almost crazy – as crazy as the flame-tip of an acetylene torch.

'I knew he was in trouble.'

Mile coughed once more, hard, possibly trying to spit up blood. Then he subsided.

'After lunch,' Connie explained grimly, 'he went to his room. He went alone, although you had instructed us to stay together. This worried me, Mr Axbrewder. I could understand his desire to numb his troubles with alcohol. But alcohol isn't selective. Numbing his troubles, he also numbed himself to danger. For that reason, I decided to watch over him.

'A short time after lunch – no more than half an hour – I went to his room to be sure that he was all right. I intended to stay with him until he awoke. Or until Ms Fistoulari returned.

'I found him as you saw him.

'I'm not acquainted with violent death, Mr Axbrewder. I write about it, certainly, but I have no personal experience with murder. Catherine Reverie was the first *victim* I've seen.

'Nonetheless no one could mistake what had happened to Mac.' Without warning her voice caught, clenched around a sob. Again she tightened her grip on herself. 'And only a fool could fail to draw the obvious conclusions. I am not a fool. Clearly, our reasoning – *your* reasoning, Mr Axbrewder – was predicated on a false premise. Clearly–'

I interrupted her. 'Did you touch anything?' I had my own panic and outrage to deal with.

She shook her head. Judging by her expression, her estimation of me sank every time I opened my mouth. 'Of course not.'

'You didn't touch him? To see what he felt like?' What violent death felt like? 'See if he was still warm?'

At least I succeeded at surprising her. 'What would be the point?'

That got a reaction out of Hardhouse. 'To find out how long he'd been dead. It might make a big difference if we knew when during that half hour he was killed.'

I sighed to myself. One of the last things I wanted in life was to have Joseph Hardhouse on my side. But the issue had to be faced. I looked at Sam.

Sam shrugged. 'I examined the body.' He had his own brand of bitterness, which he made no effort to conceal. 'Without an autopsy, I can't be sure of much. I can't even be sure he was killed by a broken neck. For all I know, that was done to him after he died, just to confuse us.

'In addition, the gradient along which a body loses warmth – like the rate of rigor mortis – varies widely from one individual to the next, one situation to the next.

'If he was cold, we could've been reasonably sure he was killed early in that half hour. But he was still warm – warm enough. It could've happened any time.'

'Which brings us,' Rock put in unexpectedly, 'to the question of alibis.'

I stared at him. So did Sam and Queenie and Hardhouse. Connie, Lara, and the rest kept their attention on me.

'We all know the killer is one of us.' From his tone, you would've thought that we held guns to his head, forcing him to explain leveraged buy-outs to morons. 'Right? The doors are all locked. There is no one else to suspect. We all had the means to kill Mr Westward. Who had the opportunity?'

He faced me. He still looked like ashes and defeat, but he'd been cursed with a brain that continued to function.

'I had the opportunity. I was here' – he indicated the den – 'alone. And my wife had the opportunity. She was in our room, also alone.'

Buffy bit her thin lips in distress.

Rock glanced around the room, mutely asking, Who else?

'But you didn't have any reason,' Maryanne put in timidly. 'Did you? You've run mystery camps for years now. Why would you suddenly start killing your guests? And Thornton Foal is famous. Once people find out Mac was killed here, they'll never come to another Murder On Cue camp.'

'That's right,' Buffy breathed from the bottom of her heart. 'We don't have any motive. We don't–'

I stopped her. 'One thing at a time. If we're going to make sense out of this, let's do it by the numbers.

'Buffy and Rock had opportunity. Connie had opportunity. Lara and I didn't. We were together.' When I said that, Lara looked so grateful that I couldn't resist adding, 'Unless she did it during the first ten minutes after lunch.

'Maryanne, what about you and Mile?' I would've loved to ask Mile himself, but he was in no condition to answer.

Maryanne's expression made me feel like a child molester. Her fear went right to the core. 'I didn't do it.' Her voice wobbled like a frail chair with too much weight in it.

'That isn't what I asked you.'

Her fellow guests seemed to hold their collective breath while Maryanne groped for courage.

Thinly she replied, 'Houston sent me to our room. I thought he wanted to look for those guns. But he didn't tell me that. He didn't say anything about it.

'He came back after fifteen or twenty minutes. I was alone that long.' She shot me a pleading gaze and repeated, 'I didn't do it.'

I ignored her insistence. 'Sam? Queenie?'

Queenie shrugged. 'Sam and I were together the whole time.'

'So if you did it,' Hardhouse remarked like he was having fun, 'you did it together. That's clever. I wonder how much easier it is to commit murder when you have a partner. You sure as hell don't have to worry about alibis, do you?'

'One thing at a time,' I said again. I spoke harshly, mostly because I hated Hardhouse. 'You're the only one left. What's *your* alibi?'

He faced me with fire in his eyes and a range of interesting emotions on his mouth. 'What do you mean, I'm the only one left? What about them?' He indicated the Carbones and Faith Jerrick.

Amalia snorted in disgust. But she responded before I could prompt her. 'Petruchio chose to prepare boards to repair the wall in the workshop. We were instructed to remain indoors, but then he cannot do his work. He left and returned through the kitchen. Faith and I saw him. We washed dishes together.'

Which wasn't the best defence I'd ever heard. If anyone had keys to the doors, Truchi did. He could've gone out, let himself in another door, killed Mac, and retreated the way he came. But Reeson had already pointed out the absurdity of accusing the Carbones or Faith. Rock and Buffy were better candidates.

I returned to Hardhouse. 'Like I say' – friendly as a bucksaw – 'you're the only one left. Tell us why we should cross you off the list.'

The Draytons, Rock, and Maryanne all turned to study him.

He spread his hands as if to show us how clean they were. Despite his animation, his artificially slick hair made him resemble one of the animal trophies. 'I was alone, too. No alibi. I was in my room, trying to get some sleep. After all the exercise I've had' – I couldn't mistake his point – 'I need rest.'

Lara bit her lips and scrutinized the floorboards.

Silence answered him. The only sound was the soft rush of the wind past the chimneys and the faint crackle of the fires.

'Which brings us,' Sam said suddenly, in the hard brittle voice I'd heard earlier, 'to the question of motive.'

'Why look at me?' Hardhouse retorted, facing Sam now.

Sam didn't hesitate. 'Because I think you killed him.'

Hardhouse widened his eyes as if he were actively surprised. 'Me? Why me?' A second later he added, 'What about Connie?'

No one so much as glanced at Connie. Stiffly Sam said, 'You killed him because he had an affair with your wife.'

Lara did her best to melt into the floor or the tree trunk, but neither of them accepted her.

Hardhouse laughed confidently. 'Don't be absurd.' His tone mocked Sam's accusation. 'She's had dozens of affairs. So have I. That's how we keep our marriage fresh. It turns us on. It makes us excited about each other. Isn't that right, Lara?'

His wife went on trying to melt. She didn't respond.

'Lara?' he asked again. He had so much confidence that he didn't need to threaten her.

For another moment she didn't reply. Then she said in a muffled voice, 'Joseph is right. We've done it for years. If he wanted to kill my lovers, he should have started a long time ago.'

'But that's *sick*,' Buffy protested.

Lara looked up. Sudden fire showed in her eyes. She may've been uncomfortable about being exposed, but her behaviour didn't embarrass her. 'How do you know? Have you ever tried it?'

'If it works,' Hardhouse put in, 'it isn't sick. What gives you the right to judge? Look at you, sitting there half dead. You and Rock' – he sneered the name – 'probably haven't touched each other for decades. But whenever Lara goes to bed with another man, I know I'm being tested. Before and after. I'm being given the chance to prove I'm the best she's ever had.

'That doesn't scare me. It doesn't intimidate me. I *like* a challenge. The rest of you talk about it, but you don't mean it. The kind of challenge you like is a mystery camp, where everyone *pretends* the issues are serious. There's no pretence about what Lara and I do. Every time we have sex, we're on the line with each other, we're being tested, we have to prove ourselves in the most intimate way there is.

'You only think it's sick,' he finished almost triumphantly, 'because you couldn't handle it.'

'No,' Connie said into the silence, as flat and sure as the blade of a knife, 'that isn't the reason.'

Personally I couldn't think of an answer. Knowing the real reason that Lara had wanted sex with me made me feel demeaned and helpless. Ultimately I was irrelevant to her. I'd endured the distress of her attempted seduction for nothing. But Connie didn't have that problem.

I hadn't seen her stand. Nevertheless she was on her feet, facing Hardhouse as if this were a contest between the two of them and none of the rest of us mattered.

'You and I, Mr Hardhouse,' Connie said. 'Only we have any apparent motive for killing Mac, you because he slept with your wife, I for essentially the same reason, because he was my partner, perhaps my lover, and he was unfaithful. I'm the one who says it, Mr Hardhouse – I who have the right. What you and Lara do is sick.'

Hardhouse probably wanted to retort. But Connie had too much dignity. Her controlled indignation kept him quiet.

'Mac was a *writer*, Mr Hardhouse. He understood, as every artist must, that there is no such thing as a contest between persons. Oh, competitions exist, competitions for jobs or advancement, athletic competitions. A murder mystery is a competition. But the *writer* of the mystery must know better.

'It is impossible to *create*, Mr Hardhouse – ultimately it is impossible to live – on the assumption that any contest can exist between persons. All characters must have the same distinctive worth, the same individual value, the same right to life, or else they have been poorly created, and the artist has failed.

'Mac understood this, I say.' She spoke as if tremors rose in her bones. 'I consider him a *writer* in the best sense, a good writer. We didn't work together because we were weak apart, but because we were stronger together. And I tell you plainly that he did not have sex with your wife in order to measure himself against you. Nor did he have sex with her in order to measure her against me.

'*That* is why I have no motive. There was no contest between Lara and me – or between Mac himself and me. Nothing that either of them did reduced me in any way. But *you*, Mr Hardhouse – you perceive a contest. Any motive here is yours, just as any failure is yours.'

I wanted to applaud. It was a wonderful speech. Queenie's eyes shone with appreciation, and Sam nodded approval. Maryanne's face had gone all soft and child-like, and even Rock and Buffy looked like they'd felt the brief butterfly kiss of grace. But you had to give Hardhouse credit. He wasn't an easy man to get around.

He didn't try to argue. Instead he simply bowed to Connie and grinned. 'I surrender,' he said humorously. Then he looked across at me. 'Since I'm the only one with means, opportunity, *and* motive, you'd better lock me up. In fact, you'd better put handcuffs on me. That way I'll be safe.' His eyes flashed. 'Just like Simon.'

Just like that, he paralysed me. With one insidious little remark, he made me realize what was wrong with my theory about Simon being alive.

Who broke Simon out of the wine cellar? Mac's killer, presumably. Why? To make Simon look guilty. And to get at the rat poison. But if Mac's killer did all that, he couldn't afford to let Simon live. Simon knew who he was. So if the killer was still outside, being chased by Ginny – which was impossible, how could he have killed Mac? – Simon was dead. And if the killer was here – which was also impossible, who else could've left that trail into the hills? – Simon was still dead.

If I did anything to imprison Hardhouse and turned out to be wrong, he might become the next victim.

None of this made any *sense*.

I didn't turn away from the problem. I didn't even wince. But in the back of my brain, panic began to gibber.

I was out of my depth.

I needed Ginny.

Chapter Nineteen

'**W**hat are we going to do?' Buffy asked.

She spoke to Rock, not to me. That was a good thing, because I had no idea. The effect of Sam's miracle drugs faded by the moment, and fever left my brain flopping around loose in my skull. Simon was dead, innocent Simon, and Hardhouse couldn't have killed Cat because he was with Ginny at the time, yet he was the only obvious candidate for Mac's murderer.

'I don't know,' Rock said like a shrug. 'It's up to Axbrewder.'

I should've paid attention, but I didn't. I didn't hear the threat gathering in the room. Instead I made a positively heroic effort to face Hardhouse's grin.

He could only be the killer if he and Ginny worked together.

Wonderful. The perfect solution. It all fitted. Together they could've shot Cat and planted the rifle and broken Simon out of the wine cellar and hidden his body and stuffed rat poison down the chimney and killed Mac. People can do amazing things when they work together.

Without her I wasn't even a whole person.

'Brew' – Queenie echoed Buffy's question – 'what're we going to do?'

'All of a sudden,' Mile growled, 'you don't look so good, do you, boy?'

That brought me back. Until then I hadn't grasped how much my credibility depended on the idea that I was the intended victim. But if I were irrelevant to Cat's death – a deduction which followed logically from the angle of Mac's neck – I was irrelevant to everything. My relationship to the whole group changed. And Houston Mile, for one, had no more use for me.

'You like to strut, don't you?' he continued. He didn't appear to notice as Maryanne shifted away from him. Pain still marked his face, leaving hints of congested crimson around his bad teeth, but he'd had enough time to recover his natural charm. 'You like to wave that cannon around, and punch innocent folks in the back when they ain't lookin', and carry on like the almighty Law of God. But you been wrong about everythin' so far, ain't you, boy?

'You and that fuckin' partner of yours, issuin' orders, thinks she a man, and she ain't got better sense than to go off huntin' a boy who ain't killed his first horsefly yet, never mind an actual woman. Unless she's on the run herself, leavin' us to get picked off one at a time while you stand there refusin' to let us defend ourself.'

Rock nodded as if he agreed with all this.

'You're a pitiful excuse for a detective, boy, and you're finished.' Mile's anger gave him confidence. 'Ah ain't takin' your orders no more, and the rest of us ain't either.' He waggled a pudgy hand at me. 'You pass over that cannon before anybody else gets killed, and Ah'll show you how to do your job.'

'What would you do with it, Houston?' Sam put in, at the limit of his patience. 'Shoot Joseph?'

'For a start,' Mile retorted. 'The way Ah got this thin' figured, there's only two possibilities, and givin' him a little ol' third eye in the middle of that nice face eliminates one of 'em.'

Lara made a small noise that might've been a giggle before she swallowed it.

Hardhouse glanced at her, back at me. 'In that case,' he said equably, 'I think I'll vote to leave Brew in charge.'

Mile ignored him. 'After that, pretty boy,' he snarled at Sam, 'Ah'll make you and this flouncin' bitch' – he meant Queenie – 'tell us what you're really doin' here.'

Just for a second, I thought Sam might haul off and deck Mile. Or maybe that was just wishful thinking. In any case, he didn't do it. Instead he tightened his grip on his wife. 'I think,' he said between his teeth, 'you had better explain that before I make you eat it.'

No. Absolutely not. I felt sure that I knew what Mile was about to say, and I didn't want to hear it. Deliberately I picked up the .45. I meant to cock it – I meant to fire it, if I had to, to shut him up.

Unfortunately I couldn't. I lacked the strength to work the slide. The room had started into a lazy spin, and there wasn't enough air, and as soon as Mile said anything about Ginny and Hardhouse working together I'd cackle my brains out.

Fortunately something else interrupted him.

A muffled pounding.

A distant sound like a doorknob being rattled.

More pounding.

Maybe a voice. I couldn't be sure.

But everyone else heard it, too. The whole room went still, as stiff as a corpse. Maryanne covered her mouth. Buffy's face turned as pale as her eyes. Sam and Mile cut off their argument. Lara jerked around.

The sound seemed to come from one of the bedroom wings.

'Somebody is at the back door,' Hardhouse said clearly. He was already on his way to answer the pounding.

From somewhere I dredged up the energy to shout at him. '*No!*' When he paused and turned, he saw the .45 in my fist, aimed right at him.

No one else moved a muscle.

I pushed away from the mantel, leaned into motion. Locking my knees so that I wouldn't fall, I went around the furniture and the tree to Hardhouse. He studied me in an intense but non-committal way, almost disinterested, as if for purely scientific reasons he wanted to know how much further I could go.

'It's still *my* job,' I said past the muzzle of the gun. 'The rest of you, stay here. If you want something to do, watch each other. You're all safe as long as you watch each other.'

I waited for a reaction, not from anyone else, but from Hardhouse.

'Don't worry,' he said in a friendly tone. 'I'll make sure they don't hurt themselves.'

Instead of jamming the .45 up one of his nostrils, I stumbled away into the hall.

I couldn't actually tell which hall the pounding came from. But I'd entered the one Hardhouse had headed towards. Down an aisle of tight floorboards padded by an expensive runner. Past bedrooms and the parlour. If I'd been in better shape, I would've seen immediately that this was the right hall. A shape showed through the panes of the door ahead, and the knob rattled again. I was halfway there, however, before I registered any of this information. And I'd nearly reached the door before I recognized Ginny's coat under its camouflage of snow.

I didn't hurry. The gibber of panic in my head had grown louder. Manic and lucid, it informed me that anyone could wear a coat.

Shattered by alarm and fever, I had to brace the .45 against my leg to cock it. Then, as if this were the scariest moment of my whole life, I twisted the deadbolt and let the door open.

Ginny staggered inside.

Details which I didn't notice immediately slipped past me. She'd obviously spent a fair amount of time stretched out in the snow. It still clung to her coat and hair. Clots of it packed the prongs of her claw. Her face had the particular pallor underlined with blue that comes from intense cold. She seemed too frozen to shiver. Her eyes were glazed, almost blind.

But all of that was secondary. Instead my attention jumped into focus on the wound on her left temple.

Snow and hair and coagulated blood disguised the injury, but it looked like a bullet-mark – the kind of furrow a slug leaves in your skin as it skims past you.

Oh, Ginny. My gun weighed too much. Ginny. I managed to uncock it. Then I left it dangling from the end of my arm and leaned my weight against the wall. I couldn't speak. Even simple words refused to come out.

'Brew,' she breathed in a soft empty voice, as if all her blood had gone to ice. 'He almost got me.'

It was like magic. As soon as I heard the need in her voice, I forgot about being weak. Quickly I picked myself off the wall, put the .45 away. Wrapping an arm around her, I drew her back from the door.

'Sam!' I called. 'Queenie!'

We only went as far as the parlour. A fire crackled in the hearth, so I steered Ginny inside, towards the nearest heat.

At the same time everyone from the den poured into the hallway like I'd uncorked a bottle.

Hardhouse led the way, of course, but Sam and Queenie followed close behind. While I fumbled at the sash of Ginny's coat, they rushed into the parlour. One glance at Ginny, and Sam wheeled away, fighting the press of people to go get his medical bag. I didn't see Hardhouse's reaction, Ginny's coat gave me too much trouble. Fortunately Queenie came straight over and helped. In a moment Rock and Buffy, with Connie and Maryanne and Lara, reached the parlour, and Mile filled the door, and the Carbones and Faith stood outside. Queenie shoved Ginny's coat off, urged her closer to the hearth.

A faint after-smell of port and blood tinged the air. They'd soaked into the rug, marking the place where Cat died. Luckily Truchi or Reeson had moved her body somewhere. And the fireplace sucked most of the odour away.

I looked around for something to warm Ginny. The decanter of port still stood on the wet bar, but I knew she hated port, so I opened the liquor cabinet. Like everything else in Deerskin Lodge, it was well stocked. I spotted a bottle of Black Bush, but I didn't touch it – I didn't think I could stand the smell of that much heaven. Instead I grabbed some vodka and a glass, poured a healthy shot, and took it to her.

Sam had already returned, shouldering Mile aside to reenter the parlour. When he saw the glass in my hand, he snapped, 'That's not a good idea. Get her something hot,' he instructed Faith or Ama, 'tea, coffee, cocoa, I don't care, something with sugar in it.' Then he hurried to examine Ginny.

Faith and Ama left together. Truchi stayed behind Mile, guarding all of us.

Now I had time to remember vodka. My stomach knotted, and I nearly dropped the glass. With an effort I put it down beside the port.

Sam poked a thermometer into Ginny's mouth, checked her pulse and blood pressure. Then he tore open a betadyne swab and started on her forehead. 'What happened?'

Around the thermometer, she mumbled, 'I got shot.'

I could hardly hear myself think through the gabble of panic in my head. Apparently she'd been shot at approximately the same time that Mac got killed.

Hardhouse noticed the same problem. 'You know,' he said conversationally, 'this is as good as one of those "locked room" puzzles. The facts are impossible. The killer must be outside, but he can't be because he's in here with us. He must be in here with us, but he can't be because he's outside.

'Congratulations.' He bowed to Buffy and Rock. 'This has to be the best mystery you've ever put on.'

Lara gazed at him as if she contemplated eviscerating him in his sleep.

Maybe Ginny wasn't as close to hypothermia as she looked. Or maybe she was too stubborn to quit. Something in Hardhouse's tone or words snagged her attention. She looked around the room, then took the thermometer out of her mouth and asked harshly, 'Where's Mac?'

Sam took the thermometer and studied it, frowning hard. He didn't answer her question. Instead he said, 'You and Brew have one thing in common, anyway. You're both lucky as hell. Whatever hit your head doesn't appear to have done any structural damage, and your temperature is only a little low. What you have to worry about now is shock. You need fluids. Force down as much as you can stand. And stay awake. Let me know if you feel drowsy. How long were you down in the snow? Do you know? Did you lose consciousness?'

Ginny was in no mood for medical details, however. Already I could see the difference in her, the recovered snap and fire. That more than anything else helped me believe her wound wasn't serious. Stiffly she repeated, 'Where's Mac?'

'Sit down,' Sam commanded as if he wanted to hit her. 'Head injuries are always dangerous. You can make this worse than it has to be if you don't take care of yourself.'

'*Brew*.' Ginny caught me with her grey gaze so hard that I almost saluted. '*Where's Mac?*'

Panic suddenly filled my throat. I forced out one word, 'Dead,' and stopped.

'He was killed,' Sam rasped in a kind of fury. 'Someone broke his neck. Sit *down*.'

She sat down.

Obediently Lara, Connie, and Maryanne sat down as well.

Ama and Faith had returned, but Mile didn't move to let them in. Truchi solved this problem with a gentle nudge which shifted Mile's position by several feet. At once Faith carried a steaming electric coffee pot and some cups into the parlour. She probably kept coffee for the guests ready all the time.

Promptly, but without any obvious hurry or concern, she filled a cup, stirred in some sugar, and handed it to Sam in its saucer.

He pushed it at Ginny. 'Drink this.'

One thing a prosthetic device doesn't do well is hold a cup and saucer. Just for a second, a look of naked helplessness crossed Ginny's face. Then Queenie saw the problem and intervened. She took the cup and saucer from Sam, kept the saucer, and turned the handle of the cup towards Ginny.

Ginny accepted it and hid her face over the coffee to recover her balance.

Calm as a saint, Faith put the coffee pot down on the wet bar and plugged it into an outlet.

'I don't understand,' Maryanne said as if she thought everyone else did. 'How could the same person shoot Ginny and kill Mac?'

Rock had been watching Sam and Ginny with a blank look that resembled catatonia. Now, however, he roused himself enough to murmur, 'Depends on how long ago she was shot. He could've hidden a hundred yards away. It's less than that up into the trees. He could've shot her and come back inside while we ate lunch. Then he could've hidden in Mac's room and waited.' Dully he finished, 'He could still be here.'

This novel idea made the guests flinch.

'Let me see if I understand you,' Hardhouse said. 'You think the killer *isn't* one of us. You're back to Axbrewder's theory about a hired gun – an outsider who wants to get rid of one or all of us for some unknown reason.'

Rock accepted this interpretation without blinking.

'There's only one problem,' Hardhouse continued. 'We locked all the doors from the inside. If our killer did what you're suggesting, he would have to have a key.'

Unless he came in through my window. I hadn't latched it. Queenie did that for me some time after Ginny left – after Sam and I returned from looking at the wine cellar.

In which case, why wasn't I dead?

So what other possibilities were there? Who had keys?

By the time I thought of an answer, Sam, Lara, and Connie had all turned to stare at Ama's husband like they feared he carried an Uzi under his shirt.

Ama may've grasped what this was about. Truchi didn't appear to. If anything, his general stoicism seemed less weary than usual, more bemused. She looked disgusted on his behalf.

'I don't believe it,' Connie pronounced as if no one else's opinion mattered.

'Tell me what happened,' Ginny demanded.

Sam dragged his attention back to her. 'You first. It's good for you to talk. It'll help you stay alert.'

Ginny looked at me. Maybe she wanted me to ignore Sam and answer her. Hell, maybe she wanted me to tell her what to do. At the moment, I didn't know, and I didn't care. I needed to sit down. My efforts to take charge of this situation had ended in panic, and I didn't feel able to continue functioning.

I had to do better.

The two armchairs and the loveseat were already occupied, so I retreated to the wall beside the wet bar and lowered myself to the floor. The rug was almost as thick as a cushion, but comfort wasn't exactly uppermost in my mind. Fighting the confusion of fever and the slow erosion of the artificial energy Sam had given me, I tried to make my brain work.

I needed to figure out what was wrong with that hole in the wall. It meant something – something I hadn't seen yet. Unfortunately reason and deduction weren't my best skills. As a rule, I lived on intuition. And at the moment I felt so hampered, so incomplete, that I couldn't think about anything except the night I got shot.

That night, when I was supposed to be in my hospital bed, I went hunting for a killer, armed only with my instincts and the .45. I found him. Naturally he insisted that he was innocent. But he'd left a window open because he couldn't afford the time to close it. That small detail should've given me the hint I needed. It should've told me that I was right, warned me to trust myself. Too bad I didn't pay attention. Instead I let him give me a glass of vodka, thinking it was water.

That mistake had nearly killed me and Ginny both.

Simon's open window was another hint. And Queenie had given me a glass of water that wasn't vodka. That felt like a hint as well, a trigger for intuition.

But why? What did either of those details have to do with the hole in the wine cellar wall?

Ginny was saying, 'Brew must've told you what I was doing.' She spoke coldly, without emotion – thinking hard, sifting information, organizing facts. 'After he warned me about Smithsonian, we discovered Simon was gone. I went after him.

'I started out assuming he was a hired gun who worked for el Señor, here to kill Brew. But once I had time to think, I realized there were other possibilities. He might be innocent. The real killer might've broken him out to get at the rat poison. In that case, he was probably dead. The killer couldn't afford to leave him alive. So I had two reasons to catch up with him. To stop him, if he was the killer. Or to save him, if he was still alive.

'I didn't see anybody.' In this kind of mood, she wasted no time on bitterness or frustration. 'I still don't know who I was after. He hit me as soon as I reached the trees. Must've been less than half an hour after I left Brew, probably no more than twenty minutes.'

She wasn't digressing, just making connections. 'He had plenty of time to come back here while you were having lunch. 'He nearly finished me. I went down, and for a minute or two I hurt so bad I thought the slug was somewhere in my head. But I don't think I passed out. Instead I waited for him to check on me, see if I was still alive. The snow covered me pretty well, and I was sure I'd hear him coming.'

Ordinarily this sort of thing made me want to yell at her. Damn woman, who did she think she was, lying there in the snow with a head wound trying to spring an ambush back on the goon who shot her?

But now I couldn't muster my usual indignation. My mind kept sliding away.

El Señor's hit man could have entered the lodge through my window. He could be here right now.

In which case, why wasn't I dead?

The back of my brain wanted to tell my something about glasses of water – or glasses of vodka – but I couldn't hear it.

'I waited a long time,' Ginny went on. 'He didn't come. When I stopped feeling cold and got sleepy, I knew I had to take a chance on standing up and coming back here.'

Sam muttered some sort of medical curse that had to do with drunks and idiots, but she didn't stop.

'It was harder than I thought it would be. I couldn't tell if I'd lost blood or was just frozen, but I kept falling down. That's how I know he wasn't watching the lodge from my side. Otherwise he would've seen me and tried again. Which was a comfort.' For a moment she let a little of her anger out. 'It helped me concentrate on getting up and going on.'

But she didn't dwell on that. 'Eventually,' she concluded, 'I got here. Now you know as much as I do. It's your turn.'

Sam scanned the group, apparently looking for volunteers. I guess he didn't feel up to providing a summary of recent events. But no one else seemed to want the job either. Lara sat in one of the armchairs, chewing on her lips so hard that I thought she might draw blood. Her husband frowned studiously to himself like an entrepreneur deciding how to take advantage of a competitor's mistakes. Beside Connie on the loveseat, Maryanne looked too frightened to explain anything to anyone. To my surprise, Rock and Buffy stood together with their arms actually around each other, as grey as two halves of one lost soul. Mile's eyes flicked piggy malice all around the parlour, but he didn't speak.

'Somebody?' Ginny asked acerbically. 'Anybody?'

I didn't offer. In my struggle for insight, I was trying to be logical, even methodical. Which doesn't usually work with intuition – but what the hell, I had to try something.

Abruptly Connie said, 'I'll do it.'

Scrutinizing the stained rug as if she needed to understand its pattern, Mac's collaborator gave a clear, accurate, and concise account of events since Ginny had gone after Simon.

I suppose I should've been impressed, considering the fact that

Connie herself was one of the chief suspects, but most of the time I couldn't make myself listen.

Ginny absorbed the information intently. When she asked a question, it amplified Connie's explanation without distracting her. Then she thought for a while, scowling into the air.

Everyone waited for her. The atmosphere in the parlour was tense with expectation or dread, but no one wanted to interrupt the professional investigator at work.

'So,' she said finally, 'we need to reconcile two apparently irreconcilable crimes. We have somebody with a gun outside, and somebody with strong fingers inside, and we don't know how they fit together.' She emptied her cup and handed it to Queenie. 'First we need to consider timing and access.'

Rock and the Hardhouses nodded sharply. Even Connie nodded. To himself, Mile growled something I couldn't make out.

Queenie moved across the room to get more coffee. I followed her with my eyes simply because she was moving. When she picked up the coffee pot, I saw the decanter of port on the wet bar.

A shiver ran through my head. Queenie had given me a glass of water. Which had reminded me of drinking vodka. Which now felt like a hint.

A hint of what?

What else, I thought because I'd just noticed it on the wet bar, what else besides Cat's port?

'Timing.' Ginny clicked her claw experimentally. 'As far as I can tell, Mac could've been killed as much as half an hour after lunch. And you didn't go to lunch right after I left. You talked in the den for a while. Whoever shot me obviously had time to come back here and kill Mac.

'Another point. If we start from the assumption that one of you killed Mac, we'll have a terrible time figuring out who was able to get away long enough to put rat poison in the fire, break Simon out of the wine cellar, leave that trail up into the hills, dispose of the body, shoot me, and come back without being missed. That doesn't sound possible. If we assume the killer is an outsider, we're at least dealing with things that are possible.'

This made a certain mount of sense. Rock regained a bit of colour, and Maryanne's eyes brightened. With an air of concentration, Queenie took a fresh cup of coffee to Ginny, then stepped out of the way. Sam's frown relaxed slightly. The idea of an unknown killer was bad enough, but it was better than the possibility that one of us, *someone in this room*, did it.

For the time being, however, I left that stuff to Ginny. A completely different question troubled me. On what conceivable basis did a decanter of port accidentally left on a wet bar constitute a hint?

Because Catherine Reverie, rest her poor lonely soul, had made such a point out of it. She was an actress, and she'd been downright ostentatious about her taste for port.

Why would she do such a thing? What did it imply?

'But,' Hardhouse said to Ginny, 'that brings us back to the question of access. Your hypothetical outsider had to get into the lodge somehow. He had to have a key. Or help.'

For a moment Ginny seemed to accept this assertion. Once again, heads turned towards Truchi. But then she said, 'Wait a minute. Did anybody relock the wine cellar after I left?'

Considering his air of vagueness, Truchi's prompt reply came as a surprise. 'Me,' he said distantly. 'The key was in the lock.' He rummaged in his pocket and produced a key. 'The kitchen was cold, and we were told to lock all the doors.'

'Shee-it,' Mile pronounced profoundly.

So what, I asked myself, did Cat's display of fondness for port suggest? For one thing, anyone who wanted her dead didn't need to shoot her. All he had to do was spike her port. No one else drank the stuff.

'Anything else?' Ginny asked the group. 'Can you think of any way somebody could get in here without a key?'

Abruptly Queenie gave a low gasp. 'Brew's window.'

I should've expected this. Failing that, I should've reacted to it. But I was obsessed by nameless possibilities, and I wanted to talk to Rock. Or Buffy.

I wanted to ask them how Simon was supposed to kill Cat.

Heads swivelled from Truchi to Queenie. In a startled voice, Sam said, 'That's right.'

Everyone waited for Queenie to explain.

'It wasn't latched,' she said awkwardly. She looked at me with misery in her eyes. She may've been asking me to forgive her. 'I guess he forgot. I latched it for him.'

'When was this?' Ginny demanded.

'Right before lunch. Brew talked to us in the den. He asked Faith and Ama to get lunch ready. Then he and Sam and Rock went to look at the wine cellar from the outside. When they came back in, we went to his room. That's when I noticed the window.'

Ginny made a musing noise. 'That complicates things. If the man who shot me got in through Brew's window, he had to do it well before lunch. Was there enough time? Did any of you happen to see the time? How long did Brew talk?'

Unfortunately that distracted me. It was too implausible. I simply couldn't imagine a killer, presumably a professional, shooting Ginny and then running back along his trail to the lodge in plain daylight, risking being seen, encountering someone, all for the unlikely chance that he'd find a door or window unlocked.

I shouldn't have let my attention shift. I should've finished thinking about port.

No one answered Ginny's question. No one said anything. Except Queenie. In a worried tone she murmured, 'I need a drink.'

For the second time she crossed the parlour to the wet bar.

I'd left a glass of vodka handy, but she ignored it. Instead she picked up the decanter and poured herself a hefty slug of port. Holding the decanter in one hand and her glass in the other, she turned back to the group.

'Anyone else want anything?'

Too late, I caught up with myself. I didn't believe that Truchi had killed anyone. And I didn't believe that he'd given his keys to a killer. Therefore –

If the outsider theory were true, the killer must've entered the lodge through my window. And I sure as hell didn't believe *that*. No one who knew what he was doing would take that risk.

Therefore the killer was one of us. Someone who wanted a random assortment of us dead. Cat, me, Simon, Mac – and who else? Surely he wouldn't stop there?

'No,' I choked out, 'don't.' But Queenie didn't hear me. Or she didn't know I meant her. Before I could stop her, she lifted her glass and took a deep swig.

I'd nearly reached my feet when she started gagging.

The sound she made was horrible to hear. Her own muscles strangled her. As she went into convulsions, she dropped her glass and the decanter. Sweet purple splashed the rug like blood. I tried to catch her, but she was too far away, I had too much of my weight braced on the wall. Flailing wildly, she went down in a pile of limbs and spasms.

'*Queenie!*' Sam cried, a hoarse wail from the depths of his heart. Then he vaulted past Ginny's chair and dived at his wife.

For some reason, I noticed that a blue marble rolled out of the decanter into the middle of the puddle on the rug.

Chapter Twenty

The puddle soaked in slowly, staining the rug a nauseous colour, blurring the ambiguous design, while Sam fought to save Queenie's life.

Ginny took his bag to him before he called for it – before he finished his first quick check of Queenie's vital signs. Then she knelt to help hold Queenie still while he worked.

The way Ginny moved made her look like she'd never needed help in her life.

Strain mottled Queenie's face. The seizure closed her throat, sealed her chest, she wasn't breathing. Spasms exploded fired in her muscles. She thrashed like a madwoman. Ginny couldn't control her. Sam needed someone to clamp down Queenie's legs.

It should've been me, but Joseph Hardhouse and Amalia Carbone got there ahead of me. They reached Queenie at the same moment and put their weight on her legs.

Instead of pushing either of them aside, I lowered myself back down the wall and crawled on my hands and knees after the marble.

Sam tore open a disposable needle, fixed it to a syringe. He snapped the top off an ampoule and filled the syringe. Every line of his face and arms clenched around the necessity of keeping his hands steady.

As soon as he had the injection ready, he snapped, 'I need a vein!'

Ginny didn't seem to understand.

No, that wasn't it. She simply couldn't pull either of Queenie's arms away from her chest.

She released Queenie's shoulders to work on one arm. But when she did that, the convulsive wrenching of Queenie's body went wild.

I picked up the marble, closed it in my fist. My hands were sticky

633

with port from the damp rug. At this rate, I'd smell like port for the rest of my days.

In tandem Hardhouse and Ama moved. He shifted himself on to Queenie's legs while she leaned against Queenie's shoulders. That enabled Ginny to concentrate on freeing one arm so that Sam could reach a vein.

Ginny still wasn't strong enough. She had only one useful hand. And the seizure gripped Queenie like iron, inhuman and unbreakable.

But she wasn't breathing, she couldn't breathe, and oxygen starvation eroded her strength. As she lost consciousness, her muscles weakened.

Sam helped as much as he could with his free hand. An inch at a time, Ginny broke the clench of Queenie's arm.

'Brew!' she panted. 'Get them out of here. Give us room.'

I knew that tone. It compelled me, in spite of all my mistakes and obsessions. The blue marble I followed in my mind would have to wait. With a heave, I got my legs under me and pitched upright. 'Come on!' I barked at the group. 'Everyone out! Back to the den!'

I didn't have Ginny's talent for command. No one reacted. Matched like twins, Rock and Buffy looked like they might faint. Connie had her hands up over her mouth, uncharacteristically aghast. Maryanne's whole face stretched for a scream that refused to come out, paralysed by terror. Mile muttered to himself, words I couldn't hear and didn't want to. Only Lara glanced at me. The light in her gaze had the shining intensity of an orgasm.

Without hesitation I pulled the .45 out of my pocket, worked the slide, and fired at the ceiling.

That got everyone's attention, no question about it. Even Ginny gaped for a second as if she thought I'd lost my mind. But she didn't loosen her grip. Sam concentrated on his syringe as if the .45 and I didn't exist.

'I'm only going to say this one more time,' I remarked. 'Everyone out. Back to the den.'

This time people moved. Taking Maryanne by the hand like a frightened schoolgirl, Connie stood up and started for the door. For reasons of his own, Truchi put a hand on Mile's arm and tugged him in the same direction.

Then everyone else complied – the Altars, Lara, Faith Jerrick. To Ama, Ginny panted, 'Joseph can do it.' Ama seemed to know that tone as well as I did. Without hesitation she joined her husband. At once Hardhouse stretched out across most of Queenie's torso.

Still clinging to the .45, I herded the depleted group back to the den.

Queenie's plight seemed to claw at my back as I left. I still hadn't heard her breathe. How long could she go without air? How long before she suffered brain damage? Or died?

It would be my fault. Another failure, like my failure with Simon. I couldn't have known the port was poisoned, of course. But once again I'd recognized the potential danger too late. If I'd been faster, I could've saved her.

To make matters worse, Mile was waiting for me in the den.

Buffy and Rock had collapsed on one of the couches, and Connie and Maryanne sat as well, holding on to each other as if one of them, anyway, couldn't go on without the other. Too tense for anything as helpless as sitting, Lara had begun to pace around the tree, repeating the circle to calm herself. Truchi had moved to the nearest hearth to build up the fire. His wife and Faith stood together, their arms folded across their bellies at exactly the same angle, but with very different effects. Ama looked like she was restraining a visceral outrage. Faith seemed to cradle her trust in salvation, using it to warm her heart.

In contrast, Houston Mile confronted me with his fists braced on his hips and a flush of fat anger on his face.

'This is your doin', Axbrewder,' he rasped. 'You know that? She's goin' to die. You know why? You didn't listen to me. Ah tried to tell you, and you wouldn't listen. You wouldn't even *listen*, never mind give me a gun and let me try to save us. How many more of us got to become corpses before you *wake up*?'

I glared at him and didn't say anything.

'Sam is a doctor,' Connie put in as if she'd taken on the job of reassuring everyone. 'I expect he's a good doctor. He may be able to treat her. Especially if he can guess what kind of poison it is.'

'No,' Mile snarled. 'You left the wrong people with him. They'll make damn sure she dies.'

There it was in a nutshell – Mile's solution to the mystery. After all, he had his reputation to maintain – the one who always solved the crime, the best player at Murder On Cue's camps. Now he intended to explain it to us. Judging by appearances, he didn't plan on letting anybody stop him.

I didn't give a shit. In my own way, I was as lost as Queenie, as far gone. If I didn't do something to treat myself soon, I'd never recover.

I followed the blue marble.

Ignoring Mile, I moved to the couch and stopped in front of Rock and Buffy. They didn't notice me at first, but I stood there until they both raised their heads and looked at me.

'Tell me something,' I said. I wanted to sound casual, detached, I wanted to sound like I had everything under control, but my voice twitched. 'How was Simon supposed to kill Cat?'

In unison Buffy and Rock blinked at me. Their mouths hung open.

'You're stallin', boy,' Mile put in. 'This ain't no mystery camp now. We ain't in no mood to waste our time figurin' out a pretend crime that never had no chance to happen anyway.'

I still ignored him. I ignored Connie and Maryanne and the Carbones and Faith and Lara. And I ignored common sense, too. Common sense suggested that I wasn't in a particularly good position to make promises or bank on my credibility.

I did it anyway.

'Trust me,' I told the Altars. 'This isn't irrelevant.'

Rock closed his mouth and cleared his throat. Buffy answered me. 'We aren't sure.'

That wasn't what I wanted to hear. 'What do you mean, you aren't sure? This is your camp. You hired Simon and Cat. You designed this whole experience. How could you not know what they had planned?'

Buffy nodded. 'We designed it, yes. But only in a general way. We couldn't know what the rest of you would do, so we couldn't be too rigid. Otherwise the actors couldn't adjust it to fit the circumstances. It might go wrong. You might say we' – she glanced at her husband – 'I designed the theory, but Simon and Cat were responsible for the application.'

'Tell him the truth,' Rock murmured heavily. 'You're just confusing him.'

Buffy ducked her head. As if she were ashamed of something, she admitted, 'I used to plan out the whole thing. I liked doing that. It was like writing a mystery novel myself, except better. I had live characters to work with.

'But then' – her voice was so grey and small that I could hardly hear her – 'Rock started tampering with the clues. After that, the camps didn't go the way I planned. So I stopped planning them. All the details, I mean. I wanted to make it harder for him to interfere.'

Now she looked up at me, almost gallantly daring me to doubt her. 'And when I didn't plan everything, I could be surprised myself. That made our camps fun in a different way. Instead of being like a writer, I was more of a participant. And Rock had to work harder, if he wanted to tamper. He had to pay more attention. I liked that, too.'

For some reason she needed to make me understand that she didn't resent her husband.

But that wasn't the point. Clinging to my reasons for asking the question, I pursued, 'So you had no idea what Simon and Cat cooked up between them? Her taste for port wasn't your idea?'

Again Rock cleared his throat. 'Actually, it was my idea.'

Huh?

'Part of the planning,' he explained, 'involved creating opportunities for a murder. We didn't tell Simon what to do, but we did help invent circumstances he could use. And I still wanted to interfere. I thought if I planted a suggestion, and Simon used it, I'd have the upper hand. So I suggested the port. And I told Cat it would be clever to get herself poisoned at a time when it would be hard to connect the port and Simon.' For instance, while Cat and I were alone – and Simon had gone out for a walk. 'I meant to smuggle the marble out of the port after she collapsed. Then no one would know how she was killed.' He shrugged limply. 'But when she was shot I forgot all about it.'

'You done yet, Axbrewder?' Mile demanded. 'You ready to start facin' some facts for a change?'

With an effort, I pulled myself away from the Altars. In an odd way, I was ready for Mile now. What Buffy and Rock said changed nothing, at least as far as Cat's murder, and Simon's, and Mac's were concerned. But it affected the tissue of hints inside my head. Hints don't kill anybody. They don't prove anything. But they help make intuitive connections. And on that level Cat's port told me as much as any fact.

'Oh, sure,' I said across the den at Mile. 'If you have some facts that need facing, you might as well mention them now.'

'Fine,' he growled, 'fine,' trying for assurance. If nothing else, my attention to the marble question unsettled him. He didn't know what I had in mind.

'Take your time,' I retorted harshly. 'We've got all day.'

Lara had stopped pacing. She stood opposite Mile, facing me. Her burning eyes gave the impression that she'd remembered why she wanted to go to bed with me.

Truchi finished with the fires and moved to stand beside his wife. Both of them watched me, too. But Connie and Maryanne had turned in their seats to look at Mile. Maryanne concentrated on him as if he hypnotized her the way a snake does a bird.

'What you all ain't thinkin' about,' he began, 'what you been refusin' to listen to, Axbrewder, is that we ain't got one killer here. We got two.'

I nodded, trying to project a confidence I didn't feel.

'You been workin' too hard to figure out how one man shoots Cat and plants that gun on Abel and gets him out of the wine cellar and breaks Westward's neck and still has an alibi. It don't wash. There ain't enough leeway. There ain't no way one of us could do all that.

'But if you're goin' to claim we got us an outside killer, you got the same problem. There ain't no way the man who shot Fistoulari is goin' to come back here to snuff Westward 'less he knows he's got a way in he can count on. He ain't goin' to sneak around here in broad daylight just *hopin'* there's a window open. He's got to have him an accomplice. Just like any one of us got to have an alibi.

'That means there's two of 'em.

'But if there's two of 'em, we don't need to take no notice of this outside killer idea. Ain't none of us here got that kind of enemies 'cept you, Axbrewder – and you ain't dead. All we got to do is look for two of us who've always got the same alibi. They're the ones lyin'. That don't include none of us.'

He waved a fat hand around the room. 'Sometimes we got alibis, sometimes we don't.' He indicated Connie pointedly. 'When we got more than one, they ain't the same.' This may've been a reference to Lara Hardhouse, or to me – or to himself. 'But you can't say that about good ol' Dr Sam Drayton, or his floozy wife neither.'

'On the other hand,' Connie put in with the kind of sarcasm that wilts house plants, 'Queenie Drayton is the one dying right now.'

'So that lets 'em out,' Mile went on fiercely. 'But it don't let out Joseph Hardhouse' – he faced me with his teeth bared – 'and that bitch you call your partner.'

Before I could protest, he snapped, 'They say they was together when Cat got shot. We know they was together when that rat poison went down the chimney. He got no alibi for killing Westward, he admitted that. She don't either. And for all we know she went after Abel so she could kill him. Maybe she and Hardhouse didn't have time when they broke him out. Then she clubbed herself over the head – or she got Abel to do it for her before she killed him – so she could look innocent.

'Queenie Drayton is goin' to end up dead' – his teeth resembled the fangs on a dog with distemper – 'because you let two killers help her husband save her.'

Lara wanted to say something. Once again, however, Connie was the first to speak.

'Houston Mile,' she pronounced firmly, 'you are out of your mind.'

'Why would they do that?' Maryanne's question came out like a little wail. 'People don't just kill for no reason. Joseph and Ginny didn't even know each other before we came here. Why do they want Cat and Mac dead? Why did they try to kill Brew? They must have had a *reason*.'

'How the hell should Ah know?' Mile shouted back at her. 'Ah ain't God! Ah don't see inside their heads. There just ain't nobody else got the means and the opportunity to kill us like this!'

Out of the empty air, Rock mumbled, 'It's possible, I suppose.'

In an incredulous tone, I demanded, 'Say what?'

'Well,' he replied without focusing on any of us, 'suppose there's an investor who wants to buy Deerskin Lodge, but the owners don't want to sell. One way to get a property under those conditions is to devalue it in some way. Perhaps by making it the site of multiple murders. So the investor hires Ms Fistoulari. But she can't rely on her partner due to his injuries, so she turns to Joseph for help. Perhaps they were already lovers. Or perhaps he's the investor. Together they come here and begin killing the rest of us.

'Of course, this won't work unless they appear innocent at the end. Otherwise they wouldn't escape arrest. That may be your role, Mr Axbrewder. You'll vouch for Ms Fistoulari. You'll explain about el Señor. But it's possible.' He glanced, not at me, but at Buffy. 'Isn't it?'

His theory must've sounded plausible to Connie. Turning to Lara, she asked, 'Is your husband capable of such a thing, Mrs Hardhouse?'

Whatever Lara thought about the situation, she thought it intensely. She kept it to herself, however. Instead she flared, 'Anything is possible. Joseph is capable of anything. But he isn't the only possibility here.' Facing Rock and Buffy, she demanded, 'You're an investor yourself, aren't you, Mr Altar? Who would be better placed than you are to set up such a scheme?'

Rock didn't react, but Buffy seemed to gag on something horrible. When she could get words out, she admitted thinly, 'That's one of the scenarios we considered. A series of murders to lower the value of the Lodge. I rejected it because it was too – too abstract. The murderer would be too difficult to catch because the motive was so impersonal.' In a sickened tone, she added, 'It was Rock's idea.'

Rock nodded dully.

'You *see*?' Lara insisted, facing Mile now. 'You can't pin this on Joseph. There are other possibilities.'

'No.' Mile didn't waver. '*You* care about *reasons*. *Ah* don't. All Ah want is to stay alive. All this couldn't happen 'less two people did it.

And the only two people could've done it are your husband and Fistoulari. You want a reason, try holdin' a gun to one of 'em's *head*. Maybe that'll make 'em talk.'

'No,' I said myself. This had gone on long enough. 'You weren't listening, Mile. You missed the point.'

'The point?' he rasped. 'What point?'

'Catherine Reverie was the only one who drank port. We all knew that. She made an issue out of it, she made sure we all knew. And Ginny *is* my partner. She doesn't want me dead. If she did, she could've left me in the hospital, come on this case alone. I would've been too vulnerable to defend myself. Her only reason to bring me along was to keep me alive.

'But if you're right, her reason was to make the idea of an outside killer believable. Because el Señor really does want me dead. So she still can't afford to kill me. If someone else gets killed after I'm dead, the whole plan goes out the window. Therefore whoever shot Cat was *not* aiming at me. She was the intended victim all along. That pretty well destroys your accomplice theory, doesn't it.'

I was too far ahead of him. His lips flapped on his teeth before he managed to ask, 'How?'

'Because' – I wanted to shout at him, but my stomach hurt too much – 'Cat didn't need to be shot.' I was *goddamned* if I'd let anyone else die because I didn't think fast enough. 'The port was already poisoned. Why would Ginny and Hardhouse – or anyone with an accomplice – bother shooting a woman who was already as good as dead?'

That did it. I'd finally said something effective against Houston Mile. In fact, I'd scared him down to his socks. His attack on Ginny was his way of fighting off his fear. Without it, he looked suddenly defenceless – as frightened as Maryanne.

'Axbrewder,' he murmured thickly, 'give me a gun. Ah got to have me a gun.'

Everyone ignored him. He might as well have made himself irrelevant. Even Maryanne turned away.

'So what you're saying,' Lara proposed in a thoughtful tone, 'is that none of our theories is any good. These crimes must have been committed by someone working alone – but they couldn't have been committed by anyone working alone. Nothing makes any sense.'

'Not quite. All I'm really saying is that Cat must've been killed by accident. That shot was aimed at me. Which lets Ginny out.' And Hardhouse as well, since he'd been with her when Cat died. 'Everything else is still open to question.'

'Axbrewder,' Mile begged, nearly blubbering. 'Ah *got* to have a gun.'

'Perhaps we're going about this in the wrong way,' Connie offered. 'We're attempting to reason from opportunity or motive to guilt. That's the method of most novels. It's easier. But perhaps we should try to reason from *capacity* to guilt. Certainly those of us who are *incapable* of committing any of these crimes can be dismissed from consideration.' She made this sound like a reference to Maryanne. 'We may be able to go further, however. We're intelligent people, and we've spent some rather concentrated time together. We may be able to evaluate who among us is sufficiently determined, desperate, or unscrupulous to have done these things.'

'But how can we do that?' Buffy protested plaintively. 'You want us to figure out who *isn't* capable of murder. Until now, I would have said I've never met anyone who *is*.'

'*Axbrewder!*' Mile came at me before I noticed the white craziness in his eyes, the frenzy in his movements. '*Ah got to have a GUN.*'

He was fast when he thought his life depended on it. And my own special brand of desperation clogged my reflexes. He came past the couches at a run and threw himself at me before I could do anything more than gape at him.

I went down hard.

Which was just what I needed, a fall like that, with him on top. I didn't even know whether he knocked the air out of me. Too many other kinds of pain happened at once. The impact and his weight lit napalm in my guts, sudden flame splashed along my nerves, I blazed from head to foot. The way he scrabbled at the .45 in my pocket felt like he'd cut into me with a welding torch. The walls and the tree crackled like the hearth, and the ceiling blurred.

Somehow I remained conscious. Distinctly I heard Ginny yell, '*Stop it or I'll blow your fucking head off!*'

Now I could see her. She crouched over me with her .357 jammed into Mile's ear. Sam hadn't bandaged her forehead yet. Blood oozed from her wound, staining her pale skin. But the wound itself didn't look especially deep or dangerous.

Hardhouse must've come in with her. When Mile froze, Hardhouse heaved him off me.

I still had the gun.

Mile sounded like he was whimpering for his life, but it didn't come out in sentences.

As soon as his weight left, I began to take fractured little gasps, trying to sneak pieces of air past the voiceless howl of the fire.

'Brew.' Ginny knelt beside me. 'Are you all right? Can you stand?'

I croaked, 'Sam.'

What I meant was, I need Sam. But that wasn't what she heard, so she said, 'He's taken Queenie to their room. He doesn't know yet whether she'll make it. He finally got enough IV valium into her to ease the seizure. But by then she'd been unconscious for a while. She may be in a coma. And she could have another attack any time. Her heart could stop. He's doing what he can to stabilize her. But he can't tell how much poison she swallowed, or how powerful it is, or whether she'll ever wake up. Can you stand?'

Fire filled my chest. I had too many things to say, but the words had been burned away.

'Help me,' I croaked.

'Sure.' She braced her arm under my shoulders.

Hardhouse didn't help her. Maybe he was still busy with Mile. But Rock seemed to appear out of the air at Ginny's side. The two of them got me on to my feet.

The difference between up and down confused me. And I couldn't hear anyone except Ginny. Only her voice penetrated my distress.

'I'll get you to Sam's room,' she told me. 'He can take care of you there. Maybe the distraction will do him good. Then I'll organize a search. If we have a killer hiding here, we'd better find him. Anybody who doesn't want to help I'll send to you.'

Did that make sense? I had no way of knowing. As far as I could tell, I was being taken in the direction of Sam's room. At the moment nothing else felt important.

One step at a time. Across the den to the hallway. The people behind me seemed to do too much moving around. General panic? Struggling to control Mile? Whatever it was, I couldn't do anything about it.

Ginny knocked on Sam's door before we went in. A wasted precaution. He sat on the bed beside his wife without turning his head to see who we were. Instead he gripped both her hands as if he wanted to anchor her somehow. The strain left his knuckles white. From time to time a tremor ran down his shoulders. If he kept holding her like that, he might crush her fingers.

Her pallor made her look like she'd already lost too much blood, and her limbs sprawled, limp as a corpse's. Her eyes were closed. Her breathing seemed too shallow to sustain her life.

Ginny steered me to a chair and propped me there. She didn't try to talk to Sam. Instead she asked Rock if he wanted to stay with me.

He took a deep breath. Without looking at her, he said, 'This is your job. You're being paid for it. But you're here because of me. I'm responsible for this whole camp. Buffy and I. And I'm the one who didn't mention Lawrence Smithsonian. I won't let you risk searching the lodge without help.'

She didn't comment on his unexpected determination. She just accepted it with a nod and turned to me.

I managed a nod of my own.

A moment later she and Rock left me alone with the Draytons.

Sam still didn't glance in my direction. After a minute or two, I realized that I'd better attract his attention somehow, so I wheezed his name.

That made him turn his head. He couldn't refuse the sound of need. Slowly he focused on me. 'Brew,' he said dully, almost like he'd become stupid. 'What happened to you?'

This didn't seem like a good time to go into detail. 'Mile jumped me,' I answered weakly.

To my surprise, he released Queenie's hands and got to his feet. At once he came over to me, began checking my pulse and respiration. If I'd only watched the way he moved and hadn't looked at the darkness on his face or the hollow helplessness in his eyes, I would've thought that he knew what he was doing. But as he went through the motions of examining me – a thermometer in my mouth, a blood-pressure cuff on my arm, a flashlight at my pupils – he asked me nothing about my condition.

'Do you know how long we've been married?' He sounded like he'd worn out his voice shouting for help in a wasteland. 'A year.' He checked the gauge on the blood-pressure cuff as if he had no idea what it indicated. 'That's all. A year.'

Next the thermometer. Maybe he never actually saw it.

'You may not realize it, but doctors have a hard time meeting eligible women. Oh, we meet lots of nurses. But they're deadly to marry. They can't forget we're doctors, and then the marriage doesn't work. Or they forget too easily, and then the profession doesn't work. And who else is there? Secretaries? Most of them work in billing. They can't afford to remember that the patients who have no money are still people. Or in personnel. If you work in personnel, you aren't allowed to use your brain. Or in publicity. If you work in publicity, you don't have a brain.

'I have no *time* for singles bars.'

Out of habit he put the thermometer and blood-pressure cuff and flashlight away in his bag.

'But the one thing a doctor should absolutely never do is marry a patient. It's better if we don't even know their names. That sounds callous, but it isn't. It avoids confusing the illness and the person. When you know your patient is a scuzball, you have a hard time treating him. It's hard to make painful decisions about an illness when the woman who has it is someone you love.

'And patients make lousy wives. They think you're magic. They think you can save them from their problems for the rest of their lives. They confuse the treatment and the person.'

Next he filled a syringe. I didn't know what was in it, and maybe he didn't either. But I didn't care. I was listening too hard. His wasted face and worn-out voice made everything he said personal, poignant.

'Queenie was a patient.'

Sudden fury bared his teeth. Nevertheless he slid his needle into me as gently as a caress. Almost at once, a soothing sensation eased along my veins.

'She should've died. Pure neglect. She's as bad as a drunk when it comes to her own health. She didn't think those lumps and all that discomfort were worth worrying about. We did a radical mastectomy on both sides and pumped her full of enough chemo to fry her brains, and she still should've died. But she didn't.

'In the middle of all that, during one of her lucid moments, I had to tell her breasts were gone.' Tears streamed down his face. He could only talk by biting down on the words and snarling. Yet his movements were pure calm as he put down the first syringe and filled another one. 'When she understood what I'd said, she gave me such a smile – I wanted to die for that smile. And she said–'

For a moment his throat and chest locked. He couldn't breathe or talk. But he kept on filling the syringe. Then he held it up to the light and cleared out the air. Like a farewell kiss, he planted the needle's little pain in my arm.

'She said, "Thanks, Sam. That helps."

'I think she was trying to do me a favour when she let me talk her into plastic surgery – implants and so on to give her a normal figure. She wasn't confused about me. She wasn't in love with my power or wisdom. She just wanted to let me help her again if I felt like it. If helping her felt good to me. She didn't need it. She didn't need breasts. She didn't even need me to save her. She loved being alive too much to need that. But she had room in her heart for everything I wanted to give.'

Then he was done. Without another glance at me, he repacked his bag and closed it. Returned to the bed. Sat down again. Took hold of Queenie's hands.

At the same time I felt an artificial strength returning. Any minute now I'd be able to stand up and go do something about my rage and grief and guilt.

'Why was she poisoned, Brew?' he asked as if he'd given me all the strength he had – as if that worn-out whisper was the only cry for help he could manage. 'Who wants her dead?'

'No one.' If he'd been more alert, he could've heard black murder in my voice. 'It was an accident. That stuff was aimed at Cat. It was put in the port before she was shot. She just never got a chance to drink it.

'That bullet was aimed at me.'

He didn't react. Maybe he didn't hear me. Or maybe he knew there was nothing I could say that would change anything.

'Sam,' I asked unsteadily, 'is she going to make it?'

I barely heard his answer. 'I'm not magic, Brew. I don't know.'

I sat with him for a while longer. But he didn't move or speak again. Every ounce of him concentrated on Queenie. Eventually I knew that I had to go.

Leaving the room quietly, I went back to the den.

Chapter Twenty-one

In the den, the situation hadn't improved any. Only four people remained, Faith Jerrick, Sue-Rose Altar, Maryanne Green – and Houston Mile. None of them noticed my arrival. Buffy sat on one of the couches with her hands over her face and her shoulders shaking noiselessly, gripped by revulsion or grief. Beside her knelt Faith. Art Reeson's girl friend held her crucifix and moved her lips like a woman in prayer, but she didn't make a sound. I couldn't tell whether she prayed for herself or for Buffy.

In fact, Maryanne was the only one talking.

She'd pulled a chair so close to Mile that their knees touched. Leaning forward with her weight braced on her elbows, she spoke softly, urgently, almost pleading with him.

'You have to understand, Houston, dear.' She seemed to be repeating herself, not for the first time. 'This is for your own good. You've had a breakdown – like a nervous breakdown. You're more sensitive than anyone realizes. All this violence has upset you, and you want to defend yourself. You want to defend me. That's why you attacked Brew. But we can't let you do that. I can't. If Brew is honest, we need him. He's used to violence. He doesn't have your sensitive nature. And if he isn't honest, he might kill you. I couldn't bear that. Dear Houston, it's for your own good.'

For some reason, a moment or two passed before I noticed that Mile had been tied to his chair, trussed like a turkey. He even had a gag between his teeth. He struggled to spit it out so that he could yell something – hell, he looked like he wanted to froth at the mouth – but whenever he worked the wad of cloth loose, Maryanne pushed it back into place. Behind her gentle, pleading tone, I heard an edge that sounded, not like hysteria or fear, but like retribution. No matter what else happened, she meant to keep him tied and gagged just as long as she could.

I approved.

I didn't want to listen to it, however. I needed something more direct and bloody, more like a bullet in the head than poison masked by sweet port. Roughly I demanded, 'Where's everyone else? What happened here?'

Buffy and Faith ignored me. Maryanne glanced up, a bit startled, but she didn't answer right away. Instead she whispered to her prisoner, 'It's Brew, Houston, dear. He's right behind you. He has his gun. Please sit still. Don't provoke him. I'll try to protect you.'

When she stood up, I saw triumph in her eyes, plain as a placard.

She drew me a few steps away. 'We couldn't get him to stop,' she told me softly. 'Ginny sent Truchi for some rope. She wanted us to join you with Sam, so you could guard us. But Houston wouldn't stop, and Joseph said it wasn't a good idea to put him in with Queenie. So Ginny told us to stay here. Stay together. The others are searching the lodge.

'Buffy didn't want Rock to go, but he insisted.' Maryanne grimaced sympathetically. 'She got a little frantic, so Faith offered to stay with her. And I wouldn't be any good at searching. I'm too timid.' She did her best to look timid, but at the moment she was enjoying herself too much. 'Ginny said I could keep an eye on Houston.'

That made sense. Unfortunately it didn't shed any light on what I should do next. I had to ask, 'Did anyone tell her what he said about her?'

Maryanne looked blank for a second, then shook her head. 'I don't think anybody believed it.'

So Ginny still believed that we had an outsider on our hands. Someone hidden in the building. She'd gone looking for him with the remaining survivors – the Hardhouses and the Carbones, Connie and Rock. She hadn't heard Mile's reasons for thinking that no one killer could've done all this alone.

I liked the outsider theory myself. It explained Smithsonian's phone calls. But it had problems. For one thing, Mile was right. The murders would be easier to explain if the killer had an accomplice. For another, I simply couldn't imagine why the same killer would want me and Cat and Mac and Simon all dead. Which in turn suggested that the murders had nothing to do with any one of us personally – which made nonsense out of those calls from Smithsonian.

And for another – for another – there was definitely another problem, but at the moment I couldn't put my finger on it.

But the insider theory was just as bad. According to Mile, it required two insiders. And I had only ten candidates, leaving out the Draytons. Seven, if I ignored the Carbones and Faith Jerrick. Five if I crossed Mile and Maryanne off the list. Four discounting Buffy.

That left the Hardhouses, Rock, and Connie.

The same people helping Ginny with her search.

When I made that connection, apprehension tingled down my back, and the skin of my scrotum tightened. Now I knew what I should be doing.

Ginny needed backup, in case she opened a closet or turned a corner and found herself facing the missing guns.

'Which way did she go?' I asked Maryanne.

Apparently she hadn't expected that question. 'What do you mean?'

I made an effort to control my sudden impatience. 'How did Ginny organize the search? Where was she going?'

'Oh.' Now Maryanne understood. 'She paired the Hardhouses together. Lara didn't kill Mac, and Joseph didn't kill Cat, so she said they were safe. She told them to search Rock's and Buffy's room, and Connie's, and Mac's. And she put Connie and Rock together. To keep an eye on each other. They're supposed to search Simon's and Cat's rooms, and yours, and hers. She's going to start with Mile's and my room. Then she's going to do the Hardhouses'. And the Draytons'.

'She sent Truchi and Ama to check the dining room and kitchen, the storerooms. When they're all done, they're supposed to come back here. Then they'll tackle the attic.'

I didn't have time to be impressed by the clarity of Maryanne's grasp on these details. 'Ginny's working alone?'

'Yes.'

Great. Wonderful. Over my shoulder, I said, 'I'll go help her.' I was already on my way.

Faith stopped me. She must've been paying attention after all. As I left Maryanne, she rose from Buffy's side.

'Mr Axbrewder.'

I wanted to brush past her. Alarms of all kinds sounded in my head. Some of them started quietly, but they were turning into klaxons, inarticulate squalls of warning.

Nevertheless Faith's assertiveness held me. She looked pale and determined, as if God had instructed her to prevent me from leaving the den until she'd made one last effort to save my soul.

I didn't understand why she hadn't joined the search. Ginny would've been a hell of a lot safer with a companion, any companion.

'What do you want?' I demanded harshly. 'I'm in a hurry.'

'Murder is offensive to God,' she said with soft intensity. 'It is a crime against the souls of those who die. If they are not among the redeemed, they are deprived of their hope of Heaven. And it is a crime against the souls of those who kill. Life and death and hope belong to the Lord, not to men. A man who kills damns himself by claiming powers which belong to God.'

'When will these crimes stop?'

I heard an implied accusation which may or may not have been intended – and I was in no mood for it. 'If you're so eager to see them stop,' I growled, 'why aren't you helping Ginny?'

No, Faith hadn't intended any accusation. She wasn't thinking about me or my competence – or my culpability. She had a dilemma of her own. Just for a second, her gaze flicked across my face, almost met my eyes. Then she said simply, 'Because I'm afraid. I have a horror of violence, Mr Axbrewder. It is true, certainly, that the Lord does not ask violence of me. But at need He asks all who serve Him to enter the presence of violence, to accept the sight and the risk of bloodshed. We are asked to love others as He loves them – and if we love them we must serve them as well as we can. It may be necessary to serve them by standing between them and murder.

'You have done that, Mr Axbrewder. But I cannot. God's Will is plain, yet I cannot obey it. I can only pray that He will pity me and forgive.'

Without transition, my irritation evaporated. Instead of the contempt she probably expected me to feel, she forced me to respect her. She may've been a religious fanatic, deaf and blind with thoughts of God, but she didn't make excuses. Which made her braver than I was. Like her, I'd been deaf and blind for a good part of my adult life, but I'd never hesitated to use my drinking as an excuse.

'Don't worry about it,' I muttered. 'We're all scared. If God doesn't understand that, He doesn't deserve to be worshipped anyway.'

Driven by klaxons, I headed past Faith towards the bedrooms.

Too late. As usual. Before I reached the nearest doorway, I heard Lara Hardhouse cry out, *'Ginny! Oh my God!'*

I forgot Faith and Buffy, Maryanne and Mile. I forgot pain and fever and weakness. And my gun. Empty-handed, I jumped at the door and hauled it open.

Gloom filled the hall. Bulbs had burned out – or someone had switched them off. For an instant I saw only the dim air, the condensed darkness of wooden doors, the black stretch of the carpet – and a couple of shapes where the gloom solidified.

As I ran towards them, they turned into Lara and Ginny.

Lara stood against the wall with her hands over her mouth, braced to scream again. The dimness hid her features, but her whole body looked like panic.

'*Brew!*' she cried. 'Oh my God! *Come quick.*'

Ginny sprawled almost at Lara's feet. She might've been trying to bury her face in the carpet. I couldn't see her move. The rug under her looked dark as blood, and she lay motionless, as if she'd been nailed there.

Another fraction of a second passed before I made out the shape jutting from her right shoulder.

A knife.

I slammed to my knees beside her. But then I froze. She had a knife in her back – down in her right shoulder at an angle towards her heart. I couldn't decide what to do. Turn her over to see if she was still breathing? Just pull the knife out? How deeply had she been stabbed? The knife didn't look particularly long. A couple of inches of the blade hadn't gone in. How badly would she bleed if I pulled it out?

While I dithered, she lifted the stump of her left arm and thumped her claw sideways against the wall. In a voice muffled by pain and fury, she started cursing.

'Ginny,' I panted, 'Ginny, don't move. You've got a knife in your back.' As if she couldn't tell what had happened to her. 'I don't know how deep it goes.'

'Brew,' she gasped. 'Christ! Get that thing out of me.'

'Wait,' I insisted, 'wait, we need Sam, I don't know how bad it is, when it comes out you're going to lose blood.'

Her claw hit the wall again. Squirming against the pain, she twisted her head up. '*Get that thing out of me.*'

I looked around. No one appeared. Where were they all when I needed them? Surely everyone in the lodge had heard Lara's yell? But Maryanne and Faith and Buffy kept to the illusory safety of the den. The Carbones might not have heard Lara from the distance of the kitchen. Sam probably wouldn't leave Queenie for anything. Connie and Rock and Hardhouse –

When Ginny gave me orders, I was supposed to obey.

'*Damn* it, woman!' I snapped, 'hold still! You need a *doctor*. I don't want to make a mistake about this.'

Then Hardhouse materialized out of the gloom, soundless on the tight floorboards. Practically skidding to his knees opposite me, he barked, 'Have you lost your mind? Pull it out!'

Before I could react, he tugged the blade loose, slapped it into my hands, and immediately jammed the heel of his palm on to the wound to staunch the bleeding.

Over Ginny's cursing, he commanded, 'Get moving, Axbrewder! We need Sam.'

The knife was slick and warm with blood – it felt almost hot on my shocked fingers. No one would've called it long, a five-inch blade at most. And it hadn't gone all the way in. Her attacker hadn't been very strong. Or the blade had struck on her scapula and skidded aside.

I had enough experience with knives and wounds to see that Ginny wasn't about to die.

Dumbly I got to my feet. The warmth of her blood seemed to burn into me like a splash of acid. Every beat of my heart carried concentrated sulphuric. I didn't care whether I was on my knees or standing or stark mad. I had the knife in my right hand, the handle wedged into my palm. With my left, I grabbed at Lara's blouse so hard that her head flopped against the wall.

Aiming the knife at her face, I demanded, *'Who did it?'*

Unmistakable panic glistened in her eyes. As soon as she saw the knife she started to babble.

'Brew, no, don't hurt me, I didn't do it, *I didn't do it*, I swear it, she was like that when I found her, don't hurt me!'

I shifted my left hand from her blouse to her chin. Hunching over her, I forced her head up. Almost softly, as if I weren't too savage to care what I did next, I repeated, *'Who did it?'*

'I didn't see.' Her eyes were about to melt with fear. Nevertheless she stopped babbling. 'Honest to God, Brew, I didn't see. I didn't see it happen. The hall's too dark. She was like that when I found her.

'Joseph and I finished the rooms – the ones she told us to search. We didn't find anything. He sent me to tell her we were done. He went to help Rock and Connie.

'I heard her fall. The way she groaned – God, I thought she was dead! But I didn't see it happen. He was gone when I got here. I didn't see anyone. There isn't enough light.'

That left Connie and Rock.

Constance Bebb, who might not be able to drive a five-inch blade hard enough.

Roderick Altar, who might not know how to drive it at all.

'Whose is it?' Hardhouse put in tightly. 'If we knew that, we might be able to figure out who did it.'

Ginny coughed something that sounded like, 'How?'

The pressure he put on her shoulder showed in his voice. 'Whoever searched the room where that knife was is probably the killer. If we find out whose knife it is, we'll know who searched that room.'

Which made sense, but I didn't care. I had other priorities. Another hint –

Just to be on the safe side, I waggled the knife and asked Lara, 'Is this yours?'

She didn't look at it. 'I've never seen it before. I don't like knives. I don't know whose it is.'

I let her go. 'All right,' I grated. 'Go get Sam. Make him come. Tell him to bring his bag. Hit him if you have to.'

She glanced at her husband for confirmation. When he nodded sharply, she moved away.

Another hint. Not a piece of evidence, just an idea. Imagine someone – Connie, Rock, I didn't know who – searching rooms. Pretending to hunt for a killer, but really on the skulk for some way to attack Ginny without getting caught. Would this someone be willing to wing it – to take a chance on a random knife and unpredictable hallway lighting? Or would he require a more reliable combination of means and opportunity?

Would whoever had shot Ginny come back to the lodge without being sure that he could get in?

One interesting difference between professional and amateur killers is that professionals don't like chance.

I didn't get to pursue the question, however. Before Lara reached the doorway, Sam came into the hall from the den.

He had his bag with him.

Connie held him by one arm as if she were leading him along.

As soon as I saw him, I forgot knives and hints. Suddenly I cared about nothing except what Sam could do for Ginny.

He came forward with the unsteady gait and aimless movements of a man who'd lost his essential balance. In some way, he seemed dependent on Connie's grip. But none of us had to tell him what Ginny needed. As he reached her, he said in a husky voice, 'Get some light.' Then he pushed Hardhouse aside to kneel beside her.

No one else moved, so Hardhouse went looking for a light switch.

To no one in particular, Connie said, 'Mr Altar and I heard Mrs Hardhouse cry out. We didn't know what had happened, of course, but we could guess that Dr Drayton would be required. It was difficult to persuade him to leave his wife. But Mr Altar volunteered to stay with her while I brought Dr Drayton here. He's there now.'

Alibis again. Connie and Rock could vouch for each other. If they weren't both guilty, they were both innocent.

At the end of the hall, Hardhouse found a switch. When he flipped it, the lights came on. The gloom disappeared so fast that the hallway seemed to blaze.

No burned-out bulbs. Someone had deliberately ditched the lights.

Sam inspected Ginny's back. To improve his view, he stuck two fingers through the cut in her shirt and ripped the material away. Because of Hardhouse's pressure – or because the knife hadn't hit anything vital – she'd stopped bleeding, and her shirt had soaked up the blood. I had a good view of the wound. It looked minor and insidious, too small to be dangerous, too ugly to be ignored.

It pulled me down to the floor again, on my knees across from Sam, as if I might see what it meant if I looked at it hard enough.

Whoever had tried to kill her was definitely an amateur.

Tearing open swabs and syringes, Sam asked, 'Is that the knife?'

I still had it in my hand. Instead of answering, I showed it to him.

His eyes were dull, pulled down at the corners by anguish, and his skin had a cheesy colour that didn't suit his handsome features. But he was still a doctor. After a glance at the knife, he muttered, 'Doesn't look like it went in deep enough,' and began to work.

'Don't you want to know what I think?' Ginny rasped. 'I think it went in fucking far enough.'

Sam ignored her. She swore under her breath for a moment. Then he used a syringe to squeeze antiseptic down into the cut, and she flinched involuntarily. But she didn't protest.

'Ginny.' I knew she was in no position to answer questions, but I had to try. 'Did you see anything? Hear anything? When did the lights go off? Do you know who stabbed you?'

'No!' she gasped as Sam probed at her shoulder. 'The light was out the whole time. I didn't mind. I thought I could use the cover. But that sonofabitch got me easy. Like I was one of the Ladies Auxiliary. All I had to do was turn around, and this damn case would be over.'

'If you'd turned around,' Sam retorted with unexpected vehemence, 'the knife might've gone straight into your heart. You're already luckier than you deserve.'

'So that proves it,' Hardhouse commented as if we were all talking to him. 'The killer isn't one of us. It has to be someone we don't know – someone still hiding in the lodge.'

'Perhaps you would care to explain yourself, Mr Hardhouse.' Connie's tone didn't express confidence. Her own anger ran deep, and she made it clear that she meant to draw her own conclusions. 'How do you arrive at that deduction?'

'Simple.' The worse the situation got, the more assurance he seemed to feel. 'We don't need to consider the Carbones or Faith Jerrick. Reeson explained why we can trust them. That leaves the rest of us. In fact, it only leaves those of us right here. Maryanne, Houston, and Buffy are together in the den – with Faith. None of them could have stabbed Ginny. And Brew was in the den as well. Weren't you, Brew?'

He didn't wait for an answer. 'Sam's an unlikely candidate in any case,' he continued. 'And you and Rock can vouch for him. He was in his room when you went to get him. Similarly, the rest of us can vouch for you. Assuming you attacked Ginny, there are only two ways you could have reached Sam's room from here – the two exits from the hall. One would take you through the den. Past Brew. The other would take you outside. You didn't have time for that.

'As for Lara and me – neither of us could have committed the other murders. And we were together until just moments before she found Ginny. I can tell you she didn't have time to stab Ginny. In fact, I can tell you she didn't have a knife with her.

'That's everybody.' Hardhouse spread his hands. 'We're all accounted for. The killer isn't one of us.' He paused suggestively. 'He must be hiding in one of the rooms in this wing. Unless he's opened a window and gone outside.'

His explanation sounded too persuasive – so persuasive that I dismissed it completely. But I didn't have time to react. Before I could take hold of what the back of my brain was trying to tell me, we all heard a pounding noise. Again.

A noise like someone knocking on a door.

Knocking hard.

It came from the direction of the den.

At the same instant Buffy let out a squeal of fright.

Connie and Lara turned to the sound. Growling, 'Now what?' Hardhouse started towards the den. Even Sam raised his head. He looked confused, as if he'd forgotten what he was doing.

Ginny twisted over on to her side. 'Brew.' Her right hand clamped on to my wrist. 'Stay close,' she whispered. 'I need to talk to you.'

Then she added, 'Find my gun. I dropped it.'

Somehow I hadn't realized that I was kneeling virtually on top of her .357.

I picked it up. With her hand on my wrist and my arm across her back, we climbed to our feet. I wanted to stop there, put both arms around her, let the acid burn through me. But my fists were full of weapons, and the pounding hadn't stopped.

Leaning on each other, we stumbled into motion.

'I'm not done,' Sam remarked as if he didn't expect either of us to care.

'Come on,' I told him over my shoulder. I didn't want him left alone. But Ginny and I kept moving.

By the time we reached the den, Hardhouse had already taken it on himself to open the door.

Arthur Reeson stood outside.

He looked like he'd just completed a forty-mile trek through four feet of snow.

Chapter Twenty-two

He didn't come in. When he saw me with the .357 in one hand and a bloody knife in the other, he stopped on the doorsill.

All in all, we must've presented an interesting picture. Ginny was obviously injured. Sam did a pretty convincing imitation of a derelict. Mile hadn't stopped struggling against his bonds. The gag made him look apoplectic. Maryanne was obviously delighted to see Reeson, who represented rescue, but Buffy gaped at him as if she didn't know if he came from heaven or hell. And I couldn't manage anything more intelligent than to drop my jaw and stare. Only Connie, Lara, and Joseph didn't appear to have been traumatized during Reeson's absence.

'Art!' Faith cried. She ran to him, flung herself into his arms, and kissed him ravenously.

'Did you get through?' Hardhouse demanded with aggressive good cheer. 'Is help on the way? We're dropping like flies around here.'

Reeson eyed me past Faith's shoulder. Still hugging her, he opened his hands to show me they were empty. As soon as she finished kissing him, he gave me a quizzical smile – which reminded me I'd never liked his smile.

'May I come in?'

Behind him wind blew across the valley. The sky had stayed clear, but the light was fading. Dusk cast Deerskin Lodge into shadow. He'd been gone for less than a day.

Like Hardhouse, I wondered if he'd summoned help.

'If you don't' – Ginny's voice was almost as hoarse as Reeson's – 'we'll all freeze to death.'

Hell, I'd freeze to death if I just had to look at Reeson's smile much longer.

He nodded. Disentangling himself from Faith, he shrugged the pack off his shoulders and dropped it on the porch. Still watching Ginny and me, he dusted most of the snow off his legs.

Then he came in.

Faith closed the door for him. With tears bright in her eyes and an uncharacteristic flush on her cheeks, she hung at his side.

He unbuttoned his coat smoothly. 'Maybe,' he said, trying to be helpful, 'you'd better tell me what's happened.'

'Maybe,' Ginny retorted harshly, 'you'd better tell us if you got through. You're back early.'

His smile had a faintly maniacal twist, but his voice remained steady. 'If you think I'd come back without doing what I said I would, you don't know me very well. Ordinarily I'd take offence. But I can see you haven't been having an easy time.

'Yes, I got through. There's a cabin five miles from here. Some city guy – an artist, I think – uses it in the summer.' He shrugged. 'I broke in to check the phone. It worked. The sheriff is on his way. He'll be here as soon as a plough opens the road.'

Buffy gasped a sob of relief. Maryanne sat down suddenly, as if the strings of fear which kept her on her feet had been cut. Staring like he couldn't believe his ears, Mile stopped trying to work the gag loose.

'Thank God,' Connie said succinctly.

'There's a lot of road to clear,' Reeson warned. 'Help won't arrive until some time tomorrow.'

We were still in trouble.

Apparently Hardhouse didn't realize that. Hurrying for some other reason, he took Lara by the arm and drew her away from the door. 'We'll go tell Rock and Queenie the good news.' Without any sign of protest from his wife, he swept her out of the den.

'Are they–?' Sam had to struggle to clear his throat. 'Are they bringing an ambulance? Paramedics? I need more IV valium. She's still in a coma.'

Reeson started to ask a question, but he thought better of it when he looked at Sam. 'An ambulance, yes,' he answered, 'for the woman who got shot. Catherine Reverie. I don't know about paramedics.'

Then he added, 'The sheriff has a radio. So do the ploughs. When they arrive, the road will be open. They can get what you need up here in an hour.'

Faith gripped his arm so tightly that the cords in the backs of her hands showed. She seemed to consider him a better anchor than her religion.

'I need them today.' Sam didn't look at any of us. 'By tomorrow she might be dead.'

That was too much for Reeson. 'Who?' he demanded. 'What's happened? I can't do anything about it if you don't tell me what's going on.'

Out of the corner of my eye, I saw Mile's gag drop free.

'*God*, Reeson!' he spat at once, 'you took your sweet time gettin' here. We got us a killer on the loose. Broke Westward's neck, ditched Abel somewhere, took a shot at Fistoulari, poisoned Drayton's wife. And these sons a bitches won't let me defend mahself. Get these ropes off me! Tomorrow ain't near fast enough. We need *guns*. Before he tries again.'

Reflexively we all watched Reeson. He had that kind of effect on people – he made us want to see what he would do.

He was surprised, I'll give him that. He couldn't have known what had happened to us, and he showed it. At least we got his frown back, which relieved my sense that he was about to explode. His eyebrows did a quirky little dance, up and down, up and down. 'My, my.' His voice sounded like someone had tried to strangle him a while back, and he hadn't fully recovered. 'We do live in interesting times, don't we? And you don't have any idea who did all this?'

For some reason Mile let his question pass. In unison, Buffy and Maryanne shook their heads. But Ginny's face was blank – studiously blank, like a mask – and I kept my thoughts to myself.

'Off-hand,' Reeson commented to me, 'I'd say the ghouls and beasties are coming out of the woodwork.' Like an acknowledgement of Buffy's distress and Sam's shock, he added, 'With a vengeance.'

Vengeance. Another unexpected hint. Not that Reeson meant to hint at anything, of course. He was just talking. Nevertheless a little shiver of recognition ran through my brain.

As far as I knew, no one here had anything to do with vengeance. Except me.

El Señor's revenge.

Reeson scanned the room again. 'Where are the Carbones?'

Faith started to answer, but right on cue Ama and Truchi appeared from the dining room. Neither of them indicated any surprise at Reeson's arrival. Truchi simply nodded. Ama muttered quietly, 'It's about time,' and folded her arms under her bosom. Together, she and her husband took up their deferential stations against one of the walls.

'We need to talk about this,' Ginny told Reeson abruptly. As if she'd reached a decision, she stopped leaning on me. 'I'm in no mood for an audience. Let's go to the office.'

Deliberately, so that everyone could see her, she took her .357 from me. Ignoring the pain in her shoulder – never mind the fact that Sam wasn't done with her – she hefted the gun, checked to be sure it was loaded.

Just for a second, Reeson's frown flicked into a smile. Then he resumed his dark contented scowl and nodded. 'Sure.'

To Faith, he said, 'These people want supper. They just don't know it yet. Maybe you'd better get started.'

He and I both knew she wouldn't argue with him. A woman who looked at him like that wasn't about to argue.

'Let's go,' he said to Ginny.

'Good.' Without hesitation, she headed across the den towards the office.

I followed. The shiver in my brain grew stronger. It seemed to feed on anger and medication.

After two steps, however, Ginny turned back. Pointing her claw at Mile, she commanded Maryanne, 'Don't untie him. I don't want him loose. If he drives you crazy, gag him again.'

Then she left the den.

Reeson and I didn't hang around to hear Mile's response.

To all appearances, no one had been in the office since Rock and I sat there the first night of the camp – except, of course, to latch and cover the window. I raised the blind for confirmation, saw that the latch remained securely shut. I didn't know where the light switches were, so I left the blind up for a little extra illumination.

The room itself smelled vaguely musty, disused. When Reeson snapped on the lights, we could see that nothing had been disturbed – no covert ransacking of the filing cabinets, no scrabbling through the desk. Apparently none of our murderers needed to know the things they could've learned here.

The artificial light emphasized the mismatch between the dark desk and chairs and the blond panelling and floorboards. That discrepancy reminded me of my strange conversation here with Rock – listening to him tell me that he didn't want to stir up trouble about the guns – hearing him talk about Smithsonian –

The back of my brain churned, bitter as bile. I wanted something to hit.

I should've pulled the blind down again, but I forgot.

Emphasizing her authority, Ginny went around the desk and sat in the big armchair. That left Reeson and me to argue over the less comfortable seating arrangements.

He pulled up a chair in front of the desk. I thought about doing the same, but the pressure of Sam's injection kept me on my feet. Instead of sitting, I went to the wall behind Ginny, beside the window, and propped myself there. Reminding Reeson that I was on her side.

Reeson still wore his coat. Under it he had on a bulky insulated vest that all by itself looked warm enough to keep out a blizzard. Facing Ginny, he unpopped several of the snaps. His hands seemed to function independent of his attention.

'So,' he said, 'this Houston Mile had something to do with it.'

Ginny rolled her chair forward so that she could lean her arms on the desk top. With that wound in her shoulder, her gun must've been hard to hold. As if to let Reeson know that the .357 wasn't intended for him, she put it down on the big blotter that covered half the desk.

'No.' She did her best to sound clear, but I heard the strain in her voice. 'If anything, I'm sure he *isn't* involved. He's just dangerous. He's a coward. He wants to blow people away before they get a chance to threaten him.'

'Does that mean you don't know anything?' Reeson asked. Somehow he managed not to sound critical. 'You don't have any ideas? You haven't found any' – despite his careful tone, his pause gave the word a little sneer – 'clues?'

'Oh, we have enough evidence to convict a truckload of murderers.' From where I stood, I couldn't see Ginny's face, but her tense posture made her look like she was engaged in some kind of contest with Reeson. 'We just don't know what it all means.'

He lifted his shoulders in a small shrug. 'I can't help if you don't tell me about it.'

She nodded curtly. 'I'll give you the short form.'

Outside night came down fast as the mountains cut off the light.

'A while after you left, Brew took a nap in the den. Someone dropped rat poison in the fireplace. Nearly asphyxiated him.'

The world was growing as dark as when Cat was shot. The lights in the office seemed unnatural, fragile somehow, like you couldn't trust them.

'When we checked the wine cellar, Simon Abel was gone. Someone broke him out through the wall. We haven't seen him since. But he left a trail in the snow, so I followed it. Got shot for my trouble.' She pointed at her temple.

'While I was gone, Mac Westward had too much to drink at lunch.

He went to his room to sleep it off. Someone went into his room and broke his neck. When I–'

'Wait a minute,' Reeson interrupted. '*While* you were gone? How could somebody shoot you outside, and still be inside breaking Westward's neck?'

'Interesting question,' Ginny drawled acerbically. 'If you think of an answer, let me know.'

Soon the light inside and the dark outside blinded the window. The glass looked opaque, like the surface of a black pool. Anything could happen out there now, and we wouldn't be able to do anything about it.

'When I got back,' she continued, 'Queenie Drayton decided she needed a drink. It was poisoned. She went into a seizure.'

Obliquely I noticed that Ginny didn't identify the drink. Her caution may've been unnecessary, but I approved anyway.

'We thought the killer had to be somewhere in the lodge, so we organized a search. While we were doing that, someone came up behind me and stuck a knife in my shoulder. So far we've lost Cat, Simon, and Mac, and Queenie may die.'

Ginny stopped.

Reeson's eyebrows did their dance on his forehead. The moral equivalent of whistling in surprise. First he said, 'None of this makes sense.' Then he asked, 'What's your "evidence"?'

'I'll give you an example.' Shock and loss of blood frayed her voice. She sounded like she had the same fever I did. 'Brew, this is what I wanted to talk to you about.' She didn't glance at me. 'I think I know how Queenie was poisoned.'

Reeson and I both listened. Judging by appearances, however, he paid more attention than I did. Fury and chemicals made a witch's brew in my blood, and the cauldron's seething consumed most of my brain. I'd already missed my chance to save Queenie. If I didn't start to think effectively, I'd continue missing vital connections and clues until we all died for it.

'Before I was stabbed, I had time to search two rooms, Mile's and Lara's. I didn't find anything useful in his. But in hers' – she paused to focus her anger – 'I found cocaine. A lot of it.'

The cauldron bubbled and spat. Coke might explain a lot of Lara Hardhouse's behaviour.

'Do you know what happens,' Ginny demanded, 'when you get a massive overdose of cocaine? You go into seizure. Every one of your muscles locks up. You can't even breathe. Even if your heart doesn't fail from shock, you die because you get no air. Or you collapse into a coma because of the brain damage.'

She sounded quietly savage, too angry to suffer her own despair. 'But we know Lara isn't the killer. Brew was with her when Mac died.'

I couldn't suffer it myself. My heart felt as black and blind as the window, and I'd come to the end of what I could endure. Window latches and port. Vengeance and wine cellars. And something else that might boil to the surface any second now.

'I'll give you another example,' I said harshly. 'Another useful bit of "evidence". We know that shot wasn't aimed at Cat. It was aimed at me.'

Reeson cocked his head. His scowl flickered on the edge of a smile.

'A goon called el Señor wants me dead. And he's got his hooks into a private investigator named Lawrence Smithsonian. You've heard of Smithsonian. He arranged this job for us. He even called me while I was in the hospital, trying to scare us into taking this job.

'Why do you suppose he did that? I think he wanted to set us up. He knew el Señor could have me killed when I got here.'

'I wouldn't know anything about that,' Reeson answered non-committally. 'But it doesn't make sense. It doesn't explain why Westward was killed, or why Mrs Drayton was poisoned.'

He didn't mention Simon. I noticed that.

'Because,' I said.

Window-latches and port. Vengeance and wine cellars. Coke aimed at Cat had poisoned Queenie, I couldn't argue with that. And Lara Hardhouse had cocaine. But it was an amateur job, dependent on chance. The dose had to be enough, or the treatment had to be wrong, or the treatment had to come too late. And Mac's murder relied on chance. Connie could've walked into the room at any moment. And the knife in Ginny's back was another amateur job, rank with chance and luck.

But –

Any killer hired by el Señor wouldn't trust chance. He wouldn't shoot Ginny and then run down to the lodge in broad daylight just *hoping* that someone had left a window unlatched. Too many things could go wrong. First he'd make sure Ginny was dead. If she hadn't played dead trying to trap him, he would've finished her. Then he'd take all the time he needed to come back carefully.

'Because,' I said, 'we have more than one killer.'

Instinctively Ginny twisted in her chair to stare at me.

A smile twitched Reeson's mouth, and his eyebrows worked.

'One of them is el Señor's hit man,' I told her. 'He shot Cat and you, broke Simon out of the wine cellar, put rat poison down the chimney. The other killed Mac and doped Cat's drink and stabbed you.'

Out of an obscure sympathy for vulnerable women, I added, 'It doesn't have to be Lara. Anyone who searched her room could've found that coke and used it. Or someone could've planted it in her room. Like the rifle in Simon's closet.

'But there have to be two of them. Mile is right about that. An amateur and a professional. The pro wants me. The amateur is just trying to take advantage of the confusion.'

Then I had it. The cauldron spat in my face so hard that I nearly went blind, and the room started turning on its axis, changing the meaning of everything. But I had it.

Facing Reeson with blood in my throat and no strength left, I said, 'You never went for help. There's no help coming. After you tried to shoot me and hit Cat, you decided to get away from the scene so that we wouldn't connect you with whatever happened next. And you wanted to keep your freedom of movement. But you didn't go anywhere. You freed Simon from the wine cellar and ditched his body and shot Ginny, and now you're back to finish the job.'

Until I saw Ginny's stunned expression, I didn't understand how much trouble – personal trouble – she'd had with this case. It wasn't just a matter of being shot and stabbed. Or of having her wounded partner wander around like the universal victim. Her fear of el Señor and her involvement with Hardhouse got in her way. She actually didn't seem to grasp the implications of what I said.

'Axbrewder,' Reeson murmured gently, 'the ghouls and beasties are getting the better of you. You'll look pretty foolish when the sheriff gets here.'

Ginny swivelled slowly to face him. He didn't take his eyes off me, however, and a moment later she swivelled back. Her gaze was fractured and uncertain. It reminded me of the way she'd looked after she first lost her hand. Uneasily she asked, 'How do you know all that?'

Pain throbbed through my stomach. I wanted to jump Reeson, but I knew I couldn't. I didn't let myself meet his gaze.

'The killer has to be someone who works here. Someone with inside information about the lodge. That's obvious.' So obvious that it hadn't occurred to me until a moment ago. 'But the Carbones and Faith never go anywhere. El Señor couldn't use a hired killer who lived up here all the time. That leaves Reeson. He takes vacations and doesn't even tell Faith where he's going.'

Ginny shook her head. 'Slow down. Back up. Why is it obvious? Even if you're right about two killers, why does either of them need inside information?'

The throb expanded. I heard an odd rushing noise like a gale chewing on the trees around Deerskin Lodge. Too much pain and infection and anger – too much medication. The gale seemed to crowd the edges of my vision, contracting my field of view.

'Because of the rat poison.'

Ginny's mouth shaped the words, *rat poison*, but no sound came out.

'No one knew it was there except the people who work here. Anyone who wasn't personally familiar with Deerskin Lodge on a day-to-day basis wouldn't have known there was rat poison available. Or known where to find it.

'Reeson is the only candidate.'

Darkness tightened around my vision like a noose, but I still saw Reeson get to his feet. Ginny flung her chair back to face him, but she was too slow. He picked up her revolver. Just for a second, he smiled at it disapprovingly, as if it weren't good enough for him. Then he reached into his vest and brought out his own gun.

I recognized it right away. It was one of the guns missing from the dining room, a Ruger .357 Magnum. The kind of weapon that can powder your bones and spray your blood for ten yards in all directions.

When he pointed it at her, Ginny froze. I would've frozen myself, but I was already immobilized. If I took my weight off the wall, I'd crumble.

'You don't think very highly of my intelligence, Axbrewder,' he commented amiably. 'I'm the one who first suggested the wine cellar. Why did I do that, if I wanted something out of it? Why didn't I get the rat poison before I let you put Abel in there?'

'You didn't know you'd need it.' My voice came out of the wind. 'But that's not the main reason. Mostly you wanted to frame Simon – make him look guilty when he broke out, so that we wouldn't think of anything else. And if we hadn't already locked him up, you couldn't have broken through the wall to get the poison. That would've been too obvious.

'Professionals don't usually take chances, but of course that isn't always true.' Now that I'd started talking, I couldn't stop, even if I wanted to. Once the room began to turn, I had to ride the spin until it ended. 'They need opportunity, just like the rest of us. When you saw Simon go out for a walk, you grabbed an opportunity.

'You were already outside with that rifle, watching the lodge for a shot at me. You'd already taken the guns, mostly to create confusion, make everyone look guilty – but also so that your weapon couldn't be traced to you. The random assortment was a smoke screen. You wanted the killer to look like someone who didn't really know what he was doing, an amateur.

'Simon gave you part of your chance. You knew he was one of the actors – you handled the reservations for Murder On Cue. Once you saw Cat and me in the parlour, you had everything you needed.'

With every angle and muscle, Ginny focused on Reeson.

'But Simon's window was latched,' I continued. 'That didn't leave you much time. You had to run inside by one of the back doors and go out through his window. Then you shot at me and hit Cat instead. So you dumped the rifle in Simon's closet and left again, leaving the window open – another ploy to make him look guilty. And you didn't have time to do anything else.

'So you took a chance. That's OK. You're smart – you took a smart chance. You're just not a very good shot. So now you had to arrange another opportunity.

'That's why you pulled down the phone line, disabled the vehicles. To give yourself an excuse to go for help. Only you didn't go anywhere. You hiked out of sight and then sneaked back. When you were sure the way was clear, you reached the lodge and got up on the roof. From the roof, there's probably a way into the attic – and from the attic there are probably knotholes and gaps that let you watch some of the rooms. The den, anyway. The way this place is built, nothing creaks. We wouldn't hear you up there.'

Reeson did me the courtesy of looking mildly impressed.

'My nap in the den gave you another opportunity. You broke Simon out of the wine cellar, killed him, and took the rat poison. You dropped the box down the chimney and packed it with snow. Then you carried Simon up into the hills, leaving a nice plain trail to make us think he was on the run. After that, you waited to see if you were followed. You wanted me, of course, but you didn't mind getting Ginny out of the way while you had the chance. El Señor sure as hell wouldn't object.

'Unfortunately after you shot her you didn't get any more opportunities. You were out in the hills, and I was here. You waited for a while in case you got lucky again, like you did with Simon, but when the day was almost over and nothing solved your problem for you, you came back to tell us that we were about to be rescued. That way, you could be sure that you'd get another chance at me.'

Then I was finished. I'd come to the end of words. And I had no other weapons. The gale rushed closer, stalking me by increments, and I knew that I wouldn't be on my feet much longer.

Fortunately Ginny took up the struggle. I'd given her time to recover her grasp of the situation. 'Too bad you're stuck now,' she put in grimly. 'Everybody knows where you are. When you shoot us, they won't need to guess who did it. Then you'll have to kill them all. Or go on the run. And a hit man on the run won't be much use to el Señor. In fact, he may decide to have *you* killed, just in case you think the cops might trade immunity for testimony.

'You're out of opportunities, Reeson. Put the guns down. Give it up while you still can.'

'Oh, I don't think so.' His frown looked as secure as grip on the guns. 'After I shoot you, I'll just yell for help. I'll say you were shot through the window. Luckily Axbrewder was kind enough to pull up the blind. Before anybody questions me, I'll go after the killer. When I come back with Abel's body – not to mention his fingerprints on this gun' – he indicated the Ruger – 'there won't be anyone around to contradict me.

'Look at it this way. After wrestling for all these years with the things that haunt you, and not doing very well at it, you'll finally be at peace.'

He had a point. I couldn't deny that. If he gave a shout and then jumped out through the window, no one would ever know that the glass had no bullet-holes. The rest would be easy.

I had to do something. This was my job, the work Ginny paid me for – this was why she had a partner in the first place. Whether she still loved me or not didn't matter any more. I was sick of all the things I blamed myself for, sick of being pushed around by circumstances, sick of making excuses. And I'd made a promise to myself.

I'd promised that I would *get* this bastard.

I had to do *something*.

Nevertheless I was helpless – which nearly broke my heart. At my best, I couldn't have pulled out the .45 and shot Reeson before he killed both of us. On top of that, I didn't have the strength to fight him, even if I could've reached him before he fired. The gale gathered in the room, and darkness squeezed my vision down to a tunnel barely big enough to include both Reeson and Ginny, and I was helpless.

Ginny was about to die because of me.

At that moment I stopped being angry. The spin of the room

carried all the fury out of my bones. El Señor and Smithsonian and Reeson no longer enraged me. I wasn't even angry at myself.

I simply couldn't endure letting Ginny die.

She slid her hand and her claw off the desktop into her lap and bowed forward as if she were beaten and couldn't hide it any more. I did the only thing I could think of.

I collapsed.

Rolling my eyes, I toppled towards the corner of the desk like a man in a dead faint.

It worked.

Damn near got us both blown away.

My tumble caught Reeson's attention, snagged his eyes away from Ginny. Instinctively he lined up both guns on me. If I hadn't been falling, he would've shot me then.

I only distracted him for an instant. But during that instant Ginny reached under the desk, found the Smith & Wesson .44 I'd discovered four days ago, and hauled it out.

In a voice like a gunshot, she yelled, '*Stop!*'

Reeson stopped. His weapons were directed at me, and she had an absolutely unobstructed shot at the centre of his chest. That .44 was no Magnum, but at this range it had the power to drive his heart out through his back.

He didn't know what I knew.

Too bad she didn't, either. I hadn't told her that the gun was empty – that I'd taken out the shells.

But *he* didn't know, that was the crucial thing. With any luck at all, he might take five or ten seconds to figure it out. The .44 was a revolver. As soon as he got a good look at it, he would see that the cylinder held no shells.

Ginny and I had that long to live.

Fortunately I was moving faster than I could think.

Snatching up my hands, I caught myself on the corner of the desk. But from there I didn't go around the desk at Reeson. If I tried that, he'd shoot me, no matter what Ginny did. A survival reflex. And then he'd be safe.

Instead I shoved my weight backwards with every atom of stubbornness and need I could muster.

Whirling, I dived head-first through the window.

Out into the dark and the deep snow.

Chapter Twenty-three

I landed in a shower of shattered glass and a splash of cold, but I didn't notice either of them. The impact drove the air out of my lungs and turned my guts into a howling blast of pain.

Would've been worse if the snow hadn't been so thick.

Familiar, all of it. Just a few days ago, I'd gone through a window into snow to get at Muy Estobal – and I'd done it so that I could save Ginny. Even the gale exploding inside me, raking my nerves with agony, was the same.

And we were up against more than one killer. That was similar too.

Everything else had changed.

For one thing, Reeson probably wouldn't let me sneak up behind him and crush his larynx.

For another – any second now, he'd lean out the window and blow my head off. I had to get moving right now, *right now*.

I scrabbled my legs and arms under me. Shedding clumps of snow as if I'd climbed out of a winter grave, I heaved myself upright. I still couldn't breathe, but I didn't have time to worry about that. *Get out of the light*. The glow from the window seemed to etch me where I stood – a dummy set out for target practice. Stumbling frantically, I flung myself at the wall and collided my way along it as fast as I could go.

Towards the front of the lodge.

'*Axbrewder!*'

Reeson's shout hit me hard. I almost stopped.

If I'd stopped, he would've gotten me. He must've known where I was. He could see my trail – he could probably hear me against the wall.

But the light of the office and the dark outside blinded him temporarily, just for a couple of heartbeats.

I plunged ahead.

Then I dropped back into the snow around the corner of the porch and lay there gasping for breath, retching at the pain.

He hadn't fired.

'*Axbrewder!*' His hoarse shout sounded like a cry of despair. '*Come back! I've got her! Come back or I'll kill her!*'

Ginny –

Wait your fucking turn, you sonofabitch!

I got up again. Supporting myself on the edge of the porch, I went for the front door.

I knew exactly what I had to do. You've got to draw the line somewhere. I drew it at letting him shoot Ginny.

Which might not be under my control, of course. I'd killed Muy Estobal. I'd brought el Señor's vengeance here without understanding it. Those things had consequences.

But Reeson's real violence was directed at me, not Ginny. He held her hostage to get at me.

While he did that, I had a chance.

He could kill her at any time. Under the circumstances, he might decide to do his job by eliminating the survivors, the witnesses. Naturally he'd start with her.

I had to get to him before he made that decision.

And I had one advantage that he probably didn't realize.

He knew I was hurt, but he didn't know *me*. He couldn't begin to guess how far I was willing to go.

He might let Ginny live a little longer because he wasn't afraid of me.

Your turn is coming, Reeson. Just wait for it.

I reached the front steps. The way I went up them should've made a racket, but the snow muffled my feet.

Ginny needed to do a hell of a balancing act. She had to convince Reeson that he needed a hostage. Make him think that I still had the strength to threaten him. If I were unconscious out in the snow somewhere, he could afford to kill her. At the same time, however, she didn't want to rush him into a decision – which meant she had to give him the impression that I was too stupid, or too crazy, to surprise him. If she could find that balance, she might buy herself a little time.

I skidded gracelessly across the porch and hauled at the front door.

Thank God and all His Angels, no one had thought to relock the door after Reeson came in.

A rush of heat nearly dropped me to my knees. Maybe because he didn't know what else to do with himself while his wife and Faith prepared supper, Truchi had built up the fires to a roar. Compared to the cold outside, the den felt like an oven.

But I didn't have time for warmth. Swinging the door shut hard to preserve my momentum, I headed through the den as fast as I could, approximately running.

The place seemed unusually empty. Only Carbone and Mile and Maryanne were there. I didn't try to guess where everyone else was, but I could see why Houston Mile and his 'filly' had remained. No one had untied him. And Maryanne had shoved the gag back in his mouth. She'd resumed talking to him, sitting knee to knee with him as if this were an insidious form of torture.

Now, however, what she said brought an entirely different expression to his piggy eyes. Her hands were on his thighs, and her fingers seemed to be probing his crotch.

Apparently she was trying to get back into his good graces the only way she knew how.

I'd already passed the tree and had almost reached the dining room hallway when I heard her cry, 'Brew?' Not scared yet, not the way she used to be. Nevertheless a little lift of panic in her voice betrayed her fragility. 'Why did you come in that way? What's going on?'

'Later.'

I didn't wait to see how she took my rebuff. The last thing I needed right then was people following me, asking frightened questions.

The hallway. The dining room. Both empty.

The hall to the kitchen.

There I found Faith Jerrick.

Alone.

She stood at the cook top, stirring a big four-quart soup kettle. The air held a persistent suggestion of gas. I'd expected to find Amalia as well, but apparently she had other duties. Desperately I hoped that she and Truchi would stay out of my way. I needed people out of my way. Especially the Carbones, who were probably sane. Anyone who retained a substantial amount of sanity wouldn't like what I had in mind.

Faith absolutely wouldn't like it.

I did it anyway.

The fluorescent lighting made the counter tops and appliances gleam feverishly, like an hallucination. All the utensils looked sharp as knives, and the huge Hobart resembled a gas chamber for roasting martyrs. Bracing myself from surface to surface, I advanced around the counters towards Faith.

She raised a brief glance as high as my chin, then returned her gaze to her soup. Cream of tomato. It had the sickly reddish shade you get when you don't put in enough milk.

'Mr Axbrewder,' she said, 'where's Art?' Only her voice betrayed the fact that she didn't give a damn about the soup. Her real attention was fixed on me. 'I thought you would be done talking by now. I've made some soup.' The pot steamed, full of simmering. 'I can make sandwiches in a minute. What is Art doing?'

Her appearance – the deferential and passionate line of her neck, the clarity of her skin, the self-contained extravagance in her eyes – made me think that what I had in mind just might be terrible enough to succeed.

'Faith.'

In an odd way, she daunted me. Just for a second, I couldn't go on. She was one of the innocent. She didn't deserve the kind of damage I intended.

But I had no choice. I needed help. Too many people had already died, most of them innocent. And more might follow.

'Yes?' she offered.

Groping for a way to approach her, I asked the first question that came into my head. 'Do you ever talk to Art about the guests? Did you tell him that Catherine Reverie liked port?'

'No.' She allowed herself to look mildly startled. 'Why would I? He has his own concerns. And the guests have a right to their privacy. Ama feels the same way. We haven't discussed Miss Reverie's habits with anyone.'

So. Arthur Reeson hadn't poisoned Queenie. He hadn't killed Mac or stabbed Ginny. At some point – if I lived long enough – I'd have to face that problem. But not now. First things first.

Ginny always said that. She believed in tackling crises in some kind of logical order.

'You told me once,' I floundered on as if I weren't changing the subject, 'that Art doesn't take you when he goes on vacation. And you don't know what he does when he's away.'

Well, at least we were talking about Art. That relieved her chagrin at my strange manner. Softly she said, 'That's right.'

'How often does he go? How many vacations does he take a year?'

For a woman who had God's company during Reeson's absences, she was remarkably prompt with the answer. 'Never more than eight.

Usually five or six.' Then she let her curiosity get the better of her. 'Why do you ask?'

Five or six *vacations* a year. Christ! How many people had he hit?

'Faith,' I repeated. I didn't falter now – but I didn't attack her either. I was as gentle as my pain, and my fear that I'd hear shots, allowed. 'Arthur Reeson shot Cat. He tried to kill me. He tried to kill Ginny. Now he's holding her hostage in the office. He's been hired to kill me. If I don't go back in there, he'll kill her. I want you to come talk to him.'

Be *my* hostage, Faith. Give me something I can trade for Ginny's life.

She didn't flush. She had blood and passion in her, but not for that. And she didn't turn pale. She was already about as pale as she could get. And she didn't look at me. She had no need to see who I was. She just went completely still, like a small animal in a corner. Her hand stopped stirring the soup. As far as I could tell, she stopped breathing.

'You never asked him what he does with his vacations. Or why he needs so *many* of them.' Urgently I pleaded with her. 'You never asked him why he's content with a job like this – a man like him isolated out here, with so much competence and so little need for it.

'I'll tell you why. He's a professional killer. When he goes on vacation, he kills people. And then he comes back here because it's isolated and safe, and no one questions him.

'I told you about el Señor. You were there when I talked about him. He wants me dead, I told you why. He hired Art to kill me.' I wasn't on a first-name basis with Reeson. I faked it for her. 'When he shot Cat, he was trying to hit me. She got in the way.

'He doesn't want Ginny. She's not his target. But he'll gladly kill her to get at me.'

Would Faith ever breathe again? I couldn't tell. In her shocked stillness, she might've been transformed to alabaster, or a pillar of salt, or whatever it is you turn into when you look back on degradation and ruin. She should've prayed, clutched her crucifix and beseeched God. Or at least called me a liar, yelled at me somehow. But she didn't. The soup under her ladle seethed in spots. Before long, it would boil, and if she didn't stir it it would scald. Without moving a muscle, she gave the impression that I'd kicked out the bottom of her heart.

'I need your help.' I didn't raise my voice, despite my desperation. I feared that I'd miss the sound of his Ruger. And I didn't want to treat Faith like an enemy, responsible in some way for Reeson's violence. I drew the line at letting Ginny get killed – but I drew it here, too. 'I want you to talk to him. If he knows that you know what he's doing, he might stop.'

No, that wasn't enough, it wasn't the truth. And she deserved the truth. Now more than ever before in her life she deserved it.

'You're the only one here he cares about. I want to use you to save Ginny. I want to trade you for her.'

A quiver plucked at the corner of her mouth. She couldn't accuse me of lying about her lover. She didn't know *how*. Lies had no place in her life with God. To me the little spasm in her cheek looked like the first faint tremor of an earthquake, a shattering upheaval. She was so still, so needy – that minor vibration would be enough to break her.

I fought for quietness, kept my voice gentle. I didn't intend to browbeat her with my own need.

'If you can't help me,' I said, 'I don't know what else to do. He's only keeping Ginny alive so that he can use her against me. If I don't give him what he wants, he'll kill her. But even if I let him have me, he'll kill her. She's a witness. He can't let her go.

'And that isn't the end of it. He'll have to kill everyone. When I escaped from the office, I doomed you all. He doesn't know where I've been, who I've talked to. He can't trust anyone now. Not even Truchi and Ama.' I choked convulsively. 'Not even you.'

Abruptly the quiver spread across her cheek, ran down her neck to her shoulders. Her hands began to shake. Twitching, she let go of the ladle. It clattered dully against the side of the kettle – her distress only made that one sound, and most of it was muffled by the soup.

With the least amount of movement possible, using only the parts of her that were absolutely necessary, she turned away.

Between the counters, she headed for the back door.

Away from the office.

Towards her cottage.

Oh, Ginny.

If I were sane, I wouldn't have told Faith anything. I would've simply said that Reeson wanted to see her in the office. But if I were sane, I wouldn't have been here in the first place. I would've found a better answer to my life, one that didn't involve asking the innocent to pay for my mistakes. Turning her back on me, Faith abandoned Ginny as well, but I had no right to complain. I had nothing to complain about.

She went slowly towards the door. For a moment I couldn't move. Darkness filled my head, and pain cramped my heart, and walking away she used up all the movement in the room, all the decision.

Reeson might shoot Ginny any time now.

I stumbled after Faith.

Distress clogged her steps, held her back. I caught her several paces from the door. When I put my hand on her shoulder, she flinched so hard that her own dismay turned her around. Tears pouring from her eyes, she faced me, and her lips quivered.

'I can't endure violence.' Her voice trembled like her lips. 'You know that. I can't.'

'Faith,' I murmured softly, as if I were her friend and counsellor instead of her doom, 'you love God. You love Art. You don't want him to kill Ginny. Not at the cost of his soul.

'I need to save her, but I can't let him kill the rest of you. If you won't help me, I'll have to let her die. So that I can hunt him down before he kills anyone else.'

I didn't mention the obvious fact that I couldn't hope to out-hunt Reeson. There didn't seem to be any point.

'Please help me.'

'Brew.' Lara spoke quietly, but her voice hit me between the shoulder blades like an ice pick. 'I need to talk to you.'

Oh God, not now. Not *now*.

Ignoring the woman behind me, I concentrated everything I had left on Faith. 'Please,' I repeated as if that were my last argument, and my best. 'Please.'

'You're the only one who can help me, Brew,' Lara insisted.

I felt so close to the edge that I nearly whimpered. What was that damn woman doing here now anyway? And how had she chosen *this* moment for whatever she had in mind? Couldn't she see that I was fighting for Ginny's life?

Faith watched me. Her eyes spilled water like wells, but she watched me. Her gaze seemed to study me, measuring me by the way I responded to Lara.

'Later,' I coughed against a mounting wave of panic. 'Ask me later.'

'*Brew.*'

Lara's tone cut through my alarm. Suddenly I heard something like hysteria in it – and something like glee. She may've been a coke addict after all, submerged in so many artificial substances that her brain had gone to mush and wildness. She sounded on the verge of ecstasy or a breakdown, which ever came first.

'*What did Ginny find in my room?*'

I snapped, staggering like a ship in a long wind when the cables that tied it to its the berth parted. With a howl rising from my torn-up guts, I wheeled on Lara Hardhouse – and froze. Stricken, my howl came out as a strangled groan.

Lara held a gun.

She pointed it at my sternum from a distance of less than ten yards. Her finger curled on the trigger. She'd already advanced past the stove where Faith's soup steamed. At this range she was never going to miss.

Her eyes glittered intensely. Exaltation limned her face. Quietly now because she knew she didn't need to shout, she repeated, 'What did Ginny find in my room?'

My head felt like a discus. Some great mother of an athlete whirled me around and around, and any second now he would let me go, send me sailing into the empty air and the dark. I couldn't tell whether Faith pulled away from me, headed for the door again. She found coke in your room, the coke you used to poison Cat. You didn't know Queenie would drink it instead. None of this makes sense. Who killed Mac?

I wanted to turn my head, catch some sign of Faith, but if I looked around at all, released my focus on Lara's gun, the spin would carry me away. It was a little .22, a plinking gun you could hide in a clutch purse. But it was as good as artillery from this distance.

'Ask her yourself,' I croaked. 'She's in the office. With Reeson.'

Lara shook her head. 'I don't want to ask her, Brew. I want to ask you.' She sounded strangely sure of herself. 'And you're going to tell me.

'Do you know why? Have you figured out why I come to you? Why I'm attracted to you? Why I want you to go to bed with me?

'It's because you're a *cripple*, because you're *flawed*. You're only half a human being, Brew – and I like that. I like having sex with crippled men.'

She seemed to expand in front of me, her underlying passion made her tower over me. Or maybe it just made me shrink.

'Sex with me would make you feel like you aren't crippled. Like you aren't as pathetic as you look and feel. I like having that much power, Brew.

'And I like knowing it won't make any difference. When you fuck me, you feel like a man again, you feel alive again – and it doesn't make any difference. Because I know as soon as you start to feel that way you're going to die. I can take you to the top of the mountain, Brew, and I enjoy it because I know you'll fall off. You're going to end up dead.'

I saw movement behind her. For a moment I couldn't fix on it. I couldn't do anything except watch the .22 and shrink. If I took my eyes off the gun, I might warn her.

Then the background clarified, and I saw Connie.

She eased forward carefully, so carefully that she hardly seemed to move. Her gaze flicked back and forth between Lara and me, hunting for some hint of what was going on.

Lara didn't know Connie was there. 'That's *power*, Brew,' she said. 'You can't say no to me, you really can't. You're a cripple, and cripples can't say no. They never can.'

'What did Ginny find in my room?'

'You can't shoot me,' I replied thinly. 'You poisoned Queenie. I figured that out.' I spoke for Connie's benefit, explaining to her, giving her time. But I couldn't answer Lara's question. If I did, she wouldn't have any reason left to hold back. 'And you probably stabbed Ginny. But who killed Mac?'

Lara's finger clenched on the trigger. 'Brew,' she warned, 'I asked you a question.'

Connie hadn't advanced far enough. Her features were pure and hard, she didn't intend to let anything stop her. The anger which had held her since Mac's death impelled her. But she'd never reach Lara in time.

'No. You can't shoot me.' I wanted to sound casual, but my voice twanged like a snapping rubber band. 'Don't you smell it?'

Lara frowned. 'Smell what?'

'Gas.' Personally I couldn't smell it at all now. Just soup. 'There's a leak in here somewhere. I first caught a whiff of it a couple of days ago, but it's getting stronger.

'If you shoot me, the muzzle flash will set it off. This entire kitchen will blow. Do you know what that kind of fire does to you? Even if you live, it'll char the skin from your bones.'

Lara hesitated. 'You're lying.' Just a small falter – a tiny decrease of pressure in the trigger – but it sufficed. 'I don't smell any gas.'

You're going to end up dead.

In that instant a wild and unholy look like a glimpse of the abyss crossed Connie's face. With both hands she picked up the kettle and poured soup on to Lara's head.

The shock saved me. Lara didn't shoot. She didn't manage to fire at all. The .22 flipped out of her grasp as she screamed and clutched at her scalded flesh.

Still screaming in short mad bursts, she dropped to the floor. Her

676

hands clawed at the back of her dress, fighting to tear the burn away, but she couldn't rip the fabric.

'Oh, my Lord,' Faith moaned. 'God help me.'

Connie looked stricken, as if she'd terrified herself unexpectedly, but she went and retrieved the .22. She'd written enough novels about violence. She knew what to do. When she had the gun, she met my gaze. Shadows shifted like ghosts across the depths of her eyes. 'Second degree burns,' she announced as if she were sure. 'She'll live.'

I didn't thank her. I didn't have time. Quickly I said, 'Reeson killed Cat and Simon. He wants to kill me. He's holding Ginny hostage in the office.'

Then I said, 'Faith is going to help me rescue her.'

Both Connie and I turned towards Faith.

'You can't get away from it,' I breathed softly, gently. 'No one ever gets away from violence. No one is ever safe. That isn't the way God works. If you want these murders to stop, you have to make that happen yourself.'

She didn't respond. Her eyes were riveted on Lara. But her hands were where they belonged, holding her crucifix, and her mouth shaped prayers I couldn't hear.

When I took hold of her arm, she didn't resist. Clinging to the delicate silver remnant of her beliefs, she let me steer her in the direction of the office.

None of us tried to help Lara.

As we left I told Connie, 'Get everyone together in Sam's room. Even Mile. But don't let him have the gun.'

The way she said, 'Leave it to me,' was good enough.

Faith and I moved along the halls like martyrs on their way to the stake. Although she didn't know it, she actually kept me on my feet, supporting me through my grip on her arm. Under her breath she murmured prayers that went nowhere.

Dazed by our separate fears, we reached the office.

I couldn't hear voices, which scared me so badly that I nearly let everything else go and charged inside by myself.

But I still hadn't heard a shot. I clutched that fact the same way Faith clutched her crucifix.

Trying not to shake like a drunk with the DTs, I took out the .45 for the first time in what seemed like for ever. Bracing my arm, I worked the slide.

As a kind of apology, I muttered to Faith, 'I have to make this look good.' Then I put the gun behind her and pointed the muzzle at the back of her skull.

God help me.

'*Reeson!*'

My voice cracked. I swallowed, nearly choking. The silence from the office was absolute.

'I've got Faith!'

Absolute.

'I'll trade you! Her for Ginny!'

Not a sound. Nothing. Reeson had already killed Ginny. He'd gone out through the window. By now he'd probably positioned himself right behind me.

'I have a gun on her! You've got five seconds! Then I'm going to blow her head off!'

From somewhere I heard an odd thunk. It sounded like Ginny's claw hitting the desktop.

'*Faith.*' Reeson didn't shout, but his hoarse whisper carried like a cry. 'Get away from him. He won't shoot you.'

An inarticulate sob burst from Faith's throat.

Praying as hard as she did, I reached past her to the doorknob, turned it, pushed the door open. While it swung aside, I pulled her in front of me, giving Reeson a blocked target if he decided to fire.

He stood at one end of the desk. His hands knew what to do without help. One held the Ruger on Ginny, steady as death. The other aimed her .357 at Faith and me.

Directly at Faith's heart.

Ginny's face was pale iron, as stiff as a mask. She didn't so much as nod at me. She held both arms braced on the desktop where Reeson could watch them – where they were helpless. She loathed helplessness as much as I did, but she didn't excuse it with alcohol. When she accepted her claw, she'd given up excuses. Nevertheless her grim mask kept her loathing secret, away from Reeson. She'd given him nothing of herself, nothing he could use.

'Art,' Faith murmured brokenly, 'oh, Art.' Now she saw that I'd told the truth. Reeson didn't try to hide it. He had nowhere to go. 'Don't do this.'

'Get away from him.' Reeson's face looked like it was about to crack, split open by murder and love. Seeing Faith brought him face to face with his own ghouls and beasties. He knew too much about death. He shouldn't have allowed himself to care for her. 'I'll shoot you if I have to. Don't make me do it.'

Faith moved – but not away. Instead she took a step towards him. As if she thought that she might still be able to convince him, she said, 'Oh, Art, killing is evil. Life and death belong to the Lord.'

'*Stop*. Don't.' Despair ached unmistakably in Reeson's voice. 'I don't want to kill you.'

She took another step. 'This has to end. Don't you see that? Everybody knows what you've done. God knows. This is a crime against your own soul.'

Another step.

'Art, please.'

Reeson actually backed away from the desk, retreated to the wall. He no longer covered Ginny. Instead he held both guns aligned on Faith, and his fingers hugged the triggers.

Ginny still didn't move, however. She knew better. Anything sudden might set him off.

'No,' he rasped. 'No.'

Yes.

Maybe he wasn't that desperate. Maybe he wouldn't shoot her. I didn't know how much power his demons had with him. But I couldn't take the risk. She was worth too much.

As soon as I had a clear shot past her shoulder, I raised the .45 and fired.

For once in my life, I hit my target. The .45 made a sound like a stick of dynamite in the enclosed space, and bright red burst from the centre of Reeson's chest.

When she saw him fall, Faith lifted her voice and began wailing.

Chapter Twenty-four

An hour or so later, the rest of the group gathered in the Draytons' room, those of us who were still alive, or functional, or who didn't have better things to do.

My own ability to function was open to question. Sam's second injection, the jolt of artificial energy, didn't last as long as the first. The blood had gone leaden in my veins, which forced my heart to beat overtime, and fever filled my head again. To keep myself out of everyone's way – out of trouble – I sat on the floor beside the window with my back against the wall and my face towards the door. In that position, I did what I could to prevent my mind from merging with the woodwork.

Just to be on the safe side, I had the .45 on the floor between my legs, in easy reach. But I didn't believe that I'd ever be able to shoot straight again.

Nevertheless I was in a hell of a lot better shape than Queenie. As far as I could tell, she hadn't moved a muscle for hours. Her coma had shut down on her like the lid of a coffin.

But I would've given several of my remaining body-parts to see her smile again.

Sam sat on the bed beside her, clenching her hand as if he'd never left. Now he faced in the opposite direction, however, out towards the rest of us rather than down at Queenie. In that position I could see his face too well. He looked altogether haunted and fragile, as if he had all Art Reeson's ghouls and beasties caterwauling loose inside his head. The fact that we'd caught the woman who poisoned his wife didn't give him any noticeable relief.

Lara Hardhouse wasn't among us, naturally. We'd left her in her room, handcuffed face-down to her bed so that she wouldn't get away.

Sam had wrapped her burns in damp gauze. The cracks and blisters punctuating her red skin he'd treated with silvadene. Then he'd given her a sedative against the shock – a gesture which I considered remarkably charitable under the circumstances. Like Connie, he thought that she had only superficial burns.

Like Connie, he didn't seem to care.

Faith Jerrick was absent as well. Sam had sedated her, too, and she slept a frail heart-breaking sleep in Cat's bed. I didn't trust this. I doubted that any mere sedative could contain her distress for long. When she woke up, she'd be more alone than she'd ever been in her life. So I was glad that Amalia had decided to stay with her.

Meanwhile Truchi had gone to search Reeson's cottage for the missing rotors, at Ginny's suggestion. Like me, she found it impossible to imagine the Carbones guilty of anything.

As for the rest – counting Queenie, there were ten of us. More than half of the fourteen we'd started with – which was a pretty good survival rate for a guerrilla war, but just plain shitty for a mystery camp. In a characteristic display of Texas chivalry, Mile had commandeered one of the two original chairs. Buffy creaked away in the other, rocking herself determinedly for comfort. But Rock had brought two more chairs from some other room. With more weakness than she usually let herself show, Ginny accepted one of them. When Connie refused the other, Maryanne sat down beside Mile. They'd resumed holding hands. From my angle, I couldn't tell whether that was her idea or his.

Rock, Connie, and Hardhouse remained standing. Rock occupied the corner of the room closest to Buffy. Apparently he wanted to keep an eye on all of us – but especially on her. Connie stood at the head of Queenie's bed across from Sam. I didn't see any sign of the .22. She'd put it out of sight somewhere.

Against the wall near the door, Hardhouse lounged with his arms folded over his chest and his aggressive chin jutting. He didn't look exactly chipper, but his eyes were bright and clear, and his attention remained sharp, as if he had unlimited resources of adrenaline to call on.

I couldn't say the same for the rest of the group.

After what Ginny had endured, her exhaustion showed in the blurred colour of her eyes and the deep lines on either side of her pale nose. At odd moments she shook her head and scowled angrily, as if she couldn't forgive herself for failing to recognize Reeson's guilt earlier.

Superficially, at least, Mile and Maryanne concentrated on each other. But his gaze when he glanced at her was strangely baleful and lost, confused by lust or loathing. And her relief at Reeson's death and Lara's capture only made her seem morose. Maybe she'd had a taste of power, of her own kind of vengeance, and didn't want to resume her familiar role with Mile. On the other hand, she had no idea what else to do.

If they felt any relief, Buffy and Rock didn't show it. For better or worse, they both knew too much about murder. Rocking hard looked like her only defence against hysteria. By degrees, he inched deeper into the corner like a man who stood there because he wanted to escape his responsibilities.

As for Connie, nothing in her face or posture suggested anything except vigilance and unrelenting anger. Nevertheless I had the impression that she'd come to some kind of limit inside herself. More than most of the people here, she knew what she was doing. She thought clearly, she understood the consequences of her actions. And she was a novelist who preached the importance of sympathizing with all her characters, even the criminals. Scalding Lara was probably the most hurtful thing she'd ever done. It may've been the most hurtful thing she could ever do.

For a while no one spoke. Our own thoughts occupied our attention. Murder does that to you. It forces you to look at your life. And most of the time you can't honestly say that you like what you see. But eventually Buffy gave her rocker a vehement swing and protested in a frayed voice, 'I don't understand.'

'What is there to understand?' Maryanne asked plaintively. 'Houston was right all along. There were two killers – and now they've both been caught. We're safe at last.' She looked around the room for confirmation. 'Aren't we?'

Connie shook her head. 'Mrs Altar is right.' She sounded unkind, but she was only angry. 'The pieces don't add up. Who killed Mac?'

Even though I'd been doing my best to meditate on that question, I still felt a chill to hear it stated. As long as we didn't know the answer, we could be wrong about any number of other things as well. Lara Hardhouse, for instance.

'Why, Art Reeson, of course,' Maryanne countered a shade frantically. 'Didn't he? He and Lara were working together, just like Houston said. She opened a window for him, and he came in and killed Mac. Then he went out again and pretended to come back for the first time.' She turned to Mile. 'Isn't that right?'

He glared at her without answering. However, he didn't make her let go of his fingers.

'But *why*?' Buffy insisted. '*Why* were they working together? *Why* would they kill Mac? *Why* did they want to kill Cat?' Too much weeping had tattered her voice, but now she'd used up all her tears. 'I don't understand.'

'All right,' Ginny said heavily. This was her job. For some reason she didn't want to do it. But she did it anyway. 'We'll start with what we know.

'The idea that Lara and Reeson are in this together has too many practical problems. According to your theory, he would've had to return here while I was playing dead outside. If he did that, I probably would've heard him. He didn't have time to go around the hills to the other side of the lodge. He would've had to pass fairly close to me.

'According to your theory again, he must've been the one who stabbed me. As Joseph pointed out, Lara was the only other possibility – and she didn't have a knife. So Reeson was still in the building. He stabbed me and then went out through a window. Maybe she closed it after him to cover his trail.

'But he's a professional killer. If *he'd* stabbed me, I wouldn't be here talking about it.

'What we do know about him is *why*.' He was in the business of death. That's how he proved himself against his demons. 'He worked for el Señor – and el Señor wanted him to kill Brew. We know that. Otherwise he would've shot me while he had the chance, instead of holding me to use against Brew.

'That means he had no reason to kill Mac.

'And,' she asserted, 'he couldn't have poisoned Cat if he'd wanted to.' I'd explained this detail to her before we gathered in Sam's room. 'Faith never told him about her taste for port.

'Another thing,' she continued. 'I can't really believe that a man like him would work with a woman like Lara. He was a professional. She's too unreliable for him.

'And he loved Faith. Otherwise Brew and I would both be dead.'

'So Mrs Hardhouse acted on her own,' Connie said flatly. 'And she must've intended murder almost from the first. The port was poisoned before Cat was shot. If she didn't arrive here meaning to kill, she conceived the idea soon after we settled in.

'She put cocaine in the port because she had some reason for wanting Cat dead. And she stabbed you' – Ginny – 'for the same reason.

'What reason, I wonder?'

The way she asked the question brought back an odd memory. When Lara had entered the parlour with Mac right after Cat's murder, her first words had been directed at her husband.

Joseph. What have you done?

She hadn't just jumped to the conclusion that he was responsible. She'd been offended by it.

And he'd answered, *I didn't do it.* As if he owed her that particular reassurance.

And I'd seen them kissing like lovers at a time when they were both busy fucking everyone they could get their hands on.

You're going to end up dead.

In a tone of exhaustion, Ginny said, 'Maybe it was the same reason for both of us.'

'You're scaring me,' Maryanne protested. 'What are you talking about?'

'Maybe Lara wanted Cat and me dead because we both had sex with her husband.'

That was it, of course – the only possible connection between Catherine Reverie and Ginny Fistoulari, the only thing they had in common.

Suddenly everyone in the room stared at Hardhouse.

He unfolded his arms, shoved his hands deep into his pockets. Apparently making an effort of self-control. His gaze flicked around at us as if we'd all accused him of something and he didn't know who to defend himself against first.

'Is that possible, Mr Hardhouse?' Connie sounded like she'd already made up her mind. 'Is your wife that possessive? Why does she kill your lovers instead of you?'

He opened his mouth, closed it again. His hands started up out of his pockets, then went down again. Whatever he saw when he looked at us steadied him.

'It's the damn coke,' he said harshly. 'She wasn't like that when I married her. But the coke changed her. It made her paranoid. After that I couldn't stand her. Our marriage was effectively over. But she didn't want a divorce. And I couldn't divorce her. She owned most of the business – it was her money in the first place. I couldn't afford to divorce her.'

Sam followed this with a hollow expression, as if he didn't understand a word of it.

'She had the idea,' Hardhouse growled, 'that if she got rid of every woman I went to bed with, I'd come back to her. I'd have to. That was her delusion.

'But she never killed anybody. Not until now.' His voice was a snarl of sincerity or violence. 'I would've turned her over to the police if she had. But until now she just drove my women away. As soon as I found someone I liked, she made her leave.

'It's a tragedy, really. She was a wonderful wife before she started on coke.'

He watched all of us for our reaction.

Ginny answered him. She sounded tired to the bone, worn down to her essential marrow. But she didn't back away.

'I don't think so.'

He gauged her with his eyes. 'What do you mean?'

'Your wife had no reason to kill Mac. He was her lover, not yours. And anyway she couldn't have done it. She was with Brew. Trying to seduce him. Which doesn't make her sound like a possessive lunatic.'

'I agree,' Connie put in, as stiff as a teacher's paddle.

Buffy continued rocking as if she wanted to achieve escape velocity. Rock had shrunk so far into the corner that he nearly disappeared. Mile and Maryanne held on to each other. Neither of them moved a muscle.

Ginny shifted her weight in the chair. Her purse lay on the floor beside her, close to her right hand. 'On top of that,' she sighed, 'you said she didn't have a knife. But she must've had one. How else could she stab me? Either she had it when she was with you. Or else you weren't together. In either case, you're lying. You must've known what she was doing.'

Hardhouse's gaze burned. 'You'd better say what you mean.' His hands fisted in his pockets, holding on to his self-control. His voice was as hard as a hammer, but he used it carefully. 'I can't answer you until I know what you're accusing me of.'

'I'm accusing you,' Ginny replied with a hint of her old ferocity, 'of murdering Mac.'

Maryanne choked. No one else made a sound.

'I'm accusing you and Lara of plotting together to murder Mac and Cat and me.' Ginny's voice held more than just weariness and anger. I heard something else as well – something that sounded like loss. 'That's what you do, both of you. You have affairs with as many different people as you can manage. Then you kill each other's lovers. That's what holds your marriage together. That's how you get your kicks. It isn't cocaine. It's blood.'

685

You're going to end up dead.

Hoping that Hardhouse couldn't see me, I reached between my legs and closed my hand around the butt of the .45.

'That's crazy,' he murmured as if he were honestly astonished. 'You think I'm crazy.'

Ginny didn't hesitate. She was prepared to pay the price of her mistakes. 'I've been in bed with you. I know what turns you on. At the time I thought something was strange, but I couldn't identify it. I didn't realize what it was until you told Brew my claw was sexy. I *know* you're crazy.'

'How long have you been doing this? How many' – she snarled the word – '*damaged* women have you fucked so Lara could kill them?'

I like having sex with crippled men.

'How many of her lovers have you killed?'

In a sane world, Hardhouse would've panicked. He would've realized that he was caught, trapped, he would've broken. But the world wasn't sane – or he wasn't. Instead of panicking, he threw back his head and laughed.

The sheer unexpectedness of his reaction paralysed all of us.

Connie hesitated a fraction of a second too long. His laugh disrupted her concentration. And she asked too much of herself. After scalding Lara she didn't know how to make herself go further.

For that fraction of a second, she faltered. Then she drove her hand under Queenie's pillow and came out with the .22.

Too late.

Maryanne screamed as Hardhouse snatched a gun out of his pocket.

A flat automatic of some kind, I didn't have time to recognize it. He aimed it right into Ginny's face and yelled at Connie, '*Drop it!*'

Pandemonium.

Connie's desperation to get rid of the .22 before he fired flung it from her. It bounced away across the carpet and skidded against the wall.

Instinctively she crouched behind the bed.

At the same time I hauled up the .45. I'd already started squeezing the trigger.

Before I could get a bead on Hardhouse, Mile and Maryanne jumped in front of me. He bounded out of his chair, scrambled for escape. Still screaming, she clung to him as if even now she thought he might protect her. They collided and grappled with each other frantically, blocking my shot.

Simultaneously, Rock burst out of the corner. In a wild rush he grabbed Buffy, heaved her and her rocker to the floor. Then he dived on top of her, covering her body, muffling her wails.

'You, too, Axbrewder!' Hardhouse roared. 'Drop it!'

Ginny hadn't moved a muscle. He'd never miss her at that range. No matter what else happened, she'd be shot. And her .357 was in her purse, out of reach.

Somehow I managed to catch myself before I made a mistake.

'Don't shoot!' I shouted back urgently. 'I'll drop it!'

Trying to be obvious about it, I tossed the .45 away.

Damn near brained Rock with it, but Hardhouse didn't seem to notice.

'All of you, stop!' His aim at Ginny never wavered. I recognized the gun now – a lightweight Star BKM 9mm. Not part of the Lodge collection, as far as I knew. Hardhouse must've brought it with him. It held nine rounds. He had nine of us to kill. 'Hold still!'

Even Mile and Maryanne froze. Rock held Buffy down. Connie shrank into her crouch behind the bed.

'Well, well.' Hardhouse breathed heavily, mostly from adrenaline, but he still managed to sound conversational. 'It looks like we'll get away with it after all. Lara always says anticipation is the best part. Knowing what's about to happen. Personally, I like this part best. Getting away with it.'

'No, don't, Joseph,' Maryanne pleaded in a whimper, 'don't kill me, oh my God, don't kill me.'

'Rock,' Buffy panted, a thin whisper, as if he were suffocating her. 'Rock, please.'

I distinctly heard him say, 'All right.'

A heavy shudder ran through him, and he sighed. As if he were surrendering her to be murdered, he rolled off her. Then he came up on to his knees with his back towards Hardhouse.

In both fists he clutched my .45.

He probably knew that he didn't stand a chance in hell of turning fast enough to fire at Hardhouse before Hardhouse shot Ginny. He didn't try – he was no hunter. Instead he did what he could to make himself the target instead of her.

Concealing the .45 with his pudgy frame, he jerked one heavy slug into the wall. For the second time in less than two hours, my gun went off like gelignite.

Involuntarily Hardhouse flinched.

In that instant, Sam moved. With a shout of recognition, as if he'd finally identified an outlet for his anguish, he hurled himself at Hardhouse.

I couldn't see clearly, Mile and Maryanne were in my way. A shot went off as Sam dived into Hardhouse. Ginny recoiled like she'd been hit. Galvanized by panic, I pitched to the side, got my legs under me, came to my feet almost on top of Buffy. Practically in the same movement, I ripped the .45 out of Rock's fists and fumbled the butt into my palm.

Sam landed on Hardhouse, fighting like a schoolyard brawl – all fury and fists, no skill. They collapsed to the floor and thrashed from side to side, blundered against the wall. Hardhouse couldn't force Sam away. But he still had the 9mm.

He brought it around to shoot Sam.

In one long hard movement like the punch of a piston, Ginny stood up from her chair, swept forward, and stamped the heel of her boot down on Hardhouse's wrist.

I didn't know whether she broke his wrist or not. I couldn't hear any bones snap, Maryanne was making too much noise. But the 9mm skidded away from his fingers.

Before he could do anything else, Ginny dropped her other knee into the centre of his chest and jabbed her claw at the base of his throat.

'*Stop*,' she hissed. 'Stop, or I'll tear out your larynx.'

He stopped. Gagging slightly, he lay still.

Sam retreated to his feet, panting hugely. His skin burned with exertion, but his eyes were full of fight instead of ruin. If Hardhouse had so much as twitched, Sam would've jumped back into the fray without hesitation.

Panting like Sam, but for a completely different reason, I stumbled forward. Almost falling, I landed on my knees beside Ginny. Just to be on the safe side, I poked the .45 at Hardhouse's nose.

'You all right?' I gasped out. 'Did he hit you?'

She didn't turn her head or answer. She didn't need to. I could see a scorch mark spreading from the corner of her mouth in a fan along her cheek. Sam had deflected Hardhouse enough. The shot had only given her a powder burn.

By some miracle, the slug hadn't hit anyone at all.

When Maryanne quit screaming, I heard Connie murmur, 'I'm sorry. I'm sorry. I couldn't do it. I panicked.'

Ginny ignored her. Also Mile and Maryanne and Buffy and Rock. Leaning over Hardhouse, pushing her claw at the base of his throat, she demanded softly, 'Why? What do you get out of it?' She didn't sound angry. She sounded close to tears. 'Why did you make love to me?'

As far as I could tell, Hardhouse still wasn't scared. He didn't look caught or beaten. As much as possible with that dark aggressive face, he seemed happy, almost beatified, as if he'd finally achieved a climax that released him from himself.

Swallowing against the pressure, he said, 'Because it works.'

Ginny and I stared at him and waited. She made no effort to wipe the black pain off her cheek.

'Life is sex. You don't understand that. You think sex is just fucking. But it's more than that, much more. It's passion and dominion and *life*.' The words came out half choked, but he didn't ask her to ease back. 'When you understand that, nothing ordinary works. Fucking doesn't work. It isn't enough. Women are just women. They don't mean anything. But a woman who needs me – a broken, maimed woman who needs me to make her whole – *that's* sex.

'When I learned that, I started living for the first time. I started looking for damaged women, women with physical and emotional injuries. Because they needed me.

'But it didn't help me with Lara. She didn't need me, not like that. And when you give people what they need, they stop needing you. I wanted more. *More.* I wanted sex that would make my whole body and mind flame with life.

'Part of what makes sex so potent is that you can give it or take it away. At first, I thought I wanted women who were going to die anyway. Women in the first stages of some terminal illness. Women who would lose what I gave them. That helped, but it wasn't enough. It didn't let me choose. And it still didn't help me with Lara.

'But *she* understood. She *understood*. She was the one who thought of killing my lovers.'

Maryanne took one horrified breath. Buffy moaned softly.

Hardhouse's grin made him look like a malign saint. 'Do you have any idea how sexy it is to know that the woman you're fucking is about to die? That she's going to die *because* you fucked her? That you can make her whole and doom her at the same time? When we started doing that, I had everything I could ever want. Damaged women, emotional and physical cripples – sex with them was vindication. And sex with Lara afterward was absolution.

'It's Heaven.

'For her, the only problem was that we had to be so careful. Getting caught would ruin everything. That's what kills you. But for me, getting away with it is the crowning touch, the ultimate victory – the best part of being alive. And the more we lived, the more we wanted to live.

'When we heard about this mystery camp, we decided to risk it. The chance was too good to miss – the chance to do what we wanted in a camp full of "detectives" and get away with it.

'You think you're so tough,' he said straight to Ginny, 'and you don't even know how maimed you are. Sex with you was the best I've ever had.'

Her claw began trembling against his throat. Her shoulders shook, taken by sobs. His words hurt her worse than any bullet.

'You sonofabitch,' she whispered back in the kind of husky voice lovers use. 'I trusted you.'

Nevertheless she fought to keep her grief to herself. Biting down on the unsteadiness of her voice, she asked, 'Sam, have you got any tape?'

Sam's bag sat on the end table beside Queenie. He went to it promptly and came back with a wide roll of bandage tape. As he handed it to Ginny, he said harshly, 'Tape his mouth shut. I don't want to listen to him any more.'

She nodded once, stiffly. That was all the acknowledgement she gave any of us.

Behind me, Rock and Buffy got to their feet. She looked like she wanted to sob, but that wasn't what she did. Facing him with tears in her eyes, she murmured, 'Thank you.'

He made a gentle shushing noise as if she'd asked him to comfort her.

'Is it over?' Maryanne asked like a frightened doll.

Connie stood up from behind the bed. 'Yes,' she answered. 'It's over.'

'Shee-it,' Mile muttered thinly. 'Shee-it.' Then he growled at Maryanne, 'Fool woman, you damn near got me killed.'

'No, she didn't,' Connie retorted. Apparently she'd had all she could stand of Houston Mile. 'She pulled you out of the line of fire. She saved your life.'

That may or may not have been true. In either case, it shut Mile up.

Ginny gave me the roll of tape and took my gun to cover Hardhouse. It wobbled in her grasp, but she didn't need to worry about missing him. Against her pale skin, the powder burn looked dark and permanent, like a stain on her spirit.

With more strength than I knew I had, I flopped Hardhouse over on to his face so I wouldn't have to suffer his belligerent happy smile. Apparently his wrist wasn't broken after all – he didn't show any special pain when I strapped his forearms together. Then I did his ankles. I didn't stop until I'd immobilized him for good.

Because I agreed with Sam, I put a big strip of tape over Hardhouse's mouth. Maliciously I hoped that he was one of those people who had trouble breathing through his nose.

You think you're so tough, and you don't even know how maimed you are.

I like having sex with crippled men.

As I pried myself upright, I felt more than a bit stained myself.

As soon as I regained my feet, Ginny handed me the .45. Without a word to anyone, she left the room.

I wanted to follow her. In fact, I had to follow her. But when I looked around, I forgot that for a moment. The eight of us who remained were a shambles, no question about it. Too much fear had turned Maryanne's face raw and homely. Mile resembled a porker on the way to the slaughter-house. Buffy and Rock lay on the floor again, cradling each other like lost kids.

As if she weren't aware of what she did, Connie picked up Buffy's rocker and sat in it. Her failure with Hardhouse had brought her anger to an end, or degraded it somehow. She didn't want it any more. Mumbling to herself like an old woman, she closed her eyes.

Only Sam looked like he'd come through the experience with his soul intact. He'd saved Ginny and stopped Hardhouse. And struck a blow for his wife.

I envied him.

Through everything that had happened, Queenie slept on like the dead. If I hadn't seen the blanket move over her chest, I wouldn't have known that she was still alive.

I went to her side. I didn't ask Sam's permission. I didn't think I needed it. As if I were alone with her, I spent a moment studying her sweet unseeing face, waiting for her smile even though I knew that I might never see it again. Then I bent over her and kissed her on the mouth.

She'd told me once I owed her the story of my life. This was as close as I could get.

After that I went to find Ginny.

Chapter Twenty-five

During the night Queenie regained consciousness.

Sam couldn't assess how badly she'd been damaged, of course. Only time would reveal how much of her brain still worked right. When she woke up, however, she smiled at him – just a ghost of her former vitality, but a smile anyway, a recognition. And like a good girl she drank the glass of water he put to her lips. Those were encouraging signs.

At about the same time, Truchi returned with a handful of distributor rotors. He'd found them in a chest in Reeson's attic, along with the missing guns and enough other munitions to equip a platoon.

Shortly after sunrise he left Deerskin Lodge on the snowmobile – and came back a couple of hours later with a heavy diesel plough chugging along behind him. He wasn't exactly elaborate in his explanation, but he let us know that he'd met the county road crew on its regular run up the mountain. The run hadn't been made sooner because this road wasn't used enough to be a high priority.

When he heard Truchi's story, the plough's operator had used his radio to call for help. Before another hour passed the sheriff and several cars full of deputies arrived at Deerskin Lodge, along with two ambulances.

One of the ambulances left promptly, carrying a load of corpses for the coroner – Catherine Reverie, Mac Westward, Arthur Reeson. The other took Lara Hardhouse, Queenie Drayton, and Sam to the nearest hospital.

The sheriff arrested Joseph Hardhouse, naturally. He also impounded Reeson's chest and Lara's cocaine, and asked the rest of us a lot of questions.

Those questions could've gotten me into trouble pretty quickly.

Hours earlier, however – in fact, right after Truchi left on the snowmobile – Ginny had called the survivors together and told them how she wanted to save my life.

We didn't need much time, she explained. Just a few days, say until Sunday. For that long, she asked the Altars and Sam and Mile and Maryanne and Connie to tell the cops the same lie she did. On Sunday they could switch to the truth. They could even explain why they'd been lying. Unless the cops found Simon first, in which case the whole question would become academic.

Only Mile objected. He had a score to settle with Ginny and me – but mostly me – and betraying us to el Señor sounded fine to him. But Maryanne worked on him for a while. She spent the credit she'd gained by apparently saving his life. And when that didn't work, she let him know that if he refused Ginny she'd lose respect for him – which, she hinted broadly, would involve telling his friends back home about his sexual practices.

He gave in with his usual grace.

So Ginny introduced me to the sheriff as Simon Abel, and no one contradicted her. Under questioning, we all agreed that Mick Axbrewder had gone up into the hills tracking Reeson and hadn't returned. No one mentioned locking Abel in the wine cellar. Or the hole in Axbrewder's stomach, for that matter. The sheriff had no immediate reason to doubt us.

Which meant the police reports and newspapers would tell el Señor that I was missing and presumed dead. He wouldn't send anyone else after me until he learned the truth.

Ginny and I had that long to get out of the state.

Unless one of the Hardhouses decided to talk. But neither of them knew what we were doing. And they had both apparently concluded that silence was their best defence, at least until they could bring in some legal talent. Since they didn't say anything, they didn't give me away.

Some of the deputies started a search for the body. They weren't organized or equipped for the job, however, and the snow hampered them. Our lie might well last until Sunday.

While the sheriff asked baffled questions, groping to make sense out of what we told him, one of the deputies drove away with Joseph Hardhouse. On his way out to the unit, he passed Ginny and me in the den. As charming as ever, he paused under the heads of dead animals to tell her, 'You still don't understand. That claw really is the most desirable thing about you.'

693

His smile radiated happy malice in all directions.

I watched the muscles bunch and release at the corner of her jaw, but she didn't retort. He'd already had all the response he was ever going to get out of her.

I wouldn't have had any idea what was going on with her myself if we hadn't talked about it earlier.

When I followed her out of Sam's room after Hardhouse's confession, I'd found her in the kitchen, making a sandwich as well as she could with one hand and a prosthetic device, and munching vitamins like candy. She still hadn't tried to clean the powder burn off her cheek, and that impacted mark accentuated the pallor of her face, the vulnerability in her gaze. The damaged skin probably hurt too much to touch. Fortunately the wound in her shoulder hadn't resumed bleeding. Only her eyes bled. Tears streaked her face while she chewed.

Despite my own exhaustion, her distress went through my heart. Years had passed since the Ginny Fistoulari I knew had let me see her in a state like this – let me this close to her. For the time being, however, I'd apparently used up my fear of her. Of her and for her. I was willing to take risks that would've scared me to the core of my bones a day ago.

Propping my pain and fever on the edge of a counter, I said, 'I don't think much of your taste in men.'

A snarl twisted her mouth. 'Is that your subtle way of reminding me that I made a mistake with Joseph, or are you just putting yourself down again?'

I shrugged. 'Some of both, probably. I'm not terribly impressed with my contribution to this case. I've been in such a sweat about losing you that I couldn't think.' I groped for the description I wanted. 'Which is an expensive problem. I should've taken Connie's advice years ago.'

And Sam's.

I guess I was being cryptic again. Ginny glared at me and demanded, 'Huh?'

'I forgot, you weren't there. While you were out, Connie made a hell of a speech. To Joseph, of all people. If I heard her right, I've been treating everything you and I do together like a contest. I had to prove I needed you so much that you wouldn't have the heart to ditch me. And I had to prove I didn't deserve you so that I wouldn't hate you for letting me fear you'd ditch me anyway.

'But she said' – I remembered it exactly – ' "It is impossible to live on the assumption that any contest can exist between persons." ' Then I

694

shrugged again. 'I know what the words mean. I need to learn what it means to live like that.'

Ginny's eyes continued to spill tears. The effort of seeing through them made her look furious. 'And you think I don't?'

Well, at least she was listening. I shifted my weight against the counter, trying to find a more comfortable position. 'Ginny, I don't give a shit whether you do or not. I've got enough problems of my own. I can't tell you what to do with yours. All I'm trying to say is, I intend to stop. I want to stop treating you like you're the enemy.'

A quiver she couldn't control in her lower lip. 'What for?'

I faced her straight. 'You and I will never get back to where we were. We used to love each other – it all used to seem pretty simple. We'll never get that back. But I can think of reasons to go on.'

Her voice was so small that I almost missed the words. 'Like what?'

'Like' – I paused to be sure that I was ready – 'your claw isn't the most desirable thing about you.' She flinched when I took that chance, but I didn't back down. Instead I stroked the tears on her undamaged cheek and showed her my wet fingers. 'Neither is this. The most desirable thing about you is that you aren't Lara or Maryanne. You aren't Cat. You sure as hell aren't Faith, and you also aren't Connie or Buffy. You're Ginny by God Fistoulari, and no one can take your place.'

That was honest, anyway.

Fortunately I didn't expect a gratified response. If anything, my assertion had the opposite effect. 'Stop it,' she murmured, fighting distress. 'I can't deal with that right now. You're too far ahead of me. I thought I'd have to carry your self-pity and your stupid drinking around on my back for the rest of my life. I wanted to believe I was strong enough, but I knew I wasn't. I couldn't do it. That's why I didn't see what was wrong with Joseph. I felt like such a failure around you. He offered me a way out. He wanted me – and Lara wanted you, so that was all right. At least for a few days, I could stop carrying you around.

'I was helpless to really look at him. At what I was getting myself into.

'I don't know what to do with you if this isn't a contest.'

I lowered my head. It felt too heavy anyway, and besides I couldn't pretend that what she said didn't hurt.

But I was braced for it. And the time had come to put up or shut up. If 'no contest can exist between persons', I had nothing to lose. Sure, she could walk out of my life – but she couldn't take my life with her.

And she couldn't take away the fact that I'd told her the truth at least once or twice.

When I felt ready to say it without sounding bitter, I looked back up at her and asked, 'So what do you want to do?'

She didn't meet my gaze. With the same disdain she had for the burn on her cheek, she didn't wipe her eyes or her nose.

'You want the truth?'

'No,' I said. 'I prefer comfortable lies. The truth hurts. But I finally figured out that lies kill.' Sam told me, actually. 'I'd rather we both stayed alive, if we can manage it.'

She nodded hard enough to hurt her neck. Harshly she answered, 'The truth is, I don't know what I want. I don't know how I feel about you. I don't like *cripples*.' She couldn't say the word without turning it into a curse. 'I don't like being one, and I don't like you when you're one.'

Then, before I could accept the implications and let her go, she added, 'No, that isn't the truth. I mean, it is, but it isn't. It isn't enough.'

Abruptly she raised her eyes. Tears blurred her grey gaze, confusing everything she saw. In a tight voice, she said, 'I want you to go away with me. Somewhere out of el Señor's reach. Somewhere we can *think*. If we have reasons to go on, I don't know it right now. And if we're finished, I'm not going to admit it until I've had a chance to *think*.'

Well, by God. And just when I was getting set to ride off into the sunset, too.

I was no Queenie Drayton, but I smiled with everything I had. 'You devil. You always could sweet-talk me into anything.'

That was honest, too.

For a while she dropped her gaze. Without saying anything, she chewed on her ragged sandwich.

When she looked up again, her eyes had cleared.

'In that case, we need a better way to keep you alive. Doing security for mystery camps obviously isn't the answer.'

Which wasn't exactly the same thing as a sign from God. But it sufficed.

After she finished eating, I went to my room for some sleep.

I remembered to take my pills before I climbed into bed. And again when I got up to see Truchi off.

The sheriff wasn't much fun to deal with. He had too much stubbornness, and not enough imagination to back it up. But eventually he allowed us to go home.

696

We were all ready by then. While the sheriff interrogated one or another of us, the rest made our preparations. Connie had packed the Draytons' stuff. Truchi put our bags in the van.

Ginny and I stood on the porch as if we were still in charge, supervising Murder On Cue's departure. We'd preceded the others by a minute or two, but the Carbones were out in the cold with us, sharing a brief vigil for the dead – and the living.

'Will you be all right with Faith?' Ginny asked Ama. 'We could take her into town with us. If she has any family, we could get in touch with them.'

Ama had worn a stony expression for days, but now her face softened. 'I am the one to care for her,' she replied. 'I have known her long. And I have known Mr Reeson.' Apparently she'd never been on a first name basis with her boss. 'I can assure her that she was not wrong in him. His love was a thing to be trusted. Perhaps it will redeem him in her God's sight.'

Ginny shrugged and let go of Faith's fate.

Houston Mile and Maryanne Green left first. He was in a hurry and didn't give her a chance to speak to anyone.

After them the Altars emerged from the lodge. In a forlorn murmur, Sue-Rose said a few words of thanks, but she didn't wait to see how Ginny and I took them. As if she'd aged a decade in the past few days, she went stiffly down the steps and climbed into the van. In the passenger seat.

Her husband scanned the hills to avoid our faces. Distantly he asked, 'Where should I send your cheque?'

Ginny grimaced. 'I don't want a cheque. I need cash.'

This didn't surprise him. He knew what we were doing, and why. 'I have money at home.'

'That's fine,' she answered. 'We'll follow you there from the Camelot.' Where we'd left her car.

He paused a moment longer, still gazing away. Then he said, 'I don't know how to pick up the pieces after something like this. I think we're going to need help.'

Mostly because I knew how he felt, I said, 'There's nothing wrong with needing help.'

He sighed. 'I know. I'm just not used to it.'

Stooped and grey, he trudged out to the van.

Constance Bebb came last. For both of us, Ginny asked her, 'Will you be all right? I mean, without Mac? What are you going to do?'

Connie dismissed the first question. To the second, she answered,

'I'll try to write another Thornton Foal novel. It will be difficult without him. He was always the better writer. But I've learned a few things I can use.'

On impulse I leaned down and kissed her cheek.

The way she pulled back made me think that I'd frightened her. Then I saw her blush.

Nevertheless her dignity didn't forsake her. 'Thank you, Mr Abel,' she said firmly. With a slight smile, she added, 'Try to take better care of yourself on your next assignment.'

With her head high and her back straight, she descended the steps.

Ginny nudged my arm. 'Let's go.'

I looked over at Petruchio Carbone. The antique droop of his moustache reminded me of our only conversation. As a way of saying goodbye, I remarked, 'You were right. Everyone who comes here is crazy.'

He looked at me with a mixture of sadness and contentment, like a man whose heart had been broken and healed so long ago that the cost no longer mattered.

'Not you,' he said distinctly. After a moment he nodded towards Ginny. 'Not her.'

He surprised me. But when I considered, I thought he might be right. Maybe Ginny and I were finally on our way to sanity.

Past my shoulder, she told him, 'If you think that, you're loonier than he is.'

I wanted to laugh. 'I hope so.'

Together she and I went to the van to make our getaway.